DASHIELL HAMMETT &

DASHIELL HAMMETT

CRIME STORIES AND
OTHER WRITINGS

THE LIBRARY OF AMERICA

F
Hamm

STEVEN MARCUS
SELECTED THE CONTENTS AND WROTE THE NOTES
FOR THIS VOLUME

Contents

CRIME STORIES

Arson Plus 3
Slippery Fingers 22
Crooked Souls 35
The Tenth Clew 52
Zigzags of Treachery 84
The House in Turk Street 123
The Girl with the Silver Eyes 146
Women, Politics and Murder 191
The Golden Horseshoe 219
Nightmare Town 264
The Whosis Kid 310
The Scorched Face 356
Dead Yellow Women 395
The Gutting of Couffignal 450
The Assistant Murderer 483
Creeping Siamese 522
The Big Knock-Over 538
$106,000 Blood Money 592
The Main Death 636
This King Business 659
Fly Paper 711
The Farewell Murder 745
Woman in the Dark 783
Two Sharp Knives 829

OTHER WRITINGS

The Thin Man: An Early Typescript 847
From the Memoirs of a Private Detective 905
"Suggestions to Detective Story Writers" 910

Chronology 915
Note on the Texts 926
Notes 932

CRIME STORIES

Arson Plus

Jim Tarr picked up the cigar I rolled across his desk, looked at the band, bit off an end, and reached for a match.

"Fifteen cents straight," he said. "You must want me to break a *couple* of laws for you this time."

I had been doing business with this fat sheriff of Sacramento County for four or five years—ever since I came to the Continental Detective Agency's San Francisco office—and I had never known him to miss an opening for a sour crack; but it didn't mean anything.

"Wrong both times," I told him. "I get two of them for a quarter; and I'm here to do you a favor instead of asking for one. The company that insured Thornburgh's house thinks somebody touched it off."

"That's right enough, according to the fire department. They tell me the lower part of the house was soaked with gasoline, but God knows how they could tell—there wasn't a stick left standing. I've got McClump working on it, but he hasn't found anything to get excited about yet."

"What's the layout? All I know is that there was a fire."

Tarr leaned back in his chair, turned his red face to the ceiling, and bellowed:

"Hey, Mac!"

The pearl push-buttons on his desk are ornaments as far as he is concerned. Deputy sheriffs McHale, McClump and Macklin came to the door together—MacNab apparently wasn't within hearing.

"What's the idea?" the sheriff demanded of McClump. "Are you carrying a bodyguard around with you?"

The two other deputies, thus informed as to who "Mac" referred to this time, went back to their cribbage game.

"We got a city slicker here to catch our firebug for us," Tarr told his deputy. "But we got to tell him what it's all about first."

McClump and I had worked together on an express robbery, several months before. He's a rangy, tow-headed youngster of twenty-five or six, with all the nerve in the world—and most of the laziness.

"Ain't the Lord good to us?"

He had himself draped across a chair by now—always his first objective when he comes into a room.

"Well, here's how she stands: This fellow Thornburgh's house was a couple miles out of town, on the old county road—an old frame house. About midnight, night before last, Jeff Pringle—the nearest neighbor, a half-mile or so to the east—saw a glare in the sky from over that way, and phoned in the alarm; but by the time the fire wagons got there, there wasn't enough of the house left to bother about. Pringle was the first of the neighbors to get to the house, and the roof had already fell in then.

"Nobody saw anything suspicious—no strangers hanging around or nothing. Thornburgh's help just managed to save themselves, and that was all. They don't know much about what happened—too scared, I reckon. But they did see Thornburgh at his window just before the fire got him. A fellow here in town—name of Handerson—saw that part of it too. He was driving home from Wayton, and got to the house just before the roof caved in.

"The fire department people say they found signs of gasoline. The Coonses, Thornburgh's help, say they didn't have no gas on the place. So there you are."

"Thornburgh have any relatives?"

"Yeah. A niece in San Francisco—a Mrs. Evelyn Trowbridge. She was up yesterday, but there wasn't nothing she could do, and she couldn't tell us nothing much, so she went back home."

"Where are the servants now?"

"Here in town. Staying at a hotel on I Street. I told 'em to stick around for a few days."

"Thornburgh own the house?"

"Uh-huh. Bought it from Newning & Weed a couple months ago."

"You got anything to do this morning?"

"Nothing but this."

"Good! Let's get out and dig around."

We found the Coonses in their room at the hotel on I Street. Mr. Coons was a small-boned, plump man with the smooth, meaningless face, and the suavity of the typical male house-servant.

His wife was a tall, stringy woman, perhaps five years older than her husband—say, forty—with a mouth and chin that seemed shaped for gossiping. But he did all the talking, while she nodded her agreement to every second or third word.

"We went to work for Mr. Thornburgh on the fifteenth of June, I think," he said, in reply to my first question. "We came to Sacramento, around the first of the month, and put in applications at the Allis Employment Bureau. A couple of weeks later they sent us out to see Mr. Thornburgh, and he took us on."

"Where were you before you came here?"

"In Seattle, sir, with a Mrs. Comerford; but the climate there didn't agree with my wife—she has bronchial trouble—so we decided to come to California. We most likely would have stayed in Seattle, though, if Mrs. Comerford hadn't given up her house."

"What do you know about Thornburgh?"

"Very little, sir. He wasn't a talkative gentleman. He hadn't any business that I know of. I think he was a retired seafaring man. He never said he was, but he had that manner and look. He never went out or had anybody in to see him, except his niece once, and he didn't write or get any mail. He had a room next to his bedroom fixed up as a sort of workshop. He spent most of his time in there. I always thought he was working on some kind of invention, but he kept the door locked, and wouldn't let us go near it."

"Haven't you any idea at all what it was?"

"No, sir. We never heard any hammering or noises from it, and never smelt anything either. And none of his clothes were ever the least bit soiled, even when they were ready to go out to the laundry. They would have been if he had been working on anything like machinery."

"Was he an old man?"

"He couldn't have been over fifty, sir. He was very erect, and his hair and beard were thick, with no grey hairs."

"Ever have any trouble with him?"

"Oh, no, sir! He was, if I may say it, a very peculiar gentleman in a way; and he didn't care about anything except having his meals fixed right, having his clothes taken care of—he was very particular about them—and not being disturbed. Except early in the morning and at night, we'd hardly see him all day."

"Now about the fire. Tell us the whole thing—everything you remember."

"Well, sir, I and my wife had gone to bed about ten o'clock, our regular time, and had gone to sleep. Our room was on the second floor, in the rear. Some time later—I never did exactly know what time it was—I woke up, coughing. The room was all full of smoke, and my wife was sort of strangling. I jumped up, and dragged her down the back stairs and out the back door, not thinking of anything but getting her out of there.

"When I had her safe in the yard, I thought of Mr. Thornburgh, and tried to get back in the house; but the whole first floor was just flames. I ran around front then, to see if he had got out, but didn't see anything of him. The whole yard was as light as day by then. Then I heard him scream—a horrible scream, sir—I can hear it yet! And I looked up at his window—that was the front second-story room—and saw him there, trying to get out the window. But all the woodwork was burning, and he screamed again and fell back, and right after that the roof over his room fell in.

"There wasn't a ladder or anything that I could have put up to the window for him—there wasn't anything I could have done.

"In the meantime, a gentleman had left his automobile in the road, and come up to where I was standing; but there wasn't anything we could do—the house was burning everywhere and falling in here and there. So we went back to where I had left my wife, and carried her farther away from the fire, and brought her to—she had fainted. And that's all I know about it, sir."

"Hear any noises earlier that night? Or see anybody hanging around?"

"No, sir."

"Have any gasoline around the place?"

"No, sir. Mr. Thornburgh didn't have a car."

"No gasoline for cleaning?"

"No, sir, none at all, unless Mr. Thornburgh had it in his workshop. When his clothes needed cleaning, I took them to town, and all his laundry was taken by the grocer's man, when he brought our provisions."

"Don't know anything that might have some bearing on the fire?"

"No, sir. I was surprised when I heard that somebody had set the house afire. I could hardly believe it. I don't know why anybody should want to do that."

"What do you think of them?" I asked McClump, as we left the hotel.

"They might pad the bills, or even go South with some of the silver, but they don't figure as killers in my mind."

That was my opinion, too; but they were the only persons known to have been there when the fire started except the man who had died. We went around to the Allis Employment Bureau and talked to the manager.

He told us that the Coonses had come into his office on June second, looking for work; and had given Mrs. Edward Comerford, 45 Woodmansee Terrace, Seattle, Washington, as reference. In reply to a letter—he always checked up the references of servants—Mrs. Comerford had written that the Coonses had been in her employ for a number of years, and had been "extremely satisfactory in every respect." On June thirteenth, Thornburgh had telephoned the bureau, asking that a man and his wife be sent out to keep house for him; and Allis had sent two couples that he had listed. Neither had been employed by Thornburgh, though Allis considered them more desirable than the Coonses, who were finally hired by Thornburgh.

All that would certainly seem to indicate that the Coonses hadn't deliberately maneuvered themselves into the place, unless they were the luckiest people in the world—and a detective can't afford to believe in luck or coincidence, unless he has unquestionable proof of it.

At the office of the real estate agents, through whom Thornburgh had bought the house—Newning & Weed—we were told that Thornburgh had come in on the eleventh of June, and had said that he had been told that the house was for sale, had looked it over, and wanted to know the price.

The deal had been closed the next morning, and he had paid for the house with a check for $4,500 on the Seamen's Bank of San Francisco. The house was already furnished.

After luncheon, McClump and I called on Howard Handerson—the man who had seen the fire while driving home from Wayton. He had an office in the Empire Building, with his name and the title "Northern California Agent, Instant-Sheen Cleanser Company," on the door. He was a big, care-less-looking man of forty-five or so, with the professionally jovial smile that belongs to the salesman.

He had been in Wayton on business the day of the fire, he said, and had stayed there until rather late, going to dinner and afterward playing pool with a grocer named Hammer-smith—one of his customers. He had left Wayton in his machine, at about ten-thirty, and set out for Sacramento. At Tavender he had stopped at the garage for oil and gas and to have one of his tires blown up.

Just as he was about to leave the garage, the garage-man had called his attention to a red glare in the sky, and had told him that it was probably from a fire somewhere along the old county road that paralleled the State road into Sacramento; so Handerson had taken the county road, and had arrived at the burning house just in time to see Thornburgh try to fight his way through the flames that enveloped him.

It was too late to make any attempt to put out the fire, and the man upstairs was beyond saving by then—undoubtedly dead even before the roof collapsed; so Handerson had helped Coons revive his wife, and stayed there watching the fire until it had burned itself out. He had seen no one on that county road while driving to the fire.

"What do you know about Handerson?" I asked McClump, when we were on the street.

"Came here, from somewhere in the East, I think, early in the summer to open that Cleanser agency. Lives at the Garden Hotel. Where do we go next?"

"We get a machine, and take a look at what's left of the Thornburgh house."

An enterprising incendiary couldn't have found a lovelier spot in which to turn himself loose, if he looked the whole county over. Tree-topped hills hid it from the rest of the world, on three sides; while away from the fourth, an uninhabited plain rolled down to the river. The county road that passed the front gate was shunned by automobiles, so McClump said, in favor of the State Highway to the north.

Where the house had been, was now a mound of blackened ruins. We poked around in the ashes for a few minutes—not that we expected to find anything, but because it's the nature of man to poke around in ruins.

A garage in the rear, whose interior gave no evidence of recent occupation, had a badly scorched roof and front, but was otherwise undamaged. A shed behind it, sheltering an ax, a shovel, and various odds and ends of gardening tools, had escaped the fire altogether. The lawn in front of the house, and the garden behind the shed—about an acre in all—had been pretty thoroughly cut and trampled by wagon wheels, and the feet of the firemen and the spectators.

Having ruined our shoe-shines, McClump and I got back in our machine and swung off in a circle around the place, calling at all the houses within a mile radius, and getting little besides jolts for our trouble.

The nearest house was that of Pringle, the man who had turned in the alarm; but he not only knew nothing about the dead man, but said he had never seen him. In fact, only one of the neighbors had ever seen him: a Mrs. Jabine, who lived about a mile to the south.

She had taken care of the key to the house while it was vacant; and a day or two before he bought it, Thornburgh had come to her house, inquiring about the vacant one. She had gone over there with him and showed him through it, and he had told her that he intended buying it, if the price, of which neither of them knew anything, wasn't too high.

He had been alone, except for the chauffeur of the hired car in which he had come from Sacramento, and, save that he had no family, he had told her nothing about himself.

Hearing that he had moved in, she went over to call on him several days later—"just a neighborly visit"—but had been told by Mrs. Coons that he was not at home. Most of the neighbors had talked to the Coonses, and had got the impression that Thornburgh did not care for visitors, so they had let him alone. The Coonses were described as "pleasant enough to talk to when you meet them," but reflecting their employer's desire not to make friends.

McClump summarized what the afternoon had taught us as we pointed our machine toward Tavender: "Any of these folks could have touched off the place, but we got nothing to show that any of 'em even knew Thornburgh, let alone had a bone to pick with him."

Tavender turned out to be a crossroads settlement of a general store and post office, a garage, a church, and six dwellings, about two miles from Thornburgh's place. McClump knew the storekeeper and postmaster, a scrawny little man named Philo, who stuttered moistly.

"I n-n-never s-saw Th-thornburgh," he said, "and I n-n-never had any m-mail for him. C-coons"—it sounded like one of these things butterflies come out of—"used to c-come in once a week t-to order groceries—they d-didn't have a phone. He used to walk in, and I'd s-send the stuff over in my c-c-car. Th-then I'd s-see him once in a while, waiting f-for the stage to S-s-sacramento."

"Who drove the stuff out to Thornburgh's?"

"M-m-my b-boy. Want to t-talk to him?"

The boy was a juvenile edition of the old man, but without the stutter. He had never seen Thornburgh on any of his visits, but his business had taken him only as far as the kitchen. He hadn't noticed anything peculiar about the place.

"Who's the night man at the garage?" I asked him, after we had listened to the little he had to tell.

"Billy Luce. I think you can catch him there now. I saw him go in a few minutes ago."

We crossed the road and found Luce.

"Night before last—the night of the fire down the road—was there a man here talking to you when you first saw it?"

He turned his eyes upward in that vacant stare which people use to aid their memory.

"Yes, I remember now! He was going to town, and I told him that if he took the county road instead of the State Road he'd see the fire on his way in."

"What kind of looking man was he?"

"Middle-aged—a big man, but sort of slouchy. I think he had on a brown suit, baggy and wrinkled."

"Medium complexion?"

"Yes."

"Smile when he talked?"

"Yes, a pleasant sort of fellow."

"Curly brown hair?"

"Have a heart!" Luce laughed. "I didn't put him under a magnifying glass."

From Tavender, we drove over to Wayton. Luce's description had fit Handerson all right; but while we were at it, we thought we might as well check up to make sure that he had been coming from Wayton.

We spent exactly twenty-five minutes in Wayton; ten of them finding Hammersmith, the grocer with whom Handerson had said he dined and played pool; five minutes finding the proprietor of the pool-room; and ten verifying Handerson's story.

"What do you think of it now, Mac?" I asked, as we rolled back toward Sacramento.

Mac's too lazy to express an opinion, or even form one, unless he's driven to it; but that doesn't mean they aren't worth listening to, if you can get them.

"There ain't a hell of a lot to think," he said cheerfully. "Handerson is out of it, if he ever was in it. There's nothing to show that anybody but the Coonses and Thornburgh were there when the fire started—but there may have been a regiment there. Them Coonses ain't too honest looking, maybe, but they ain't killers, or I miss my guess. But the fact remains that they're the only bet we got so far. Maybe we ought to try to get a line on them."

"All right," I agreed. "I'll get a wire off to our Seattle office asking them to interview Mrs. Comerford, and see what she can tell about them as soon as we get back in town. Then I'm going to catch a train for San Francisco, and see Thornburgh's niece in the morning."

Next morning, at the address McClump had given me—a rather elaborate apartment building on California Street—I had to wait three-quarters of an hour for Mrs. Evelyn Trowbridge to dress. If I had been younger, or a social caller, I suppose I'd have felt amply rewarded when she finally came in—a tall, slender woman of less than thirty; in some sort of clinging black affair; with a lot of black hair over a very white face, strikingly set off by a small red mouth and big hazel eyes that looked black until you got close to them.

But I was a busy, middle-aged detective, who was fuming over having his time wasted; and I was a lot more interested in finding the bird who struck the match than I was in feminine beauty. However, I smothered my grouch, apologized for disturbing her at such an early hour, and got down to business.

"I want you to tell me all you know about your uncle—his family, friends, enemies, business connections, everything."

I had scribbled on the back of the card I had sent into her what my business was.

"He hadn't any family," she said; "unless I might be it. He was my mother's brother, and I am the only one of that family now living."

"Where was he born?"

"Here in San Francisco. I don't know the date, but he was about fifty years old, I think—three years older than my mother."

"What was his business?"

"He went to sea when he was a boy, and, so far as I know, always followed it until a few months ago."

"Captain?"

"I don't know. Sometimes I wouldn't see or hear from him for several years, and he never talked about what he was doing; though he would mention some of the places he had visited—Rio de Janeiro, Madagascar, Tobago, Christiania. Then, about three months ago—some time in May—he came here and told me that he was through with wandering; that he was going to take a house in some quiet place where he could work undisturbed on an invention in which he was interested.

"He lived at the Francisco Hotel while he was in San Francisco. After a couple of weeks, he suddenly disappeared. And then, about a month ago, I received a telegram from him, asking me to come to see him at his house near Sacramento. I went up the very next day, and I thought that he was acting very queerly—he seemed very excited over something. He gave me a will that he had just drawn up and some life insurance policies in which I was beneficiary.

"Immediately after that he insisted that I return home, and hinted rather plainly that he did not wish me to either visit him again or write until I heard from him. I thought all that rather peculiar, as he had always seemed fond of me. I never saw him again."

"What was this invention he was working on?"

"I really don't know. I asked him once, but he became so excited—even suspicious—that I changed the subject, and never mentioned it again."

"Are you sure that he really did follow the sea all those years?"

"No, I am not. I just took it for granted; but he may have been doing something altogether different."

"Was he ever married?"

"Not that I know of."

"Know any of his friends or enemies?"

"No, none."

"Remember anybody's name that he ever mentioned?"

"No."

"I don't want you to think this next question insulting, though I admit it is. But it has to be asked. Where were you the night of the fire?"

"At home; I had some friends here to dinner, and they stayed until about midnight. Mr. and Mrs. Walker Kellogg, Mrs. John Dupree, and a Mr. Killmer, who is a lawyer. I can give you their addresses, or you can get them from the phone book, if you want to question them."

From Mrs. Trowbridge's apartment I went to the Francisco Hotel. Thornburgh had been registered there from May tenth to June thirteenth, and hadn't attracted much attention. He had been a tall, broad-shouldered, erect man of about fifty, with rather long brown hair brushed straight back; a short, pointed brown beard, and healthy, ruddy complexion—grave, quiet, punctilious in dress and manner; his hours had been regular and he had had no visitors that any of the hotel employes remembered.

At the Seamen's Bank—upon which Thornburgh's check, in payment of the house, had been drawn—I was told that he had opened an account there on May fifteenth, having been introduced by W. W. Jeffers & Sons, local stock brokers. A balance of a little more than four hundred dollars remained to his credit. The cancelled checks on hand were all to the order of various life insurance companies; and for amounts that, if they represented premiums, testified to rather large policies. I jotted down the names of the life insurance companies, and then went to the offices of W. W. Jeffers & Sons.

Thornburgh had come in, I was told, on the tenth of May with $4,000 worth of Liberty bonds that he wanted sold. During one of his conversations with Jeffers, he had asked the broker to recommend a bank, and Jeffers had given him a letter of introduction to the Seamen's Bank.

That was all Jeffers knew about him. He gave me the numbers of the bonds, but tracing Liberty bonds isn't the easiest thing in the world.

The reply to my Seattle telegram was waiting for me at the Agency when I arrived.

MRS. EDWARD COMERFORD RENTED APARTMENT AT ADDRESS YOU GIVE ON MAY TWENTY-FIVE GAVE IT UP JUNE SIX TRUNKS TO SAN FRANCISCO SAME DAY CHECK NUMBERS GN FOUR FIVE TWO FIVE EIGHT SEVEN AND EIGHT AND NINE

Tracing baggage is no trick at all, if you have the dates and check numbers to start with—as many a bird who is wearing somewhat similar numbers on his chest and back, because he overlooked that detail when making his getaway, can tell you—and twenty-five minutes in a baggage-room at the Ferry and half an hour in the office of a transfer company gave me my answer.

The trunks had been delivered to Mrs. Evelyn Trowbridge's apartment!

I got Jim Tarr on the phone and told him about it.

"Good shooting!" he said, forgetting for once to indulge his wit. "We'll grab the Coonses here and Mrs. Trowbridge there, and that's the end of another mystery."

"Wait a minute!" I cautioned him. "It's not all straightened out yet! There's still a few kinks in the plot."

"It's straight enough for me. I'm satisfied."

"You're the boss, but I think you're being a little hasty. I'm going up and talk with the niece again. Give me a little time before you phone the police here to make the pinch. I'll hold her until they get there."

Evelyn Trowbridge let me in this time, instead of the maid who had opened the door for me in the morning, and she led me to the same room in which we had had our first talk. I let her pick out a seat, and then I selected one that was closer to either door than hers was.

On the way up I had planned a lot of innocent-sounding questions that would get her all snarled up; but after taking a good look at this woman sitting in front of me, leaning comfortably back in her chair, coolly waiting for me to speak my piece, I discarded the trick stuff and came out cold-turkey.

"Ever use the name Mrs. Edward Comerford?"

"Oh, yes." As casual as a nod on the street.

"When?"

"Often. You see, I happen to have been married not so long ago to Mr. Edward Comerford. So it's not really strange that I should have used the name."

"Use it in Seattle recently?"

"I would suggest," she said sweetly, "that if you are leading up to the references I gave Coons and his wife, you might save time by coming right to it?"

"That's fair enough," I said. "Let's do that."

There wasn't a half-tone, a shading, in voice, manner, or expression to indicate that she was talking about anything half so serious or important to her as a possibility of being charged with murder. She might have been talking about the weather, or a book that hadn't interested her particularly.

"During the time that Mr. Comerford and I were married, we lived in Seattle, where he still lives. After the divorce, I left Seattle and resumed my maiden name. And the Coonses *were* in our employ, as you might learn if you care to look it up. You'll find my husband—or former husband—at the Chelsea apartments, I think.

"Last summer, or late spring, I decided to return to Seattle. The truth of it is—I suppose all my personal affairs will be aired anyhow—that I thought perhaps Edward and I might patch up our differences; so I went back and took an apartment on Woodmansee Terrace. As I was known in Seattle as Mrs. Edward Comerford, and as I thought my using his name might influence him a little, perhaps, I used it while I was there.

"Also I telephoned the Coonses to make tentative arrangements in case Edward and I should open our house again; but Coons told me that they were going to California, and so I gladly gave them an excellent recommendation when, some days later, I received a letter of inquiry from an employment bureau in Sacramento. After I had been in Seattle for about two weeks, I changed my mind about the reconciliation— Edward's interest, I learned, was all centered elsewhere; so I returned to San Francisco."

"Very nice! But—"

"If you will permit me to finish," she interrupted. "When I went to see my uncle in response to his telegram, I was surprised to find the Coonses in his house. Knowing my uncle's peculiarities, and finding them now increased, and remembering his extreme secretiveness about his mysterious invention, I cautioned the Coonses not to tell him that they had been in my employ.

"He certainly would have discharged them, and just as certainly would have quarreled with me—he would have thought that I was having him spied upon. Then, when Coons telephoned me after the fire, I knew that to admit that the Coonses had been formerly in my employ, would, in view of the fact that I was my uncle's heir, cast suspicion on all three of us. So we foolishly agreed to say nothing about it and carry on the deception."

That didn't sound all wrong, but it didn't sound all right. I wished Tarr had taken it easier and let us get a better line on these people, before having them thrown in the coop.

"The coincidence of the Coonses stumbling into my uncle's house is, I fancy, too much for your detecting instincts," she went on, as I didn't say anything. "Am I to consider myself under arrest?"

I'm beginning to like this girl; she's a nice, cool piece of work.

"Not yet," I told her. "But I'm afraid it's going to happen pretty soon."

She smiled a little mocking smile at that, and another when the door-bell rang.

It was O'Hara from police headquarters. We turned the apartment upside down and inside out, but didn't find anything of importance except the will she had told me about, dated July eighth, and her uncle's life insurance policies. They were all dated between May fifteenth and June tenth, and added up to a little more than $200,000.

I spent an hour grilling the maid after O'Hara had taken Evelyn Trowbridge away, but she didn't know any more than I did. However, between her, the janitor, the manager of the apartments, and the names Mrs. Trowbridge had given me, I learned that she had really been entertaining friends on the night of the fire—until after eleven o'clock, anyway—and that was late enough.

Half an hour later I was riding the Short Line back to Sacramento. I was getting to be one of the line's best customers, and my anatomy was on bouncing terms with every bump in the road; and the bumps, as "Rubberhead" Davis used to say about the flies and mosquitoes in Alberta in summer, "is freely plentiful."

Between bumps I tried to fit the pieces of this Thornburgh puzzle together. The niece and the Coonses fit in somewhere, but not just where we had them. We had been working on the job sort of lop-sided, but it was the best we could do with it. In the beginning we had turned to the Coonses and Evelyn Trowbridge because there was no other direction to go; and now we had something on them—but a good lawyer could make hash of our case against them.

The Coonses were in the county jail when I got to Sacramento. After some questioning they had admitted their connection with the niece, and had come through with stories that matched hers in every detail.

Tarr, McClump, and I sat around the sheriff's desk and argued.

"Those yarns are pipe-dreams," the sheriff said. "We got all three of 'em cold, and there's nothing else to it. They're as good as convicted of murder!"

McClump grinned derisively at his superior, and then turned to me.

"Go on! You tell him about the holes in his little case. He ain't your boss, and can't take it out on you later for being smarter than he is!"

Tarr glared from one of us to the other.

"Spill it, you wise guys!" he ordered.

"Our dope is," I told him, figuring that McClump's view of it was the same as mine, "that there's nothing to show that even Thornburgh knew he was going to buy that house before the tenth of June, and that the Coonses were in town looking for work on the second. And besides, it was only by luck that they got the jobs. The employment office sent two couples out there ahead of them."

"We'll take a chance on letting the jury figure that out."

"Yes? You'll also take a chance on them figuring out that Thornburgh, who seems to have been a nut all right, might have touched off the place himself! We've got something on these people, Jim, but not enough to go into court with them! How are you going to prove that when the Coonses were planted in Thornburgh's house—if you can even prove they were—they and the Trowbridge woman knew he was going to load up with insurance policies?"

The sheriff spat disgustedly.

"You guys are the limit! You run around in circles, digging up the dope on these people until you get enough to hang 'em, and then you run around hunting for outs! What the hell's the matter with you now?"

I answered him from half-way to the door—the pieces were beginning to fit together under my skull.

"Going to run some more circles! Come on, Mac!"

McClump and I held a conference on the fly, and then I got a machine from the nearest garage and headed for Tavender. We made time going out, and got there before the general store had closed for the night. The stuttering Philo separated himself from the two men with whom he had been talking Hiram Johnson, and followed me to the rear of the store.

"Do you keep an itemized list of the laundry you handle?"

"N-n-no; just the amounts."

"Let's look at Thornburgh's."

He produced a begrimed and rumpled account book and we picked out the weekly items I wanted: $2.60, $3.10, $2.25, and so on.

"Got the last batch of laundry here?"

"Y-yes," he said. "It j-just c-c-came out from the city t-to-day."

I tore open the bundle—some sheets, pillow-cases, table-cloths, towels, napkins; some feminine clothing; some shirts, collars, underwear, sox that were unmistakably Coons's. I thanked Philo while running back to my machine.

Back in Sacramento again, McClump was waiting for me at the garage where I had hired the car.

"Registered at the hotel on June fifteenth, rented the office on the sixteenth. I think he's in the hotel now," he greeted me.

We hurried around the block to the Garden Hotel.

"Mr. Handerson went out a minute or two ago," the night clerk told us. "He seemed to be in a hurry."

"Know where he keeps his car?"

"In the hotel garage around the corner."

We were within two pavements of the garage, when Handerson's automobile shot out and turned up the street.

"Oh, Mr. Handerson!" I cried, trying to keep my voice level and smooth.

He stepped on the gas and streaked away from us.

"Want him?" McClump asked; and, at my nod, stopped a passing roadster by the simple expedient of stepping in front of it.

We climbed aboard, McClump flashed his star at the bewildered driver, and pointed out Handerson's dwindling tail-light. After he had persuaded himself that he wasn't being boarded by a couple of bandits, the commandeered driver did his best, and we picked up Handerson's tail-light after two or three turnings, and closed in on him—though his machine was going at a good clip.

By the time we reached the outskirts of the city, we had crawled up to within safe shooting distance, and I sent a bullet over the fleeing man's head. Thus encouraged, he managed to get a little more speed out of his car; but we were definitely overhauling him now.

Just at the wrong minute Handerson decided to look over his shoulder at us—an unevenness in the road twisted his wheels—his machine swayed—skidded—went over on its side. Almost immediately, from the heart of the tangle, came a flash and a bullet moaned past my ear. Another. And then, while I was still hunting for something to shoot at in the pile of junk we were drawing down upon, McClump's ancient and battered revolver roared in my other ear.

Handerson was dead when we got to him—McClump's bullet had taken him over one eye.

McClump spoke to me over the body.

"I ain't an inquisitive sort of fellow, but I hope you don't mind telling me why I shot this lad."

"Because he was Thornburgh."

He didn't say anything for about five minutes. Then: "I reckon that's right. How'd you guess it?"

We were sitting beside the wreckage now, waiting for the police that we had sent our commandeered chauffeur to phone for.

"He had to be," I said, "when you think it all over. Funny we didn't hit on it before! All that stuff we were told about Thornburgh had a fishy sound. Whiskers and an unknown profession, immaculate and working on a mysterious invention, very secretive and born in San Francisco—where the fire wiped out all the old records—just the sort of fake that could be cooked up easily.

"Then nobody but the Coonses, Evelyn Trowbridge and Handerson ever saw him except between the tenth of May and the middle of June, when he bought the house. The Coonses and the Trowbridge woman were tied up together in this affair somehow, we knew—so that left only Handerson to consider. You had told me he came to Sacramento sometime early this summer—and the dates you got tonight show that he didn't come until after Thornburgh had bought his house. All right! Now compare Handerson with the descriptions we got of Thornburgh.

"Both are about the same size and age, and with the same color hair. The differences are all things that can be manufactured—clothes, a little sunburn, and a month's growth of beard, along with a little acting, would do the trick. Tonight

I went out to Tavender and took a look at the last batch of laundry, and there wasn't any that didn't fit the Coonses— and none of the bills all the way back were large enough for Thornburgh to have been as careful about his clothes as we were told he was."

"It must be great to be a detective!" McClump grinned as the police ambulance came up and began disgorging policemen. "I reckon somebody must have tipped Handerson off that I was asking about him this evening." And then, regretfully: "So we ain't going to hang them folks for murder after all."

"No, but we oughtn't have any trouble convicting them of arson plus conspiracy to defraud, and anything else that the Prosecuting Attorney can think up."

Slippery Fingers

"Y ou are already familiar, of course, with the particulars of my father's—ah—death?"

"The papers are full of it, and have been for three days," I said, "and I've read them; but I'll have to have the whole story first-hand."

"There isn't very much to tell."

This Frederick Grover was a short, slender man of something under thirty years, and dressed like a picture out of *Vanity Fair*. His almost girlish features and voice did nothing to make him more impressive, but I began to forget these things after a few minutes. He wasn't a sap. I knew that downtown, where he was rapidly building up a large and lively business in stocks and bonds without calling for too much help from his father's millions, he was considered a shrewd article; and I wasn't surprised later when Benny Forman, who ought to know, told me that Frederick Grover was the best poker player west of Chicago. He was a cool, well-balanced, quick-thinking little man.

"Father has lived here alone with the servants since mother's death, two years ago," he went on. "I am married, you know, and live in town. Last Saturday evening he dismissed Barton—Barton was his butler-valet, and had been with father for quite a few years—at a little after nine, saying that he did not want to be disturbed during the evening.

"Father was here in the library at the time, looking through some papers. The servants' rooms are in the rear, and none of the servants seem to have heard anything during the night.

"At seven-thirty the following morning—Sunday—Barton found father lying on the floor, just to the right of where you are sitting, dead, stabbed in the throat with the brass paper-knife that was always kept on the table here. The front door was ajar.

"The police found bloody finger-prints on the knife, the table, and the front door; but so far they have not found the man who left the prints, which is why I am employing your agency. The physician who came with the police placed the time of father's death at between eleven o'clock and midnight.

"Later, on Monday, we learned that father had drawn $10,000 in hundred-dollar bills from the bank Saturday morning. No trace of the money has been found. My fingerprints, as well as the servants', were compared with the ones found by the police, but there was no similarity. I think that is all."

"Do you know of any enemies your father had?"

He shook his head.

"I know of none, though he may have had them. You see, I really didn't know my father very well. He was a very reticent man and, until his retirement, about five years ago, he spent most of his time in South America, where most of his mining interests were. He may have had dozens of enemies, though Barton—who probably knew more about him than anyone—seems to know of no one who hated father enough to kill him."

"How about relatives?"

"I was his heir and only child, if that is what you are getting at. So far as I know he had no other living relatives."

"I'll talk to the servants," I said.

The maid and the cook could tell me nothing, and I learned very little more from Barton. He had been with Henry Grover since 1912, had been with him in Yunnan, Peru, Mexico, and Central America, but apparently he knew little or nothing of his master's business or acquaintances.

He said that Grover had not seemed excited or worried on the night of the murder, and that nearly every night Grover dismissed him at about the same time, with orders that he not be disturbed; so no importance was to be attached to that part of it. He knew of no one with whom Grover had communicated during the day, and he had not seen the money Grover had drawn from the bank.

I made a quick inspection of the house and grounds, not expecting to find anything; and I didn't. Half the jobs that come to a private detective are like this one: three or four days—and often as many weeks—have passed since the crime was committed. The police work on the job until they are stumped; then the injured party calls in a private sleuth, dumps him down on a trail that is old and cold and badly trampled, and expects— Oh, well! I picked out this way of making a living, so . . .

I looked through Grover's papers—he had a safe and a desk full of them—but didn't find anything to get excited about. They were mostly columns of figures.

"I'm going to send an accountant out here to go over your father's books," I told Frederick Grover. "Give him everything he asks for, and fix it up with the bank so they'll help him."

I caught a street-car and went back to town, called at Ned Root's office, and headed him out toward Grover's. Ned is a human adding machine with educated eyes, ears, and nose. He can spot a kink in a set of books farther than I can see the covers.

"Keep digging until you find something, Ned, and you can charge Grover whatever you like. Give me something to work on—quick!"

The murder had all the earmarks of one that had grown out of blackmail, though there was—there always is—a chance that it might have been something else. But it didn't look like the work of an enemy or a burglar: either of them would have packed his weapon with him, would not have trusted to finding it on the grounds. Of course, if Frederick Grover, or one of the servants, had killed Henry Grover . . . but the finger-prints said "No."

Just to play safe, I put in a few hours getting a line on Frederick. He had been at a ball on the night of the murder; he had never, so far as I could learn, quarreled with his father; his father was liberal with him, giving him everything he wanted; and Frederick was taking in more money in his brokerage office than he was spending. No motive for a murder appeared on the surface there.

At the city detective bureau I hunted up the police sleuths who had been assigned to the murder; Marty O'Hara and George Dean. It didn't take them long to tell me what they knew about it. Whoever had made the bloody finger-prints was not known to the police here: they had not found the prints in their files. The classifications had been broadcast to every large city in the country, but with no results so far.

A house four blocks from Grover's had been robbed on the night of the murder, and there was a slim chance that the same man *might* have been responsible for both jobs. But the burglary had occurred after one o'clock in the morning, which made the connection look not so good. A burglar who had killed a man, and perhaps picked up $10,000 in the bargain, wouldn't be likely to turn his hand to another job right away.

I looked at the paper-knife with which Grover had been killed, and at the photographs of the bloody prints, but they couldn't help me much just now. There seemed to be nothing to do but get out and dig around until I turned up something somewhere.

Then the door opened, and Joseph Clane was ushered into the room where O'Hara, Dean and I were talking.

Clane was a hard-bitten citizen, for all his prosperous look; fifty or fifty-five, I'd say, with eyes, mouth and jaw that held plenty of humor but none of what is sometimes called the milk of human kindness.

He was a big man, beefy, and all dressed up in a tight-fitting checkered suit, fawn-colored hat, patent-leather shoes with buff uppers, and the rest of the things that go with that sort of combination. He had a harsh voice that was as empty of expression as his hard red face, and he held his body stiffly, as if he was afraid the buttons on his too-tight clothes were about to pop off. Even his arms hung woodenly at his sides, with thick fingers that were lifelessly motionless.

He came right to the point. He had been a friend of the murdered man's, and thought that perhaps what he could tell us would be of value.

He had met Henry Grover—he called him "Henny"—in 1894, in Ontario, where Grover was working a claim: the gold mine that had started the murdered man along the road to wealth. Clane had been employed by Grover as foreman, and the two men had become close friends. A man named Denis Waldeman had a claim adjoining Grover's and a dispute had arisen over their boundaries. The dispute ran on for some time—the men coming to blows once or twice—but finally Grover seems to have triumphed, for Waldeman suddenly left the country.

Clane's idea was that if we could find Waldeman we might find Grover's murderer, for considerable money had been involved in the dispute, and Waldeman was "a mean cuss, for a fact," and not likely to have forgotten his defeat.

Clane and Grover had kept in touch with each other, corresponding or meeting at irregular intervals, but the murdered man had never said or written anything that would throw a light on his death. Clane, too, had given up mining, and now had a small string of race-horses which occupied all his time.

He was in the city for a rest between racing-meets, had arrived two days before the murder, but had been too busy with his own affairs—he had discharged his trainer and was trying to find another—to call upon his friend. Clane was staying at the Marquis hotel, and would be in the city for a week or ten days longer.

"How come you've waited three days before coming to tell us all this?" Dean asked him.

"I wasn't noways sure I had ought to do it. I wasn't never sure in my mind but what maybe Henny done for that fellow Waldeman—he disappeared sudden-like. And I didn't want to do nothing to dirty Henny's name. But finally I decided to do the right thing. And then there's another thing: you found some finger-prints in Henny's house, didn't you? The newspapers said so."

"We did."

"Well, I want you to take mine and match them up. I was out with a girl the night of the murder"—he leered suddenly, boastingly—"all night! And she's a good girl, got a husband and a lot of folks; and it wouldn't be right to drag her into this to prove that I wasn't in Henny's house when he was killed, in case you'd maybe think I killed him. So I thought I better come down here, tell you all about it, and get you to take my finger-prints, and have it all over with."

We went up to the identification bureau and had Clane's prints taken. They were not at all like the murderer's.

After we pumped Clane dry I went out and sent a telegram to our Toronto office, asking them to get a line on the Waldeman angle. Then I hunted up a couple of boys who eat, sleep, and breathe horse racing. They told me that Clane was well known in racing circles as the owner of a small string of near-horses that ran as irregularly as the stewards would permit.

At the Marquis hotel I got hold of the house detective, who is a helpful chap so long as his hand is kept greased. He verified my information about Clane's status in the sporting world, and told me that Clane had stayed at the hotel for several days at a time, off and on, within the past couple years.

He tried to trace Clane's telephone calls for me but—as usual when you want them—the records were jumbled. I arranged to have the girls on the switchboard listen in on any talking he did during the next few days.

Ned Root was waiting for me when I got down to the office the next morning. He had worked on Grover's accounts all night, and had found enough to give me a start. Within the past year—that was as far back as Ned had gone—Grover had drawn out of his bank-accounts nearly fifty thousand dollars that couldn't be accounted for; nearly fifty thousand exclusive of the ten thousand he had drawn the day of the murder. Ned gave me the amounts and the dates:

May 6, 1922,	$15,000
June 10,	5,000
August 1,	5,000
October 10,	10,000
January 3, 1923,	12,500

Forty-seven thousand, five hundred dollars! Somebody was getting fat off him!

The local managers of the telegraph companies raised the usual howl about respecting their patrons' privacy, but I got an order from the Prosecuting Attorney and put a clerk at work on the files of each office.

Then I went back to the Marquis hotel and looked at the old registers. Clane had been there from May 4th to 7th, and from October 8th to 15th last year. That checked off two of the dates upon which Grover had made his withdrawals.

I had to wait until nearly six o'clock for my information from the telegraph companies, but it was worth waiting for. On the third of last January Henry Grover had telegraphed $12,500 to Joseph Clane in San Diego. The clerks hadn't found anything on the other dates I had given them, but I wasn't at all dissatisfied. I had Joseph Clane fixed as the man who had been getting fat off Grover.

I sent Dick Foley—he is the Agency's shadow-ace—and Bob Teal—a youngster who will be a world-beater some day—over to Clane's hotel.

"Plant yourselves in the lobby," I told them. "I'll be over in a few minutes to talk to Clane, and I'll try to bring him down in the lobby where you can get a good look at him. Then I want him shadowed until he shows up at police head-quarters tomorrow. I want to know where he goes and who he talks to. And if he spends much time talking to any one person, or their conversation seems very important, I want one of you boys to trail the other man, to see who he is and what he does. If Clane tries to blow town, grab him and have him thrown in the can, but I don't think he will."

I gave Dick and Bob time enough to get themselves placed, and then went to the hotel. Clane was out, so I waited. He came in a little after eleven and I went up to his room with him. I didn't hem-and-haw, but came out cold-turkey:

"All the signs point to Grover's having been blackmailed. Do you know anything about it?"

"No," he said.

"Grover drew a lot of money out of his banks at different times. You got some of it, I know, and I suppose you got most of it. What about it?"

He didn't pretend to be insulted, or even surprised by my talk. He smiled a little grimly, maybe, but as if he thought it the most natural thing in the world—and it was, at that—for me to suspect him.

"I told you that me and Henny were pretty chummy, didn't I? Well, you ought to know that all us fellows that fool with the bang-tails have our streaks of bad luck. Whenever I'd get up against it I'd hit Henny up for a stake; like at Tiajuana last winter where I got into a flock of bad breaks. Henny lent me twelve or fifteen thousand and I got back on my feet again. I've done that often. He ought to have some of my let-ters and wires in his stuff. If you look through his things you'll find them."

I didn't pretend that I believed him.

"Suppose you drop into police headquarters at nine in the morning and we'll go over everything with the city dicks," I told him.

And then, to make my play stronger:

"I wouldn't make it much later than nine—they might be out looking for you."

"Uh-huh," was all the answer I got.

I went back to the Agency and planted myself within reach of a telephone, waiting for word from Dick and Bob. I thought I was sitting pretty. Clane had been blackmailing Grover—I didn't have a single doubt of that—and I didn't think he had been very far away when Grover was killed. That woman alibi of his sounded all wrong!

But the bloody finger-prints were not Clane's—unless the police identification bureau had pulled an awful boner—and the man who had left the prints was the bird I was setting my cap for. Clane had let three days pass between the murder and his appearance at headquarters. The natural explanation for that would be that his partner, the actual murderer, had needed nearly that much time to put himself in the clear.

My present game was simple: I had stirred Clane up with the knowledge that he was still suspected, hoping that he would have to repeat whatever precautions were necessary to protect his accomplice in the first place.

He had taken three days then. I was giving him about nine hours now: time enough to do something, but not too much time, hoping that he would have to hurry things along and that in his haste he would give Dick and Bob a chance to turn up his partner: the owner of the fingers that had smeared blood on the knife, the table, and the door.

At a quarter to one in the morning Dick telephoned that Clane had left the hotel a few minutes behind me, had gone to an apartment house on Polk Street, and was still there.

I went up to Polk Street and joined Dick and Bob. They told me that Clane had gone in apartment number 27, and that the directory in the vestibule showed this apartment was occupied by George Farr. I stuck around with the boys until about two o'clock, when I went home for some sleep.

At seven I was with them again, and was told that our man had not appeared yet. It was a little after eight when he came out and turned down Geary Street, with the boys trailing him, while I went into the apartment house for a talk with the manager. She told me that Farr had been living there for four or five months, lived alone, and was a photographer by trade, with a studio on Market Street.

I went up and rang his bell. He was a husky of thirty or thirty-two with bleary eyes that looked as if they hadn't had much sleep that night. I didn't waste any time with him.

"I'm from the Continental Detective Agency and I am interested in Joseph Clane. What do you know about him?"

He was wide awake now.

"Nothing."

"Nothing at all?"

"No," sullenly.

"Do you know him?"

"No."

What can you do with a bird like that?

"Farr," I said, "I want you to go down to headquarters with me."

He moved like a streak and his sullen manner had me a little off my guard; but I turned my head in time to take the punch above my ear instead of on the chin. At that, it carried me off my feet and I wouldn't have bet a nickel that my skull wasn't dented; but luck was with me and I fell across the doorway, holding the door open, and managed to scramble up, stumble through some rooms, and catch one of his feet as it was going through the bathroom window to join its mate on the fire-escape. I got a split lip and a kicked shoulder in the scuffle, but he behaved after a while.

I didn't stop to look at his stuff—that could be done more regularly later—but put him in a taxicab and took him to the Hall of Justice. I was afraid that if I waited too long Clane would take a run-out on me.

Clane's mouth fell open when he saw Farr, but neither of them said anything.

I was feeling pretty chirp in spite of my bruises.

"Let's get this bird's finger-prints and get it over with," I said to O'Hara.

Dean was not in.

"And keep an eye on Clane. I think maybe he'll have another story to tell us in a few minutes."

We got in the elevator and took our men up to the identification bureau, where we put Farr's fingers on the pad. Phels—he is the department's expert—took one look at the results and turned to me.

"Well, what of it?"

"What of what?" I asked.

"This isn't the man who killed Henry Grover!"

Clane laughed, Farr laughed, O'Hara laughed, and Phels laughed. I didn't! I stood there and pretended to be thinking, trying to get myself in hand.

"Are you sure you haven't made a mistake?" I blurted, my face a nice, rosy red.

You can tell how badly upset I was by that: it's plain suicide to say a thing like that to a finger-print expert!

Phels didn't answer; just looked me up and down.

Clane laughed again, like a crow cawing, and turned his ugly face to me.

"Do you want to take my prints again, Mr. Slick Private Detective?"

"Yeah," I said, "just that!"

I had to say something.

Clane held his hands out to Phels, who ignored them, speaking to me with heavy sarcasm.

"Better take them yourself this time, so you'll be sure it's been done right."

I was mad clean through—of course it was my own fault—but I was pig-headed enough to go through with anything, particularly anything that would hurt somebody's feelings; so I said:

"That's not a bad idea!"

I walked over and took hold of one of Clane's hands. I'd never taken a finger-print before, but I had seen it done often enough to throw a bluff. I started to ink Clane's fingers and found that I was holding them wrong—my own fingers were in the way.

Then I came back to earth. The balls of Clane's fingers were too smooth—or rather, too slick—without the slight clinging feeling that belongs to flesh. I turned his hand over so fast that I nearly upset him and looked at the fingers. I don't know what I had expected to find but I didn't find anything—not anything that I could name.

"Phels," I called, "look here!"

He forgot his injured feelings and bent to look at Clane's hand.

"I'll be—" he began, and then the two of us were busy for a few minutes taking Clane down and sitting on him, while O'Hara quieted Farr, who had also gone suddenly into action.

When things were peaceful again Phels examined Clane's hands carefully, scratching the fingers with a finger-nail.

He jumped up, leaving me to hold Clane, and paying no attention to my, "What is it?" got a cloth and some liquid, and washed the fingers thoroughly. We took his prints again. They matched the bloody ones taken from Grover's house!

Then we all sat down and had a nice talk.

"I told you about the trouble Henny had with that fellow Waldeman," Clane began, after he and Farr had decided to come clean: there was nothing else they could do. "And how he won out in the argument because Waldeman disappeared. Well, Henny done for him—shot him one night and buried him—and I saw it. Grover was one bad actor in them days, a tough *hombre* to tangle with, so I didn't try to make nothing out of what I knew.

"But after he got older and richer he got soft—a lot of men go like that—and must have begun worrying over it; because when I ran into him in New York accidentally about four years ago it didn't take me long to learn that he was pretty well tamed, and he told me that he hadn't been able to forget the look on Waldeman's face when he drilled him.

"So I took a chance and braced Henny for a couple thousand. I got them easy, and after that, whenever I was flat I either went to him or sent him word, and he always came across. But I was careful not to crowd him too far. I knew what a terror he was in the old days, and I didn't want to push him into busting loose again.

"But that's what I did in the end. I 'phoned him Friday that I needed money and he said he'd call me up and let me know where to meet him the next night. He called up around half past nine Saturday night and told me to come out to the house. So I went out there and he was waiting for me on the porch and took me upstairs and gave me the ten thousand. I told him this was the last time I'd ever bother him—I always told him that—it had a good effect on him.

"Naturally I wanted to get away as soon as I had the money but he must have felt sort of talkative for a change, because he kept me there for half an hour or so, gassing about men we used to know up in the province.

"After awhile I began to get nervous. He was getting a look in his eyes like he used to have when he was young. And then all of a sudden he flared up and tied into me. He had me by the throat and was bending me back across the table when my hand touched that brass knife. It was either me or him—so I let him have it where it would do the most good.

"I beat it then and went back to the hotel. The newspapers were full of it next day, and had a whole lot of stuff about bloody finger-prints. That gave me a jolt! I didn't know nothing about finger-prints, and here I'd left them all over the dump.

"And then I got to worrying over the whole thing, and it seemed like Henny must have my name written down somewheres among his papers, and maybe had saved some of my letters or telegrams—though *they* were wrote in careful enough language. Anyway I figured the police would want to be asking me some questions sooner or later; and there I'd be with fingers that fit the bloody prints, and nothing for what Farr calls a alibi.

"That's when I thought of Farr. I had his address and I knew he had been a finger-print sharp in the East, so I decided to take a chance on him. I went to him and told him the whole story and between us we figured out what to do.

"He said he'd dope my fingers, and I was to come here and tell the story we'd fixed up, and have my finger-prints taken, and then I'd be safe no matter what leaked out about me and Henny. So he smeared up the fingers and told me to be careful not to shake hands with anybody or touch anything, and I came down here and everything went like three of a kind.

"Then that little fat guy"—meaning me—"came around to the hotel last night and as good as told me that he thought I had done for Henny and that I better come down here this morning. I beat it for Farr's right away to see whether I ought to run for it or sit tight, and Farr said, 'Sit tight!' So I stayed there all night and he fixed up my hands this morning. That's my yarn!"

Phels turned to Farr.

"I've seen faked prints before, but never any this good. How'd you do it?"

These scientific birds are funny. Here was Farr looking a nice, long stretch in the face as "accessory after the fact," and yet he brightened up under the admiration in Phel's tone and answered with a voice that was chock-full of pride.

"It's simple! I got hold of a man whose prints I knew weren't in any police gallery—I didn't want any slip up there—and took his prints and put them on a copper plate, using the ordinary photo-engraving process, but etching it pretty deep. Then I coated Clane's fingers with gelatin—just enough to cover all his markings—and pressed them against the plates. That way I got everything, even to the pores, and . . ."

When I left the bureau ten minutes later Farr and Phels were still sitting knee to knee, jabbering away at each other as only a couple of birds who are cuckoo on the same subject can.

Crooked Souls

H ARVEY GATEWOOD had issued orders that I was to be admitted as soon as I arrived, so it only took me a little less than fifteen minutes to thread my way past the door-keepers, office boys, and secretaries who filled up most of the space between the Gatewood Lumber Corporation's front door and the president's private office. His office was large, all mahogany and bronze and green plush, with a mahogany desk as big as a bed in the center of the floor.

Gatewood, leaning across the desk, began to bark at me as soon as the obsequious clerk who had bowed me in bowed himself out.

"My daughter was kidnapped last night! I want the . . . that did it if it takes every cent I got!"

"Tell me about it," I suggested, drawing up the chair that he hadn't thought to offer me.

But he wanted results, it seemed, and not questions, and so I wasted nearly an hour getting information that he could have given me in fifteen minutes.

He's a big bruiser of a man, something over two hundred pounds of hard red flesh, and a czar from the top of his bullet head to the toes of his shoes that would have been at least number twelves if they hadn't been made to measure.

He had made his several millions by sandbagging everybody that stood in his way, and the rage that he's burning up with now doesn't make him any easier to deal with.

His wicked jaw is sticking out like a knob of granite and his eyes are filmed with blood—he's in a lovely frame of mind. For a while it looks as if the Continental Detective Agency is going to lose a client; because I've made up my mind that he's going to tell me all I want to know, or I'm going to chuck up the job. But finally I got the story out of him.

His daughter Audrey had left their house on Clay street at about seven o'clock the preceding evening, telling her maid that she was going for a walk. She had not returned that night—though Gatewood had not known that until after he had read the letter that came this morning.

The letter had been from someone who said that she had been kidnapped. It demanded fifty thousand dollars for her release; and instructed Gatewood to get the money ready in hundred dollar bills, so that there might be no delay when he is told in what manner it is to be paid over to his daughter's captors. As proof that the demand was not a hoax, a lock of the girl's hair, a ring she always wore, and a brief note from her, asking her father to comply with the demands, had been enclosed.

Gatewood had received the letter at his office, and had telephoned to his house immediately. He had been told that the girl's bed had not been slept in the previous night, and that none of the servants had seen her since she started out for her walk. He had then notified the police, turning the letter over to them; and, a few minutes later, he had decided to employ private detectives also.

"Now," he burst out, after I had wormed these things out of him, and he had told me that he knew nothing of his daughter's associates or habits, "go ahead and do something! I'm not paying you to sit around and talk about it!"

"What are you going to do?" I asked.

"Me? I'm going to put those . . . behind the bars if it takes every cent I've got in the world!"

"Sure! But first you can get that fifty thousand ready, so you can give it to them when they ask for it."

He clicked his jaw shut and thrust his face into mine.

"I've never been clubbed into doing anything in my life! And I'm too old to start now!" he said. "I'm going to call these people's bluff!"

"That's going to make it lovely for your daughter. But, aside from what it'll do to her, it's the wrong play. Fifty thousand isn't a whole lot to you, and paying it over will give us two chances that we haven't got now. One when the payment is made—a chance to either nab whoever comes for it or get a line on them. And the other when your daughter is returned. No matter how careful they are it's a cinch that she'll be able to tell us something that will help us grab them."

He shook his head angrily, and I was tired of arguing with him. So I left him, hoping that he'd see the wisdom of the course I had advised before too late.

At the Gatewood residence I found butlers, second men, chauffeurs, cooks, maids, upstairs girls, downstairs girls, and a raft of miscellaneous flunkies—he had enough servants to run a hotel.

What they told me amounted to this: The girl had not received a phone call, note by messenger, or telegram—the time-honored devices for luring a victim out to a murder or abduction—before she left the house. She had told her maid that she would be back within an hour or two; but the maid had not been alarmed when her mistress failed to return all that night.

Audrey was the only child, and since her mother's death she had come and gone to suit herself. She and her father didn't hit it off very well together—their natures were too much alike, I gathered—and he never knew where she was; and there was nothing unusual about her remaining away all night, as she seldom bothered to leave word when she was going to stay overnight with friends.

She was nineteen years old, but looked several years older; about five feet five inches tall, and slender. She had blue eyes, brown hair,—very thick and long,—was pale and very nervous. Her photographs, of which I took a handful, showed that her eyes were large, her nose small and regular, and her chin obstinately pointed.

She was not beautiful, but in the one photograph where a smile had wiped off the sullenness of her mouth, she was at least pretty.

When she left the house she had worn a light tweed skirt and jacket with a London tailor's labels in them, a buff silk shirtwaist with stripes a shade darker, brown wool stockings, low-heeled brown oxfords, and an untrimmed grey felt hat.

I went up to her rooms—she had three on the third floor—and looked through all her stuff. I found nearly a bushel of photographs of men, boys, and girls; and a great stack of letters of varying degrees of intimacy, signed with a wide assortment of names and nicknames. I made notes of all the addresses I found.

Nothing there seemed to have any bearing on her abduction, but there was a chance that one of the names and addresses might be of someone who had served as a decoy. Also, some of her friends might be able to tell us something of value.

I dropped in at the Agency and distributed the names and addresses among the three operatives who were idle, sending them out to see what they could dig up.

Then I reached the police detectives who were working on the case—O'Gar and Thode—by telephone, and went down to the Hall of Justice to meet them. Lusk, a post office inspector, was also there. We turned the job around and around, looking at it from every angle, but not getting very far. We were all agreed, however, that we couldn't take a chance on any publicity, or work in the open, until the girl was safe.

They had had a worse time with Gatewood than I—he had wanted to put the whole thing in the newspapers, with the offer of a reward, photographs and all. Of course, Gatewood was right in claiming that this was the most effective way of catching the kidnappers—but it would have been tough on his daughter if her captors happened to be persons of sufficiently hardened character. And kidnappers as a rule aren't lambs.

I looked at the letter they had sent. It was printed with pencil on ruled paper of the kind that is sold in pads by every stationery dealer in the world. The envelope was just as common, also addressed in pencil, and post-marked "San Francisco, September 20, 9 P.M." That was the night she had been seized.

The letter reads:

"SIR:

WE HAVE YOUR CHARMING DAUGHTER AND PLACE A VALUE OF $50,000 UPON HER. YOU WILL GET THE MONEY READY IN $100 BILLS AT ONCE SO THERE WILL BE NO DELAY WHEN WE TELL YOU HOW IT IS TO BE PAID OVER TO US.

WE BEG TO ASSURE YOU THAT THINGS WILL GO BADLY WITH YOUR DAUGHTER SHOULD YOU NOT DO AS YOU ARE TOLD, OR SHOULD YOU BRING THE POLICE INTO THIS MATTER, OR SHOULD YOU DO ANYTHING FOOLISH.

$50,000 IS ONLY A SMALL FRACTION OF WHAT YOU STOLE WHILE WE WERE LIVING IN MUD AND BLOOD IN

FRANCE FOR YOU, AND WE MEAN TO GET THAT MUCH
OR . . . . !

> THREE."

A peculiar note in several ways. They are usually written
with a great pretense of partial illiterateness. Almost always
there's an attempt to lead suspicion astray. Perhaps the ex-
service stuff was there for that purpose . . . or perhaps not.
Then there was a postscript:

"WE KNOW A CHINAMAN WHO WILL BUY HER EVEN
AFTER WE ARE THROUGH WITH HER—IN CASE YOU
WON'T LISTEN TO REASON."

The letter from the girl was written jerkily on the same kind
of paper, apparently with the same pencil.

> "Daddy—
> Please do as they ask! I am so afraid—
> Audrey"

A door at the other end of the room opened, and a head
came through.

"O'Gar! Thode! Gatewood just called up. Get up to his office right away!"

The four of us tumbled out of the Hall of Justice and into
a machine.

Gatewood was pacing his office like a maniac when we
pushed aside enough hirelings to get to him. His face was hot
with blood and his eyes had an insane glare in them.

"She just phoned me!" he cried thickly, when he saw us.

It took a minute or two to get him calm enough to tell us
about it.

"She called me on the phone. Said, 'Oh, daddy! Do something! I can't stand this—they're killing me!' I asked her if
she knew where she was, and she said, 'No, but I can see
Twin Peaks from here. There's three men and a woman,
and—' And then I heard a man curse, and a sound as if he
had struck her, and the phone went dead. I tried to get central to give me the number, but she couldn't! It's a damned
outrage the way the telephone system is run. We pay enough
for service, God knows, and we . . . ."

O'Gar scratched his head and turned away from Gatewood. "In sight of Twin Peaks! There are hundreds of houses that are!"

Gatewood meanwhile had finished denouncing the telephone company and was pounding on his desk with a paperweight to attract our attention.

"Have you people done anything at all?" he demanded.

I answered him with another question: "Have you got the money ready?"

"No," he said, "I won't be held up by anybody!"

But he said it mechanically, without his usual conviction—the talk with his daughter had shaken him out of some of his stubbornness. He was thinking of her safety a little now instead of altogether of his own fighting spirit.

We went at him hammer and tongs for a few minutes, and after a while he sent a clerk out for the money.

We split up the field then. Thode was to take some men from headquarters and see what he could find in the Twin Peaks end of town; but we weren't very optimistic over the prospects there—the territory was too large.

Lusk and O'Gar were to carefully mark the bills that the clerk brought from the bank, and then stick as close to Gatewood as they could without attracting attention. I was to go out to Gatewood's house and stay there.

The abductors had plainly instructed Gatewood to get the money ready immediately so that they could arrange to get it on short notice—not giving him time to communicate with anyone or make any plans.

Gatewood was to get hold of the newspapers, give them the whole story, with the $10,000 reward he was offering for the abductors' capture, to be published as soon as the girl was safe—so that we would get the help of publicity at the earliest moment possible without jeopardizing the girl.

The police in all the neighboring towns had already been notified—that had been done before the girl's phone message had assured us that she was held in San Francisco.

Nothing happened at the Gatewood residence all that evening. Harvey Gatewood came home early; and after dinner he paced his library floor and drank whiskey until bedtime, demanding every few minutes that we, the detectives in the case, do something besides sit around like a lot of damned mummies. O'Gar, Lusk and Thode were out in the street, keeping an eye on the house and neighborhood.

At midnight Harvey Gatewood went to bed. I declined a bed in favor of the library couch, which I dragged over beside the telephone, an extension of which was in Gatewood's bedroom.

At two-thirty the bell rang. I listened in while Gatewood talked from his bed.

A man's voice, crisp and curt: "Gatewood?"

"Yes."

"Got the dough?"

"Yes."

Gatewood's voice was thick and blurred—I could imagine the boiling that was going on inside him.

"Good!" came the brisk voice. "Put a piece of paper around it, and leave the house with it, right away! Walk down Clay street, keeping on the same side as your house. Don't walk too fast and keep walking. If everything's all right, and there's no elbows tagging along, somebody'll come up to you between your house and the water-front. They'll have a handkerchief up to their face for a second, and then they'll let it fall to the ground.

"When you see that, you'll lay the money on the pavement, turn around and walk back to your house. If the money isn't marked, and you don't try any fancy tricks, you'll get your daughter back in an hour or two. If you try to pull anything—remember what we wrote you about the Chink! Got it straight?"

Gatewood sputtered something that was meant for an affirmative, and the telephone clicked silent.

I didn't waste any of my precious time tracing the call—it would be from a public telephone, I knew—but yelled up the stairs to Gatewood:

"You do as you were told, and don't try any foolishness!"

Then I ran out into the early morning air to find the police detectives and the post office inspector.

They had been joined by two plainclothes men, and had two automobiles waiting. I told them what the situation was, and we laid hurried plans.

O'Gar was to drive in one of the machines down Sacramento street, and Thode, in the other, down Washington street. These streets parallel Clay, one on each side. They were to drive slowly, keeping pace with Gatewood, and stopping at each cross street to see that he passed.

When he failed to cross within a reasonable time they were to turn up to Clay street—and their actions from then on would have to be guided by chance and their own wits.

Lusk was to wander along a block or two ahead of Gatewood, on the opposite side of the street, pretending to be mildly intoxicated, and keeping his eyes and ears open.

I was to shadow Gatewood down the street, with one of the plainclothes men behind me. The other plainclothes man was to turn in a call at headquarters for every available man to be sent to Clay street. They would arrive too late, of course, and as likely as not it would take them some time to find us; but we had no way of knowing what was going to turn up before the night was over.

Our plan was sketchy enough, but it was the best we could do—we were afraid to grab whoever got the money from Gatewood. The girl's talk with her father that afternoon had sounded too much as if her captors were desperate for us to take any chances on going after them rough-shod until she was out of their hands.

We had hardly finished our plans when Gatewood, wearing a heavy overcoat, left his house and turned down the street.

Farther down, Lusk, weaving along, talking to himself, was almost invisible in the shadows. There was no one else in sight. That meant that I had to give Gatewood at least two blocks' lead, so that the man who came for the money wouldn't tumble to me. One of the plainclothes men was half a block behind me, on the other side of the street.

Two blocks down we walked, and then a little chunky man in a derby hat came into sight. He passed Gatewood, passed me, went on.

Three blocks more.

A touring-car, large, black, powerfully engined, and with lowered curtains, came from the rear, passed us, went on. Possibly a scout! I scrawled its license number down on my pad without taking my hand out of my overcoat pocket.

Another three blocks.

A policeman passed, strolling along in ignorance of the game being played under his nose; and then a taxicab with a single male passenger. I wrote down its license number.

Four blocks with no one in sight ahead of me but Gatewood—I couldn't see Lusk any more.

Just ahead of Gatewood a man stepped out of a black door-way—turned around—called up to a window for someone to come down and open the door for him.

We went on.

Coming from nowhere, a woman stood on the sidewalk fifty feet ahead of Gatewood, a handkerchief to her face. It fluttered to the pavement.

Gatewood stopped, standing stiff-legged. I could see his right hand come up, lifting the side of the overcoat in which it was pocketed—and I knew the hand was gripped around a pistol.

For perhaps half a minute he stood like a statue. Then his left hand came out of his pocket, and the bundle of money fell to the sidewalk in front of him, where it made a bright blur in the darkness. Gatewood turned abruptly, and began to retrace his steps homeward.

The woman had recovered her handkerchief. Now she ran to the bundle, picked it up, and scuttled to the black mouth of an alley, a few feet distant—a rather tall woman, bent, and in dark clothes from head to feet.

In the black mouth of the alley she vanished.

I had been compelled to slow up while Gatewood and the woman stood facing each other, and I was more than a block away now. As soon as the woman disappeared I took a chance, and started pounding my rubber soles against the pavement.

The alley was empty when I reached it.

It ran all the way through to the next street, but I knew that the woman couldn't have reached the other end before I got to this one. I carry a lot of weight these days, but I can still step a block or two in good time. Along both sides of the alley were the rears of apartment buildings, each with its back door looking blankly, secretively at me.

The plainclothes man who had been trailing behind me came up, then O'Gar and Thode in their machines, and soon,

Lusk. O'Gar and Thode rode off immediately to wind through the neighboring streets, hunting for the woman. Lusk and the plainclothes man each planted himself on a corner from which two of the streets enclosing the block could be watched.

I went through the alley, hunting vainly for an unlocked door, an open window, a fire-escape that would show recent use—any of the signs that a hurried departure from the alley might leave.

Nothing!

O'Gar came back shortly with some reinforcements from headquarters that he had picked up, and Gatewood.

Gatewood was burning.

"Bungled the damn thing again! I won't pay your agency a nickel, and I'll see that some of these so-called detectives get put back in a uniform and set to walking beats!"

"What'd the woman look like?" I asked him.

"I don't know! I thought you were hanging around to take care of her! She was old and bent, kind of, I guess, but I couldn't see her face for her veil. I don't know! What the hell were you men doing? It's a damned outrage the way . . ."

I finally got him quieted down and took him home, leaving the city men to keep the neighborhood under surveillance. There was fourteen or fifteen of them on the job now, and every shadow held at least one.

The girl would naturally head for home as soon as she was released and I wanted to be there to pump her. There was an excellent chance of catching her abductors before they got very far if she could tell us anything at all about them.

Home, Gatewood went up against the whiskey bottle again, while I kept one ear cocked at the telephone and the other at the front door. O'Gar or Thode phoned every half hour or so to ask if we'd heard from the girl. They had still found nothing.

At nine o'clock they, with Lusk, arrived at the house. The woman in black had turned out to be a man, and had gotten away.

In the rear of one of the apartment buildings that touched the alley—just a foot or so within the back-door—they found a woman's skirt, long coat, hat and veil—all black. Investigating the occupants of the house, they had learned that an apartment had been rented to a young man named Leighton three days before.

Leighton was not at home when they went up to his apartment. His rooms held a lot of cold cigarette butts, and an empty bottle, and nothing else that had not been there when he rented it.

The inference was clear: he had rented the apartment so that he might have access to the building. Wearing woman's clothes over his own, he had gone out of the back door—leaving it unlatched behind him—to meet Gatewood.

Then he had run back into the building, discarded his disguise, and hurried through the building, out the front door, and away before we had our feeble net around the block; perhaps dodging into dark doorways here and there to avoid O'Gar and Thode in their automobiles.

Leighton, it seemed, was a man of about thirty, slender, about five feet eight or nine inches tall, with dark hair and eyes; rather good-looking, and well-dressed, on the two occasions when people living in the building had seen him, in a brown suit and a light brown felt hat.

There was no possibility, according to the opinions of both of the detectives and the post office inspector, that the girl might have been held, even temporarily, in Leighton's apartment.

Ten o'clock came, and no word from the girl.

Gatewood had lost his domineering bull-headedness by now and was breaking up. The suspense was getting him, and the liquor he had put away wasn't helping him. I didn't like him either personally or by reputation, but at that I felt sorry for him this morning.

I talked to the agency over the phone and got the reports of the operatives who had been looking up Audrey's friends. The last person to see her had been an Agnes Dangerfield, who had seen her walking down Market street near Sixth, alone, on the night of her abduction—some time between 8:15 and 8:45. Audrey had been too far away for the Dangerfield girl to speak to her.

For the rest, the boys had learned nothing except that Audrey was a wild, spoiled youngster who hadn't shown any great care in selecting her friends—just the sort of girl who could easily fall into the hands of a mob of highbinders!

Noon struck. No sign of the girl. We told the newspapers to turn loose the story, with the added developments of the past few hours.

Gatewood was broken; he sat with his head in his hands, looking at nothing. Just before I left to follow a hunch I had, he looked up at me, and I'd never have recognized him if I hadn't seen the change take place.

"What do you think is keeping her away?" he asked.

I didn't have the heart to tell him what I was beginning to suspect, now that the money had been paid and she had failed to show up. So I stalled with some vague assurances, and left.

I caught a street-car and dropped off down in the shopping district. I visited the five largest department stores, going to all the women's wear departments from shoes to hats, and trying to learn if a man—perhaps one answering Leighton's description—had been buying clothes that would fit Audrey Gatewood within the past couple days.

Failing to get any results, I turned the rest of the local stores over to one of the boys from the agency, and went across the bay to canvass the Oakland stores.

At the first one I got action. A man who might easily have been Leighton had been in the day before, buying clothes that could easily fit Audrey. He had bought lots of them, everything from lingerie to a cloak, and—my luck was hitting on all its cylinders—had had his purchases delivered to T. Offord, at an address on Fourteenth street.

At the Fourteenth street address, an apartment house, I found Mr. and Mrs. Theodore Offord's names under the vestibule telephone for apartment 202.

I had just found them when the front door opened and a stout, middle-aged woman in a gingham house-dress came out. She looked at me a bit curiously, so I asked:

"Do you know where I can find the manager?"

"I'm the manager," she said.

I handed her a card and stepped indoors with her.

"I'm from the bonding department of the North American Casualty Company"—a repetition of the lie that was printed on the card I had given her—"and a bond for Mr. Offord has been applied for. Is he all right so far as you know?" With the slightly apologetic air of one going through with a necessary but not too important formality.

She frowned.

"A bond? That's funny! He is going away tomorrow."

"Well, I can't say what the bond is for," I said lightly. "We investigators just get the names and addresses. It may be for his present employer, or perhaps the man he is going to work for wherever he's going has applied for it. Or some firms have us look up prospective employees before they hire them, just to be safe."

"Mr. Offord, so far as I know, is a very nice young man," she said, "but he has been here only a week."

"Not staying long, then?"

"No. They came here from Denver, intending to stay, but the low altitude doesn't agree with Mrs. Offord, so they are going back."

"Are you sure they came from Denver?"

"Well," she said, "they told me they did."

"How many of them are there?"

"Only the two of them; they're young people."

"Well, how do they impress you?" I asked, trying to get the impression that I thought her a woman of shrewd judgment over.

"They seem to be a very nice young couple. You'd hardly know they were in their apartment most of the time, they are so quiet. I am sorry they can't stay."

"Do they go out much?"

"I really don't know. They have their keys, and unless I should happen to pass them going in or out I'd never see them."

"Then, as a matter of fact, you couldn't say whether they stayed away all night some nights or not. Could you?"

She eyed me doubtfully—I was stepping way over my pretext now, but I didn't think it mattered—and shook her head.

"No, I couldn't say."

"They have many visitors?"

"I don't know. Mr. Offord is not—"

She broke off as a man came in quietly from the street, brushed past me, and started to mount the steps to the second floor.

"Oh, dear!" she whispered. "I hope he didn't hear me talking about him. That's Mr. Offord."

A slender man in brown, with a light brown hat—Leighton perhaps.

I hadn't seen anything of him except his back, nor he anything except mine. I watched him as he climbed the stairs. If he had heard the manager mention his name he would use the turn at the head of the stairs to sneak a look at me.

He did. I kept my face stolid, but I knew him. He was "Penny" Quayle, a con man who had been active in the East four or five years before. His face was as expressionless as mine. But he knew me.

A door on the second floor shut. I left the manager and started for the stairs.

"I think I'll go up and talk to him," I told her.

Coming silently to the door of apartment 202, I listened. Not a sound. This was no time for hesitation. I pressed the bell-button.

As close together as the tapping of three keys under the fingers of an expert typist, but a thousand times more vicious, came three pistol shots. And waist-high in the door of apartment 202 were three bullet holes.

The three bullets would have been in my fat carcass if I hadn't learned years ago to stand to one side of strange doors when making uninvited calls.

Inside the apartment sounded a man's voice, sharp, commanding.

"Cut it, kid! For God's sake, not that!"

A woman's voice, shrill, bitter, spiteful screaming blasphemies.

Two more bullets came through the door.

"Stop! No! No!" The man's voice had a note of fear in it now.

The woman's voice, cursing hotly. A scuffle. A shot that didn't hit the door.

I hurled my foot against the door, near the knob, and the lock broke away.

On the floor of the room, a man—Quayle—and a woman were tussling. He was bending over her, holding her wrists, trying to keep her down. A smoking automatic pistol was in one of her hands. I got to it in a jump and tore it loose.

"That's enough!" I called to them when I was planted. "Get up and receive company."

Quayle released his antagonist's wrists, whereupon she struck at his eyes with curved, sharp-nailed fingers, tearing his cheek open. He scrambled away from her on hands and knees, and both of them got to their feet.

He sat down on a chair immediately, panting and wiping his bleeding cheek with a handkerchief.

She stood, hands on hips, in the center of the room, glaring at me.

"I suppose," she spat, "you think you've raised hell!"

I laughed—I could afford to.

"If your father is in his right mind," I told her, "he'll do it with a razor strop when he gets you home again. A fine joke you picked out to play on him!"

"If *you'd* been tied to him as long as I have, and had been bullied and held down as much, I guess *you'd* do most anything to get enough money so that you could go away and live your own life."

I didn't say anything to that. Remembering some of the business methods Harvey Gatewood had used—particularly some of his war contracts that the Department of Justice was still investigating—I suppose the worst that could be said about Audrey was that she was her father's own daughter.

"How'd you rap to it?" Quayle asked me, politely.

"Several ways," I said. "First, I'm a little doubtful about grown persons being kidnapped in cities. Maybe it really happens sometimes, but at least nine-tenths of the cases you hear about are fakes. Second, one of Audrey's friends saw her on Market street between 8:15 and 8:45 the night she disappeared; and your letter to Gatewood was post-marked 9 P.M. Pretty fast work. You should have waited a while before mailing it, even if it had to miss the first morning delivery. I suppose she dropped it in the post office on her way over here?"

Quayle nodded.

"Then third," I went on, "there was that phone call of hers. She knew it took anywhere from ten to fifteen minutes to get her father on the wire at the office. If time had been as valuable as it would have been if she had gotten to a phone while imprisoned, she'd have told her story to the first person she got hold of—the phone girl, most likely. So that made it look as if, besides wanting to throw out that Twin Peaks line, she wanted to stir the old man out of his bull-headedness.

"When she failed to show up after the money was paid I figured it was a sure bet that she had kidnapped herself. I knew that if she came back home after faking this thing we'd find it out before we'd talked to her very long—and I figured she knew that too, and would stay away.

"The rest was easy, as I got some good breaks. We knew a man was working with her after we found the woman's clothes you left behind, and I took a chance on there being no one else in it. Then I figured she'd need clothes—she couldn't have taken any from home without tipping her mitt—and there was an even chance that she hadn't laid in a stock beforehand. She's got too many girl friends of the sort that do a lot of shopping to make it safe for her risk showing herself in stores. Maybe, then, the man would buy what she needed for her. And it turned out that he did, and that he was too lazy to carry away his purchases, or perhaps there was too many of them, and so he had them sent out. That's the story."

Quayle nodded again.

"I was damned careless," he said, and then, jerking a contemptuous thumb toward the girl. "But what can you expect? She's had a skin full of hop ever since we started. Took all my time and attention keeping her from running wild and gumming the works. Just now was a sample—I told her you were coming up and she goes crazy and tries to add your corpse to the wreck!"

The Gatewood reunion took place in the office of the captain of inspectors, on the second floor of the Oakland City Hall, and it was a merry little party. For an hour it was a toss-up whether Harvey Gatewood would die of apoplexy, strangle his daughter, or send her off to the state reformatory until she was of age. But Audrey licked him. Besides being a chip off the old block, she was young enough to be careless of consequences, while her father, for all his bullheadedness, had had some caution hammered into him.

The card she beat him with was a threat of spilling everything she knew about him to the newspapers, and at least one of the San Francisco papers had been trying to get his scalp for years. I don't know what she had on him, and I don't think he was any too sure himself; but, with his war contracts even then being investigated by the Department of Justice, he couldn't afford to take a chance. There was no doubt at all that she would have done as she threatened.

And so, together, they left for home, sweating hate for each other at every pore.

We took Quayle upstairs and put him in a cell, but he was too experienced to let that worry him. He knew that if the girl was to be spared, he himself couldn't very easily be convicted of anything.

The Tenth Clew

CHAPTER I

"Do you know . . . Emil Bonfils?"

"M R. LEOPOLD GANTVOORT is not at home," the servant who opened the door said, "but his son, Mr. Charles, is—if you wish to see him."

"No. I had an appointment with Mr. Leopold Gantvoort for nine or a little after. It's just nine now. No doubt he'll be back soon. I'll wait."

"Very well, sir."

He stepped aside for me to enter the house, took my overcoat and hat, guided me to a room on the second floor—Gantvoort's library—and left me. I picked up a magazine from the stack on the table, pulled an ash tray over beside me, and made myself comfortable.

An hour passed. I stopped reading and began to grow impatient. Another hour passed—and I was fidgeting.

A clock somewhere below had begun to strike eleven when a young man of twenty-five or -six, tall and slender, with remarkably white skin and very dark hair and eyes, came into the room.

"My father hasn't returned yet," he said. "It's too bad that you should have been kept waiting all this time. Isn't there anything I could do for you? I am Charles Gantvoort."

"No, thank you." I got up from my chair, accepting the courteous dismissal. "I'll get in touch with him tomorrow."

"I'm sorry," he murmured, and we moved toward the door together.

As we reached the hall an extension telephone in one corner of the room we were leaving buzzed softly, and I halted in the doorway while Charles Gantvoort went over to answer it.

His back was toward me as he spoke into the instrument.

"Yes. Yes. Yes!"—sharply—"*What?* Yes"—very weakly—"Yes."

He turned slowly around and faced me with a face that was gray and tortured, with wide shocked eyes and gaping mouth—the telephone still in his hand.

"Father," he gasped, "is dead—killed!"

"Where? How?"

"I don't know. That was the police. They want me to come down at once."

He straightened his shoulders with an effort, pulling himself together, put down the telephone, and his face fell into less strained lines.

"You will pardon my—"

"Mr. Gantvoort," I interrupted his apology, "I am connected with the Continental Detective Agency. Your father called up this afternoon and asked that a detective be sent to see him tonight. He said his life had been threatened. He hadn't definitely engaged us, however, so unless you—"

"Certainly! You are employed! If the police haven't already caught the murderer I want you to do everything possible to catch him."

"All right! Let's get down to headquarters."

Neither of us spoke during the ride to the Hall of Justice. Gantvoort bent over the wheel of his car, sending it through the streets at a terrific speed. There were several questions that needed answers, but all his attention was required for his driving if he was to maintain the pace at which he was driving without piling us into something. So I didn't disturb him, but hung on and kept quiet.

Half a dozen police detectives were waiting for us when we reached the detective bureau. O'Gar—a bullet-headed detective-sergeant who dresses like the village constable in a movie, wide-brimmed black hat and all, but who isn't to be put out of the reckoning on that account—was in charge of the investigation. He and I had worked on two or three jobs together before, and hit it off excellently.

He led us into one of the small offices below the assembly room. Spread out on the flat top of a desk there were a dozen or more objects.

"I want you to look these things over carefully," the detective-sergeant told Gantvoort, "and pick out the ones that belonged to your father."

"But where is he?"

"Do this first," O'Gar insisted, "and then you can see him."

I looked at the things on the table while Charles Gantvoort made his selections. An empty jewel case; a memoranda book; three letters in slit envelopes that were addressed to the dead man; some other papers; a bunch of keys; a fountain pen; two white linen handkerchiefs; two pistol cartridges; a gold watch, with a gold knife and a gold pencil attached to it by a gold-and-platinum chain; two black leather wallets, one of them very new and the other worn; some money, both paper and silver; and a small portable typewriter, bent and twisted, and matted with hair and blood. Some of the other things were smeared with blood and some were clean.

Gantvoort picked out the watch and its attachments, the keys, the fountain pen, the memoranda book, the handkerchiefs, the letters and other papers, and the older wallet.

"These were father's," he told us. "I've never seen any of the others before. I don't know, of course, how much money he had with him tonight, so I can't say how much of this is his."

"You're sure none of the rest of this stuff was his?" O'Gar asked.

"I don't think so, but I'm not sure. Whipple could tell you." He turned to me. "He's the man who let you in tonight. He looked after father, and he'd know positively whether any of these other things belonged to him or not."

One of the police detectives went to the telephone to tell Whipple to come down immediately.

I resumed the questioning.

"Is anything that your father usually carried with him missing? Anything of value?"

"Not that I know of. All of the things that he might have been expected to have with him seem to be here."

"At what time tonight did he leave the house?"

"Before seven-thirty. Possibly as early as seven."

"Know where he was going?"

"He didn't tell me, but I supposed he was going to call on Miss Dexter."

The faces of the police detectives brightened, and their eyes grew sharp. I suppose mine did, too. There are many, many

actively engaged in the management of

village constable hat back and scratched his
tively for a moment. Then he looked at me.
se you want to ask?"

Gantvoort, do you know, or did you ever hear
or anyone else speak of an Emil Bonfils?"

our father ever tell you that he had received a threat-
tter? Or that he had been shot at on the street?"
o."

Vas your father in Paris in 1902?"

"Very likely. He used to go abroad every year up until the
ime of his retirement from business."

CHAPTER II

"That's Something!"

O'Gar and I took Gantvoort around to the morgue to see his
father, then. The dead man wasn't pleasant to look at, even to
O'Gar and me, who hadn't known him except by sight. I remembered him as a small wiry man, always smartly tailored,
and with a brisk springiness that was far younger than his
years.

He lay now with the top of his head beaten into a red and
pulpy mess.

We left Gantvoort at the morgue and set out afoot for the
Hall of Justice.

"What's this deep stuff you're pulling about Emil Bonfils
and Paris in 1902?" the detective-sergeant asked as soon as we
were out in the street.

"This: the dead man phoned the Agency this afternoon and
said he had received a threatening letter from an Emil Bonfils
with whom he had had trouble in Paris in 1902. He also said
that Bonfils had shot at him the previous evening, in the
street. He wanted somebody to come around and see him
about it tonight. And he said that under no circumstances
were the police to be let in on it—that he'd rather have

murders with never a w...
a very conspicuous killi...

"Who's this Miss D...

"She's well—" Ch...
was on very friendl...
ally called on ther...
I suspected that...

"Who and w...

"Father be...
ago. I've met th...
well. Miss Dexter—...
twenty-three years old, ...
Madden is four or five years ol...
on his way there, to transact some bu...

"Did your father tell you he was go...
O'Gar hammered away at the woman angle.

"No; but it was pretty obvious that he was very
ah—infatuated. We had some words over it a few days a...
last week. Not a quarrel, you understand, but words. From
the way he talked I feared that he meant to marry her."

"What do you mean 'feared'?" O'Gar snapped at that
word.

Charles Gantvoort's pale face flushed a little, and he cleared
his throat embarrassedly.

"I don't want to put the Dexters in a bad light to you. I
don't think—I'm sure they had nothing to do with father's—
with this. But I didn't care especially for them—didn't like
them. I thought they were—well—fortune hunters, perhaps.
Father wasn't fabulously wealthy, but he had considerable
means. And, while he wasn't feeble, still he was past fifty-
seven, old enough for me to feel that Creda Dexter was more
interested in his money than in him."

"How about your father's will?"

"The last one of which I have any knowledge—drawn up
two or three years ago—left everything to my wife and me
jointly. Father's attorney, Mr. Murray Abernathy, could tell
you if there was a later will, but I hardly think there was."

"Your father had retired from business, hadn't he?"

"Yes; he turned his import and export business over to me
about a year ago. He had quite a few investments scattered

Bonfils get him than have the trouble made public. That's all
he would say over the phone; and that's how I happened to
be on hand when Charles Gantvoort was notified of his father's death."

O'Gar stopped in the middle of the sidewalk and whistled
softly.

"That's something!" he exclaimed. "Wait till we get back
to headquarters—I'll show you something."

Whipple was waiting in the assembly room when we arrived
at headquarters. His face at first glance was as smooth and
mask-like as when he had admitted me to the house on
Russian Hill earlier in the evening. But beneath his perfect
servant's manner he was twitching and trembling.

We took him into the little office where we had questioned
Charles Gantvoort.

Whipple verified all that the dead man's son had told us. He
was positive that neither the typewriter, the jewel case, the two
cartridges, or the newer wallet had belonged to Gantvoort.

We couldn't get him to put his opinion of the Dexters in
words, but that he disapproved of them was easily seen. Miss
Dexter, he said, had called up on the telephone three times
this night at about eight o'clock, at nine, and at nine-thirty.
She had asked for Mr. Leopold Gantvoort each time, but she
had left no message. Whipple was of the opinion that she was
expecting Gantvoort, and he had not arrived.

He knew nothing, he said, of Emil Bonfils or of any threatening letters. Gantvoort had been out the previous night
from eight until midnight. Whipple had not seen him closely
enough when he came home to say whether he seemed excited or not. Gantvoort usually carried about a hundred dollars in his pockets.

"Is there anything that you know of that Gantvoort had on
his person tonight which isn't among these things on the
desk?" O'Gar asked.

"No, sir. Everything seems to be here—watch and chain,
money, memorandum book, wallet, keys, handkerchiefs,
fountain pen—everything that I know of."

"Did Charles Gantvoort go out tonight?"

"No, sir. He and Mrs. Gantvoort were at home all
evening."

"Positive?"

Whipple thought a moment.

"Yes, sir, I'm fairly certain. But I know Mrs. Gantvoort wasn't out. To tell the truth, I didn't see Mr. Charles from about eight o'clock until he came downstairs with this gentleman"—pointing to me—"at eleven. But I'm fairly certain he was home all evening. I think Mrs. Gantvoort said he was."

Then O'Gar put another question—one that puzzled me at the time.

"What kind of collar buttons did Mr. Gantvoort wear?"

"You mean Mr. Leopold?"

"Yes."

"Plain gold ones, made all in one piece. They had a London jeweler's mark on them."

"Would you know them if you saw them?"

"Yes, sir."

We let Whipple go home then.

"Don't you think," I suggested when O'Gar and I were alone with this desk-load of evidence that didn't mean anything at all to me yet, "it's time you were loosening up and telling me what's what?"

"I guess so—listen! A man named Lagerquist, a grocer, was driving through Golden Gate Park tonight, and passed a machine standing on a dark road, with its lights out. He thought there was something funny about the way the man in it was sitting at the wheel, so he told the first patrolman he met about it.

"The patrolman investigated and found Gantvoort sitting at the wheel—dead—with his head smashed in and this dingus"—putting one hand on the bloody typewriter—"on the seat beside him. That was at a quarter of ten. The doc says Gantvoort was killed—his skull crushed—with this typewriter.

"The dead man's pockets, we found, had all been turned inside out; and all this stuff on the desk, except this new wallet, was scattered about in the car—some of it on the floor and some on the seats. This money was there too—nearly a hundred dollars of it. Among the papers was this."

He handed me a sheet of white paper upon which the following had been typewritten:

L. F. G.—

I want what is mine. 6,000 miles and 21 years
are not enough to hide you from the victim of
your treachery. I mean to have what you stole.

E. B.

"L. F. G. could be Leopold F. Gantvoort," I said. "And
E. B. could be Emil Bonfils. Twenty-one years is the time
from 1902 to 1923, and 6,000 miles is, roughly, the distance
between Paris and San Francisco."

I laid the letter down and picked up the jewel case. It was
a black imitation leather one, lined with white satin, and un-
marked in any way.

Then I examined the cartridges. There were two of them,
S. W. .45-caliber, and deep crosses had been cut in their soft
noses—an old trick that makes the bullet spread out like a
saucer when it hits.

"These in the car, too?"

"Yep—and this."

From a vest pocket O'Gar produced a short tuft of blond
hair—hairs between an inch and two inches in length. They
had been cut off, not pulled out by the roots.

"Any more?"

There seemed to be an endless stream of things.

He picked up the new wallet from the desk—the one that
both Whipple and Charles Gantvoort had said did not belong
to the dead man—and slid it over to me.

"That was found in the road, three or four feet from the
car."

It was of a cheap quality, and had neither manufacturer's
name nor owner's initials on it. In it were two ten-dollar bills,
three small newspaper clippings, and a typewritten list of six
names and addresses, headed by Gantvoort's.

The three clippings were apparently from the Personal
columns of three different newspapers—the type wasn't the
same—and they read:

GEORGE—

Everything is fixed. Don't wait too long.

D. D. D.

R. H. T.—
    They do not answer.
                            FLO.

CAPPY.—
    Twelve on the dot and look sharp.
                            BINGO.

The names and addresses on the typewritten list, under Ganvoort's, were:

Quincy Heathcote, 1223 S. Jason Street, Denver; B. D. Thornton, 96 Hughes Circle, Dallas; Luther G. Randall, 615 Columbia Street, Portsmouth; J. H. Boyd Willis, 4544 Harvard Street, Boston; Hannah Hindmarsh, 218 E. 79th Street, Cleveland.

"What else?" I asked when I had studied these.

The detective-sergeant's supply hadn't been exhausted yet.

"The dead man's collar buttons—both front and back—had been taken out, though his collar and tie were still in place. And his left shoe was gone. We hunted high and low all around, but didn't find either shoe or collar buttons."

"Is that all?"

I was prepared for anything now.

"What the hell do you want?" he growled. "Ain't that enough?"

"How about fingerprints?"

"Nothing stirring! All we found belonged to the dead man."

"How about the machine he was found in?"

"A coupe belonging to a Doctor Wallace Girargo. He phoned in at six this evening that it had been stolen from near the corner of McAllister and Polk Streets. We're checking up on him—but I think he's all right."

The things that Whipple and Charles Gantvoort had identified as belonging to the dead man told us nothing. We went over them carefully, but to no advantage. The memoranda book contained many entries, but they all seemed totally foreign to the murder. The letters were quite as irrelevant.

The serial number of the typewriter with which the murder had been committed had been removed, we found—apparently filed out of the frame.

"Well, what do you think?" O'Gar asked when we had given up our examination of our clews and sat back burning tobacco.

"I think we want to find Monsieur Emil Bonfils."

"It wouldn't hurt to do that," he grunted. "I guess our best bet is to get in touch with these five people on the list with Gantvoort's name. Suppose that's a murder list? That this Bonfils is out to get all of them?"

"Maybe. We'll get hold of them anyway. Maybe we'll find that some of them have already been killed. But whether they have been killed or are to be killed or not, it's a cinch they have some connection with this affair. I'll get off a batch of telegrams to the Agency's branches, having the names on the list taken care of. I'll try to have the three clippings traced, too."

O'Gar looked at his watch and yawned.

"It's after four. What say we knock off and get some sleep? I'll leave word for the department's expert to compare the typewriter with that letter signed E. B. and with that list to see if they were written on it. I guess they were, but we'll make sure. I'll have the park searched all around where we found Gantvoort as soon as it gets light enough to see, and maybe the missing shoe and the collar buttons will be found. And I'll have a couple of the boys out calling on all the typewriter shops in the city to see if they can get a line on this one."

I stopped at the nearest telegraph office and got off a wad of messages. Then I went home to dream of nothing even remotely connected with crime or the detecting business.

CHAPTER III

"A sleek kitten that dame!"

At eleven o'clock that same morning, when, brisk and fresh with five hours' sleep under my belt, I arrived at the police detective bureau, I found O'Gar slumped down at his desk, staring dazedly at a black shoe, half a dozen collar buttons, a rusty flat key, and a rumpled newspaper—all lined up before him.

"What's all this? Souvenir of your wedding?"

"Might as well be." His voice was heavy with disgust. "Listen to this: one of the porters of the Seamen's National Bank found a package in the vestibule when he started cleaning up this morning. It was this shoe—Gantvoort's missing one—wrapped in this sheet of a five-day-old *Philadelphia Record,* and with these collar buttons and this old key in it. The heel of the shoe, you'll notice, has been pried off, and is still missing. Whipple identifies it all right, as well as two of the collar buttons, but he never saw the key before. These other four collar buttons are new, and common gold-rolled ones. The key don't look like it had had much use for a long time. What do you make of all that?"

I couldn't make anything out of it.

"How did the porter happen to turn the stuff in?"

"Oh, the whole story was in the morning papers—all about the missing shoe and collar buttons and all."

"What did you learn about the typewriter?" I asked.

"The letter and the list were written with it, right enough; but we haven't been able to find where it came from yet. We checked up the doc who owns the coupe, and he's in the clear. We accounted for all his time last night. Lagerquist, the grocer who found Gantvoort, seems to be all right, too. What did you do?"

"Haven't had any answers to the wires I sent last night. I dropped in at the Agency on my way down this morning, and got four operatives out covering the hotels and looking up all the people named Bonfils they can find—there are two or three families by that name listed in the directory. Also I sent our New York branch a wire to have the steamship records searched to see if an Emil Bonfils had arrived recently; and I put a cable through to our Paris correspondent to see what he could dig up over there."

"I guess we ought to see Gantvoort's lawyer—Abernathy— and that Dexter woman before we do anything else," the detective-sergeant said.

"I guess so," I agreed, "let's tackle the lawyer first. He's the most important one, the way things now stand."

Murray Abernathy, attorney-at-law, was a long, stringy, slow-spoken old gentleman who still clung to starched-bosom shirts. He was too full of what he thought were professional ethics to give us as much help as we had expected; but by letting him talk—letting him ramble along in his own way—we did get a little information from him. What we got amounted to this:

The dead man and Creda Dexter had intended being married the coming Wednesday. His son and her brother were both opposed to the marriage, it seemed, so Gantvoort and the woman had planned to be married secretly in Oakland, and catch a boat for the Orient that same afternoon; figuring that by the time their lengthy honeymoon was over they could return to a son and brother who had become resigned to the marriage.

A new will had been drawn up, leaving half of Gantvoort's estate to his new wife and half to his son and daughter-in-law. But the new will had not been signed yet, and Creda Dexter knew it had not been signed. She knew—and this was one of the few points upon which Abernathy would make a positive statement—that under the old will, still in force, everything went to Charles Gantvoort and his wife.

The Gantvoort estate, we estimated from Abernathy's roundabout statements and allusions, amounted to about a million and a half in cash value. The attorney had never heard of Emil Bonfils, he said, and had never heard of any threats or attempts at murder directed toward the dead man. He knew nothing—or would tell us nothing—that threw any light upon the nature of the thing that the threatening letter had accused the dead man of stealing.

From Abernathy's office we went to Creda Dexter's apartment, in a new and expensively elegant building only a few minutes' walk from the Gantvoort residence.

Creda Dexter was a small woman in her early twenties. The first thing you noticed about her were her eyes. They were large and deep and the color of amber, and their pupils were never at rest. Continuously they changed size, expanded and contracted—slowly at times, suddenly at others—ranging incessantly from the size of pinheads to an extent that threatened to blot out the amber irides.

With the eyes for a guide, you discovered that she was pronouncedly feline throughout. Her every movement was the

slow, smooth, sure one of a cat; and the contours of her
rather pretty face, the shape of her mouth, her small nose, the
set of her eyes, the swelling of her brows, were all cat-like.
And the effect was heightened by the way she wore her hair,
which was thick and tawny.

"Mr. Gantvoort and I," she told us after the preliminary
explanations had been disposed of, "were to have been married the day after tomorrow. His son and daughter-in-law
were both opposed to the marriage, as was my brother
Madden. They all seemed to think that the difference between our ages was too great. So to avoid any unpleasantness,
we had planned to be married quietly and then go abroad for
a year or more, feeling sure that they would all have forgotten their grievances by the time we returned.

"That was why Mr. Gantvoort persuaded Madden to go to
New York. He had some business there—something to do
with the disposal of his interest in a steel mill—so he used it
as an excuse to get Madden out of the way until we were off
on our wedding trip. Madden lived here with me, and it
would have been nearly impossible for me to have made any
preparations for the trip without him seeing them."

"Was Mr. Gantvoort here last night?" I asked her.

"No. I expected him—we were going out. He usually
walked over—it's only a few blocks. When eight o'clock
came and he hadn't arrived, I telephoned his house, and
Whipple told me that he had left nearly an hour before. I
called up again, twice, after that. Then, this morning, I
called up again before I had seen the papers, and I was told
that he—"

She broke off with a catch in her voice—the only sign of
sorrow she displayed throughout the interview. The impression of her we had received from Charles Gantvoort and
Whipple had prepared us for a more or less elaborate display
of grief on her part. But she disappointed us. There was nothing crude about her work—she didn't even turn on the tears
for us.

"Was Mr. Gantvoort here night before last?"

"Yes. He came over at a little after eight and stayed until
nearly twelve. We didn't go out."

"Did he walk over and back?"

"Yes, so far as I know."

"Did he ever say anything to you about his life being threatened?"

"No."

She shook her head decisively.

"Do you know Emil Bonfils?"

"No."

"Ever hear Mr. Gantvoort speak of him?"

"No."

"At what hotel is your brother staying in New York?"

The restless black pupils spread out abruptly, as if they were about to overflow into the white areas of her eyes. That was the first clear indication of fear I had seen. But, outside of those tell-tale pupils, her composure was undisturbed.

"I don't know."

"When did he leave San Francisco?"

"Thursday—four days ago."

O'Gar and I walked six or seven blocks in thoughtful silence after we left Creda Dexter's apartment, and then he spoke.

"A sleek kitten—that dame! Rub her the right way, and she'll purr pretty. Rub her the wrong way—and look out for the claws!"

"What did that flash of her eyes when I asked about her brother tell you?" I asked.

"Something—but I don't know what! It wouldn't hurt to look him up and see if he's really in New York. If he is there today it's a cinch he wasn't here last night—even the mail planes take twenty-six or twenty-eight hours for the trip."

"We'll do that," I agreed. "It looks like this Creda Dexter wasn't any too sure that her brother wasn't in on the killing. And there's nothing to show that Bonfils didn't have help. I can't figure Creda being in on the murder, though. She knew the new will hadn't been signed. There'd be no sense in her working herself out of that three-quarters of a million berries."

We sent a lengthy telegram to the Continental's New York branch, and then dropped in at the Agency to see if any replies had come to the wires I had got off the night before.

They had.

None of the people whose names appeared on the typewritten list with Gantvoort's had been found; not the least trace had been found of any of them. Two of the addresses given were altogether wrong. There were no houses with those numbers on those streets—and there never had been.

CHAPTER IV

"Maybe that ain't so foolish!"

What was left of the afternoon, O'Gar and I spent going over the street between Gantvoort's house on Russian Hill and the building in which the Dexters lived. We questioned everyone we could find—man, woman and child—who lived, worked, or played along any of the three routes the dead man could have taken.

We found nobody who had heard the shots that had been fired by Bonfils on the night before the murder. We found nobody who had seen anything suspicious on the night of the murder. Nobody who remembered having seen him picked up in a coupe.

Then we called at Gantvoort's house and questioned Charles Gantvoort again, his wife, and all the servants—and we learned nothing. So far as they knew, nothing belonging to the dead man was missing—nothing small enough to be concealed in the heel of a shoe.

The shoes he had worn the night he was killed were one of three pairs made in New York for him two months before. He could have removed the heel of the left one, hollowed it out sufficiently to hide a small object in it, and then nailed it on again; though Whipple insisted that he would have noticed the effects of any tampering with the shoe unless it had been done by an expert repairman.

This field exhausted, we returned to the Agency. A telegram had just come from the New York branch, saying that none of the steamship companies' records showed the arrival of an Emil Bonfils from either England, France, or Germany within the past six months.

The operatives who had been searching the city for Bonfils had all come in empty-handed. They had found and investigated eleven persons named Bonfils in San Francisco, Oakland, Berkeley, and Alameda. Their investigations had definitely cleared all eleven. None of these Bonfilses knew an Emil Bonfils. Combing the hotels had yielded nothing.

O'Gar and I went to dinner together—a quiet, grouchy sort of meal during which we didn't speak six words apiece—and then came back to the Agency to find that another wire had come in from New York.

> Madden Dexter arrived McAlpin Hotel this morning with Power of Attorney to sell Gantvoort interest in B. F. and F. Iron Corporation. Denies knowledge of Emil Bonfils or of murder. Expects to finish business and leave for San Francisco tomorrow.

I let the sheet of paper upon which I had decoded the telegram slide out of my fingers, and we sat listlessly facing each other across my desk, looking vacantly each at the other, listening to the clatter of charwomen's buckets in the corridor.

"It's a funny one," O'Gar said softly to himself at last.

I nodded. It was.

"We got nine clews," he spoke again presently, "and none of them have got us a damned thing.

"Number one: the dead man called up you people and told you that he had been threatened and shot at by an Emil Bonfils that he'd had a run-in with in Paris a long time ago.

"Number two: the typewriter he was killed with and that the letter and list were written on. We're still trying to trace it, but with no breaks so far. What the hell kind of a weapon was that, anyway? It looks like this fellow Bonfils got hot and hit Gantvoort with the first thing he put his hand on. But what was the typewriter doing in a stolen car? And why were the numbers filed off it?"

I shook my head to signify that I couldn't guess the answer, and O'Gar went on enumerating our clews.

"Number three: the threatening letter, fitting in with what Gantvoort had said over the phone that afternoon.

"Number four: those two bullets with the crosses in their snoots.

"Number five: the jewel case.

"Number six: that bunch of yellow hair.

"Number seven: the fact that the dead man's shoe and collar buttons were carried away.

"Number eight: the wallet, with two ten-dollar bills, three clippings, and the list in it, found in the road.

"Number nine: finding the shoe next day, wrapped up in a five-day-old Philadelphia paper, and with the missing collar buttons, four more, and a rusty key in it.

"That's the list. If they mean anything at all, they mean that Emil Bonfils whoever he is—was flimflammed out of something by Gantvoort in Paris in 1902, and that Bonfils came to get it back. He picked Gantvoort up last night in a stolen car, bringing his typewriter with him—for God knows what reason! Gantvoort put up an argument, so Bonfils bashed in his noodle with the typewriter, and then went through his pockets, apparently not taking anything. He decided that what he was looking for was in Gantvoort's left shoe, so he took the shoe away with him. And then—but there's no sense to the collar button trick, or the phoney list, or—"

"Yes there is!" I cut in, sitting up, wide awake now. "That's our tenth clew—the one we're going to follow from now on. That list was, except for Gantvoort's name and address, a fake. Our people would have found at least one of the five people whose names were on it if it had been on the level. But they didn't find the least trace of any of them. And two of the addresses were of street numbers that didn't exist!

"That list was faked up, put in the wallet with the clippings and twenty dollars—to make the play stronger—and planted in the road near the car to throw us off-track. And if that's so, then it's a hundred to one that the rest of the things were cooked up too.

"From now on I'm considering all those nine lovely clews as nine bum steers. And I'm going just exactly contrary to them. I'm looking for a man whose name isn't Emil Bonfils, and whose initials aren't either E or B; who isn't French, and who wasn't in Paris in 1902. A man who hasn't light hair, doesn't carry a .45-calibre pistol, and has no interest in Personal advertisements in newspapers. A man who didn't kill Gantvoort to recover anything that could have been hidden in a shoe or on a collar button. That's the sort of a guy I'm hunting for now!"

The detective-sergeant screwed up his little green eyes reflectively and scratched his head.

"Maybe that ain't so foolish!" he said. "You might be right at that. Suppose you are—what then? That Dexter kitten didn't do it—it cost her three-quarters of a million. Her brother didn't do it—he's in New York. And, besides, you don't croak a guy just because you think he's too old to marry your sister. Charles Gantvoort? He and his wife are the only ones who make any money out of the old man dying before the new will was signed. We have only their word for it that Charles was home that night. The servants didn't see him between eight and eleven. You were there, and you didn't see him until eleven. But me and you both believe him when he says he *was* home all that evening. And neither of us think he bumped the old man off—though of course he might. Who then?"

"This Creda Dexter," I suggested, "was marrying Gantvoort for his money, wasn't she? You don't think she was in love with him, do you?"

"No. I figure, from what I saw of her, that she was in love with the million and a half."

"All right," I went on. "Now she isn't exactly homely—not by a long shot. Do you reckon Gantvoort was the only man who ever fell for her?"

"I got you! I got you!" O'Gar exclaimed. "You mean there might have been some young fellow in the running who didn't have any million and a half behind him, and who didn't take kindly to being nosed out by a man who did. Maybe—maybe."

"Well, suppose we bury all this stuff we've been working on and try out that angle."

"Suits me," he said. "Starting in the morning, then, we spend our time hunting for Gantvoort's rival for the paw of this Dexter kitten."

CHAPTER V

"Meet Mr. Smith"

Right or wrong, that's what we did. We stowed all those lovely clews away in a drawer, locked the drawer, and forgot them. Then we set out to find Creda Dexter's masculine acquaintances and sift them for the murderer.

But it wasn't as simple as it sounded.

All our digging into her past failed to bring to light one man who could be considered a suitor. She and her brother had been in San Francisco three years. We traced them back the length of that period, from apartment to apartment. We questioned everyone we could find who even knew her by sight. And nobody could tell us of a single man who had shown an interest in her besides Gantvoort. Nobody, apparently, had ever seen her with any man except Gantvoort or her brother.

All of which, while not getting us ahead, at least convinced us that we were on the right trail. There must have been, we argued, at least one man in her life in those three years besides Gantvoort. She wasn't—unless we were very much mistaken— the sort of woman who would discourage masculine attention; and she was certainly endowed by nature to attract it. And if there was another man, then the very fact that he had been kept so thoroughly under cover strengthened the probability of him having been mixed up in Gantvoort's death.

We were unsuccessful in learning where the Dexters had lived before they came to San Francisco, but we weren't so very interested in their earlier life. Of course it was possible that some old-time lover had come upon the scene again recently; but in that case it should have been easier to find the recent connection than the old one.

There was no doubt, our explorations showed, that Gantvoort's son had been correct in thinking the Dexters were fortune hunters. All their activities pointed to that, although there seemed to be nothing downright criminal in their pasts.

I went up against Creda Dexter again, spending an entire afternoon in her apartment, banging away with question after question, all directed toward her former love affairs. Who had she thrown over for Gantvoort and his million and a half? And the answer was always *nobody*—an answer that I didn't choose to believe.

We had Creda Dexter shadowed night and day—and it carried us ahead not an inch. Perhaps she suspected that she was being watched. Anyway, she seldom left her apartment, and then on only the most innocent of errands. We had her apartment watched whether she was in it or not. Nobody visited it. We tapped her telephone—and all our listening-in netted us nothing. We had her mail covered—and she didn't receive a single letter, not even an advertisement.

Meanwhile, we had learned where the three clippings found in the wallet had come from—from the Personal columns of a New York, a Chicago, and a Portland newspaper. The one in the Portland paper had appeared two days before the murder, the Chicago one four days before, and the New York one five days before. All three of those papers would have been on the San Francisco newsstands the day of the murder—ready to be purchased and cut out by anyone who was looking for material to confuse detectives with.

The Agency's Paris correspondent had found no less than six Emil Bonfilses—all bloomers so far as our job was concerned—and had a line on three more.

But O'Gar and I weren't worrying over Emil Bonfils any more—that angle was dead and buried. We were plugging away at our new task—the finding of Gantvoort's rival.

Thus the days passed, and thus the matter stood when Madden Dexter was due to arrive home from New York.

Our New York branch had kept an eye on him until he left that city, and had advised us of his departure, so I knew what train he was coming on. I wanted to put a few questions to him before his sister saw him. He could tell me what I wanted to know, and he might be willing to if I could get to him before his sister had an opportunity to shut him up.

If I had known him by sight I could have picked him up when he left his train at Oakland, but I didn't know him; and I didn't want to carry Charles Gantvoort or anyone else along with me to pick him out for me.

So I went up to Sacramento that morning, and boarded his train there. I put my card in an envelope and gave it to a messenger boy in the station. Then I followed the boy through the train, while he called out:

"Mr. Dexter! Mr. Dexter!"

In the last car—the observation-club car—a slender, dark-haired man in well-made tweeds turned from watching the station platform through a window and held out his hand to the boy.

I studied him while he nervously tore open the envelope and read my card. His chin trembled slightly just now, emphasizing the weakness of a face that couldn't have been strong at its best. Between twenty-five and thirty, I placed him; with his hair parted in the middle and slicked down; large, too-expressive brown eyes; small well-shaped nose; neat brown mustache; very red, soft lips—that type.

I dropped into the vacant chair beside him when he looked up from the card.

"You are Mr. Dexter?"

"Yes," he said. "I suppose it's about Mr. Gantvoort's death that you want to see me?"

"Uh-huh. I wanted to ask you a few questions, and since I happened to be in Sacramento, I thought that by riding back on the train with you I could ask them without taking up too much of your time."

"If there's anything I can tell you," he assured me, "I'll be only too glad to do it. But I told the New York detectives all I knew, and they didn't seem to find it of much value."

"Well, the situation has changed some since you left New York." I watched his face closely as I spoke. "What we thought of no value then may be just what we want now."

I paused while he moistened his lips and avoided my eyes. He may not know anything, I thought, but he's certainly jumpy. I let him wait a few minutes while I pretended deep thoughtfulness. If I played him right, I was confident I could turn him inside out. He didn't seem to be made of very tough material.

We were sitting with our heads close together, so that the four or five other passengers in the car wouldn't overhear our talk; and that position was in my favor. One of the things that every detective knows is that it's often easy to get information—even a confession—out of a feeble nature simply by putting your face close to his and talking in a loud tone. I couldn't talk loud here, but the closeness of our faces was by itself an advantage.

"Of the men with whom your sister was acquainted," I came out with it at last, "who, outside of Mr. Gantvoort, was the most attentive?"

He swallowed audibly, looked out of the window, fleetingly at me, and then out of the window again.

"Really, I couldn't say."

"All right. Let's get at it this way. Suppose we check off one by one all the men who were interested in her and in whom she was interested."

He continued to stare out of the window.

"Who's first?" I pressed him.

His gaze flickered around to meet mine for a second, with a sort of timid desperation in his eyes.

"I know it sounds foolish, but I, her brother, couldn't give you the name of even one man in whom Creda was interested before she met Gantvoort. She never, so far as I know, had the slightest feeling for any man before she met him. Of course it is possible that there may have been someone that I didn't know anything about, but—"

It did sound foolish, right enough! The Creda Dexter I had talked to—a sleek kitten, as O'Gar had put it—didn't impress me as being at all likely to go very long without having at least one man in tow. This pretty little guy in front of me was lying. There couldn't be any other explanation.

I went at him tooth and nail. But when he reached Oakland early that night he was still sticking to his original statement—that Gantvoort was the only one of his sister's suitors that he knew anything about. And I knew that I had blundered, had underrated Madden Dexter, had played my hand wrong in trying to shake him down too quickly—in driving too directly at the point I was interested in. He was either a lot stronger than I had figured him, or his interest in concealing Gantvoort's murderer was much greater than I had thought it would be.

But I had this much: if Dexter was lying—and there

couldn't be much doubt of that—then Gantvoort *had* had a rival, and Madden Dexter believed or knew that this rival had killed Gantvoort.

When we left the train at Oakland I knew I was licked, that he wasn't going to tell me what I wanted to know—not this night, anyway. But I clung to him, stuck at his side when we boarded the ferry for San Francisco, in spite of the obviousness of his desire to get away from me. There's always a chance of something unexpected happening; so I continued to ply him with questions as our boat left the slip.

Presently a man came toward where we were sitting—a big burly man in a light overcoat, carrying a black bag.

"Hello, Madden!" he greeted my companion, striding over to him with outstretched hand. "Just got in and was trying to remember your phone number," he said, setting down his bag, as they shook hands warmly.

Madden Dexter turned to me.

"I want you to meet Mr. Smith," he told me, and then gave my name to the big man, adding, "he's with the Continental Detective Agency here."

That tag—clearly a warning for Smith's benefit—brought me to my feet, all watchfulness. But the ferry was crowded—a hundred persons were within sight of us, all around us. I relaxed, smiled pleasantly, and shook hands with Smith. Whoever Smith was, and whatever connection he might have with the murder—and if he hadn't any, why should Dexter have been in such a hurry to tip him off to my identity?—he couldn't do anything here. The crowd around us was all to my advantage.

That was my second mistake of the day.

Smith's left hand had gone into his overcoat pocket—or rather, through one of those vertical slits that certain styles of overcoats have so that inside pockets may be reached without unbuttoning the overcoat. His hand had gone through that slit, and his coat had fallen away far enough for me to see a snub-nosed automatic in his hand—shielded from everyone's sight but mine—pointing at my waist-line.

"Shall we go on deck?" Smith asked—and it was an order.

I hesitated. I didn't like to leave all these people who were so blindly standing and sitting around us. But Smith's face wasn't the face of a cautious man. He had the look of one who might easily disregard the presence of a hundred witnesses.

I turned around and walked through the crowd. His right hand lay familiarly on my shoulder as he walked behind me; his left hand held his gun, under the overcoat, against my spine.

The deck was deserted. A heavy fog, wet as rain,—the fog of San Francisco Bay's winter nights,—lay over boat and water, and had driven everyone else inside. It hung about us, thick and impenetrable; I couldn't see so far as the end of the boat, in spite of the lights glowing overhead.

I stopped.

Smith prodded me in the back.

"Farther away, where we can talk," he rumbled in my ear.

I went on until I reached the rail.

The entire back of my head burned with sudden fire . . . tiny points of light glittered in the blackness before me . . . grew larger . . . came rushing toward me. . . .

CHAPTER VI

"Those damned horns!"

Semi-consciousness! I found myself mechanically keeping afloat somehow and trying to get out of my overcoat. The back of my head throbbed devilishly. My eyes burned. I felt heavy and logged, as if I had swallowed gallons of water.

The fog hung low and thick on the water—there was nothing else to be seen anywhere. By the time I had freed myself of the encumbering overcoat my head had cleared somewhat, but with returning consciousness came increased pain.

A light glimmered mistily off to my left, and then vanished. From out of the misty blanket, from every direction, in a dozen different keys, from near and far, fog-horns sounded. I stopped swimming and floated on my back, trying to determine my whereabouts.

After a while I picked out the moaning, evenly spaced blasts of the Alcatraz siren. But they told me nothing. They came to me out of the fog without direction—seemed to beat down upon me from straight above.

I was somewhere in San Francisco Bay, and that was all I knew, though I suspected the current was sweeping me out toward the Golden Gate.

A little while passed, and I knew that I had left the path of the Oakland ferries—no boat had passed close to me for some time. I was glad to be out of that track. In this fog a boat was a lot more likely to run me down than to pick me up.

The water was chilling me, so I turned over and began swimming, just vigorously enough to keep my blood circulating while I saved my strength until I had a definite goal to try for.

A horn began to repeat its roaring note nearer and nearer, and presently the lights of the boat upon which it was fixed came into sight. One of the Sausalito ferries, I thought.

It came quite close to me, and I halloed until I was breathless and my throat was raw. But the boat's siren, crying its warning, drowned my shouts.

The boat went on and the fog closed in behind it.

The current was stronger now, and my attempts to attract the attention of the Sausalito ferry had left me weaker. I floated, letting the water sweep me where it would, resting.

Another light appeared ahead of me suddenly—hung there for an instant—disappeared.

I began to yell, and worked my arms and legs madly, trying to drive myself through the water to where it had been.

I never saw it again.

Weariness settled upon me, and a sense of futility. The water was no longer cold. I was warm with a comfortable, soothing numbness. My head stopped throbbing; there was no feeling at all in it now. No lights, now, but the sound of fog-horns . . . fog-horns . . . fog-horns ahead of me, behind me, to either side; annoying me, irritating me.

But for the moaning horns I would have ceased all effort. They had become the only disagreeable detail of my situation—the water was pleasant, fatigue was pleasant. But the horns tormented me. I cursed them petulantly and decided to swim until I could no longer hear them, and then, in the quiet of the friendly fog, go to sleep. . . .

Now and then I would doze, to be goaded into wakefulness by the wailing voice of a siren.

"Those damned horns! Those damned horns!" I complained aloud, again and again.

One of them, I found presently, was bearing down upon me from behind, growing louder and stronger. I turned and waited. Lights, dim and steaming, came into view.

With exaggerated caution to avoid making the least splash, I swam off to one side. When this nuisance was past I could go to sleep. I sniggered softly to myself as the lights drew abreast, feeling a foolish triumph in my cleverness in eluding the boat. Those damned horns. . . .

Life—the hunger for life—all at once surged back into my being.

I screamed at the passing boat, and with every iota of my being struggled toward it. Between strokes I tilted up my head and screamed. . . .

CHAPTER VII

"You have a lot of fun, don't you?"

When I returned to consciousness for the second time that evening, I was lying on my back on a baggage truck, which was moving. Men and women were crowding around, walking beside the truck, staring at me with curious eyes.

I sat up.

"Where are we?" I asked.

A little red-faced man in uniform answered my question.

"Just landing in Sausalito. Lay still. We'll take you over to the hospital."

I looked around

"How long before this boat goes back to San Francisco?"

"Leaves right away."

I slid off the truck and started back aboard the boat.

"I'm going with it," I said.

Half an hour later, shivering and shaking in my wet clothes, keeping my mouth clamped tight so that my teeth wouldn't sound like a dice-game, I climbed into a taxi at the Ferry Building and went to my flat.

There, I swallowed half a pint of whisky, rubbed myself with a coarse towel until my skin was sore, and, except for an enormous weariness and a worse headache, I felt almost human again.

I reached O'Gar by phone, asked him to come up to my flat right away, and then called up Charles Gantvoort.

"Have you seen Madden Dexter yet?" I asked him.

"No, but I talked to him over the phone. He called me up as soon as he got in. I asked him to meet me in Mr. Abernathy's office in the morning, so we could go over that business he transacted for father."

"Can you call him up now and tell him him that you have been called out of town—will have to leave early in the morning—and that you'd like to run over to his apartment and see him tonight?"

"Why yes, if you wish."

"Good! Do that. I'll call for you in a little while and go over to see him with you."

"What is—"

"I'll tell you about it when I see you," I cut him off.

O'Gar arrived as I was finishing dressing.

"So he told you something?" he asked, knowing of my plan to meet Dexter on the train and question him.

"Yes," I said with sour sarcasm, "but I came near forgetting what it was. I grilled him all the way from Sacramento to Oakland, and couldn't get a whisper out of him. On the ferry coming over he introduces me to a man he calls Mr. Smith, and he tells Mr. Smith that I'm a gum-shoe. This, mind you, all happens in the middle of a crowded ferry! Mr. Smith puts a gun in my belly, marches me out on deck, raps me across the back of the head, and dumps me into the bay."

"You have a lot of fun, don't you?" O'Gar grinned, and then wrinkled his forehead. "Looks like Smith would be the man we want then—the buddy who turned the Gantvoort trick. But what the hell did he want to give himself away by chucking you overboard for?"

"Too hard for me," I confessed, while trying to find which of my hats and caps would sit least heavily upon my bruised head. "Dexter knew I was hunting for one of his sister's former lovers, of course. And he must have thought I knew a whole lot more than I do, or he wouldn't have made that raw play—tipping my mitt to Smith right in front of me.

"It may be that after Dexter lost his head and made that break on the ferry, Smith figured that I'd be on to him soon, if not right away; and so he'd take a desperate chance on putting me out of the way. But we'll know all about it in a little while," I said, as we went down to the waiting taxi and set out for Gantvoort's.

"You ain't counting on Smith being in sight, are you?" the detective-sergeant asked.

"No. He'll be holed up somewhere until he sees how things are going. But Madden Dexter will have to be out in the open to protect himself. He has an alibi, so he's in the clear so far as the actual killing is concerned. And with me supposed to be dead, the more he stays in the open, the safer he is. But it's a cinch that he knows what this is all about, though he wasn't necessarily involved in it. As near as I could see, he didn't go out on deck with Smith and me tonight. Anyway he'll be home. And this time he's going to talk—he's going to tell his little story!"

Charles Gantvoort was standing on his front steps when we reached his house. He climbed into our taxi and we headed for the Dexters' apartment. We didn't have time to answer any of the questions that Gantvoort was firing at us with every turning of the wheels.

"He's home and expecting you?" I asked him.

"Yes."

Then we left the taxi and went into the apartment building.

"Mr. Gantvoort to see Mr. Dexter," he told the Philippine boy at the switchboard.

The boy spoke into the phone.

"Go right up," he told us.

At the Dexters' door I stepped past Gantvoort and pressed the button.

Creda Dexter opened the door. Her amber eyes widened and her smile faded as I stepped past her into the apartment.

I walked swiftly down the little hallway and turned into the first room through whose open door a light showed.

And came face to face with Smith!

We were both surprised, but his astonishment was a lot more profound than mine. Neither of us had expected to see the other; but I had known he was still alive, while he had every reason for thinking me at the bottom of the bay.

I took advantage of his greater bewilderment to the extent of two steps toward him before he went into action.

One of his hands swept down.

I threw my right fist at his face—threw it with every ounce of my 180 pounds behind it, re-enforced by the memory of every second I had spent in the water, and every throb of my battered head.

His hand, already darting down for his pistol, came back up too late to fend off my punch.

Something clicked in my hand as it smashed into his face, and my hand went numb.

But he went down—and lay where he fell.

I jumped across his body to a door on the opposite side of the room, pulling my gun loose with my left hand.

"Dexter's somewhere around!" I called over my shoulder to O'Gar, who with Gantvoort and Creda, was coming through the door by which I had entered. "Keep your eyes open!"

I dashed through the four other rooms of the apartment, pulling closet doors open, looking everywhere—and I found nobody.

Then I returned to where Creda Dexter was trying to revive Smith, with the assistance of O'Gar and Gantvoort.

The detective-sergeant looked over his shoulder at me.

"Who do you think this joker is?" he asked.

"My friend Mr. Smith."

"Gantvoort says he's Madden Dexter."

I looked at Charles Gantvoort, who nodded his head.

"This is Madden Dexter," he said.

CHAPTER VIII

"I hope you swing!"

We worked upon Dexter for nearly ten minutes before he opened his eyes.

As soon as he sat up we began to shoot questions and accusations at him, hoping to get a confession out of him before he recovered from his shakiness—but he wasn't that shaky.

All we could get out of him was:

"Take me in if you want to. If I've got anything to say I'll say it to my lawyer, and to nobody else."

Creda Dexter, who had stepped back after her brother came to, and was standing a little way off, watching us, suddenly came forward and caught me by the arm.

"What have you got on him?" she demanded, imperatively.

"I wouldn't want to say," I countered, "but I don't mind telling you this much. We're going to give him a chance in a nice modern court-room to prove that he didn't kill Leopold Gantvoort."

"He was in New York!"

"He was not! He had a friend who went to New York as Madden Dexter and looked after Gantvoort's business under that name. But if this is the real Madden Dexter then the closest he got to New York was when he met his friend on the ferry to get from him the papers connected with the B. F. & F. Iron Corporation transaction; and learned that I had stumbled upon the truth about his alibi—even if I didn't know it myself at the time."

She jerked around to face her brother.

"Is that on the level?" she asked him.

He sneered at her, and went on feeling with the fingers of one hand the spot on his jaw where my fist had landed.

"I'll say all I've got to say to my lawyer," he repeated.

"You will?" she shot back at him. "Well, I'll say what I've got to say right now!"

She flung around to face me again.

"Madden is not my brother at all! My name is Ives. Madden and I met in St. Louis about four years ago, drifted around together for a year or so, and then came to Frisco. He was a con man—still is. He made Mr. Gantvoort's acquaintance six or seven months ago, and was getting him all ribbed up to unload a fake invention on him. He brought him here a couple of times, and introduced me to him as his sister. We usually posed as brother and sister.

"Then, after Mr. Gantvoort had been here a couple times, Madden decided to change his game. He thought Mr. Gantvoort liked me, and that we could get more money out of him by working a fancy sort of badger-game on him. I was to lead the old man on until I had him wrapped around my finger—until we had him tied up so tight he couldn't get away—had something on him—something good and strong. Then we were going to shake him down for plenty of money.

"Everything went along fine for a while. He fell for me— fell hard. And finally he asked me to marry him. We had never figured on that. Blackmail was our game. But when he asked me to marry him I tried to call Madden off. I admit the old man's money had something to do with it—it influenced me—but I had come to like him a little for himself. He was mighty fine in lots of ways—nicer than anybody I had ever known.

"So I told Madden all about it, and suggested that we drop the other plan, and that I marry Gantvoort. I promised to see that Madden was kept supplied with money—I knew I could get whatever I wanted from Mr. Gantvoort. And I was on the level with Madden. I liked Mr. Gantvoort, but Madden had found him and brought him around to me; and so I wasn't going to run out on Madden. I was willing to do all I could for him.

"But Madden wouldn't hear of it. He'd have got more money in the long run by doing as I suggested—but he wanted his little handful right away. And to make him more unreasonable he got one of his jealous streaks. He beat me one night!

"That settled it. I made up my mind to ditch him. I told Mr. Gantvoort that my brother was bitterly opposed to our marrying, and he could see that Madden was carrying a grouch. So he arranged to send Madden East on that steel business, to get him out of the way until we were off on our wedding trip. And we thought Madden was completely deceived—but I should have known that he would see through our scheme. We planned to be gone about a year, and by that time I thought Madden would have forgotten me—or I'd be fixed to handle him if he tried to make any trouble.

"As soon as I heard that Mr. Gantvoort had been killed I had a hunch that Madden had done it. But then it seemed like a certainty that he was in New York the next day, and I thought I had done him an injustice. And I was glad he was out of it. But now—"

She whirled around to her erstwhile confederate.

"Now I hope you swing, you big sap!"

She spun around to me again. No sleek kitten, this, but a furious, spitting cat, with claws and teeth bared.

"What kind of looking fellow was the one who went to New York for him?"

I described the man I had talked to on the train.

"Evan Felter," she said, after a moment of thought. "He used to work with Madden. You'll probably find him hiding in Los Angeles. Put the screws on him and he'll spill all he knows—he's a weak sister! The chances are he didn't know what Madden's game was until it was all over."

"How do you like that?" she spat at Madden Dexter. "How do you like that for a starter? You messed up my little party, did you? Well, I'm going to spend every minute of my time from now until they pop you off helping them pop you!"

And she did, too—with her assistance it was no trick at all to gather up the rest of the evidence we needed to hang him. And I don't believe her enjoyment of her three-quarters of a million dollars is spoiled a bit by any qualms over what she did to Madden. She's a very respectable woman *now*, and glad to be free of the con-man.

Zigzags of Treachery

"ALL I know about Dr. Estep's death," I said, "is the stuff in the papers."

Vance Richmond's lean gray face took on an expression of distaste.

"The newspapers aren't always either thorough or accurate. I'll give you the salient points as I know them; though I suppose you'll want to go over the ground for yourself, and get your information first-hand."

I nodded, and the attorney went on, shaping each word precisely with his thin lips before giving it sound.

"Dr. Estep came to San Francisco in '98 or '99—a young man of twenty-five, just through qualifying for his license. He opened an office here, and, as you probably know, became in time a rather excellent surgeon. He married two or three years after he came here. There were no children. He and his wife seem to have been a bit happier together than the average.

"Of his life before coming to San Francisco, nothing is known. He told his wife briefly that he had been born and raised in Parkersburg, W. Va., but that his home life had been so unpleasant that he was trying to forget it, and that he did not like to talk—or even think—about it. Bear that in mind.

"Two weeks ago—on the third of the month—a woman came to his office, in the afternoon. His office was in his residence on Pine Street. Lucy Coe, who was Dr. Estep's nurse and assistant, showed the woman into his office, and then went back to her own desk in the reception room.

"She didn't hear anything the doctor said to the woman, but through the closed door she heard the woman's voice now and then—a high and anguished voice, apparently pleading. Most of the words were lost upon the nurse, but she heard one coherent sentence. 'Please! Please!' she heard the woman cry. 'Don't turn me away!' The woman was with Dr. Estep for about fifteen minutes, and left sobbing into a handkerchief. Dr. Estep said nothing about the caller either to his nurse or to his wife, who didn't learn of it until after his death.

"The next day, toward evening, while the nurse was putting on her hat and coat preparatory to leaving for home, Dr. Estep came out of his office, with his hat on and a letter in his hand. The nurse saw that his face was pale—'white as my uniform,' she says—and he walked with the care of one who takes pains to keep from staggering.

"She asked him if he was ill. 'Oh, it's nothing!' he told her. 'I'll be all right in a very few minutes.' Then he went on out. The nurse left the house just behind him, and saw him drop the letter he had carried into the mail box on the corner, after which he returned to the house.

"Mrs. Estep, coming downstairs ten minutes later,—it couldn't have been any later than that,—heard, just as she reached the first floor, the sound of a shot from her husband's office. She rushed into it, meeting nobody. Her husband stood by his desk, swaying, with a hole in his right temple and a smoking revolver in his hand. Just as she reached him and put her arms around him, he fell across the desk—dead."

"Anybody else—any of the servants, for instance—able to say that Mrs. Estep didn't go to the office until after the shot?" I asked.

The attorney shook his head sharply.

"No, damn it! That's where the rub comes in!"

His voice, after this one flare of feeling, resumed its level, incisive tone, and he went on with his tale.

"The next day's papers had accounts of Dr. Estep's death, and late that morning the woman who had called upon him the day before his death came to the house. She is Dr. Estep's first wife—which is to say, his legal wife! There seems to be no reason—not the slightest—for doubting it, as much as I'd like to. They were married in Philadelphia in '96. She has a certified copy of the marriage record. I had the matter investigated in Philadelphia, and it's a certain fact that Dr. Estep and this woman—Edna Fife was her maiden name—were really married.

"She says that Estep, after living with her in Philadelphia for two years, deserted her. That would have been in '98, or just before he came to San Francisco. She has sufficient proof of her identity—that she really is the Edna Fife who married him; and my agents in the East found positive proof that Estep had practiced for two years in Philadelphia.

"And here is another point. I told you that Estep had said he was born and raised in Parkersburg. I had inquiries made there, but found nothing to show that he had ever lived there, and found ample to show that he had never lived at the address he had given his wife. There is, then, nothing for us to believe except that his talk of an unhappy early life was a ruse to ward off embarrassing questions."

"Did you do anything toward finding out whether the doctor and his first wife had ever been divorced?" I asked.

"I'm having that taken care of now, but I hardly expect to learn that they had. That would be too crude. To get on with my story: This woman—the first Mrs. Estep—said that she had just recently learned her husband's whereabouts, and had come to see him in an attempt to effect a reconciliation. When she called upon him the afternoon before his death, he asked for a little time to make up his mind what he should do. He promised to give her his decision in two days. My personal opinion, after talking to the woman several times, is that she had learned that he had accumulated some money, and that her interest was more in getting the money than in getting him. But that, of course, is neither here nor there.

"At first the authorities accepted the natural explanation of the doctor's death—suicide. But after the first wife's appearance, the second wife—my client—was arrested and charged with murder.

"The police theory is that after his first wife's visit, Dr. Estep told his second wife the whole story; and that she, brooding over the knowledge that he had deceived her, that she was not his wife at all, finally worked herself up into a rage, went to the office after his nurse had left for the day, and shot him with the revolver that she knew he always kept in his desk.

"I don't know, of course, just what evidence the prosecution has, but from the newspapers I gather that the case against her will be built upon her finger prints on the revolver with which he was killed; an upset inkwell on his desk; splashes of ink on the dress she wore; and an inky print of her hand on a torn newspaper on his desk.

"Unfortunately, but perfectly naturally, one of the first things she did was to take the revolver out of her husband's hand. That accounts for her prints on it. He fell—as I told you—just as she put her arms around him, and, though her memory isn't very clear on this point, the probabilities are that he dragged her with him when he fell across the desk. That accounts for the upset inkwell, the torn paper, and the splashes of ink. But the prosecution will try to persuade the jury that those things all happened before the shooting—that they are proofs of a struggle."

"Not so bad," I gave my opinion.

"Or pretty damned bad—depending on how you look at it. And this is the worst time imaginable for a thing like this to come up! Within the past few months there have been no less than five widely-advertised murders of men by women who were supposed to have been betrayed, or deceived, or one thing or another.

"Not one of those five women was convicted. As a result, we have the press, the public, and even the pulpit, howling for a stricter enforcement of justice. The newspapers are lined up against Mrs. Estep as strongly as their fear of libel suits will permit. The woman's clubs are lined up against her. Everybody is clamoring for an example to be made of her.

"Then, as if all that isn't enough, the Prosecuting Attorney has lost his last two big cases, and he'll be out for blood this time—election day isn't far off."

The calm, even, precise voice was gone now. In its place was a passionate eloquence.

"I don't know what you think," Richmond cried. "You're a detective. This is an old story to you. You're more or less callous, I suppose, and skeptical of innocence in general. But I *know* that Mrs. Estep didn't kill her husband. I don't say it because she's my client! I was Dr. Estep's attorney, and his friend, and if I thought Mrs. Estep guilty, I'd do everything in my power to help convict her. But I know as well as I know anything that she didn't kill him—couldn't have killed him.

"She's innocent. But I know too that if I go into court with no defense beyond what I now have, she'll be convicted! There has been too much leniency shown feminine criminals, public sentiment says. The pendulum will swing the other way—Mrs. Estep, if convicted, will get the limit. I'm putting it up to you! Can you save her?"

"Our best mark is the letter he mailed just before he died," I said, ignoring everything he said that didn't have to do with the facts of the case. "It's good betting that when a man writes and mails a letter and then shoots himself, that the letter isn't altogether unconnected with the suicide. Did you ask the first wife about the letter?"

"I did, and she denies having received one."

"That wasn't right. If the doctor had been driven to suicide by her appearance, then according to all the rules there are, the letter should have been addressed to her. He might have written one to his second wife, but he would hardly have mailed *it*."

"Would she have any reason for lying about it?"

"Yes," the lawyer said slowly, "I think she would. His will leaves everything to the second wife. The first wife, being the only legal wife, will have no difficulty in breaking that will, of course; but if it is shown that the second wife had no knowledge of the first one's existence—that she really believed herself to be Dr. Estep's legal wife—then I think that she will receive at least a portion of the estate. I don't think any court would, under the circumstances, take everything away from her. But if she should be found guilty of murdering Dr. Estep, then no consideration will be shown her, and the first wife will get every penny."

"Did he leave enough to make half of it, say, worth sending an innocent person to the gallows for?"

"He left about half a million, roughly; $250,000 isn't a mean inducement."

"Do you think it would be enough for the first wife—from what you have seen of her?"

"Candidly, I do. She didn't impress me as being a person of many very active scruples."

"Where does this first wife live?" I asked.

"She's staying at the Montgomery Hotel now. Her home is in Louisville, I believe. I don't think you will gain anything by talking to her, however. She has retained Somerset, Somerset, and Quill to represent her—a very reputable firm, by the way—and she'll refer you to them. They will tell you nothing. But if there's anything dishonest about her affairs—such as the concealing of Dr. Estep's letter—I'm confident that Somerset, Somerset and Quill know nothing of it."

"Can I talk to the second Mrs. Estep—your client?"

"Not at present, I'm afraid; though perhaps in a day or two. She is on the verge of collapse just now. She has always been delicate; and the shock of her husband's death, followed by her own arrest and imprisonment, has been too much for her. She's in the city jail, you know, held without bail. I've tried to have her transferred to the prisoner's ward of the City Hospital, even; but the authorities seem to think that her illness is simply a ruse. I'm worried about her. She's really in a critical condition."

His voice was losing its calmness again, so I picked up my hat, said something about starting to work at once, and went out. I don't like eloquence: if it isn't effective enough to pierce your hide, it's tiresome; and if it is effective enough, then it muddles your thoughts.

II

I spent the next couple of hours questioning the Estep servants, to no great advantage. None of them had been near the front of the house at the time of the shooting, and none had seen Mrs. Estep immediately prior to her husband's death.

After a lot of hunting, I located Lucy Coe, the nurse, in an apartment on Vallejo Street. She was a small, brisk, business-like woman of thirty or so. She repeated what Vance Richmond had told me, and could add nothing to it.

That cleaned up the Estep end of the job; and I set out for the Montgomery Hotel, satisfied that my only hope for success—barring miracles, which usually don't happen—lay in finding the letter that I believed Dr. Estep had written to his first wife.

My drag with the Montgomery Hotel management was pretty strong—strong enough to get me anything I wanted that wasn't too far outside the law. So as soon as I got there, I hunted up Stacey, one of the assistant managers.

"This Mrs. Estep who's registered here," I asked, "what do you know about her?"

"Nothing, myself, but if you'll wait a few minutes I'll see what I can learn."

The assistant manager was gone about ten minutes.

"No one seems to know much about her," he told me when he came back. "I've questioned the telephone girls, bell-boys, maids, clerks, and the house detective; but none of them could tell me much.

"She registered from Louisville, on the second of the month. She has never stopped here before, and she seems unfamiliar with the city—asks quite a few questions about how to get around. The mail clerks don't remember handling any mail for her, nor do the girls on the switchboard have any record of phone calls for her.

"She keeps regular hours—usually goes out at ten or later in the morning, and gets in before midnight. She doesn't seem to have any callers or friends."

"Will you have her mail watched—let me know what postmarks and return addresses are on any letters she gets?"

"Certainly."

"And have the girls on the switchboard put their ears up against any talking she does over the wire?"

"Yes."

"Is she in her room now?"

"No, she went out a little while ago."

"Fine! I'd like to go up and take a look at her stuff."

Stacey looked sharply at me, and cleared his throat.

"Is it as—ah—important as all that? I want to give you all the assistance I can, but—"

"It's this important," I assured him, "that another woman's life depends on what I can learn about this one."

"All right!" he said. "I'll tell the clerk to let us know if she comes in before we are through; and we'll go right up."

The woman's room held two valises and a trunk, all unlocked, and containing not the least thing of importance—no letters—nothing. So little, in fact, that I was more than half convinced that she had expected her things to be searched.

Downstairs again, I planted myself in a comfortable chair within sight of the key rack, and waited for a view of this first Mrs. Estep.

She came in at 11:15 that night. A large woman of forty-five or fifty, well dressed, and carrying herself with an air of assurance. Her face was a little too hard as to mouth and chin, but not enough to be ugly. A capable looking woman—a woman who would get what she went after.

III

Eight o'clock was striking as I went into the Montgomery lobby the next morning and picked out a chair, this time, within eye-range of the elevators.

At 10:30 Mrs. Estep left the hotel, with me in her wake. Her denial that a letter from her husband, written immediately before his death, had come to her didn't fit in with the possibilities as I saw them. And a good motto for the detective business is, "When in doubt—shadow 'em."

After eating breakfast at a restaurant on O'Farrell Street, she turned toward the shopping district; and for a long, long time—though I suppose it was a lot shorter than it seemed to me—she led me through the most densely packed portions of the most crowded department stores she could find.

She didn't buy anything, but she did a lot of thorough looking, with me muddling along behind her, trying to act like a little fat guy on an errand for his wife; while stout women bumped me and thin ones prodded me and all sorts got in my way and walked on my feet.

Finally, after I had sweated off a couple of pounds, she left the shopping district, and cut up through Union Square, walking along casually, as if out for a stroll.

Three-quarters way through, she turned abruptly, and retraced her steps, looking sharply at everyone she passed. I was on a bench, reading a stray page from a day-old newspaper, when she went by. She walked on down Post Street to Kearny, stopping every now and then to look—or to pretend to look—in store windows; while I ambled along sometimes beside her, sometimes almost by her side, and sometimes in front.

She was trying to check up the people around her, trying to determine whether she was being followed or not. But here, in the busy part of town, that gave me no cause for worry. On a less crowded street it might have been different, though not necessarily so.

There are four rules for shadowing: Keep behind your subject as much as possible; never try to hide from him; act in a natural manner no matter what happens; and never meet his eye. Obey them, and, except in unusual circumstances, shadowing is the easiest thing that a sleuth has to do.

Assured, after a while, that no one was following her, Mrs. Estep turned back toward Powell Street, and got into a taxicab at the St. Francis stand. I picked out a modest touring car from the rank of hire-cars along the Geary Street side of Union Square, and set out after her.

Our route was out Post Street to Laguna, where the taxi presently swung into the curb and stopped. The woman got out, paid the driver, and went up the steps of an apartment building. With idling engine my own car had come to rest against the opposite curb in the block above.

As the taxicab disappeared around a corner, Mrs. Estep came out of the apartment building doorway, went back to the sidewalk, and started down Laguna Street.

"Pass her," I told my chauffeur, and we drew down upon her.

As we came abreast, she went up the front steps of another building, and this time she rang a bell. These steps belonged to a building apparently occupied by four flats, each with its separate door, and the button she had pressed belonged to the right-hand second-story flat.

Under cover of my car's rear curtains, I kept my eye on the doorway while my driver found a convenient place to park in the next block.

I kept my eye on the vestibule until 5:35 P.M., when she came out, walked to the Sutter Street car line, returned to the Montgomery, and went to her room.

I called up the Old Man—the Continental Detective Agency's San Francisco manager—and asked him to detail an operative to learn who and what were the occupants of the Laguna Street flat.

That night Mrs. Estep ate dinner at her hotel, and went to a show afterward, and she displayed no interest in possible shadowers. She went to her room at a little after eleven, and I knocked off for the day.

IV

The following morning I turned the woman over to Dick Foley, and went back to the Agency to wait for Bob Teale, the operative who had investigated the Laguna Street flat. He came in at a little after ten.

"A guy named Jacob Ledwich lives there," Bob said. "He's a crook of some sort, but I don't know just what. He and 'Wop' Healey are friendly, so he must be a crook! 'Porky' Grout says he's an ex-bunco man who is in with a gambling ring now; but 'Porky' would tell you a bishop was a safe-ripper if he thought it would mean five bucks for himself.

"This Ledwich goes out mostly at night, and he seems to be pretty prosperous. Probably a high-class worker of some sort. He's got a Buick—license number 645-221—that he keeps in a garage around the corner from his flat. But he doesn't seem to use the car much."

"What sort of looking fellow is he?"

"A big guy—six feet or better—and he'll weigh a couple hundred easy. He's got a funny mug on him. It's broad and heavy around the cheeks and jaw, but his mouth is a little one that looks like it was made for a smaller man. He's no youngster—middle-aged."

"Suppose you tail him around for a day or two, Bob, and see what he's up to. Try to get a room or apartment in the neighborhood—a place that you can cover his front door from."

V

Vance Richmond's lean face lighted up as soon as I mentioned Ledwich's name to him.

"Yes!" he exclaimed. "He was a friend, or at least an acquaintance, of Dr. Estep's. I met him once—a large man with a peculiarly inadequate mouth. I dropped in to see the doctor one day, and Ledwich was in the office. Dr. Estep introduced us."

"What do you know about him?"

"Nothing."

"Don't you know whether he was intimate with the doctor, or just a casual acquaintance?"

"No. For all I know, he might have been a friend, a patient, or almost anything. The doctor never spoke of him to me, and nothing passed between them while I was there that afternoon. I simply gave the doctor some information he had asked for and left. Why?"

"Dr. Estep's first wife—after going to a lot of trouble to see that she wasn't followed—connected with Ledwich yesterday afternoon. And from what we can learn, he seems to be a crook of some sort."

"What would that indicate?"

"I'm not sure what it means, but I can do a lot of guessing. Ledwich knew both the doctor and the doctor's first wife; then it's not a bad bet that *she* knew where her husband was all the time. If she did, then it's another good bet that she was getting money from him right along. Can you check up his accounts and see whether he was passing out any money that can't be otherwise accounted for?"

The attorney shook his head.

"No, his accounts are in rather bad shape, carelessly kept. He must have had more than a little difficulty with his income tax statements."

"I see. To get back to my guesses: If she knew where he was all the time, and was getting money from him, then why did his first wife finally come to see her husband? Perhaps because—"

"I think I can help you there," Richmond interrupted. "A fortunate investment in lumber nearly doubled Dr. Estep's wealth two or three months ago."

"That's it, then! She learned of it through Ledwich. She demanded, either through Ledwich, or by letter, a rather large share of it—more than the doctor was willing to give. When he refused, she came to see him in person, to demand the money under threat—we'll say—of instant exposure. He thought she was in earnest. Either he couldn't raise the money she demanded, or he was tired of leading a double life. Anyway, he thought it all over, and decided to commit suicide. This is all a guess, or a series of guesses—but it sounds reasonable to me."

"To me, too," the attorney said. "What are you going to do now?"

"I'm still having both of them shadowed—there's no other way of tackling them just now. I'm having the woman looked up in Louisville. But, you understand, I might dig up a whole flock of things on them, and when I got through still be as far as ever from finding the letter Dr. Estep wrote before he died.

"There are plenty of reasons for thinking that the woman destroyed the letter—that would have been her wisest play. But if I can get enough on her, even at that, I can squeeze her into admitting that the letter was written, and that it said something about suicide—if it did. And that will be enough to spring your client. How is she today—any better?"

His thin face lost the animation that had come to it during our discussion of Ledwich, and became bleak.

"She went completely to pieces last night, and was removed to the hospital, where she should have been taken in the first place. To tell you the truth, if she isn't liberated soon, she won't need our help. I've done my utmost to have her released on bail—pulled every wire I know—but there's little likelihood of success in that direction.

"Knowing that she is a prisoner—charged with murdering her husband—is killing her. She isn't young, and she has always been subject to nervous disorders. The bare shock of her husband's death was enough to prostrate her—but now— You've *got* to get her out—and quickly!"

He was striding up and down his office, his voice throbbing with feeling. I left quickly.

VI

From the attorney's office, I returned to the Agency, where I was told that Bob Teale had phoned in the address of a furnished apartment he had rented on Laguna Street. I hopped on a street car, and went up to take a look at it.

But I didn't get that far.

Walking down Laguna Street, after leaving the car, I spied Bob Teale coming toward me. Between Bob and me—also coming toward me—was a big man whom I recognized as Jacob Ledwich: a big man with a big red face around a tiny mouth.

I walked on down the street, passing both Ledwich and Bob, without paying any apparent attention to either. At the next corner I stopped to roll a cigarette, and steal a look at the pair.

And then I came to life!

Ledwich had stopped at a vestibule cigar stand up the street to make a purchase. Bob Teale, knowing his stuff, had passed him and was walking steadily up the street.

He was figuring that Ledwich had either come out for the purpose of buying cigars or cigarettes, and would return to his flat with them; or that after making his purchase the big man would proceed to the car line, where, in either event, Bob would wait.

But as Ledwich had stopped before the cigar stand, a man across the street had stepped suddenly into a doorway, and stood there, back in the shadows. This man, I now remembered, had been on the opposite side of the street from Bob and Ledwich, and walking in the same direction.

He, too, was following Ledwich.

By the time Ledwich had finished his business at the stand, Bob had reached Sutter Street, the nearest car line. Ledwich started up the street in that direction. The man in the doorway stepped out and went after him. I followed that one.

A ferry-bound car came down Sutter Street just as I reached the corner. Ledwich and I got aboard together. The mysterious stranger fumbled with a shoe-string several pavements from the corner until the car was moving again, and then he likewise made a dash for it.

He stood beside me on the rear platform, hiding behind a large man in overalls, past whose shoulder he now and then peeped at Ledwich. Bob had gone to the corner above, and was already seated when Ledwich, this amateur detective,—there was no doubting his amateur status,—and I got on the car.

I sized up the amateur while he strained his neck peeping at Ledwich. He was small, this sleuth, and scrawny and frail. His most noticeable feature was his nose—a limp organ that twitched nervously all the time. His clothes were old and shabby, and he himself was somewhere in his fifties.

After studying him for a few minutes, I decided that he hadn't tumbled to Bob Teale's part in the game. His attention had been too firmly fixed upon Ledwich, and the distance had been too short thus far for him to discover that Bob was also tailing the big man.

So when the seat beside Bob was vacated presently, I chucked my cigarette away, went into the car, and sat down, my back toward the little man with the twitching nose.

"Drop off after a couple of blocks and go back to the apartment. Don't shadow Ledwich any more until I tell you. Just watch his place. There's a bird following him, and I want to see what he's up to," I told Bob in an undertone.

He grunted that he understood, and, after few minutes, left the car.

At Stockton Street, Ledwich got off, the man with the twitching nose behind him, and me in the rear. In that formation we paraded around town all afternoon.

The big man had business in a number of pool rooms, cigar stores, and soft drink parlors—most of which I knew for places where you can get a bet down on any horse that's running in North America, whether at Tanforan, Tijuana, or Timonium.

Just what Ledwich did in these places, I didn't learn. I was bringing up the rear of the procession, and my interest was centered upon the mysterious little stranger. He didn't enter any of the places behind Ledwich, but loitered in their neighborhoods until Ledwich reappeared.

He had a rather strenuous time of it—laboring mightily to keep out of Ledwich's sight, and only succeeding because we were downtown, where you can get away with almost any sort of shadowing. He certainly made a lot of work for himself, dodging here and there.

After a while, Ledwich shook him.

The big man came out of a cigar store with another man. They got into an automobile that was standing beside the curb, and drove away; leaving my man standing on the edge of the sidewalk twitching his nose in chagrin. There was a taxi stand just around the corner, but he either didn't know it or didn't have enough money to pay the fare.

I expected him to return to Laguna Street then, but he didn't. He led me down Kearney Street to Portsmouth Street, where he stretched himself out on the grass, face down, lit a black pipe, and lay looking dejectedly at the Stevenson monument, probably without seeing it.

I sprawled on a comfortable piece of sod some distance away—between a Chinese woman with two perfectly round children and an ancient Portuguese in a gaily checkered suit—and we let the afternoon go by.

When the sun had gone low enough for the ground to become chilly, the little man got up, shook himself, and went back up Kearney Street to a cheap lunch-room, where he ate meagerly. Then he entered a hotel a few doors away, took a key from the row of hooks, and vanished down a dark corridor.

Running through the register, I found that the key he had taken belonged to a room whose occupant was "John Boyd, St. Louis, Mo.," and that he had arrived the day before.

This hotel wasn't of the sort where it is safe to make inquiries, so I went down to the street again, and came to rest on the least conspicuous nearby corner.

Twilight came, and the street and shop lights were turned on. It got dark. The night traffic of Kearney Street went up and down past me: Filipino boys in their too-dapper clothes, bound for the inevitable black-jack game; gaudy women still heavy-eyed from their day's sleep; plain clothes men on their way to headquarters, to report before going off duty; Chinese going to or from Chinatown; sailors in pairs, looking for action of any sort; hungry people making for the Italian and French restaurants; worried people going into the bail bond broker's office on the corner to arrange for the release of friends and relatives whom the police had nabbed; Italians on their homeward journeys from work; odds and ends of furtive-looking citizens on various shady errands.

Midnight came, and no John Boyd, and I called it a day, and went home.

Before going to bed, I talked with Dick Foley over the wire. He said that Mrs. Estep had done nothing of any importance all day, and had received neither mail nor phone calls. I told him to stop shadowing her until I solved John Boyd's game.

I was afraid Boyd might turn his attention to the woman, and I didn't want him to discover that she was being shadowed. I had already instructed Bob Teale to simply watch Ledwich's flat—to see when he came in and went out, and with whom—and now I told Dick to do the same with the woman.

My guess on this Boyd person was that he and the woman were working together—that she had him watching Ledwich for her, so that the big man couldn't double-cross her. But that was only a guess—and I don't gamble too much on my guesses.

VII

The next morning I dressed myself up in an army shirt and shoes, an old faded cap, and a suit that wasn't downright ragged, but was shabby enough not to stand out too noticeably beside John Boyd's old clothes.

It was a little after nine o'clock when Boyd left his hotel and had breakfast at the grease-joint where he had eaten the night before. Then he went up to Laguna Street, picked himself a corner, and waited for Jacob Ledwich.

He did a lot of waiting. He waited all day; because Ledwich didn't show until after dark. But the little man was well-stocked with patience—I'll say that for him. He fidgeted, and stood on one foot and then the other, and even tried sitting on the curb for awhile, but he stuck it out.

I took it easy, myself. The furnished apartment Bob Teale had rented to watch Ledwich's flat from was a ground floor one, across the street, and just a little above the corner where Boyd waited. So we could watch him and the flat with one eye.

Bob and I sat and smoked and talked all day, taking turns watching the fidgeting man on the corner and Ledwich's door.

Night had just definitely settled when Ledwich came out and started up toward the car line. I slid out into the street, and our parade was under way again—Ledwich leading, Boyd following him, and we following *him*.

Half a block of this, and I got an idea!

I'm not what you'd call a brilliant thinker—such results as I get are usually the fruits of patience, industry, and unimaginative plugging, helped out now and then, maybe, by a little luck—but I do have my flashes of intelligence. And this was one of them.

Ledwich was about a block ahead of me; Boyd half that distance. Speeding up, I passed Boyd, and caught up with Ledwich. Then I slackened my pace so as to walk beside him, though with no appearance from the rear of having any interest in him.

"Jake," I said, without turning my head, "there's a guy following you!"

The big man almost spoiled my little scheme by stopping dead still, but he caught himself in time, and, taking his cue from me, kept walking.

"Who the hell are you?" he growled.

"Don't get funny!" I snapped back, still looking and walking ahead. "It ain't my funeral. But I was coming up the street when you came out, and I seen this guy duck behind a pole until you was past, and then follow you up."

That got him.

"You sure?"

"Sure! All you got to do to prove it is turn the next corner and wait."

I was two or three steps ahead of him by this time, I turned the corner, and halted, with my back against the brick building front. Ledwich took up the same position at my side.

"Want any help?" I grinned at him—a reckless sort of grin, unless my acting was poor.

"No."

His little lumpy mouth was set ugly, and his blue eyes were hard as pebbles.

I flicked the tail of my coat aside to show him the butt of my gun.

"Want to borrow the rod?" I asked.

"No."

He was trying to figure me out, and small wonder.

"Don't mind if I stick around to see the fun, do you?" I asked, mockingly.

There wasn't time for him to answer that. Boyd had quickened his steps, and now he came hurrying around the corner, his nose twitching like a tracking dog's.

Ledwich stepped into the middle of the sidewalk, so suddenly that the little man thudded into him with a grunt. For a moment they stared at each other, and there was recognition between them.

Ledwich shot one big hand out and clamped the other by a shoulder.

"What are you snooping around me for, you rat? Didn't I tell you to keep away from 'Frisco?"

"Aw, Jake!" Boyd begged. "I didn't mean no harm. I just thought that—"

Ledwich silenced him with a shake that clicked his mouth shut, and turned to me.

"A friend of mine," he sneered.

His eyes grew suspicious and hard again, and ran up and down me from cap to shoes.

"How'd you know my name?" he demanded.

"A famous man like you?" I asked, in burlesque astonishment.

"Never mind the comedy!" He took a threatening step toward me. "How'd you know my name?"

"None of your damned business," I snapped.

My attitude seemed to reassure him. His face became less suspicious.

"Well," he said slowly, "I owe you something for this trick, and— How are you fixed?"

"I have been dirtier." Dirty is Pacific Coast argot for prosperous.

He looked speculatively from me to Boyd, and back.

"Know 'The Circle'?" he asked me.

I nodded. The underworld calls "Wop" Healey's joint 'The Circle.'

"If you'll meet me there tomorrow night, maybe I can put a piece of change your way."

"Nothing stirring!" I shook my head with emphasis. "I ain't circulating that prominent these days."

A fat chance I'd have of meeting him there! "Wop" Healey and half his customers knew me as a detective. So there was nothing to do but to try to get the impression over that I was a crook who had reasons for wanting to keep away from the more notorious hang-outs for a while. Apparently it got over. He thought a while, and then gave me his Laguna Street number.

"Drop in this time tomorrow and maybe I'll have a proposition to make you—if you've got the guts."

"I'll think it over," I said noncommittally, and turned as if to go down the street.

"Just a minute," he called, and I faced him again. "What's your name?"

"Wisher," I said, "Shine, if you want a front one."

"Shine Wisher," he repeated. "I don't remember ever hearing it before."

It would have surprised me if he had—I had made it up only about fifteen minutes before.

"You needn't yell it," I said sourly, "so that everybody in the burg *will* remember hearing it."

And with that I left him, not at all dissatisfied with myself. By tipping him off to Boyd, I had put him under obligations to me, and had led him to accept me, at least tentatively, as a fellow crook. And by making no apparent effort to gain his good graces, I had strengthened my hand that much more.

I had a date with him for the next day, when I was to be given a chance to earn—illegally, no doubt—"a piece of change."

There was a chance that this proposition he had in view for me had nothing to do with the Estep affair, but then again it might; and whether it did or not, I had my entering wedge at least a little way into Jake Ledwich's business.

I strolled around for about half an hour, and then went back to Bob Teale's apartment.

"Ledwich come back?"

"Yes," Bob said, "with that little guy of yours. They went in about half an hour ago."

"Good! Haven't seen a woman go in?"

"No."

I expected to see the first Mrs. Estep arrive sometime during the evening, but she didn't. Bob and I sat around and talked and watched Ledwich's doorway, and the hours passed.

At one o'clock Ledwich came out alone.

"I'm going to tail him, just for luck," Bob said, and caught up his cap.

Ledwich vanished around a corner, and then Bob passed out of sight behind him.

Five minutes later Bob was with me again.

"He's getting his machine out of the garage."

I jumped for the telephone and put in a rush order for a fast touring car.

Bob, at the window, called out, "Here he is!"

I joined Bob in time to see Ledwich going into his vestibule. His car stood in front of the house. A very few minutes, and Boyd and Ledwich came out together. Boyd was leaning heavily on Ledwich, who was supporting the little man with an arm across his back. We couldn't see their faces in the dark, but the little man was plainly either sick, drunk, or drugged!

Ledwich helped his companion into the touring car. The red tail-light laughed back at us for a few blocks, and then disappeared. The automobile I had ordered arrived twenty minutes later, so we sent it back unused.

At a little after three in the morning, Ledwich, alone and afoot, returned from the direction of his garage. He had been gone exactly two hours.

VIII

Neither Bob nor I went home that night, but slept in the Laguna Street apartment.

Bob went down to the corner grocer's to get what we needed for breakfast in the morning, and he brought a morning paper back with him.

I cooked breakfast while he divided his attention between Ledwich's front door and the newspaper.

"Hey!" he called suddenly, "look here!"

I ran out of the kitchen with a handful of bacon.

"What is it?"

"Listen! 'Park murder mystery!' " he read. " 'Early this morning the body of an unidentified man was found near a driveway in Golden Gate Park. His neck had been broken, according to the police, who say that the absence of any considerable bruises on the body, as well as the orderly condition of the clothes and the ground nearby, show that he did not come to his death through falling, or being struck by an automobile. It is believed that he was killed and then carried to the Park in an automobile, to be left there.'"

"Boyd!" I said.

"I bet you!" Bob agreed.

And at the morgue a very little while later, we learned that we were correct. The dead man was John Boyd.

"He was dead when Ledwich brought him out of the house," Bob said.

I nodded.

"He was! He was a little man, and it wouldn't have been much of a stunt for a big bruiser like Ledwich to have dragged him along with one arm the short distance from the door to the curb, pretending to be holding him up, like you do with a drunk. Let's go over to the Hall of Justice and see what the police have got on it—if anything."

At the detective bureau we hunted up O'Gar, the detective-sergeant in charge of the Homicide Detail, and a good man to work with.

"This dead man found in the park," I asked, "know anything about him?"

O'Gar pushed back his village constable's hat—a big black hat with a floppy brim that belongs in vaudeville—scratched his bullet-head, and scowled at me as if he thought I had a joke up my sleeve.

"Not a damned thing except that he's dead!" he said at last.

"How'd you like to know who he was last seen with?"

"It wouldn't hinder me any in finding out who bumped him off, and that's a fact."

"How do you like the sound of this?" I asked. "His name was John Boyd and he was living at a hotel down in the next block. The last person he was seen with was a guy who is tied up with Dr. Estep's first wife. You know—the Dr. Estep whose second wife is the woman you people are trying to prove a murder on. Does that sound interesting?"

"It does," he said. "Where do we go first?"

"This Ledwich—he's the fellow who was last seen with Boyd—is going to be a hard bird to shake down. We better try to crack the woman first—the first Mrs. Estep. There's a chance that Boyd was a pal of hers, and in that case when she finds out that Ledwich rubbed him out, she may open up and spill the works to us.

"On the other hand, if she and Ledwich are stacked up against Boyd together, then we might as well get her safely placed before we tie into him. I don't want to pull him before night, anyway. I got a date with him, and I want to try to rope him first."

Bob Teale made for the door.

"I'm going up and keep my eye on him until you're ready for him," he called over his shoulder.

"Good," I said. "Don't let him get out of town on us. If he tries to blow have him chucked in the can."

In the lobby of the Montgomery Hotel, O'Gar and I talked to Dick Foley first. He told us that the woman was still in her room—had had her breakfast sent up. She had received neither letters, telegrams, or phone calls since we began to watch her.

I got hold of Stacey again.

"We're going up to talk to this Estep woman, and maybe we'll take her away with us. Will you send up a maid to find out whether she's up and dressed yet? We don't want to announce ourselves ahead of time, and we don't want to burst in on her while she's in bed, or only partly dressed."

He kept us waiting about fifteen minutes, and then told us that Mrs. Estep was up and dressed.

We went up to her room, taking the maid with us.

The maid rapped on the door.

"What is it?" an irritable voice demanded.

"The maid; I want to—"

The key turned on the inside, and an angry Mrs. Estep jerked the door open. O'Gar and I advanced, O'Gar flashing his "buzzer."

"From headquarters," he said. "We want to talk to you."

O'Gar's foot was where she couldn't slam the door on us, and we were both walking ahead, so there was nothing for her to do but to retreat into the room, admitting us—which she did with no pretense of graciousness.

We closed the door, and then I threw our big load at her.

"Mrs. Estep, why did Jake Ledwich kill John Boyd?"

The expressions ran over her face like this: Alarm at Ledwich's name, fear at the word "kill," but the name John Boyd brought only bewilderment.

"Why did what?" she stammered meaninglessly, to gain time.

"Exactly," I said. "Why did Jake kill him last night in his flat, and then take him in the park and leave him?"

Another set of expressions: Increased bewilderment until I had almost finished the sentence, and then the sudden understanding of something, followed by the inevitable groping for poise. These things weren't as plain as billboards, you understand, but they were there to be read by anyone who had ever played poker—either with cards or people.

What I got out of them was that Boyd hadn't been working with or for her, and that, though she knew Ledwich had killed somebody at some time, it wasn't Boyd and it wasn't last night. Who, then? And when? Dr. Estep? Hardly! There wasn't a chance in the world that—if he had been murdered—anybody except his wife had done it—his second wife. No possible reading of the evidence could bring any other answer.

Who, then, had Ledwich killed before Boyd? Was he a wholesale murderer?

These things are flitting through my head in flashes and odd scraps while Mrs. Estep is saying:

"This is absurd! The idea of your coming up here and—"

She talked for five minutes straight, the words fairly sizzling from between her hard lips; but the words themselves didn't mean anything. She was talking for time—talking while she tried to hit upon the safest attitude to assume.

And before we could head her off, she had hit upon it—silence!

We got not another word out of her; and that is the only way in the world to beat the grilling game. The average suspect tries to talk himself out of being arrested; and it doesn't matter how shrewd a man is, or how good a liar, if he'll talk to you, and you play your cards right, you can hook him—can make him help you convict him. But if he won't talk you can't do a thing with him.

And that's how it was with this woman. She refused to pay any attention to our questions—she wouldn't speak, nod, grunt, or wave an arm in reply. She gave us a fine assortment of facial expressions, true enough, but we wanted verbal information—and we got none.

We weren't easily licked, however. Three beautiful hours of it we gave her without rest. We stormed, cajoled, threatened, and at times I think we danced; but it was no go. So in the end we took her away with us. We didn't have anything on her, but we couldn't afford to have her running around loose until we nailed Ledwich.

At the Hall of Justice we didn't book her; but simply held her as a material witness, putting her in an office with a matron and one of O'Gar's men, who were to see what they could do with her while we went after Ledwich. We had had her frisked as soon as she reached the Hall, of course; and, as we expected, she hadn't a thing of importance on her.

O'Gar and I went back to the Montgomery and gave her room a thorough overhauling—and found nothing.

"Are you sure you know what you're talking about?" the detective-sergeant asked as we left the hotel. "It's going to be a pretty joke on somebody if you're mistaken."

I let that go by without an answer.

"I'll meet you at 6:30," I said, "and we'll go up against Ledwich."

He grunted an approval, and I set out for Vance Richmond's office.

IX

The attorney sprang up from his desk as soon as his stenographer admitted me. His face was leaner and grayer than ever; its lines had deepened, and there was a hollowness around his eyes.

"You've *got* to do something!" he cried huskily. "I have just come from the hospital. Mrs. Estep is on the point of death! A day more of this—two days at the most—and she will—"

I interrupted him, and swiftly gave him an account of the day's happenings, and what I expected, or hoped, to make out of them. But he received the news without brightening, and shook his head hopelessly.

"But don't you see," he exclaimed when I had finished, "that that won't do? I know you can find proof of her innocence in time. I'm not complaining—you've done all that could be expected, and more! But all that's no good! I've got to have—well—a miracle, perhaps.

"Suppose that you do finally get the truth out of Ledwich and the first Mrs. Estep or it comes out during their trials for Boyd's murder? Or that you even get to the bottom of the matter in three or four days? That will be too late! If I can go to Mrs. Estep and tell her she's free now, she may pull herself together, and come through. But another day of imprisonment—two days, or perhaps even two hours—and she won't need anybody to clear her. Death will have done it! I tell you, she's—"

I left Vance Richmond abruptly again. This lawyer was bound upon getting me worked up; and I like my jobs to be simply jobs—emotions are nuisances during business hours.

X

At a quarter to seven that evening, while O'Gar remained down the street, I rang Jacob Ledwich's bell. As I had stayed with Bob Teale in our apartment the previous night, I was still wearing the clothes in which I had made Ledwich's acquaintance as Shine Wisher.

Ledwich opened the door.

"Hello, Wisher!" he said without enthusiasm, and led me upstairs.

His flat consisted of four rooms, I found, running the full length and half the breadth of the building, with both front and rear exits. It was furnished with the ordinary none-too-spotless appointments of the typical moderately priced furnished flat—alike the world over.

In his front room we sat down and talked and smoked and sized one another up. He seemed a little nervous. I thought he would have been just as well satisfied if I had forgotten to show up.

"About this job you mentioned?" I asked presently.

"Sorry," he said, moistening his little lumpy mouth, "but it's all off." And then he added, obviously as an afterthought, "for the present, at least."

I guessed from that that my job was to have taken care of Boyd—but Boyd had been taken care of for good.

He brought out some whisky after a while, and we talked over it for some time, to no purpose whatever. He was trying not to appear too anxious to get rid of me, and I was cautiously feeling him out.

Piecing together things he let fall here and there, I came to the conclusion that he was a former con man who had fallen into an easier game of late years. That was in line, too, with what "Porky" Grout had told Bob Teale.

I talked about myself with the evasiveness that would have been natural to a crook in my situation; and made one or two carefully planned slips that would lead him to believe that I had been tied up with the "Jimmy the Riveter" hold-up mob, most of whom were doing long hitches at Walla Walla then.

He offered to lend me enough money to tide me over until I could get on my feet again. I told him I didn't need chicken feed so much as a chance to pick up some real jack.

The evening was going along, and we were getting nowhere.

"Jake," I said casually—outwardly casual, that is, "you took a big chance putting that guy out of the way like you did last night."

I meant to stir things up, and I succeeded.

His face went crazy.

A gun came out of his coat.

Firing from my pocket, I shot it out of his hand.

"Now behave!" I ordered.

He sat rubbing his benumbed hand and staring with wide eyes at the smouldering hole in my coat.

Looks like a great stunt—this shooting a gun out of a man's hand, but it's a thing that happens now and then. A man who is a fair shot (and that is exactly what I am—no more, no less), naturally and automatically shoots pretty close to the spot upon which his eyes are focused. When a man goes for his gun in front of you, you shoot at *him*—not at any particular part of him. There isn't time for that—you shoot at *him*. However, you are more than likely to be looking at his gun, and in that case it isn't altogether surprising if your bullet should hit his gun—as mine had done. But it looks impressive.

I beat out the fire around the bullet-hole in my coat, crossed the room to where his revolver had been knocked, and picked it up. I started to eject the bullets from it, but, instead, I snapped it shut again and stuck it in my pocket. Then I returned to my chair, opposite him.

"A man oughtn't to act like that," I kidded him, "he's likely to hurt somebody."

His little mouth curled up at me.

"An elbow, huh?" putting all the contempt he could in his voice; and somehow any synonym for detective seems able to hold a lot of contempt.

I might have tried to talk myself back into the Wisher role. It could have been done, but I doubted that it would be worth it; so I nodded my confession.

His brain was working now, and the passion left his face, while he sat rubbing his right hand, and his little mouth and eyes began to screw themselves up calculatingly.

I kept quiet, waiting to see what the outcome of his thinking would be. I knew he was trying to figure out just what my place in this game was. Since, to his knowledge, I had come into it no later than the previous evening, then the Boyd murder hadn't brought me in. That would leave the Estep affair—unless he was tied up in a lot of other crooked stuff that I didn't know anything about.

"You're not a city dick, are you?" he asked finally; and his voice was on the verge of friendliness now: the voice of one who wants to persuade you of something, or sell you something.

The truth, I thought, wouldn't hurt.

"No," I said, "I'm with the Continental."

He hitched his chair a little closer to the muzzle of my automatic.

"What are you after, then? Where do you come in on it?"

I tried the truth again.

"The second Mrs. Estep. She didn't kill her husband."

"You're trying to dig up enough dope to spring her?"

"Yes."

I waved him back as he tried to hitch his chair still nearer.

"How do you expect to do it?" he asked, his voice going lower and more confidential with each word.

I took still another flier at the truth.

"He wrote a letter before he died."

"Well?"

But I called a halt for the time.

"Just that," I said.

He leaned back in his chair, and his eyes and mouth grew small in thought again.

"What's your interest in the man who died last night?" he asked slowly.

"It's something on you," I said, truthfully again. "It doesn't do the second Mrs. Estep any direct good, maybe; but you and the first wife are stacked up together against her. Anything, therefore, that hurts you two will help her, somehow. I admit I'm wandering around in the dark; but I'm going ahead wherever I see a point of light—and I'll come through to daylight in the end. Nailing you for Boyd's murder is one point of light."

He leaned forward suddenly, his eyes and mouth popping open as far as they would go.

"You'll come out all right," he said very softly, "if you use a little judgment."

"What's that supposed to mean?"

"Do you think," he asked, still very softly, "that you can nail me for Boyd's murder—that you can convict me of murder?"

"I do."

But I wasn't any too sure. In the first place, though we were morally certain of it, neither Bob Teale nor I could swear that the man who had got in the machine with Ledwich was John Boyd.

We knew it was, of course, but the point is that it had been too dark for us to see his face. And, again, in the dark, we had thought him alive; it wasn't until later that we knew he had been dead when he came down the steps.

Little things, those, but a private detective on the witness stand—unless he is absolutely sure of every detail—has an unpleasant and ineffectual time of it.

"I do," I repeated, thinking these things over, "and I'm satisfied to go to the bat with what I've got on you and what I can collect between now and the time you and your accomplice go to trial."

"Accomplice?" he said, not very surprised. "That would be Edna. I suppose you've already grabbed her?"

"Yes."

He laughed.

"You'll have one sweet time getting anything out of her. In the first place, she doesn't know much, and in the second— well, I suppose you've tried, and have found out what a helpful sort she is! So don't try the old gag of pretending that she has talked!"

"I'm not pretending anything."

Silence between us for a few seconds, and then—

"I'm going to make you a proposition," he said. "You can take it or leave it. The note Dr. Estep wrote before he died was to me, and it is positive proof that he committed suicide. Give me a chance to get away—just a chance—a half-hour start—and I'll give you my word of honor to send you the letter."

"I know I can trust you," I said sarcastically.

"I'll trust you, then!" he shot back at me. "I'll turn the note over to you if you'll give me your word that I'm to have half an hour's start."

"For what?" I demanded. "Why shouldn't I take both you and the note?"

"If you can get them! But do I look like the kind of sap who would leave the note where it would be found? Do you think it's here in the room maybe?"

I didn't, but neither did I think that because he had hidden it, it couldn't be found.

"I can't think of any reason why I should bargain with you," I told him. "I've got you cold, and that's enough."

"If I can show you that your only chance of freeing the second Mrs. Estep is through my voluntary assistance, will you bargain with me?"

"Maybe—I'll listen to your persuasion, anyway."

"All right," he said, "I'm going to come clean with you. But most of the things I'm going to tell you can't be proven

in court without my help; and if you turn my offer down I'll
have plenty of evidence to convince the jury that these things
are all false, that I never said them, and that you are trying to
frame me."

That part was plausible enough. I've testified before juries
all the way from the City of Washington to the State of
Washington, and I've never seen one yet that wasn't anxious
to believe that a private detective is a double-crossing special
ist who goes around with a cold deck in one pocket, a complete forger's outfit in another, and who counts that day lost
in which he railroads no innocent to the hoosgow.

XI

"There was once a young doctor in a town a long way from
here," Ledwich began. "He got mixed up in a scandal—a
pretty rotten one—and escaped the pen only by the skin of
his teeth. The state medical board revoked his license.

"In a large city not far away, this young doc, one night
when he was drunk,—as he usually was in those days,—told
his troubles to a man he had met in a dive. The friend was a
resourceful sort; and he offered, for a price, to fix the doc up
with a fake diploma, so he could set up in practice in some
other state.

"The young doctor took him up, and the friend got the
diploma for him. The doc was the man you know as Dr.
Estep, and I was the friend. The real Dr. Estep was found
dead in the park this morning!"

That was news—if true!

"You see," the big man went on, "when I offered to get
the phoney diploma for the young doc—whose real name
doesn't matter—I had in mind a forged one. Nowadays
they're easy to get—there's a regular business in them,—but
twenty-five years ago, while you could manage it, they were
hard to get. While I was trying to get one, I ran across a
woman I used to work with—Edna Fife. That's the woman
you know as the first Mrs. Estep.

"Edna had married a doctor—the real Dr. Humbert Estep.
He was a hell of a doctor, though; and after starving with him
in Philadelphia for a couple of years, she made him close up

his office, and she went back to the bunko game, taking him with her. She was good at it, I'm telling you—a real cleaner—and, keeping him under her thumb all the time, she made him a pretty good worker himself.

"It was shortly after that that I met her, and when she told me all this, I offered to buy her husband's medical diploma and other credentials. I don't know whether he wanted to sell them or not—but he did what she told him, and I got the papers.

"I turned them over to the young doc, who came to San Francisco and opened an office under the name of Humbert Estep. The real Esteps promised not to use that name any more—not much of an inconvenience for them, as they changed names every time they changed addresses.

"I kept in touch with the young doctor, of course, getting my regular rake-off from him. I had him by the neck, and I wasn't foolish enough to pass up any easy money. After a year or so, I learned that he had pulled himself together and was making good. So I jumped on a train and came to San Francisco. He was doing fine; so I camped here, where I could keep my eye on him and watch out for my own interests.

"He got married about then, and, between his practice and his investments, he began to accumulate a roll. But he tightened up on me—damn him! He wouldn't be bled. I got a regular percentage of what he made, and that was all.

"For nearly twenty-five years I got it—but not a nickel over the percentage. He knew I wouldn't kill the goose that laid the golden eggs, so no matter how much I threatened to expose him, he sat tight, and I couldn't budge him. I got my regular cut, and not a nickel more.

"That went along, as I say, for years. I was getting a living out of him, but I wasn't getting any big money. A few months ago I learned that he had cleaned up heavily in a lumber deal so I made up my mind to take him for what he had.

"During all these years I had got to know the Doc pretty well. You do when you're bleeding a man—you get a pretty fair idea of what goes on in his head, and what he's most likely to do if certain things should happen. So I knew the doc pretty well.

"I knew for instance, that he had never told his wife the truth about his past; that he had stalled her with some lie about being born in West Virginia. That was fine—for me! Then I knew that he kept a gun in his desk, and I knew why. It was kept there for the purpose of killing himself if the truth ever came out about his diploma. He figured that if, at the first hint of exposure, he wiped himself out, the authorities, out of respect for the good reputation he had built up, would hush things up.

"And his wife—even if she herself learned the truth—would be spared the shame of a public scandal. I can't see myself dying just to spare some woman's feeling, but the doc was a funny guy in some ways—and he was nutty about his wife.

"That's the way I had him figured out, and that's the way things turned out.

"My plan might sound complicated, but it was simple enough. I got hold of the real Esteps—it took a lot of hunting, but I found them at last. I brought the woman to San Francisco, and told the man to stay away.

"Everything would have gone fine if he had done what I told him; but he was afraid that Edna and I were going to double-cross him, so he came here to keep an eye on us. But I didn't know that until you put the finger on him for me.

"I brought Edna here and, without telling her any more than she had to know, drilled her until she was letter-perfect in her part.

"A couple days before she came I had gone to see the doc, and had demanded a hundred thousand cool smacks. He laughed at me, and I left, pretending to be as hot as hell.

"As soon as Edna arrived, I sent her to call on him. She asked him to perform an illegal operation on her daughter. He, of course, refused. Then she pleaded with him, loud enough for the nurse or whoever else was in the reception-room to hear. And when she raised her voice she was careful to stick to words that could be interpreted the way we wanted them to. She ran off her end to perfection, leaving in tears.

"Then I sprung my other trick! I had a fellow—a fellow who's a whiz at that kind of stuff—make me a plate: an imitation of newspaper printing. It was all worded like the real article, and said that the state authorities were investigating information that a prominent surgeon in San Francisco was practising under a license secured by false credentials. This plate measured four and an eighth by six and three-quarter inches. If you'll look at the first inside page of the *Evening Times* any day in the week you'll see a photograph just that size.

"On the day after Edna's call, I bought a copy of the first edition of the *Times*—on the street at ten in the morning. I had this scratcher friend of mine remove the photograph with acid, and print this fake article in its place.

"That evening I substituted a 'home edition' outer sheet for the one that had come with the paper we had cooked up, and made a switch as soon as the doc's newsboy made his delivery. There was nothing to that part of it. The kid just tossed the paper into the vestibule. It's simply a case of duck into the doorway, trade papers, and go on, leaving the loaded one for the doc to read."

I was trying not to look too interested, but my ears were cocked for every word. At the start, I had been prepared for a string of lies. But I knew now that he was telling me the truth! Every syllable was a boast; he was half-drunk with appreciation of his own cleverness—the cleverness with which he had planned and carried out his program of treachery and murder.

I knew that he was telling the truth, and I suspected that he was telling more of it than he had intended. He was fairly bloated with vanity—the vanity that fills the crook almost invariably after a little success, and makes him ripe for the pen.

His eyes glistened, and his little mouth smiled triumphantly around the words that continued to roll out of it.

"The doc read the paper, all right—and shot himself. But first he wrote and mailed a note—to me. I didn't figure on his wife's being accused of killing him. That was plain luck.

"I figured that the fake piece in the paper would be overlooked in the excitement. Edna would then go forward, claiming to be his first wife; and his shooting himself after her first call, with what the nurse had overheard, would make his death seem a confession that Edna *was* his wife.

"I was sure that she would stand up under any sort of an investigation. Nobody knew anything about the doc's real past; except what he had told them, which would be found false.

"Edna had really married a Dr. Humbert Estep in Philadelphia in '96; and the twenty-seven years that had passed since then would do a lot to hide the fact that that Dr. Humbert Estep wasn't this Dr. Humbert Estep.

"All I wanted to do was convince the doc's real wife and her lawyers that she wasn't really his wife at all. And we did that! Everybody took it for granted that Edna was the legal wife.

"The next play would have been for Edna and the real wife to have reached some sort of an agreement about the estate, whereby Edna would have got the bulk—or at least half—of it; and nothing would have been made public.

"If worst came to worst, we were prepared to go to court. We were sitting pretty! But I'd have been satisfied with half the estate. It would have come to a few hundred thousand at the least, and that would have been plenty for me—even deducting the twenty thousand I had promised Edna.

"But when the police grabbed the doc's wife and charged her with his murder, I saw my way into the whole roll. All I had to do was sit tight and wait until they convicted her. Then the court would turn the entire pile over to Edna.

"I had the only evidence that would free the doc's wife: the note he had written me. But I couldn't—even if I had wanted to—have turned it in without exposing my hand. When he read that fake piece in the paper, he tore it out, wrote his message to me across the face of it, and sent it to me. So the note is a dead give-away. However, I didn't have any intention of publishing it, anyhow.

"Up to this point everything had gone like a dream. All I had to do was wait until it was time to cash in on my brains. And that's the time that the real Humbert Estep picked out to mess up the works.

"He shaved his mustache off, put on some old clothes, and came snooping around to see that Edna and I didn't run out on him. As if he could have stopped us! After you put the finger on him for me, I brought him up here.

"I intended salving him along until I could find a place to keep him until all the cards had been played. That's what I was going to hire you for—to take care of him.

"But we got to talking, and wrangling, and I had to knock him down. He didn't get up, and I found that he was dead. His neck was broken. There was nothing to do but take him out to the park and leave him.

"I didn't tell Edna. She didn't have a lot of use for him, as far as I could see, but you can't tell how women will take things. Anyhow, she'll stick, now that it's done. She's on the up and up all the time. And if she should talk, she can't do a lot of damage. She only knows her own part of the lay.

"All this long-winded story is so you'll know just exactly what you're up against. Maybe you think you can dig up the proof of these things I have told you. You can this far. You can prove that Edna wasn't the doc's wife. You can prove that I've been blackmailing him. But you can't prove that the doc's wife didn't *believe* that Edna was his real wife! It's her word against Edna's and mine.

"We'll swear that we had convinced her of it, which will give her a motive. You can't prove that the phoney news article I told you about ever existed. It'll sound like a hop-head's dream to a jury.

"You can't tie last night's murder on me—I've got an alibi that will knock your hat off! I can prove that I left here with a friend of mine who was drunk, and that I took him to his hotel and put him to bed, with the help of a night clerk and a bellboy. And what have you got against that? The word of two private detectives. Who'll believe you?

"You can convict me of conspiracy to defraud, or something—maybe. But, regardless of that, you can't free Mrs. Estep without my help.

"Turn me loose and I'll give you the letter the doc wrote me. It's the goods, right enough! In his own handwriting, written across the face of the fake newspaper story—which ought to fit the torn place in the paper that the police are supposed to be holding—and he wrote that he was going to kill himself, in words almost that plain."

That would turn the trick—there was no doubt of it. And I believed Ledwich's story. The more I thought it over the better I liked it. It fit into the facts everywhere. But I wasn't enthusiastic about giving this big crook his liberty.

"Don't make me laugh!" I said. "I'm going to put you away and free Mrs. Estep—both."

"Go ahead and try it! You're up against it without the letter; and you don't think a man with brains enough to plan a job like this one would be foolish enough to leave the note where it could be found, do you?"

I wasn't especially impressed with the difficulty of convicting this Ledwich and freeing the dead man's widow. His scheme—that cold-blooded zigzag of treachery for everybody he had dealt with, including his latest accomplice, Edna Estep—wasn't as airtight as he thought it. A week in which to run out a few lines in the East, and— But a week was just what I didn't have!

Vance Richmond's words were running through my head: "But another day of imprisonment—two days, or perhaps even two hours—and she won't need anybody to clear her. Death will have done it!"

If I was going to do Mrs. Estep any good, I had to move quick. Law or no law, her life was in my fat hands. This man before me—his eyes bright and hopeful now and his mouth anxiously pursed—was thief, blackmailer, double-crosser, and at least twice a murderer. I hated to let him walk out. But there was the woman dying in a hospital. . . .

XII

Keeping my eye on Ledwich, I went to the telephone, and got Vance Richmond on the wire at his residence.

"How is Mrs. Estep?" I asked.

"Weaker! I talked with the doctor half an hour ago, and he says—"

I cut in on him; I didn't want to listen to the details.

"Get over to the hospital, and be where I can reach you by phone. I may have news for you before the night is over."

"What— Is there a chance? Are you—"

I didn't promise him anything. I hung up the receiver and spoke to Ledwich. "I'll do this much for you. Slip me the note, and I'll give you your gun and put you out the back door. There's a bull on the corner out front, and I can't take you past him."

He was on his feet, beaming.

"Your word on it?" he demanded.

"Yes—get going!"

He went past me to the phone, gave a number (which I made a note of), and then spoke hurriedly into the instrument.

"This is Shuler. Put a boy in a taxi with that envelope I gave you to hold for me, and send him out here right away."

He gave his address, said "Yes" twice and hung up.

There was nothing surprising about his unquestioning acceptance of my word. He couldn't afford to doubt that I'd play fair with him. And, also, all successful bunko men come in time to believe that the world—except for themselves—is populated by a race of human sheep who may be trusted to conduct themselves with true sheep-like docility.

Ten minutes later the door-bell rang. We answered it together, and Ledwich took a large envelope from a messenger boy, while I memorized the number on the boy's cap. Then we went back to the front room.

Ledwich slit the envelope and passed its contents to me: a piece of rough-torn newspaper. Across the face of the fake article he had told me about was written a message in a jerky hand.

> I wouldn't have suspected you, Ledwich, of such profound stupidity. My last thought will be—this bullet that ends my life also ends your years of leisure. You'll have to go to work now.
>
> ESTEP.

The doctor had died game!

I took the envelope from the big man, put the death note in it, and put them in my pocket. Then I went to a front window, flattening a cheek against the glass until I could see O'Gar, dimly outlined in the night, patiently standing where I had left him hours before.

"The city dick is still on the corner," I told Ledwich. "Here's your gat"—holding out the gun I had shot from his fingers a little while back—"take it, and blow through the back door. Remember, that's all I'm offering you—the gun and a fair start. If you play square with me, I'll not do anything to help find you—unless I have to keep myself in the clear."

"Fair enough!"

He grabbed the gun, broke it to see that it was still loaded, and wheeled toward the rear of the flat. At the door he pulled up, hesitated, and faced me again. I kept him covered with my automatic.

"Will you do me a favor I didn't put in the bargain?" he asked.

"What is it?"

"That note of the doc's is in an envelope with my handwriting and maybe my fingerprints on it. Let me put it in a fresh envelope, will you? I don't want to leave any broader trail behind than I have to."

With my left hand—my right being busy with the gun—I fumbled for the envelope and tossed it to him. He took a plain envelope from the table, wiped it carefully with his handkerchief, put the note in it, taking care not to touch it with the balls of his fingers, and passed it back to me; and I put it in my pocket.

I had a hard time to keep from grinning in his face.

That fumbling with the handkerchief told me that the envelope in my pocket was empty, that the death-note was in Ledwich's possession—though I hadn't seen it pass there. He had worked one of his bunko tricks upon me.

"Beat it!" I snapped, to keep from laughing in his face.

He spun on his heel. His feet pounded against the floor. A door slammed in the rear.

I tore into the envelope he had given me. I needed to be sure he had double-crossed me.

The envelope was empty.

Our agreement was wiped out.

I sprang to the front window, threw it wide open, and leaned out. O'Gar saw me immediately—clearer than I could see him. I swung my arm in a wide gesture toward the rear of the house. O'Gar set out for the alley on the run. I dashed back through Ledwich's flat to the kitchen, and stuck my head out of an already open window.

I could see Ledwich against the white-washed fence—throwing the back gate open, plunging through it into the alley.

O'Gar's squat bulk appeared under a light at the end of the alley.

Ledwich's revolver was in his hand. O'Gar's wasn't—not quite.

Ledwich's gun swung up—the hammer clicked.

O'Gar's gun coughed fire.

Ledwich fell with a slow revolving motion over against the white fence, gasped once or twice, and went down in a pile.

I walked slowly down the stairs to join O'Gar; slowly, because it isn't a nice thing to look at a man you've deliberately sent to his death. Not even if it's the surest way of saving an innocent life, and if the man who dies is a Jake Ledwich—altogether treacherous.

"Howcome?" O'Gar asked, when I came into the alley, where he stood looking down at the dead man.

"He got out on me," I said simply.

"He must've."

I stooped and searched the dead man's pockets until I found the suicide note, still crumpled in the handkerchief. O'Gar was examining the dead man's revolver.

"Lookit!" he exclaimed. "Maybe this ain't my lucky day! He snapped at me once, and his gun missed fire. No wonder! Somebody must've been using an ax on it—the firing pin's broke clean off!"

"Is that so?" I asked; just as if I hadn't discovered, when I first picked the revolver up, that the bullet which had knocked it out of Ledwich's hand had made it harmless.

The House in Turk Street

I HAD been told that the man for whom I was hunting lived in a certain Turk Street block, but my informant hadn't been able to give me his house number. Thus it came about that late one rainy afternoon I was canvassing this certain block, ringing each bell, and reciting a myth that went like this:

"I'm from the law office of Wellington and Berkeley. One of our clients—an elderly lady—was thrown from the rear platform of a street car last week and severely injured. Among those who witnessed the accident, was a young man whose name we don't know. But we have been told that he lives in this neighborhood." Then I would describe the man I wanted, and wind up: "Do you know of anyone who looks like that?"

All down one side of the block the answers were:

"No," "No," "No."

I crossed the street and started to work the other side. The first house: "No."

The second: "No."

The third. The fourth.

The fifth—

No one came to the door in answer to my first ring. After a while, I rang again. I had just decided that no one was at home, when the knob turned slowly and a little old woman opened the door. She was a very fragile little old woman, with a piece of grey knitting in one hand, and faded eyes that twinkled pleasantly behind gold-rimmed spectacles. She wore a stiffly starched apron over a black dress and there was white lace at her throat.

"Good evening," she said in a thin friendly voice. "I hope you didn't mind waiting. I always have to peep out to see who's here before I open the door—an old woman's timidity."

She laughed with a little gurgling sound in her throat.

"Sorry to disturb you," I apologized. "But—"

"Won't you come in, please?"

"No; I just want a little information. I won't take much of your time."

"I wish you would come in," she said, and then added with mock severity, "I'm sure my tea is getting cold."

She took my damp hat and coat, and I followed her down a narrow hall to a dim room, where a man got up as we entered. He was old too, and stout, with a thin white beard that fell upon a white vest that was as stiffly starched as the woman's apron.

"Thomas," the little fragile woman told him; "this is Mr.—"

"Tracy," I said, because that was the name I had given the other residents of the block; but I came as near blushing when I said it, as I have in fifteen years. These folks weren't made to be lied to.

Their name, I learned, was Quarre; and they were an affectionate old couple. She called him "Thomas" every time she spoke to him, rolling the name around in her mouth as if she liked the taste of it. He called her "my dear" just as frequently, and twice he got up to adjust a cushion more comfortably to her frail back.

I had to drink a cup of tea with them and eat some little spiced cookies before I could get them to listen to a question. Then Mrs. Quarre made little sympathetic clicking sounds with her tongue and teeth, while I told about the elderly lady who had fallen off a street car. The old man rumbled in his beard that it was "a damn shame," and gave me a fat and oily cigar. I had to assure them that the fictitious elderly lady was being taken care of and was coming along nicely—I was afraid they were going to insist upon being taken to see her.

Finally I got away from the accident itself, and described the man I wanted.

"Thomas," Mrs. Quarre said; "isn't that the young man who lives in the house with the railing—the one who always looks so worried?"

The old man stroked his snowy beard and pondered.

"But, my dear," he rumbled at last; "hasn't he got dark hair?"

She beamed upon her husband and then upon me.

"Thomas is *so* observant," she said with pride. "I had forgotten; but the young man I spoke of does have dark hair, so he couldn't be the one who saw the accident at all."

The old man then suggested that one who lived in the block below might be my man. They discussed this one at some length before they decided that he was too tall and too old. Mrs. Quarre suggested another. They discussed that one, and voted against him. Thomas offered a candidate; he was weighed and discarded. They chattered on:

"But don't you think, Thomas . Yes, my dear, but . . . Of course you're right, Thomas, but. . . ."

Two old folks enjoying a chance contact with the world that they had dropped out of.

Darkness settled. The old man turned on a light in a tall lamp that threw a soft yellow circle upon us, and left the rest of the room dim. The room was a large one, and heavy with the thick hangings and bulky horse-hair furniture of a generation ago. I burned the cigar the old man had given me, and slumped comfortably down in my chair, letting them run on, putting in a word or two whenever they turned to me. I didn't expect to get any information here; but I was comfortable, and the cigar was a good one. Time enough to go out into the drizzle when I had finished my smoke.

Something cold touched the nape of my neck.

"Stand up!"

I didn't stand up: I couldn't. I was paralyzed. I sat and blinked at the Quarres.

And looking at them, I knew that something cold *couldn't* be against the back of my neck; a harsh voice *couldn't* have ordered me to stand up. It wasn't possible!

Mrs. Quarre still sat primly upright against the cushions her husband had adjusted to her back; her eyes still twinkled with friendliness behind her glasses; her hands were still motionless in her lap, crossed at the wrists over the piece of knitting. The old man still stroked his white beard, and let cigar smoke drift unhurriedly from his nostrils.

They would go on talking about the young men in the neighborhood who might be the man I wanted. Nothing had happened. I had dozed.

"Get up!"

The cold thing against my neck jabbed deep into the flesh. I stood up.

"Frisk him," the harsh voice came from behind.

The old man carefully laid his cigar down, came to me, and ran his hands over my body. Satisfied that I was unarmed, he emptied my pockets, dropping the contents upon the chair that I had just left.

Mrs. Quarre was pouring herself some more tea.

"Thomas," she said; "you've overlooked that little watch pocket in the trousers."

He found nothing there.

"That's all," he told the man behind me, and returned to his chair and cigar.

"Turn around, you!" the harsh voice ordered.

I turned and faced a tall, gaunt, raw-boned man of about my own age, which is thirty-five. He had an ugly face— hollow-cheeked, bony, and spattered with big pale freckles. His eyes were of a watery blue, and his nose and chin stuck out abruptly.

"Know me?" he asked.

"No."

"You're a liar!"

I didn't argue the point: he was holding a level gun in one big freckled hand.

"You're going to know me pretty well before you're through with me," this big ugly man threatened. "You're going to—"

"Hook!" a voice came from a portièred doorway—the doorway through which the ugly man had no doubt crept up behind me. "Hook, come here!"

The voice was feminine—young, clear, and musical.

"What do you want?" the ugly man called over his shoulder.

"*He's* here."

"All right!" He turned to Thomas Quarre. "Keep this joker safe."

From somewhere among his whiskers, his coat, and his stiff white vest, the old man brought out a big black revolver, which he handled with no signs of either weakness or unfamiliarity.

The ugly man swept up the things that had been taken from my pockets, and carried them through the portières with him.

Mrs. Quarre smiled brightly up at me.

"Do sit down, Mr. Tracy," she said.

I sat.

Through the portières a new voice came from the next room; a drawling baritone voice whose accent was unmistakably British; cultured British.

"What's up, Hook?" this voice was asking.

The harsh voice of the ugly man:

"Plenty's up, I'm telling you! They're onto us! I started out a while ago; and as soon as I got to the street, I seen a man I knowed on the other side. He was pointed out to me in Philly five-six years ago. I don't know his name, but I remembered his mug—he's a Continental Detective Agency man. I came back in right away, and me and Elvira watched him out of the window. He went to every house on the other side of the street, asking questions or something. Then he came over and started to give this side a whirl, and after a while he rings the bell. I tell the old woman and her husband to get him in, stall him along, and see what he says for himself. He's got a song and dance about looking for a guy what seen an old woman bumped by a street car—but that's the bunk! He's gunning for us. There ain't nothing else to it. I went in and stuck him up just now. I meant to wait till you come, but I was scared he'd get nervous and beat it. Here's his stuff if you want to give it the once over."

The British voice:

"You shouldn't have shown yourself to him. The others could have taken care of him."

Hook:

"What's the diff? Chances is he knows us all anyway. But supposing he didn't, what diff does it make?"

The drawling British voice:

"It may make a deal of difference. It was stupid."

Hook, blustering:

"Stupid, huh? You're always bellyaching about other people being stupid. To hell with you, I say! If you don't like my style, to hell with you! Who does all the work? Who's the guy that swings all the jobs? Huh? Where—"

The young feminine voice:

"Now, Hook, for God's sake don't make that speech again. I've listened to it until I know it by heart!"

A rustle of papers, and the British voice:

"I say, Hook, you're correct about his being a detective. Here is an identification card among his things."

The Quarres were listening to the conversation in the next room with as much interest as I, but Thomas Quarre's eyes never left me, and his fat fingers never relaxed about the gun in his lap. His wife sipped tea, with her head cocked on one side in the listening attitude of a bird.

Except for the weapon in the old man's lap, there was not a thing to persuade the eye that melodrama was in the room; the Quarres were in every other detail still the pleasant old couple who had given me tea and expressed sympathy for the elderly lady who had been injured.

The feminine voice from the next room:

"Well, what's to be done? What's our play?"

Hook:

"That's easy to answer. We're going to knock this sleuth off, first thing!"

The feminine voice:

"And put our necks in the noose?"

Hook, scornfully:

"As if they ain't there if we don't! You don't think this guy ain't after us for the L.A. job, do you?"

The British voice:

"You're an ass, Hook, and a quite hopeless one. Suppose this chap is interested in the Los Angeles affair, as is probable; what then? He is a Continental operative. Is it likely that his organization doesn't know where he is? Don't you think they know he was coming up here? And don't they know as much about us—chances are—as he does? There's no use killing him. That would only make matters worse. The thing to do is to tie him up and leave him here. His associates will hardly come looking for him until tomorrow—and that will give us all night to manage our disappearance."

My gratitude went out to the British voice! Somebody was in my favor, at least to the extent of letting me live. I hadn't been feeling very cheerful these last few minutes. Somehow, the fact that I couldn't see these people who were deciding whether I was to live or die, made my plight seem all the more desperate. I felt better now, though far from gay; I had confidence in the drawling British voice; it was the voice of a man who habitually carries his point.

Hook, bellowing:

"Let me tell you something, brother: that guy's going to be knocked off! That's flat! I'm taking no chances. You can jaw all you want to about it, but I'm looking out for my own neck and it'll be a lot safer with that guy where he can't talk. That's flat. He's going to be knocked off!"

The feminine voice, disgustedly:

"Aw, Hook, be reasonable!"

The British voice, still drawling, but dead cold:

"There's no use reasoning with you, Hook, you've the instincts and the intellect of a troglodyte. There is only one sort of language that you understand; and I'm going to talk that language to you, my son. If you are tempted to do anything silly between now and the time of our departure, just say this to yourself two or three times: 'If he dies, I die. If he dies, I die.' Say it as if it were out of the Bible—because it's that true."

There followed a long space of silence, with a tenseness that made my not particularly sensitive scalp tingle. Beyond the portière, I knew, two men were matching glances in a battle of wills, which might any instant become a physical struggle, and my chances of living were tied up in that battle.

When, at last, a voice cut the silence, I jumped as if a gun had been fired; though the voice was low and smooth enough.

It was the British voice, confidently victorious, and I breathed again.

"We'll get the old people away first," the voice was saying. "You take charge of our guest, Hook. Tie him up neatly. But remember—no foolishness. Don't waste time questioning him—he'll lie. Tie him up while I get the bonds, and we'll be gone in less than half an hour."

The portières parted and Hook came into the room—a scowling Hook whose freckles had a greenish tinge against the sallowness of his face. He pointed a revolver at me, and spoke to the Quarres:

"He wants you."

They got up and went into the next room, and for a while an indistinguishable buzzing of whispers came from that room.

Hook, meanwhile, had stepped back to the doorway, still menacing me with his revolver; and pulled loose the plush ropes that were around the heavy curtains. Then he came around behind me, and tied me securely to the high-backed chair; my arms to the chair's arms, my legs to the chair's legs, my body to the chair's back and seat; and he wound up by gagging me with the corner of a cushion that was too well-stuffed for my comfort. The ugly man was unnecessarily rough throughout; but I was a lamb. He wanted an excuse for drilling me, and I wanted above all else that he should have no excuse.

As he finished lashing me into place, and stepped back to scowl at me, I heard the street door close softly, and then light footsteps ran back and forth overhead.

Hook looked in the direction of those footsteps, and his little watery blue eyes grew cunning.

"Elvira!" he called softly.

The portières bulged as if someone had touched them, and the musical feminine voice came through.

"What?"

"Come here."

"I'd better not. He wouldn't—"

"Damn him!" Hook flared up. "Come here!"

She came into the room and into the circle of light from the tall lamp; a girl in her early twenties, slender and lithe, and dressed for the street, except that she carried her hat in one hand. A white face beneath a bobbed mass of flame-colored hair. Smoke-grey eyes that were set too far apart for trustworthiness—though not for beauty—laughed at me; and her red mouth laughed at me, exposing the edges of little sharp animal-teeth. She was beautiful; as beautiful as the devil, and twice as dangerous.

She laughed at me—a fat man all trussed up with red plush rope, and with the corner of a green cushion in my mouth—and she turned to the ugly man.

"What do you want?"

He spoke in an undertone, with a furtive glance at the ceiling, above which soft steps still padded back and forth.

"What say we shake him?"

Her smoke-grey eyes lost their merriment and became hard and calculating.

"There's a hundred thousand he's holding—a third of it's mine. You don't think I'm going to take a Mickey Finn on that, do you?"

"Course not! Supposing we get the hundred-grand?"

"How?"

"Leave it to me, kid; leave it to me! If I swing it, will you go with me? You know I'll be good to you."

She smiled contemptuously, I thought—but he seemed to like it.

"You're whooping right you'll be good to me," she said. "But listen, Hook: we couldn't get away with it—not unless you *get him*. I know him! I'm not running away with anything that belongs to him unless he is fixed so that he can't come after it."

Hook moistened his lips and looked around the room at nothing. Apparently he didn't like the thought of tangling with the owner of the British drawl. But his desire for the girl was too strong for his fear of the other man.

"I'll do it!" he blurted. "I'll get him! Do you mean it, kid? If I get him, you'll go with me?"

She held out her hand.

"It's a bet," she said, and he believed her.

His ugly face grew warm and red and utterly happy, and he took a deep breath and straightened his shoulders. In his place, I might have believed her myself—all of us have fallen for that sort of thing at one time or another—but sitting tied up on the side-lines, I knew that he'd have been better off playing with a gallon of nitro than with this baby. She was dangerous! There was a rough time ahead for this Hook!

"This is the lay—" Hook began, and stopped, tongue-tied. A step had sounded in the next room.

Immediately the British voice came through the portières, and there was an edge of exasperation to the drawl now:

"This is really too much! I can't"—he said *reahly* and *cawnt*—"leave for a moment without having things done all wrong. Now just what got into you, Elvira, that you must go in and exhibit yourself to our detective friend?"

Fear flashed into her smoke-grey eyes, and out again, and she spoke airily:

"Don't be altogether yellow," she said. "Your precious neck can get along all right without so much guarding."

The portières parted, and I twisted my head around as far as I could get it for my first look at this man who was responsible for my still being alive. I saw a short fat man, hatted and coated for the street, and carrying a tan traveling bag in one hand.

Then his face came into the yellow circle of light, and I saw that it was a Chinese face. A short fat Chinese, immaculately clothed in garments that were as British as his accent.

"It isn't a matter of color," he told the girl—and I understood now the full sting of her jibe; "it's simply a matter of ordinary wisdom."

His face was a round yellow mask, and his voice was the same emotionless drawl that I had heard before; but I knew that he was as surely under the girl's sway as the ugly man—or he wouldn't have let her taunt bring him into the room. But I doubted that she'd find this Anglicized oriental as easily handled as Hook.

"There was no particular need," the Chinese was still talking, "for this chap to have seen any of us." He looked at me now for the first time, with little opaque eyes that were like two black seeds. "It's quite possible that he didn't know any of us, even by description. This showing ourselves to him is the most arrant sort of nonsense."

"Aw, hell, Tai!" Hook blustered. "Quit your bellyaching, will you? What's the diff? I'll knock him off, and that takes care of that!"

The Chinese set down his tan bag and shook his head.

"There will be no killing," he drawled, "or there will be quite a bit of killing. You don't mistake my meaning, do you, Hook?"

Hook didn't. His Adam's apple ran up and down with the effort of his swallowing, and behind the cushion that was choking me, I thanked the yellow man again.

Then this red-haired she-devil put her spoon in the dish.

"Hook's always offering to do things that he has no intention of doing," she told the Chinese.

Hook's ugly face blazed red at this reminder of his promise to *get* the Chinese, and he swallowed again, and his eyes looked as if nothing would have suited him better than an opportunity to crawl under something. But the girl had him; her influence was stronger than his cowardice.

He suddenly stepped close to the Chinese, and from his advantage of a full head in height scowled down into the round yellow face that was as expressionless as a clock without hands.

"Tai," the ugly man snarled; "you're done. I'm sick and tired of all this dog you put on—acting like you was a king or something. I've took all the lip I'm going to take from a Chink! I'm going to—"

He faltered, and his words faded away into silence. Tai looked up at him with eyes that were as hard and black and inhuman as two pieces of coal. Hook's lips twitched and he flinched away a little.

I stopped sweating. The yellow man had won again. But I had forgotten the red-haired she-devil.

She laughed now—a mocking laugh that must have been like a knife to the ugly man.

A bellow came from deep in his chest, and he hurled one big fist into the round blank face of the yellow man.

The force of the punch carried Tai all the way across the room, and threw him on his side in one corner.

But he had twisted his body around to face the ugly man even as he went hurtling across the room—a gun was in his hand before he went down—and he was speaking before his legs had settled upon the floor—and his voice was a cultured British drawl.

"Later," he was saying; "we will settle this thing that is between us. Just now you will drop your pistol and stand very still while I get up."

Hook's revolver—only half out of his pocket when the oriental had covered him—thudded to the rug. He stood rigidly still while Tai got to his feet, and Hook's breath came out noisily, and each freckle stood ghastily out against the dirty scared white of his face.

I looked at the girl. There was contempt in the eyes with which she looked at Hook, but no disappointment.

Then I made a discovery: *something had changed in the room near her!*

I shut my eyes and tried to picture that part of the room as it had been before the two men had clashed. Opening my eyes suddenly, I had the answer.

On the table beside the girl had been a book and some magazines. They were gone now. Not two feet from the girl was the tan bag that Tai had brought into the room. Suppose the bag had held the bonds from the Los Angeles job that they had mentioned. It probably had. What then? It probably now held the book and magazines that had been on the table! The girl had stirred up the trouble between the two men to distract their attention while she made a switch. Where would the loot be, then? I didn't know, but I suspected that it was too bulky to be on the girl's slender person.

Just beyond the table was a couch, with a wide red cover that went all the way down to the floor. I looked from the couch to the girl. She was watching me, and her eyes twinkled with a flash of mirth as they met mine coming from the couch. The couch it was!

By now the Chinese had pocketed Hook's revolver, and was talking to him:

"If I hadn't a dislike for murder, and if I didn't think that you will perhaps be of some value to Elvira and me in effecting our departure, I should certainly relieve us of the handicap of your stupidity now. But I'll give you one more chance. I would suggest, however, that you think carefully before you give way to any more of your violent impulses." He turned to the girl. "Have you been putting foolish ideas in our Hook's head?"

She laughed.

"Nobody could put any kind in it."

"Perhaps you're right," he said, and then came over to test the lashings about my arms and body.

Finding them satisfactory, he picked up the tan bag, and held out the gun he had taken from the ugly man a few minutes before.

"Here's your revolver, Hook, now try to be sensible. We may as well go now. The old man and his wife will do as they were told. They are on their way to a city that we needn't

mention by name in front of our friend here, to wait for us
and their share of the bonds. Needless to say, they will wait a
long while—they are out of it now. But between ourselves
there must be no more treachery. If we're to get clear, we
must help each other."

According to the best dramatic rules, these folks should
have made sarcastic speeches to me before they left, but they
didn't. They passed me without even a farewell look, and
went out of sight into the darkness of the hall.

Suddenly the Chinese was in the room again, running tiptoe—an open knife in one hand, a gun in the other. This was
the man I had been thanking for saving my life!

He bent over me.

The knife moved on my right side, and the rope that held
that arm slackened its grip. I breathed again, and my heart
went back to beating.

"Hook will be back," Tai whispered, and was gone.

On the carpet, three feet in front of me, lay a revolver.

The street door closed, and I was alone in the house for a
while.

You may believe that I spent that while struggling with the
red plush ropes that bound me. Tai had cut one length, loos
ening my right arm somewhat and giving my body more play,
but I was far from free. And his whispered "Hook will be
back" was all the spur I needed to throw my strength against
my bonds.

I understood now why the Chinese had insisted so strongly
upon my life being spared. I was the weapon with which
Hook was to be removed. The Chinese figured that Hook
would make some excuse as soon as they reached the street,
slip back into the house, knock me off, and rejoin his confederates. If he didn't do it on his own initiative, I suppose the
Chinese would suggest it.

So he had put a gun within reach—in case I could get
loose—and had loosened my ropes as much as he could, not
to have me free before he himself got away.

This thinking was a side-issue. I didn't let it slow up my efforts to get loose. The *why* wasn't important to me just
now—the important thing was to have that revolver in my
hand when the ugly man came into this room again.

Just as the front door opened, I got my right arm completely free, and plucked the strangling cushion from my mouth. The rest of my body was still held by the ropes—held loosely—but held. There was no time for more.

I threw myself, chair and all, forward, breaking the fall with my free arm. The carpet was thick. I went down on my face, with the heavy chair atop me, all doubled up any which way; but my right arm was free of the tangle, and my right hand grasped the gun.

My left side—the wrong side—was toward the hall door. I twisted and squirmed and wrestled under the bulky piece of furniture that sat on my back.

An inch—two inches—six inches, I twisted. Another inch. Feet were at the hall door. Another inch.

The dim light hit upon a man hurrying into the room—a glint of metal in his hand.

I fired.

He caught both hands to his belly, bent double, and slid out across the carpet.

That was over. But that was far from being all. I wrenched at the plush ropes that held me, while my mind tried to sketch what lay ahead.

The girl had switched the bonds, hiding them under the couch—there was no question of that. She had intended coming back for them before I had time to get free. But Hook had come back first, and she would have to change her plan. What more likely than that she would now tell the Chinese that Hook had made the switch? What then? There was only one answer: Tai would come back for the bonds—both of them would come. Tai knew that I was armed now, but they had said that the bonds represented a hundred thousand dollars. That would be enough to bring them back!

I kicked the last rope loose and scrambled to the couch. The bonds were beneath it: four thick bundles of Liberty Bonds, done up with heavy rubber bands. I tucked them under one arm, and went over to the man who was dying near the door. His gun was under one of his legs. I pulled it out, stepped over him, and went into the dark hall.

Then I stopped to consider.

The girl and the Chinese would split to tackle me. One would come in the front door and the other in the rear. That would be the safest way for them to handle me. My play, obviously, was to wait just inside one of those doors for them. It would be foolish for me to leave the house. That's exactly what they would be expecting at first—and they would be lying in ambush.

Decidedly, my play was to lie low within sight of this front door and wait until one of them came through it—as one of them surely would, when they had tired of waiting for me to come out.

Toward the street door, the hall was lighted with the glow that filtered through the glass from the street lights. The stairway leading to the second-story threw a triangular shadow across part of the hall—a shadow that was black enough for any purpose. I crouched low in this three-cornered slice of night, and waited.

I had two guns: the one the Chinese had given me, and the one I had taken from Hook. I had fired one shot; that would leave me eleven still to use—unless one of the weapons had been used since it was loaded. I broke the gun Tai had given me, and in the dark ran my fingers across the back of the cylinder. My fingers touched *one* shell—under the hammer. Tai had taken no chances; he had given me one bullet—the bullet with which I had dropped Hook.

I put that gun down on the floor, and examined the one I had taken from Hook. It was *empty*. The Chinese had taken no chances at all! He had emptied Hook's gun before returning it to him after their quarrel.

I was in a hole! Alone, unarmed, in a strange house that would presently hold two who were hunting me—and that one of them was a woman didn't soothe me any—she was none the less deadly on that account.

For a moment I was tempted to make a dash for it; the thought of being out in the street again was pleasant; but I put the idea away. That would be foolishness, and plenty of it. Then I remembered the bonds under my arm. They would have to be my weapon; and if they were to serve me, they would have to be concealed.

I slipped out of my triangular shadow and went up the

stairs. Thanks to the street lights, the upstairs rooms were not too dark for me to move around. Around and around I went through the rooms, hunting for a place to hide the Liberty Bonds.

But when suddenly a window rattled, as if from the draught created by the opening of an outside door somewhere, I still had the loot in my hands.

There was nothing to do now but to chuck them out of a window and trust to luck. I grabbed a pillow from a bed, stripped off the white case, and dumped the bonds into it. Then I leaned out of an already open window and looked down into the night, searching for a desirable dumping place: I didn't want the bonds to land on an ash-can or a pile of bottles, or anything that would make a racket.

And, looking out of the window, I found a better hiding-place. The window opened into a narrow court, on the other side of which was a house of the same sort as the one I was in. That house was of the same height as this one, with a flat tin roof that sloped down the other way. The roof wasn't far from me—not too far to chuck the pillow-case. I chucked it. It disappeared over the edge of the roof and crackled softly on the tin.

If I had been a movie actor or something of the sort, I suppose I'd have followed the bonds; I suppose I'd have jumped from the sill, caught the edge of the roof with my fingers, swung a while, and then pulled myself up and away. But dangling in space doesn't appeal to me; I preferred to face the Chinese and the red-head.

Then I did another not at all heroic thing. I turned on all the lights in the room, lighted a cigarette (we all like to pose a little now and then), and sat down on the bed to await my capture. I might have stalked my enemies through the dark house, and possibly have nabbed them; but most likely I would simply have succeeded in getting myself shot. And I don't like to be shot.

The girl found me.

She came creeping up the hall, an automatic in each hand, hesitated for an instant outside the door, and then came in on the jump. And when she saw me sitting peacefully on the side of the bed, her eyes snapped scornfully at me, as if I had done something mean. I suppose she thought I should have given her an opportunity to put lead in me.

"I got him, Tai," she called, and the Chinese joined us.

"What did Hook do with the bonds?" he asked point blank.

I grinned into his round yellow face and led my ace.

"Why don't you ask the girl?"

His face showed nothing, but I imagined that his fat body stiffened a little within its fashionable British clothing. That encouraged me, and I went on with my little lie that was meant to stir things up.

"Haven't you rapped to it," I asked; "that they were fixing up to ditch you?"

"You dirty liar!" the girl screamed, and took a step toward me.

Tai halted her with an imperative gesture. He stared through her with his opaque black eyes, and as he stared the blood slid out of her face. She had this fat yellow man on her string, right enough, but he wasn't exactly a harmless toy.

"So that's how it is?" he said slowly, to no one in particular. "So that's how it is?" Then to me: "Where did they put the bonds?"

The girl went close to him and her words came out tumbling over each other:

"Here's the truth of it, Tai, so help me God! I switched the stuff myself. Hook wasn't in it. I was going to run out on both of you. I stuck them under the couch downstairs, but they're not there now. That's the God's truth!"

He was eager to believe her, and her words had the ring of truth to them. And I knew that—in love with her as he was—he'd more readily forgive her treachery with the bonds than he would forgive her for planning to run off with Hook; so I made haste to stir things up again. The old timer who said *"Divide to conquer,"* or something of the sort, knew what he was talking about.

"Part of that is right enough," I said. "She did stick the bonds under the couch—but Hook was in on it. They fixed it up between them while you were upstairs. He was to pick a fight with you, and during the argument she was to make the switch, and that is exactly what they did."

I had him!

As she wheeled savagely toward me, he stuck the muzzle of an automatic in her side—a smart jab that checked the angry words she was hurling at me.

"I'll take your guns, Elvira," he said, and took them.

There was a purring deadliness in his voice that made her surrender them without a word.

"Where are the bonds now?" he asked me.

I grinned.

"I'm not with you, Tai. I'm against you."

He studied me with his little eyes that were like black seeds for a while, and I studied him; and I hope that his studying was as fruitless as mine.

"I don't like violence," he said slowly, "and I believe you are a sensible person. Let us traffic, my friend."

"You name it," I suggested.

"Gladly! As a basis for our bargaining, we will stipulate that you have hidden the bonds where they cannot be found by anyone else; and that I have you completely in my power, as the shilling shockers used to have it."

"Reasonable enough," I said, "go on."

"The situation, then, is what gamblers call a standoff. Neither of us has the advantage. As a detective, you want us; but we have you. As thieves, we want the bonds; but you have them. I offer you the girl in exchange for the bonds, and that seems to me an equitable offer. It will give me the bonds and a chance to get away. It will give you no small degree of success in your task as a detective. Hook is dead. You will have the girl. All that will remain is to find me and the bonds again—by no means a hopeless task. You will have turned a defeat into more than half of a victory, with an excellent chance to make it complete one."

"How do I know that you'll give me the girl?"

He shrugged.

"Naturally, there can be no guarantee. But, knowing that she planned to desert me for the swine who lies dead below, you can't imagine that my feelings for her are the most friendly. Too, if I take her with me, she will want a share in the loot."

I turned the lay-out over in my mind, and looked at it from this side and that and the other.

"This is the way it looks to me," I told him at last. "You aren't a killer. I'll come through alive no matter what happens. All right; why should I swap? You and the girl will be easier to find again than the bonds, and they are the most important part of the job anyway. I'll hold on to them, and take my chances on finding you folks again. Yes, I'm playing it safe."

And I meant it, for the time being, at least.

"No, I'm not a killer," he said, very softly; and he smiled the first smile I had seen on his face. It wasn't a pleasant smile: and there was something in it that made you want to shudder. "But I am other things, perhaps, of which you haven't thought. But this talking is to no purpose. Elvira!"

The girl, who had been standing a little to one side, watching us, came obediently forward.

"You will find sheets in one of the bureau drawers," he told her. "Tear one or two of them into strips strong enough to tie up your friend securely."

The girl went to the bureau. I wrinkled my head, trying to find a not too disagreeable answer to the question in my mind. The answer that came first wasn't nice: *torture.*

Then a faint sound brought us all into tense motionlessness.

The room we were in had two doors: one leading into the hall, the other into another bedroom. It was through the hall door that the faint sound had come—the sound of creeping feet.

Swiftly, silently, Tai moved backward to a position from which he could watch the hall door without losing sight of the girl and me—and the gun poised like a live thing in his fat hand was all the warning we needed to make no noise.

The faint sound again, just outside the door.

The gun in Tai's hand seemed to quiver with eagerness.

Through the other door—the door that gave to the next room—popped Mrs. Quarre, an enormous cocked revolver in her thin hand.

"Let go it, you nasty heathen," she screeched.

Tai dropped his pistol before he turned to face her, and he held his hands up high—all of which was very wise.

Thomas Quarre came through the hall door then; he also

held a cocked revolver—the mate of his wife's—though, in front of his bulk, his didn't look so enormously large.

I looked at the old woman again, and found little of the friendly fragile one who had poured tea and chatted about the neighbors. This was a witch if there ever was one—a witch of the blackest, most malignant sort. Her little faded eyes were sharp with ferocity, her withered lips were taut in a wolfish snarl, and her thin body fairly quivered with hate.

"I knew it," she was shrilling. "I told Tom as soon as we got far enough away to think things over. I knew it was a frame-up! I knew this supposed detective was a pal of yours! I knew it was just a scheme to beat Thomas and me out of our shares! Well, I'll show you, you yellow monkey! And the rest of you too! I'll show the whole caboodle of you! Where are them bonds? Where are they?"

The Chinese had recovered his poise, if he had ever lost it.

"Our stout friend can tell you perhaps," he said. "I was about to extract the information from him when you so—ah—dramatically arrived."

"Thomas, for goodness sakes don't stand there dreaming," she snapped at her husband, who to all appearances was still the same mild old man who had given me an excellent cigar. "Tie up this Chinaman! I don't trust him an inch, and I won't feel easy until he's tied up. Tie him up, and then we'll see what's to be done."

I got up from my seat on the side of the bed, and moved cautiously to a spot that I thought would be out of the line of fire if the thing I expected happened.

Tai had dropped the gun that had been in his hand, but he hadn't been searched. The Chinese are a thorough people; if one of them carries a gun at all, he usually carries two or three or more. (I remember picking up one in Oakland during the last tong war, who had five on him—one under each armpit, one on each hip, and one in his waistband.) One gun had been taken from Tai, and if they tried to truss him up without frisking him, there was likely to be fireworks. So I moved off to one side.

Fat Thomas Quarre went phlegmatically up to the Chinese to carry out his wife's orders—and bungled the job perfectly.

He put his bulk between Tai and the old woman's gun.

Tai's hands moved.

An automatic was in each.

Once more Tai ran true to racial form. When a Chinese shoots, he keeps on shooting until his gun is empty.

When I yanked Tai over backward by his fat throat, and slammed him to the floor, his guns were still barking metal; and they clicked empty as I got a knee on one of his arms. I didn't take any chances. I worked on his throat until his eyes and tongue told me that he was out of things for a while.

Then I looked around.

Thomas Quarre was huddled against the bed, plainly dead, with three round holes in his starched white vest—holes that were brown from the closeness of the gun that had put them there.

Across the room, Mrs. Quarre lay on her back. Her clothes had somehow settled in place around her fragile body, and death had given her once more the gentle friendly look she had worn when I first saw her. One thin hand was on her bosom, covering, I found later, the two bullet-holes that were there.

The red-haired girl Elvira was gone.

Presently Tai stirred, and, after taking another gun from his clothes, I helped him sit up. He stroked his bruised throat with one fat hand, and looked coolly around the room.

"So this is how it came out?" he said.

"Uh-huh!"

"Where's Elvira?"

"Got away—for the time being."

He shrugged.

"Well, you can call it a decidedly successful operation. The Quarres and Hook dead; the bonds and I in your hands."

"Not so bad," I admitted, "but will you do me a favor?"

"If I may."

"Tell me what the hell this is all about!"

"All about?" he asked.

"Exactly! From what you people have let me overhear, I gather that you pulled some sort of job in Los Angeles that netted you a hundred-thousand-dollars' worth of Liberty Bonds; but I can't remember any recent job of that size down there."

"Why, that's preposterous!" he said with what, for him, was almost wild-eyed amazement. "Preposterous! Of course you know all about it!"

"I do not! I was trying to find a young fellow named Fisher who left his Tacoma home in anger a week or two ago. His father wants him found on the quiet, so that he can come down and try to talk him into going home again. I was told that I might find Fisher in this block of Turk Street, and that's what brought me here."

He didn't believe me. He never believed me. He went to the gallows thinking me a liar.

When I got out into the street again (and Turk Street was a lovely place when I came free into it after my evening in that house!) I bought a newspaper that told me most of what I wanted to know.

A boy of twenty—a messenger in the employ of a Los Angeles stock and bond house—had disappeared two days before, while on his way to a bank with a wad of Liberty Bonds. That same night this boy and a slender girl with bobbed red hair had registered at a hotel in Fresno as *J. M. Riordan and wife*. The next morning the boy had been found in his room—murdered. The girl was gone. The bonds were gone.

That much the paper told me. During the next few days, digging up a little here and a little there, I succeeded in piecing together most of the story.

The Chinese—whose full name was Tai Choon Tau—had been the brains of the mob. Their game had been a variation of the always-reliable badger game. Tai selected the victims, and he must have been a good judge of humans, for he seems never to have picked a bloomer. He would pick out some youth who was messenger or runner for a banker or broker— one who carried either cash or negotiable securities in large quantities around the city.

The girl Elvira would then *make* this lad, get him all fussed up over her—which shouldn't have been very hard for her— and then lead him gently around to running away with her and whatever he could grab in the way of his employer's bonds or currency.

Wherever they spent the first night of their flight, there Hook would appear—foaming at the mouth and loaded for

bear. The girl would plead and tear her hair and so forth, trying to keep Hook—in his rôle of irate husband—from
butchering the youth. Finally she would succeed, and in the
end the youth would find himself without either girl or the
fruits of his thievery.

Sometimes he had surrendered to the police. Two we
found had committed suicide. The Los Angeles lad had been
built of tougher stuff than the others. He had put up a fight,
and Hook had had to kill him. You can measure the girl's skill
in her end of the game by the fact that not one of the half
dozen youths who had been trimmed had said the least thing
to implicate her; and some of them had gone to great trouble
to keep her out of it.

The house in Turk Street had been the mob's retreat, and,
that it might be always a safe one, they had not worked their
game in San Francisco. Hook and the girl were supposed by
the neighbors to be the Quarres' son and daughter—and Tai
was the Chinese cook. The Quarres' benign and respectable
appearances had also come in handy when the mob had securities to be disposed of.

The Chinese went to the gallows. We threw out the widest
and finest-meshed of drag-nets for the red-haired girl; and we
turned up girls with bobbed red hair by the scores. But the
girl Elvira was not among them.

I promised myself that some day. . . .

The Girl with the Silver Eyes

A BELL jangled me into wakefulness. I rolled to the edge of my bed and reached for the telephone. The neat voice of the Old Man—the Continental Detective Agency's San Francisco manager—came to my ears:

"Sorry to disturb you, but you'll have to go up to the Glenton Apartments on Leavenworth Street. A man named Burke Pangburn, who lives there, phoned me a few minutes ago asking to have someone sent up to see him at once. He seemed rather excited. Will you take care of it? See what he wants."

I said I would and, yawning, stretching and cursing Pangburn—whoever he was—got my fat body out of pajamas and into street clothes.

The man who had disturbed my Sunday morning sleep—I found when I reached the Glenton—was a slim, white-faced person of about twenty-five, with big brown eyes that were red-rimmed just now from either sleeplessness or crying, or both. His long brown hair was rumpled when he opened the door to admit me; and he wore a mauve dressing-robe spotted with big jade parrots over wine-colored silk pajamas.

The room into which he led me resembled an auctioneer's establishment just before the sale—or maybe one of these alley tea-rooms. Fat blue vases, crooked red vases, lanky yellow vases, vases of various shapes and colors; marble statuettes, ebony statuettes, statuettes of any material; lanterns, lamps and candlesticks; draperies, hangings and rugs of all sorts; odds and ends of furniture that were all somehow queerly designed; peculiar pictures hung here and there in unexpected places. A hard room to feel comfortable in.

"My fiancée," he began immediately in a high-pitched voice that was within a notch of hysteria, "has disappeared! Something has happened to her! Foul play of some horrible sort! I want you to find her—to save her from this terrible thing that. . . ."

I followed him this far and then gave it up. A jumble of words came out of his mouth—"spirited away . . . mysterious

146

something . . . lured into a trap"—but they were too disconnected for me to make anything out of them. So I stopped
trying to understand him, and waited for him to babble himself empty of words.

I have heard ordinarily reasonable men, under stress of excitement, run on even more crazily than this wild-eyed youth;
but his dress—the parroted robe and gay pajamas—and his
surroundings—this deliriously furnished room—gave him too
theatrical a setting; made his words sound utterly unreal.

He himself, when normal, should have been a rather nice-
looking lad: his features were well spaced and, though his
mouth and chin were a little uncertain, his broad forehead
was good. But standing there listening to the occasional
melodramatic phrase that I could pick out of the jumbled
noises he was throwing at me, I thought that instead of parrots on his robe he should have had cuckoos.

Presently he ran out of language and was holding his long,
thin hands out to me in an appealing gesture, saying,

"Will you?" over and over. "Will you? Will you?"

I nodded soothingly, and noticed that tears were on his
thin cheeks.

"Suppose we begin at the beginning," I suggested, sitting
down carefully on a carved bench affair that didn't look any
too strong.

"Yes! Yes!" He was standing legs apart in front of me, running his fingers through his hair. "The beginning. I had a
letter from her every day until—"

"That's not the beginning," I objected. "Who is she? What
is she?"

"She's Jeanne Delano!" he exclaimed in surprise at my ignorance. "And she is my fiancée. And now she is gone, and I
know that—"

The phrases *"victim of foul play," "into a trap"* and so on
began to flow hysterically out again.

Finally I got him quieted down and, sandwiched in between occasional emotional outbursts, got a story out of him
that amounted to this:

This Burke Pangburn was a poet. About two months before, he had received a note from a Jeanne Delano—forwarded
from his publishers—praising his latest book of rhymes. Jeanne

Delano happened to live in San Francisco, too, though she hadn't known that he did. He had answered her note, and had received another. After a little of this they met. If she really was as beautiful as he claimed, then he wasn't to be blamed for falling in love with her. But whether or not she was really beautiful, he thought she was, and he had fallen hard.

This Delano girl had been living in San Francisco for only a little while, and when the poet met her she was living alone in an Ashbury Avenue apartment. He did not know where she came from or anything about her former life. He suspected— from certain indefinite suggestions and peculiarities of conduct which he couldn't put in words—that there was a cloud of some sort hanging over the girl; that neither her past nor her present were free from difficulties. But he hadn't the least idea what those difficulties might be. He hadn't cared. He knew absolutely nothing about her, except that she was beautiful, and he loved her, and she had promised to marry him.

Then, on the third of the month—exactly twenty-one days before this Sunday morning—the girl had suddenly left San Francisco. He had received a note from her, by messenger.

This note, which he showed me after I had insisted point blank on seeing it, read:

Burkelove:
    Have just received a wire, and must go East on next train. Tried to get you on the phone, but couldn't. Will write you as soon as I know what my address will be. If anything. (*These two words were erased and could be read only with great difficulty.*) Love me until I'm back with you forever.
                                        Your JEANNE.

Nine days later he had received another letter from her, from Baltimore, Maryland. This one, which I had a still harder time getting a look at, read:

Dearest Poet:
    It seems like two years since I have seen you, and I have a fear that it's going to be between one and two months before I see you again.
    I can't tell you now, beloved, about what brought me here. There are things that can't be written. But as

soon as I'm back with you, I shall tell you the whole wretched story.

If anything should happen—I mean to me—you'll go on loving me forever, won't you, beloved? But that's foolish. Nothing is going to happen. I'm just off the train, and tired from traveling.

Tomorrow I shall write you a long, long letter to make up for this.

My address here is 215 N. Stricker St. Please, Mister, at least one letter a day!

Your own JEANNE.

For nine days he had had a letter from her each day—with two on Monday to make up for the none on Sunday—and then her letters had stopped. And the daily letters he had sent to the address she gave—215 N. Stricker Street—had begun to come back to him, marked "Not known."

He had sent a telegram, and the telegraph company had informed him that its Baltimore office had been unable to find a Jeanne Delano at the North Stricker Street address.

For three days he had waited, expecting hourly to hear from the girl, and no word had come. Then he had bought a ticket for Baltimore.

"But," he wound up, "I was afraid to go. I know she's in some sort of trouble—I can feel that—but I'm a silly poet. I can't deal with mysteries. Either I would find nothing at all or, if by luck I did stumble on the right track, the probabilities are that I would only muddle things; add fresh complications, perhaps endanger her life still further. I can't go blundering at it in that fashion, without knowing whether I am helping or harming her. It's a task for an expert in that sort of thing. So I thought of your agency. You'll be careful, won't you? It may be—I don't know—that she won't want assistance. It may be that you can help her without her knowing anything about it. You are accustomed to that sort of thing; you can do it, can't you?"

II

I turned the job over and over in my mind before answering him. The two great bugaboos of a reputable detective agency are the persons who bring in a crooked plan or a piece of

divorce work all dressed up in the garb of a legitimate operation, and the irresponsible person who is laboring under wild
and fanciful delusions—who wants a dream run out.

This poet—sitting opposite me now twining his long, white
fingers nervously together—was, I thought, sincere; but I
wasn't so sure of his sanity.

"Mr. Pangburn," I said after a while, "I'd like to handle
this thing for you, but I'm not sure that I can. The
Continental is rather strict, and, while I believe this thing is
on the level, still I am only a hired man and have to go by the
rules. Now if you could give us the endorsement of some firm
or person of standing—a reputable lawyer, for instance, or any
legally responsible party—we'd be glad to go ahead with the
work. Otherwise, I am afraid—"

"But I know she's in danger!" he broke out. "I know
that— And I can't be advertising her plight—airing her affairs—to everyone."

"I'm sorry, but I can't touch it unless you can give me
some such endorsement." I stood up. "But you can find
plenty of detective agencies that aren't so particular."

His mouth worked like a small boy's, and he caught his
lower lip between his teeth. For a moment I thought he was
going to burst into tears. But instead he said slowly:

"I dare say you are right. Suppose I refer you to my
brother-in-law, Roy Axford. Will his word be sufficient?"

"Yes."

Roy Axford—R. F. Axford—was a mining man who had a
finger in at least half of the big business enterprises of the
Pacific Coast; and his word on anything was commonly considered good enough for anybody.

"If you can get in touch with him now," I said, "and
arrange for me to see him today, I can get started without
much delay."

Pangburn crossed the room and dug a telephone out from
among a heap of his ornaments. Within a minute or two he
was talking to someone whom he called "Rita."

"Is Roy home? . . . Will he be home this afternoon? . . .
No, you can give him a message for me, though. . . . Tell
him I'm sending a gentleman up to see him this afternoon on
a personal matter—personal with me—and that I'll be very

grateful if he'll do what I want. . . . Yes. . . . You'll find out, Rita. . . . It isn't a thing to talk about over the phone. . . . Yes, thanks!"

He pushed the telephone back into its hiding place and turned to me.

"He'll be at home until two o'clock. Tell him what I told you and if he seems doubtful, have him call me up. You'll have to tell him the whole thing; he doesn't know anything at all about Miss Delano."

"All right. Before I go, I want a description of her."

"She's beautiful!" he exclaimed. "The most beautiful woman in the world!"

That would look nice on a reward circular.

"That isn't exactly what I want," I told him. "How old is she?"

"Twenty-two."

"Height?"

"About five feet eight inches, or possibly nine."

"Slender, medium or plump?"

"She's inclined toward slenderness, but she—"

There was a note of enthusiasm in his voice that made me fear he was about to make a speech, so I cut him off with another question.

"What color hair?"

"Brown—so dark that it's almost black—and it's soft and thick and—"

"Yes, yes. Long or bobbed?"

"Long and thick and—"

"What color eyes?"

"You've seen shadows on polished silver when—"

I wrote down *grey eyes* and hurried on with the interrogation.

"Complexion?"

"Perfect!"

"Uh-huh. But is it light, or dark, or florid, or sallow, or what?"

"Fair."

"Face oval, or square, or long and thin, or what shape?"

"Oval."

"What shaped nose? Large, small, turned-up—"

"Small and regular!" There was a touch of indignation in his voice.

"How did she dress? Fashionably? And did she favor bright or quiet colors?"

"Beaut—" And then as I opened my mouth to head him off he came down to earth with:

"Very quietly—usually dark blues and browns."

"What jewelry did she wear?"

"I've never seen her wear any."

"Any scars, or moles?" The horrified look on his white face urged me on to give him a full shot. "Or warts, or deformities that you know?"

He was speechless, but he managed to shake his head.

"Have you a photograph of her?"

"Yes, I'll show you."

He bounded to his feet, wound his way through the room's excessive furnishings and out through a curtained doorway. Immediately he was back with a large photograph in a carved ivory frame. It was one of these artistic photographs—a thing of shadows and hazy outlines—not much good for identification purposes. She was beautiful—right enough—but that meant nothing; that's the purpose of an artistic photograph.

"This the only one you have?"

"Yes."

"I'll have to borrow it, but I'll get it back to you as soon as I have my copies made."

"No! No!" he protested against having his ladylove's face given to a lot of gumshoes. "That would be terrible!"

I finally got it, but it cost me more words than I like to waste on an incidental.

"I want to borrow a couple of her letters, or something in her writing, too," I said.

"For what?"

"To have photostatic copies made. Handwriting specimens come in handy—give you something to go over hotel registers with. Then, even if going under fictitious names, people now and then write notes and make memorandums."

We had another battle, out of which I came with three envelopes and two meaningless sheets of paper, all bearing the girl's angular writing.

"She have much money?" I asked, when the disputed photograph and handwriting specimens were safely tucked away in my pocket.

"I don't know. It's not the sort of thing that one would pry into. She wasn't poor; that is, she didn't have to practice any petty economies; but I haven't the faintest idea either as to the amount of her income or its source. She had an account at the Golden Gate Trust Company, but naturally I don't know anything about its size."

"Many friends here?"

"That's another thing I don't know. I think she knew a few people here, but I don't know who they were. You see, when we were together we never talked about anything but ourselves. You know what I mean: there was nothing we were interested in but each other. We were simply—"

"Can't you even make a guess at where she came from, who she was?"

"No. Those things didn't matter to me. She was Jeanne Delano, and that was enough for me."

"Did you and she ever have any financial interests in common? I mean, was there ever any transaction in money or other valuables in which both of you were interested?"

What I meant, of course, was had she got into him for a loan, or had she sold him something, or got money out of him in any other way.

He jumped to his feet, and his face went fog-grey. Then he sat down again—slumped down—and blushed scarlet.

"Pardon me," he said thickly. "You didn't know her, and of course you must look at the thing from all angles. No, there was nothing like that. I'm afraid you are going to waste time if you are going to work on the theory that she was an adventuress. There was nothing like that! She was a girl with something terrible hanging over her; something that called her to Baltimore suddenly; something that has taken her away from me. Money? What could money have to do with it? I love her!"

III

R. F. Axford received me in an office-like room in his Russian Hill residence: a big blond man, whose forty-eight or -nine years had not blurred the outlines of an athlete's body. A big, full-blooded man with the manner of one whose self-confidence is complete and not altogether unjustified.

"What's our Burke been up to now?" he asked amusedly when I told him who I was. His voice was a pleasant vibrant bass.

I didn't give him all the details.

"He was engaged to marry a Jeanne Delano, who went East about three weeks ago and then suddenly disappeared. He knows very little about her; thinks something has happened to her; and wants her found."

"Again?" His shrewd blue eyes twinkled. "And to a Jeanne this time! She's the fifth within a year, to my knowledge, and no doubt I missed one or two who were current while I was in Hawaii. But where do I come in?"

"I asked him for responsible endorsement. I think he's all right, but he isn't, in the strictest sense, a responsible person. He referred me to you."

"You're right about his not being, in the strictest sense, a responsible person." The big man screwed up his eyes and mouth in thought for a moment. Then: "Do you think that something has really happened to the girl? Or is Burke imagining things?"

"I don't know. I thought it was a dream at first. But in a couple of her letters there are hints that something was wrong."

"You might go ahead and find her then," Axford said. "I don't suppose any harm will come from letting him have his Jeanne back. It will at least give him something to think about for a while."

"I have your word for it then, Mr. Axford, that there will be no scandal or anything of the sort connected with the affair?"

"Assuredly! Burke is all right, you know. It's simply that he is spoiled. He has been in rather delicate health all his life; and then he has an income that suffices to keep him modestly, with a little over to bring out books of verse and buy doo-daws for his rooms. He takes himself a little too solemnly—is too much the poet—but he's sound at bottom."

"I'll go ahead with it, then," I said, getting up. "By the way, the girl has an account at the Golden Gate Trust

Company, and I'd like to find out as much about it as possible, especially where her money came from. Clement, the cashier, is a model of caution when it comes to giving out information about depositors. If you could put in a word for me it would make my way smoother."

"Be glad to."

He wrote a couple of lines across the back of a card and gave it to me; and, promising to call on him if I needed further assistance, I left.

IV

I telephoned Pangburn that his brother-in-law had given the job his approval. I sent a wire to the agency's Baltimore branch, giving what information I had. Then I went up to Ashbury Avenue, to the apartment house in which the girl had lived.

The manager—an immense Mrs. Clute in rustling black—knew little, if any, more about the girl than Pangburn. The girl had lived there for two and a half months; she had had occasional callers, but Pangburn was the only one that the manager could describe to me. The girl had given up the apartment on the third of the month, saying that she had been called East, and she had asked the manager to hold her mail until she sent her new address. Ten days later Mrs. Clute had received a card from the girl instructing her to forward her mail to 215 N. Stricker Street, Baltimore, Maryland. There had been no mail to forward.

The single thing of importance that I learned at the apartment house was that the girl's two trunks had been taken away by a green transfer truck. Green was the color used by one of the city's largest transfer companies.

I went then to the office of this transfer company, and found a friendly clerk on duty. (A detective, if he is wise, takes pains to make and keep as many friends as possible among transfer company, express company and railroad employees.) I left the office with a memorandum of the transfer company's check numbers and the Ferry baggage-room to which the two trunks had been taken.

At the Ferry Building, with this information, it didn't take me many minutes to learn that the trunks had been checked to Baltimore. I sent another wire to the Baltimore branch, giving the railroad check numbers.

Sunday was well into night by this time, so I knocked off and went home.

V

Half an hour before the Golden Gate Trust Company opened for business the next morning I was inside, talking to Clement, the cashier. All the traditional caution and conservatism of bankers rolled together wouldn't be one-two-three to the amount usually displayed by this plump, white-haired old man. But one look at Axford's card, with *"Please give the bearer all possible assistance"* inked across the back of it, made Clement even eager to help me.

"You have, or have had, an account here in the name of Jeanne Delano," I said. "I'd like to know as much as possible about it: to whom she drew checks, and to what amounts; but especially all you can tell me about where her money came from."

He stabbed one of the pearl buttons on his desk with a pink finger, and a lad with polished yellow hair oozed silently into the room. The cashier scribbled with a pencil on a piece of paper and gave it to the noiseless youth, who disappeared. Presently he was back, laying a handful of papers on the cashier's desk.

Clement looked through the papers and then up at me.

"Miss Delano was introduced here by Mr. Burke Pangburn on the sixth of last month, and opened an account with eight hundred and fifty dollars in cash. She made the following deposits after that: four hundred dollars on the tenth; two hundred and fifty on the twenty-first; three hundred on the twenty-sixth; two hundred on thirtieth; and twenty thousand dollars on the second of this month. All of these deposits except the last were made with cash. The last one was a check—which I have here."

He handed it to me: a Golden Gate Trust Company check.

Pay to the order of Jeanne Delano, twenty thousand dollars.

(Signed) BURKE PANGBURN.

It was dated the second of the month.

"Burke Pangburn!" I exclaimed, a little stupidly. "Was it usual for him to draw checks to that amount?"

"I think not. But we shall see."

He stabbed the pearl button again, ran his pencil across another slip of paper, and the youth with the polished yellow hair made a noiseless entrance, exit, entrance, and exit.

The cashier looked through the fresh batch of papers that had been brought to him.

"On the first of the month, Mr. Pangburn deposited twenty thousand dollars—a check against Mr. Axford's account here."

"Now how about Miss Delano's withdrawals?" I asked.

He picked up the papers that had to do with her account again.

"Her statement and canceled checks for last month haven't been delivered to her yet. Everything is here. A check for eighty-five dollars to the order of H. K. Clute on the fifteenth of last month; one 'to cash' for three hundred dollars on the twentieth, and another of the same kind for one hundred dollars on the twenty-fifth. Both of these checks were apparently cashed here by her. On the third of this month she closed out her account, with a check to her own order for twenty-one thousand, five hundred and fifteen dollars."

"And that check?"

"Was cashed here by her."

I lighted a cigarette, and let these figures drift around in my head. None of them—except those that were fixed to Pangburn's and Axford's signatures—seemed to be of any value to me. The Clute check—the only one the girl had drawn in anyone else's favor—had almost certainly been for rent.

"This is the way of it," I summed up aloud. "On the first of the month, Pangburn deposited Axford's check for twenty thousand dollars. The next day he gave a check to that amount to Miss Delano, which she deposited. On the following day she closed her account, taking between twenty-one and twenty-two thousand dollars in currency."

"Exactly," the cashier said.

VI

Before going up to the Glenton Apartments to find out why Pangburn hadn't come clean with me about the twenty thousand dollars, I dropped in at the agency, to see if any word had come from Baltimore. One of the clerks had just finished decoding a telegram.

It read:

> Baggage arrived Mt. Royal Station on eighth. Taken away same day. Unable to trace. 215 North Stricker Street is Baltimore Orphan Asylum. Girl not known there. Continuing our efforts to find her.

The Old Man came in from luncheon as I was leaving. I went back into his office with him for a couple of minutes. "Did you see Pangburn?" he asked.

"Yes. I'm working on his job now—but I think it's a bust."

"What is it?"

"Pangburn is R. F. Axford's brother-in-law. He met a girl a couple of months ago, and fell for her. She sizes up as a worker. He doesn't know anything about her. The first of the month he got twenty thousand dollars from his brother-in-law and passed it over to the girl. She blew, telling him she had been called to Baltimore, and giving him a phoney address that turns out to be an orphan asylum. She sent her trunks to Baltimore, and sent him some letters from there— but a friend could have taken care of the baggage and could have remailed her letters for her. Of course, she would have needed a ticket to check the trunks on, but in a twenty-thousand-dollar game that would be a small expense. Pangburn held out on me; he didn't tell me a word about the money. Ashamed of being easy pickings, I reckon. I'm going to the bat with him on it now."

The Old Man smiled his mild smile that might mean anything, and I left.

VII

Ten minutes of ringing Pangburn's bell brought no answer. The elevator boy told me he thought Pangburn hadn't been in all night. I put a note in his box and went down to the rail-road company's offices, where I arranged to be notified if an unused Baltimore–San Francisco ticket was turned in for re-demption.

That done, I went up to the *Chronicle* office and searched the files for weather conditions during the past month, mak-ing a memorandum of four dates upon which it had rained steadily day and night. I carried my memorandum to the of-fices of the three largest taxicab companies.

That was a trick that had worked well for me before. The girl's apartment was some distance from the street car line, and I was counting upon her having gone out—or having had a caller—on one of those rainy dates. In either case, it was very likely that she—or her caller—had left in a taxi in prefer-ence to walking through the rain to the car line. The taxicab companies' daily records would show any calls from her ad-dress, and the fares' destinations.

The ideal trick, of course, would have been to have the records searched for the full extent of the girl's occupancy of the apartment; but no taxicab company would stand for having that amount of work thrust upon them, unless it was a matter of life and death. It was difficult enough for me to persuade them to turn clerks loose on the four days I had selected.

I called up Pangburn again after I left the last taxicab office, but he was not at home. I called up Axford's residence, think-ing that the poet might have spent the night there, but was told that he had not.

Late that afternoon I got my copies of the girl's photo-graph and handwriting, and put one of each in the mail for Baltimore. Then I went around to the three taxicab compa-nies' offices and got my reports. Two of them had nothing for me. The third's records showed two calls from the girl's apartment.

On one rainy afternoon a taxi had been called, and one passenger had been taken to the Glenton Apartments. That passenger, obviously, was either the girl or Pangburn. At half-past twelve one night another call had come in, and this passenger had been taken to the Marquis Hotel.

The driver who had answered this second call remembered it indistinctly when I questioned him, but he thought that his fare had been a man. I let the matter rest there for the time; the Marquis isn't a large hotel as San Francisco hotels go, but it is too large to make canvassing its guests for the one I wanted practicable.

I spent the evening trying to reach Pangburn, with no success. At eleven o'clock I called up Axford, and asked him if he had any idea where I might find his brother-in-law.

"Haven't seen him for several days," the millionaire said. "He was supposed to come up for dinner last night, but didn't. My wife tried to reach him by phone a couple times today, but couldn't."

VIII

The next morning I called Pangburn's apartment before I got out of bed, and got no answer. Then I telephoned Axford and made an appointment for ten o'clock at his office.

"I don't know what he's up to now," Axford said good-naturedly when I told him that Pangburn had apparently been away from his apartment since Sunday, "and I suppose there's small chance of guessing. Our Burke is nothing if not erratic. How are you progressing with your search for the damsel in distress?"

"Far enough to convince me that she isn't in a whole lot of distress. She got twenty thousand dollars from your brother-in-law the day before she vanished."

"Twenty thousand dollars from Burke? She must be a wonderful girl! But wherever did he get that much money?"

"From you."

Axford's muscular body straightened in his chair.

"From me?"

"Yes—your check."

"He did not."

There was nothing argumentative in his voice; it simply stated a fact.

"You didn't give him a check for twenty thousand dollars on the first of the month?"

"No."

"Then," I suggested, "perhaps we'd better take a run over to the Golden Gate Trust Company."

Ten minutes later we were in Clement's office.

"I'd like to see my cancelled checks," Axford told the cashier.

The youth with the polished yellow hair brought them in presently—a thick wad of them—and Axford ran rapidly through them until he found the one he wanted. He studied that one for a long while, and when he looked up at me he shook his head slowly but with finality.

"I've never seen it before."

Clement mopped his head with a white handkerchief, and tried to pretend that he wasn't burning up with curiosity and fears that his bank had been gypped.

The millionaire turned the check over and looked at the endorsement.

"Deposited by Burke," he said in the voice of one who talks while he thinks of something entirely different, "on the first."

"Could we talk to the teller who took in the twenty-thousand-dollar check that Miss Delano deposited?" I asked Clement.

He pressed one of his desk's pearl buttons with a fumbling pink finger, and in a minute or two a little sallow man with a hairless head came in.

"Do you remember taking a check for twenty thousand from Miss Jeanne Delano a few weeks ago?" I asked him.

"Yes, sir! Yes, sir! Perfectly."

"Just what do you remember about it?"

"Well, sir, Miss Delano came to my window with Mr. Burke Pangburn. It was his check. I thought it was a large check for him to be drawing, but the bookkeepers said he had enough money in his account to cover it. They stood there—Miss Delano and Mr. Pangburn—talking and laughing while I entered the deposit in her book, and then they left, and that was all."

"This check," Axford said slowly, after the teller had gone back to his cage, "is a forgery. But I shall make it good, of course. That ends the matter, Mr. Clement, and there must be no more to-do about it."

"Certainly, Mr. Axford. Certainly."

Clement was all enormously relieved smiles and head-noddings, with this twenty-thousand-dollar load lifted from his bank's shoulders.

Axford and I left the bank then and got into his coupé, in which we had come from his office. But he did not immediately start the engine. He sat for a while staring at the traffic of Montgomery Street with unseeing eyes.

"I want you to find Burke," he said presently, and there was no emotion of any sort in his bass voice. "I want you to find him without risking the least whisper of scandal. If my wife knew of all this— She mustn't know. She thinks her brother is a choice morsel. I want you to find him for me. The girl doesn't matter any more, but I suppose that where you find one you will find the other. I'm not interested in the money, and I don't want you to make any special attempt to recover that; it could hardly be done, I'm afraid, without publicity. I want you to find Burke before he does something else."

"If you want to avoid the wrong kind of publicity," I said, "your best bet is to spread the right kind first. Let's advertise him as missing, fill the papers up with his pictures and so forth. They'll play him up strong. He's your brother-in-law and he's a poet. We can say that he has been ill—you told me that he had been in delicate health all his life—and that we fear he has dropped dead somewhere or is suffering under some mental derangement. There will be no necessity of mentioning the girl or the money, and our explanation may keep people—especially your wife—from guessing the truth when the fact that he is missing leaks out. It's bound to leak out somehow."

He didn't like my idea at first, but I finally won him over.

We went up to Pangburn's apartment then, easily securing admittance on Axford's explanation that we had an engagement with him and would wait there for him. I went through the rooms inch by inch, prying into each hole and hollow and crack; reading everything that was written anywhere, even down to his manuscripts; and I found nothing that threw any light on his disappearance.

I helped myself to his photographs—pocketing five of the dozen or more that were there. Axford did not think that any of the poet's bags or trunks were missing from the pack room. I did not find his Golden Gate Trust Company deposit book.

I spent the rest of the day loading the newspapers up with what we wished them to have; and they gave my ex-client one grand spread: first-page stuff with photographs and all possible trimmings. Anyone in San Francisco who didn't know that Burke Pangburn—brother-in-law of R. F. Axford and author of *Sandpatches and Other Verse*—was missing, either couldn't read or wouldn't.

IX

This advertising brought results. By the following morning, reports were rolling in from all directions, from dozens of people who had seen the missing poet in dozens of places. A few of these reports looked promising—or at least possible— but the majority were ridiculous on their faces.

I came back to the agency from running out one that had—until run out—looked good, to find a note on my desk asking me to call up Axford.

"Can you come down to my office now?" he asked when I got him on the wire.

There was a lad of twenty-one or -two with Axford when I was ushered into his office: a narrow-chested, dandified lad of the sporting clerk type.

"This is Mr. Fall, one of my employees," Axford told me. "He says he saw Burke Sunday night."

"Where?" I asked Fall.

"Going into a roadhouse near Halfmoon Bay."

"Sure it was him?"

"Absolutely! I've seen him come in here to Mr. Axford's office to know him. It was him all right."

"How'd you come to see him?"

"I was coming up from further down the shore with some friends, and we stopped in at the roadhouse to get something to eat. As we were leaving, a car drove up and Mr. Pangburn and a girl or woman—I didn't notice her particularly—got out and went inside. I didn't think anything of it until I saw in the paper last night that he hadn't been seen since Sunday. So then I thought to myself that—"

"What roadhouse was this?" I cut in, not being interested in his mental processes.

"The White Shack."

"About what time?"

"Somewhere between eleven-thirty and midnight, I guess."

"He see you?"

"No. I was already in our car when he drove up. I don't think he'd know me anyway."

"What did the woman look like?"

"I don't know. I didn't see her face, and I can't remember how she was dressed or even if she was short or tall."

That was all Fall could tell me.

We shooed him out of the office, and I used Axford's telephone to call up "Wop" Healey's dive in North Beach and leave word that when "Porky" Grout came in he was to call up "Jack." That was a standing arrangement by which I got word to Porky whenever I wanted to see him, without giving anybody a chance to tumble to the connection between us.

"Know the White Shack?" I asked Axford, when I was through phoning.

"I know where it is, but I don't know anything about it."

"Well, it's a tough hole. Run by 'Tin-Star' Joplin, an ex-yegg who invested his winnings in the place when Prohibition made the roadhouse game good. He makes more money now than he ever heard of in his piking safe-ripping days. Retailing liquor is a side-line with him; his real profit comes from acting as a relay station for the booze that comes through Halfmoon Bay for points beyond; and the dope is that half the booze put ashore by the Pacific rum fleet is put ashore in Halfmoon Bay.

"The White Shack is a tough hole, and it's no place for your brother-in-law to be hanging around. I can't go down there myself without stirring things up; Joplin and I are old friends. But I've got a man I can put in there for a few nights. Pangburn may be a regular visitor, or he may even be staying there. He wouldn't be the first one Joplin had ever let hide-out there. I'll put this man of mine in the place for a week, anyway, and see what he can find."

"It's all in your hands," Axford said. "Find Burke without scandal—that's all I ask."

X

From Axford's office I went straight to my rooms, left the outer door unlocked, and sat down to wait for Porky Grout. I had waited an hour and a half when he pushed the door open and came in.

" 'Lo! How's tricks?"

He swaggered to a chair, leaned back in it, put his feet on the table and reached for a pack of cigarettes that lay there.

That was Porky Grout. A pasty-faced man in his thirties, neither large nor small, always dressed flashily—even if sometimes dirtily—and trying to hide an enormous cowardice behind a swaggering carriage, a blustering habit of speech, and an exaggerated pretense of self-assurance.

But I had known him for three years; so now I crossed the room and pushed his feet roughly off the table, almost sending him over backward.

"What's the idea?" He came to his feet, crouching and snarling. "Where do you get that stuff? Do you want a smack in the—"

I took a step toward him. He sprang away, across the room.

"Aw, I didn't mean nothin'. I was only kiddin'!"

"Shut up and sit down," I advised him.

I had known this Porky Grout for three years, and had been using him for nearly that long, and I didn't know a single thing that could be said in his favor. He was a coward. He was a liar. He was a thief, and a hophead. He was a traitor to his kind and, if not watched, to his employers. A nice bird to deal with! But detecting is a hard business, and you use whatever tools come to hand. This Porky was an effective tool if handled right, which meant keeping your hand on his throat all the time and checking up every piece of information he brought in.

His cowardice was—for my purpose—his greatest asset. It was notorious throughout the criminal Coast; and though nobody—crook or not—could possibly think him a man to be trusted, nevertheless he was not actually distrusted. Most of his fellows thought him too much the coward to be dangerous; they thought he would be afraid to betray them; afraid of the summary vengeance that crookdom visits upon the squealer. But they didn't take into account Porky's gift for convincing himself that he was a lion-hearted fellow, when no danger was near. So he went freely where he desired and where I sent him, and brought me otherwise unobtainable bits of information upon matters in which I was interested.

For nearly three years I had used him with considerable success, paying him well, and keeping him under my heel. *Informant* was the polite word that designated him in my reports; the underworld has even less lovely names than the common *stool-pigeon* to denote his kind.

"I have a job for you," I told him, now that he was seated again, with his feet on the floor.

His loose mouth twitched up at the left corner, pushing that eye into a knowing squint.

"I thought so."

He always says something like that.

"I want you to go down to Halfmoon Bay and stick around Tin-Star Joplin's joint for a few nights. Here are two photos" —sliding one of Pangburn and one of the girl across the table. "Their names and descriptions are written on the backs. I want to know if either of them shows up down there, what they're doing, and where they're hanging out. It may be that Tin-Star is covering them up."

Porky was looking knowingly from one picture to the other.

"I think I know this guy," he said out of the corner of his mouth that twitches.

That's another thing about Porky. You can't mention a name or give a description that won't bring that same remark, even though you make them up.

"Here's some money." I slid some bills across the table. "If you're down there more than a couple of nights, I'll get some more to you. Keep in touch with me, either over this phone or the under-cover one at the office. And—remember this— lay off the stuff! If I come down there and find you all snowed up, I promise that I'll tip Joplin off to you."

He had finished counting the money by now—there wasn't a whole lot to count—and he threw it contemptuously back on the table.

"Save that for newspapers," he sneered. "How am I goin' to get anywheres if I can't spend no money in the joint?"

"That's plenty for a couple of days' expenses; you'll probably knock back half of it. If you stay longer than a couple of days, I'll get more to you. And you get your pay when the job is done, and not before."

He shook his head and got up.

"I'm tired of pikin' along with you. You can turn your own jobs. I'm through!"

"If you don't get down to Halfmoon Bay tonight, you *are* through," I assured him, letting him get out of the threat whatever he liked.

After a little while, of course, he took the money and left. The dispute over expense money was simply a preliminary that went with every job I sent him out on.

XI

After Porky had cleared out, I leaned back in my chair and burned half a dozen Fatimas over the job. The girl had gone first with the twenty thousand dollars, and then the poet had gone; and both had gone, whether permanently or not, to the White Shack. On its face, the job was an obvious affair. The girl had given Pangburn the *work* to the extent of having him forge a check against his brother-in-law's account; and then, after various moves whose value I couldn't determine at the time, they had gone into hiding together.

There were two loose ends to be taken care of. One of them—the finding of the confederate who had mailed the letters to Pangburn and who had taken care of the girl's baggage—was in the Baltimore branch's hands. The other was: Who had ridden in the taxicab that I had traced from the girl's apartment to the Marquis Hotel?

That might not have any bearing upon the job, or it might. Suppose I could find a connection between the Marquis Hotel and the White Shack. That would make a completed chain of some sort. I searched the back of the telephone directory and found the roadhouse number. Then I went up to the Marquis Hotel.

The girl on duty at the hotel switchboard, when I got there, was one with whom I had done business before.

"Who's been calling Halfmoon Bay numbers?" I asked her.

"My God!" She leaned back in her chair and ran a pink hand gently over the front of her rigidly waved red hair. "I got enough to do without remembering every call that goes through. This ain't a boarding-house. We have more'n one call a week."

"You don't have many Halfmoon Bay calls," I insisted, leaning an elbow on the counter and letting a folded five-spot peep out between the fingers of one hand. "You ought to remember any you've had lately."

"I'll see," she sighed, as if willing to do her best on a hopeless task.

She ran through her tickets.

"Here's one—from room 522, a couple weeks ago."

"What number was called?"

"Halfmoon Bay 51."

That was the roadhouse number. I passed over the five-spot.

"Is 522 a permanent guest?"

"Yes. Mr. Kilcourse. He's been here three or four months."

"What is he?"

"I don't know. A perfect gentleman, if you ask me."

"That's nice. What does he look like?"

"Tall and elegant."

"Be yourself," I pleaded. "What does he look like?"

"He's a young man, but his hair is turning gray. He's dark and handsome. Looks like a movie actor."

"Bull Montana?" I asked, as I moved off toward the desk.

The key to 522 was in its place in the rack. I sat down where I could keep an eye on it. Perhaps an hour later a clerk took it out and gave it to a man who did look somewhat like an actor. He was a man of thirty or so, with dark skin, and dark hair that showed grey around the ears. He stood a good six feet of fashionably dressed slenderness.

Carrying the key, he disappeared into an elevator.

I called up the agency then and asked the Old Man to send Dick Foley over. Ten minutes later Dick arrived. He's a little shrimp of a Canadian—there isn't a hundred and ten pounds of him—who is the smoothest shadow I've ever seen, and I've seen most of them.

"I have a bird in here I want tailed," I told Dick. "His name is Kilcourse and he's in room 522. Stick around outside, and I'll give you the spot on him."

I went back to the lobby and waited some more.

At eight o'clock Kilcourse came down and left the hotel. I went after him for half a block—far enough to turn him over to Dick—and then went home, so that I would be within reach of a telephone if Porky Grout tried to get in touch with me. No call came from him that night.

XII

When I arrived at the agency the next morning, Dick was waiting for me.

"What luck?" I asked.

"Damndest!" The little Canadian talks like a telegram when his peace of mind is disturbed, and just now he was decidedly peevish. "Took me two blocks. Shook me. Only taxi in sight."

"Think he made you?"

"No. Wise head. Playing safe."

"Try him again, then. Better have a car handy, in case he tries the same trick again."

My telephone jingled as Dick was going out. It was Porky Grout, talking over the agency's unlisted line.

"Turn up anything?" I asked.

"Plenty," he bragged.

"Good! Are you in town?"

"Yes."

"I'll meet you in my rooms in twenty minutes," I said.

The pasty-faced informant was fairly bloated with pride in himself when he came through the door I had left unlocked for him. His swagger was almost a cake-walk; and the side of his mouth that twitches was twisted into a knowing leer that would have fit a Solomon.

"I knocked it over for you, kid," he boasted. "Nothin' to it—for me! I went down there and talked to ever'body that knowed anything, seen ever'thing there was to see, and put the X-ray on the whole dump. I made a—"

"Uh-huh," I interrupted. "Congratulations and so forth. But just what did you turn up?"

"Now le'me tell you." He raised a dirty hand in a traffic-cop sort of gesture, and blew a stream of cigarette smoke at the ceiling. "Don't crowd me. I'll give you all the dope."

"Sure," I said. "I know. You're great, and I'm lucky to have you to knock off my jobs for me, and all that! But is Pangburn down there?"

"I'm gettin' around to that. I went down there and—"

"Did you see Pangburn?"

"As I was sayin', I went down there and—"

"Porky," I said, "I don't give a damn what you did! Did you see Pangburn?"

"Yes. I seen him."

"Fine! Now what did you see?"

"He's camping down there with Tin-Star. Him and the broad that you give me a picture of are both there. She's been there a month. I didn't see her, but one of the waiters told me about her. I seen Pangburn myself. They don't show themselves much—stick back in Tin-Star's part of the joint—where he lives—most of the time. Pangburn's been there since Sunday. I went down there and—"

"Learn who the girl is? Or anything about what they're up to?"

"No. I went down there and—"

"All right! *Went down there* again tonight. Call me up as soon as you know positively Pangburn is there—that he hasn't gone out. Don't make any mistakes. I don't want to come down there and scare them up on a false alarm. Use the agency's under-cover line, and just tell whoever answers that you won't be in town until late. That'll mean that Pangburn is there; and it'll let you call up from Joplin's without giving the play away."

"I got to have more dough," he said, as he got up. "It costs—"

"I'll file your application," I promised. "Now beat it, and let me hear from you tonight, the minute you're sure Pangburn is there."

Then I went up to Axford's office.

"I think I have a line on him," I told the millionaire. "I hope to have him where you can talk to him tonight. My man says he was at the White Shack last night, and is probably living there. If he's there tonight, I'll take you down, if you want."

"Why can't we go now?"

"No. The place is too dead in the daytime for my man to hang around without making himself conspicuous, and I don't want to take any chances on either you or me showing ourselves there until we're sure we're coming face to face with Pangburn."

"What do you want me to do then?"

"Have a fast car ready tonight, and be ready to start as soon as I get word to you."

"Righto. I'll be at home after five-thirty. Phone me as soon as you're ready to go, and I'll pick you up."

XIII

At nine-thirty that evening I was sitting beside Axford on the front seat of a powerfully engined foreign car, and we were roaring down a road that led to Halfmoon Bay. Porky's telephone call had come.

Neither of us talked much during that ride, and the imported monster under us made it a rather short ride. Axford sat comfortable and relaxed at the wheel, but I noticed for the first time that he had a rather heavy jaw.

The White Shack is a large building, square-built, of imitation stone. It is set away back from the road, and is approached by two curving driveways, which, together, make a semi-circle whose diameter is the public road. The center of this semi-circle is occupied by sheds under which Joplin's patrons stow their cars, and here and there around the sheds are flower-beds and clumps of shrubbery.

We were still going at a fair clip when we turned into one end of this semi-circular driveway, and—

Axford slammed on his brakes, and the big machine threw us into the windshield as it jolted into an abrupt stop—barely in time to avoid smashing into a cluster of people who had suddenly loomed up before us.

In the glow from our headlights faces stood sharply out; white, horrified faces, furtive faces, faces that were callously curious. Below the faces, white arms and shoulders showed, and bright gowns and jewelry, against the duller background of masculine clothing.

This was the first impression I got, and then, by the time I had removed my face from the windshield, I realized that this cluster of people had a core, a thing about which it centered. I stood up, trying to look over the crowd's heads, but I could see nothing.

Jumping down to the driveway, I pushed through the crowd.

Face down on the white gravel a man sprawled—a thin man in dark clothes—and just above his collar, where the head and neck join, was a hole. I knelt to peer into his face.

Then I pushed through the crowd again, back to where Axford was just getting out of the car, the engine of which was still running.

"Pangburn is dead—shot!"

XIV

Methodically, Axford took off his gloves, folded them and put them in a pocket. Then he nodded his understanding of what I had told him, and walked toward where the crowd stood around the dead poet. I looked after him until he had vanished in the throng. Then I went winding through the outskirts of the crowd, hunting for Porky Grout.

I found him standing on the porch, leaning against a pillar. I passed where he could see me, and went on around to the side of the roadhouse that afforded most shadow.

In the shadows Porky joined me. The night wasn't cool, but his teeth were chattering.

"Who got him?" I demanded.

"I don't know," he whined, and that was the first thing of which I had ever known him to confess complete ignorance. "I was inside, keepin' an eye on the others."

"What others?"

"Tin-Star, and some guy I never seen before, and the broad. I didn't think the kid was going out. He didn't have no hat."

"What *do* you know about it?"

"A little while after I phoned you, the girl and Pangburn came out from Joplin's part of the joint and sat down at a table around on the other side of the porch, where it's fairly dark. They eat for a while and then this other guy comes over and sits down with 'em. I don't know his name, but I think I've saw him around town. He's a tall guy, all rung up in fancy rags."

That would be Kilcourse.

"They talk for a while and then Joplin joins 'em. They sit around the table laughin' and talkin' for maybe a quarter of a hour. Then Pangburn gets up and goes indoors. I got a table that I can watch 'em from, and the place is crowded, and I'm afraid I'll lose my table if I leave it, so I don't follow the kid. He ain't got no hat; I figure he ain't goin' nowhere. But he must of gone through the house and out front, because pretty soon there's a noise that I thought was a auto backfire, and then the sound of a car gettin' away quick. And then some guy squawks that there's a dead man outside. Ever'body runs out here, and it's Pangburn."

"You dead sure that Joplin, Kilcourse and the girl were all at the table when Pangburn was killed?"

"Absolutely," Porky said, "if this dark guy's name is Kilcourse."

"Where are they now?"

"Back in Joplin's hang-out. They went up there as soon as they seen Pangburn had been croaked."

I had no illusions about Porky. I knew he was capable of selling me out and furnishing the poet's murderer with an alibi. But there was this about it: if Joplin, Kilcourse or the girl had fixed him, and had fixed my informant, then it was hopeless for me to try to prove that they weren't on the rear porch when the shot was fired. Joplin had a crowd of hangers-on who would swear to anything he told them without batting an eye. There would be a dozen supposed witnesses to their presence on the rear porch.

Thus the only thing for me to do was to take it for granted that Porky was coming clean with me.

"Have you seen Dick Foley?" I asked, since Dick had been shadowing Kilcourse.

"No."

"Hunt around and see if you can find him. Tell him I've gone up to talk to Joplin, and tell him to come on up. Then you can stick around where I can get hold of you if I want you."

I went in through a French window, crossed an empty dance-floor and went up the stairs that lead to Tin-Star Joplin's living quarters in the rear second story. I knew the way, having been up there before. Joplin and I were old friends.

I was going up now to give him and his friends a shake-down on the off-chance that some good might come of it, though I knew that I had nothing on any of them. I could have tied something on the girl, of course, but not without advertising the fact that the dead poet had forged his brother-in-law's signature to a check. And that was no go.

"Come in," a heavy, familiar voice called when I rapped on Joplin's living-room door.

I pushed the door open and went in.

Tin-Star Joplin was standing in the middle of the floor: a big-bodied ex-yegg with inordinately thick shoulders and an expressionless horse face. Beyond him Kilcourse sat dangling one leg from the corner of a table, alertness hiding behind an amused half-smile on his handsome dark face. On the other side of a room a girl whom I knew for Jeanne Delano sat on the arm of a big leather chair. And the poet hadn't exaggerated when he told me she was beautiful.

"You!" Joplin grunted disgustedly as soon as he recognized me. "What the hell do *you* want?"

"What've you got?"

My mind wasn't on this sort of repartee, however; I was studying the girl. There was something vaguely familiar about her—but I couldn't place her. Perhaps I hadn't seen her before; perhaps much looking at the picture Pangburn had given me was responsible for my feeling of recognition. Pictures will do that.

Meanwhile, Joplin had said:

"Time to waste is one thing I ain't got."

And I had said:

"If you'd saved up all the time different judges have given you, you'd have plenty."

I had seen the girl somewhere before. She was a slender girl in a glistening blue gown that exhibited a generous spread of front, back and arms that were worth showing. She had a mass of dark brown hair above an oval face of the color that pink ought to be. Her eyes were wide-set and of a grey shade that wasn't altogether unlike the shadows on polished silver that the poet had compared them to.

I studied the girl, and she looked back at me with level eyes, and still I couldn't place her. Kilcourse still sat dangling a leg from the table corner.

Joplin grew impatient,

"Will you stop gandering at the girl, and tell me what you want of me?" he growled.

The girl smiled then, a mocking smile that bared the edges of razor-sharp little animal teeth. And with the smile I knew her!

Her hair and skin had fooled me. The last time I had seen her—the only time I had seen her before—her face had been marble-white, and her hair had been short and the color of fire. She and an older woman and three men and I had played hide-and-seek one evening in a house in Turk Street over a matter of the murder of a bank messenger and the theft of a hundred thousand dollars' worth of Liberty Bonds. Through her intriguing three of her accomplices had died that evening, and the fourth—the Chinese—had eventually gone to the gallows at Folsom prison. Her name had been Elvira then, and since her escape from the house that night we had been fruitlessly hunting her from border to border, and beyond.

Recognition must have shown in my eyes in spite of the effort I made to keep them blank, for, swift as a snake, she had left the arm of the chair and was coming forward, her eyes more steel than silver.

I put my gun in sight.

Joplin took a half-step toward me.

"What's the idea?" he barked.

Kilcourse slid off the table, and one of his thin dark hands hovered over his necktie.

"This is the idea," I told them. "I want the girl for a murder a couple months back, and maybe—I'm not sure—for tonight's. Anyway, I'm—"

The snapping of a light-switch behind me, and the room went black.

I moved, not caring where I went so long as I got away from where I had been when the lights went out.

My back touched a wall and I stopped, crouching low.

"Quick, kid!" A hoarse whisper that came from where I thought the door should be.

But both of the room's doors, I thought, were closed, and could hardly be opened without showing gray rectangles. People moved in the blackness, but none got between me and the lighter square of windows.

Something clicked softly in front of me—too thin a click for the cocking of a gun—but it could have been the opening of a spring-knife, and I remembered that Tin-Star Joplin had a fondness for that weapon.

"Let's go! Let's go!" A harsh whisper that cut through the dark like a blow.

Sounds of motion, muffled, indistinguishable . . . one sound not far away. . . .

Abruptly a strong hand clamped one of my shoulders, a hard-muscled body strained against me. I stabbed out with my gun, and heard a grunt.

The hand moved up my shoulder toward my throat.

I snapped up a knee, and heard another grunt.

A burning point ran down my side.

I stabbed again with my gun—pulled it back until the muzzle was clear of the soft obstacle that had stopped it, and squeezed the trigger.

The crash of the shot. Joplin's voice in my ear—a curiously matter-of-fact voice:

"God damn! That got me."

XV

I spun away from him then, toward where I saw the dim yellow of an open door. I had heard no sounds of departure. I had been too busy. But I knew that Joplin had tied into me while the others made their get-away.

Nobody was in sight as I jumped, slid, tumbled down the steps—any number at a time. A waiter got in my path as I plunged toward the dance-floor. I don't know whether his interference was intentional or not. I didn't ask. I slammed the flat of my gun in his face and went on. Once I jumped a leg that came out to trip me; and at the outer door I had to smear another face.

Then I was out in the semi-circular driveway, from one end of which a red tail light was turning east into the county road.

While I sprinted for Axford's car I noticed that Pangburn's body had been removed. A few people still stood around the spot where he had lain, and they gaped at me now with open mouths.

The car was as Axford had left it, with idling engine. I swung it through a flower-bed and pointed it east on the public road. Five minutes later I picked up the red point of a tail-light again.

The car under me had more power than I would ever need, more than I would have known how to handle. I don't know how fast the one ahead was going, but I closed in as if it had been standing still.

A mile and a half, or perhaps two—

Suddenly a man was in the road ahead—a little beyond the reach of my lights. The lights caught him, and I saw that it was Porky Grout!

Porky Grout standing facing me in the middle of the road, the dull metal of an automatic in each hand.

The guns in his hands seemed to glow dimly red and then go dark in the glare of my headlights—glow and then go dark, like two bulbs in an automatic electric sign.

The windshield fell apart around me.

Porky Grout—the informant whose name was a synonym for cowardice the full length of the Pacific Coast—stood in the center of the road shooting at a metal comet that rushed down upon him. . . .

I didn't see the end.

I confess frankly that I shut my eyes when his set white face showed close over my radiator. The metal monster under me trembled—not very much—and the road ahead was empty except for the fleeing red light. My windshield was gone. The wind tore at my uncovered hair and brought tears to my squinted-up eyes.

Presently I found that I was talking to myself, saying, "That was Porky. That was Porky." It was an amazing fact. It was no surprise that he had double-crossed me. That was to be expected. And for him to have crept up the stairs behind me and turned off the lights wasn't astonishing. But for him to have stood straight up and died—

An orange streak from the car ahead cut off my wonderment. The bullet didn't come near me—it isn't easy to shoot accurately from one moving car into another—but at the pace I was going it wouldn't be long before I was close enough for good shooting.

I turned on the searchlight above the dashboard. It didn't quite reach the car ahead, but it enabled me to see that the girl was driving, while Kilcourse sat screwed around beside her, facing me. The car was a yellow roadster.

I eased up a little. In a duel with Kilcourse here I would have been at a disadvantage, since I would have had to drive as well as shoot. My best play seemed to be to hold my distance until we reached a town, as we inevitably must. It wasn't midnight yet. There would be people on the streets of any town, and policemen. Then I could close in with a better chance of coming off on top.

A few miles of this and my prey tumbled to my plan. The yellow roadster slowed down, wavered, and came to rest with its length across the road. Kilcourse and the girl were out immediately and crouching in the road on the far side of their barricade.

I was tempted to dive pell-mell into them, but it was a weak temptation, and when its short life had passed I put on the brakes and stopped. Then I fiddled with my searchlight until it bore full upon the roadster.

A flash came from somewhere near the roadster's wheels, and the searchlight shook violently, but the glass wasn't touched. It would be their first target, of course, and . . .

Crouching in my car, waiting for the bullet that would smash the lens, I took off my shoes and overcoat.

The third bullet ruined the light.

I switched off the other lights, jumped to the road, and when I stopped running I was squatting down against the near side of the yellow roadster. As easy and safe a trick as can be imagined.

The girl and Kilcourse had been looking into the glare of a powerful light. When that light suddenly died, and the weaker ones around it went, too, they were left in pitch unseeing blackness, which must last for the minute or longer that their eyes would need to readjust themselves to the gray-black of the night. My stockinged feet had made no sound on the macadam road, and now there was only a roadster between us; and I knew it and they didn't.

From near the radiator Kilcourse spoke softly:

"I'm going to try to knock him off from the ditch. Take a shot at him now and then to keep him busy."

"I can't see him," the girl protested.

"Your eyes'll be all right in a second. Take a shot at the car anyway."

I moved toward the radiator as the girl's pistol barked at the empty touring car.

Kilcourse, on hands and knees, was working his way toward the ditch that ran along the south side of the road. I gathered my legs under me, intent upon a spring and a blow with my gun upon the back of his head. I didn't want to kill him, but I wanted to put him out of the way quick. I'd have the girl to take care of, and she was at least as dangerous as he.

As I tensed for the spring, Kilcourse, guided perhaps by some instinct of the hunted, turned his head and saw me— saw a threatening shadow.

Instead of jumping I fired.

I didn't look to see whether I had hit him or not. At that range there was little likelihood of missing. I bent double and slipped back to the rear of the roadster, keeping on my side of it.

Then I waited.

The girl did what I would perhaps have done in her place. She didn't shoot or move toward the place the shot had come from. She thought I had forestalled Kilcourse in using the ditch and that my next play would be to circle around behind her. To offset this, she moved around the rear of the roadster, so that she could ambush me from the side nearest Axford's car.

Thus it was that she came creeping around the corner and poked her delicately chiseled nose plunk into the muzzle of the gun that I held ready for her.

She gave a little scream.

Women aren't always reasonable: they are prone to disregard trifles like guns held upon them. So I grabbed her gun hand, which was fortunate for me. As my hand closed around the weapon, she pulled the trigger, catching a chunk of my forefinger between hammer and frame. I twisted the gun out of her hand; released my finger.

But she wasn't done yet.

With me standing there holding a gun not four inches from her body, she turned and bolted off toward where a clump of trees made a jet-black blot to the north.

When I recovered from my surprise at this amateurish procedure, I stuck both her gun and mine in my pockets, and set out after her, tearing the soles of my feet at every step.

She was trying to get over a wire fence when I caught her.

XVI

"Stop playing, will you?" I said crossly, as I set the fingers of my left hand around her wrist and started to lead her back to the roadster. "This is a serious business. Don't be so childish!"

"You are hurting my arm."

I knew I wasn't hurting her arm, and I knew this girl for the direct cause of four, or perhaps five, deaths; yet I loosened my grip on her wrist until it wasn't much more than a friendly clasp. She went back willingly enough to the roadster, where, still holding her wrist, I switched on the lights.

Kilcourse lay just beneath the headlight's glare, huddled on his face, with one knee drawn up under him.

I put the girl squarely in the line of light.

"Now stand there," I said, "and behave. The first break you make, I'm going to shoot a leg out from under you," and I meant it.

I found Kilcourse's gun, pocketed it, and knelt beside him.

He was dead, with a bullet-hole above his collar-bone.

"Is he—" her mouth trembled.

"Yes."

She looked down at him, and shivered a little.

"Poor Fag," she whispered.

I've gone on record as saying that this girl was beautiful,

and, standing there in the dazzling white of the headlights, she was more than that. She was a thing to start crazy thoughts even in the head of an unimaginative middle-aged thief-catcher. She was—

Anyhow, I suppose that is why I scowled at her and said:

"Yes, poor Fag, and poor Hook, and poor Tai, and poor kind of a Los Angeles bank messenger, and poor Burke," calling the roll, so far as I knew it, of men who had died loving her.

She didn't flare up. Her big grey eyes lifted, and she looked at me with a gaze that I couldn't fathom, and her lovely oval face under the mass of brown hair—which I knew was phoney—was sad.

"I suppose you do think—" she began.

But I had had enough of this; I was uncomfortable along the spine.

"Come on," I said. "We'll leave Kilcourse and the roadster here for the present."

She said nothing, but went with me to Axford's big machine, and sat in silence while I laced my shoes. I found a robe on the back seat and gave it to her.

"Better wrap this around your shoulders. The windshield is gone. It'll be cool."

She followed my suggestion without a word, but when I had edged our vehicle around the rear of the roadster, and had straightened out in the road again, going east, she laid a hand on my arm.

"Aren't we going back to the White Shack?"

"No. Redwood City—the county jail."

A mile perhaps, during which, without looking at her, I knew she was studying my rather lumpy profile. Then her hand was on my forearm again and she was leaning toward me so that her breath was warm against my cheek.

"Will you stop for a minute? There's something—some things I want to tell you."

I brought the car to a halt in a cleared space of hard soil off to one side of the road, and screwed myself a little around in the seat to face her more directly.

"Before you start," I told her, "I want you to understand that we stay here for just so long as you talk about the

Pangburn affair. When you get off on any other line—then we finish our trip to Redwood City."

"Aren't you even interested in the Los Angeles affair?"

"No. That's closed. You and Hook Riordan and Tai Choon Tau and the Quarres were equally responsible for the messenger's death, even if Hook did the actual killing. Hook and the Quarres passed out the night we had our party in Turk Street. Tai was hanged last month. Now I've got you. We had enough evidence to swing the Chinese, and we've even more against you. That is done—finished—completed. If you want to tell me anything about Pangburn's death, I'll listen. Otherwise—"

I reached for the self-starter.

A pressure of her fingers on my arm stopped me.

"I do want to tell you about it," she said earnestly. "I want you to know the truth about it. You'll take me to Redwood City, I know. Don't think that I expect—that I have any foolish hopes. But I'd like you to know the truth about this thing. I don't know why I should care especially what you think, but—"

Her voice dwindled off to nothing.

XVII

Then she began to talk very rapidly—as people talk when they fear interruptions before their stories are told—and she sat leaning slightly forward, so that her beautiful oval face was very close to mine.

"After I ran out of the Turk Street house that night—while you were struggling with Tai—my intention was to get away from San Francisco. I had a couple of thousand dollars, enough to carry me any place. Then I thought that going away would be what you people would expect me to do, and that the safest thing for me to do would be to stay right here. It isn't hard for a woman to change her appearance. I had bobbed red hair, white skin, and wore gay clothes. I simply dyed my hair, bought these transformations to make it look long, put color on my face, and bought some dark clothes. Then I took an apartment on Ashbury Avenue under the name of Jeanne Delano, and I was an altogether different person.

"But, while I knew I was perfectly safe from recognition anywhere, I felt more comfortable staying indoors for a while, and, to pass the time, I read a good deal. That's how I happened to run across Burke's book. Do you read poetry?"

I shook my head. An automobile going toward Halfmoon Bay came into sight just then—the first one we'd seen since we left the White Shack. She waited until it had passed before she went on, still talking rapidly.

"Burke wasn't a genius, of course, but there was something about some of his things that—something that got inside me. I wrote him a little note, telling him how much I had enjoyed these things, and sent it to his publishers. A few days later I had a note from Burke, and I learned that he lived in San Francisco. I hadn't known that.

"We exchanged several notes, and then he asked if he could call, and we met. I don't know whether I was in love with him or not, even at first. I did like him, and, between the ardor of his love for me and the flattery of having a fairly well-known poet for a suitor, I really thought that I loved him. I promised to marry him.

"I hadn't told him anything about myself, though now I know that it wouldn't have made any difference to him. But I was afraid to tell him the truth, and I wouldn't lie to him, so I told him nothing.

"Then Fag Kilcourse saw me one day on the street, and knew me in spite of my new hair, complexion and clothes. Fag hadn't much brains, but he had eyes that could see through anything. I don't blame Fag. He acted according to his code. He came up to my apartment, having followed me home; and I told him that I was going to marry Burke and be a respectable housewife. That was dumb of me. Fag was square. If I had told him that I was ribbing Burke up for a trimming, Fag would have let me alone, would have kept his hands off. But when I told him that I was through with the graft, had 'gone queer,' that made me his meat. You know how crooks are: everyone in the world is either a fellow crook or a prospective victim. So if I was no longer a crook, then Fag considered me fair game.

"He learned about Burke's family connections, and then he put it up to me—twenty thousand dollars, or he'd turn me up. He knew about the Los Angeles job, and he knew how badly I was wanted. I was up against it then. I knew I couldn't hide from Fag or run away from him. I told Burke I had to have twenty thousand dollars. I didn't think he had that much, but I thought he could get it. Three days later he gave me a check for it. I didn't know at the time how he had raised it, but it wouldn't have mattered if I had known. I had to have it.

"But that night he told me where he got the money; that he had forged his brother-in-law's signature. He told me because, after thinking it over, he was afraid that when the forgery was discovered I would be caught with him and considered equally guilty. I'm rotten in spots, but I wasn't rotten enough to let him put himself in the pen for me, without knowing what it was all about. I told him the whole story. He didn't bat an eye. He insisted that the money be paid Kilcourse, so that I would be safe, and began to plan for my further safety.

"Burke was confident that his brother-in-law wouldn't send him over for forgery, but, to be on the safe side, he insisted that I move and change my name again and lay low until we knew how Axford was going to take it. But that night, after he had gone, I made some plans of my own. I did like Burke—I liked him too much to let him be the goat without trying to save him, and I didn't have a great deal of faith in Axford's kindness. This was the second of the month. Barring accidents, Axford wouldn't discover the forgery until he got his cancelled checks early the following month. That gave me practically a month to work in.

"The next day I drew all my money out of the bank, and sent Burke a letter, saying that I had been called to Baltimore, and I laid a clear trail to Baltimore, with baggage and letters and all, which a pal there took care of for me. Then I went down to Joplin's and got him to put me up. I let Fag know I was there, and when he came down I told him I expected to have the money for him in a day or two.

"He came down nearly every day after that, and I stalled him from day to day, and each time it got easier. But my time was getting short. Pretty soon Burke's letters would be coming back from the phoney address I had given him, and I wanted to be on hand to keep him from doing anything fool-ish. And I didn't want to get in touch with him until I could give him the twenty thousand, so he could square the forgery before Axford learned of it from his cancelled checks.

"Fag was getting easier and easier to handle, but I still didn't have him where I wanted him. He wasn't willing to give up the twenty thousand dollars—which I was, of course, holding all this time—unless I'd promise to stick with him for good. And I still thought I was in love with Burke, and I didn't want to tie myself up with Fag, even for a little while.

"Then Burke saw me on the street one Sunday night. I was careless, and drove into the city in Joplin's roadster—the one back there. And, as luck would have it, Burke saw me. I told him the truth, the whole truth. And he told me that he had just hired a private detective to find me. He was like a child in some ways: it hadn't occurred to him that the sleuth would dig up anything about the money. But I knew the forged check would be found in a day or two at the most. I knew it!

"When I told Burke that he went to pieces. All his faith in his brother-in-law's forgiveness went. I couldn't leave him the way he was. He'd have babbled the whole thing to the first person he met. So I brought him back to Joplin's with me. My idea was to hold him there for a few days, until we could see how things were going. If nothing appeared in the papers about the check, then we could take it for granted that Axford had hushed the matter up, and Burke could go home and try to square himself. On the other hand, if the papers got the whole story, then Burke would have to look for a per-manent hiding-place, and so would I.

"Tuesday evening's and Wednesday morning's papers were full of the news of his disappearance, but nothing was said about the check. That looked good, but we waited another day for good measure. Fag Kilcourse was in on the game by this time, of course, and I had had to pass over the twenty thousand dollars, but I still had hopes of getting it—or most of it—back, so I continued to string him along. I had a hard time keeping him off Burke, though, because he had begun to think he had some sort of right to me, and jealousy made him wicked. But I got Tin-Star to throw a scare into him, and I thought Burke was safe.

"Tonight one of Tin-Star's men came up and told us that a man named Porky Grout, who had been hanging around the place for a couple of nights, had made a couple of cracks that might mean he was interested in us. Grout was pointed out to me, and I took a chance on showing myself in the public part of the place, and sat at a table close to his. He was plain rat— as I guess you know—and in less than five minutes I had him at my table, and half an hour later I knew that he had tipped you off that Burke and I were in the White Shack. He didn't tell me all this right out, but he told me more than enough for me to guess the rest.

"I went up and told the others. Fag was for killing both Grout and Burke right away. But I talked him out of it. That wouldn't help us any, and I had Grout where he would jump in the ocean for me. I thought I had Fag convinced, but— We finally decided that Burke and I would take the roadster and leave, and that when you got here Porky Grout was to pretend he was hopped up, and point out a man and a woman—any who happened to be handy—as the ones he had taken for us. I stopped to get a cloak and gloves, and Burke went on out to the car alone—and Fag shot him. I didn't know he was going to! I wouldn't have let him! Please believe that! I wasn't as much in love with Burke as I had thought, but please believe that after all he had done for me I wouldn't have let them hurt him!

"After that it was a case of stick with the others whether I liked it or not, and I stuck. We ribbed Grout to tell you that all three of us were on the back porch when Burke was killed, and we had any number of others primed with the same story. Then you came up and recognized me. Just my luck that it had to be you—the only detective in San Francisco who knew me!

"You know the rest: how Porky Grout came up behind you and turned off the lights, and Joplin held you while we ran for the car; and then, when you closed in on us, Grout offered to stand you off while we got clear, and now. . . ."

XVIII

Her voice died, and she shivered a little. The robe I had given her had fallen away from her white shoulders. Whether or not it was because she was so close against my shoulder, I shivered, too. And my fingers, fumbling in my pocket for a cigarette, brought it out twisted and mashed.

"That's all there is to the part you promised to listen to," she said softly, her face turned half away. "I wanted you to know. You're a hard man, but somehow I—"

I cleared my throat, and the hand that held the mangled cigarette was suddenly steady.

"Now don't be crude, sister," I said. "Your work has been too smooth so far to be spoiled by rough stuff now."

She laughed—a brief laugh that was bitter and reckless and just a little weary, and she thrust her face still closer to mine, and the grey eyes were soft and placid.

"Little fat detective whose name I don't know"—her voice had a tired huskiness in it, and a tired mockery—"you think I am playing a part, don't you? You think I am playing for liberty. Perhaps I am. I certainly would take it if it were offered me. But— Men have thought me beautiful, and I have played with them. Women are like that. Men have loved me and, doing what I liked with them, I have found men contemptible. And then comes this little fat detective whose name I don't know, and he acts as if I were a hag—an old squaw. Can I help then being piqued into some sort of feeling for him? Women are like that. Am I so homely that any man has a right to look at me without even interest? Am I ugly?"

I shook my head.

"You're quite pretty," I said, struggling to keep my voice as casual as the words.

"You beast!" she spat, and then her smile grew gentle again. "And yet it is because of that attitude that I sit here and turn myself inside out for you. If you were to take me in your arms and hold me close to the chest that I am already leaning against, and if you were to tell me that there is no jail ahead for me just now, I would be glad, of course. But, though for a while you might hold me, you would then be only one of the men with which I am familiar: men who love and are used and are succeeded by other men. But because you do none of these things, because you are a wooden block of a man, I find myself wanting you. Would I tell you this, little fat detective, if I were playing a game?"

I grunted noncommittally, and forcibly restrained my tongue from running out to moisten my dry lips.

"I'm going to this jail tonight if you are the same hard man who has goaded me into whining love into his uncaring ears, but before that, can't I have one whole-hearted assurance that you think me a little more than 'quite pretty'? Or at least a hint that if I were not a prisoner your pulse might beat a little faster when I touch you? I'm going to this jail for a long while—perhaps to the gallows. Can't I take my vanity there not quite in tatters to keep me company? Can't you do some slight thing to keep me from the afterthought of having bleated all this out to a man who was simply bored?"

Her lids had come down half over the silver-grey eyes; her head had tilted back so far that a little pulse showed throbbing in her white throat; her lips were motionless over slightly parted teeth, as the last word had left them. My fingers went deep into the soft white flesh of her shoulders. Her head went further back, her eyes closed, one hand came up to my shoulder.

"You're beautiful as all hell!" I shouted crazily into her face, and flung her against the door.

It seemed an hour that I fumbled with starter and gears before I had the car back in the road and thundering toward the San Mateo County jail. The girl had straightened herself up in the seat again, and sat huddled within the robe I had given her. I squinted straight ahead into the wind that tore at my hair and face, and the absence of the windshield took my thoughts back to Porky Grout.

Porky Grout, whose yellowness was notorious from Seattle to San Diego, standing rigidly in the path of a charging metal monster, with an inadequate pistol in each hand. She had done that to Porky Grout—this woman beside me! She had done that to Porky Grout, and he hadn't even been human! A slimy reptile whose highest thought had been a skinful of dope had gone grimly to death that she might get away— she—this woman whose shoulders I had gripped, whose mouth had been close under mine!

I let the car out another notch, holding the road somehow.

We went through a town: a scurrying of pedestrians for safety, surprised faces staring at us, street lights glistening on the moisture the wind had whipped from my eyes. I passed blindly by the road I wanted, circled back to it, and we were out in the country again.

XIX

At the foot of a long, shallow hill I applied the brakes and we snapped to motionlessness.

I thrust my face close to the girl's.

"Furthermore, you are a liar!" I knew I was shouting foolishly, but I was powerless to lower my voice. "Pangburn never put Axford's name on that check. He never knew anything about it. You got in with him because you knew his brother-in-law was a millionaire. You pumped him, finding out everything he knew about his brother-in-law's account at the Golden Gate Trust. You stole Pangburn's bank book—it wasn't in his room when I searched it—and deposited the forged Axford check to his credit, knowing that under those circumstances the check wouldn't be questioned. The next day you took Pangburn into the bank, saying you were going to make a deposit. You took him in because with him standing beside you the check to which *his* signature had been forged wouldn't be questioned. You knew that, being a gentleman, he'd take pains not to see what you were depositing.

"Then you framed the Baltimore trip. He told the truth to me—the truth so far as he knew it. Then you met him Sunday night—maybe accidentally, maybe not. Anyway, you took him down to Joplin's, giving him some wild yarn that he would swallow and that would persuade him to stay there for a few days. That wasn't hard, since he didn't know anything about either of the twenty-thousand-dollar checks. You and your pal Kilcourse knew that if Pangburn disappeared nobody would ever know that he hadn't forged the Axford check, and nobody would ever suspect that the second check was phoney. You'd have killed him quietly, but when Porky tipped you off that I was on my way down you had to move quick—so you shot him down. That's the truth of it!" I yelled.

All this while she had watched me with wide grey eyes that were calm and tender, but now they clouded a little and a pucker of pain drew her brows together.

I yanked my head away and got the car in motion.

Just before we swept into Redwood City one of her hands came up to my forearm, rested there for a second, patted the arm twice, and withdrew.

I didn't look at her, nor, I think, did she look at me, while she was being booked. She gave her name as Jeanne Delano, and refused to make any statement until she had seen an attorney. It all took a very few minutes.

As she was being led away, she stopped and asked if she might speak privately with me.

We went together to a far corner of the room.

She put her mouth close to my ear so that her breath was warm again on my cheek, as it had been in the car, and whispered the vilest epithet of which the English language is capable.

Then she walked out to her cell.

Women, Politics and Murder

A PLUMP maid with bold green eyes and a loose, full-lipped mouth led me up two flights of steps and into an elaborately furnished boudoir, where a woman in black sat at a window. She was a thin woman of a little more than thirty, this murdered man's widow, and her face was white and haggard.

"You are from the Continental Detective Agency?" she asked before I was two steps inside the room.

"Yes."

"I want you to find my husband's murderer." Her voice was shrill, and her dark eyes had wild lights in them. "The police have done nothing. Four days, and they have done nothing. They say it was a robber, but they haven't found him. They haven't found anything!"

"But, Mrs. Gilmore," I began, not exactly tickled to death with this explosion, "you must—"

"I know! I know!" she broke in. "But they have done nothing, I tell you—nothing. I don't believe they've made the slightest effort. I don't believe they want to find h-him!"

"Him?" I asked, because she had started to say *her.* "You think it was a man?"

She bit her lip and looked away from me, out of the window to where San Francisco Bay, the distance making toys of its boats, was blue under the early afternoon sun.

"I don't know," she said hesitantly; "it might have—"

Her face spun toward me—a twitching face—and it seemed impossible that anyone could talk so fast, hurl words out so rapidly one after the other.

"I'll tell you. You can judge for yourself. Bernard wasn't faithful to me. There was a woman who calls herself Cara Kenbrook. She wasn't the first. But I learned about her last month. We quarreled. Bernard promised to give her up. Maybe he didn't. But if he did, I wouldn't put it past her— A woman like that would do anything—anything. And down in my heart I really believe she did it!"

"And you think the police don't want to arrest her?"

"I didn't mean exactly that. I'm all unstrung, and likely to say anything. Bernard was mixed up in politics, you know; and if the police found, or thought, that politics had anything to do with his death, they might—I don't know just what I mean. I'm a nervous, broken woman, and full of crazy notions." She stretched a thin hand out to me. "Straighten this tangle out for me! Find the person who killed Bernard!"

I nodded with empty assurance, still not any too pleased with my client.

"Do you know this Kenbrook woman?" I asked.

"I've seen her on the street, and that's enough to know what sort of person she is!"

"Did you tell the police about her?"

"No-o." She looked out of the window again, and then, as I waited, she added, defensively:

"The police detectives who came to see me acted as if they thought I might have killed Bernard. I was afraid to tell them that I had cause for jealousy. Maybe I shouldn't have kept quiet about that woman, but I didn't think she had done it until afterward, when the police failed to find the murderer. Then I began to think she had done it; but I couldn't make myself go to the police and tell them that I had withheld information. I knew what they'd think. So I— You can twist it around so it'll look as if I hadn't known about the woman, can't you?"

"Possibly. Now as I understand it, your husband was shot on Pine Street, between Leavenworth and Jones, at about three o'clock Tuesday morning. That right?"

"Yes."

"Where was he going?"

"Coming home, I suppose; but I don't know where he had been. Nobody knows. The police haven't found out, if they have tried. He told me Monday evening that he had a business engagement. He was a building contractor, you know. He went out at about half-past eleven, saying he would probably be gone four or five hours."

"Wasn't that an unusual hour to be keeping a business engagement?"

"Not for Bernard. He often had men come to the house at midnight."

"Can you make any guess at all where he was going that night?"

She shook her head with emphasis.

"No. I knew nothing at all about his business affairs, and even the men in his office don't seem to know where he went that night."

That wasn't unlikely. Most of the B. F. Gilmore Construction Company's work had been on city and state contracts, and it isn't altogether unheard-of for secret conferences to go with that kind of work. Your politician-contractor doesn't always move in the open.

"How about enemies?" I asked.

"I don't know anybody that hated him enough to kill him."

"Where does this Kenbrook woman live, do you know?"

"Yes—in the Garford Apartments on Bush Street."

"Nothing you've forgotten to tell me, is there?" I asked, stressing the *me* a little.

"No, I've told you everything I know—every single thing."

CHAPTER II

Walking over to California Street, I shook down my memory for what I had heard here and there of Bernard Gilmore. I could remember a few things—the opposition papers had been in the habit of exposing him every election year—but none of them got me anywhere. I had known him by sight: a boisterous, red-faced man who had hammered his way up from hod-carrier to the ownership of a half-a-million-dollar business and a pretty place in local politics. "A roughneck with a manicure," somebody had called him; a man with a lot of enemies and more friends; a big, good-natured, hard-hitting rowdy.

Odds and ends of a dozen graft scandals in which he had been mixed up, without anybody ever really getting anything on him, flitted through my head as I rode downtown on the too-small outside seat of a cable-car. Then there had been some talk of a bootlegging syndicate of which he was supposed to be the head. . . .

I left the car at Kearny Street and walked over to the Hall of Justice. In the detectives' assembly-room I found O'Gar, the detective-sergeant in charge of the Homicide Detail: a squat man of fifty who goes in for wide-brimmed hats of the movie-sheriff sort, but whose little blue eyes and bullet head aren't handicapped by the trick headgear.

"I want some dope on the Gilmore killing," I told him.

"So do I," he came back. "But if you'll come along I'll tell you what little I know while I'm eating. I ain't had lunch yet."

Safe from eavesdroppers in the clatter of a Sutter Street lunchroom, the detective-sergeant leaned over his clam chowder and told me what he knew about the murder, which wasn't much.

"One of the boys, Kelly, was walking his beat early Tuesday morning, coming down the Jones Street hill from California Street to Pine. It was about three o'clock—no fog or nothing—a clear night. Kelly's within maybe twenty feet of Pine Street when he hears a shot. He whisks around the corner, and there's a man dying on the north sidewalk of Pine Street, halfway between Jones and Leavenworth. Nobody else is in sight. Kelly runs up to the man and finds it's Gilmore. Gilmore dies before he can say a word. The doctors say he was knocked down and then shot; because there's a bruise on his forehead, and the bullet slanted upward in his chest. See what I mean? He was lying on his back when the bullet hit him, with his feet pointing toward the gun it came from. It was a .38."

"Any money on him?"

O'Gar fed himself two spoons of chowder and nodded.

"Six hundred smacks, a coupla diamonds and a watch. Nothing touched."

"What was he doing on Pine Street at that time in the morning?"

"Damned if I know, brother. Chances are he was going home, but we can't find out where he'd been. Don't even know what direction he was walking in when he was knocked over. He was lying across the sidewalk with his feet to the curb; but that don't mean nothing—he could of turned around three or four times after he was hit."

"All apartment buildings in that block, aren't there?"

"Uh-huh. There's an alley or two running off from the south side; but Kelly says he could see the mouths of both

alleys when the shot was fired—before he turned the corner—
and nobody got away through them."

"Reckon somebody who lives in that block did the shooting?" I asked.

O'Gar tilted his bowl, scooped up the last drops of the
chowder, put them in his mouth, and grunted.

"Maybe. But we got nothing to show that Gilmore knew
anybody in that block."

"Many people gather around afterward?"

"A few. There's always people on the street to come running if anything happens. But Kelly says there wasn't anybody
that looked wrong—just the ordinary night crowd. The boys
gave the neighborhood a combing, but didn't turn up anything."

"Any cars around?"

"Kelly says there wasn't, that he didn't see any, and couldn't
of missed seeing it if there'd been one."

"What do you think?" I asked.

He got to his feet, glaring at me.

"I don't think," he said disagreeably; "I'm a police detective."

I knew by that that somebody had been panning him for
not finding the murderer.

"I have a line on a woman," I told him. "Want to come
along and talk to her with me?"

"I want to," he growled, "but I can't. I got to be in court
this afternoon—in half an hour."

CHAPTER III

In the vestibule of the Garford Apartments, I pressed the button tagged Miss Cara Kenbrook several times before the door
clicked open. Then I mounted a flight of stairs and walked
down a hall to her door. It was opened presently by a tall girl
of twenty-three or -four in a black and white crepe dress.

"Miss Cara Kenbrook?"

"Yes."

I gave her a card—one of those that tell the truth about
me.

"I'd like to ask you a few questions; may I come in?"

"Do."

Languidly she stepped aside for me to enter, closed the door behind me, and led me back into a living-room that was littered with newspapers, cigarettes in all stages of consumption from unlighted freshness to cold ash, and miscellaneous articles of feminine clothing. She made room for me on a chair by dumping off a pair of pink silk stockings and a hat, and herself sat on some magazines that occupied another chair.

"I'm interested in Bernard Gilmore's death," I said, watching her face.

It wasn't a beautiful face, although it should have been. Everything was there—perfect features; smooth, white skin; big, almost enormous, brown eyes—but the eyes were dead-dull, and the face was as empty of expression as a china door-knob, and what I said didn't change it.

"Bernard Gilmore," she said without interest. "Oh, yes."

"You and he were pretty close friends, weren't you?" I asked, puzzled by her blankness.

"We had been—yes."

"What do you mean by *had been*?"

She pushed back a lock of her short-cut brown hair with a lazy hand.

"I gave him the air last week," she said casually, as if speaking of something that had happened years ago.

"When was the last time you saw him?"

"Last week—Monday, I think—a week before he was killed."

"Was that the time when you broke off with him?"

"Yes."

"Have a row, or part friends?"

"Not exactly either. I just told him that I was through with him."

"How did he take it?"

"It didn't break his heart. I guess he'd heard the same thing before."

"Where were you the night he was killed?"

"At the Coffee Cup, eating and dancing with friends until about one o'clock. Then I came home and went to bed."

"Why did you split with Gilmore?"

"Couldn't stand his wife."

"Huh?"

"She was a nuisance." This without the faintest glint of either annoyance or humor. "She came here one night and raised a racket; so I told Bernie that if he couldn't keep her away from me he'd have to find another playmate."

"Have you any idea who might have killed him?" I asked.

"Not unless it was his wife—these excitable women are always doing silly things."

"If you had given her husband up, what reason would she have for killing him, do you think?"

"I'm sure I don't know," she replied with complete indifference. "But I'm not the only girl that Bernie ever looked at."

"Think there were others, do you? Know anything, or are you just guessing?"

"I don't know any names," she said, "but I'm not just guessing."

I let that go at that and switched back to Mrs. Gilmore, wondering if this girl could be full of dope.

"What happened the night his wife came here?"

"Nothing but that. She followed Bernie here, rang the bell, rushed past me when I opened the door, and began to cry and call Bernie names. Then she started on me, and I told him that if he didn't take her away I'd hurt her, so he took her home."

Admitting I was licked for the time, I got up and moved to the door. I couldn't do anything with this baby just now. I didn't think she was telling the whole truth, but on the other hand it wasn't reasonable to believe that anybody would lie so woodenly—with so little effort to be plausible.

"I may be back later," I said as she let me out.

"All right."

Her manner didn't even suggest that she hoped I wouldn't.

CHAPTER IV

From this unsatisfactory interview I went to the scene of the killing, only a few blocks away, to get a look at the neighborhood. I found the block just as I had remembered it and as

O'Gar had described it: lined on both sides by apartment buildings, with two blind alleys—one of which was dignified with a name, Touchard Street—running from the south side.

The murder was four days old; I didn't waste any time snooping around the vicinity; but, after strolling the length of the block, boarded a Hyde Street car, transferred at California Street, and went up to see Mrs. Gilmore again. I was curious to know why she hadn't told me about her call on Cara Kenbrook.

The same plump maid who had admitted me earlier in the afternoon opened the door.

"Mrs. Gilmore is not at home," she said. "But I think she'll be back in half an hour or so."

"I'll wait," I decided.

The maid took me into the library, an immense room on the second floor, with barely enough books in it to give it that name. She switched on a light—the windows were too heavily curtained to let in much daylight—crossed to the door, stopped, moved over to straighten some books on a shelf, looked at me with a half-questioning, half-inviting look in her green eyes, started for the door again, and halted.

By that time I knew she wanted to say something, and needed encouragement. I leaned back in my chair and grinned at her, and decided I had made a mistake—the smile into which her slack lips curved held more coquetry than anything else. She came over to me, walking with an exaggerated swing of the hips, and stood close in front of me.

"What's on your mind?" I asked.

"Suppose—suppose a person knew something that nobody else knew; what would it be worth to them?"

"That," I stalled, "would depend on how valuable it was."

"Suppose I knew who killed the boss?" She bent her face close down to mine, and spoke in a husky whisper. "What would that be worth?"

"The newspapers say that one of Gilmore's clubs has offered a thousand-dollar reward. You'd get that."

Her green eyes went greedy, and then suspicious.

"If *you* didn't."

I shrugged. I knew she'd go through with it—whatever it was—now; so I didn't even explain to her that the Continental doesn't touch rewards, and doesn't let its hired men touch them.

"I'll give you my word," I said; "but you'll have to use your own judgment about trusting me."

She licked her lips.

"You're a good fellow, I guess. I wouldn't tell the police, because I know they'd beat me out of the money. But you look like I can trust you." She leered into my face. "I used to have a gentleman friend who was the very image of you, and he was the grandest—"

"Better speak your piece before somebody comes in," I suggested.

She shot a look at the door, cleared her throat, licked her loose mouth again, and dropped on one knee beside my chair.

"I was coming home late Monday night—the night the boss was killed—and was standing in the shadows saying good night to my friend, when the boss came out of the house and walked down the street. And he had hardly got to the corner, when she—Mrs. Gilmore—came out, and went down the street after him. Not trying to catch up with him, you understand; but following him. What do you think of that?"

"What do *you* think of it?"

"*I* think that she finally woke up to the fact that all of her Bernie's dates didn't have anything to do with the building business."

"Do you know that they didn't?"

"Do I know it? I knew that man! He liked 'em—liked 'em all." She smiled into my face, a smile that suggested all evil. "I found *that* out soon after I first came here."

"Do you know when Mrs. Gilmore came back that night—what time?"

"Yes," she said; "at half-past three."

"Sure?"

"Absolutely! After I got undressed I got a blanket and sat at the head of the front stairs. My room's in the rear of the top floor. I wanted to see if they came home together, and if there was a fight. After she came in alone I went back to my room, and it was just twenty-five minutes to four then. I looked at my alarm clock."

"Did you see her when she came in?"

"Just the top of her head and shoulders when she turned toward her room at the landing."

"What's your name?" I asked.

"Lina Best."

"All right, Lina," I told her. "If this is the goods I'll see that you collect on it. Keep your eyes open, and if anything else turns up you can get in touch with me at the Continental office. Now you'd better beat it, so nobody will know we've had our heads together."

Alone in the library, I cocked an eye at the ceiling and considered the information Lina Best had given me. But I soon gave that up—no use trying to guess at things that will work out for themselves in a while. I found a book, and spent the next half-hour reading about a sweet young she-chump and a big strong he-chump and all their troubles.

Then Mrs. Gilmore came in, apparently straight from the street.

I got up and closed the doors behind her, while she watched me with wide eyes.

"Mrs. Gilmore," I said, when I faced her again, "why didn't you tell me that you followed your husband the night he was killed?"

"That's a lie!" she cried; but there was no truth in her voice. "That's a lie!"

"Don't you think you're making a mistake?" I urged. "Don't you think you'd better tell me the whole thing?"

She opened her mouth, but only a dry sobbing sound came out; and she began to sway with a hysterical rocking motion, the fingers of one black-gloved hand plucking at her lower lip, twisting and pulling it.

I stepped to her side and set her down in the chair I had been sitting in, making foolish clucking sounds—meant to soothe her—with my tongue. A disagreeable ten minutes— and gradually she pulled herself together; her eyes lost their glassiness, and she stopped clawing at her mouth.

"I did follow him." It was a hoarse whisper, barely audible.

Then she was out of the chair, kneeling, with arms held up to me, and her voice was a thin scream.

"But I didn't kill him! I didn't! Please believe that I didn't!"

I picked her up and put her back in the chair.

"I didn't say you did. Just tell me what did happen."

"I didn't believe him when he said he had a business engagement," she moaned. "I didn't trust him. He had lied to me before. I followed him to see if he went to that woman's rooms."

"Did he?"

"No. He went into an apartment house on Pine Street, in the block where he was killed. I don't know exactly which house it was—I was too far behind him to make sure. But I saw him go up the steps and into one—near the middle of the block."

"And then what did you do?"

"I waited, hiding in a dark doorway across the street. I knew the woman's apartment was on Bush Street, but I thought she might have moved, or be meeting him here. I waited a long time shivering and trembling. It was chilly and I was frightened—afraid somebody would come into the vestibule where I was. But I made myself stay. I wanted to see if he came out alone, or if that woman came out. I had a right to do it—he had deceived me before.

"It was terrible, horrible—crouching there in the dark—cold and scared. Then—it must have been about half-past two—I couldn't stand it any longer. I decided to telephone the woman's apartment and find out if she were home. I went down to an all-night lunchroom on Ellis Street and called her up."

"Was she home?"

"No! I tried for fifteen minutes, or maybe longer, but nobody answered the phone. So I knew she was in that Pine Street building."

"And what did you do then?"

"I went back there, determined to wait until he came out. I walked up Jones Street. When I was between Bush and Pine I heard a shot. I thought it was a noise made by an automobile then, but now I know that it was the shot that killed Bernie.

"When I reached the corner of Pine and Jones, I could see a policeman bending over Bernie on the sidewalk, and I saw people gathering around. I didn't know then that it was

Bernie lying on the sidewalk. In the dark and at that distance I couldn't even see whether it was a man or a woman.

"I was afraid that Bernard would come out to see what was going on, or look out of a window, and discover me; so I didn't go down that way. I was afraid to stay in the neighborhood now, for fear the police would ask me what I was doing loitering in the street at three in the morning—and have it come out that I had been following my husband. So I kept on walking up Jones Street, to California, and then straight home."

"And then what?" I led her on.

"Then I went to bed. I didn't go to sleep—lay there worrying over Bernie; but still not thinking it was he I had seen lying in the street. At nine o'clock that morning two police detectives came and told me Bernie had been killed. They questioned me so sharply that I was afraid to tell them the whole truth. If they had known I had reason for being jealous, and had followed my husband that night, they would have accused me of shooting him. And what could I have done? Everybody would have thought me guilty.

"So I didn't say anything about the woman. I thought they'd find the murderer, and then everything would be all right. I didn't think *she* had done it then, or I would have told you the whole thing the first time you were here. But four days went by without the police finding the murderer, and I began to think they suspected *me!* It was terrible! I couldn't go to them and confess that I had lied to them, and I was sure that the woman had killed him and that the police had failed to suspect her because I hadn't told them about her.

"So I employed you. But I was afraid to tell even you the whole truth. I thought that if I just told you there had been another woman and who she was, you could do the rest without having to know that I had followed Bernie that night. I was afraid *you* would think I had killed him, and would turn me over to the police if I told you everything. And now you *do* believe it! And you'll have me arrested! And they'll hang me! I know it! I know it!"

She began to rock crazily from side to side in her chair.

"Sh-h-h," I soothed her. "You're not arrested yet. Sh-h-h."

I didn't know what to make of her story. The trouble with these nervous, hysterical women is that you can't possibly tell when they're lying and when telling the truth unless you have outside evidence—half of the time they themselves don't know.

"When you heard the shot," I went on when she had quieted down a bit, "you were walking north on Jones, between Bush and Pine? You could see the corner of Pine and Jones?"

"Yes—clearly."

"See anybody?"

"No not until I reached the corner and looked down Pine Street. Then I saw a policeman bending over Bernie, and two men walking toward them."

"Where were the two men?"

"On Pine Street east of Jones. They didn't have hats on— as if they had come out of a house when they heard the shot."

"Any automobiles in sight either before or after you heard the shot?"

"I didn't see or hear any."

"I have some more questions, Mrs. Gilmore," I said; "but I'm in a hurry now. Please don't go out until you hear from me again."

"I won't," she promised; "but—"

I didn't have any answers for anybody's questions, so I ducked my head and left the library.

Near the street door Lina Best appeared out of a shadow, her eyes bright and inquisitive.

"Stick around," I said without any meaning at all, stepped around her, and went on out into the street.

CHAPTER V

I returned then to the Garford Apartments, walking, because I had a lot things to arrange in my mind before I faced Cara Kenbrook again. And, even though I walked slowly, they weren't all exactly filed in alphabetical order when I got there. She had changed the black and white dress for a plush-like gown of bright green, but her empty doll's face hadn't changed.

"Some more questions," I explained when she opened her door.

She admitted me without word or gesture, and led me back into the room where we had talked before.

"Miss Kenbrook," I asked, standing beside the chair she had offered me, "why did you tell me you were home in bed when Gilmore was killed?"

"Because it's so." Without the flicker of a lash.

"And you wouldn't answer the doorbell?"

I had to twist the facts to make my point. Mrs. Gilmore had phoned, but I couldn't afford to give this girl a chance to shunt the blame for her failure to answer off on central.

She hesitated for a split second.

"No—because I didn't hear it."

One cool article, this baby! I couldn't figure her. I didn't know then, and I don't know now, whether she was the owner of the world's best poker face or was just naturally stupid. But whichever she was, she was thoroughly and completely it!

I stopped trying to guess, and got on with my probing.

"And you wouldn't answer the phone either?"

"It didn't ring—or not enough to awaken me."

I chuckled—an artificial chuckle—because central could have been ringing the wrong number. However . . .

"Miss Kenbrook," I lied, "your phone rang at 2:30 and at 2:40 that morning. And your doorbell rang almost continually from about 2:50 until after 3:00."

"Perhaps," she said; "but I wonder who'd be trying to get me at that hour."

"You didn't hear either?"

"No."

"But you were here?"

"Yes—who was it?" carelessly.

"Get your hat," I bluffed, "and I'll show them to you down at headquarters."

She glanced down at the green gown and walked toward an open bedroom door.

"I suppose I'd better get a cloak, too," she said.

"Yes," I advised her; "and bring your toothbrush."

She turned around then and looked at me, and for a moment it seemed that some sort of expression—surprise maybe—was about to come into her big brown eyes; but none actually came. The eyes stayed dull and empty.

"You mean you're arresting me?"

"Not exactly. But if you stick to your story about being home in bed at 3:00 last Tuesday morning I can promise you you *will* be arrested. If I were you I'd think up another story while we're riding down to the Hall of Justice."

She left the doorway slowly and came back into the room, as far as a chair that stood between us, put her hands on its back, and leaned over it to look at me. For perhaps a minute neither of us spoke—just stood there staring at each other, while I tried to keep my face as expressionless as hers.

"Do you really think," she asked at last, "that I wasn't here when Bernie was killed?"

"I'm a busy man, Miss Kenbrook." I put all the certainty I could fake into my voice. "If you want to stick to your funny story, it's all right with me. But please don't expect me to stand here and argue about it. Get your hat and cloak."

She shrugged, and came around the chair on which she had been leaning.

"I suppose you *do* know something," she said, sitting down. "Well, it's tough on Stan, but women and children first."

My ears twitched at the name *Stan*, but I didn't interrupt her.

"I *was* in the Coffee Cup until one o'clock," she was saying, her voice still flat and emotionless. "And I *did* come home afterward. I'd been drinking *vino* all evening, and it always makes me blue. So after I came home I got to worrying over things. Since Bernie and I split finances haven't been so good. I took stock that night—or morning—and found only four dollars in my purse. The rent was due, and the world looked pretty damned blue.

"Half-lit on Dago wine as I was, I decided to run over and see Stan, tell him all my troubles, and make a touch. Stan is a good egg and he's always willing to go the limit for me. Sober, I wouldn't have gone to see him at three in the morning; but it seemed a perfectly sensible thing to do at the time.

"It's only a few minutes' walk from here to Stan's. I went down Bush Street to Leavenworth, and up Leavenworth to Pine. I was in the middle of that last block when Bernie was shot—I heard it. And when I turned the corner into Pine

Street I saw a copper bending over a man on the pavement right in front of Stan's. I hesitated for a couple of minutes, standing in the shadow of a pole, until three or four men had gathered around the man on the sidewalk. Then I went over.

"It was Bernie. And just as I got there I heard the copper tell one of the men that he had been shot. It was an awful shock to me. You know how things like that will hit you!"

I nodded; though God knows there was nothing in this girl's face, manner, or voice to suggest shock. She might have been talking about the weather.

"Dumfounded, not knowing what to do," she went on, "I didn't even stop. I went on, passing as close to Bernie as I am to you now, and rang Stan's bell. He let me in. He had been half-undressed when I rang. His rooms are in the rear of the building, and he hadn't heard the shot, he said. He didn't know Bernie had been killed until I told him. It sort of knocked the wind out of him. He said Bernie had been there—in Stan's rooms—since midnight, and had just left.

"Stan asked me what I was doing there, and I told him my tale of woe. That was the first time Stan knew that Bernie and I were so thick. I met Bernie through Stan, but Stan didn't know we had got so chummy.

"Stan was worried for fear it would come out that Bernie had been to see him that night, because it would make a lot of trouble for him—some sort of shady deal they had on, I guess. So he didn't go out to see Bernie. That's about all there is to it. I got some money from Stan, and stayed in his rooms until the police had cleared out of the neighborhood; because neither of us wanted to get mixed up in anything. Then I came home. That's straight—on the level."

"Why didn't you get this off your chest before?" I demanded, knowing the answer.

It came.

"I was afraid. Suppose I told about Bernie throwing me down, and said I was close to him—a block or so away—when he was killed, and was half-full of vino? The first thing everybody would have said was that I had shot him! I'd lie about it still if I thought you'd believe me."

"So Bernie was the one who broke off, and not you?"

"Oh, yes," she said lightly.

CHAPTER VI

I lit a Fatima and breathed smoke in silence for a while, and the girl sat placidly watching me.

Here I had two women—neither normal. Mrs. Gilmore was hysterical, abnormally nervous. This girl was dull, subnormal. One was the dead man's wife; the other his mistress; and each with reason for believing she had been thrown down for the other. Liars, both; and both finally confessing that they had been near the scene of the crime at the time of the crime, though neither admitted seeing the other. Both, by their own accounts, had been at that time even further from normal than usual—Mrs. Gilmore filled with jealousy; Cara Kenbrook half-drunk.

What was the answer? Either could have killed Gilmore; but hardly both—unless they had formed some sort of crazy partnership, and in that event—

Suddenly all the facts I had gathered—true and false—clicked together in my head. I had the answer—the one simple, satisfying answer!

I grinned at the girl, and set about filling in the gaps in my solution.

"Who is Stan?" I asked.

"Stanley Tennant—he has something to do with the city."

Stanley Tennant. I knew him by reputation, a—

A key rattled in the hall door.

The hall door opened and closed, and a man's footsteps came toward the open doorway of the room in which we were. A tall, broad-shouldered man in tweeds filled the doorway—a ruddy-faced man of thirty-five or so, whose appearance of athletic blond wholesomeness was marred by close-set eyes of an indistinct blue.

Seeing me, he stopped—a step inside the room.

"Hello, Stan!" the girl said lightly. "This gentleman is from the Continental Detective Agency. I've just emptied myself to him about Bernie. Tried to stall him at first, but it was no good."

The man's vague eyes switched back and forth between the girl and me. Around the pale irises his eyeballs were pink.

He straightened his shoulders and smiled too jovially.

"And what conclusion have you come to?" he inquired.

The girl answered for me.

"I've already had *my* invitation to take a ride."

Tennant bent forward. With an unbroken swing of his arms, he swept a chair up from the floor into my face. Not much force behind it, but quick.

I went back against the wall, fending off the chair with both arms—threw it aside—and looked into the muzzle of a nickeled revolver.

A table drawer stood open—the drawer from which he had grabbed the gun while I was busy with the chair. The revolver, I noticed, was of .38 caliber.

"Now," his voice was thick, like a drunk's, "turn around."

I turned my back to him, felt a hand moving over my body, and my gun was taken away.

"All right," he said, and I faced him again.

He stepped back to the girl's side, still holding the nickel-plated revolver on me. My own gun wasn't in sight—in his pocket perhaps. He was breathing noisily, and his eyeballs had gone from pink to red. His face, too, was red, with veins bulging in the forehead.

"You know me?" he snapped.

"Yes, I know you. You're Stanley Tennant, assistant city engineer, and your record is none too lovely." I chattered away on the theory that conversation is always somehow to the advantage of the man who is looking into the gun. "You're supposed to be the lad who supplied the regiment of well-trained witnesses who turned last year's investigation of graft charges against the engineer's office into a comedy. Yes, Mr. Tennant, I know you. You're the answer to why Gilmore was so lucky in landing city contracts with bids only a few dollars beneath his competitors'. Yes, Mr. Tennant, I know you. You're the bright boy who—"

I had a lot more to tell him, but he cut me off.

"That will do out of you!" he yelled. "Unless you want me to knock a corner off your head with this gun."

Then he addressed the girl, not taking his eyes from me.

"Get up, Cara."

She got out of her chair and stood beside him. His gun was in his right hand, and that side was toward her. He moved around to the other side.

The fingers of his left hand hooked themselves inside of the girl's green gown where it was cut low over the swell of her breasts. His gun never wavered from me. He jerked his left hand, ripping her gown down to the waistline.

"*He* did that, Cara," Tennant said.

She nodded.

His fingers slid inside of the flesh-colored undergarment that was now exposed, and he tore that as he had torn the gown.

"*He* did that."

She nodded again.

His bloodshot eyes darted little measuring glances at her face—swift glances that never kept his eyes from me for the flash of time I would have needed to tie into him.

Then—eyes and gun on me—he smashed his left fist into the girl's blank white face.

One whimper—low and not drawn out—came from her as she went down in a huddle against the wall. Her face—well, there wasn't *much* change in it. She looked dumbly up at Tennant from where she had fallen.

"*He* did that," Tennant was saying.

She nodded, got up from the floor, and returned to her chair.

"Here's our story." The man talked rapidly, his eyes alert on me. "Gilmore was never in my rooms in his life, Cara, and neither were you. The night he was killed you were home shortly after one o'clock, and stayed there. You were sick—probably from the wine you had been drinking—and called a doctor. His name is Howard. I'll see that he's fixed. He got here at 2:30 and stayed until 3:30.

"Today, this gum-shoe, learning that you had been intimate with Gilmore, came here to question you. He knew you hadn't killed Gilmore, but he made certain suggestions to you—you can play them up as strong as you like; maybe say that he's been annoying you for months—and when you turned him down he threatened to frame you.

"You refused to have anything to do with him, and he grabbed you, tearing your clothes, and bruising your face when you resisted. I happened to come along then, having an engagement with you, and heard you scream. Your front door was unlocked, so I rushed in, pulled this fellow away, and disarmed him. Then we held him until the police—whom we will phone for—came. Got that?"

"Yes, Stan."

"Good! Now listen: When the police get here this fellow will spill all he knows, of course, and the chances are that all three of us will be taken in. That's why I want you to know what's what right now. I ought to have enough pull to get you and me out on bail tonight, or, if worst comes to worst, to see that my lawyer gets to me tonight—so I can arrange for the witnesses we'll need. Also I ought to be able to fix it so our little fat friend will be held for a day or two, and not allowed to see anybody until late tomorrow—which will give us a good start on him. I don't know how much he knows, but between your story and the stories of a couple of other smart little ladies I have in mind, I'll fix him up with a rep that will keep any jury in the world from ever believing him about anything."

"How do you like that?" he asked me, triumphantly.

"You big clown," I laughed at him, "I think it's funny!"

But I didn't really think so. In spite of what I thought I knew about Gilmore's murder—in spite of my simple, satisfactory solution—something was crawling up my back, my knees felt jerky, and my hands were wet with sweat. I had had people try to frame me before—no detective stays in the business long without having it happen—but I had never got used to it. There's a peculiar deadliness about the thing—especially if you know how erratic juries can be—that makes your flesh crawl, no matter how safe your judgment tells you you are.

"Phone the police," Tennant told the girl; "and for God's sake keep your story straight!"

As he tried to impress that necessity on the girl his eyes left me.

I was perhaps five feet from him and his level gun.

A jump—not straight at him—off to one side—put me close.

The gun roared under my arm. I was surprised not to feel the bullet. It seemed that he *must* have hit me.

There wasn't a second shot.

I looped my right fist over as I jumped. It landed when I landed. It took him too high—up on the cheekbone—but it rocked him back a couple of steps.

I didn't know what had happened to his gun. It wasn't in his hand any more. I didn't stop to look for it. I was busy, crowding him back—not letting him set himself—staying close to him—driving at him with both hands.

He was a head taller than I, and had longer arms, but he wasn't any heavier or stronger. I suppose he hit me now and then as I hammered him across the room. He must have. But I didn't feel anything.

I worked him into a corner. Jammed him back in a corner with his legs cramped under him—which didn't give him much leverage to hit from. I got my left arm around his body, holding him where I wanted him. And I began to throw my right fist into him.

I liked that. His belly was flabby, and it got softer every time I hit it. I hit it often.

He was chopping at my face, but by digging my nose into his chest and holding it there I kept my beauty from being altogether ruined. Meanwhile I threw my right fist into him.

Then I became aware that Cara Kenbrook was moving around behind me; and I remembered the revolver that had fallen somewhere when I had charged Tennant. I didn't like that; but there was nothing I could do about it—except put more weight in my punches. My own gun, I thought, was in one of his pockets. But neither of us had time to hunt for it now.

Tennant's knees sagged the next time I hit him.

Once more, I said to myself, and then I'll step back, let him have one on the button, and watch him fall.

But I didn't get that far.

Something that I knew was the missing revolver struck me on the top of the head. An ineffectual blow—not clean enough to stun me—but it took the steam out of my punches.

Another.

They weren't hard, these taps, but to hurt a skull with a hunk of metal you don't have to hit it hard.

I tried to twist away from the next bump, and failed. Not only failed, but let Tennant wiggle away from me.

That was the end.

I wheeled on the girl just in time to take another rap on the head, and then one of Tennant's fists took me over the ear.

I went down in one of those falls that get pugs called quitters—my eyes were open, my mind was alive, but my legs and arms wouldn't lift me up from the floor.

Tennant took my own gun out of a pocket, and with it held on me, sat down in a Morris chair, to gasp for the air I had pounded out of him. The girl sat in another chair; and I, finding I could manage it, sat up in the middle of the floor and looked at them.

Tennant spoke, still panting.

"This is fine—all the signs of a struggle we need to make our story good!"

"If they don't believe you were in a fight," I suggested sourly, pressing my aching head with both hands, "you can strip and show them your little tummy."

"And you can show them this!"

He leaned down and split my lip with a punch that spread me on my back.

Anger brought my legs to life. I got up on them. Tennant moved around behind the Morris chair. My black gun was steady in his hand.

"Go easy," he warned me. "My story will work if I have to kill you—maybe work better."

That was sense. I stood still.

"Phone the police, Cara," he ordered.

She went out of the room, closing the door behind her; and all I could hear of her talk was a broken murmur.

CHAPTER VII

Ten minutes later three uniformed policemen arrived. All three knew Tennant, and they treated him with respect. Tennant reeled off the story he and the girl had cooked up, with a few changes to take care of the shot that had been fired from the nickeled gun and our rough-house. She nodded her head vigorously whenever a policeman looked at her. Tennant turned both guns over to the white-haired sergeant in charge.

I didn't argue, didn't deny anything, but told the sergeant: "I'm working with Detective Sergeant O'Gar on a job. I want to talk to him over the phone and then I want you to take all three of us down to the detective bureau."

Tennant objected to that, of course; not because he expected to gain anything, but on the off chance that he might. The white-haired sergeant looked from one of us to the other in puzzlement. Me, with my skinned face and split lip; Tennant, with a red lump under one eye where my first wallop had landed; and the girl, with most of the clothes above the waistline ripped off and a bruised cheek.

"It has a queer look, this thing," the sergeant decided aloud; "and I shouldn't wonder but what the detective bureau was the place for the lot of you."

One of the patrolmen went into the hall with me, and I got O'Gar on the phone at his home. It was nearly ten o'clock by now, and he was preparing for bed.

"Cleaning up the Gilmore murder," I told him. "Meet me at the Hall. Will you get hold of Kelly, the patrolman who found Gilmore, and bring him down there? I want him to look at some people."

"I will that," O'Gar promised, and I hung up.

The "wagon" in which the three policemen had answered Cara Kenbrook's call carried us down to the Hall of Justice, where we all went into the captain of detectives' office. McTighe, a lieutenant, was on duty.

I knew McTighe, and we were on pretty good terms; but I wasn't an influence in local politics, and Tennant was. I don't mean that McTighe would have knowingly helped Tennant frame me; but with me stacked up against the assistant city engineer, I knew who would get the benefit of any doubt there might be.

My head was thumping and roaring just now, with knots all over it where the girl had beaned me. I sat down, kept quiet, and nursed my head while Tennant and Cara Kenbrook, with a lot of details that they had not wasted on the uniformed men, told their tale and showed their injuries.

Tennant was talking—describing the terrible scene that had met his eyes when, drawn by the girl's screams, he had rushed into her apartment—when O'Gar came into the office. He recognized Tennant with a lifted eyebrow, and came over to sit beside me.

"What the hell is all this?" he muttered.

"A lovely mess," I whispered back. "Listen—in that nickel gun on the desk there's an empty shell. Get it for me."

He scratched his head doubtfully, listened to the next few words of Tennant's yarn, glanced at me out of the corner of his eye, and then went over to the desk and picked up the revolver.

McTighe looked at him—a sharp, questioning look.

"Something on the Gilmore killing," the detective-sergeant said, breaking the gun.

The lieutenant started to speak, changed his mind, and O'Gar brought the shell over and handed it to me.

"Thanks," I said, putting it in my pocket. "Now listen to my friend there. It's a good act, if you like it."

Tennant was winding up his history.

". . . Naturally a man who tried a thing like that on an unprotected woman would be yellow; so it wasn't very hard to handle him after I got his gun away from him. I hit him a couple of times, and he quit—begging me to stop, getting down on his knees. Then we called the police."

McTighe looked at me with eyes that were cold and hard. Tennant had made a believer of him, and not only of him—the police-sergeant and his two men were glowering at me. I suspected that even O'Gar—with whom I had been through a dozen storms—would have been half-convinced if the engineer hadn't added the neat touches about my kneeling.

"Well, what have *you* got to say?" McTighe challenged me in a tone which suggested that it didn't make much difference what I said.

"I've got nothing to say about this dream," I said shortly. "I'm interested in the Gilmore murder—not in this stuff." I turned to O'Gar. "Is the patrolman here?"

The detective-sergeant went to the door, and called: "Oh, Kelly!"

Kelly came in—a big, straight-standing man, with iron-gray hair and an intelligent fat face.

"You found Gilmore's body?" I asked.

"I did."

I pointed at Cara Kenbrook.

"Ever see her before?"

His gray eyes studied her carefully.

"Not that I remember," he answered.

"Did she come up the street while you were looking at Gilmore, and go into the house he was lying in front of?"

"She did not."

I took out the empty shell O'Gar had got for me, and chucked it down on the desk in front of the patrolman.

"Kelly," I asked, *why did you kill Gilmore?*"

Kelly's right hand went under his coat-tail at his hip.

I jumped for him.

Somebody grabbed me by the neck. Somebody else piled on my back. McTighe aimed a big fist at my face, but it missed. My legs had been suddenly kicked from under me, and I went down hard with men all over me.

When I was yanked to my feet again, big Kelly stood straight up by the desk, weighing his service revolver in his hand. His clear eyes met mine, and he laid the weapon on the desk. Then he unfastened his shield and put it with the gun.

"It was an accident," he said simply.

By this time the birds who had been manhandling me woke up to the fact that maybe they were missing part of the play—that maybe I wasn't a maniac. Hands dropped off me; and presently everybody was listening to Kelly.

He told his story with unhurried evenness, his eyes never wavering or clouding. A deliberate man, though unlucky.

"I was walkin' my beat that night, an' as I turned the corner of Jones into Pine I saw a man jump back from the steps of a buildin' into the vestibule. A burglar, I thought, an' cat-footed it down there. It was a dark vestibule, an' deep, an' I saw somethin' that looked like a man in it, but I wasn't sure.

" 'Come out o' there!' I called, but there was no answer. I took my gun in my hand an' started up the steps. I saw him move just then, comin' out. An' then my foot slipped. It was worn smooth, the bottom step, an' my foot slipped. I fell forward, the gun went off, an' the bullet hit him. He had come out a ways by then, an' when the bullet hit him he toppled over frontwise, tumblin' down the steps onto the sidewalk.

"When I looked at him I saw it was Gilmore. I knew him to say 'howdy' to, an' he knew me—which is why he must o' ducked out of sight when he saw me comin' around the corner. He didn't want me to see him comin' out of a buildin' where I knew Mr. Tennant lived, I suppose, thinkin' I'd put two an' two together, an' maybe talk.

"I don't say that I did the right thing by lyin', but it didn't hurt anybody. It was an accident; but he was a man with a lot of friends up in high places, an'—accident or no—I stood a good chance of bein' broke, an' maybe sent over for a while. So I told my story the way you people know it. I couldn't say I'd seen anything suspicious without maybe puttin' the blame on some innocent party, an' I didn't want that. I'd made up my mind that if anybody was arrested for the murder, an' things looked bad for them, I'd come out an' say I'd done it. Home, you'll find a confession all written out—written out in case somethin' happened to me—so nobody else'd ever be blamed.

"That's why I had to say I'd never seen the lady here. I did see her—saw her go into the buildin' that night—the buildin' Gilmore had come out of. But I couldn't say so without makin' it look bad for her; so I lied. I could have thought up a better story if I'd had more time, I don't doubt; but I had to think quick. Anyways, I'm glad it's all over."

CHAPTER VIII

Kelly and the other uniformed policeman had left the office, which now held McTighe, O'Gar, Cara Kenbrook, Tennant and me. Tennant had crossed to my side, and was apologizing.

"I hope you'll let me square myself for this evening's work. But you know how it is when somebody you care for is in a jam. I'd have killed you if I had thought it would help Cara—on the level. Why didn't you tell us that you didn't suspect her?"

"But I did suspect the pair of you," I said. "It looked as if Kelly had to be the guilty one; but you people carried on so much that I began to feel doubtful. For a while it was funny—you thinking she had done it, and she thinking you had, though I suppose each had sworn to his or her innocence. But after a time it stopped being funny. You carried it too far."

"How did you rap to Kelly?" O'Gar, at my shoulder, asked.

"Miss Kenbrook was walking north on Leavenworth—and was half-way between Bush and Pine—when the shot was fired. She saw nobody, no cars, until she rounded the corner. Mrs. Gilmore, walking north on Jones, was about the same distance away when *she* heard the shot, and she saw nobody until she reached Pine Street. If Kelly had been telling the truth, she would have seen him on Jones Street. He said he didn't turn the corner until after the shot was fired.

"Either of the women could have killed Gilmore, but hardly both; and I doubted that either could have shot him and got away without running into Kelly or the other. Suppose both of them were telling the truth—what then? Kelly must have been lying! He was the logical suspect anyway—the nearest known person to the murdered man when the shot was fired.

"To back all this up, he had let Miss Kenbrook go into the apartment building at 3:00 in the morning, in front of which a man had just been killed, without questioning her or mentioning her in his report. That looked as if he *knew* who had done the killing. So I took a chance with the empty shell trick, it being a good bet that he would have thrown his away, and would think that—"

McTighe's heavy voice interrupted my explanation.

"How about this assault charge?" he asked, and had the decency to avoid my eye when I turned toward him with the others.

Tennant cleared his throat.

"Er—ah—in view of the way things have turned out, and knowing that Miss Kenbrook doesn't want the disagreeable publicity that would accompany an affair of this sort, why, I'd suggest that we drop the whole thing." He smiled brightly from McTighe to me. "You know nothing has gone on the records yet."

"Make the big heap play his hand out," O'Gar growled in my ear. "Don't let him drop it."

"Of course if Miss Kenbrook doesn't want to press the charge," McTighe was saying, watching me out of the tail of his eye, "I suppose—"

"If everybody understands that the whole thing was a plant," I said, "and if the policemen who heard the story are brought in here now and told by Tennant and Miss Kenbrook that it was all a lie—then I'm willing to let it go at that. Otherwise, I won't stand for a hush-up."

"You're a damned fool!" O'Gar whispered. "Put the screws on them!"

But I shook my head. I didn't see any sense in making a lot of trouble for myself just to make some for somebody else— and suppose Tennant *proved* his story . . .

So the policemen were found, and brought into the office again, and told the truth.

And presently Tennant, the girl, and I were walking together like three old friends through the corridors toward the door, Tennant still asking me to let him make amends for the evening's work.

"You've *got* to let me do something!" he insisted. "It's only right!"

His hand dipped into his coat, and came out with a thick bill-fold.

"Here," he said; "let me—"

We were going, at that happy moment, down the stone vestibule steps that lead to Kearny Street—six or seven steps there are.

"No," I said; "let me—"

He was on the next to the top step, when I reached up and let go.

He settled in a rather limp pile at the bottom.

Leaving his empty-faced lady love to watch over him, I strolled up through Portsmouth Square toward a restaurant where the steaks come thick.

The Golden Horseshoe

I HAVEN'T anything very exciting to offer you this time," Vance Richmond said as we shook hands. "I want you to find a man for me—a man who is not a criminal."

There was an apology in his voice. The last couple of jobs this lean, grey-faced attorney had thrown my way had run to gun-play and other forms of rioting, and I suppose he thought anything less than that would put me to sleep. Was a time when he might have been right—when I was a young sprout of twenty or so, newly attached to the Continental Detective Agency. But the fifteen years that had slid by since then had dulled my appetite for rough stuff. I don't mean that I shuddered whenever I considered the possibility of some bird taking a poke at me; but I didn't call that day a total loss in which nobody tried to puncture my short, fat carcass.

"The man I want found," the lawyer went on, as we sat down, "is an English architect named Norman Ashcraft. He is a man of about thirty-seven, five feet ten inches tall, well built, and fair-skinned, with light hair and blue eyes. Four years ago he was a typical specimen of the clean-cut blond Britisher. He may not be like that now—those four years have been rather hard ones for him, I imagine.

"I want to find him for Mrs. Ashcraft, his wife. I know your Agency's rule against meddling with family affairs, but I can assure you that no matter how things turn out there will be no divorce proceedings in which you will be involved.

"Here is the story. Four years ago the Ashcrafts were living together in England, in Bristol. It seems that Mrs. Ashcraft is of a very jealous disposition, and he was rather high-strung. Furthermore, he had only what money he earned at his profession, while she had inherited quite a bit from her parents. Ashcraft was rather foolishly sensitive about being the husband of a wealthy woman—was inclined to go out of his way to show that he was not dependent upon her money, that he wouldn't be influenced by it. Foolish, of course, but just the sort of attitude a man of his temperament would assume. One night she accused him of paying too much attention to another woman. They quarreled, and he packed up and left.

"She was repentant within a week—especially repentant since she had learned that her suspicion had had no foundation outside of her own jealousy—and she tried to find him. But he was gone. It became manifest that he had left England. She had him searched for in Europe, in Canada, in Australia, and in the United States. She succeeded in tracing him from Bristol to New York, and then to Detroit, where he had been arrested and fined for disturbing the peace in a drunken row of some sort. After that he dropped out of sight until he bobbed up in Seattle ten months later."

The attorney hunted through the papers on his desk and found a memorandum.

"On May 23, 1923, he shot and killed a burglar in his room in a hotel there. The Seattle police seem to have suspected that there was something funny about the shooting, but had nothing to hold Ashcraft on. The man he killed was undoubtedly a burglar. Then Ashcraft disappeared again, and nothing was heard of him until just about a year ago. Mrs. Ashcraft had advertisements inserted in the personal columns of papers in the principal American cities.

"One day she received a letter from him, from San Francisco. It was a very formal letter, and simply requested her to stop advertising. Although he was through with the name Norman Ashcraft, he wrote, he disliked seeing it published in every newspaper he read.

"She mailed a letter to him at the General Delivery window here, and used another advertisement to tell him about it. He answered it, rather caustically. She wrote him again, asking him to come home. He refused, though he seemed less bitter toward her. They exchanged several letters, and she learned that he had become a drug addict, and what was left of his pride would not let him return to her until he looked—and was at least somewhat like—his former self. She persuaded him to accept enough money from her to straighten himself out. She sent him this money each month, in care of General Delivery, here.

"Meanwhile she closed up her affairs in England—she had no close relatives to hold her there—and came to San Fran-

cisco, to be on hand when her husband was ready to return
to her. A year has gone. She still sends him money each
month. She still waits for him to come back to her. He has repeatedly refused to see her, and his letters are evasive— filled
with accounts of the struggle he is having, making headway
against the drug one month, slipping back the next.

"She suspects by now, of course, that he has no intention
of ever coming back to her; that he does not intend giving up
the drug; that he is simply using her as a source of income. I
have urged her to discontinue the monthly allowance for a
while. That would at least bring about an interview, I think,
and she could learn definitely what to expect. But she will not
do that. You see, she blames herself for his present condition.
She thinks her foolish flare of jealousy is responsible for his
plight, and she is afraid to do anything that might either hurt
him or induce him to hurt himself further. Her mind is un-
changeably made up in that respect. She wants him back,
wants him straightened out; but if he will not come, then she
is content to continue the payments for the rest of his life.
But she wants to know what she is to expect. She wants to
end this devilish uncertainty in which she has been living.

"What we want, then, is for you to find Ashcraft. We want
to know whether there is any likelihood of his ever becoming
a man again, or whether he is gone beyond redemption.
There is your job. Find him, learn whatever you can about
him, and then, after we know something, we will decide
whether it is wiser to force an interview between them—in
hopes that she will be able to influence him—or not."

"I'll try it," I said. "When does Mrs. Ashcraft send him his
monthly allowance?"

"On the first of each month."

"Today is the twenty-eighth. That'll give me three days to
wind up a job I have on hand. Got a photo of him?"

"Unfortunately, no. In her anger immediately after their
row, Mrs. Ashcraft destroyed everything she had that would
remind her of him. But I don't think a photograph would be
of any great help at the post office. Without consulting me,
Mrs. Ashcraft watched for her husband there on several occasions, and did not see him. It is more than likely that he has
someone else call for his mail."

I got up and reached for my hat.

"See you around the second of the month," I said, as I left the office.

II

On the afternoon of the first, I went down to the post office and got hold of Lusk, the inspector in charge of the division at the time.

"I've got a line on a scratcher from up north," I told Lusk, "who is supposed to be getting his mail at the window. Will you fix it up so I can get a spot on him?"

Post office inspectors are all tied up with rules and regulations that forbid their giving assistance to private detectives except on certain criminal matters. But a friendly inspector doesn't have to put you through the third degree. You lie to him—so that he will have an alibi in case there's a kick-back—and whether he thinks you're lying or not doesn't matter.

So presently I was downstairs again, loitering within sight of the A to D window, with the clerk at the window instructed to give me the office when Ashcraft's mail was called for. There was no mail for him there at the time. Mrs. Ashcraft's letter would hardly get to the clerks that afternoon, but I was taking no chances. I stayed on the job until the windows closed at eight o'clock, and then went home.

At a few minutes after ten the next morning I got my action. One of the clerks gave me the signal. A small man in a blue suit and a soft gray hat was walking away from the window with an envelope in his hand. A man of perhaps forty years, though he looked older. His face was pasty, his feet dragged, and, although his clothes were fairly new, they needed brushing and pressing.

He came straight to the desk in front of which I stood fiddling with some papers. Out of the tail of my eye I saw that he had not opened the envelope in his hand—was not going to open it. He took a large envelope from his pocket, and I got just enough of a glimpse of its front to see that it was already stamped and addressed. I twisted my neck out of joint trying to read the address, but failed. He kept the addressed side against his body, put the letter he had got from the window in it, and licked the flap backward, so that there was no possible way for anybody to see the front of the envelope. Then he rubbed the flap down carefully and turned toward the mailing slots. I went after him. There was nothing to do but to pull the always reliable stumble.

I overtook him, stepped close and faked a fall on the marble floor, bumping into him, grabbing him as if to regain my balance. It went rotten. In the middle of my stunt my foot really did slip, and we went down on the floor like a pair of wrestlers, with him under me. To botch the trick thoroughly, he fell with the envelope pinned under him.

I scrambled up, yanked him to his feet, mumbled an apology and almost had to push him out of the way to beat him to the envelope that lay face down on the floor. I had to turn it over as I handed it to him in order to get the address:

Mr. Edward Bohannon,
Golden Horseshoe Cafe,
Tijuana, Baja California, Mexico.

I had the address, but I had tipped my mitt. There was no way in God's world for this little man in blue to miss knowing that I had been trying to get that address.

I dusted myself off while he put his envelope through a slot. He didn't come back past me, but went on down toward the Mission Street exit. I couldn't let him get away with what he knew. I didn't want Ashcraft tipped off before I got to him. I would have to try another trick as ancient as the one the slippery floor had bungled for me. I set out after the little man again.

Just as I reached his side he turned his head to see if he was being followed.

"Hello, Micky!" I hailed him. "How's everything in Chi?"

"You got me wrong." He spoke out of the side of his gray-lipped mouth, not stopping. "I don't know nothin' about Chi."

His eyes were pale blue, with needle-point pupils—the eyes of a heroin or morphine user.

"Quit stalling." I walked along at his side. We had left the building by this time and were going down Mission Street. "You fell off the rattler only this morning."

He stopped on the sidewalk and faced me.

"Me? Who do you think I am?"

"You're Micky Parker. The Dutchman gave us the rap that you were headed here. They got him—if you don't already know it."

"You're cuckoo," he sneered. "I don't know what the hell you're talkin' about!"

That was nothing—neither did I. I raised my right hand in my overcoat pocket.

"Now I'll tell one," I growled at him. "And keep your hands away from your clothes or I'll let the guts out of you."

He flinched away from my bulging pocket.

"Hey, listen, brother!" he begged. "You got me wrong— on the level. My name ain't Micky Parker, an' I ain't been in Chi in six years. I been here in Frisco for a solid year, an' that's the truth."

"You got to show me."

"I can do it," he exclaimed, all eagerness. "You come down the drag with me, an' I'll show you. My name's Ryan, an' I been livin' aroun' the corner here on Sixth Street for six or eight months."

"Ryan?" I asked.

"Yes—John Ryan."

I chalked that up against him. Of course there have been Ryans christened John, but not enough of them to account for the number of times that name appears in criminal records. I don't suppose there are three old-time yeggs in the country who haven't used the name at least once; it's the John Smith of yeggdom.

This particular John Ryan led me around to a house on Sixth Street, where the landlady—a rough-hewn woman of fifty, with bare arms that were haired and muscled like the village smithy's—assured me that her tenant had to her positive knowledge been in San Francisco for months, and that she remembered seeing him at least once a day for a couple of weeks back. If I had been really suspicious that this Ryan was my mythical Micky Parker from Chicago, I wouldn't have taken the woman's word for it, but as it was I pretended to be satisfied.

That seemed to be all right then. Mr. Ryan had been led astray, had been convinced that I had mistaken him for

another crook, and that I was not interested in the Ashcraft
letter. I would be safe—reasonably safe—in letting the situation go as it stood. But loose ends worry me. And you can't
always count on people doing and thinking what you want.
This bird was a hop-head, and he had given me a phoney-
sounding name, so . . .

"What do you do for a living?" I asked him.

"I ain't been doin' nothin' for a coupla months," he pattered,
"but I expec' to open a lunch room with a fella nex' week."

"Let's go up to your room," I suggested. "I want to talk to
you."

He wasn't enthusiastic, but he took me up. He had two
rooms and a kitchen on the third floor. They were dirty, foul-
smelling rooms. I dangled a leg from the corner of a table and
waved him into a squeaky rocking chair in front of me. His
pasty face and dopey eyes were uneasy.

"Where's Ashcraft?" I threw at him.

He jerked, and then looked at the floor.

"I don't know what you're talkin' about," he mumbled.

"You'd better figure it out," I advised him, "or there's a
nice cool cell down in the booby-hutch that will be wrapped
around you."

"You ain't got nothin' on me."

"What of that? How'd you like to do a thirty or a sixty on
a vag charge?"

"Vag, hell!" he snarled, looking up at me. "I got five hundred smacks in my kick. Does that look like you can vag me?"

I grinned down at him.

"You know better than that, Ryan. A pocketful of money'll
get you nothing in California. You've got no job. You can't
show where your money comes from. You're made to order
for the vag law."

I had this bird figured as a dope pedler. If he was—or was
anything else off color that might come to light when he was
vagged—the chances were that he would be willing to sell
Ashcraft out to save himself; especially since, so far as I knew,
Ashcraft wasn't on the wrong side of the criminal law.

"If I were you," I went on while he stared at the floor and
thought, "I'd be a nice, obliging fellow and do my talking
now. You're—"

He twisted sidewise in his chair and one of his hands went behind him.

I kicked him out of his chair.

The table slipped under me or I would have stretched him. As it was, the foot that I aimed at his jaw took him on the chest and carried him over backward, with the rocking-chair piled on top of him. I pulled the chair off and took his gun— a cheap nickel-plated .32. Then I went back to my seat on the corner of the table.

He had only that one flash of fight in him. He got up sniveling.

"I'll tell you. I don't want no trouble, an' it ain't nothin' to me. I didn't know there was nothin' wrong. This Ashcraft told me he was jus' stringin' his wife along. He give me ten bucks a throw to get his letter ever' month an' send it to him in Tijuana. I knowed him here, an' when he went south six months ago—he's got a girl down there—I promised I'd do it for him. I knowed it was money—he said it was his 'alimony'—but I didn't know there was nothin' wrong."

"What sort of a hombre is this Ashcraft? What's his graft?"

"I don't know. He could be a con man—he's got a good front. He's a Englishman, an' mostly goes by the name of Ed Bohannon. He hits the hop. I don't use it myself"—that was a good one—"but you know how it is in a burg like this, a man runs into all kinds of people. I don't know nothin' about what he's up to. I jus' send the money ever' month an' get my ten."

That was all I could get out of him. He couldn't—or wouldn't—tell me where Ashcraft had lived in San Francisco or who he had mobbed up with. However, I had learned that Bohannon was Ashcraft, and not another go-between, and that was something.

Ryan squawked his head off when he found that I was going to vag him anyway. For a moment it looked like I would have to kick him loose from his backbone again.

"You said you'd spring me if I talked," he wailed.

"I did not. But if I had—when a gent flashes a rod on me I figure it cancels any agreement we might have had. Come on."

I couldn't afford to let him run around loose until I got in touch with Ashcraft. He would have been sending a telegram before I was three blocks away, and my quarry would be on his merry way to points north, east, south and west.

It was a good hunch I played in nabbing Ryan. When he was finger-printed at the Hall of Justice he turned out to be one Fred Rooney, alias "Jamocha," a pedler and smuggler who had crushed out of the Federal Prison at Leavenworth, leaving eight years of a tenner still unserved.

"Will you sew him up for a couple of days?" I asked the captain of the city jail. "I've got work to do that will go smoother if he can't get any word out for a while."

"Sure," the captain promised. "The federal people won't take him off our hands for two or three days. I'll keep him air-tight till then."

III

From the jail I went up to Vance Richmond's office and turned my news over to him.

"Ashcraft is getting his mail in Tijuana. He's living down there under the name of Ed Bohannon, and maybe has a woman there. I've just thrown one of his friends—the one who handled the mail and an escaped con—in the cooler."

"Was that necessary?" Richmond asked. "We don't want to work any hardships. We're really trying to help Ashcraft, you know."

"I could have spared this bird," I admitted. "But what for. He was all wrong. If Ashcraft can be brought back to his wife, he's better off with some of his shady friends out of the way. If he can't, what's the difference? Anyway, we've got one line on him safely stowed away where we can find it when we want it."

The attorney shrugged, and reached for the telephone.

He called a number. "Is Mrs. Ashcraft there? . . . This is Mr. Richmond. . . . No, we haven't exactly found him, but I think we know where he is. . . . Yes. . . . In about fifteen minutes."

He put down the telephone and stood up.

"We'll run up to Mrs. Ashcraft's house and see her."

Fifteen minutes later we were getting out of Richmond's car in Jackson Street near Gough. The house was a three-story white stone building, set behind a carefully sodded little lawn with an iron railing around it.

Mrs. Ashcraft received us in a drawing-room on the second floor. A tall woman of less than thirty, slimly beautiful in a gray dress. Clear was the word that best fits her; it described the blue of her eyes, the pink-white of her skin, and the light brown of her hair.

Richmond introduced me to her, and then I told her what I had learned, omitting the part about the woman in Tijuana. Nor did I tell her that the chances were her husband was a crook nowadays.

"Mr. Ashcraft is in Tijuana, I have been told. He left San Francisco about six months ago. His mail is being forwarded to him in care of a cafe there, under the name of Edward Bohannon."

Her eyes lighted up happily, but she didn't throw a fit. She wasn't that sort. She addressed the attorney.

"Shall I go down? Or will you?"

Richmond shook his head.

"Neither. You certainly shouldn't go, and I cannot—not at present. I must be in Eureka by the day after tomorrow, and shall have to spend several days there." He turned to me. "You'll have to go. You can no doubt handle it better than I could. You will know what to do and how to do it. There are no definite instructions I can give you. Your course will have to depend on Mr. Ashcraft's attitude and condition. Mrs. Ashcraft doesn't wish to force herself on him, but neither does she wish to leave anything undone that might help him."

Mrs. Ashcraft held a strong, slender hand out to me.

"You will do whatever you think wisest."

It was partly a question, partly an expression of confidence.

"I will," I promised.

I liked this Mrs. Ashcraft.

IV

Tijuana hadn't changed much in the two years I had been away. Still the same six or seven hundred feet of dusty and dingy street running between two almost solid rows of saloons,—perhaps thirty-five of them to a row,—with dirtier side streets taking care of the dives that couldn't find room on the main street.

The automobile that had brought me down from San Diego dumped me into the center of the town early in the afternoon, and the day's business was just getting under way. That is, there were only two or three drunks wandering around among the dogs and loafing Mexicans in the street, although there was already a bustle of potential drunks moving from one saloon to the next. But this was nothing like the crowd that would be here the following week, when the season's racing started.

In the middle of the next block I saw a big gilded horseshoe. I went down the street and into the saloon behind the sign. It was a fair sample of the local joint. A bar on your left as you came in, running half the length of the building, with three or four slot machines on one end. Across from the bar, against the right-hand wall, a dance floor that ran from the front wall to a raised platform, where a greasy orchestra was now preparing to go to work. Behind the orchestra was a row of low stalls or booths, with open fronts and a table and two benches apiece. Opposite them, in the space between the bar and the rear of the building, a man with a hair-lip was shaking pills out of a keno goose.

It was early in the day, and there were only a few buyers present, so the girls whose business it is to speed the sale of drinks charged down on me in a flock.

"Buy me a drink? Let's have a little drink? Buy a drink, honey?"

I shooed them away—no easy job—and caught a bartender's eye. He was a beefy, red-faced Irishman, with sorrel hair plastered down in two curls that hid what little forehead he had.

"I want to see Ed Bohannon," I told him confidentially.

He turned blank fish-green eyes on me.

"I don't know no Ed Bohannon."

Taking out a piece of paper and a pencil I scribbled, *Jamocha is copped*, and slid the paper over to the bartender.

"If a man who says he's Ed Bohannon asks for that, will you give it to him?"

"I guess so."

"Good," I said. "I'll hang around a while."

I walked down the room and sat at a table in one of the stalls. A lanky girl who had done something to her hair that made it purple was camped beside me before I had settled in my seat.

"Buy me a little drink?" she asked.

The face she made at me was probably meant for a smile. Whatever it was, it beat me. I was afraid she'd do it again, so I surrendered.

"Yes," I said, and ordered a bottle of beer for myself from the waiter who was already hanging over my shoulder.

The beer wasn't bad, for green beer; but at four bits a bottle it wasn't anything to write home about. This Tijuana happens to be in Mexico—by about a mile—but it's an American town, run by Americans, who sell American artificial booze at American prices. If you know your way around the United States you can find lots of places—especially near the Canadian line—where good booze can be bought for less than you are soaked for poison in Tijuana.

The purple-haired woman at my side downed her shot of whiskey, and was opening her mouth to suggest that we have another drink,—hustlers down there don't waste any time at all,—when a voice spoke from behind me.

"Cora, Frank wants you."

Cora scowled, looking over my shoulder.

Then she made that damned face at me again, said "All right, Kewpie. Will you take care of my friend here?" and left me.

Kewpie slid into the seat beside me. She was a little chunky girl of perhaps eighteen—not a day more than that. Just a kid. Her short hair was brown and curly over a round, boyish face with laughing, impudent eyes. Rather a cute little trick.

I bought her a drink and got another bottle of beer.

"What's on your mind?" I asked her.

"Hooch." She grinned at me—a grin that was as boyish as the straight look of her brown eyes. "Gallons of it."

"And besides that?"

I knew this switching of girls on me hadn't been purposeless.

"I hear you're looking for a friend of mine," Kewpie said.

"That might be. What friends have you got?"

"Well, there's Ed Bohannon for one. You know Ed?"

I shook my head.

"No—not yet."

"But you're looking for him?"

"Uh-huh."

"Maybe I could tell you how to find him, if I knew you were all right."

"It doesn't make any difference to me," I said carelessly. "I've a few more minutes to waste, and if he doesn't show up by then it's all one to me."

She cuddled against my shoulder.

"What's the racket? Maybe I could get word to Ed."

I stuck a cigarette in her mouth, one in my own, and lit them.

"Let it go," I bluffed. "This Ed of yours seems to be as exclusive as all hell. Well, it's no skin off *my* face. I'll buy you another drink and then trot along."

She jumped up.

"Wait a minute. I'll see if I can get him. What's your name?"

"Parker will do as well as any other," I said, the name I had used on Ryan popping first into my mind.

"You wait," she called back as she moved toward the back door. "I think I can find him."

"I think so too," I agreed.

Ten minutes went by, and a man came to my table from the front of the establishment. He was a blond Englishman of less than forty, with all the marks of the gentleman gone to pot on him. Not altogether on the rocks yet, but you could see evidence of the downhill slide plainly in the dullness of his blue eyes, in the pouches under his eyes, in the blurred lines around his mouth and the mouth's looseness, and in the grayish tint of his skin. He was still fairly attractive in appearance—enough of his former wholesomeness remained for that.

He sat down facing me across the table.

"You're looking for me?"

There was only a hint of the Britisher in his accent.

"You're Ed Bohannon?"

He nodded.

"Jamocha was picked up a couple of days ago," I told him, "and ought to be riding back to the Kansas big house by now. He got word out for me to give you the rap. He knew I was heading this way."

"How did they come to get him?"

His blue eyes were suspicious on my face.

"Don't know," I said. "Maybe they picked him up on a circular."

He frowned at the table and traced a meaningless design with a finger in a puddle of beer. Then he looked sharply at me again.

"Did he tell you anything else?"

"*He* didn't tell me anything. He got word out to me by somebody's mouthpiece. I didn't see him."

"You're staying down here a while?"

"Yes, for two or three days," I said. "I've got something on the fire."

He stood up and smiled, and held out his hand.

"Thanks for the tip, Parker," he said. "If you'll take a walk with me I'll give you something real to drink."

I didn't have anything against that. He led me out of the Golden Horseshoe and down a side street to an adobe house set out where the town fringed off into the desert. In the front room he waved me to a chair and went into the next room.

"What do you fancy?" he called through the door. "Rye, gin, tequila, Scotch—"

"The last one wins," I interrupted his catalog.

He brought in a bottle of Black and White, a siphon and some glasses, and we settled down to drinking. When that bottle was empty there was another to take its place. We drank and talked, drank and talked, and each of us pretended to be drunker than he really was—though before long we were both as full as a pair of goats.

It was a drinking contest pure and simple. He was trying to drink me into a pulp—a pulp that would easily give up all of its secrets—and I was trying the same game on him. Neither of us made much progress. Neither he nor I was young enough in the world to blab much when we were drunk that wouldn't have come out if we had been sober. Few grown men do, unless they get to boasting, or are very skilfully handled.

All that afternoon we faced each other over the table in the center of the room, drank and entertained each other.

"Y' know," he was saying somewhere along toward dark, "I've been a damn' ass. Got a wife—the nicesh woman in the worl'. Wantsh me t' come back to her, an' all tha' short of thing. Yet I hang around here, lappin' up this shtuff—hittin' the pipe—when I could be shomebody. Arc—architec', y' un'ershtand—good one, too. But I got in rut—got mixsh up with theshe people. C-can't sheem to break 'way. Goin' to, though—no spoofin'. Goin' back to li'l wife, nicesh woman in the worl'. Don't you shay anything t' Kewpie. She'd raishe hell 'f she knew I wash goin' t' shake her. Nishe girl, K-kewpie, but tough. S-shtick a bloomin' knife in me. Good job, too! But I'm goin' back to wife. Breakin' 'way from p-pipe an' ever'thing. Look at me. D' I look like a hop-head? Course not! Curin' m'self, tha's why. I'll show you—take a smoke now—show you I can take it or leave it alone."

Pulling himself dizzily up out of his chair, he wandered into the next room, bawling a song at the top of his voice:

> "A dimber mort with a quarter-stone slum,
> A-bubbin' of max with her cove—
> A bingo fen in a crack-o'-dawn drum,
> A-waitin' for—"

He came staggering into the room again carrying an elaborate opium layout—all silver and ebony—on a silver tray. He put it on the table and flourished a pipe at me.

"Have a li'l rear on me, Parker."

I told him I'd stick to the Scotch.

"Give y' shot of C. 'f y'd rather have it," he invited me.

I declined the cocaine, so he sprawled himself comfortably on the floor beside the table, rolled and cooked a pill, and our party went on—with him smoking his hop and me punishing the liquor—each of us still talking for the other's benefit, and trying to get the other to talk for our own.

I was holding down a lovely package by the time Kewpie came in, at midnight.

"Looks like you folks are enjoying yourselves," she laughed, leaning down to kiss the Englishman's rumpled hair as she stepped over him.

She perched herself on the table and reached for the Scotch.

"Everything's lovely," I assured her, though probably I didn't say it that clear.

I was fighting a battle with myself just about then. I had an idea that I wanted to dance. Down in Yucatan, four or five months before—hunting for a lad who had done wrong by the bank that employed him—I had seen some natives dance the *naual*. And that naual dance was the one thing in the world I wanted to do just then. (I was carrying a beautiful bun!) But I knew that if I sat still—as I had been sitting all evening—I could keep my cargo in hand, while it wasn't going to take much moving around to knock me over.

I don't remember whether I finally conquered the desire to dance or not. I remember Kewpie sitting on the table, grinning her boy's grin at me, and saying:

"You ought to stay oiled all the time, Shorty; it improves you."

I don't know whether I made any answer to that or not. Shortly afterward, I know, I spread myself beside the Englishman on the floor and went to sleep.

v

The next two days were pretty much like the first one. Ashcraft and I were together twenty-four hours each of the days, and usually the girl was with us, and the only time we weren't drinking was when we were sleeping off what we had been drinking. We spent most of those three days in either the adobe house or the Golden Horseshoe, but we found time to take in most of the other joints in town now and then. I had only a hazy idea of some of the things that went on around me, though I don't think I missed anything entirely. On the second day someone added a first name to the alias I had given the girl—and thereafter I was "Painless" Parker to Tijuana, and still am to some of them. I don't know who christened me, or why.

Ashcraft and I were as thick as thieves, on the surface, but neither of us ever lost his distrust of the other, no matter how drunk we got—and we got plenty drunk. He went up against his mud-pipe regularly. I don't think the girl used the stuff, but she had a pretty capacity for hard liquor. I would go to sleep not knowing whether I was going to wake up or not; but I had nothing on me to give me away, so I figured that I was safe unless I talked myself into a jam. I didn't worry much,—bedtime usually caught me in a state that made worry impossible.

Three days of this, and then, sobering up, I was riding back to San Francisco, making a list of what I knew and guessed about Norman Ashcraft, alias Ed Bohannon.

The list went something like this:

(1) He suspected, if he didn't know, that I had come down to see him on his wife's account: he had been too smooth and had entertained me too well for me to doubt that; (2) he apparently had decided to return to his wife, though there was no guarantee that he would actually do so; (3) he was not incurably addicted to drugs; he merely smoked opium and, regardless of what the Sunday supplements say, an opium smoker is little, if any, worse off than a tobacco smoker; (4) he might pull himself together under his wife's influence, but it was doubtful: physically he hadn't gone to the dogs, but he had had his taste of the gutter and seemed to like it; (5) the girl Kewpie was crazily in love with him, while he liked her, but wasn't turning himself inside out over her.

A good night's sleep on the train between Los Angeles and San Francisco set me down in the Third and Townsend Street station with nearly normal head and stomach and not too many kinks in my nerves. I put away a breakfast that was composed of more food than I had eaten in three days, and went up to Vance Richmond's office.

"Mr. Richmond is still in Eureka," his stenographer told me. "I don't expect him back until the first of the week."

"Can you get him on the phone for me?"

She could, and did.

Without mentioning any names, I told the attorney what I knew and guessed.

"I see," he said. "Suppose you go out to Mrs. A's house and tell her. I will write her tonight, and I probably shall be back in the city by the day after tomorrow. I think we can safely delay action until then."

I caught a street car, transferred at Van Ness Avenue, and went out to Mrs. Ashcraft's house. Nothing happened when I rang the bell. I rang it several times before I noticed that there were two morning newspapers in the vestibule. I looked at the dates—this morning's and yesterday morning's.

An old man in faded overalls was watering the lawn next door.

"Do you know if the people who live here have gone away?" I called to him.

"I don't guess so. The back door's open, I seen this mornin'."

He returned his attention to his hose, and then stopped to scratch his chin.

"They may of gone," he said slowly. "Come to think of it, I ain't seen any of 'em for—I don't remember seein' any of 'em yesterday."

I left the front steps and went around the house, climbed the low fence in back and went up the back steps. The kitchen door stood about a foot open. Nobody was visible in the kitchen, but there was a sound of running water.

I knocked on the door with my knuckles, loudly. There was no answering sound. I pushed the door open and went in. The sound of water came from the sink. I looked in the sink.

Under a thin stream of water running from one of the faucets lay a carving knife with nearly a foot of keen blade. The knife was clean, but the back of the porcelain sink—where water had splashed with only small, scattered drops—was freckled with red-brown spots. I scraped one of them with a finger-nail—dried blood.

Except for the sink, I could see nothing out of order in the kitchen. I opened a pantry door. Everything seemed all right there. Across the room another door led to the front of the house. I opened the door and went into a passageway. Not enough light came from the kitchen to illuminate the passageway. I fumbled in the dusk for the light-button that I knew should be there. I stepped on something soft.

Pulling my foot back, I felt in my pocket for matches, and struck one. In front of me, his head and shoulders on the floor, his hips and legs on the lower steps of a flight of stairs, lay a Filipino boy in his underclothes.

He was dead. One eye was cut, and his throat was gashed straight across, close up under his chin. I could see the killing without even shutting my eyes. At the top of the stairs—the killer's left hand dashing into the Filipino's face—thumb-nail gouging into eye—pushing the brown face back—tightening the brown throat for the knife's edge—the slash—and the shove down the steps.

The light from my second match showed me the button. I clicked on the lights, buttoned my coat, and went up the steps. Dried blood darkened them here and there, and at the second-floor landing the wall paper was stained with a big blot. At the head of the stairs I found another light-button, and pressed it.

I walked down the hall, poked my head into two rooms that seemed in order, and then turned a corner—and pulled up with a jerk, barely in time to miss stumbling over a woman who lay there.

She was huddled on the floor, face down, with knees drawn up under her and both hands clasped to her stomach. She wore a nightgown, and her hair was in a braid down her back.

I put a finger on the back of her neck. Stone-cold.

Kneeling on the floor—to avoid the necessity of turning her over—I looked at her face. She was the maid who had admitted Richmond and me four days ago.

I stood up again and looked around. The maid's head was almost touching a closed door. I stepped around her and pushed the door open. A bedroom, and not the maid's. It was an expensively dainty bedroom in cream and gray, with French prints on the walls. Nothing in the room was disarranged except the bed. The bed clothes were rumpled and tangled, and piled high in the center of the bed—in a pile that was too large. . . .

Leaning over the bed, I began to draw the covers off. The second piece came away stained with blood. I yanked the rest off.

Mrs. Ashcraft was dead there.

Her body was drawn up in a little heap, from which her head hung crookedly, dangling from a neck that had been cut clean through to the bone. Her face was marked with four deep scratches from temple to chin. One sleeve had been torn from the jacket of her blue silk pajamas. Bedding and pajamas were soggy with the blood that the clothing piled over her head kept from drying.

I put the blanket over her again, edged past the dead woman in the hall, and went down the front stairs, switching on more lights, hunting for the telephone. Near the foot of the stairs I found it. I called the police detective bureau first, and then Vance Richmond's office.

"Get word to Mr. Richmond that Mrs. Ashcraft has been murdered," I told his stenographer. "I'm at her house, and he can get in touch with me here any time during the next two or three hours."

Then I went out of the front door and sat on the top step, smoking a cigarette while I waited for the police.

I felt rotten. I've seen dead people in larger quantities than three in my time, and I've seen some that were hacked up pretty badly; but this thing had fallen on me while my nerves were ragged from three days of boozing.

The police automobile swung around the corner and began disgorging men before I had finished my first cigarette. O'Gar, the detective sergeant in charge of the Homicide Detail, was the first man up the steps.

"Hullo," he greeted me. "What have you got hold of this time?"

I was glad to see him. This squat, bullet-headed sergeant is as good a man as the department has, and he and I have always been lucky when we tied up together.

"I found three bodies in there before I quit looking," I told him as I led him indoors. "Maybe a regular detective like you—with a badge and everything—can find more."

"You didn't do bad—for a lad," he said.

My wooziness had passed. I was eager to get to work. These people lying dead around the house were merely counters in a game again—or almost. I remembered the feel of Mrs. Ashcraft's slim hand in mine, but I stuck that memory in the back of my mind. You hear now and then of detectives who have not become callous, who have not lost what you might call the human touch. I always feel sorry for them, and wonder why they don't chuck their jobs and find another line of work that wouldn't be so hard on their emotions. A sleuth who doesn't grow a tough shell is in for a gay life—day in and day out poking his nose into one kind of woe or another.

I showed the Filipino to O'Gar first, and then the two women. We didn't find any more. Detail work occupied all of us—O'Gar, the eight men under him, and me—for the next few hours. The house had to be gone over from roof to cellar. The neighbors had to be grilled. The employment agencies through which the servants had been hired had to be examined. Relatives and friends of the Filipino and the maid had to be traced and questioned. Newsboys, mail carriers, grocers' delivery men, laundrymen, had to be found, questioned and, when necessary, investigated.

When the bulk of the reports were in, O'Gar and I sneaked away from the others—especially away from the newspaper men, who were all over the place by now—and locked ourselves in the library.

"Night before last, huh? Wednesday night?" O'Gar grunted when we were comfortable in a couple of leather chairs, burning tobacco.

I nodded. The report of the doctor who had examined the bodies, the presence of the two newspapers in the vestibule, and the fact that neither neighbor, grocer nor butcher had seen any of them since Wednesday, combined to make Wednesday night—or early Thursday morning—the correct date.

"I'd say the killer cracked the back door," O'Gar went on, staring at the ceiling through smoke, "picked up the carving knife in the kitchen, and went upstairs. Maybe he went straight to Mrs. Ashcraft's room—maybe not. But after a bit he went in there. The torn sleeve and the scratches on her face mean that there was a tussle. The Filipino and the maid heard the noise—heard her scream maybe—and rushed to her room to find out what was the matter. The maid most likely got there just as the killer was coming out—and got hers. I guess the Filipino saw him then and ran. The killer caught him at the head of the back stairs—and finished him. Then he went down to the kitchen, washed his hands, dropped the knife, and blew."

"So far, so good," I agreed; "but I notice you skip lightly over the question of who he was and why he killed."

He pushed his hat back and scratched his bullet head.

"Don't crowd me," he rumbled; "I'll get around to that. There seem to be just three guesses to take your pick from. We know that nobody else lived in the house outside of the three that were killed. So the killer was either a maniac who did the job for the fun of it, a burglar who was discovered and ran wild, or somebody who had a reason for bumping off Mrs. Ashcraft, and then had to kill the two servants when they discovered him.

"Taking the knife from the kitchen would make the burglar guess look like a bum one. And, besides, we're pretty sure nothing was stolen. A good prowler would bring his own weapon with him if he wanted one. But the hell of it is that there are a lot of bum prowlers in the world—half-wits who would be likely to pick up a knife in the kitchen, go to pieces when the house woke up, slash everybody in sight, and then beat it without turning anything over.

"So it could have been a prowler; but my personal guess is that the job was done by somebody who wanted to wipe out Mrs. Ashcraft."

"Not so bad," I applauded. "Now listen to this: Mrs. Ashcraft has a husband in Tijuana, a mild sort of hop-head who is mixed up with a bunch of thugs. She was trying to persuade him to come back to her. He has a girl down there who is young, goofy over him, and a bad actor—one tough youngster. He was planning to run out on the girl and come back home."

"So-o-o?" O'Gar said softly.

"But," I continued, "I was with both him and the girl, in Tijuana, night before last—when this killing was done."

"So-o?"

A knock on the door interrupted our talk. It was a policeman to tell me that I was wanted on the phone. I went down to the first floor, and Vance Richmond's voice came over the wire.

"What is it? Miss Henry delivered your message, but she couldn't give me any details."

I told him the whole thing.

"I'll leave for the city tonight," he said when I had finished. "You go ahead and do whatever you want. You're to have a free hand."

"Right," I replied. "I'll probably be out of town when you get back. You can reach me through the Agency if you want to get in touch with me. I'm going to wire Ashcraft to come up—in your name."

After Richmond had hung up, I called the city jail and asked the captain if John Ryan, alias Fred Rooney, alias Jamocha, was still there.

"No. Federal officers left for Leavenworth with him and two other prisoners yesterday morning."

Up in the library again, I told O'Gar hurriedly:

"I'm catching the evening train south, betting my marbles that the job was made in Tijuana. I'm wiring Ashcraft to come up. I want to get him away from the Mexican town for a day or two, and if he's up here you can keep an eye on him. I'll give you a description of him, and you can pick him up at Vance Richmond's office. He'll probably connect there first thing."

Half an hour of the little time I had left I spent writing and sending three telegrams. The first was to Ashcraft.

> EDWARD BOHANNON,
> GOLDEN HORSESHOE CAFE,
> TIJUANA, MEXICO.
> MRS. ASHCRAFT IS DEAD. CAN YOU COME
> IMMEDIATELY?
>> VANCE RICHMOND.

The other two were in code. One went to the Continental Detective Agency's Kansas City branch, asking that an operative be sent to Leavenworth to question Jamocha. The other requested the Los Angeles branch to have a man meet me in San Diego the next day.

Then I dashed out to my rooms for a bagful of clean clothes, and went to sleep riding south again.

VI

San Diego was gay and packed when I got off the train early the next afternoon—filled with the crowd that the first Saturday of the racing season across the border had drawn. Movie folk from Los Angeles, farmers from the Imperial Valley, sailors from the Pacific Fleet, gamblers, tourists, grifters, and even regular people, from everywhere. I lunched, registered and left my bag at a hotel, and went up to the U. S. Grant Hotel to pick up the Los Angeles operative I had wired for.

I found him in the lobby—a freckle-faced youngster of twenty-two or so, whose bright gray eyes were busy just now with a racing program, which he held in a hand that had a finger bandaged with adhesive tape. I passed him and stopped at the cigar stand, where I bought a package of cigarettes and straightened out an imaginary dent in my hat. Then I went out to the street again. The bandaged finger and the business with the hat were our introductions. Somebody invented those tricks back before the Civil War, but they still worked smoothly, so their antiquity was no reason for discarding them.

I strolled up Fourth Street, getting away from Broadway— San Diego's main stem—and the operative caught up with me. His name was Gorman, and he turned out to be a pretty good lad. I gave him the lay.

"You're to go down to Tijuana and take a plant on the Golden Horseshoe Café. There's a little chunk of a girl hustling drinks in there—short curly brown hair; brown eyes; round face; rather large red mouth; square shoulders. You can't miss her; she's a nice-looking kid of about eighteen, called Kewpie. She's the target for your eye. Keep away from her. Don't try to rope her. I'll give you an hour's start. Then I'm coming down to talk to her. I want to know what she does right after I leave, and what she does for the next few days. You can get in touch with me at the"—I gave him the name of my hotel and my room number—"each night. Don't give me a tumble anywhere else. I'll most likely be in and out of the Golden Horseshoe often."

We parted, and I went down to the plaza and sat on a bench under the palms for an hour. Then I went up to the corner and fought for a seat on a Tijuana stage.

Fifteen or more miles of dusty riding—packed five in a seat meant for three—a momentary halt at the Immigration Station on the line, and I was climbing out of the stage at the entrance to the race track. The ponies had been running for some time, but the turnstiles were still spinning a steady stream of customers into the track. I turned my back on the gate and went over to the row of jitneys in front of the Monte Carlo—the big wooden casino—got into one, and was driven over to the Old Town.

The Old Town had a deserted look. Nearly everybody was over watching the dogs do their stuff. Gorman's freckled face showed over a drink of mescal when I entered the Golden Horseshoe. I hoped he had a good constitution. He needed one if he was going to do his sleuthing on a distilled cactus diet.

The welcome I got from the Horseshoers was just like a homecoming. Even the bartender with the plastered-down curls gave me a grin.

"Where's Kewpie?" I asked.

"Brother-in-lawing, Ed?" a big Swede girl leered at me. "I'll see if I can find her for you."

Kewpie came through the back door just then.

"Hello, Painless!" She climbed all over me, hugging me, rubbing her face against mine, and the Lord knows what all. "Down for another swell souse?"

"No," I said, leading her back toward the stalls. "Business this time. Where's Ed?"

"Up north. His wife kicked off and he's gone to collect the remains."

"That makes you sorry?"

She showed her big white teeth in a boy's smile of pure happiness.

"You bet! It's tough on me that papa has come into a lot of sugar."

I looked at her out of the corner of my eyes—a glance that was supposed to be wise.

"And you think Ed's going to bring the jack back to you?"

Her eyes snapped darkly at me.

"What's eating you?" she demanded.

I smiled knowingly.

"One of two things is going to happen," I predicted. "Ed's going to ditch you—he was figuring on that, anyway—or he's going to need every brownie he can scrape up to keep his neck from being—"

"You God-damned liar!"

Her right shoulder was to me, touching my left. Her left hand flashed down under her short skirt. I pushed her shoulder forward, twisting her body sharply away from me. The knife her left hand had whipped up from her leg jabbed deep into the underside of the table. A thick-bladed knife, I noticed, balanced for accurate throwing.

She kicked backward, driving one of her sharp heels into my ankle. I slid my left arm around behind her and pinned her elbow to her side just as she freed the knife from the table.

"What th' hell's all 'is?"

I looked up.

Across the table a man stood glaring at me—legs apart, fists on hips. He was a big man, and ugly. A tall, raw-boned man with wide shoulders, out of which a long, skinny yellow neck rose to support a little round head. His eyes were black shoe-buttons stuck close together at the top of a little mashed nose. His mouth looked as if it had been torn in his face, and it was stretched in a snarl now, baring a double row of crooked brown teeth.

"Where d' yuh get 'at stuff?" this lovely person roared at me.

He was too tough to reason with.

"If you're a waiter," I told him, "bring me a bottle of beer and something for the kid. If you're not a waiter—sneak."

He leaned over the table and I gathered my feet in. It looked like I was going to need them to move around on.

"I'll bring yuh a—"

The girl wriggled out of my hands and shut him up.

"Mine's liquor," she said sharply.

He snarled, looked from one of us to the other, showed me his dirty teeth again, and wandered away.

"Who's your friend?"

"You'll do well to lay off him," she advised me, not answering my question.

Then she slid her knife back in its hiding place under her skirt and twisted around to face me.

"Now what's all this about Ed being in trouble?"

"You read about the killing in the papers?"

"Yes."

"You oughtn't need a map, then," I said. "Ed's only out is to put the job on you. But I doubt if he can get away with that. If he can't, he's nailed."

"You're crazy!" she exclaimed. "You weren't too drunk to know that both of us were here with you when the killing was done."

"I'm not crazy enough to think that proves anything," I corrected her. "But I am crazy enough to expect to go back to San Francisco wearing the killer on my wrist."

She laughed at me. I laughed back and stood up.

"See you some more," I said as I strolled toward the door.

I returned to San Diego and sent a wire to Los Angeles, asking for another operative. Then I got something to eat and spent the evening lying across the bed in my hotel room smoking and scheming and waiting for Gorman.

It was late when he arrived, and he smelled of mescal from San Diego to St. Louis and back, but his head seemed level enough.

"Looked like I was going to have to shoot you loose from the place for a moment," he grinned. "Between the twist flashing the pick and the big guy loosening a sap in his pocket, it looked like action was coming."

"You let me alone," I ordered. "Your job is to see what goes on, and that's all. If I get carved, you can mention it in your report, but that's your limit. What did you turn up?"

"After you blew, the girl and the big guy put their noodles together. They seemed kind of agitated—all agog, you might say. He slid out, so I dropped the girl and slid along behind him. He came to town and got a wire off. I couldn't crowd him close enough to see who it was to. Then he went back to the joint. Things were normal when I knocked off."

"Who is the big guy? Did you learn?"

"He's no sweet dream, from what I hear. 'Gooseneck' Flinn is the name on his calling cards. He's bouncer and general utility man for the joint. I saw him in action against a couple of gobs, and he's nobody's meat—as pretty a double throw-out as I've ever seen."

So this Gooseneck party was the Golden Horseshoe's clean-up man, and he hadn't been in sight during my three-day spree? I couldn't possibly have been so drunk that I'd forget his ugliness. And it had been on one of those three days that Mrs. Ashcraft and her servants had been killed.

"I wired your office for another op," I told Gorman. "He's to connect with you. Turn the girl over to him, and you camp on Gooseneck's trail. I think we're going to hang three killings on him, so watch your step. I'll be in to stir things up a little more tomorrow; but remember, no matter what happens, everybody plays his own game. Don't ball things up trying to help me."

"Aye, aye, Cap," and he went off to get some sleep.

The next afternoon I spent at the race track, fooling around with the bangtails while I waited for night. The track was jammed with the usual Sunday crowd. I ran into any number of old acquaintances, some of them on my side of the game, some on the other, and some neutral. One of the second lot was "Trick-hat" Schultz. At our last meeting—a copper was leading him out of a Philadelphia court room toward a fifteen-year bit—he had promised to open me up from my eyebrows to my ankles the next time he saw me. He greeted me this afternoon with an eight-inch smile, bought me a shot of what they sell for gin under the grandstand, and gave me a tip on a horse named Beeswax. I'm not foolish enough to play anybody's tips, so I didn't play this one. Beeswax ran so far ahead of the others that it looked like he and his competitors were in separate races, and he paid twenty-something to one. So Trick-hat had his revenge after all.

After the last race, I got something to eat at the Sunset Inn, and then drifted over to the big casino—the other end of the same building. A thousand or more people of all sorts were jostling one another there, fighting to go up against poker, craps, chuck-a-luck, wheels of fortune, roulette and twenty-one with whatever money the race track had left or given them. I didn't buck any of the games. My playtime was over. I walked around through the crowd looking for my men.

I spotted the first one—a sunburned man who was plainly a farm hand in his Sunday clothes. He was pushing toward the door, and his face held that peculiar emptiness which belongs to the gambler who has gone broke before the end of the game. It's a look of regret that is not so much for the loss of the money as for the necessity of quitting.

I got between the farm hand and the door.

"Clean you?" I asked sympathetically when he reached me.

A sheepish sort of nod.

"How'd you like to pick up five bucks for a few minutes' work?" I tempted him.

He would like it, but what was the work?

"I want you to go over to the Old Town with me and look at a man. Then you get your pay. There are no strings to it."

That didn't exactly satisfy him, but five bucks are five bucks; and he could drop out any time he didn't like the looks of things. He decided to try it.

I put the farm hand over by a door, and went after another—a little, plump man with round, optimistic eyes and a weak mouth. He was willing to earn five dollars in the simple and easy manner I had outlined. The next man I braced was a little too timid to take a chance on a blind game. Then I got a Filipino—glorious in a fawn-colored suit, with a coat split to the neck and pants whose belled bottoms would have held a keg apiece—and a stocky young Greek who was probably either a waiter or a barber.

Four men were enough. My quartet pleased me immensely. They didn't look too intelligent for my purpose, and they didn't look like thugs or sharpers. I put them in a jitney and took them over to the Old Town.

"Now this is it," I coached them when we had arrived. "I'm going into the Golden Horseshoe Café, around the corner. Give me two or three minutes, and then come in and buy yourselves a drink." I gave the farm hand a five-dollar bill. "You pay for the drinks with that—it isn't part of your wages. There's a tall, broad-shouldered man with a long, yellow neck and a small ugly face in there. You can't miss him. I want you all to take a good look at him without letting him get wise. When you're sure you'd know him again anywhere, give me the nod, and come back here and you get your money. Be careful when you give me the nod. I don't want anybody in there to find out that you know me."

It sounded queer to them, but there was the promise of five dollars apiece, and there were the games back in the casino, where five dollars might buy a man into a streak of luck that—write the rest of it yourself. They asked questions, which I refused to answer, but they stuck.

Gooseneck was behind the bar, helping out the bartenders, when I entered the place. They needed help. The joint bulged with customers. The dance floor looked like a mob scene. Thirsts were lined up four deep at the bar. A shotgun wouldn't have sounded above the din: men and women laughing, roaring and cursing; bottles and glasses rattling and banging; and louder and more disagreeable than any of those noises was the noise of the sweating orchestra. Turmoil, uproar, stink—a Tijuana joint on Sunday night.

I couldn't find Gorman's freckled face in the crowd, but I picked out the hatchet-sharp white face of Hooper, another Los Angeles operative, who, I knew then, had been sent down in response to my second telegram. Kewpie was farther down the bar, drinking with a little man whose meek face had the devil-may-care expression of a model husband on a tear. She nodded at me, but didn't leave her client.

Gooseneck gave me a scowl and the bottle of beer I had ordered. Presently my four hired men came in. They did their parts beautifully!

First they peered through the smoke, looking from face to face, and hastily avoiding eyes that met theirs. A little of this, and one of them, the Filipino, saw the man I had described, behind the bar. He jumped a foot in the excitement of his discovery, and then, finding Gooseneck glaring at him, turned his back and fidgeted. The three others spotted Gooseneck now, and sneaked looks at him that were as conspicuously furtive as a set of false whiskers. Gooseneck glowered at them.

The Filipino turned around, looked at me, ducked his head sharply, and bolted for the street. The three who were left shot their drinks down their gullets and tried to catch my eye. I was reading a sign high on the wall behind the bar:

ONLY GENUINE PRE-WAR AMERICAN
AND BRITISH WHISKEYS SERVED HERE

I was trying to count how many lies could be found in those nine words, and had reached four, with promise of more, when one of my confederates, the Greek, cleared his throat with the noise of a gasoline engine's backfire. Gooseneck was edging down the bar, a bungstarter in one hand, his face purple.

I looked at my assistants. Their nods wouldn't have been so terrible had they come one at a time; but they were taking no chances on my looking away again before they could get their reports in. The three heads bobbed together—a signal that nobody within twenty feet could, or did, miss—and they scooted out of the door, away from the long-necked man and his bung-starter.

I emptied my glass of beer, sauntered out of the saloon and around the corner. They were clustered where I had told them to wait.

"We'd know him! We'd know him!" they chorused.

"That's fine," I praised them. "You did great. I think you're all natural-born gumshoes. Here's your pay. Now if I were you boys, I think I'd sort of avoid that place after this; because, in spite of the clever way you covered yourselves up—and you did nobly!—he might possibly suspect something. There's no use taking chances, anyway."

They grabbed their wages and were gone before I had finished my speech. I returned to the Golden Horseshoe—to be on hand in case one of them should decide to sell me out and come back there to spill the deal to Gooseneck.

Kewpie had left her model husband, and met me at the door. She stuck an arm through mine and led me toward the rear of the building. I noticed that Gooseneck was gone from behind the bar. I wondered if he was out gunning for my four ex-employees.

"Business looks good," I chattered as we pushed through the crowd. "You know, I had a tip on Beeswax this afternoon, and wouldn't play the pup." I made two or three more aimless cracks of that sort—just because I knew the girl's mind was full of something else. She paid no attention to anything I said.

But when we had dropped down in front of a vacant table, she asked:

"Who were your friends?"

"What friends?"

"The four jobbies who were at the bar when you were there a few minutes ago."

"Too hard for me, sister." I shook my head. "There were slews of men there. Oh, yes! I know who you mean! Those four gents who seemed kind of smitten with Gooseneck's looks. I wonder what attracted them to him—besides his beauty."

She grabbed my arm with both hands.

"So help me God, Painless," she swore, "if you tie anything on Ed, I'll kill you!"

Her brown eyes were big and damp. She was a hard and wise little baby—had rubbed the world's sharp corners with both shoulders—but she was only a kid, and she was worried sick over this man of hers. However, the business of a sleuth is to catch criminals, not to sympathize with their ladyloves.

I patted her hands.

"I could give you some good advice," I said as I stood up, "but you wouldn't listen to it, so I'll save my breath. It won't do any harm to tell you to keep an eye on Gooseneck, though—he's shifty."

There wasn't any special meaning to that speech, except that it might tangle things up a little more. One way of finding what's at the bottom of either a cup of coffee or a situation is to keep stirring it up until whatever is on the bottom comes to the surface. I had been playing that system thus far on this affair.

Hooper came into my room in the San Diego hotel at a little before two the next morning.

"Gooseneck disappeared, with Gorman tailing him, immediately after your first visit," he said. "After your second visit, the girl went around to a 'dobe house on the edge of town, and she was still there when I knocked off. The place was dark."

Gorman didn't show up.

VII

A bell-hop with a telegram roused me at ten o'clock in the morning. The telegram was from Mexicali:

DROVE HERE LAST NIGHT HOLED UP WITH
FRIENDS SENT TWO WIRES.

GORMAN.

That was good news. The long-necked man had fallen for
my play, had taken my four busted gamblers for four witnesses, had taken their nods for identifications. Gooseneck
was the lad who had done the actual killing, and Gooseneck
was in flight.

I had shed my pajamas and was reaching for my union suit
when the boy came back with another wire. This one was
from O'Gar, through the Agency:

ASHCRAFT DISAPPEARED YESTERDAY

I used the telephone to get Hooper out of bed.

"Get down to Tijuana," I told him. "Stick up the house
where you left the girl last night, unless you run across her at
the Golden Horseshoe. Stay there until she shows. Stay with
her until she connects with a big blond Englishman, and then
switch to him. He's a man of less than forty, tall, with blue
eyes and yellow hair. Don't let him shake you—he's the big
boy in this party just now. I'll be down. If the Englishman
and I stay together and the girl leaves us, take her, but otherwise stick to him."

I dressed, put down some breakfast and caught a stage for
the Mexican town. The boy driving the stage made fair time,
but you would have thought we were standing still to see a
maroon roadster pass us near Palm City. Ashcraft was driving
the roadster.

The roadster was empty, standing in front of the adobe
house, when I saw it again. Up in the next block, Hooper was
doing an imitation of a drunk, talking to two Indians in the
uniforms of the Mexican Army.

I knocked on the door of the adobe house.

Kewpie's voice: "Who is it?"

"Me—Painless. Just heard that Ed is back."

"Oh!" she exclaimed. A pause. "Come in."

I pushed the door open and went in. The Englishman sat
tilted back in a chair, his right elbow on the table, his right

hand in his coat pocket—if there was a gun in that pocket it was pointing at me.

"Hello," he said. "I hear you've been making guesses about me."

"Call 'em anything you like." I pushed a chair over to within a couple of feet of him, and sat down. "But don't let's kid each other. You had Gooseneck knock your wife off so you could get what she had. The mistake you made was in picking a sap like Gooseneck to do the turn—a sap who went on a killing spree and then lost his nerve. Going to read and write just because three or four witnesses put the finger on him! And only going as far as Mexicali! That's a fine place to pick! I suppose he was so scared that the five or six-hour ride over the hills seemed like a trip to the end of the world!"

The man's face told me nothing. He eased himself around in his chair an inch or two, which would have brought the gun in his pocket—if a gun *was* there—in line with my thick middle. The girl was somewhere behind me, fidgeting around. I was afraid of her. She was crazily in love with this man in front of me, and I had seen the blade she wore on one leg. I imagined her fingers itching for it now. The man and his gun didn't worry me much. He was not rattle-brained, and he wasn't likely to bump me off either in panic or for the fun of it.

I kept my chin going.

"You aren't a sap, Ed, and neither am I. I want to take you riding north with bracelets on, but I'm in no hurry. What I mean is, I'm not going to stand up and trade lead with you. This is all in my daily grind. It isn't a matter of life or death with me. If I can't take you today, I'm willing to wait until to-morrow. I'll get you in the end, unless somebody beats me to you—and that won't break my heart. There's a rod between my vest and my belly. If you'll have Kewpie get it out, we'll be all set for the talk I want to make."

He nodded slowly, not taking his eyes from me. The girl came close to my back. One of her hands came over my shoulder, went under my vest, and my old black gun left me. Before she stepped away she laid the point of her knife against the nape of my neck for an instant—a gentle reminder. I managed not to squirm or jump.

"Good," I said when she gave my gun to the Englishman, who pocketed it with his left hand. "Now here's my proposition. You and Kewpie ride across the border with me—so we won't have to fool with extradition papers—and I'll have you locked up. We'll do our fighting in court. I'm not absolutely certain that I can tie the killings on either of you, and if I flop, you'll be free. If I make the grade—as I hope to—you'll swing, of course. But there's always a good chance of beating the courts—especially if you're guilty—and that's the only chance you have that's worth a damn.

"What's the sense of scooting? Spending the rest of your life dodging bulls? Only to be nabbed finally—or bumped off trying to get away? You'll maybe save your neck, but what of the money your wife left? That money is what you are in the game for—it's what you had your wife killed for. Stand trial and you've a chance to collect it. Run—and you kiss it good-by. Are you going to ditch it—throw it away just because your cat's-paw bungled the deal? Or are you going to stick to the finish—win everything or lose everything?"

A lot of these boys who make cracks about not being taken alive have been wooed into peaceful surrender with that kind of talk. But my game just now was to persuade Ed and his girl to bolt. If they let me throw them in the can I might be able to convict one of them, but my chances weren't any too large. It depended on how things turned out later. It depended on whether I could prove that Gooseneck had been in San Francisco on the night of the killings, and I imagined that he would be well supplied with all sorts of proof to the contrary. We had not been able to find a single finger-print of the killer's in Mrs. Ashcraft's house. And if I *could* convince a jury that he was in San Francisco at the time, then I would have to show that he had done the killing. And after that I would have the toughest part of the job still ahead of me—to prove that he had done the killing for one of these two, and not on his own account. I had an idea that when we picked Gooseneck up and put the screws to him he would talk. But that was only an idea.

What I was working for was to make this pair dust out. I didn't care where they went or what they did, so long as they scooted. I'd trust to luck and my own head to get profit out of their scrambling—I was still trying to stir things up.

The Englishman was thinking hard. I knew I had him worried, chiefly through what I had said about Gooseneck Flinn. If I had pulled the moth-eaten stuff—said that Gooseneck had been picked up and had squealed—this Englishman would have put me down as a liar; but the little I had said was bothering him.

He bit his lip and frowned. Then he shook himself and chuckled.

"You're balmy, Painless," he said. "But you—"

I don't know what he was going to say—whether I was going to win or lose.

The front door slammed open, and Gooseneck Flinn came into the room.

His clothes were white with dust. His face was thrust forward to the full length of his long, yellow neck.

His shoe-button eyes focused on me. His hands turned over. That's all you could see. They simply turned over—and there was a heavy revolver in each.

"Your paws on the table, Ed," he snarled.

Ed's gun—if that is what he had in his pocket—was blocked from a shot at the man in the doorway by a corner of the table. He took his hand out of his pocket, empty, and laid both palms down on the table-top.

"Stay where y'r at!" Gooseneck barked at the girl.

She was standing on the other side of the room. The knife with which she had pricked the back of my neck was not in sight.

Gooseneck glared at me for nearly a minute, but when he spoke it was to Ed and Kewpie.

"So this is what y' wired me to come back for, huh? A trap! Me the goat for yur! I'll be y'r goat! I'm goin' to speak my piece, an' then I'm goin' out o' here if I have to smoke my way through the whole damn' Mex army! I killed y'r wife all right— an' her help, too. Killed 'em for the thousand bucks—"

The girl took a step toward him, screaming:

"Shut up, damn you!"

Her mouth was twisting and working like a child's, and there was water in her eyes.

"Shut up, yourself!" Gooseneck roared back at her, and his thumb raised the hammer of the gun that threatened her. "I'm doin' the talkin'. I killed her for—"

Kewpie bent forward. Her left hand went under the hem of her skirt. The hand came up—empty. The flash from Gooseneck's gun lit on a flying steel blade.

The girl spun back across the room—hammered back by the bullets that tore through her chest. Her back hit the wall. She pitched forward to the floor.

Gooseneck stopped shooting and tried to speak. The brown haft of the girl's knife stuck out of his yellow throat. He couldn't get his words past the blade. He dropped one gun and tried to take hold of the protruding haft. Half-way up to it his hand came, and dropped. He went down slowly— to his knees—hands and knees—rolled over on his side—and lay still.

I jumped for the Englishman. The revolver Gooseneck had dropped turned under my foot, spilling me sidewise. My hand brushed the Englishman's coat, but he twisted away from me, and got his guns out.

His eyes were hard and cold and his mouth was shut until you could hardly see the slit of it. He backed slowly across the floor, while I lay still where I had tumbled. He didn't make a speech. A moment of hesitation in the doorway. The door jerked open and shut. He was gone.

I scooped up the gun that had thrown me, sprang to Gooseneck's side, tore the other gun out of his dead hand, and plunged into the street. The maroon roadster was trailing a cloud of dust into the desert behind it. Thirty feet from me stood a dirt-caked black touring car. That would be the one in which Gooseneck had driven back from Mexicali.

I jumped for it, climbed in, brought it to life, and pointed it at the dust-cloud ahead.

VIII

The car under me, I discovered, was surprisingly well engined for its battered looks—its motor was so good that I knew it was a border-runner's car. I nursed it along, not pushing it. There were still four or five hours of daylight left, and while there was any light at all I couldn't miss the cloud of dust from the fleeing roadster.

I didn't know whether we were following a road or not. Sometimes the ground under me looked like one, but mostly it didn't differ much from the rest of the desert. For half an hour or more the dust-cloud ahead and I held our respective positions, and then I found that I was gaining.

The going was roughening. Any road that we might originally have been using had petered out. I opened up a little, though the jars it cost me were vicious. But if I was going to avoid playing Indian among the rocks and cactus, I would have to get within striking distance of my man before he deserted his car and started a game of hide and seek on foot. I'm a city man. I have done my share of work in the open spaces, but I don't like it. My taste in playgrounds runs more to alleys, backyards and cellars than to canyons, mesas and arroyos.

I missed a boulder that would have smashed me up—missed it by a hair—and looked ahead again to see that the maroon roadster was no longer stirring up the grit. It had stopped.

The roadster was empty. I kept on.

From behind the roadster a pistol snapped at me, three times. It would have taken good shooting to plug me at that instant. I was bounding and bouncing around in my seat like a pellet of quicksilver in a nervous man's palm.

He fired again from the shelter of his car, and then dashed for a narrow arroyo—a sharp-edged, ten-foot crack in the earth—off to the left. On the brink, he wheeled to snap another cap at me—and jumped down out of sight.

I twisted the wheel in my hands, jammed on the brakes and slid the black touring car to the spot where I had seen him last. The edge of the arroyo was crumbling under my front wheels. I released the brake. Tumbled out. Shoved.

The car plunged down into the gully after him.

Sprawled on my belly, one of Gooseneck's guns in each hand, I wormed my head over the edge. On all fours, the Englishman was scrambling out of the way of the car. The car was mangled, but still sputtering. One of the man's fists was bunched around a gun—mine.

"Drop it and stand up, Ed!" I yelled.

Snake-quick, he flung himself around in a sitting position on the arroyo bottom, swung his gun up—and I smashed his forearm with my second shot.

He was holding the wounded arm with his left hand when I slid down beside him, picked up the gun he had dropped, and frisked him to see if he had any more.

He grinned at me.

"You know," he drawled, "I fancy your true name isn't Painless Parker at all. You don't act like it."

Twisting a handkerchief into a tourniquet of a sort, I knotted it around his wounded arm, which was bleeding.

"Let's go upstairs and talk," I suggested, and helped him up the steep side of the gully.

We climbed into his roadster.

"Out of gas," he said. "We've got a nice walk ahead of us."

"We'll get a lift. I had a man watching your house, and another one shadowing Gooseneck. They'll be coming out after me, I reckon. Meanwhile, we have time for a nice heart-to-heart talk."

"Go ahead, talk your head off," he invited; "but don't expect me to add much to the conversation. You've got nothing on me." (I'd like to have a dollar, or even a nickel, for every time I've heard that remark!) "You saw Kewpie bump Gooseneck off to keep him from peaching on her."

"So that's your play?" I inquired. "The girl hired Gooseneck to kill your wife—out of jealousy—when she learned that you were planning to shake her and return to your own world?"

"Exactly."

"Not bad, Ed, but there's one rough spot in it."

"Yes?"

"Yes," I repeated. "You are not Ashcraft!"

He jumped, and then laughed.

"Now your enthusiasm is getting the better of your judgment," he kidded me. "Could I have deceived another man's wife? Don't you think her lawyer, Richmond, made me prove my identity?"

"Well, I'll tell you, Ed, I think I'm a smarter baby than either of them. Suppose you had a lot of stuff that belonged to Ashcraft—papers, letters, things in his handwriting? If you were even a fair hand with a pen, you could have fooled his wife. She thought her husband had had four tough years and had become a hop-head. That would account for irregularities in his writing. And I don't imagine you ever got very familiar in your letters—not enough so to risk any missteps. As for the lawyer—his making you identify yourself was only a matter of form. It never occurred to him that you weren't Ashcraft. Identification is easy, anyway. Give me a week and I'll prove that I'm the Sultan of Turkey."

He shook his head sadly.

"That comes from riding around in the sun."

I went on.

"At first your game was to bleed Mrs. Ashcraft for an allowance—to take the cure. But after she closed out her affairs in England and came here, you decided to wipe her out and take everything. You knew she was an orphan and had no close relatives to come butting in. You knew it wasn't likely that there were many people in America who could say you were not Ashcraft. Now if you want to you can do your stalling for just as long as it takes us to send a photograph of you to England—to be shown to the people that knew him there. But you understand that you will do your stalling in the can, so I don't see what it will get you."

"Where do you think Ashcraft would be while I was spending his money?"

There were only two possible guesses. I took the more reasonable one.

"Dead."

I imagined his mouth tightened a little, so I took another shot, and added:

"Up north."

That got to him, though he didn't get excited. But his eyes became thoughtful behind his smile. The United States is all "up north" from Tijuana, but it was even betting that he thought I meant Seattle, where the last record of Ashcraft had come from.

"You may be right, of course," he drawled. "But even at that, I don't see just how you expect to hang me. Can you prove that Kewpie didn't think I was Ashcraft? Can you prove that she knew why Mrs. Ashcraft was sending me money? Can you prove that she knew anything about my game? I rather think not. There are still any number of reasons for her to have been jealous of this other woman.

"I'll do my bit for fraud, Painless, but you're not going to swing me. The only two who could possibly tie anything on me are dead behind us. Maybe one of them told you something. What of it? You know damned well that you won't be allowed to testify to it in court. What someone who is now dead may have told you—unless the person it affects was present—isn't evidence, and you know it."

"You may get away with it," I admitted. "Juries are funny, and I don't mind telling you that I'd be happier if I knew a few things about those murders that I don't know. Do you mind telling me about the ins and outs of your switch with Ashcraft—in Seattle?"

He squinted his blue eyes at me.

"You're a puzzling chap, Painless," he said. "I can't tell whether you know everything, or are just sharp-shooting." He puckered his lips and then shrugged. "I'll tell you. It won't matter greatly. I'm due to go over for this impersonation, so a confession to a little additional larceny won't matter."

IX

"The hotel-sneak used to be my lay," the Englishman said after a pause. "I came to the States after England and the Continent got uncomfortable. I was rather good at it. I had the proper manner—the front. I could do the gentleman without sweating over it, you know. In fact there was a day, not so long ago, when I wasn't 'Liverpool Ed.' But you don't want to hear me brag about the select blood that flows through these veins.

"To get back to our knitting: I had rather a successful tour on my first American voyage. I visited most of the better hotels between New York and Seattle, and profited nicely. Then, one night in a Seattle hotel, I worked the tarrel and put myself into a room on the fourth floor. I had hardly closed the door behind me before another key was rattling in it. The room was night-dark. I risked a flash from my light, picked out a closet door, and got behind it just in time.

"The clothes closet was empty; rather a stroke of luck, since there was nothing in it for the room's occupant to come for. He—it was a man—had switched on the lights by then.

"He began pacing the floor. He paced it for three solid hours—up and down, up and down, up and down—while I stood behind the closet door with my gun in my hand, in case he should pull it open. For three solid hours he paced that damned floor. Then he sat down and I heard a pen scratching on paper. Ten minutes of that and he was back at his pacing; but he kept it up for only a few minutes this time. I heard the latches of a valise click. And a shot!

"I bounded out of my retreat. He was stretched on the floor, with a hole in the side of his head. A bad break for me, and no mistake! I could hear excited voices in the corridor. I stepped over the dead chap, found the letter he had been writing on the writing-desk. It was addressed to Mrs. Norman Ashcraft, at a Wine Street number in Bristol, England. I tore it open. He had written that he was going to kill himself, and it was signed Norman. I felt better. A murder couldn't be made out of it.

"Nevertheless, I was here in this room with a flashlight, skeleton keys, and a gun—to say nothing of a handful of jewelry that I had picked up on the next floor. Somebody was knocking on the door.

" 'Get the police!' I called through the door, playing for time.

"Then I turned to the man who had let me in for all this. I would have pegged him for a fellow Britisher even if I hadn't seen the address on his letter. There are thousands of us on the same order—blond, fairly tall, well set up. I took the only chance there was. His hat and topcoat were on a chair where he had tossed them. I put them on and dropped my hat beside him. Kneeling, I emptied his pockets, and my own, gave him all my stuff, pouched all of his. Then I traded guns with him and opened the door.

"What I had in mind was that the first arrivals might not know him by sight, or not well enough to recognize him immediately. That would give me several seconds to arrange my disappearance in. But when I opened the door I found that my idea wouldn't work out as I had planned. The house detective was there, and a policeman, and I knew I was licked. There would be little chance of sneaking away from them. But I played my hand out. I told them I had come up to my room and found this chap on the floor going through my belongings. I had seized him, and in the struggle had shot him.

"Minutes went by like hours, and nobody denounced me. People were calling me Mr. Ashcraft. My impersonation was succeeding. It had me gasping then, but after I learned more about Ashcraft it wasn't so surprising. He had arrived at the hotel only that afternoon, and no one had seen him except in his hat and coat—the hat and coat I was wearing. We were of the same size and type—typical blond Englishmen.

"Then I got another surprise. When the detective examined the dead man's clothes he found that the maker's labels had been ripped out. When I got a look at his diary, later, I found the explanation of that. He had been tossing mental coins with himself, alternating between a determination to kill himself, and another to change his name and make a new place for himself in the world—putting his old life behind him. It was while he was considering the second plan that he had removed the markers from all of his clothing.

"But I didn't know that while I stood there among those people. All I knew was that miracles were happening. I met the miracles half-way, not turning a hair, accepting everything as a matter of course. I think the police smelled something wrong, but they couldn't put their hands on it. There was the dead man on the floor, with a prowler's outfit in his pockets, a pocketful of stolen jewelry, and the labels gone from his clothes—a burglar's trick. And there I was—a well-to-do Englishman whom the hotel people recognized as the room's rightful occupant.

"I had to talk small just then, but after I went through the dead man's stuff I knew him inside and outside, backward and forward. He had nearly a bushel of papers, and a diary that had everything he had ever done or thought in it. I put in the first night studying those things—memorizing them—and practicing his signature. Among the other things I had taken from his pockets were fifteen hundred dollars' worth of traveler's checks, and I wanted to be able to get them cashed in the morning.

"I stayed in Seattle for three days—as Norman Ashcraft. I had tumbled into something rich and I wasn't going to throw it away. The letter to his wife would keep me from being charged with murder if anything slipped, and I knew I was safer seeing the thing through than running. When the excitement had quieted down I packed up and came down to San Francisco, resuming my own name—Edward Bohannon. But I held onto all of Ashcraft's property, because I had learned from it that his wife had money, and I knew I could get some of it if I played my cards right.

"She saved me the trouble of figuring out a deal for myself. I ran across one of her advertisements in the *Examiner*, answered it, and—here we are."

I looked toward Tijuana. A cloud of yellow dust showed in a notch between two low hills. That would be the machine in which Gorman and Hooper were tracking me. Hooper would have seen me set out after the Englishman, would have waited for Gorman to arrive in the car in which he had followed Gooseneck from Mexicali—Gorman would have had to stay some distance in the rear—and then both of the operatives would have picked up my trail.

I turned to the Englishman.

"But you didn't have Mrs. Ashcraft killed?"

He shook his head.

"You'll never prove it."

"Maybe not," I admitted.

I took a package of cigarettes out of my pocket and put two of them on the seat between us.

"Suppose we play a game. This is just for my own satisfaction. It won't tie anybody to anything—won't prove anything. If you did a certain thing, pick up the cigarette that is nearer me. If you didn't do that thing, pick up the one nearer you. Will you play?"

"No, I won't," he said emphatically. "I don't like your game. But I do want a cigarette."

He reached out his uninjured arm and picked up the cigarette nearer *me*.

"Thanks, Ed," I said. "Now I hate to tell you this, but I'm going to swing you."

"You're balmy, my son."

"You're thinking of the San Francisco job, Ed," I explained. "I'm talking about Seattle. You, a hotel sneak-thief, were discovered in a room with a man who had just died with a bullet in his head. What do you think a jury will make out of that, Ed?"

He laughed at me. And then something went wrong with the laugh. It faded into a sickly grin.

"Of course you did," I said. "When you started to work out your plan to inherit all of Mrs. Ashcraft's wealth by having her killed, the first thing you did was to destroy that suicide letter of her husband's. No matter how carefully you guarded it, there was always a chance that somebody would stumble into it and knock your game on the head. It had served its purpose—you wouldn't need it. It would be foolish to take a chance on it turning up.

"I can't put you up for the murders you engineered in San Francisco; but I can sock you with the one you didn't do in Seattle—so justice won't be cheated. You're going to Seattle, Ed, to hang for Ashcraft's suicide."

And he did.

Nightmare Town

CHAPTER I

A Sensational Arrival

A FORD—whitened by desert travel until it was almost indistinguishable from the dust-clouds that swirled around it—came down Izzard's Main Street. Like the dust, it came swiftly, erratically, zigzagging the breadth of the roadway.

A small woman—a girl of twenty in tan flannel—stepped into the street. The wavering Ford missed her by inches, missing her at all only because her backward jump was bird-quick. She caught her lower lip between white teeth, dark eyes flashed annoyance at the rear of the passing machine, and she essayed the street again.

Near the opposite curb the Ford charged down upon her once more. But turning had taken some of its speed. She escaped it this time by scampering the few feet between her and the sidewalk ahead.

Out of the moving automobile a man stepped. Miraculously he kept his feet, stumbling, sliding, until an arm crooked around an iron awning-post jerked him into an abrupt halt. He was a large man in bleached khaki, tall, broad and thick-armed; his gray eyes were bloodshot; face and clothing were powdered heavily with dust. One of his hands clutched a thick, black stick, the other swept off his hat, and he bowed with exaggerated lowness before the girl's angry gaze.

The bow completed, he tossed his hat carelessly into the street, and grinned grotesquely through the dirt that masked his face—a grin that accented the heaviness of a begrimed and hair-roughened jaw.

"I *beg* y'r par'on," he said. "'F I hadn't been careful I believe I'd a'most hit you. 'S unreli'ble, tha' wagon. Borr'ed it from an engi—eng'neer. Don't ever borrow one from eng'neer. They're unreli'ble."

The girl looked at the place where he stood as if no one stood there, as if, in fact, no one had ever stood there, turned her small back on him, and walked very precisely down the street.

He stared after her with stupid surprise in his eyes until she had vanished through a doorway in the middle of the block. Then he scratched his head, shrugged, and turned to look across the street, where his machine had pushed its nose into the red brick side wall of the Bank of Izzard and now shook and clattered as if in panic at finding itself masterless.

"Look at the son-of-a-gun," he exclaimed.

A hand fastened upon his arm. He turned his head, and then, though he stood a good six feet himself, had to look up to meet the eyes of the giant who held his arm.

"We'll take a little walk," the giant said.

The man in bleached khaki examined the other from the tips of his broad-toed shoes to the creased crown of his black hat, examined him with a whole-hearted admiration that was unmistakable in his red-rimmed eyes. There were nearly seven massive feet of the speaker. Legs like pillars held up a great hogshead of a body, with wide shoulders that sagged a little, as if with their own excessive weight. He was a man of perhaps forty-five, and his face was thick-featured, phlegmatic, with sun-lines around small light eyes—the face of a deliberate man.

"My God, you're big!" the man in khaki exclaimed when he had finished his examination; and then his eyes brightened. "Let's wrestle. Bet you ten bucks against fifteen I can throw you. Come on!"

The giant chuckled deep in his heavy chest, took the man in khaki by the nape of the neck and an arm, and walked down the street with him.

CHAPTER II

Justice and a Slapped Face

Steve Threefall awakened without undue surprise at the unfamiliarity of his surroundings, as one who has awakened in strange places before. Before his eyes were well open he knew the essentials of his position. The feel of the shelf-bunk on which he lay and the sharp smell of disinfectant in his nostrils told him that he was in jail. His head and his mouth told him that he had been drunk; and the three-day growth of beard on his face told him he had been very drunk.

As he sat up and swung his feet down to the floor details came back to him. The two days of steady drinking in Whitetufts on the other side of the Nevada-California line, with Harris, the hotel proprietor, and Whiting, an irrigation engineer. The boisterous arguing over desert travel, with his own Gobi experience matched against the American experiences of the others. The bet that he could drive from Whitetufts to Izzard in daylight with nothing to drink but the especially bitter white liquor they were drinking at the time. The start in the grayness of imminent dawn, in Whiting's Ford, with Whiting and Harris staggering down the street after him, waking the town with their drunken shouts and roared-out mocking advice, until he had reached the desert's edge. Then the drive through the desert, along the road that was hotter than the rest of the desert, with— He chose not to think of the ride. He had made it, though— had won the bet. He couldn't remember the amount of the latter.

"So you've come out of it at last?" a rumbling voice inquired.

The steel-slated door swung open and a man filled the cell's door. Steve grinned up at him. This was the giant who would not wrestle. He was coatless and vestless now, and loomed larger than before. One suspender strap was decorated with a shiny badge that said "Marshal."

"Feel like breakfast?" he asked.

"I could do things to a can of black coffee," Steve admitted.

"All right. But you'll have to gulp it. Judge Denvir is waiting to get a crack at you, and the longer you keep him waiting, the tougher it'll be for you."

The room in which Tobin Denvir, J. P., dealt justice was a large one on the third floor of a wooden building. It was scantily furnished with a table, an ancient desk, a steel engraving of Daniel Webster, a shelf of books sleeping under the dust of weeks, a dozen uncomfortable chairs, and half as many cracked and chipped china cuspidors.

The judge sat between desk and table, with his feet on the latter. They were small feet, and he was a small man. His face was filled with little irritable lines, his lips were thin and tight, and he had the bright, lidless eyes of a bird.

"Well, what's he charged with?" His voice was thin, harshly metallic. He kept his feet on the table.

The marshal drew a deep breath, and recited:

"Driving on the wrong side of the street, exceeding the speed limit, driving while under the influence of liquor, driving without a driver's license, endangering the lives of pedestrians by taking his hands off the wheel, and parking improperly— on the sidewalk up against the bank."

The marshal took another breath, and added, with manifest regret:

"There was a charge of attempted assault, too, but that Vallance girl won't appear, so that'll have to be dropped."

The justice's bright eyes turned upon Steve.

"What's your name?" he growled.

"Steve Threefall."

"Is that your real name?" the marshal asked.

"Of course it is," the justice snapped. "You don't think anybody'd be damn fool enough to give a name like that unless it was his, do you?" Then to Steve: "What have you got to say—guilty or not?"

"I was a little—"

"Are you guilty or not?"

"Oh, I suppose I did—"

"That's enough! You're fined a hundred and fifty dollars and costs. The costs are fifteen dollars and eighty cents, making a total of a hundred and sixty-five dollars and eighty cents. Will you pay it or will you go to jail?"

"I'll pay it if I've got it," Steve said, turning to the marshal. "You took my money. Have I got that much?"

The marshal nodded his massive head.

"You have," he said, "exactly—to the nickel. Funny it should have come out like that—huh?"

"Yes—funny," Steve repeated.

While the justice of the peace was making out a receipt for the fine, the marshal restored Steve's watch, tobacco and matches, pocket-knife, keys, and last of all the black walking-stick. The big man weighed the stick in his hand and examined it closely before he gave it up. It was thick and of ebony, but heavy even for that wood, with a balanced weight that hinted at loaded ferrule and knob. Except for a space the breadth of a man's hand in its middle, the stick was roughened, cut and notched with the marks of hard use—marks that much careful polishing had failed to remove or conceal. The unscarred hand's-breadth was of a softer black than the rest—as soft a black as the knob—as if it had known much contact with a human palm.

"Not a bad weapon in a pinch," the marshal said meaningly as he handed the stick to its owner.

Steve took it with the grasp a man reserves for a favorite and constant companion.

"Not bad," he agreed. "What happened to the flivver?"

"It's in the garage around the corner on Main Street. Pete said it wasn't altogether ruined, and he thinks he can patch it up if you want."

The justice held out the receipt.

"Am I all through here now?" Steve asked.

"I hope so," Judge Denvir said sourly.

"Both of us," Steve echoed, put on his hat, tucked the black stick under his arm, nodded to the big marshal, and left the room.

Steve Threefall went down the wooden stairs toward the street in as cheerful a frame of mind as his body—burnt out inwardly with white liquor and outwardly by a day's scorching desert-riding—would permit. That justice had emptied his pockets of every last cent disturbed him little. That, he knew, was the way of justice everywhere with the stranger, and he had left the greater part of his money with the hotel proprietor in Whitetufts. He had escaped a jail sentence, and he counted himself lucky. He would wire Harris to send him some of his money, wait here until the Ford was repaired, and then drive back to Whitetufts—but not on a whisky ration this time.

"You will not!" a voice cried in his ear.

He jumped, and then laughed at his alcohol-jangled nerves. The words had not been meant for him. Beside him, at a turning of the stairs, was an open window, and opposite it, across a narrow alley, a window in another building was open.

This window belonged to an office in which two men stood facing each other across a flat-topped desk.

One of them was middle-aged and beefy, in a black broadcloth suit out of which a white-vested stomach protruded. His face was purple with rage. The man who faced him was younger—a man of perhaps thirty, with a small dark mustache, finely chiseled features, and satiny brown hair. His slender athlete's body was immaculately clothed in gray suit, gray shirt, gray and silver tie, and on the desk before him lay a Panama hat with gray band. His face was as white as the other's was purple.

The beefy man spoke—a dozen words pitched too low for Steve to catch.

The younger man slapped the speaker viciously across the face with an open hand—a hand that then flashed back to its owner's coat and flicked out a snub-nosed automatic pistol.

"You big lard-can," the younger man cried, his voice sibilant; "you'll lay off or I'll spoil your vest for you!"

He stabbed the protuberant vest with the automatic, and laughed into the scared fat face of the beefy man—laughed with a menacing flash of even teeth and dark slitted eyes. Then he picked up his hat, pocketed the pistol, and vanished from Steve's sight. The fat man sat down.

Steve went on down to the street.

CHAPTER III

Izzard Gains a Citizen

Steve unearthed the garage to which the Ford had been taken, found a greasy mechanic who answered to the name of Pete, and was told that Whiting's automobile would be in condition to move under its own power within two days.

"A beautiful snootful you had yesterday," Pete grinned.

Steve grinned back and went on out. He went down to the telegraph office, next door to the Izzard Hotel, pausing for a moment on the sidewalk to look at a glowing cream-colored Vauxhall-Velox roadster that stood at the curb—as out of place in this grimy factory town as a harlequin opal in a grocer's window.

In the doorway of the telegraph office Steve paused again, abruptly this time.

Behind the counter was a girl in tan flannel—the girl he had nearly run down twice the previous afternoon—the "Vallance girl" who had refrained from adding to justice's account against Steve Threefall. In front of the counter, leaning over it, talking to her with every appearance of intimacy, was one of the two men he had seen from the staircase window half an hour before—the slender dandy in gray who had slapped the other's face and threatened him with an automatic.

The girl looked up, recognized Steve, and stood very erect. He took off his hat, and advanced smiling.

"I'm awfully sorry about yesterday," he said. "I'm a crazy fool when I—"

"Do you wish to send a telegram?" she asked frigidly.

"Yes," Steve said; "I also wish to—"

"There are blanks and pencils on the desk near the window," and she turned her back on him.

Steve felt himself coloring, and since he was one of the men who habitually grin when at a loss, he grinned now, and found himself looking into the dark eyes of the man in gray.

That one smiled back under his little brown mustache, and said:

"Quite a time you had yesterday."

"Quite," Steve agreed, and went to the table the girl had indicated.

He wrote his telegram:

> HENRY HARRIS,
>   HARRIS HOTEL, WHITETUFTS:
> ARRIVED RIGHT SIDE UP, BUT AM IN HOCK. WIRE
> ME TWO HUNDRED DOLLARS. WILL BE BACK
> SATURDAY.
>
>   THREEFALL.

But he did not immediately get up from the desk. He sat there holding the piece of paper in his fingers, studying the man and girl, who were again engaged in confidential conversation over the counter. Steve studied the girl most.

She was quite a small girl, no more than five feet in height, if that; and she had that peculiar rounded slenderness which gives a deceptively fragile appearance. Her face was an oval of skin whose find whiteness had thus far withstood the grimy winds of Izzard; her nose just missed being upturned, her violet-black eyes just missed being too theatrically large, and her black-brown hair just missed being too bulky for the small head it crowned; but in no respect did she miss being as beautiful as a figure from a Monticelli canvas.

All these things Steve Threefall, twiddling his telegram in sun-brown fingers, considered and as he considered them he came to see the pressing necessity of having his apologies accepted. Explain it as you will—he carefully avoided trying to explain it to himself—the thing was there. One moment there was nothing, in the four continents he knew, of any bothersome importance to Steve Threefall; the next moment he was under an unescapable compulsion to gain the favor of this small person in tan flannel with brown ribbons at wrists and throat.

At this point the man in gray leaned farther over the counter, to whisper something to the girl. She flushed, and her eyes flinched. The pencil in her hand fell to the counter, and she picked it up with small fingers that were suddenly incongruously awkward. She made a smiling reply, and went on with her writing, but the smile seemed forced.

Steve tore up his telegram and composed another:

I MADE IT, SLEPT IT OFF IN THE COOLER, AND
AM GOING TO SETTLE HERE A WHILE. THERE ARE
THINGS ABOUT THE PLACE I LIKE. WIRE MY MONEY
AND SEND MY CLOTHES TO HOTEL HERE. BUY
WHITING'S FORD FROM HIM AS CHEAP AS YOU CAN
FOR ME.

He carried the blank to the counter and laid it down. The girl ran her pencil over it, counting the words.

"Forty-seven," she said, in a tone that involuntarily rebuked the absence of proper telegraphic brevity.

"Long, but it's all right," Steve assured her. "I'm sending it collect."

She regarded him icily.

"I can't accept a collect message unless I know that the sender can pay for it if the addressee refuses it. It's against the rules."

"You'd better make an exception this time," Steve told her solemnly, "because if you don't, you'll have to lend me the money to pay for it."

"I'll have—?"

"You will," he insisted. "You got me into this jam, and it's up to you to help get me out. The Lord knows you've cost me enough as it is—nearly two hundred dollars! The whole thing was your fault."

"*My fault?*"

"It was! Now I'm giving you a chance to square yourself. Hurry it off, please, because I'm hungry and I need a shave. I'll be waiting on the bench outside."

And he spun on his heel and left the office.

CHAPTER IV

A Thin, Sad-Faced Man

One end of the bench in front of the telegraph office was oc-cupied when Steve, paying no attention to the man who sat there, made himself comfortable on the other. He put his black stick between his legs and rolled a cigarette with thoughtful slowness, his mind upon the just completed scene in the office.

Why, he wondered, whenever there was some special reason for gravity, did he always find himself becoming flippant? Why, whenever he found himself face to face with a situation that was important, that meant something to him, did he slip uncontrollably into banter—play the clown? He lit his ciga-rette and decided scornfully—as he had decided a dozen times before—that it all came from a childish attempt to con-ceal his self-consciousness; that for all his thirty-three years of life and his eighteen years of rubbing shoulders with the world—its rough corners as well as its polished—he was still a green boy underneath—a big kid.

"A neat package you had yesterday," the man who sat on the other end of the bench remarked.

"Yeah," Steve admitted without turning his head. He supposed he'd be hearing about his crazy arrival as long as he stayed in Izzard.

"I reckon old man Denvir took you to the cleaner's as usual?"

"Uh-huh!" Steve said, turning now for a look at the other.

He saw a very tall and very lean man in rusty brown, slouched down on the small of his back, angular legs thrust out across the sidewalk. A man past forty, whose gaunt melancholy face was marked with lines so deep that they were folds in the skin rather than wrinkles. His eyes were the mournful chestnut eyes of a basset hound, and his nose was as long and sharp as a paper knife. He puffed on a black cigar, getting from it a surprising amount of smoke, which he exhaled upward, his thin nose splitting the smoke into two gray plumes.

"Ever been to our fair young city before?" this melancholy individual asked next. His voice held a monotonous rhythm that was not unpleasant to the ear.

"No, this is my first time."

The thin man nodded ironically.

"You'll like it if you stay," he said. "It's very interesting."

"What's it all about?" Steve asked, finding himself mildly intrigued by his benchmate.

"Soda niter. You scoop it up off the desert, and boil and otherwise cook it, and sell it to fertilizer manufacturers, and nitric acid manufacturers, and any other kind of manufacturers who can manufacture something out of soda niter. The factory in which, for which, and from which you do all this lies yonder, beyond the railroad tracks."

He waved a lazy arm down the street, to where a group of square concrete buildings shut out the desert at the end of the thoroughfare.

"Suppose you don't play with this soda?" Steve asked, more to keep the thin man talking than to satisfy any thirst for local knowledge. "What do you do then?"

The thin man shrugged his sharp shoulders.

"That depends," he said, "on who you are. If you're Dave Brackett"—he wiggled a finger at the red bank across the street—"you gloat over your mortgages, or whatever it is a banker does; if you're Grant Fernie, and too big for a man without being quite big enough for a horse, you pin a badge on your bosom and throw rough-riding strangers into the can until they sober up; or if you're Larry Ormsby, and your old man owns the soda works, then you drive trick cars from across the pond"—nodding at the cream Vauxhall—"and spend your days pursuing beautiful telegraph operators. But I take it that you're broke, and have just wired for money, and are waiting for the more or less doubtful results. Is that it?"

"It is," Steve answered absent-mindedly. So the dandy in gray was named Larry Ormsby and was the factory owner's son.

The thin man drew in his feet and stood upon them.

"In that case it's lunch time, and my name is Roy Kamp, and I'm hungry, and I don't like to eat alone, and I'd be glad to have you face the greasy dangers of a meal at the Finn's with me."

Steve got up and held out his hand.

"I'll be glad to," he said. "The coffee I had for breakfast could stand company. My name's Steve Threefall."

They shook hands, and started up the street together. Coming toward them were two men in earnest conversation; one of them was the beefy man whose face Larry Ormsby had slapped. Steve waited until they had passed, and then questioned Kamp casually:

"And who are those prominent looking folks?"

"The little round one in the checkered college boy suit is Conan Elder, real estate, insurance, and securities. The Wallingford looking personage at his side is W. W. himself—the town's founder, owner, and whatnot—W. W. Ormsby, the Hon. Larry's papa."

The scene in the office, with its slapping of a face and flourish of a pistol, had been a family affair, then; a matter between father and son, with the son in the more forcible rôle. Steve, walking along with scant attention just now for the words Kamp's barytone voice was saying, felt a growing dissatisfaction in the memory of the girl and Larry Ormsby talking over the counter with their heads close together.

The Finn's lunchroom was little more than a corridor squeezed in between a poolroom and a hardware store, of barely sufficient width for a counter and a row of revolving stools. Only one customer was there when the two men entered.

"Hello, Mr. Rymer," said Kamp.

"How are you, Mr. Kamp?" the man at the counter said, and as he turned his head toward them, Steve saw that he was blind. His large blue eyes were filmed over with a gray curtain which gave him the appearance of having dark hollows instead of eyes.

He was a medium-sized man who looked seventy, but there was a suggestion of fewer years in the suppleness of his slender white hands. He had a thick mane of white hair above a face that was crisscrossed with wrinkles, but it was a calm face, the face of a man at peace with his world. He was just finishing his meal, and left shortly, moving to the door with the slow accuracy of the blind man in familiar surroundings.

"Old man Rymer," Kamp told Steve, "lives in a shack behind where the new fire house is going to be, all alone. Supposed to have tons of gold coins under his floor—thus local gossip. Some day we're going to find him all momicked up. But he won't listen to reason. Says nobody would hurt him. Says that in a town as heavy with assorted thugs as this!"

"A tough town, is it?" Steve asked.

"Couldn't help being! It's only three years old—and a desert boom town draws the tough boys."

Kamp left Steve after their meal, saying he probably would run across him later in the evening, and suggesting that there were games of a sort to be found in the next-door poolroom.

"I'll see you there then," Steve said, and went back to the telegraph office.

The girl was alone.

"Anything for me?" he asked her.

She put a green check and a telegram on the counter and returned to her desk.

The telegram read:

COLLECTED BET. PAID WHITING TWO HUNDRED
FOR FORD. SENDING BALANCE SIX HUNDRED FORTY.
SHIPPING CLOTHES. WATCH YOUR STEP.
                                   HARRIS.

"Did you send the wire collect, or do I owe—"

"Collect." She did not look up.

Steve put his elbows on the counter and leaned over; his jaw, still exaggerated by its growth of hair, although he had washed the dirt from it, jutted forward with his determination to maintain a properly serious attitude until he had done this thing that had to be done.

"Now listen, Miss Vallance," he said deliberately. "I was all kinds of a damned fool yesterday, and I'm sorrier than I can say. But, after all, nothing terrible happened, and—"

"Nothing terrible!" she exploded. "Is it nothing to be humiliated by being chased up and down the street like a rabbit by a drunken man with a dirty face in a worse car?"

"I wasn't chasing you. I came back that second time to apologize. But, anyway"—in the uncomfortable face of her uncompromising hostility his determination to be serious went for nothing, and he relapsed into his accustomed defensive mockery—"no matter how scared you were you ought to accept my apology now and let bygones be bygones."

"Scared? Why—"

"I wish you wouldn't repeat words after me," he complained. "This morning you did it, and now you're at it again. Don't you ever think of anything to say on your own account?"

She glared at him, opened her mouth, shut it with a little click. Her angry face bent sharply over the papers on the desk, and she began to add a column of figures.

Steve nodded with pretended approval, and took his check across the street to the bank.

The only man in sight in the bank when Steve came in was a little plump fellow with carefully trimmed salt-and-pepper whiskers hiding nearly all of a jovial round face except the eyes—shrewd, friendly eyes.

This man came to the window in the grille, and said: "Good afternoon. Can I do something for you?"

Steve laid down the telegraph company's check.

"I want to open an account."

The banker picked up the slip of green paper and flicked it with a fat finger.

"You are the gentleman who assaulted my wall with an automobile yesterday?"

Steve grinned. The banker's eyes twinkled, and a smile ruffled his whiskers.

"Are you going to stay in Izzard?"

"For a while."

"Can you give me references?" the banker asked.

"Maybe Judge Denvir or Marshal Fernie will put in a word for me," Steve said. "But if you'll write the Seaman's Bank in San Francisco they'll tell you that so far as they know I'm all right."

The banker stuck a plump hand through the window in the grille.

"I'm very glad to make your acquaintance. My name is David Brackett, and anything I can do to help you get established—call on me."

Outside of the bank ten minutes later, Steve met the huge marshal, who stopped in front of him.

"You still here?" Fernie asked.

"I'm an Izzardite now," Steve said. "For a while, anyhow. I like your hospitality."

"Don't let old man Denvir see you coming out of a bank," Fernie advised him, "or he'll soak you plenty next time."

"There isn't going to be any next time."

"There always is—in Izzard," the marshal said enigmatically as he got his bulk in motion again.

CHAPTER V

A Man Leaves Izzard

That night, shaved and bathed, though still wearing his bleached khaki, Steve, with his black stick beside him, played stud poker with Roy Kamp and four factory workers. They played in the poolroom next door to the Finn's lunchroom. Izzard apparently was a wide-open town. Twelve tables given to craps, poker, red dog, and twenty-one occupied half of the poolroom, and white-hot liquor was to be had at the cost of fifty cents and a raised finger. There was nothing surreptitious about the establishment; obviously its proprietor—a bullet-headed Italian whose customers called him "Gyp"—was in favor with the legal powers of Izzard.

The game in which Steve sat went on smoothly and swiftly,
as play does when adepts participate. Though, as most games
are, always potentially crooked, it was, in practice, honest.
The six men at the table were, without exception, men who
knew their way around—men who played quietly and watch-
fully, winning and losing without excitement or inattention.
Not one of the six—except Steve, and perhaps Kamp—would
have hesitated to favor himself at the expense of honesty had
the opportunity come to him; but where knowledge of trickery is evenly distributed honesty not infrequently prevails.

Larry Ormsby came into the poolroom at a little after eleven
and sat at a table some distance from Steve. Faces he had seen
in the street during the day were visible through the smoke. At
five minutes to twelve the four factory men at Steve's table left
for work—they were in the "graveyard" shift—and the game
broke up with their departure. Steve, who had kept about even
throughout the play, found that he had won something less
than ten dollars; Kamp had won fifty some.

Declining invitations to sit in another game, Steve and
Kamp left together, going out into the dark and night-cool
street, where the air was sweet after the smoke and alcohol of
the poolroom. They walked slowly down the dim thoroughfare toward the Izzard Hotel, neither in a hurry to end their
first evening together; for each knew by now that the unpainted bench in front of the telegraph office had given him
a comrade. Not a thousand words had passed between the
two men, but they had as surely become brothers-in-arms as
if they had tracked a continent together.

Strolling thus, a dark doorway suddenly vomited men upon
them.

Steve rocked back against a building front from a blow on
his head, arms were around him, the burning edge of a knife
blade ran down his left arm. He chopped his black stick up
into a body, freeing himself from encircling grip. He used the
moment's respite this gave him to change his grasp on the
stick; so that he held it now horizontal, his right hand grasp-
ing its middle, its lower half flat against his forearm, its upper
half extending to the left.

He put his left side against the wall, and the black stick became a whirling black arm of the night. The knob darted

down at a man's head. The man threw an arm up to fend the blow. Spinning back on its axis, the stick reversed—the ferruled end darted up under warding arm, hit jawbone with a click, and no sooner struck than slid forward, jabbing deep into throat. The owner of that jaw and throat turned his broad, thick-featured face to the sky; went backward out of the fight, and was lost to sight beneath the curbing.

Kamp, struggling with two men in the middle of the sidewalk, broke loose from them, whipped out a gun; but before he could use it his assailants were on him again.

Lower half of stick against forearm once more, Steve whirled in time to take the impact of a blackjack-swinging arm upon it. The stick spun sidewise with thud of knob on temple—spun back with loaded ferrule that missed opposite temple only because the first blow had brought its target down on knees. Steve saw suddenly that Kamp had gone down. He spun his stick and battered a passage to the thin man, kicked a head that bent over the prone, thin form, straddled it; and the ebony stick whirled swifter in his hand—spun as quarter staves once spun in Sherwood Forest. Spun to the clicking tune of wood on bone, on metal weapons; to the duller rhythm of wood on flesh. Spun never in full circles, but always in short arcs—one end's recovery from a blow adding velocity to the other's stroke. Where an instant ago knob had swished from left to right, now weighted ferrule struck from right to left—struck under up-thrown arms, over low-thrown arms—put into space a forty-inch sphere, whose radii were whirling black flails.

Behind his stick that had become a living part of him, Steve Threefall knew happiness—that rare happiness which only the expert ever finds—the joy in doing a thing that he can do supremely well. Blows he took—blows that shook him, staggered him—but he scarcely noticed them. His whole consciousness was in his right arm and the stick it spun. A revolver, tossed from a smashed hand, exploded ten feet over his head, a knife tinkled like a bell on the brick sidewalk, a man screamed as a stricken horse screams.

As abruptly as it had started, the fight stopped. Feet thudded away, forms vanished into the more complete darkness of a side street; and Steve was standing alone—alone except for the man stretched out between his feet and the other man who lay still in the gutter.

Kamp crawled from beneath Steve's legs and scrambled briskly to his feet.

"Your work with a bat is what you might call adequate," he drawled.

Steve stared at the thin man. This was the man he had accepted on an evening's acquaintance as a comrade! A man who lay on the street and let his companion do the fighting for both! Hot words formed in Steve's throat.

"You—"

The thin man's face twisted into a queer grimace, as if he were listening to faint, far-off sounds. He caught his hands to his chest, pressing the sides together. Then he turned half around, went down on one knee, went over backward with a leg bent under him.

"Get—word—to—"

The fourth word was blurred beyond recognition. Steve knelt beside Kamp, lifted his head from the bricks, and saw that Kamp's thin body was ripped open from throat to waistline.

"Get—word—to—" the thin man tried desperately to make the last word audible.

A hand gripped Steve's shoulder.

"What the hell's all this?" the roaring voice of Marshal Grant Fernie blotted out Kamp's words.

"Shut up a minute!" Steve snapped, and put his ear again close to Kamp's mouth.

But now the dying man could achieve no articulate sound. He tried with an effort that bulged his eyes; then he shuddered horribly, coughed, the slit in his chest gaped open, and he died.

"What's all this?" the marshal repeated.

"Another reception committee," Steve said bitterly, easing the dead body to the sidewalk, and standing up. "There's one of them in the street; the others beat it around the corner."

He tried to point with his left hand, then let it drop to his side. Looking at it, he saw that his sleeve was black with blood.

The marshal bent to examine Kamp, grunted, "He's dead, all right," and moved over to where the man Steve had knocked into the gutter lay.

"Knocked out," the marshal said, straightening up; "but he'll be coming around in a while. How'd you make out?"

"My arm's slashed, and I've got some sore spots, but I'll live through it."

Fernie took hold of the wounded arm.

"Not bleeding so bad," he decided. "But you better get it patched up. Doc MacPhail's is only a little way up the street. Can you make it, or do you want me to give you a lift?"

"I can make it. How do I find the place?"

"Two blocks up this street, and four to the left. You can't miss it—it's the only house in town with flowers in front of it. I'll get in touch with you when I want you."

CHAPTER VI

The House with Flowers

Steve Threefall found Dr. MacPhail's house without difficulty —a two-story building set back from the street, behind a garden that did its best to make up in floral profusion for Izzard's general barrenness. The fence was hidden under twining virgin's bower, clustered now with white blossoms, and the narrow walk wound through roses, trillium, poppies, tulips, and geraniums that were ghosts in the starlight. The air was heavily sweet with the fragrance of saucerlike moon flowers, whose vines covered the doctor's porch.

Two steps from the latter Steve stopped, and his right hand slid to the middle of his stick. From one end of the porch had come a rustling, faint but not of the wind, and a spot that was black between vines had an instant before been paler, as if framing a peeping face.

"Who is—" Steve began, and went staggering back.

From the vine-blackened porch a figure had flung itself on his chest.

"Mr. Threefall," the figure cried in the voice of the girl of the telegraph office, "there's somebody in the house!"

"You mean a burglar?" he asked stupidly, staring down into the small white face that was upturned just beneath his chin.

"Yes! He's upstairs—in Dr. MacPhail's room!"

"Is the doctor up there?"

"No, no! He and Mrs. MacPhail haven't come home yet."

He patted her soothingly on a velvet-coated shoulder, selecting a far shoulder, so that he had to put his arm completely around her to do the patting.

"We'll fix that," he promised. "You stick here in the shadows, and I'll be back as soon as I have taken care of our friend."

"No, no!" She clung to his shoulder with both hands. "I'll go with you. I couldn't stay here alone; but I won't be afraid with you."

He bent his head to look into her face, and cold metal struck his chin, clicking his teeth together. The cold metal was the muzzle of a big nickel-plated revolver in one of the hands that clung to his shoulder.

"Here, give me that thing," he exclaimed; "and I'll let you come with me."

She gave him the gun and he put it in his pocket.

"Hold on to my coat tails," he ordered; "keep as close to me as you can, and when I say, 'Down,' let go, drop flat on the floor, and stay there."

Thus, the girl whispering guidance to him, they went through the door she had left open, into the house, and mounted to the second floor. From their right, as they stood at the head of the stairs, came cautious rustlings.

Steve put his face down until the girl's hair was on his lips. "How do you get to that room?" he whispered.

"Straight down the hall. It ends there."

They crept down the hall. Steve's outstretched hand touched a door frame.

"Down!" he whispered to the girl.

Her fingers released his coat. He flung the door open, jumped through, slammed it behind him. A head-sized oval was black against the gray of a window. He spun his stick at it. Something caught the stick overhead, glass crashed, showering him with fragments. The oval was no longer visible against the window. He wheeled to the left, flung out an arm toward a sound of motion. His fingers found a neck—a thin neck with skin as dry and brittle as paper.

A kicking foot drove into his shin just below the knee. The paperish neck slid out of his hand. He dug at it with desperate fingers, but his fingers, weakened by the wound in his forearm, failed to hold. He dropped his stick and flashed his right hand to the left's assistance. Too late. The weakened hand had fallen away from the paperish neck, and there was nothing for the right to clutch.

A misshapen blot darkened the center of an open window, vanished with a thud of feet on the roof of the rear porch. Steve sprang to the window in time to see the burglar scramble up from the ground, where he had slid from the porch roof, and make for the low back fence. One of Steve's legs was over the sill when the girl's arms came around his neck.

"No, no!" she pleaded. "Don't leave me! Let him go!"

"All right," he said reluctantly, and then brightened.

He remembered the gun he had taken from the girl, got it out of his pocket as the fleeing shadow in the yard reached the fence; and as the shadow, one hand on the fence top, vaulted high over it, Steve squeezed the trigger. The revolver clicked. Again—another click. Six clicks, and the burglar was gone into the night.

Steve broke the revolver in the dark, and ran his fingers over the back of the cylinder—six empty chambers.

"Turn on the lights," he said brusquely.

CHAPTER VII

Blind Rymer

When the girl had obeyed Steve stepped back into the room, and looked first for his ebony stick. That in his hand, he faced the girl. Her eyes were jet black with excitement and pale lines of strain were around her mouth. As they stood looking into each other's eyes something of bewilderment began to show through her fright. He turned away abruptly and gazed around the room.

The place had been ransacked thoroughly if not expertly. Drawers stood out, their contents strewn on the floor; the bed had been stripped of clothing, and pillows had been dumped out of their cases. Near the door a broken wall light—the obstruction that had checked Steve's stick—hung crookedly. In the center of the floor lay a gold watch and half a length of gold chain. He picked them up and held them out to the girl.

"Dr. MacPhail's?"

She shook her head in denial before she took the watch, and then, examining it closely, she gave a little gasp.

"It's Mr. Rymer's!"

"Rymer?" Steve repeated, and then he remembered. Rymer was the blind man who had been in the Finn's lunchroom, and for whom Kamp had prophesied trouble.

"Yes! Oh, I know something has happened to him!"

She put a hand on Steve's left arm.

"We've got to go see! He lives all alone, and if any harm has—"

She broke off, and looked down at the arm under her hand.

"Your arm! You're hurt!"

"Not as bad as it looks," Steve said. "That's what brought me here. But it has stopped bleeding. Maybe by the time we get back from Rymer's the doctor will be home."

They left the house by the back door, and the girl led him through dark streets and across darker lots. Neither of them spoke during the five minute walk. The girl hurried at a pace that left her little breath for conversation, and Steve was occupied with uncomfortable thinking.

The blind man's cabin was dark when they reached it, but the front door was ajar. Steve knocked his stick against the frame, got no answer, and struck a match. Rymer lay on the floor, sprawled on his back, his arms outflung.

The cabin's one room was topsy turvy. Furniture lay in up-ended confusion, clothing was scattered here and there, and boards had been torn from the floor. The girl knelt beside the unconscious man while Steve hunted for a light. Presently he found an oil lamp that had escaped injury, and got it burning just as Rymer's filmed eyes opened and he sat up. Steve righted an overthrown rocking chair and, with the girl, assisted the blind man to it, where he sat panting.

He had recognized the girl's voice at once, and he smiled bravely in her direction.

"I'm all right, Nova," he said; "not hurt a bit. Some one

knocked at the door, and when I opened it I heard a swishing sound in my ear—and that was all I knew until I came to to find you here."

He frowned with sudden anxiety, got to his feet, and moved across the room. Steve pulled a chair and an upset table from his path, and the blind man dropped on his knees in a corner, fumbling beneath the loosened floor boards. His hands came out empty, and he stood up with a tired droop to his shoulders.

"Gone," he said softly.

Steve remembered the watch then, took it from his pocket, and put it into one of the blind man's hands.

"There was a burglar at our house," the girl explained. "After he had gone we found that on the floor. This is Mr. Threefall."

The blind man groped for Steve's hand, pressed it, then his flexible fingers caressed the watch, his face lighting up happily.

"I'm glad," he said, "to have this back—gladder than I can say. The money wasn't so much—less than three hundred dollars. I'm not the Midas I'm said to be. But this watch was my father's."

He tucked it carefully into his vest, and then, as the girl started to straighten up the room, he remonstrated.

"You'd better run along home, Nova; it's late, and I'm all right. I'll go to bed now, and let the place go as it is until tomorrow."

The girl demurred, but presently she and Steve were walking back to the MacPhails' house, through the black streets; but they did not hurry now. They walked two blocks in silence, Steve looking ahead into dark space with glum thoughtfulness, the girl eying him covertly.

"What is the matter?" she asked abruptly.

Steve smiled pleasantly down at her.

"Nothing. Why?"

"There is," she contradicted him. "You're thinking of something unpleasant, something to do with me."

He shook his head.

"That's wrong, wrong on the face of it—they don't go together."

But she was not to be put off with compliments.

"You're—you're—" She stood still in the dim street, searching for the right word. "You're on your guard—you don't trust me—that's what it is!"

Steve smiled again, but with narrowed eyes. This reading of his mind might have been intuitive, or it might have been something else.

He tried a little of the truth:

"Not distrustful—just wondering. You know you *did* give me an empty gun to go after the burglar with, and you know you *wouldn't* let me chase him."

Her eyes flashed, and she drew herself up to the last inch of her slender five feet.

"So you think," she began indignantly. Then she drooped toward him, her hands fastening upon the lapels of his coat. "Please, please, Mr. Threefall, you've got to believe that I didn't know the revolver was empty. It was Dr. MacPhail's. I took it when I ran out of the house, never dreaming that it wasn't loaded. And as for not letting you chase the burglar—I was afraid to be left alone again. I'm a little coward. I—I—Please believe in me, Mr. Threefall. Be friends with me. I need friends. I—"

Womanhood had dropped from her. She pleaded with the small white face of a child of twelve—a lonely, frightened child. And because his suspicions would not capitulate immediately to her appeal, Steve felt dumbly miserable, with an obscure shame in himself, as if he were lacking in some quality he should have had.

She went on talking, very softly, so that he had to bend his head to catch the words. She talked about herself, as a child would talk.

"It's been terrible! I came here three months ago because there was a vacancy in the telegraph office. I was suddenly alone in the world, with very little money, and telegraphy was all I knew that could be capitalized. It's been terrible here! The town—I can't get accustomed to it. It's so bleak. No children play in the streets. The people are different from those I've known—cruder, more brutal. Even the houses—street after street of them without curtains in the windows, without flowers. No grass in the yards, no trees.

"But I had to stay—there was nowhere else to go. I

thought I could stay until I had saved a little money—enough to take me away. But saving money takes so long. Dr. MacPhail's garden has been like a piece of paradise to me. If it hadn't been for that I don't think I could have—I'd have gone crazy! The doctor and his wife have been nice to me; some people have been nice to me, but most of them are people I can't understand. And not all have been nice. At first it was awful. Men would say things, and women would say things, and when I was afraid of them they thought I was stuck up. Larry—Mr. Ormsby—saved me from that. He made them let me alone, and he persuaded the MacPhails to let me live with them. Mr. Rymer has helped me, too, given me courage; but I lose it again as soon as I'm away from the sight of his face and the sound of his voice.

"I'm scared—scared of everything! Of Larry Ormsby especially! And he's been wonderfully helpful to me. But I can't help it. I'm afraid of him—of the way he looks at me sometimes, of things he says when he has been drinking. It's as if there was something inside of him waiting for something. I shouldn't say this—because I owe him gratitude for— But I'm so afraid! I'm afraid of every person, of every house, of every doorstep even. It's a nightmare!"

Steve found that one of his hands was cupped over the white cheek that was not flat against his chest, and that his other arm was around her shoulders, holding her close.

"New towns are always like this, or worse," he began to tell her. "You should have seen Hopewell, Virginia, when the DuPonts first opened it. It takes time for the undesirables who come with the first rush to be weeded out. And, stuck out here in the desert, Izzard would naturally fare a little worse than the average new town. As for being friends with you—that's why I stayed here instead of going back to Whitetufts. We'll be great friends. We'll—"

He never knew how long he talked, or what he said; though he imagined afterward that he must have made a very long-winded and very stupid speech. But he was not talking for the purpose of saying anything; he was talking to soothe the girl, and to keep her small face between his hand and chest, and her small body close against his for as long a time as possible.

So he talked on and on and on—

CHAPTER VIII

A Pair of Threats

The MacPhails were at home when Nova Vallance and Steve came through the flowered yard again, and they welcomed the girl with evident relief. The doctor was a short man with a round bald head, and a round jovial face, shiny and rosy except where a sandy mustache drooped over his mouth. His wife was perhaps ten years younger than he, a slender blond woman with much of the feline in the set of her blue eyes and the easy grace of her movements.

"The car broke down with us about twenty miles out," the doctor explained in a mellow rambling voice with a hint of a burr lingering around the r's. "I had to perform a major operation on it before we could get going again. When we got home we found you gone, and were just about to rouse the town."

The girl introduced Steve to the MacPhails, and then told them about the burglar, and of what they had found in the blind man's cabin.

Dr. MacPhail shook his round naked head and clicked his tongue on teeth.

"Seems to me Fernie doesn't do all that could be done to tone Izzard down," he said.

Then the girl remembered Steve's wounded arm, and the doctor examined, washed, and bandaged it.

"You won't have to wear the arm in a sling," he said; "if you take a reasonable amount of care of it. It isn't a deep cut, and fortunately it went between the *supinator tongus* and the *great palmar* without injury to either. Get it from our burglar?"

"No. Got it in the street. A man named Kamp and I were walking toward the hotel to-night and were jumped. Kamp was killed. I got this."

An asthmatic clock somewhere up the street was striking three as Steve passed through the MacPhails' front gate and set out for the hotel again. He felt tired and sore in every muscle, and he walked close to the curb.

"If anything else happens to-night," he told himself, "I'm going to run like hell from it. I've had enough for one evening."

At the first cross street he had to pause to let an automobile race by. As it passed him he recognized it—Larry Ormsby's cream Vauxhall. In its wake sped five big trucks, with a speed that testified to readjusted gears. In a roar of engines, a cloud of dust, and a rattling of windows, the caravan vanished toward the desert.

Steve went on toward the hotel, thinking. The factory worked twenty-four hours a day, he knew; but surely no necessity of niter manufacturing would call for such excessive speed in its trucks—if they were factory trucks. He turned into Main Street and faced another surprise. The cream Vauxhall stood near the corner, its owner at the wheel. As Steve came abreast of it Larry Ormsby let its near door swing open, and held out an inviting hand.

Steve stopped and stood by the door.

"Jump in and I'll give you a lift as far as the hotel."

"Thanks."

Steve looked quizzically from the man's handsome, reckless face to the now dimly lighted hotel, less than two blocks away. Then he looked at the man again, and got into the automobile beside him.

"I hear you're a more or less permanent fixture among us," Ormsby said, proffering Steve cigarettes in a lacquered leather case, and shutting off his idling engine.

"For a while."

Steve declined the cigarettes and brought out tobacco and papers from his pocket, adding, "There are things about the place I like."

"I also hear you had a little excitement to-night."

"Some," Steve admitted, wondering whether the other meant the fight in which Kamp had been killed, the burglary at the MacPhails', or both.

"If you keep up the pace you've set," the factory owner's son went on, "it won't take you long to nose me out of my position as Izzard's brightest light."

Tautening nerves tickled the nape of Steve's neck. Larry Ormsby's words and tone seemed idle enough, but underneath them was a suggestion that they were not aimless—that they were leading to some definite place. It was not likely that he had circled around to intercept Steve merely to exchange meaningless chatter with him. Steve, lighting his cigarette, grinned and waited.

"The only thing I ever got from the old man, besides money," Larry Ormsby was saying, "is a deep-rooted proprietary love for my own property. I'm a regular burgher for insisting that my property is mine and must stay mine. I don't know exactly how to feel about a stranger coming in and making himself the outstanding black sheep of the town in two days. A reputation—even for recklessness—is property, you know; and I don't feel that I should give it up—*or any other rights*—without a struggle."

There it was. Steve's mind cleared. He disliked subtleties. But now he knew what the talk was about. He was being warned to keep away from Nova Vallance.

"I knew a fellow once in Onehunga," he drawled, "who thought he owned all of the Pacific south of the tropic of Capricorn—and had papers to prove it. He'd been that way ever since a Maori bashed in his head with a stone *mere*. Used to accuse us of stealing our drinking water from his ocean."

Larry Ormsby flicked his cigarette into the street and started the engine.

"But the point is"—he was smiling pleasantly—"that a man is moved to protect what he *thinks* belongs to him. He may be wrong, of course, but that wouldn't affect the—ah—vigor of his protecting efforts."

Steve felt himself growing warm and angry.

"Maybe you're right," he said slowly, with deliberate intent to bring this thing between them to a crisis, "but I've never had enough experience with property to know how I'd feel about being deprived of it. But suppose I had a —well, say— a white vest that I treasured. And suppose a man slapped my face and threatened to spoil the vest. I reckon I'd forget all about protecting the vest in my hurry to tangle with him."

Larry laughed sharply.

Steve caught the wrist that flashed up, and pinned it to Ormsby's side with a hand that much spinning of a heavy stick had muscled with steel.

"Easy," he said into the slitted, dancing eyes; "easy now."

Larry Ormsby's white teeth flashed under his mustache.

"Rightto," he smiled. "If you'll turn my wrist loose, I'd

like to shake hands with you—a sort of ante-bellum gesture. I like you, Threefall; you're going to add materially to the pleasures of Izzard."

In his room on the third floor of the Izzard Hotel, Steve Threefall undressed slowly, hampered by a stiff left arm and much thinking. Matter for thought he had in abundance. Larry Ormsby slapping his father's face and threatening him with an automatic; Larry Ormsby and the girl in confidential conversation; Kamp dying in a dark street, his last words lost in the noise of the marshal's arrival; Nova Vallance giving him an empty revolver, and persuading him to let a burglar escape; the watch on the floor and the looting of the blind man's savings; the caravan Larry Ormsby had led toward the desert; the talk in the Vauxhall, with its exchange of threats.

Was there any connection between each of these things and the others? Or were they simply disconnected happenings? If there was a connection—and the whole of that quality in mankind which strives toward simplification of life's phenomena, unification, urged him to belief in a connection—just what was it? Still puzzling, he got into bed; and then out again quickly. An uneasiness that had been vague until now suddenly thrust itself into his consciousness. He went to the door, opened, and closed it. It was a cheaply carpentered door, but it moved easily and silently on well-oiled hinges.

"I reckon I'm getting to be an old woman," he growled to himself; "but I've had all I want to-night."

He blocked the door with the dresser, put his stick where he could reach it quickly, got into bed again, and went to sleep.

CHAPTER IX

"What Next?"

A pounding on the door awakened Steve at nine o'clock the next morning. The pounder was one of Fernie's subordinates, and he told Steve that he was expected to be present at the inquest into Kamp's death within an hour. Steve found that his wounded arm bothered him little; not so much as a bruised area on one shoulder—another souvenir of the fight in the street.

He dressed, ate breakfast in the hotel café, and went up to Ross Amthor's "undertaking parlor," where the inquest was to be held.

The coroner was a tall man with high, narrow shoulders and a sallow, puffy face, who sped proceedings along regardless of the finer points of legal technicality. Steve told his story, the marshal told his, and then produced a prisoner—a thickset Austrian who seemingly neither spoke nor understood English. His throat and lower face were swathed in white bandages.

"Is this the one you knocked down?" the coroner asked.

Steve looked at as much of the Austrian's face as was visible above the bandages.

"I don't know. I can't see enough of him."

"This is the one I picked out of the gutter," Grant Fernie volunteered; "whether you knocked him there or not. I don't suppose you got a good look at him. But this is he all right."

Steve frowned doubtfully.

"I'd know him," he said, "if he turned his face up and I got a good look at him."

"Take off some of his bandages so the witness can see him," the coroner ordered.

Fernie unwound the Austrian's bandages, baring a bruised and swollen jaw.

Steve stared at the man. This fellow may have been one of his assailants, but he most certainly wasn't the one he had knocked into the street. He hesitated. Could he have confused faces in the fight?

"Do you identify him?" the coroner asked impatiently.

Steve shook his head.

"I don't remember ever seeing him."

"Look here, Threefall," the giant marshal scowled down at Steve, "this is the man I hauled out of the gutter—one of the men you said jumped you and Kamp. Now what's the game? What's the idea of forgetting?"

Steve answered slowly, stubbornly:

"I don't know. All I know is that this isn't the first one I hit, the one I knocked out. He was an American—had an American face. He was about this fellow's size, but this isn't he."

The coroner exposed broken yellow teeth in a snarl, the marshal glowered at Steve, the jurors regarded him with frank suspicion. The marshal and the coroner withdrew to a far corner of the room, where they whispered together, casting frequent glances at Steve.

"All right," the coroner told Steve when this conference was over; "that's all."

From the inquest Steve walked slowly back to the hotel, his mind puzzled by this newest addition to Izzard's mysteries. What was the explanation of the certain fact that the man the marshal had produced at the inquest was not the man he had taken from the gutter the previous night? Another thought: the marshal had arrived immediately after the fight of the men who had attacked him and Kamp, had arrived noisily, drowning the dying man's last words. That opportune arrival and the accompanying noise—were they accidental? Steve didn't know; and because he didn't know he strode back to the hotel in frowning meditation.

At the hotel he found that his bag had arrived from Whitetufts. He took it up to his room and changed his clothes. Then he carried his perplexity to the window, where he sat smoking cigarette after cigarette, staring into the alley below, his forehead knotted beneath his tawny hair. Was it possible that so many things should explode around one man in so short a time, in a small city of Izzard's size, without there being a connection between them—and between them and him? And if he was being involved in a vicious maze of crime and intrigue, what was it all about? What had started it? What was the key to it? The girl?

Confused thoughts fell away from him. He sprang to his feet.

Down the other side of the alley a man was walking—a thickset man in soiled blue—a man with bandaged throat and chin. What was visible of his face was the face Steve had seen turned skyward in the fight—the face of the man he had knocked out.

Steve sprang to the door, out of the room, down three flights of stairs, past the desk, and out of the hotel's back door. He gained the alley in time to see a blue trousers-leg disappearing into a doorway in the block below. Thither he went.

The doorway opened into an office building. He searched the corridors, upstairs and down, and did not find the bandaged man. He returned to the ground floor and discovered a sheltered corner near the back door, near the foot of the stairs. The corner was shielded from stairs and from most of the corridor by a wooden closet in which brooms and mops were kept. The man had entered through the rear of the building; he would probably leave that way; Steve waited.

Fifteen minutes passed, bringing no one within sight of his hiding place. Then from the front of the building came a woman's soft laugh, and footsteps moved toward him. He shrank back in his dusky corner. The footsteps passed—a man and a woman laughing and talking together as they walked. They mounted the stairs. Steve peeped out at them, and then drew back suddenly, more in surprise than in fear of detection, for the two who mounted the stairs were completely engrossed in each other.

The man was Elder, the insurance and real estate agent. Steve did not see his face, but the checkered suit on his round figure was unmistakable—"college boy suit," Kamp had called it. Elder's arm was around the woman's waist as they went up the steps, and her cheek leaned against his shoulder as she looked coquettishly into his face. The woman was Dr. MacPhail's feline wife.

"What next?" Steve asked himself, when they had passed from his sight. "Is the whole town wrong? What next, I wonder?"

The answer came immediately—the pounding of crazy footsteps directly over Steve's head—footsteps that might have belonged to a drunken man, or to a man fighting a phantom. Above the noise of heels on wooden floor, a scream rose—a scream that blended horror and pain into a sound that was all the more unearthly because it was unmistakably of human origin.

Steve bolted out of his corner and up the steps three at a time, pivoted into the second floor corridor on the newel, and came face to face with David Brackett, the banker.

Brackett's thick legs were far apart, and he swayed on them. His face was a pallid agony above his beard. Big spots of beard were gone, as if torn out or burned away. From his writhing lips thin wisps of vapor issued.

"They've poisoned me, the damned—"

He came suddenly up on the tips of his toes, his body arched, and he fell stiffly backward, as dead things fall.

Steve dropped on a knee beside him, but he knew nothing could be done—knew Brackett had died while still on his feet. For a moment, as he crouched there over the dead man, something akin to panic swept Steve Threefall's mind clean of reason. Was there never to be an end to this piling of mystery upon mystery, of violence upon violence? He had the sensation of being caught in a monstrous net—a net without beginning or end, and whose meshes were slimy with blood. Nausea—spiritual and physical—gripped him, held him impotent.

Then a shot crashed.

He jerked erect—sprang down the corridor toward the sound; seeking in a frenzy of physical activity escape from the sickness that had filled him.

At the end of the corridor a door was labeled "Ormsby Niter Corporation, W. W. Ormsby, President." There was no need for hesitancy before deciding that the shot had come from behind that label. Even as he dashed toward it, another shot rattled the door and a falling body thudded behind it.

Steve flung the door open—and jumped aside to avoid stepping on the man who lay just inside. Over by a window, Larry Ormsby stood facing the door, a black automatic in his hand. His eyes danced with wild merriment, and his lips curled in a tight-lipped smile.

"Hello, Threefall," he said. "I see you're still keeping close to the storm centers."

Steve looked down at the man on the floor—W. W. Ormsby. Two bullet holes were in the upper left-hand pocket of his vest. The holes, less than an inch apart, had been placed with a precision that left no room for doubting that the man was dead. Steve remembered Larry's threat to his father: "I'll spoil your vest!"

He looked up from killed to killer. Larry Ormsby's eyes were hard and bright; the pistol in his hand was held lightly, with the loose alertness peculiar to professional gunmen.

"This isn't a—ah—personal matter with you, is it?" he asked.

Steve shook his head; and heard the trampling of feet and a confusion of excited voices in the corridor behind him.

"That's nice," the killer was saying; "and I'd suggest that you—"

He broke off as men came into the office. Grant Fernie, the marshal, was one of them.

"Dead?" he asked, with a bare glance at the man on the floor.

"Rather," Larry replied.

"How come?"

Larry Ormsby moistened his lips, not nervously, but thoughtfully. Then he smiled at Steve, and told his story.

"Threefall and I were standing down near the front door talking, when we heard a shot. I thought it had been fired up here, but he said it came from across the street. Anyhow, we came up here to make sure—making a bet on it first; so Threefall owes me a dollar. We came up here, and just as we got to the head of the steps we heard another shot, and Brackett came running out of here with this gun in his hand."

He gave the automatic to the marshal, and went on:

"He took a few steps from the door, yelled, and fell down. Did you see him out there?"

"I did." Fernie said.

"Well, Threefall stopped to look at him while I came on in here to see if my father was all right—and found him dead. That's all there is to it."

CHAPTER X

"Y' Got To Get Out!"

Steve went slowly down to the street after the gathering in the dead man's office had broken up, without having either contradicted or corroborated Larry Ormsby's fiction. No one had questioned him. At first he had been too astonished by the killer's boldness to say anything; and when his wits had resumed their functions, he had decided to hold his tongue for a while.

Suppose he had told the truth? Would it have helped justice? Would anything help justice in Izzard? If he had known what lay behind this piling up of crime, he could have decided what to do; but he did not know—did not even know that there was anything behind it. So he had kept silent. The inquest would not be held until the following day—time enough to talk then, after a night's consideration.

He could not grasp more than a fragment of the affair at a time now; disconnected memories made a whirl of meaningless images in his brain. Elder and Mrs. MacPhail going up the stairs—to where? What had become of them? What had become of the man with the bandages on throat and jaw? Had those three any part in the double murder? Had Larry killed the banker as well as his father? By what chance did the marshal appear on the scene immediately after murder had been done?

Steve carried his jumbled thoughts back to the hotel, and lay across his bed for perhaps an hour. Then he got up and went to the Bank of Izzard, drew out the money he had there, put it carefully in his pocket, and returned to his hotel room to lie across the bed again.

Nova Vallance, nebulous in yellow crêpe, was sitting on the lower step of the MacPhails' porch when Steve went up the flowered walk that evening. She welcomed him warmly, concealing none of the impatience with which she had been waiting for him. He sat on the step beside her, twisting around a little for a better view of the dusky oval of her face.

"How is your arm?" she asked.

"Fine!" He opened and shut his left hand briskly. "I suppose you heard all about to-day's excitement?"

"Oh, yes! About Mr. Brackett's shooting Mr. Ormsby, and then dying with one of his heart attacks."

"Huh?" Steve demanded.

"But weren't you there?" she asked in surprise.

"I was, but suppose you tell me just what you heard."

"Oh, I've heard all sorts of things about it! But all I really know is what Dr. MacPhail, who examined both of them, said."

"And what was that?"

"That Mr. Brackett killed Mr. Ormsby—shot him—though nobody seems to know why; and then, before he could get out of the building, his heart failed him and he died."

"And he was supposed to have a bad heart?"

"Yes. Dr. MacPhail told him a year ago that he would have to be careful, that the least excitement might be fatal."

Steve caught her wrist in his hand.

"Think, now," he commanded. "Did you ever hear Dr. MacPhail speak of Brackett's heart trouble until to-day?"

She looked curiously into his face, and a little pucker of bewilderment came between her eyes.

"No," she replied slowly. "I don't think so; but, of course, there was never any reason why he should have mentioned it. Why do you ask?"

"Because," he told her, "Brackett did *not* shoot Ormsby; and any heart attack that killed Brackett was caused by poison—some poison that burned his face and beard."

She gave a little cry of horror.

"You think—" She stopped, glanced furtively over her shoulder at the front door of the house, and leaned close to him to whisper: "Didn't—didn't you say that the man who was killed in the fight last night was named Kamp?"

"Yes."

"Well, the report, or whatever it was that Dr. MacPhail made of his examination, reads Henry Cumberpatch."

"You sure? Sure it's the same man?"

"Yes. The wind blew it off the doctor's desk, and when I handed it back to him, he made some joke"—she colored with a little laugh—"some joke about it nearly being your death certificate instead of your companion's. I glanced down at it then, and saw that it was for a man named Henry Cumberpatch. What does it all mean? What is—"

The front gate clattered open, and a man swayed up the walk. Steve got up, picked up his black stick, and stepped between the girl and the advancing man. The man's face came out of the dark. It was Larry Ormsby; and when he spoke his words had a drunken thickness to match the unsteadiness—not quite a stagger, but nearly so—of his walk.

"Lis'en," he said; "I'm dam' near—"

Steve moved toward him.

"If Miss Vallance will excuse us," he said, "we'll stroll to the gate and talk."

Without waiting for a reply from either of them, Steve linked an arm through one of Ormsby's and urged him down the path. At the gate Larry broke away, pulling his arm loose, and confronting Steve.

"No time for foolishness," he snarled. "Y' got to get out! Get out o' Izzard!"

"Yes?" Steve asked. "And why?"

Larry leaned back against the fence and raised one hand in an impatient gesture.

"Your lives not worth a nickel—neither of you!"

He swayed and coughed. Steve grasped him by a shoulder and peered into his face.

"What's the matter with you?"

Larry coughed again and clapped a hand to his chest, up near the shoulder.

"Bullet—up high—Fernie's. But I got him—the big tramp. Toppled him out a window—down like a kid divin' for pennies." He laughed shrilly, and then became earnest again. "Get th' girl—beat it—now! Now! Now! Ten minutes'll be too late. They're comin'!"

"Who? What? Why?" Steve snapped. "Talk turkey! I don't trust you. I've got to have reasons."

"Reasons, my God!" the wounded man cried. "You'll get your reasons. You think I'm trying to scare you out o' town b'fore th' inquest." He laughed insanely. "Inquest! You fool! There won't be any inquest! There won't be any tomorrow—for Izzard! And you—"

He pulled himself sharply together and caught one of Steve's hands in both of his.

"Listen," he said. "I'll give it to you, but we're wasting time. But if you've got to have it—listen:"

CHAPTER XI

The Naked Soul of Izzard

"Izzard is a plant! The whole damned town is queer. Booze—that's the answer. The man I knocked off this afternoon—the one you thought was my father—originated the scheme. You make soda niter by boiling the nitrate in tanks heated with coils. He got the idea that a niter plant would make a good front for a moonshine factory. And he got the idea that if you had a whole town working together it'd be impossible for the game ever to fall down.

"You can guess how much money there is in this country in the hands of men who'd be glad to invest it in a booze game that was airtight. Not only crooks, I mean, but men who consider themselves honest. Take your guess, whatever it is, and double it, and you still won't be within millions of the right answer. There are men with— But anyway, Ormsby took his scheme East and got his backing—a syndicate that could have raised enough money to build a dozen cities.

"Ormsby, Elder and Brackett were the boys who managed the game. I was here to see that they didn't double-cross the syndicate; and then there's a flock of trusty lieutenants, like Fernie, and MacPhail, and Heman—he's postmaster—and Harker—another doctor, who got his last week—and Leslie, who posed as a minister. There was no trouble to getting the population we wanted. The word went around that the new town was a place where a crook would be safe so long as he did what he was told. The slums of all the cities in America, and half of 'em out of it, emptied themselves here. Every crook that was less than a step ahead of the police, and had car fare here, came and got cover.

"Of course, with every thug in the world blowing in here we had a lot of sleuths coming, too; but they weren't hard to handle, and if worse came to worse, we could let the law take an occasional man; but usually it wasn't hard to take care of the gum-shoes. We have bankers, and ministers, and doctors, and postmasters, and prominent men of all sorts either to tangle the sleuths up with bum leads, or, if necessary to frame them. You'll find a flock of men in the State pen who came here—most of them as narcotic agents or prohibition agents—and got themselves tied up before they knew what it was all about.

"God, there never was a bigger game! It couldn't flop—unless we spoiled it for ourselves. And that's what we've done. It was too big for us! There was too much money in it—it went to our heads! At first we played square with the syndicate. We made booze and shipped it out—shipped it in carload lots, in trucks, did everything but pipe it out, and we made money for the syndicate and for ourselves. Then we got the real idea—the big one! We kept on making the hooch; but we got the big idea going for our own profit. The syndicate wasn't in on that.

"First, we got the insurance racket under way. Elder managed that, with three or four assistants. Between them they became agents of half the insurance companies in the country, and they began to plaster Izzard with policies. Men who had never lived were examined, insured, and then killed—sometimes they were killed on paper, sometimes a real man who had died was substituted, and there were times when a man or two was killed to order. It was soft! We had the insurance agents, the doctors, the coroner, the undertaker, and all the city officials. We had the machinery to swing any deal we wanted! You were with Kamp the night he was killed! That was a good one. He was an insurance company sleuth—the companies were getting suspicious. He came here and was foolish enough to trust his reports to the mail. There aren't many letters from strangers that get through the post office without being read. We read his reports, kept them, and sent phoney ones out in their places. Then we nailed Mr. Kamp, and changed his name on the records to fit a policy in the very company he represented. A rare joke, eh?

"The insurance racket wasn't confined to men—cars, houses, furniture, everything you can insure was plastered. In the last census—by distributing the people we could count on, one in a house, with a list of five or six names—we got a population on the records of at least five times as many as are really here. That gave us room for plenty of policies, plenty of deaths, plenty of property insurance, plenty of everything. It gave us enough political influence in the county and State to strengthen our hands a hundred per cent, make the game safer.

"You'll find street after street of houses with nothing in them out of sight of the front windows. They cost money to put up, but we've made the money right along, and they'll show a wonderful profit when the clean-up comes.

"Then, after the insurance stunt was on its feet, we got the promotion game going. There's a hundred corporations in Izzard that are nothing but addresses on letterheads—but stock certificates and bonds have been sold in them from one end of these United States to the other. And they have bought goods, paid for it, shipped it out to be got rid of— maybe at a loss—and put in larger and larger orders until they've built up a credit with the manufacturers that would make you dizzy to total. Easy! Wasn't Brackett's bank here to give them all the financial references they needed? There was nothing to it; a careful building up of credit until they reached the highest possible point. Then, the goods shipped out to be sold through fences, and—bingo! The town is wiped out by fire. The stocks of goods are presumably burned; the expensive buildings that the out-of-town investors were told about are presumably destroyed; the books and records are burned.

"What a killing! I've had a hell of a time stalling off the syndicate, trying to keep them in the dark about the surprise we're going to give them. They're too suspicious as it is for us to linger much longer. But things are about ripe for the blow-off—the fire that's to start in the factory and wipe out the whole dirty town—and next Saturday was the day we picked. That's the day when Izzard becomes nothing but a pile of ashes—and a pile of collectable insurance policies.

"The rank and file in town won't know anything about the finer points of the game. Those that suspect anything take their money and keep quiet. When the town goes up in smoke there will be hundreds of bodies found in the ruins— all insured—and there will be proof of the death of hundreds of others—likewise insured—whose bodies can't be found.

"There never was a bigger game! But it was too big for us! My fault—some of it—but it would have burst anyway. We always weeded out those who came to town looking too honest or too wise, and we made doubly sure that nobody who was doubtful got into the post office, railroad depot, telegraph office, or telephone exchange. If the railroad company or the telegraph or telephone company sent somebody here to work, and we couldn't make them see things the way we wanted them seen, we managed to make the place disagreeable for them—and they usually flitted elsewhere in a hurry.

"Then the telegraph company sent Nova here and I flopped for her. At first it was just that I liked her looks. We had all sorts of women here—but they were mostly all sorts—and Nova was something different. I've done my share of dirtiness in this world, but I've never been able to get rid of a certain fastidiousness in my taste for women. I— Well, the rest of them—Brackett, Ormsby, Elder and the lot—were all for giving Nova the works. But I talked them out of it. I told them to let her alone and I'd have her on the inside in no time. I really thought I could do it. She liked me, or seemed to, but I couldn't get any further than that. I didn't make any headway. The others got impatient, but I kept putting them off, telling them that everything would be fine, that if necessary I'd marry her, and shut her up that way. They didn't like it. It wasn't easy to keep her from learning what was going on—working in the telegraph office—but we managed it somehow.

"Next Saturday was the day we'd picked for the big fireworks. Ormsby gave me the call yesterday—told me flatly that if I didn't sew Nova up at once they were going to pop her. They didn't know how much she had found out, and they were taking no chances. I told him I'd kill him if he touched her, but I knew I couldn't talk them out of it. To-day the break came. I heard he had given the word that she was to be put out of the way to-night. I went to his office for a showdown. Brackett was there. Ormsby salved me along, denied he had given any order affecting the girl, and poured out drinks for the three of us. The drink looked wrong. I waited to see what was going to happen next. Brackett gulped his down. It was poisoned. He went outside to die, and I nailed Ormsby.

"The game has blown up! It was too rich for us. Everybody is trying to slit everybody else's throat. I couldn't find Elder—but Fernie tried to pot me from a window; and he's Elder's right-hand man. Or he was—he's a stiff now. I think this thing in my chest is the big one—I'm about— But you can get the girl out. You've got to! Elder will go through with the play—try to make the killing for himself. He'll have the town touched off to-night. It's now or never with him. He'll try to—"

A shriek cut through the darkness.

"Steve! *Steve!! Steve!!!*"

CHAPTER XII

Pink Sky

Steve whirled away from the gate, leaping through flower-beds, crossed the porch in a bound, and was in the house. Behind him Larry Ormsby's feet clattered. An empty hallway, an empty room, another. Nobody was in sight on the ground floor. Steve went up the stairs. A strip of golden light lay under a door. He went through the door, not knowing or caring whether it was locked or not. He simply hurled himself shoulder first at it, and was in the room. Leaning back against a table in the center of the room, Dr. MacPhail was struggling with the girl. He was behind her, his arms around her, trying to hold her head still. The girl twisted and squirmed like a cat gone mad. In front of her Mrs. MacPhail poised an uplifted blackjack.

Steve flung his stick at the woman's white arm, flung it instinctively, without skill or aim. The heavy ebony struck arm and shoulder, and she staggered back. Dr. MacPhail, releasing the girl, dived at Steve's legs, got them, and carried him to the floor. Steve's fumbling fingers slid off the doctor's bald head, could get no grip on the back of his thick neck, found an ear, and gouged into the flesh under it.

The doctor grunted and twisted away from the digging fingers. Steve got a knee free—drove it at the doctor's face. Mrs. MacPhail bent over his head, raising the black leather billy she still held. He dashed an arm at her ankles, missed—but the down-crashing blackjack fell obliquely on his shoulder. He twisted away, scrambled to his knees and hands—and sprawled headlong under the impact of the doctor's weight on his back.

He rolled over, got the doctor under him, felt his hot breath on his neck. Steve raised his head and snapped it back—hard. Raised it again, and snapped it down, hammering

MacPhail's face with the back of his skull. The doctor's arms fell away, and Steve lurched upright to find the fight over.

Larry Ormsby stood in the doorway grinning evilly over his pistol at Mrs. MacPhail, who stood sullenly by the table. The blackjack was on the floor at Larry's feet.

Against the other side of the table the girl leaned weakly, one hand on her bruised throat, her eyes dazed and blank with fear. Steve went around to her.

"Get going, Steve! There's no time for playing. You got a car?"

Larry Ormsby's voice was rasping.

"No," Steve said.

Larry cursed bitterly—an explosion of foul blasphemies. Then:

"We'll go in mine—it can outrun anything in the State. But you can't wait here for me to get it. Take Nova over to blind Rymer's shack. I'll pick you up there. He's the only one in town you can trust. Go ahead, damn you!" he yelled.

Steve glanced at the sullen MacPhail woman, and at her husband, now getting up slowly from the floor, his face blood-smeared and battered.

"How about them?"

"Don't worry about them," Larry said. "Take the girl and make Rymer's place. I'll take care of this pair and be over there with the car in fifteen minutes. Get going!"

Steve's eyes narrowed and he studied the man in the doorway. He didn't trust him, but since all Izzard seemed equally dangerous, one place would be as safe as another—and Larry Ormsby might be honest this time.

"All right," he said, and turned to the girl. "Get a heavy coat."

Five minutes later they were hurrying through the same dark streets they had gone through on the previous night. Less than a block from the house, a muffled shot came to their ears, and then another. The girl glanced quickly at Steve but did not speak. He hoped she had not understood what the two shots meant.

They met nobody. Rymer had heard and recognized the girl's footsteps on the sidewalk, and he opened his door before they could knock.

"Come in, Nova," he welcomed her heartily, and then fumbled for Steve's hand. "This is Mr. Threefall, isn't it?"

He led them into the dark cabin, and then lighted the oil lamp on the table. Steve launched at once into a hurried summarizing of what Larry Ormsby had told him. The girl listened with wide eyes and wan face; the blind man's face lost its serenity, and he seemed to grow older and tired as he listened.

"Ormsby said he would come after us with his car," Steve wound up. "If he does, you will go with us, of course, Mr. Rymer. If you'll tell us what you want to take with you we'll get it ready; so that there will be no delay when he comes— if he comes." He turned to the girl. "What do you think, Nova? Will he come? And can we trust him if he does?"

"I—I hope so—he's not all bad, I think."

The blind man went to a wardrobe in the room's other end.

"I've nothing to take," he said, "but I'll get into warmer clothes."

He pulled the wardrobe door open, so that it screened a corner of the room for him to change in. Steve went to a window, and stood there looking between blind and frame, into the dark street where nothing moved. The girl stood close to him, between his arm and side, her fingers twined in his sleeve.

"Will we—? Will we—?"

He drew her closer and answered the whispered question she could not finish.

"We'll make it," he said, "if Larry plays square, or if he doesn't. We'll make it."

A rifle cracked somewhere in the direction of Main Street. A volley of pistol shots. The cream-colored Vauxhall came out of nowhere to settle on the sidewalk, two steps from the door. Larry Ormsby, hatless and with his shirt torn loose to expose a hole under one of his collar-bones, tumbled out of the car, and through the door that Steve threw open for him.

Larry kicked the door shut behind him, and laughed.

"Izzard's frying nicely!" he cried, and clapped his hands together. "Come, come! The desert awaits!"

Steve turned to call the blind man. Rymer stepped out from behind his screening door. In each of Rymer's hands was a heavy revolver. The film was gone from Rymer's eyes.

His eyes, cool and sharp now, held the two men and the girl.

"Put your hands up, all of you," he ordered curtly.

Larry Ormsby laughed insanely.

"Did you ever see a damned fool do his stuff, Rymer?" he asked.

"Put your hands up!"

"Rymer," Larry said, "I'm dying now. To hell with you!"

And without haste he took a black automatic pistol from an inside coat pocket.

The guns in Rymer's hands rocked the cabin with explosion after explosion.

Knocked into a sitting position on the floor by the heavy bullets that literally tore him apart, Larry steadied his back against the wall, and the crisp, sharp reports of his lighter weapon began to punctuate the roars of the erstwhile blind man's guns.

Instinctively jumping aside, pulling the girl with him, at the first shot, Steve now hurled himself upon Rymer's flank. But just as he reached him the shooting stopped. Rymer swayed, the very revolvers in his hands seemed to go limp. He slid out of Steve's clutching hands—his neck scraping one hand with the brittle dryness of paper—and became a lifeless pile on the floor.

Steve kicked the dead man's guns across the floor a way, and then went over to where the girl knelt beside Larry Ormsby. Larry smiled up at Steve with a flash of white teeth.

"I'm gone, Steve," he said. "That Rymer—fooled us all—phoney films on eyes painted on—spy for rum syndicate."

He writhed, and his smile grew stiff and strained.

"Mind shaking hands, Steve?" he asked a moment later.

Steve found his hand and squeezed it.

"You're a good guy, Larry," was the only thing he could think to say.

The dying man seemed to like that. His smile became real again.

"Luck to you—you can get a hundred and ten out of the Vauxhall," he managed to say.

And then, apparently having forgotten the girl for whom he had given up his life, he flashed another smile at Steve and died.

The front door slammed open—two heads looked in. The heads' owners came in.

Steve bounded upright, swung his stick. A bone cracked like a whip, a man reeled back holding a hand to his temple.

"Behind me—close!" Steve cried to the girl, and felt her hands on his back.

Men filled the doorway. An invisible gun roared and a piece of the ceiling flaked down. Steve spun his stick and charged the door. The light from the lamp behind him glittered and glowed on the whirling wood. The stick whipped backward and forward, from left to right, from right to left. It writhed like a live thing—seemed to fold upon its grasped middle as if spring-hinged with steel. Flashing half-circles merged into a sphere of deadliness. The rhythm of incessant thudding against flesh and clicking on bone became a tune that sang through the grunts of fighting men, the groans and oaths of stricken men. Steve and the girl went through the door.

Between moving arms and legs and bodies the cream of the Vauxhall showed. Men stood upon the automobile, using its height for vantage in the fight. Steve threw himself forward, swinging his stick against shin and thigh, toppling men from the machine. With his left hand he swept the girl around to his side. His body shook and rocked under the weight of blows from men who were packed too closely for any effectiveness except the smothering power of sheer weight.

His stick was suddenly gone from him. One instant he held and spun it; the next, he was holding up a clenched fist that was empty—the ebony had vanished as if in a puff of smoke. He swung the girl up over the car door, hammered her down into the car—jammed her down upon the legs of a man who stood there—heard a bone break; and saw the man go down. Hands gripped him everywhere; hands pounded him. He cried aloud with joy when he saw the girl, huddled on the floor of the car, working with ridiculously small hands at the car's mechanism.

The machine began to move. Holding, with his hands, he lashed both feet out behind. Got them back on the step. Struck over the girl's head with a hand that had neither thought nor time to make a fist—struck stiff-fingered into a broad red face.

The car moved. One of the girl's hands came up to grasp the wheel, holding the car straight along a street she could not see. A man fell on her. Steve pulled him off—tore pieces from him—tore hair and flesh. The car swerved, scraped a building; scraped one side clear of men. The hands that held Steve fell away from him, taking most of his clothing with them. He picked a man off the back of the seat and pushed him down into the street that was flowing past them. Then he fell into the car beside the girl.

Pistols exploded behind them. From a house a little ahead a bitter-voiced rifle emptied itself at them, sieving a mud-guard. Then the desert—white and smooth as a gigantic hospital bed—was around them. Whatever pursuit there had been was left far behind.

Presently the girl slowed down, stopped.

"Are you all right?" Steve asked.

"Yes, but you're—"

"All in one piece," he assured her. "Let me take the wheel."

"No! No!" she protested. "You're bleeding. You're—"

"No! No!" he mocked her. "We'd better keep going until we hit something. We're not far enough from Izzard yet to call ourselves safe."

He was afraid that if she tried to patch him up he would fall apart in her hands. He felt like that.

She started the car, and they went on. A great sleepiness came to him. What a fight! What a fight!

"Look at the sky!" she exclaimed.

He opened his heavy eyes. Ahead of them, above them, the sky was lightening—from blue-black to violet, to mauve, to rose. He turned his head and looked back. Where they had left Izzard, a monstrous bonfire was burning, painting the sky with jeweled radiance.

"Good-by, Izzard," he said drowsily, and settled himself more comfortably in the seat.

He looked again at the glowing pink in the sky ahead.

"My mother has primroses in her garden in Delaware that look like that sometimes," he said dreamily. "You'll like 'em."

His head slid over against her shoulder, and he went to sleep.

The Whosis Kid

IT STARTED in Boston, back in 1917. I ran into Lew Maher on the Tremont street sidewalk of the Touraine Hotel one afternoon, and we stopped to swap a few minutes' gossip in the snow.

I was telling him something or other when he cut in with:

"Sneak a look at this kid coming up the street. The one with the dark cap."

Looking, I saw a gangling youth of eighteen or so; pasty and pimply face, sullen mouth, dull hazel eyes, thick, shapeless nose. He passed the city sleuth and me without attention, and I noticed his ears. They weren't the battered ears of a pug, and they weren't conspicuously deformed, but their rims curved in and out in a peculiar crinkled fashion.

At the corner he went out of sight, turning down Boylston street toward Washington.

"There's a lad that will make a name for hisself if he ain't nabbed or rocked off too soon," Lew predicted. "Better put him on your list. The Whosis Kid. You'll be looking for him some one of these days."

"What's his racket?"

"Stick-up, gunman. He's got the makings of a good one. He can shoot, and he's plain crazy. He ain't hampered by nothing like imagination or fear of consequences. I wish he was. It's these careful, sensible birds that are easiest caught. I'd swear the Kid was in on a coupla jobs that were turned in Brookline last month. But I can't fit him to 'em. I'm going to clamp him some day, though—and that's a promise."

Lew never kept his promise. A prowler killed him in an Audubon Road residence a month later.

A week or two after this conversation I left the Boston branch of the Continental Detective Agency to try army life. When the war was over I returned to the Agency payroll in Chicago, stayed there for a couple of years, and got transferred to San Francisco.

So, all in all, it was nearly eight years later that I found myself sitting behind the Whosis Kid's crinkled ears at the Dreamland Rink.

Friday night is fight night at the Steiner Street house. This particular one was my first idle evening in several weeks. I had gone up to the rink, fitted myself to a hard wooden chair not too far from the ring, and settled down to watch the boys throw gloves at one another. The show was about a quarter done when I picked out this pair of odd and somehow familiar ears two rows ahead of me.

I didn't place them right away. I couldn't see their owner's face. He was watching Kid Cipriani and Bunny Keogh assault each other. I missed most of that fight. But during the brief wait before the next pair of boys went on, the Whosis Kid turned his head to say something to the man beside him. I saw his face and knew him.

He hadn't changed much, and he hadn't improved any. His eyes were duller and his mouth more wickedly sullen than I had remembered them. His face was as pasty as ever, if not so pimply.

He was directly between me and the ring. Now that I knew him, I didn't have to pass up the rest of the card. I could watch the boys over his head without being afraid he would get out on me.

So far as I knew, the Whosis Kid wasn't wanted anywhere—not by the Continental, anyway—and if he had been a pickpocket, or a con man, or a member of any of the criminal trades in which we are only occasionally interested, I would have let him alone. But stick-ups are always in demand. The Continental's most important clients are insurance companies of one sort or another, and robbery policies make up a good percentage of the insurance business these days.

When the Whosis Kid left in the middle of the main event—along with nearly half of the spectators, not caring what happened to either of the muscle-bound heavies who were putting on a room-mate act in the ring—I went with him.

He was alone. It was the simplest sort of shadowing. The streets were filled with departing fight fans. The Kid walked down to Fillmore street, took on a stack of wheats, bacon and coffee at a lunch room, and caught a No. 22 car.

He—and likewise I—transferred to a No. 5 car at McAllister street, dropped off at Polk, walked north one block, turned back west for a block and a fraction, and went up the front stairs of a dingy light-housekeeping room establishment that occupied the second and third floors over a repair shop on the south side of Golden Gate avenue, between Van Ness and Franklin.

That put a wrinkle in my forehead. If he had left the street car at either Van Ness or Franklin, he would have saved himself a block of walking. He had ridden down to Polk and walked back. For the exercise, maybe.

I loafed across the street for a short while, to see what—if anything—happened to the front windows. None that had been dark before the Kid went in lighted up now. Apparently he didn't have a front room—unless he was a very cautious young man. I knew he hadn't tumbled to my shadowing. There wasn't a chance of that. Conditions had been too favorable to me.

The front of the building giving me no information, I strolled down Van Ness avenue to look at the rear. The building ran through to Redwood street, a narrow back street that split the block in half. Four back windows were lighted, but they told me nothing. There was a back door. It seemed to belong to the repair shop. I doubted that the occupants of the upstairs rooms could use it.

On my way home to my bed and alarm clock, I dropped in at the office, to leave a note for the Old Man:

Tailing the Whosis Kid, stick-up, 25–27, 135, 5 foot 11 inches, sallow, br. hair, hzl. eyes, thick nose, crooked ears. Origin Boston. Anything on him? Will be vicinity Golden Gate and Van Ness.

CHAPTER II

Eight o'clock the next morning found me a block below the house in which the Kid had gone, waiting for him to appear. A steady, soaking rain was falling, but I didn't mind that. I was closed up inside a black coupé, a type of car whose tamely respectable appearance makes it the ideal one for city work.

This part of Golden Gate avenue is lined with automobile repair shops, second-hand automobile dealers, and the like. There are always dozens of cars standing idle to the block. Although I stayed there all day, I didn't have to worry over my being too noticeable.

That was just as well. For nine solid, end-to-end hours I sat there and listened to the rain on the roof, and waited for the Whosis Kid, with not a glimpse of him, and nothing to eat except Fatimas. I wasn't any too sure he hadn't slipped me. I didn't know that he lived in this place I was watching. He could have gone to his home after I had gone to mine. However, in this detective business pessimistic guesses of that sort are always bothering you, if you let them. I stayed parked, with my eye on the dingy door into which my meat had gone the night before.

At a little after five that evening, Tommy Howd, our pug-nosed office boy, found me and gave me a memorandum from the Old Man:

> Whosis Kid known to Boston branch as robbery-suspect, but have nothing definite on him. Real name believed to be Arthur Cory or Carey. May have been implicated in Tunnicliffe jewelry robbery in Boston last month. Employee killed, $60,000 unset stones taken. No description of two bandits. Boston branch thinks this angle worth running out. They authorize surveillance.

After I had read this memorandum, I gave it back to the boy,—there's no wisdom in carrying around a pocketful of stuff relating to your job,—and asked him:

"Will you call up the Old Man and ask him to send somebody up to relieve me while I get a bite of food? I haven't chewed since breakfast."

"Swell chance!" Tommy said. "Everybody's busy. Hasn't been an op in all day. I don't see why you fellas don't carry a hunk or two of chocolate in your pockets to—"

"You've been reading about Arctic explorers," I accused him. "If a man's starving he'll eat anything, but when he's just ordinarily hungry he doesn't want to clutter up his stomach with a lot of candy. Scout around and see if you can pick me up a couple of sandwiches and a bottle of milk."

He scowled at me, and then his fourteen-year-old face grew cunning.

"I tell you what," he suggested. "You tell me what this fella looks like, and which building he's in, and I'll watch while you go get a decent meal. Huh? Steak, and French fried potatoes, and pie, and coffee."

Tommy has dreams of being left on the job in some such circumstance, of having everything break for him while he's there, and of rounding up regiments of desperadoes all by himself. I don't think he'd muff a good chance at that, and I'd be willing to give him a whack at it. But the Old Man would scalp me if he knew I turned a child loose among a lot of thugs.

So I shook my head.

"This guy wears four guns and carries an ax, Tommy. He'd eat you up."

"Aw, applesauce! You ops are all the time trying to make out nobody else could do your work. These crooks can't be such tough mugs—or they wouldn't let you catch 'em!"

There was some truth in that, so I put Tommy out of the coupé into the rain.

"One tongue sandwich, one ham, one bottle of milk. And make it sudden."

But I wasn't there when he came back with the food. He had barely gone out of sight when the Whosis Kid, his overcoat collar turned up against the rain that was driving down in close-packed earnest just now, came out of the rooming-house doorway.

He turned south on Van Ness.

When the coupé got me to the corner he was not in sight. He couldn't have reached McAllister street. Unless he had gone into a building, Redwood street—the narrow one that split the block—was my best bet. I drove up Golden Gate avenue another block, turned south, and reached the corner of Franklin and Redwood just in time to see my man ducking into the back door of an apartment building that fronted on McAllister street.

I drove on slowly, thinking.

The building in which the Kid had spent the night and this building into which he had just gone had their rears on the same back street, on opposite sides, a little more than half a block apart. If the Kid's room was in the rear of his building, and he had a pair of strong glasses, he could keep a pretty sharp eye on all the windows—and probably much of the interiors—of the rooms on that side of the McAllister street building.

Last night he had ridden a block out of his way. Having seen him sneak into the back door just now, my guess was that he had not wished to leave the street car where he could be seen from this building. Either of his more convenient points of departure from the car would have been in sight of this building. This would add up to the fact that the Kid was watching someone in this building, and did not want them to be watching him.

He had now gone calling through the back door. That wasn't difficult to explain. The front door was locked, but the back door—as in most large buildings—probably was open all day. Unless the Kid ran into a janitor or someone of the sort, he could get in with no trouble. The Kid's call was furtive, whether his host was at home or not.

I didn't know what it was all about, but that didn't bother me especially. My immediate problem was to get to the best place from which to pick up the Kid when he came out.

If he left by the back door, the next block of Redwood street—between Franklin and Gough—was the place for me and my coupé. But he hadn't promised me he would leave that way. It was more likely that he would use the front door. He would attract less attention walking boldly out the front of the building than sneaking out the back. My best bet was the corner of McAllister and Van Ness. From there I could watch the front door as well as one end of Redwood street.

I slid the coupé down to that corner and waited.

Half an hour passed. Three quarters.

The Whosis Kid came down the front steps and walked toward me, buttoning his overcoat and turning up the collar as he walked, his head bent against the slant of the rain.

A curtained black Cadillac touring car came from behind me, a car I thought had been parked down near the City Hall when I took my plant here.

It curved around my coupé, slid with chainless recklessness in to the curb, skidded out again, picking up speed somehow on the wet paving.

A curtain whipped loose in the rain.

Out of the opening came pale fire-streaks. The bitter voice of a small-caliber pistol. Seven times.

The Whosis Kid's wet hat floated off his head—a slow balloon-like rising.

There was nothing slow about the Kid's moving.

Plunging, in a twisting swirl of coat-skirts, he flung into a shop vestibule.

The Cadillac reached the next corner, made a dizzy sliding turn, and was gone up Franklin street. I pointed the coupé at it.

Passing the vestibule into which the Kid had plunged, I got a one-eyed view of him, on his knees, still trying to get a dark gun untangled from his overcoat. Excited faces were in the doorway behind him. There was no excitement in the street. People are too accustomed to automobile noises nowadays to pay much attention to the racket of anything less than a six-inch gun.

By the time I reached Franklin street, the Cadillac had gained another block on me. It was spinning to the left, up Eddy street.

I paralleled it on Turk street, and saw it again when I reached the two open blocks of Jefferson Square. Its speed was decreasing. Five or six blocks further, and it crossed ahead of me—on Steiner street—close enough for me to read the license plate. Its pace was moderate now. Confident that they had made a clean getaway, its occupants didn't want to get in trouble through speeding. I slid into their wake, three blocks behind.

Not having been in sight during the early blocks of the flight, I wasn't afraid that they would suspect my interest in them now.

Out on Haight street near the park panhandle, the Cadillac stopped to discharge a passenger. A small man—short and slender—with cream-white face around dark eyes and a tiny black mustache. There was something foreign in the cut of his dark coat and the shape of his gray hat. He carried a walking-stick.

The Cadillac went on out Haight street without giving me a look at the other occupants. Tossing a mental nickel, I stuck to the man afoot. The chances always are against you being able to trace a suspicious car by its license number, but there is a slim chance.

My man went into a drug store on the corner and used the telephone. I don't know what else he did in there, if anything. Presently a taxicab arrived. He got in and was driven to the Marquis Hotel. A clerk gave him the key to room 761. I dropped him when he stepped into an elevator.

CHAPTER III

At the Marquis I am among friends.

I found Duran, the house copper, on the mezzanine floor, and asked him:

"Who is 761?"

Duran is a white-haired old-timer who looks, talks, and acts like the president of an exceptionally strong bank. He used to be captain of detectives in one of the larger Middle Western cities. Once he tried too hard to get a confession out of a safe-ripper, and killed him. The newspapers didn't like Duran. They used that accident to howl him out of his job.

"761?" he repeated in his grandfatherly manner. "That is Mr. Maurois, I believe. Are you especially interested in him?"

"I have hopes," I admitted. "What do you know about him?"

"Not a great deal. He has been here perhaps two weeks. We shall go down and see what we can learn."

We went to the desk, the switchboard, the captain of bell-hops, and upstairs to question a couple of chambermaids. The occupant of 761 had arrived two weeks ago, had registered as *Edouard Maurois, Dijon, France,* had frequent telephone calls, no mail, no visitors, kept irregular hours and tipped freely. Whatever business he was in or had was not known to the hotel people.

"What is the occasion of your interest in him, if I may ask?" Duran inquired after we had accumulated these facts. He talks like that.

"I don't exactly know yet," I replied truthfully. "He just connected with a bird who is wrong, but this Maurois may be all right himself. I'll give you a rap the minute I get anything solid on him."

I couldn't afford to tell Duran I had seen his guest snapping caps at a gunman under the eyes of the City Hall in daylight. The Marquis Hotel goes in for respectability. They would have shoved the Frenchman out in the streets. It wouldn't help me to have him scared up.

"Please do," Duran said. "You owe us something for our help, you know, so please don't withhold any information that might save us unpleasant notoriety."

"I won't," I promised. "Now will you do me another favor? I haven't had my teeth in anything except my mouth since seven-thirty this morning. Will you keep an eye on the elevators, and let me know if Maurois goes out? I'll be in the grill, near the door."

"Certainly."

On my way to the grillroom I stopped at the telephone booths and called up the office. I gave the night office man the Cadillac's license number.

"Look it up on the list and see whom it belongs to."

The answer was: "H. J. Paterson, San Pablo, issued for a Buick roadster."

That about wound up that angle. We could look up Paterson, but it was safe betting it wouldn't get us anything. License plates, once they get started in crooked ways, are about as easy to trace as Liberty Bonds.

All day I had been building up hunger. I took it into the grillroom and turned it loose. Between bites I turned the day's events over in my mind. I didn't think hard enough to spoil my appetite. There wasn't that much to think about.

The Whosis Kid lived in a joint from which some of the McAllister street apartments could be watched. He visited the apartment building furtively. Leaving, he was shot at, from a car that must have been waiting somewhere in the vicinity. Had the Frenchman's companion in the Cadillac—or his companions, if more than one—been the occupant of the apartment the Kid had visited? Had they expected him to visit it? Had they tricked him into visiting it, planning to shoot him down as he was leaving? Or were they watching the front

while the Kid watched the rear? If so, had either known that
the other was watching? And who lived there?

I couldn't answer any of these riddles. All I knew was that
the Frenchman and his companions didn't seem to like the
Whosis Kid.

Even the sort of meal I put away doesn't take forever to
eat. When I finished it, I went out to the lobby again.

Passing the switchboard, one of the girls—the one whose
red hair looks as if it had been poured into its waves and hardened—gave me a nod.

I stopped to see what she wanted.

"Your friend just had a call," she told me.

"You get it?"

"Yes. A man is waiting for him at Kearny and Broadway.
Told him to hurry."

"How long ago?"

"None. They're just through talking."

"Any names?"

"No."

"Thanks."

I went on to where Duran was stalling with an eye on the
elevators.

"Shown yet?" I asked.

"No."

"Good. The red-head on the switchboard just told me he
had a phone call to meet a man at Kearny and Broadway. I
think I'll beat him to it."

Around the corner from the hotel, I climbed into my coupé
and drove down to the Frenchman's corner.

The Cadillac he had used that afternoon was already there,
with a new license plate. I passed it and took a look at its one
occupant—a thick-set man of forty-something with a cap
pulled low over his eyes. All I could see of his features was a
wide mouth slanting over a heavy chin.

I put the coupé in a vacant space down the street a way. I
didn't have to wait long for the Frenchman. He came around
the corner afoot and got into the Cadillac. The man with the
big chin drove. They went slowly up Broadway. I followed.

CHAPTER IV

We didn't go far, and when we came to rest again, the Cadillac was placed conveniently for its occupants to watch the Venetian Café, one of the gaudiest of the Italian restaurants that fill this part of town.

Two hours went by.

I had an idea that the Whosis Kid was eating at the Venetian. When he left, the fireworks would break out, continuing the celebration from where it had broken off that afternoon on McAllister street. I hoped the Kid's gun wouldn't get caught in his coat this time. But don't think I meant to give him a helping hand in his two-against-one fight.

This party had the shape of a war between gunmen. It would be a private one as far as I was concerned. My hope was that by hovering on the fringes until somebody won, I could pick up a little profit for the Continental, in the form of a wanted crook or two among the survivors.

My guess at the Frenchman's quarry was wrong. It wasn't the Whosis Kid. It was a man and a woman. I didn't see their faces. The light was behind them. They didn't waste any time between the Venetian's door and their taxicab.

The man was big—tall, wide, and thick. The woman looked small at his side. I couldn't go by that. Anything weighing less than a ton would have seemed tiny beside him.

As the taxicab pulled away from the café, the Cadillac went after it. I ran in the Cadillac's wake.

It was a short chase.

The taxicab turned into a dark block on the edge of Chinatown. The Cadillac jumped to its side, bearing it over to the curb.

A noise of brakes, shouting voices, broken glass. A woman's scream. Figures moving in the scant space between touring car and taxicab. Both cars rocking. Grunts. Thuds. Oaths.

A man's voice: "Hey! You can't do that! Nix! Nix!"

It was a stupid voice.

I had slowed down until the coupé was barely moving toward this tussle ahead. Peering through the rain and darkness,

I tried to pick out a detail or so as I approached, but I could see little.

I was within twenty feet when the curbward door of the taxicab banged open. A woman bounced out. She landed on her knees on the sidewalk, jumped to her feet, and darted up the street.

Putting the coupé closer to the curb, I let the door swing open. My side windows were spattered with rain. I wanted to get a look at the woman when she passed. If she should take the open door for an invitation, I didn't mind talking to her.

She accepted the invitation, hurrying as directly to the car as if she had expected me to be waiting for her. Her face was a small oval above a fur collar.

"Help me!" she gasped. "Take me from here—quickly."

There was a suggestion of foreignness too slight to be called an accent.

"How about—?"

I shut my mouth. The thing she was jabbing me in the body with was a snub-nosed automatic.

"Sure! Get in," I urged her.

She bent her head to enter. I looped an arm over her neck, throwing her down across my lap. She squirmed and twisted—a small-boned, hard-fleshed body with strength in it.

I wrenched the gun out of her hand and pushed her back on the seat beside me.

Her fingers dug into my arms.

"Quick! Quick! Ah, please, quickly! Take me—"

"What about your friend?" I asked.

"Not him! He is of the others! Please, quickly!"

A man filled the open coupé door—the big-chinned man who had driven the Cadillac.

His hand seized the fur at the woman's throat.

She tried to scream—made the gurgling sound of a man with a slit throat. I smacked his chin with the gun I had taken from her.

He tried to fall into the coupé. I pushed him out.

Before his head had hit the sidewalk, I had the door closed, and was twisting the coupé around in the street.

We rode away. Two shots sounded just as we turned the first corner. I don't know whether they were fired at us or not. I turned other corners. The Cadillac did not appear again.

So far, so good. I had started with the Whosis Kid, dropped him to take Maurois, and now let him go to see who this woman was. I didn't know what this confusion was all about, but I seemed to be learning *who* it was all about.

"Where to?" I asked presently.

"To home," she said, and gave me an address.

I pointed the coupé at it with no reluctance at all. It was the McAllister street apartments the Whosis Kid had visited earlier in the evening.

We didn't waste any time getting there. My companion might know it or might not, but I knew that all the other players in this game knew that address. I wanted to get there before the Frenchman and Big Chin.

Neither of us said anything during the ride. She crouched close to me, shivering. I was looking ahead, planning how I was to land an invitation into her apartment. I was sorry I hadn't held on to her gun. I had let it fall when I pushed Big Chin out of the car. It would have been an excuse for a later call if she didn't invite me in.

I needn't have worried. She didn't invite me. She insisted that I go in with her. She was scared stiff.

"You will not leave me?" she pleaded as we drove up McAllister street. "I am in complete terror. You cannot go from me! If you will not come in, I will stay with you."

I was willing enough to go in, but I didn't want to leave the coupé where it would advertise me.

"We'll ride around the corner and park the car," I told her, "and then I'll go in with you."

I drove around the block, with an eye in each direction for the Cadillac. Neither eye found it. I left the coupé on Franklin street and we returned to the McAllister street building.

She had me almost running through the rain that had lightened now to a drizzle.

The hand with which she tried to fit a key to the front door was a shaky, inaccurate hand. I took the key and opened the door. We rode to the third floor in an automatic elevator, seeing no one. I unlocked the door to which she led me, near the rear of the building.

Holding my arm with one hand, she reached inside and snapped on the lights in the passageway.

I didn't know what she was waiting for, until she cried: "Frana! Frana! Ah, Frana!"

The muffled yapping of a small dog replied. The dog did not appear.

She grabbed me with both arms, trying to crawl up my damp coat-front.

"They are here!" she cried in the thin dry voice of utter terror. "They are here!"

CHAPTER V

"Is anybody supposed to be here?" I asked, putting her around to one side, where she wouldn't be between me and the two doors across the passageway.

"No! Just my little dog Frana, but—"

I slid my gun half out of my pocket and back again, to make sure it wouldn't catch if I needed it, and used my other hand to get rid of the woman's arms.

"You stay here. I'll see if you've got company."

Moving to the nearest door, I heard a seven-year-old voice—Lew Maher's—saying: *"He can shoot and he's plain crazy. He ain't hampered by nothing like imagination or fear of consequences."*

With my left hand I turned the first door's knob. With my left foot I kicked it open.

Nothing happened.

I put a hand around the frame, found the button, switched on the lights.

A sitting-room, all orderly.

Through an open door on the far side of the room came the muffled yapping of Frana. It was louder now and more excited. I moved to the doorway. What I could see of the next room, in the light from this, seemed peaceful and unoccupied enough. I went into it and switched on the lights.

The dog's voice came through a closed door. I crossed to it, pulled it open. A dark fluffy dog jumped snapping at my leg. I grabbed it where its fur was thickest and lifted it squirming and snarling. The light hit it. It was purple—purple as a grape! Dyed purple!

Carrying this yapping, yelping artificial hound a little away from my body with my left hand, I moved on to the next room—a bedroom. It was vacant. Its closet hid nobody. I found the kitchen and bathroom. Empty. No one was in the apartment. The purple pup had been imprisoned by the Whosis Kid earlier in the day.

Passing through the second room on my way back to the woman with her dog and my report, I saw a slitted envelope lying face-down on a table. I turned it over. The stationery of a fashionable store, it was addressed to Mrs. Inés Almad, here.

The party seemed to be getting international. Maurois was French; the Whosis Kid was Boston American; the dog had a Bohemian name (at least I remember nabbing a Czech forger a few months before whose first name was Frana); and Inés, I imagine, was either Spanish or Portuguese. I didn't know what Almad was, but she was undoubtedly foreign, and not, I thought, French.

I returned to her. She hadn't moved an inch.

"Everything seems to be all right," I told her. "The dog got himself caught in a closet."

"There is no one here?"

"No one."

She took the dog in both hands, kissing its fluffy stained head, crooning affectionate words to it in a language that made no sense to me.

"Do your friends—the people you had your row with tonight—know where you live?" I asked.

I knew they did. I wanted to see what she knew.

She dropped the dog as if she had forgotten it, and her brows puckered.

"I do not know that," she said slowly. "Yet it may be. If they do—"

She shuddered, spun on her heel, and pushed the hall door violently shut.

"They may have been here this afternoon," she went on. "Frana has made himself prisoner in closets before, but I fear everything. I am coward-like. But there is none here now?"

"No one," I assured her again.

We went into the sitting-room. I got my first good look at her when she shed her hat and dark cape.

She was a trifle under medium height, a dark-skinned woman of thirty in a vivid orange gown. She was dark as an Indian, with bare brown shoulders round and sloping, tiny feet and hands, her fingers heavy with rings. Her nose was thin and curved, her mouth full-lipped and red, her eyes— long and thickly lashed—were of an extraordinary narrowness. They were dark eyes, but nothing of their color could be seen through the thin slits that separated the lids. Two dark gleams through veiling lashes. Her black hair was disarranged just now in fluffy silk puffs. A rope of pearls hung down on her dark chest. Earrings of black iron—in a peculiar club-like design—swung beside her cheeks.

Altogether, she was an odd trick. But I wouldn't want to be quoted as saying that she wasn't beautiful—in a wild way.

She was shaking and shivering as she got rid of her hat and cloak. White teeth held her lower lip as she crossed the room to turn on an electric heater. I took advantage of this opportunity to shift my gun from my overcoat pocket to my pants. Then I took off the coat.

Leaving the room for a second, she returned with a brown-filled quart bottle and two tumblers on a bronze tray, which she put on a little table near the heater.

The first tumbler she filled to within half an inch of its rim. I stopped her when she had the other nearly half full.

"That'll do fine for me," I said.

It was brandy, and not at all hard to get down. She shot her tumblerful into her throat as if she needed it, shook her bare shoulders, and sighed in a satisfied way.

"You will think, certainly, I am lunatic," she smiled at me. "Flinging myself on you, a stranger in the street, demanding of you time and troubles."

"No," I lied seriously. "I think you're pretty level-headed for a woman who, no doubt, isn't used to this sort of stuff."

She was pulling a little upholstered bench closer to the electric heater, within reach of the table that held the brandy. She sat down now, with an inviting nod at the bench's empty half.

The purple dog jumped into her lap. She pushed it out. It started to return. She kicked it sharply in the side with the pointed toe of her slipper. It yelped and crawled under a chair across the room.

I avoided the window by going the long way around the room. The window was curtained, but not thickly enough to hide all of the room from the Whosis Kid—if he happened to be sitting at his window just now with a pair of field-glasses to his eyes.

"But I am not level-headed, really," the woman was saying as I dropped beside her. "I am coward-like, terribly. And even becoming accustomed— It is my husband, or he who was my husband. I should tell you. Your gallantry deserves the explanation, and I do not wish you should think a thing that is not so."

I tried to look trusting and credulous. I expected to disbelieve everything she said.

"He is most crazily jealous," she went on in her low-pitched, soft voice, with a peculiar way of saying words that just missed being marked enough to be called a foreign accent. "He is an old man, and incredibly wicked. These men he has sent to me! A woman there was once—tonight's men are not first. I don't know what—what they mean. To kill me, perhaps—to maim, to disfigure—I do not know."

"And the man in the taxi with you was one of them?" I asked. "I was driving down the street behind you when you were attacked, and I could see there was a man with you. He was one of them?"

"Yes! I did not know it, but it must have been that he was. He does not defend me. A pretense, that is all."

"Ever try sicking the cops on this hubby of yours?"

"It is what?"

"Ever notify the police?"

"Yes, but"—she shrugged her brown shoulders—"I would as well have kept quiet, or better. In Buffalo it was, and they—they bound my husband to keep the peace, I think you call it. A thousand dollars! Poof! What is that to him in his jealousy? And I—I cannot stand the things the newspapers say—the jesting of them. I must leave Buffalo. Yes, once I do try sicking the cops on him. But not more."

"Buffalo?" I explored a little. "I lived there for a while—on Crescent avenue."

"Oh, yes. That is out by the Delaware Park."

That was right enough. But her knowing something about Buffalo didn't prove anything about the rest of her story.

CHAPTER VI

She poured more brandy. By speaking quick I held my drink down to a size suitable for a man who has work to do. Hers was as large as before. We drank, and she offered me cigarettes in a lacquered box—slender cigarettes, hand-rolled in black paper.

I didn't stay with mine long. It tasted, smelt and scorched like gun-powder.

"You don't like my cigarettes?"

"I'm an old-fashioned man," I apologized, rubbing its fire out in a bronze dish, fishing in my pocket for my own deck. "Tobacco's as far as I've got. What's in these fireworks?"

She laughed. She had a pleasant laugh, with a sort of coo in it.

"I am so very sorry. So many people do not like them. I have a Hindu incense mixed with the tobacco."

I didn't say anything to that. It was what you would expect of a woman who would dye her dog purple.

The dog moved under its chair just then, scratching the floor with its nails.

The brown woman was in my arms, in my lap, her arms wrapped around my neck. Close-up, opened by terror, her eyes weren't dark at all. They were gray-green. The blackness was in the shadow from her heavy lashes.

"It's only the dog," I assured her, sliding her back on her own part of the bench. "It's only the dog wriggling around under the chair."

"Ah!" she blew her breath out with enormous relief.

Then we had to have another shot of brandy.

"You see, I am most awfully the coward," she said when the third dose of liquor was in her. "But, ah, I have had so much trouble. It is a wonder that I am not insane."

I could have told her she wasn't far enough from it to do much bragging, but I nodded with what was meant for sympathy.

She lit another cigarette to replace the one she had dropped in her excitement. Her eyes became normal black slits again.

"I do not think it is nice"—there was a suggestion of a dimple in her brown cheek when she smiled like that—"that I throw myself into the arms of a man even whose name I do not know, or anything of him."

"That's easy to fix. My name is Young," I lied; "and I can let you have a case of Scotch at a price that will astonish you. I think maybe I could stand it if you call me Jerry. Most of the ladies I let sit in my lap do."

"Jerry Young," she repeated, as if to herself. "That is a nice name. And you are the bootlegger?"

"Not *the*," I corrected her, "just *a*. This is San Francisco."

The going got tough after that.

Everything else about this brown woman was all wrong, but her fright was real. She was scared stiff. And she didn't intend being left alone this night. She meant to keep me there—to massage any more chins that stuck themselves at her. Her idea—she being that sort—was that I would be most surely held with affection. So she must turn herself loose on me. She wasn't hampered by any pruderies or puritanisms at all.

I also have an idea. Mine is that when the last gong rings I'm going to be leading this baby and some of her playmates to the city prison. That is an excellent reason—among a dozen others I could think of—why I shouldn't get mushy with her.

I was willing enough to camp there with her until something happened. That apartment looked like the scene of the next action. But I had to cover up my own game. I couldn't let her know she was only a minor figure in it. I had to pretend there was nothing behind my willingness to stay but a desire to protect her. Another man might have got by with a chivalrous, knight-errant, protector-of-womanhood-without-personal-interest attitude. But I don't look, and can't easily act, like that kind of person. I had to hold her off without letting her guess that my interest wasn't personal. It was no cinch. She was too damned direct, and she had too much brandy in her.

I didn't kid myself that my beauty and personality were responsible for any of her warmth. I was a thick-armed male with big fists. She was in a jam. She spelled my name P-r-o-t-e-c-t-i-o-n. I was something to be put between her and trouble.

Another complication: I am neither young enough nor old enough to get feverish over every woman who doesn't make me think being blind isn't so bad. I'm at that middle point around forty where a man puts other feminine qualities—amiability, for one—above beauty on his list. This brown woman annoyed me. She was too sure of herself. Her work was rough. She was trying to handle me as if I were a farmer boy. But in spite of all this, I'm constructed mostly of human ingredients. This woman got more than a stand-off when faces and bodies were dealt. I didn't like her. I hoped to throw her in the can before I was through. But I'd be a liar if I didn't admit that she had me stirred up inside—between her cuddling against me, giving me the come-on, and the brandy I had drunk.

The going was tough—no fooling.

A couple of times I was tempted to bolt. Once I looked at my watch—2:06. She put a ring heavy brown hand on the timepiece and pushed it down to my pocket.

"Please, Jerry!" the earnestness in her voice was real. "You cannot go. You cannot leave me here. I will not have it so. I will go also, through the streets following. You cannot leave me to be murdered here!"

I settled down again.

A few minutes later a bell rang sharply.

She went to pieces immediately. She piled over on me, strangling me with her bare arms. I pried them loose enough to let me talk.

"What bell is that?"

"The street door. Do not heed it."

I patted her shoulder.

"Be a good girl and answer it. Let's see who it is."

Her arms tightened.

"No! No! No! They have come!"

The bell rang again.

"Answer it," I insisted.

Her face was flat against my coat, her nose digging into my chest.

"No! No!"

"All right," I said. "I'll answer it myself."

I untangled myself from her, got up and went into the passageway. She followed me. I tried again to persuade her to do the talking. She would not, although she didn't object to my talking. I would have liked it better if whoever was downstairs didn't learn that the woman wasn't alone. But she was too stubborn in her refusal for me to do anything with her.

"Well?" I said into the speaking-tube.

"Who the hell are you?" a harsh, deep-chested voice asked. "What do you want?"

"I want to talk to Inés."

"Speak your piece to me," I suggested, "and I'll tell her about it."

The woman, holding one of my arms, had an ear close to the tube.

"Billie, it is," she whispered. "Tell him that he goes away."

"You're to go away," I passed the message on.

"Yeah?" the voice grew harsher and deeper. "Will you open the door, or will I bust it in?"

There wasn't a bit of playfulness in the question. Without consulting the woman, I put a finger on the button that unlocks the street door.

"Welcome," I said into the tube.

"He's coming up," I explained to the woman. "Shall I stand behind the door and tap him on the skull when he comes in? Or do you want to talk to him first?"

"Do not strike him!" she exclaimed. "It is Billie."

That suited me. I hadn't intended putting the slug to him—not until I knew who and what he was, anyway. I had wanted to see what she would say.

CHAPTER VII

Billie wasn't long getting up to us. I opened the door when he rang, the woman standing beside me. He didn't wait for an invitation. He was through the doorway before I had the door half opened. He glared at me. There was plenty of him!

A big, red-faced, red-haired bale of a man—big in any direction you measured him—and none of him was fat. The
skin was off his nose, one cheek was clawed, the other
swollen. His hatless head was a tangled mass of red hair. One
pocket had been ripped out of his coat, and a button dangled
on the end of a six-inch ribbon of torn cloth.

This was the big heaver who had been in the taxicab with
the woman.

"Who's this mutt?" he demanded, moving his big paws toward me.

I knew the woman was a goof. It wouldn't have surprised
me if she had tried to feed me to the battered giant. But she
didn't. She put a hand on one of his and soothed him.

"Do not be nasty, Billie. He is a friend. Without him I
would not this night have escaped."

He scowled. Then his face straightened out and he caught
her hand in both of his.

"So you got away it's all right," he said huskily. "I'd a done
better if we'd been outside. There wasn't no room in that taxi
for me to turn around. And one of them guys crowned me."

That was funny. This big clown was apologizing for getting
mangled up protecting a woman who had scooted, leaving
him to get out as well as he could.

The woman led him into the sitting-room, I tagging along
behind. They sat on the bench. I picked out a chair that
wasn't in line with the window the Whosis Kid ought to be
watching.

"What did happen, Billie?" She touched his grooved cheek
and skinned nose with her fingertips. "You are hurt."

He grinned with a sort of shamefaced delight. I saw that
what I had taken for a swelling in one cheek was only a big
hunk of chewing tobacco.

"I don't know all that happened," he said. "One of 'em
crowned me, and I didn't wake up till a coupla hours afterwards. The taxi driver didn't give me no help in the fight, but
he was a right guy and knowed where his money would come
from. He didn't holler or nothing. He took me around to a
doc that wouldn't squawk, and the doc straightened me out,
and then I come up here."

"Did you see each one of those men?" she asked.

"Sure! I seen 'em, and felt 'em, and maybe tasted 'em."

"They were how many?"

"Just two of 'em. A little fella with a trick tickler, and a husky with a big chin on him."

"There was no other? There was not a younger man, tall and thin?"

That could be the Whosis Kid. She thought he and the Frenchman were working together?

Billie shook his shaggy, banged-up head.

"Nope. They was only two of 'em."

She frowned and chewed her lip.

Billie looked sidewise at me—a look that said "Beat it."

The woman caught the glance. She twisted around on the bench to put a hand on his head.

"Poor Billie," she cooed; "his head most cruelly hurt saving me, and now, when he should be at his home giving it rest, I keep him here talking. You go, Billie, and when it is morning and your poor head is better, you will telephone to me?"

His red face got dark. He glowered at me.

Laughing, she slapped him lightly on the cheek that bulged around his cud of tobacco.

"Do not become jealous of Jerry. Jerry is enamored of one yellow and white lady somewhere, and to her he is most faithful. Not even the smallest liking has he for dark women." She smiled a challenge at me. "Is it not so, Jerry?"

"No," I denied. "And, besides, all women are dark."

Billie shifted his chew to the scratched cheek and bunched his shoulders.

"What the hell kind of a crack is that to be making?" he rumbled.

"That means nothing it should not, Billie," she laughed at him. "It is only an epigram."

"Yeah?" Billie was sour and truculent. I was beginning to think he didn't like me. "Well, tell your little fat friend to keep his smart wheezes to himself. I don't like 'em."

That was plain enough. Billie wanted an argument. The woman, who held him securely enough to have steered him off, simply laughed again. There was no profit in trying to find the reason behind any of her actions. She was a nut.

Maybe she thought that since we weren't sociable enough for her to keep both on hand, she'd let us tangle, and hold on to the one who rubbed the other out of the picture.

Anyway, a row was coming. Ordinarily I am inclined to peace. The day is past when I'll fight for the fun of it. But I've been in too many rumpuses to mind them much. Usually nothing very bad happens to you, even if you lose. I wasn't going to back down just because this big stiff was meatier than I. I've always been lucky against the large sizes. He had been banged up earlier in the evening. That would cut down his steam some. I wanted to hang around this apartment a little longer, if it could be managed. If Billie wanted to tussle— and it looked as if he did—he could.

It was easy to meet him half-way: anything I said would be used against me.

I grinned at his red face, and suggested to the woman, solemnly:

"I think if you'd dip him in blueing he'd come out the same color as the other pup."

As silly as that was, it served. Billie reared up on his feet and curled his paws into fists.

"Me and you'll take a walk," he decided; "out where there's space enough."

I got up, pushed my chair back with a foot, and quoted "Red" Burns to him: "If you're close enough, there's room enough."

He wasn't a man you had to talk to much. We went around and around.

It was fists at first. He started it by throwing his right at my head. I went in under it and gave him all I had in a right and left to the belly. He swallowed his chew of tobacco. But he didn't bend. Few big men are as strong as they look. Billie was.

He didn't know anything at all. His idea of a fight was to stand up and throw fists at your head—right, left, right, left. His fists were as large as wastebaskets. They wheezed through the air. But always at the head—the easiest part to get out of the way.

There was room enough for me to go in and out. I did that. I hammered his belly. I thumped his heart. I mauled his belly again. Every time I hit him he grew an inch, gained a pound and picked up another horsepower. I don't fool when I hit, but nothing I did to this human mountain—not even making him swallow his hunk of tobacco—had any visible effect on him.

I've always had a reasonable amount of pride in my ability to sock. It was disappointing to have this big heaver take the best I could give him without a grunt. But I wasn't discouraged. He couldn't stand it forever. I settled down to make a steady job of it.

Twice he clipped me. Once on the shoulder. A big fist spun me half around. He didn't know what to do next. He came in on the wrong side. I made him miss, and got clear. The other time he caught me on the forehead. A chair kept me from going down. The smack hurt me. It must have hurt him more. A skull is tougher than a knuckle. I got out of his way when he closed in, and let him have something to remember on the back of his neck.

The woman's dusky face showed over Billie's shoulder as he straightened up. Her eyes were shiny behind their heavy lashes, and her mouth was open to let white teeth gleam through.

Billie got tired of the boxing after that, and turned the set-to into a wrestling match, with trimmings. I would rather have kept on with the fists. But I couldn't help myself. It was his party. He grabbed one of my wrists, yanked, and we thudded chest to chest.

He didn't know any more about this than he had about that. He didn't have to. He was big enough and strong enough to play with me.

I was underneath when we tumbled down on the floor and began rolling around. I did my best. It wasn't anything. Three times I put a scissors on him. His body was too big for my short legs to clamp around. He chucked me off as if he were amusing the baby. There was no use at all in trying to do things to his legs. No hold known to man could have held them. His arms were almost as strong. I quit trying.

Nothing I knew was any good against this monster. He was out of my range. I was satisfied to spend all that was left of my strength trying to keep him from crippling me—and waiting for a chance to out-smart him.

He threw me around a lot. Then my chance came.

I was flat on my back, with everything but one or two of my most centrally located intestines squeezed out. Kneeling astride me, he brought his big hands up to my throat and fastened them there.

That's how much he didn't know!

You can't choke a man that way—not if his hands are loose and he knows a hand is stronger than a finger.

I laughed in his purple face and brought my own hands up. Each of them picked one of his little fingers out of my flesh. It wasn't a dream at that. I was all in, and he wasn't. But no man's little finger is stronger than another's hand. I twisted them back. They broke together.

He yelped. I grabbed the next—the ring fingers.

One of them snapped. The other was ready to pop when he let go.

Jerking up, I butted him in the face. I twisted from between his knees. We came on our feet together.

The doorbell rang.

CHAPTER VIII

Fight interest went out of the woman's face. Fear came in. Her fingers picked at her mouth.

"Ask who's there," I told her.

"Who—who is there?"

Her voice was flat and dry.

"Mrs. Keil," came from the corridor, the words sharp with indignation. "You will have to stop this noise immediately! The tenants are complaining—and no wonder! A pretty hour to be entertaining company and carrying on so!"

"The landlady," the dark woman whispered. Aloud: "I am sorry, Mrs. Keil. There will not be more noises."

Something like a sniff came through the door, and the sound of dimming footsteps.

Inés Almad frowned reproachfully at Billie.

"You should not have done this," she blamed him.

He looked humble, and at the floor, and at me. Looking at me, the purple began to flow back into his face.

"I'm sorry," he mumbled. "I told this fella we ought to take a walk. We'll do it now, and there won't be no more noise here."

"Billie!" her voice was sharp. She was reading the law to him. "You will go out and have attention for your hurts. If you have not won these fights, because of that am I to be left here alone to be murdered?"

The big man shuffled his feet, avoided her gaze and looked utterly miserable. But he shook his head stubbornly.

"I can't do it, Inés," he said. "Me and this guy has got to finish it. He busted my fingers, and I got to bust his jaw."

"Billie!"

She stamped one small foot and looked imperiously at him. He looked as if he'd like to roll over on his back and hold his paws in the air. But he stood his ground.

"I got to," he repeated. "There ain't no way out of it."

Anger left her face. She smiled very tenderly at him.

"Dear old Billie," she murmured, and crossed the room to a secretary in a corner.

When she turned, an automatic pistol was in her hand. Its one eye looked at Billie.

"Now, *lechón,*" she purred, "go out!"

The red man wasn't a quick thinker. It took a full minute for him to realize that this woman he loved was driving him away with a gun. The big dummy might have known that his three broken fingers had disqualified him. It took another minute for him to get his legs in motion. He went toward the door in slow bewilderment, still only half believing this thing was really happening.

The woman followed him step by step. I went ahead to open the door.

I turned the knob. The door came in, pushing me back against the opposite wall.

In the doorway stood Edouard Maurois and the man I had swatted on the chin. Each had a gun.

I looked at Inés Almad, wondering what turn her craziness would take in the face of this situation. She wasn't so crazy as I had thought. Her scream and the thud of her gun on the floor sounded together.

"Ah!" the Frenchman was saying. "The gentlemen were leaving? May we detain them?"

The man with the big chin—it was larger than ever now with the marks of my tap—was less polite.

"Back up, you birds!" he ordered, stooping for the gun the woman had dropped.

I still was holding the doorknob. I rattled it a little as I took my hand away—enough to cover up the click of the lock as I pushed the button that left it unlatched. If I needed help, and it came, I wanted as few locks as possible between me and it.

Then—Billie, the woman and I walking backward—we all paraded into the sitting-room. Maurois and his companion both wore souvenirs of the row in the taxicab. One of the Frenchman's eyes was bruised and closed—a beautiful shiner. His clothes were rumpled and dirty. He wore them jauntily in spite of that, and he still had his walking stick, crooked under the arm that didn't hold his gun.

Big Chin held us with his own gun and the woman's while Maurois ran his hand over Billie's and my clothes, to see if we were armed. He found my gun and pocketed it. Billie had no weapons.

"Can I trouble you to step back against the wall?" Maurois asked when he was through.

We stepped back as if it was no trouble at all. I found my shoulder against one of the window curtains. I pressed it against the frame, and turned far enough to drag the curtain clear of a foot or more of pane.

If the Whosis Kid was watching, he should have had a clear view of the Frenchman—the man who had shot at him earlier in the evening. I was putting it up to the Kid. The corridor door was unlocked. If the Kid could get into the building— no great trick—he had a clear path. I didn't know where he fit in, but I wanted him to join us, and I hoped he wouldn't disappoint me. If everybody got together here, maybe what- ever was going on would come out where I could see it and understand it.

Meanwhile, I kept as much of myself as possible out of the window. The Kid might decide to throw lead from across the alley.

Maurois was facing Inés. Big Chin's guns were on Billie and me.

"I do not *comprends* ze *anglais* ver' good," the Frenchman was mocking the woman. "So it is when you say you meet wit' me, I t'ink you say in New Orleans. I do not know you say San Francisc'. I am ver' sorry to make ze mistake. I am mos' sorry zat I keep you wait. But now I am here. You have ze share for me?"

"I have not." She held her hands out in an empty gesture. "The Kid took those—everything from me."

"What?" Maurois dropped his taunting smile and his vaudeville accent. His one open eye flashed angrily. "How could he, unless—?"

"He suspected us, Edouard." Her mouth trembled with earnestness. Her eyes pleaded for belief. She was lying. "He had me followed. The day after I am there he comes. He takes all. I am afraid to wait for you. I fear your unbelief. You would not—"

"*C'est incroyable!*" Maurois was very excited over it. "I was on the first train south after our—our theatricals. Could the Kid have been on that train without my knowing it? *Non!* And how else could he have reached you before I? You are playing with me, *ma petite* Inés. That you did join the Kid, I do not doubt. But not in New Orleans. You did not go there. You came here to San Francisco."

"Edouard!" she protested, fingering his sleeve with one brown hand, the other holding her throat as if she were having trouble getting the words out. "You cannot think that thing! Do not those weeks in Boston say it is not possible? For one like the Kid—or like any other—am I to betray you? You know me not more than to think I am like that?"

She was an actress. She was appealing, and pathetic, and anything else you like—including dangerous.

The Frenchman took his sleeve away from her and stepped back a step. White lines ringed his mouth below his tiny mustache, and his jaw muscles bulged. His one good eye was worried. She had got to him, though not quite enough to upset him altogether. But the game was young yet.

"I do not know what to think," he said slowly. "If I have

been wrong—I must find the Kid first. Then I will learn the truth."

"You don't have to look no further, brother. I'm right among you!"

The Whosis Kid stood in the passageway door. A black revolver was in each of his hands. Their hammers were up.

CHAPTER IX

It was a pretty tableau.

There is the Whosis Kid in the door—a lean lad in his twenties, all the more wicked-looking because his face is weak and slack-jawed and dull-eyed. The cocked guns in his hands are pointing at everybody or at nobody, depending on how you look at them.

There is the brown woman, her cheeks pinched in her two fists, her eyes open until their green-grayishness shows. The fright I had seen in her face before was nothing to the fright that is there now.

There is the Frenchman—whirled doorward at the Kid's first word—his gun on the Kid, his cane still under his arm, his face a tense white blot.

There is Big Chin, his body twisted half around, his face over one shoulder to look at the door, with one of his guns following his face around.

There is Billie—a big, battered statue of a man who hasn't said a word since Inés Almad started to gun him out of the apartment.

And, last, here I am—not feeling so comfortable as I would home in bed, but not actually hysterical either. I wasn't altogether dissatisfied with the shape things were taking. Something was going to happen in these rooms. But I wasn't friendly enough to any present to care especially what happened to whom. For myself, I counted on coming through all in one piece. Few men *get* killed. Most of those who meet sudden ends *get themselves* killed. I've had twenty years of experience at dodging that. I can count on being one of the survivors of whatever blow-up there is. And I hope to take most of the other survivors for a ride.

But right now the situation belonged to the men with guns—the Whosis Kid, Maurois and Big Chin.

The Kid spoke first. He had a whining voice that came disagreeably through his thick nose.

"This don't look nothing like Chi to me, but, anyways, we're all here."

"Chicago!" Maurois exclaimed. "You did not go to Chicago!"

The Kid sneered at him.

"Did you? Did she? What would I be going there for? You think me and her run out on you, don't you? Well, we would of if she hadn't put the two X's to me the same as she done to you, and the same as the three of us done to the boob."

"That may be," the Frenchman replied; "but you do not expect me to believe that you and Inés are not friends? Didn't I see you leaving here this afternoon?"

"You seen me, all right," the Kid agreed; "but if my rod hadn't of got snagged in my flogger you wouldn't have seen nothing else. But I ain't got nothing against you now. I thought you and her had ditched me, just as you think me and her done you. I know different now, from what I heard while I was getting in here. She twisted the pair of us, Frenchy, just like we twisted the boob. Ain't you got it yet?"

Maurois shook his head slowly.

What put an edge to this conversation was that both men were talking over their guns.

"Listen," the Kid asked impatiently. "We was to meet up in Chi for a three-way split, wasn't we?"

The Frenchman nodded.

"But she tells me," the Kid went on, "she'll connect with me in St. Louis, counting you out; and she ribs you up to meet her in New Orleans, ducking me. And then she gyps the pair of us by running out here to Frisco with the stuff.

"We're a couple of suckers, Frenchy, and there ain't no use of us getting hot at each other. There's enough of it for a fat two-way cut. What I say is let's forget what's done, and me and you make it fifty-fifty. Understand, I ain't begging you. I'm making a proposition. If you don't like it, to hell with you! You know me. You never seen the day I wouldn't shoot it out with you or anybody else. Take your pick!"

The Frenchman didn't say anything for a while. He was converted, but he didn't want to weaken his hand by coming in too soon. I don't know whether he believed the Kid's words or not, but he believed the Kid's guns. You can get a bullet out of a cocked revolver a lot quicker than out of a hammerless automatic. The Kid had the bulge there. And the Kid had him licked because the Kid had the look of one who doesn't give a damn what happens next.

Finally Maurois looked a question at Big Chin. Big Chin moistened his lips, but said nothing.

Maurois looked at the Kid again, and nodded his head.

"You are right," he said. "We will do that."

"Good!" The Kid did not move from his door. "Now who are these plugs?"

"These two"—Maurois nodded at Billie and me—"are friends of our Inés. This"—indicating Big Chin—"is a confrere of mine."

"You mean he's in with you? That's all right with me." The Kid spoke crisply. "But, you understand, his cut comes out of yours. I get half, and no trimming."

The Frenchman frowned, but he nodded in agreement.

"Half is yours, if we find it."

"Don't get no headache over that," the Kid advised him. "It's here and we'll get it."

He put one of his guns away and came into the room, the other gun hanging loosely at his side. When he walked across the room to face the woman, he managed it so that Big Chin and Maurois were never behind him.

"Where's the stuff?" he demanded.

Inés Almad wet her red mouth with her tongue and let her mouth droop a little and looked softly at the Kid, and made her play.

"One of us is as bad as are the others, Kid. We all—each of us tried to get for ourselves everything. You and Edouard have put aside what is past. Am I more wrong than you? I have them, true, but I have not them here. Until tomorrow will you wait? I will get them. We will divide them among us three, as it was to have been. Shall we not do that?"

"Not any!" The Kid's voice had finality in it.

"Is that just?" she pleaded, letting her chin quiver a bit. "Is there a treachery of which I am guilty that also you and Edouard are not? Do you—?"

"That ain't the idea at all," the Kid told her. "Me and Frenchy are in a fix where we got to work together to get anywhere. So we're together. With you it's different. We don't need you. We can take the stuff away from you. You're out! Where's the stuff?"

"Not here! Am I foolish sufficient to leave them here where so easily you could find them? You *do* need my help to find them. Without me you cannot—"

"You're silly! I might flop for that if I didn't know you. But I know you're too damned greedy to let 'em get far away from you. And you're yellower than you're greedy. If you're smacked a couple of times, you'll kick in. And don't think I got any objections to smacking you over!"

She cowered back from his upraised hand.

The Frenchman spoke quickly.

"We should search the rooms first, Kid. If we don't find them there, then we can decide what to do next."

The Whosis Kid laughed sneeringly at Maurois.

"All right. But, get this, I'm not going out of here without that stuff—not if I have to take this rat apart. My way's quicker, but we'll hunt first if you want to. Your con-what-ever-you-call-him can keep these plugs tucked in while me and you upset the joint."

They went to work. The Kid put away his gun and brought out a long-bladed spring-knife. The Frenchman unscrewed the lower two-thirds of his cane, baring a foot and a half of sword-blade.

No cursory search, theirs. They took the room we were in first. They gutted it thoroughly, carved it to the bone. Furniture and pictures were taken apart. Upholstering gave up its stuffing. Floor coverings were cut. Suspicious lengths of wallpaper were scraped loose. They worked slowly. Neither would let the other get behind him. The Kid would not turn his back on Big Chin.

The sitting-room wrecked, they went into the next room, leaving the woman, Billie and me standing among the litter. Big Chin and his two guns watched over us.

As soon as the Frenchman and the Kid were out of sight, the woman tried her stuff out on our guardian. She had a lot of confidence in her power with men, I'll say that for her.

For a while she worked her eyes on Big Chin, and then, very softly:

"Can I—?"

"You can't!" Big Chin was loud and gruff. "Shut up!"

The Whosis Kid appeared at the door.

"If nobody don't say nothing maybe nobody won't get hurt," he snarled, and went back to his work.

The woman valued herself too highly to be easily discour aged. She didn't put anything in words again, but she looked things at Big Chin—things that had him sweating and blush- ing. He was a simple man. I didn't think she'd get anywhere. If there had been no one present but the two of them, she might have put Big Chin over the jumps; but he wouldn't be likely to let her get to him with a couple of birds standing there watching the show.

Once a sharp yelp told us that the purple Frana—who had fled rearward when Maurois and Big Chin arrived—had got in trouble with the searchers. There was only that one yelp, and it stopped with a suddenness that suggested trouble for the dog.

The two men spent nearly an hour in the other rooms. They didn't find anything. Their hands, when they joined us again, held nothing but the cutlery.

CHAPTER X

"I said to you it was not here," Inés told them triumphantly. "Now will you—?"

"You can't tell me nothing I'll believe." The Kid snapped his knife shut and dropped it in his pocket. "I still think it's here."

He caught her wrist, and held his other hand, palm up, under her nose.

"You can put 'em in my hand, or I'll take 'em."

"They are not here! I swear it!"

His mouth lifted at the corner in a savage grimace.

"Liar!"

He twisted her arm roughly, forcing her to her knees. His free hand went to the shoulder-strap of her orange gown.

"I'll damn soon find out," he promised.

Billie came to life.

"Hey!" he protested, his chest heaving in and out. "You can't do that!"

"Wait, Kid!" Maurois—putting his sword-cane together again—called. "Let us see if there is not another way."

The Whosis Kid let go of the woman and took three slow steps back from her. His eyes were dead circles without any color you could name—the dull eyes of the man whose nerves quit functioning in the face of excitement. His bony hands pushed his coat aside a little and rested where his vest bulged over the sharp corners of his hip-bones.

"Let's me and you get this right, Frenchy," he said in his whining voice. "Are you with me or her?"

"You, most certainly, but—"

"All right. Then *be* with me! Don't be trying to gum every play I make. I'm going to frisk this dolly, and don't think I ain't. What are you going to do about it?"

The Frenchman pursed his mouth until his little black mustache snuggled against the tip of his nose. He puckered his eyebrows and looked thoughtfully out of his one good eye. But he wasn't going to do anything at all about it, and he knew he wasn't. Finally he shrugged.

"You are right," he surrendered. "She should be searched."

The Kid grunted contemptuous disgust at him and went toward the woman again.

She sprang away from him, to me. Her arms clamped around my neck in the habit they seemed to have.

"Jerry!" she screamed in my face. "You will not allow him! Jerry, please not!"

I didn't say anything.

I didn't think it was exactly genteel of the Kid to frisk her, but there were several reasons why I didn't try to stop him. First, I didn't want to do anything to delay the unearthing of this "stuff" there had been so much talk about. Second, I'm no Galahad. This woman had picked her playmates, and was largely responsible for this angle of their game. If they played rough, she'd have to make the best of it. And, a good strong third, Big Chin was prodding me in the side with a gun-muzzle to remind me that I couldn't do anything if I wanted to—except get myself slaughtered.

The Kid dragged Inés away. I let her go.

He pulled her over to what was left of the bench by the electric heater, and called the Frenchman there with a jerk of his head.

"You hold her while I go through her," he said.

She filled her lungs with air. Before she could turn it loose in a shriek, the Kid's long fingers had fit themselves to her throat.

"One chirp out of you and I'll tie a knot in your neck," he threatened.

She let the air wheeze out of her nose.

Billie shuffled his feet. I turned my head to look at him. He was puffing through his mouth. Sweat polished his forehead under his matted red hair. I hoped he wasn't going to turn his wolf loose until the "stuff" came to the surface. If he would wait a while I might join him.

He wouldn't wait. He went into action when—Maurois holding her—the Kid started to undress the woman.

He took a step toward them. Big Chin tried to wave him back with a gun. Billie didn't even see it. His eyes were red on the three by the bench.

"Hey, you can't do that!" he rumbled. "You can't do that!"

"No?" The Kid looked up from his work. "Watch me."

"Billie!" the woman urged the big man on in his foolishness.

Billie charged.

Big Chin let him go, playing safe by swinging both guns on me. The Whosis Kid slid out of the plunging giant's path. Maurois hurled the girl straight at Billie—and got his gun out.

Billie and Inés thumped together in a swaying tangle.

The Kid spun behind the big man. One of the Kid's hands came out of his pocket with the spring-knife. The knife clicked open as Billie regained his balance.

The Kid jumped close.

He knew knives. None of your clumsy downward strokes with the blade sticking out the bottom of his fist.

Thumb and crooked forefinger guided blade. He struck upward. Under Billie's shoulder. Once. Deep.

Billie pitched forward, smashing the woman to the floor under him. He rolled off her and was dead on his back among the furniture-stuffing. Dead, he seemed larger than ever, seemed to fill the room.

The Whosis Kid wiped his knife clean on a piece of carpet, snapped it shut, and dropped it back in his pocket. He did this with his left hand. His right was close to his hip. He did not look at the knife. His eyes were on Maurois.

But if he expected the Frenchman to squawk, he was disappointed. Maurois' little mustache twitched, and his face was white and strained, but:

"We'd better hurry with what we have to do, and get out of here," he suggested.

The woman sat up beside the dead man, whimpering. Her face was ashy under her dark skin. She was licked. A shaking hand fumbled beneath her clothes. It brought out a little flat silk bag.

Maurois—nearer than the Kid—took it. It was sewed too securely for his fingers to open. He held it while the Kid ripped it with his knife. The Frenchman poured part of the contents out in one cupped hand.

Diamonds. Pearls. A few colored stones among them.

CHAPTER XI

Big Chin blew his breath out in a faint whistle. His eyes were bright on the sparkling stones. So were the eyes of Maurois, the woman, and the Kid.

Big Chin's inattention was a temptation. I could reach his jaw. I could knock him over. The strength Billie had mauled out of me had nearly all come back by now. I could knock Big Chin over and have at least one of his guns by the time the Kid and Maurois got set. It was time for me to do something. I had let these comedians run the show long enough. The stuff had come to light. If I let the party break up there was no telling when, if ever, I could round up these folks again.

But I put the temptation away and made myself wait a bit longer. No use going off half-cocked. With a gun in my hand, facing the Kid and Maurois, I still would have less than an even break. That's not enough. The idea in this detective business is to catch crooks, not to put on heroics.

Maurois was pouring the stones back in the bag when I looked at him again. He started to put the bag in his pocket. The Whosis Kid stopped him with a hand on his arm.

"I'll pack 'em."

Maurois' eyebrows went up.

"There's two of you and one of me," the Kid explained. "I trust you, and all the like of that, but just the same I'm carrying my own share."

"But—"

The doorbell interrupted Maurois' protest.

The Kid spun to the girl.

"You do the talking—and no wise breaks!"

She got up from the floor and went to the passageway.

"Who is there?" she called.

The landlady's voice, stern and wrathful:

"Another sound, Mrs. Almad, and I shall call the police. This is disgraceful!"

I wondered what she would have thought if she had opened the unlocked door and taken a look at her apartment—furniture whittled and gutted; a dead man—the noise of whose dying had brought her up here this second time— lying in the middle of the litter.

I wondered—I took a chance.

"Aw, go jump down the sewer!" I told her.

A gasp, and we heard no more from her. I hoped she was speeding her injured feelings to the telephone. I might need the police she had mentioned.

The Kid's gun was out. For a while it was a toss-up. I would lie down beside Billie, or I wouldn't. If I could have been knifed quietly, I would have gone. But nobody was behind me. The Kid knew I wouldn't stand still and quiet while he carved me. He didn't want any more racket than necessary, now that the jewels were on hand.

"Keep your clam shut or I'll shut it for you!" was the worst I got out of it.

The Kid turned to the Frenchman again. The Frenchman had used the time spent in this side-play to pocket the gems.

"Either we divvy here and now, or I carry the stuff," the Kid announced. "There's two of you to see I don't take a Micky Finn on you."

"But, Kid, we cannot stay here! Is not the landlady even now calling the police? We will go elsewhere to divide. Why cannot you trust me when you are with me?"

Two steps put the Kid between the door and both Maurois and Big Chin. One of the Kid's hands held the gun he had flashed on me. The other was conveniently placed to his other gun.

"Nothing stirring!" he said through his nose. "My cut of them stones don't go out of here in nobody else's kick. If you want to split 'em here, good enough. If you don't, I'll do the carrying. That's flat!"

"But the police!"

"You worry about them. I'm taking one thing at a time, and it's the stones right now."

A vein came out blue in the Frenchman's forehead. His small body was rigid. He was trying to collect enough courage to swap shots with the Kid. He knew, and the Kid knew, that one of them was going to have all the stuff when the curtain came down. They had started off by double-crossing each other. They weren't likely to change their habits. One would have the stones in the end. The other would have nothing—except maybe a burial.

Big Chin didn't count. He was too simple a thug to last long in his present company. If he had known anything, he would have used one of his guns on each of them right now. Instead, he continued to cover me, trying to watch them out of the tail of his eye.

The woman stood near the door, where she had gone to talk to the landlady. She was staring at the Frenchman and the Kid. I wasted precious minutes that seemed to run into hours trying to catch her eye. I finally got it.

I looked at the light-switch, only a foot from her. I looked at her. I looked at the switch again. At her. At the switch.

She got me. Her hand crept sidewise along the wall.

I looked at the two principal players in this button-button game.

The Kid's eyes were dead—and deadly—circles. Maurois' one open eye was watery. He couldn't make the grade. He put a hand in his pocket and brought out the silk bag.

The woman's brown finger topped the light-button. God knows she was nothing to gamble on, but I had no choice. I had to be in motion when the lights went. Big Chin would pump metal. I had to trust Inés not to balk. If she did, my name was Denis.

Her nail whitened.

I went for Maurois.

Darkness—streaked with orange and blue—filled with noise.

My arms had Maurois. We crashed down on dead Billie. I twisted around, kicking the Frenchman's face. Loosened one arm. Caught one of his. His other hand gouged at my face. That told me the bag was in the one I held. Clawing fingers tore my mouth. I put my teeth in them and kept them there. One of my knees was on his face. I put my weight on it. My teeth still held his hand. Both of my hands were free to get the bag.

Not nice, this work, but effective.

The room was the inside of a black drum on which a giant was beating the long roll. Four guns worked together in a prolonged throbbing roar.

Maurois' fingernails dug into my thumb. I had to open my mouth—let his hand escape. One of my hands found the bag. He wouldn't let go. I screwed his thumb. He cried out. I had the bag.

I tried to leave him then. He grabbed my legs. I kicked at him—missed. He shuddered twice—and stopped moving. A flying bullet had hit him, I took it. Rolling over to the floor, snuggling close to him, I ran a hand over him. A hard bulge came under my hand. I put my hand in his pocket and took back my gun.

On hands and knees—one fist around my gun, the other clutching the silk sack of jewels—I turned to where the door to the next room should have been. A foot wrong, I corrected my course. As I went through the door, the racket in the room behind me stopped.

CHAPTER XII

Huddled close to the wall inside the door, I stowed the silk
bag away, and regretted that I hadn't stayed plastered to the
floor behind the Frenchman. This room was dark. It hadn't
been dark when the woman switched off the sitting-room
lights. Every room in the apartment had been lighted then.
All were dark now. Not knowing who had darkened them, I
didn't like it.

No sounds came from the room I had quit.

The rustle of gently falling rain came from an open window
that I couldn't see, off to one side.

Another sound came from behind me. The muffled tattoo
of teeth on teeth.

That cheered me. Inés the scary, of course. She had left the
sitting-room in the dark and put out the rest of the lights.
Maybe nobody else was behind me.

Breathing quietly through wide-open mouth, I waited. I
couldn't hunt for the woman in the dark without making
noises. Maurois and the Kid had strewn furniture and parts of
furniture everywhere. I wished I knew if she was holding a
gun. I didn't want to have her spraying me.

Not knowing, I waited where I was.

Her teeth clicked on for minutes.

Something moved in the sitting-room. A gun thundered.

"Inés!" I hissed toward the chattering teeth.

No answer. Furniture scraped in the sitting-room. Two
guns went off together. A groaning broke out.

"I've got the stuff," I whispered under cover of the groaning.

That brought an answer.

"Jerry! Ah, come here to me!"

The groans went on, but fainter, in the other room. I
crawled toward the woman's voice. I went on hands and
knees, bumping as carefully as possible against things. I
couldn't see anything. Midway, I put a hand down on a soggy
bundle of fur—the late purple Frana. I went on.

Inés touched my shoulder with an eager hand.

"Give them to me," were her first words.

I grinned at her in the dark, patted her hand, found her
head, and put my mouth to her ear.

"Let's get back in the bedroom," I breathed, paying no attention to her request for the loot. "The Kid will be coming." I didn't doubt that he had bested Big Chin. "We can handle him better in the bedroom."

I wanted to receive him in a room with only one door.

She led me—both of us on hands and knees—to the bedroom. I did what thinking seemed necessary as we crawled. The Kid couldn't know yet how the Frenchman and I had come out. If he guessed, he would guess that the Frenchman had survived. He would be likely to put me in the chump class with Billie, and think the Frenchman could handle me. The chances were that he had got Big Chin, and knew it by now. It was black as black in the sitting-room, but he must know by now that he was the only living thing there.

He blocked the only exit from the apartment. He would think, then, that Inés and Maurois were still alive in it, with the spoils. What would he do about it? There was no pretense of partnership now. That had gone with the lights. The Kid was after the stones. The Kid was after them alone.

I'm no wizard at guessing the other guy's next move. But my idea was that the Kid would be on his way after us, soon. He knew—he must know—that the police were coming; but I had him doped as crazy enough to disregard the police until they appeared. He'd figure that there would be only a couple of them—prepared for nothing more violent than a drinking-party. He could handle them—or he would think he could. Meanwhile, he would come after the stones.

The woman and I reached the bedroom, the room farthest back in the apartment, a room with only one door. I heard her fumbling with the door, trying to close it. I couldn't see, but I got my foot in the way.

"Leave it open," I whispered.

I didn't want to shut the Kid out. I wanted to take him in.

On my belly, I crawled back to the door, felt for my watch, and propped it on the sill, in the angle between door and frame. I wriggled back from it until I was six or eight feet away, looking diagonally across the open doorway at the watch's luminous dial.

The phosphorescent numbers could not be seen from the other side of the door. They faced me. Anybody who came through the door—unless he jumped—must, if only for a split-second, put some part of himself between me and the watch.

On my belly, my gun cocked, its butt steady on the floor, I waited for the faint light to be blotted out.

I waited a time. Pessimism: perhaps he wasn't coming; perhaps I would have to go after him; perhaps he would run out, and I would lose him after all my trouble.

Inés, beside me, breathed quaveringly in my ear, and shivered.

"Don't touch me," I growled at her as she tried to cuddle against me.

She was shaking my arm.

Glass broke in the next room.

Silence.

The luminous patches on the watch burnt my eyes. I couldn't afford to blink. A foot could pass the dial while I was blinking. I couldn't afford to blink, but I had to blink. I blinked. I couldn't tell whether something had passed the watch or not. I had to blink again. Tried to hold my eyes stiffly opened. Failed. I almost shot at the third blink. I could have sworn something had gone between me and the watch.

The Kid, whatever he was up to, made no sound.

The dark woman began to sob beside me. Throat noises that could guide bullets.

I lumped her with my eyes and cursed the lot—not aloud, but from the heart.

My eyes smarted. Moisture filmed them. I blinked it away, losing sight of the watch for precious instants. The butt of my gun was slimy with my hand's sweat. I was thoroughly uncomfortable, inside and out.

Gunpowder burned at my face.

A screaming maniac of a woman was crawling all over me.

My bullet hit nothing lower than the ceiling.

I flung, maybe kicked, the woman off, and snaked backward. She moaned somewhere to one side. I couldn't see the Kid—couldn't hear him. The watch was visible again, farther away. A rustling.

The watch vanished.

I fired at it.

Two points of light near the floor gave out fire and thunder.

My gun-barrel as close to the floor as I could hold it, I fired between those points. Twice.

Twin flames struck at me again.

My right hand went numb. My left took the gun. I sped two more bullets on their way. That left one in my gun.

I don't know what I did with it. My head filled up with funny notions. There wasn't any room. There wasn't any darkness. There wasn't anything. . . .

I opened my eyes in dim light. I was on my back. Beside me the dark woman knelt, shivering and sniffling. Her hands were busy—in my clothes.

One of them came out of my vest with the jewel-bag.

Coming to life, I grabbed her arm. She squealed as if I were a stirring corpse. I got the bag again.

"Give them back, Jerry," she wailed, trying frantically to pull my fingers loose. "They are my things. Give them!"

Sitting up, I looked around.

Beside me lay a shattered bedside lamp, whose fall—caused by carelessness with my feet, or one of the Kid's bullets—had KO'd me. Across the room, face down, arms spread in a crucified posture, the Whosis Kid sprawled. He was dead.

From the front of the apartment—almost indistinguishable from the throbbing in my head—came the pounding of heavy blows. The police were kicking down the unlocked door.

The woman went quiet. I whipped my head around. The knife stung my cheek—put a slit in the lapel of my coat. I took it away from her.

There was no sense to this. The police were already here. I humored her, pretending a sudden coming to full consciousness.

"Oh, it's you!" I said. "Here they are."

I handed her the silk bag of jewels just as the first policeman came into the room.

CHAPTER XIII

I didn't see Inés again before she was taken back East to be hit with a life-sentence in the Massachusetts big house. Neither of the policemen who crashed into her apartment that night knew me. The woman and I were separated before I ran into anyone who did know me, which gave me an opportunity to arrange that she would not be tipped off to my identity. The most difficult part of the performance was to keep myself out of the newspapers, since I had to tell the coroner's jury about the deaths of Billie, Big Chin, Maurois and the Whosis Kid. But I managed it. So far as I know, the dark woman still thinks I am Jerry Young, the bootlegger.

The Old Man talked to her before she left San Francisco. Fitting together what he got from her and what the Boston branch got, the history runs like this:

A Boston jeweler named Tunnicliffe had a trusted employee named Binder. Binder fell in with a dark woman named Inés Almad. The dark woman, in turn, had a couple of shifty friends—a Frenchman named Maurois, and a native of Boston whose name was either Carey or Cory, but who was better known as the Whosis Kid. Out of that sort of combination almost anything was more than likely to come.

What came was a scheme. The faithful Binder—part of whose duties it was to open the shop in the morning and close it at night—was to pick out the richest of the unset stones bought for the holiday trade, carry them off with him one evening, and turn them over to Inés. She was to turn them into money.

To cover up Binder's theft, the Whosis Kid and the Frenchman were to rob the jeweler's shop immediately after the door was opened the following morning. Binder and the porter—who would not notice the absence of the most valuable pieces from the stock—would be the only ones in the shop. The robbers would take whatever they could get. In addition to their pickings, they were to be paid two hundred and fifty dollars apiece, and in case either was caught later, Binder could be counted on not to identify them.

That was the scheme as Binder knew it. There were angles he didn't suspect.

Between Inés, Maurois and the Kid there was another agreement. She was to leave for Chicago with the stones as soon as Binder gave them to her, and wait there for Maurois and the Kid. She and the Frenchman would have been satisfied to run off and let Binder hold the sack. The Whosis Kid insisted that the hold-up go through as planned, and that the foolish Binder be killed. Binder knew too much about them, the Kid said, and he would squawk his head off as soon as he learned he had been double-crossed.

The Kid had his way, and he had shot Binder.

Then had come the sweet mess of quadruple and sextuple crossing that had led all three into calamity: the woman's private agreements with the Kid and Maurois—to meet one in St. Louis and the other in New Orleans—and her flight alone with the loot to San Francisco.

Billie was an innocent bystander—or almost. A lumber-handler Inés had run into somewhere, and picked up as a sort of cushion against the rough spots along the rocky road she traveled.

The Scorched Face

W E EXPECTED them home yesterday," Alfred Banbrock wound up his story. "When they had not come by this morning, my wife telephoned Mrs. Walden. Mrs. Walden said they had not been down there—had not been expected, in fact."

"On the face of it, then," I suggested, "it seems that your daughters went away of their own accord, and are staying away on their own accord?"

Banbrock nodded gravely. Tired muscles sagged in his fleshy face.

"It would seem so," he agreed. "That is why I came to your agency for help instead of going to the police."

"Have they ever disappeared before?"

"No. If you read the papers and magazines, you've no doubt seen hints that the younger generation is given to ir-regularity. My daughters came and went pretty much as they pleased. But, though I can't say I ever knew what they were up to, we always knew where they were in a general way."

"Can you think of any reason for their going like this?"

He shook his weary head.

"Any recent quarrels?" I probed.

"N—" He changed it to: "Yes—although I didn't attach any importance to it, and wouldn't have recalled it if you hadn't jogged my memory. It was Thursday evening—the evening before they went away."

"And it was about—?"

"Money, of course. We never disagreed over anything else. I gave each of my daughters an adequate allowance—perhaps a very liberal one. Nor did I keep them strictly within it. There were few months in which they didn't exceed it. Thursday evening they asked for an amount of money even more than usual in excess of what two girls should need. I wouldn't give it to them, though I finally did give them a somewhat smaller amount. We didn't exactly quarrel—not in the strict sense of the word—but there was a certain lack of friendliness between us."

"And it was after this disagreement that they said they were going down to Mrs. Walden's, in Monterey, for the week-end?"

"Possibly. I'm not sure of that point. I don't think I heard of it until the next morning, but they may have told my wife before that. I shall ask her if you wish."

"And you know of no other possible reason for their running away?"

"None. I can't think that our dispute over money—by no means an unusual one—had anything to do with it."

"What does their mother think?"

"Their mother is dead," Banbrock corrected me. "My wife is their stepmother. She is only two years older than Myra, my older daughter. She is as much at sea as I."

"Did your daughters and their stepmother get along all right together?"

"Yes! Yes! Excellently! If there was a division in the family, I usually found them standing together against me."

"Your daughters left Friday afternoon?"

"At noon, or a few minutes after. They were going to drive down."

"The car, of course, is still missing?"

"Naturally."

"What was it?"

"A Locomobile, with a special cabriolet body. Black."

"You can give me the license and engine numbers?"

"I think so."

He turned in his chair to the big roll-top desk that hid a quarter of one office wall, fumbled with papers in a compartment, and read the numbers over his shoulder to me. I put them on the back of an envelope.

"I'm going to have this car put on the police department list of stolen machines," I told him. "It can be done without mentioning your daughters. The police bulletin might find the car for us. That would help us find your daughters."

"Very well," he agreed, "if it can be done without disagreeable publicity. As I told you at first, I don't want any more advertising than is absolutely necessary—unless it becomes likely that harm has come to the girls."

I nodded understanding, and got up.

"I want to go out and talk to your wife," I said. "Is she home now?"

"Yes, I think so. I'll phone her and tell her you are coming."

II

In a big limestone fortress on top a hill in Sea Cliff, looking down on ocean and bay, I had my talk with Mrs. Banbrock. She was a tall dark girl of not more than twenty-two years, inclined to plumpness.

She couldn't tell me anything her husband hadn't at least mentioned, but she could give me finer details.

I got descriptions of the two girls:

Myra—20 years old; 5 feet 8 inches; 150 pounds; athletic; brisk, almost masculine manner and carriage; bobbed brown hair; brown eyes; medium complexion; square face, with large chin and short nose; scar over left ear, concealed by hair; fond of horses and all outdoor sports. When she left the house she wore a blue and green wool dress, small blue hat, short black seal coat, and black slippers.

Ruth—18 years; 5 feet 4 inches; 105 pounds; brown eyes; brown bobbed hair; medium complexion; small oval face; quiet, timid, inclined to lean on her more forceful sister. When last seen she had worn a tobacco-brown coat trimmed with brown fur over a grey silk dress, and a wide brown hat.

I got two photographs of each girl, and an additional snapshot of Myra standing in front of the cabriolet. I got a list of the things they had taken with them—such things as would naturally be taken on a week-end visit. What I valued most of what I got was a list of their friends, relatives, and other acquaintances, so far as Mrs. Banbrock knew them.

"Did they mention Mrs. Walden's invitation before their quarrel with Mr. Banbrock?" I asked, when I had my lists stowed away.

"I don't think so," Mrs. Banbrock said thoughtfully. "I didn't connect the two things at all. They didn't really quarrel with their father, you know. It wasn't harsh enough to be called a quarrel."

"Did you see them when they left?"

"Assuredly! They left at about half-past twelve Friday afternoon. They kissed me as usual when they went, and there was certainly nothing in their manner to suggest anything out of the ordinary."

"You've no idea at all where they might have gone?"

"None."

"Can't even make a guess?"

"I can't. Among the names and addresses I have given you are some of friends and relatives of the girls in other cities. They may have gone to one of those. Do you think we should—?"

"I'll take care of that," I promised. "Could you pick out one or two of them as the most likely places for the girls to have gone?"

She wouldn't try it.

"No," she said positively, "I could not."

From this interview I went back to the Agency, and put the Agency machinery in motion; arranging to have operatives from some of the Continental's other branches call on the out-of-town names on my list; having the missing Locomobile put on the police department list; turning one photograph of each girl over to a photographer to be copied.

That done, I set out to talk to the persons on the list Mrs. Banbrock had given me. My first call was on a Constance Delee, in an apartment building on Post Street. I saw a maid. The maid said Miss Delee was out of town. She wouldn't tell me where her mistress was, or when she would be back.

From there I went up on Van Ness Avenue and found a Wayne Ferris in an automobile salesroom: a sleek-haired young man whose very nice manners and clothes completely hid anything else—brains for instance—he might have had. He was very willing to help me, and he knew nothing. It took him a long time to tell me so. A nice boy.

Another blank: "Mrs. Scott is in Honolulu."

In a real estate office on Montgomery Street I found my next one—another sleek, stylish, smooth-haired young man with nice manners and nice clothes. His name was Raymond Elwood. I would have thought him a no more distant relative of Ferris than cousin if I hadn't known that the world—

especially the dancing, teaing world—was full of their sort. I learned nothing from him.

Then I drew some more blanks: "Out of town," "Shopping," "I don't know where you can find him."

I found one more of the Banbrock girls' friends before I called it a day. Her name was Mrs. Stewart Correll. She lived in Presidio Terrace, not far from the Banbrocks. She was a small woman, or girl, of about Mrs. Banbrock's age. A little fluffy blonde person with wide eyes of that particular blue which always looks honest and candid no matter what is going on behind it.

"I haven't seen either Ruth or Myra for two weeks or more," she said in answer to my question.

"At that time—the last time you saw them—did either say anything about going away?"

"No."

Her eyes were wide and frank. A little muscle twitched in her upper lip.

"And you've no idea where they might have gone?"

"No."

Her fingers were rolling her lace handkerchief into a little ball.

"Have you heard from them since you last saw them?"

"No."

She moistened her mouth before she said it.

"Will you give me the names and addresses of all the people you know who were also known by the Banbrock girls?"

"Why—? Is there—?"

"There's a chance that some of them may have seen them more recently than you," I explained. "Or may even have seen them since Friday."

Without enthusiasm, she gave me a dozen names. All were already on my list. Twice she hesitated as if about to speak a name she did not want to speak. Her eyes stayed on mine, wide and honest. Her fingers, no longer balling the handkerchief, picked at the cloth of her skirt.

I didn't pretend to believe her. But my feet weren't solidly enough on the ground for me to put her on the grill. I gave her a promise before I left, one that she could get a threat out of if she liked.

"Thanks, very much," I said. "I know it's hard to remember things exactly. If I run across anything that will help your memory, I'll be back to let you know about it."

"Wha—? Yes, do!" she said.

Walking away from the house, I turned my head to look back just before I passed out of sight. A curtain swung into place at a second-floor window. The street lights weren't bright enough for me to be sure the curtain had swung in front of a blonde head.

My watch told me it was nine-thirty: too late to line up any more of the girls' friends. I went home, wrote my report for the day, and turned in, thinking more about Mrs. Correll than about the girls.

She seemed worth an investigation.

III

Some telegraphic reports were in when I got to the office the next morning. None was of any value. Investigation of the names and addresses in other cities had revealed nothing. An investigation in Monterey had established reasonably—which is about as well as anything is ever established in the detecting business—that the girls had not been there recently; that the Locomobile had not been there.

The early editions of the afternoon papers were on the street when I went out to get some breakfast before taking up the grind where I had dropped it the previous night. I bought a paper to prop behind my grapefruit.

It spoiled my breakfast for me.

BANKER'S WIFE SUICIDE

Mrs. Stewart Correll, wife of the vice-president of the Golden Gate Trust Company, was found dead early this morning by the maid in her bedroom, in her home in Presidio Terrace. A bottle believed to have contained poison was on the floor beside the bed.

The dead woman's husband could give no reason for his wife's suicide. He said she had not seemed depressed or . . .

I gave my eggs and toast a quick play, put my coffee down in a lump, and got going.

At the Correll residence I had to do a lot of talking before I could get to Correll. He was a tall, slim man of less than thirty-five, with a sallow, nervous face and blue eyes that fidgeted.

"I'm sorry to disturb you at a time like this," I apologized when I had finally insisted my way into his presence. "I won't take up more of your time than necessary. I am an operative of the Continental Detective Agency. I have been trying to find Ruth and Myra Banbrock, who disappeared several days ago. You know them, I think."

"Yes," he said without interest. "I know them."

"You knew they had disappeared?"

"No." His eyes switched from a chair to a rug. "Why should I?"

"Have you seen either of them recently?" I asked, ignoring his question.

"Last week—Wednesday, I think. They were just leaving—standing at the door talking to my wife—when I came home from the bank."

"Didn't your wife say anything to you about their vanishing?"

"No. Really, I can't tell you anything about the Misses Banbrock. If you'll excuse me—"

"Just a moment longer," I said. "I wouldn't have bothered you if it hadn't been necessary. I was here last night, to question Mrs. Correll. She seemed nervous. My impression was that some of her answers to my questions were—uh—evasive. I want—"

He was up out of his chair. His face was red in front of mine.

"You!" he cried. "I can thank you for—"

"Now, Mr. Correll," I tried to quiet him, "there's no use—"

But he had himself all worked up.

"You drove my wife to her death," he accused me. "You killed her with your damned prying—with your bulldozing threats; with your—"

That was silly. I felt sorry for this young man whose wife had killed herself. Apart from that, I had work to do. I tightened the screws.

"We won't argue, Correll," I told him. "The point is that I came here to see if your wife could tell me anything about the

Banbrocks. She told me less than the truth. Later, she committed suicide. I want to know why. Come through for me,
and I'll do what I can to keep the papers and the public from
linking her death with the girls' disappearance."

"Linking her death with their disappearance?" he exclaimed. "That's absurd!"

"Maybe—but the connection is there!" I hammered away
at him. I felt sorry for him, but I had work to do. "It's there.
If you'll give it to me, maybe it won't have to be advertised.
I'm going to get it, though. You give it to me—or I'll go
after it out in the open."

For a moment I thought he was going to take a poke at
me. I wouldn't have blamed him. His body stiffened—then
sagged, and he dropped back into his chair. His eyes fidgeted
away from mine.

"There's nothing I can tell," he mumbled. "When her
maid went to her room to call her this morning, she was
dead. There was no message, no reason, nothing."

"Did you see her last night?"

"No. I was not home for dinner. I came in late and went
straight to my own room, not wanting to disturb her. I hadn't
seen her since I left the house that morning."

"Did she seem disturbed or worried then?"

"No."

"Why do you think she did it?"

"My God, man, I don't know! I've thought and thought,
but I don't know!"

"Health?"

"She seemed well. She was never ill, never complained."

"Any recent quarrels?"

"We never quarreled—never in the year and a half we have
been married!"

"Financial trouble?"

He shook his head without speaking or looking up from
the floor.

"Any other worry?"

He shook his head again.

"Did the maid notice anything peculiar in her behavior last
night?"

"Nothing."

"Have you looked through her things—for papers, letters?"

"Yes—and found nothing." He raised his head to look at me. "The only thing"—he spoke very slowly—"there was a little pile of ashes in the grate in her room, as if she had burned papers, or letters."

Correl held nothing more for me—nothing I could get out of him, anyway.

The girl at the front gate in Alfred Banbrock's Shoreman's Building suite told me he was *in conference.* I sent my name in. He came out of conference to take me into his private office. His tired face was full of questions.

I didn't keep him waiting for the answers. He was a grown man. I didn't edge around the bad news.

"Things have taken a bad break," I said as soon as we were locked in together. "I think we'll have to go to the police and newspapers for help. A Mrs. Correll, a friend of your daughters, lied to me when I questioned her yesterday. Last night she committed suicide."

"Irma Correll? Suicide?"

"You knew her?"

"Yes! Intimately! She was—that is, she was a close friend of my wife and daughters. She killed herself?"

"Yes. Poison. Last night. Where does she fit in with your daughters' disappearance?"

"Where?" he repeated. "I don't know. Must she fit in?"

"I think she must. She told me she hadn't seen your daughters for a couple of weeks. Her husband told me just now that they were talking to her when he came home from the bank last Wednesday afternoon. She seemed nervous when I questioned her. She killed herself shortly afterward. There's hardly a doubt that she fits in somewhere."

"And that means—?"

"That means," I finished for him, "that your daughters may be perfectly safe, but that we can't afford to gamble on that possibility."

"You think harm has come to them?"

"I don't think anything," I evaded, "except that with a death tied up closely with their going, we can't afford to play around."

Banbrock got his attorney on the phone—a pink-faced, white-haired old boy named Norwall, who had the reputation of knowing more about corporations than all the Morgans, but who hadn't the least idea as to what police procedure was all about—and told him to meet us at the Hall of Justice.

We spent an hour and a half there, getting the police turned loose on the affair, and giving the newspapers what we wanted them to have. That was plenty of dope on the girls, plenty of photographs and so forth; but nothing about the connection between them and Mrs. Correll. Of course we let the police in on that angle.

IV

After Banbrock and his attorney had gone away together, I went back to the detectives' assembly room to chew over the job with Pat Reddy, the police sleuth assigned to it.

Pat was the youngest member of the detective bureau—a big blond Irishman who went in for the spectacular in his lazy way.

A couple of years ago he was a new copper, pounding his feet in harness on a hillside beat. One night he tagged an automobile that was parked in front of a fireplug. The owner came out just then and gave him an argument. She was Althea Wallach, only and spoiled daughter of the owner of the Wallach Coffee Company—a slim, reckless youngster with hot eyes. She must have told Pat plenty. He took her over to the station and dumped her in a cell.

Old Wallach, so the story goes, showed up the next morning with a full head of steam and half the lawyers in San Francisco. But Pat made his charge stick, and the girl was fined. Old Wallach did everything but take a punch at Pat in the corridor afterward. Pat grinned his sleepy grin at the coffee importer, and drawled:

"You better lay off me—or I'll stop drinking your coffee."

That crack got into most of the newspapers in the country, and even into a Broadway show.

But Pat didn't stop with the snappy come-back. Three days later he and Althea Wallach went over to Alameda and got themselves married. I was in on that part. I happened to be on the ferry they took, and they dragged me along to see the deed done.

Old Wallach immediately disowned his daughter, but that didn't seem to worry anybody else. Pat went on pounding his beat, but, now that he was conspicuous, it wasn't long before his qualities were noticed. He was boosted into the detective bureau. Old Wallach relented before he died, and left Althea both of his millions.

Pat took the afternoon off to go to the funeral, and went back to work that night, catching a wagonload of gunmen. He kept on working. I don't know what his wife did with her money, but Pat didn't even improve the quality of his cigars—though he should have. He lived now in the Wallach mansion, true enough, and now and then on rainy mornings he would be driven down to the Hall in a Hispano-Suiza brougham; but there was no difference in him beyond that.

That was the big blond Irishman who sat across a desk from me in the assembly room and fumigated me with something shaped like a cigar.

He took the cigar-like thing out of his mouth presently, and spoke through the fumes.

"This Correll woman you think's tied up with the Banbrocks—she was stuck-up a couple of months back and nicked for eight hundred dollars. Know that?"

I hadn't known it.

"Lose anything besides cash?" I asked.

"No."

"You believe it?"

He grinned.

"That's the point," he said. "We didn't catch the bird who did it. With women who lose things that way—especially money—it's always a question whether it's a hold-up or a hold-out."

He teased some more poison-gas out of the cigar-thing, and added:

"The hold-up might have been on the level, though. What are you figuring on doing now?"

"Let's go up to the Agency and see if anything new has turned up. Then I'd like to talk to Mrs. Banbrock again. Maybe she can tell us something about the Correll woman."

At the office I found that reports had come in on the rest of the out-of-town names and addresses. Apparently none of these people knew anything about the girls' whereabouts. Reddy and I went on up to Sea Cliff to the Banbrock home.

Banbrock had telephoned the news of Mrs. Correll's death to his wife, and she had read the papers. She told us she could think of no reason for the suicide. She could imagine no possible connection between the suicide and her stepdaughters' vanishing.

"Mrs. Correll seemed as nearly contented and happy as usual the last time I saw her, two or three weeks ago," Mrs. Banbrock said. "Of course she was by nature inclined to be dissatisfied with things, but not to the extent of doing a thing like this."

"Do you know of any trouble between her and her husband?"

"No. So far as I know, they were happy, though—"

She broke off. Hesitancy, embarrassment showed in her dark eyes.

"Though?" I repeated.

"If I don't tell you now, you'll think I am hiding something," she said, flushing, and laughing a little laugh that held more nervousness than amusement. "It hasn't any bearing, but I was always just a little jealous of Irma. She and my husband were—well, everyone thought they would marry. That was a little before he and I married. I never let it show, and I dare say it was a foolish idea, but I always had a suspicion that Irma married Stewart more in pique than for any other reason, and that she was still fond of Alfred—Mr. Banbrock."

"Was there anything definite to make you think that?"

"No, nothing—really! I never thoroughly believed it. It was just a sort of vague feeling. Cattiness, no doubt, more than anything else."

It was getting along toward evening when Pat and I left the Banbrock house. Before we knocked off for the day, I called up the Old Man—the Continental's San Francisco branch manager, and therefore my boss—and asked him to sic an operative on Irma Correll's past.

I took a look at the morning papers—thanks to their custom of appearing almost as soon as the sun is out of sight—

before I went to bed. They had given our job a good spread. All the facts except those having to do with the Correll angle were there, plus photographs, and the usual assortment of guesses and similar garbage.

The following morning I went after the friends of the missing girls to whom I had not yet talked. I found some of them, and got nothing of value from them. Late in the morning I telephoned the office to see if anything new had turned up.

It had.

"We've just had a call from the sheriff's office at Martinez," the Old Man told me. "An Italian grapegrower near Knob Valley picked up a charred photograph a couple of days ago, and recognized it as Ruth Banbrock when he saw her picture in this morning's paper. Will you get up there? A deputy sheriff and the Italian are waiting for you in the Knob Valley marshal's office."

"I'm on my way," I said.

At the ferry building I used the four minutes before my boat left trying to get Pat Reddy on the phone, with no success.

Knob Valley is a town of less than a thousand people, a dreary, dirty town in Contra Costa county. A San Francisco–Sacramento local set me down there while the afternoon was still young.

I knew the marshal slightly—Tom Orth. I found two men in the office with him. Orth introduced us. Abner Paget, a gawky man of forty-something, with a slack chin, scrawny face, and pale intelligent eyes, was the deputy sheriff. Gio Cereghino, the Italian grapegrower, was a small, nut-brown man with strong yellow teeth that showed in an everlasting smile under his black mustache, and soft brown eyes.

Paget showed me the photograph. A scorched piece of paper the size of a half-dollar, apparently all that had not been burned of the original picture. It was Ruth Banbrock's face. There was little room for doubting that. She had a peculiarly excited—almost drunken—look, and her eyes were larger than in the other pictures of her I had seen. But it was her face.

"He says he found it day 'fore yesterday," Paget explained dryly, nodding at the Italian. "The wind blew it against his foot when he was walkin' up a piece of road near his place. He picked it up an' stuck it in his pocket, he says, for no spe cial reason, I guess, except maybe that guineas like pictures."

He paused to regard the Italian meditatively. The Italian nodded his head in vigorous affirmation.

"Anyways," the deputy sheriff went on, "he was in town this mornin', an' seen the pictures in the papers from 'Frisco. So he come in here an' told Tom about it. Tom an' me decided the best thing was to phone your agency—since the papers said you was workin' on it."

I looked at the Italian.

Paget, reading my mind, explained:

"Cereghino lives over in the hills. Got a grape-ranch there. Been around here five or six years, an' ain't killed nobody that I know of."

"Remember the place where you found the picture?" I asked the Italian.

His grin broadened under his mustache, and his head went up and down.

"For sure, I remember that place."

"Let's go there," I suggested to Paget.

"Right. Comin' along, Tom?"

The marshal said he couldn't. He had something to do in town. Cereghino, Paget and I went out and got into a dusty Ford that the deputy sheriff drove.

We rode for nearly an hour, along a county road that bent up the slope of Mount Diablo. After a while, at a word from the Italian, we left the county road for a dustier and ruttier one.

A mile of this one.

"This place," Cereghino said.

Paget stopped the Ford. We got out in a clearing. The trees and bushes that had crowded the road retreated here for twenty feet or so on either side, leaving a little dusty circle in the woods.

"About this place," the Italian was saying. "I think by this stump. But between that bend ahead and that one behind, I know for sure."

v

Paget was a countryman. I am not. I waited for him to move.

He looked around the clearing, slowly, standing still between the Italian and me. His pale eyes lighted presently. He went around the Ford to the far side of the clearing. Cereghino and I followed.

Near the fringe of brush at the edge of the clearing, the scrawny deputy stopped to grunt at the ground. The wheel-marks of an automobile were there. A car had turned around here.

Paget went on into the woods. The Italian kept close to his heels. I brought up the rear. Paget was following some sort of track. I couldn't see it, either because he and the Italian blotted it out ahead of me, or because I'm a shine Indian.

We went back quite a way.

Paget stopped. The Italian stopped.

Paget said, "Uh-huh," as if he had found an expected thing.

The Italian said something with the name of God in it.

I trampled a bush, coming beside them to see what they saw.

I saw it.

At the base of a tree, on her side, her knees drawn up close to her body, a girl was dead.

She wasn't nice to see. Birds had been at her.

A tobacco-brown coat was half on, half off her shoulders. I knew she was Ruth Banbrock before I turned her over to look at the side of her face the ground had saved from the birds.

Cereghino stood watching me while I examined the girl. His face was mournful in a calm way. The deputy sheriff paid little attention to the body. He was off in the brush, moving around, looking at the ground.

He came back as I finished my examination.

"Shot," I told him, "once in the right temple. Before that, I think, there was a fight. There are marks on the arm that was under her body. There's nothing on her—no jewelry, money—nothing."

"That goes," Paget said. "Two women got out of the car back in the clearin', an' came here. Could've been three women—if the others carried this one. Can't make out how many went back. One of 'em was larger than this one. There was a scuffle here. Find the gun?"

"No," I said.

"Neither did I. It went away in the car, then. There's what's left of a fire over there." He ducked his head to the left. "Paper an' rags burnt. Not enough left to do us any good. I reckon the photo Cereghino found blew away from the fire. Late Friday, I'd put it, or maybe Saturday mornin'. . . . No nearer than that."

I took the deputy sheriff's word for it. He seemed to know his stuff.

"Come here. I'll show you somethin'," he said, and led me over to a little black pile of ashes.

He hadn't anything to show me. He wanted to talk to me away from the Italian's ears.

"I think the guinea's all right," he said, "but I reckon I'd best hold him a while to make sure. This is some way from his place, an' he stuttered a little bit too much tellin' me how he happened to be passin' here. Course, that don't mean nothin' much. All these guineas peddle *vino*, an' I guess that's what brought him out this way. I'll hold him a day or two, anyways."

"Good," I agreed. "This is your country, and you know the people. Can you visit around and see what you can pick up? Whether anybody saw anything? Saw a Locomobile cabriolet? Or anything else? You can get more than I could."

"I'll do that," he promised.

"All right. Then I'll go back to San Francisco now. I suppose you'll want to camp here with the body?"

"Yeah. You drive the Ford back to Knob Valley, an' tell Tom what's what. He'll come or send out. I'll keep the guinea here with me."

Waiting for the next west-bound train out of Knob Valley, I got the office on the telephone. The Old Man was out. I told my story to one of the office men and asked him to get the news to the Old Man as soon as he could.

Everybody was in the office when I got back to San Francisco. Alfred Banbrock, his face a pink-grey that was deader than solid grey could have been. His pink and white old lawyer. Pat Reddy, sprawled on his spine with his feet on another chair. The Old Man, with his gentle eyes behind gold spectacles and his mild smile, hiding the fact that fifty years of sleuthing had left him without any feelings at all on any subject. (Whitey Clayton used to say the Old Man could spit icicles in August.)

Nobody said anything when I came in. I said my say as briefly as possible.

"Then the other woman—the woman who killed Ruth was—?"

Banbrock didn't finish his question. Nobody answered it.

"We don't know what happened," I said after a while. "Your daughter and someone we don't know may have gone there. Your daughter may have been dead before she was taken there. She may have—"

"But Myra!" Banbrock was pulling at his collar with a finger inside. "Where is Myra?"

I couldn't answer that, nor could any of the others.

"You are going up to Knob Valley now?" I asked him.

"Yes, at once. You will come with me?"

I wasn't sorry I could not.

"No. There are things to be done here. I'll give you a note to the marshal. I want you to look carefully at the piece of your daughter's photograph the Italian found—to see if you remember it."

Banbrock and the lawyer left.

VI

Reddy lit one of his awful cigars.

"We found the car," the Old Man said.

"Where?"

"In Sacramento. It was left in a garage there either late Friday night or early Saturday. Foley has gone up to investigate it. And Reddy has uncovered a new angle."

Pat nodded through his smoke.

"A hock-shop dealer came in this morning," Pat said, "and told us that Myra Banbrock and another girl came to his joint last week and hocked a lot of stuff. They gave him phoney names, but he swears one of them was Myra. He recognized her picture as soon as he saw it in the paper. Her companion wasn't Ruth. It was a little blonde."

"Mrs. Correll?"

"Uh-huh. The shark can't swear to that, but I think that's the answer. Some of the jewelry was Myra's, some Ruth's, and some we don't know. I mean we can't prove it belonged to Mrs. Correll—though we will."

"When did all this happen?"

"They soaked the stuff Monday before they went away."

"Have you seen Correll?"

"Uh-huh," Pat said. "I did a lot of talking to him, but the answers weren't worth much. He says he don't know whether any of her jewelry is gone or not, and doesn't care. It was hers, he says, and she could do anything she wanted with it. He was kind of disagreeable. I got along a little better with one of the maids. She says some of Mrs. Correll's pretties disappeared last week. Mrs. Correll said she had lent them to a friend. I'm going to show the stuff the hock-shop has to the maid tomorrow, to see if she can identify it. She didn't know anything else—except that Mrs. Correll was out of the picture for a while on Friday—the day the Banbrock girls went away."

"What do you mean, out of the picture?" I asked.

"She went out late in the morning and didn't show up until somewhere around three the next morning. She and Correll had a row over it, but she wouldn't tell him where she had been."

I liked that. It could mean something.

"And," Pat went on, "Correll has just remembered that his wife had an uncle who went crazy in Pittsburgh in 1902, and that she had a morbid fear of going crazy herself, and that she had often said she would kill herself if she thought she was going crazy. Wasn't it nice of him to remember those things at last? To account for her death?"

"It was," I agreed, "but it doesn't get us anywhere. It doesn't even prove that he knows anything. Now my guess is—"

"To hell with your guess," Pat said, getting up and pushing his hat in place. "Your guesses all sound like a lot of static to me. I'm going home, eat my dinner, read my Bible, and go to bed."

I suppose he did. Anyway, he left us.

We all might as well have spent the next three days in bed for all the profit that came out of our running around. No place we visited, nobody we questioned, added to our knowledge. We were in a blind alley.

We learned that the Locomobile was left in Sacramento by Myra Banbrock, and not by anyone else, but we didn't learn where she went afterward. We learned that some of the jewelry in the pawnshop was Mrs. Correll's. The Locomobile was brought back from Sacramento. Mrs. Correll was buried. Ruth Banbrock was buried. The newspapers found other mysteries. Reddy and I dug and dug, and all we brought up was dirt.

The following Monday brought me close to the end of my rope. There seemed nothing more to do but sit back and hope that the circulars with which we had plastered North America would bring results. Reddy had already been called off and put to running out fresher trails. I hung on because Banbrock wanted me to keep at it so long as there was the shadow of anything to keep at. But by Monday I had worked myself out.

Before going to Banbrock's office to tell him I was licked, I dropped in at the Hall of Justice to hold a wake over the job with Pat Reddy. He was crouched over his desk, writing a report on some other job.

"Hello!" he greeted me, pushing his report away and smearing it with ashes from his cigar. "How do the Banbrock doings?"

"They don't," I admitted. "It doesn't seem possible, with the stack-up what it is, that we should have come to a dead stop! It's there for us, if we can find it. The need of money before both the Banbrock and the Correll calamities: Mrs. Correll's suicide after I had questioned her about the girls; her burning things before she died and the burning of things immediately before or after Ruth Banbrock's death."

"Maybe the trouble is," Pat suggested, "that you're not such a good sleuth."

"Maybe."

We smoked in silence for a minute or two after that insult.

"You understand," Pat said presently, "there doesn't have to be any connection between the Banbrock death and disappearance and the Correll death."

"Maybe not. But there has to be a connection between the Banbrock death and the Banbrock disappearance. There was a connection—in a pawnshop—between the Banbrock and Correll actions before these things. If there is that connection, then—"

I broke off, all full of ideas.

"What's the matter?" Pat asked. "Swallow your gum?"

"Listen!" I let myself get almost enthusiastic. "We've got what happened to three women hooked up together. If we could tie up some more in the same string—I want the names and addresses of all the women and girls in San Francisco who have committed suicide, been murdered, or have disappeared within the past year."

"You think this is a wholesale deal?"

"I think the more we can tie up together, the more lines we'll have to run out. And they can't all lead nowhere. Let's get our list, Pat!"

We spent all the afternoon and most of the night getting it. Its size would have embarrassed the Chamber of Commerce. It looked like a hunk of the telephone book. Things happen in a city in a year. The section devoted to strayed wives and daughters was the largest; suicides next; and even the smallest division—murders—wasn't any too short.

We could check off most of the names against what the police department had already learned of them and their motives, weeding out those positively accounted for in a manner nowise connected with our present interest. The remainder we split into two classes; those of unlikely connection, and those of more possible connection. Even then, the second list was longer than I had expected, or hoped

There were six suicides in it, three murders, and twenty-one disappearances.

Reddy had other work to do. I put the list in my pocket and went calling.

VII

For four days I ground at the list. I hunted, found, questioned, and investigated friends and relatives of the women and girls on my list. My questions all hit in the same direction. Had she been acquainted with Myra Banbrock? Ruth? Mrs. Correll? Had she been in need of money before her death or disappearance? Had she destroyed anything before her death or disappearance? Had she known any of the other women on my list?

Three times I drew yeses.

Sylvia Varney, a girl of twenty, who had killed herself on November 5th, had drawn six hundred dollars from the bank the week before her death. No one in her family could say what she had done with the money. A friend of Sylvia Varney's—Ada Youngman, a married woman of twenty-five or -six—had disappeared on December 2nd, and was still gone. The Varney girl had been at Mrs. Youngman's home an hour before she—the Varney girl—killed herself.

Mrs. Dorothy Sawdon, a young widow, had shot herself on the night of January 13th. No trace was found of either the money her husband had left her or the funds of a club whose treasurer she was. A bulky letter her maid remembered having given her that afternoon was never found.

These three women's connection with the Banbrock-Correll affair was sketchy enough. None of them had done anything that isn't done by nine out of ten women who kill themselves or run away. But the troubles of all three had come to a head within the past few months—and all three were women of about the same financial and social position as Mrs. Correll and the Banbrocks.

Finishing my list with no fresh leads, I came back to these three.

I had the names and addresses of sixty-two friends of the Banbrock girls. I set about getting the same sort of catalogue on the three women I was trying to bring into the game. I didn't have to do all the digging myself. Fortunately, there were two or three operatives in the office with nothing else to do just then.

We got something.

Mrs. Sawdon had known Raymond Elwood. Sylvia Varney had known Raymond Elwood. There was nothing to show Mrs. Youngman had known him, but it was likely she had. She and the Varney girl had been thick.

I had already interviewed this Raymond Elwood in connection with the Banbrock girls, but had paid no especial attention to him. I had considered him just one of the sleek-headed, high-polished young men of whom there was quite a few listed.

I went back at him, all interest now. The results were promising.

He had, as I have said, a real estate office on Montgomery Street. We were unable to find a single client he had ever served, or any signs of one's existence. He had an apartment out in the Sunset District, where he lived alone. His local record seemed to go back no farther than ten months, though we couldn't find its definite starting point. Apparently he had no relatives in San Francisco. He belonged to a couple of fashionable clubs. He was vaguely supposed to be "well connected in the East." He spent money.

I couldn't shadow Elwood, having too recently interviewed him. Dick Foley did. Elwood was seldom in his office during the first three days Dick tailed him. He was seldom in the financial district. He visited his clubs, he danced and tea'd and so forth, and each of those three days he visited a house on Telegraph Hill.

The first afternoon Dick had him, Elwood went to the Telegraph Hill house with a tall fair girl from Burlingame. The second day—in the evening—with a plump young woman who came out of a house out on Broadway. The third evening with a very young girl who seemed to live in the same building as he.

Usually Elwood and his companion spent from three to four hours in the house on Telegraph Hill. Other people—all apparently well-to-do—went in and out of the house while it was under Dick's eye.

I climbed Telegraph Hill to give the house the up-and-down. It was a large house—a big frame house painted egg-yellow. It hung dizzily on a shoulder of the hill, a shoulder that was sharp where rock had been quarried away. The house seemed about to go ski-ing down on the roofs far below.

It had no immediate neighbors. The approach was screened by bushes and trees.

I gave that section of the hill a good strong play, calling at all the houses within shooting distance of the yellow one. Nobody knew anything about it, or about its occupants. The folks on the Hill aren't a curious lot—perhaps because most of them have something to hide on their own account.

My climbing uphill and downhill got me nothing until I succeeded in learning who owned the yellow house. The owner was an estate whose affairs were in the hands of the West Coast Trust Company.

I took my investigations to the trust company, with some satisfaction. The house had been leased eight months ago by Raymond Elwood, acting for a client named T. F. Maxwell.

We couldn't find Maxwell. We couldn't find anybody who knew Maxwell. We couldn't find any evidence that Maxwell was anything but a name.

One of the operatives went up to the yellow house on the hill, and rang the bell for half an hour with no result. We didn't try that again, not wanting to stir things up at this stage.

I made another trip up the hill, house-hunting. I couldn't find a place as near the yellow house as I would have liked, but I succeeded in renting a three-room flat from which the approach to it could be watched.

Dick and I camped in the flat—with Pat Reddy, when he wasn't off on other duties—and watched machines turn into the screened path that led to the egg-tinted house. Afternoon and night there were machines. Most of them carried women. We saw no one we could place as a resident of the house. Elwood came daily, once alone, the other time with women whose faces we couldn't see from our window.

We shadowed some of the visitors away. They were without exception reasonably well off financially, and some were socially prominent. We didn't go up against any of them with talk. Even a carefully planned pretext is as likely as not to tip your mitt when you're up against a blind game.

Three days of this—and our break came.

It was early evening, just dark. Pat Reddy had phoned that he had been up on a job for two days and a night, and was going to sleep the clock around. Dick and I were sitting at the window of our flat, watching automobiles turn toward the yellow house, writing down their license numbers as they passed through the blue-white patch of light an arc-lamp put in the road just beyond our window.

A woman came climbing the hill, afoot. She was a tall woman, strongly built. A dark veil, not thick enough to advertise the fact that she wore it to hide her features, never-theless did hide them. Her way was up the hill, past our flat, on the other side of the roadway.

A night-wind from the Pacific was creaking a grocer's sign down below, swaying the arc-light above. The wind caught the woman as she passed out of our building's sheltered area. Coat and skirts tangled. She put her back to the wind, a hand to her hat. Her veil whipped out straight from her face.

Her face was a face from a photograph—Myra Banbrock's face.

Dick made her with me.

"Our Baby!" he cried, bouncing to his feet.

"Wait," I said. "She's going into the joint on the edge of the hill. Let her go. We'll go after her when she's inside. That's our excuse for frisking the joint."

I went into the next room, where our telephone was, and called Pat Reddy's number.

"She didn't go in," Dick called from the window. "She went past the path."

"After her!" I ordered. "There's no sense to that! What's the matter with her?" I felt sort of indignant about it. "She's got to go in! Tail her. I'll find you after I get Pat."

Dick went.

Pat's wife answered the telephone. I told her who I was.

"Will you shake Pat out of the covers and send him up here? He knows where I am. Tell him I want him in a hurry."

"I will," she promised. "I'll have him there in ten min-utes—wherever it is."

Outdoors, I went up the road, hunting for Dick and Myra Banbrock. Neither was in sight. Passing the bushes that masked the yellow house, I went on, circling down a stony path to the left. No sign of either.

I turned back in time to see Dick going into our flat. I followed.

"She's in," he said when I joined him. "She went up the road, cut across through some bushes, came back to the edge of the cliff, and slid feet-first through a cellar window."

That was nice. The crazier the people you are sleuthing act, as a rule, the nearer you are to an ending of your troubles.

Reddy arrived within a minute or two of the time his wife had promised. He came in buttoning his clothes.

"What the hell did you tell Althea?" he growled at me. "She gave me an overcoat to put over my pajamas, dumped the rest of my clothes in the car, and I had to get in them on the way over."

"I'll cry with you after awhile," I dismissed his troubles. "Myra Banbrock just went into the joint through a cellar window. Elwood has been there an hour. Let's knock it off."

Pat is deliberate.

"We ought to have papers, even at that," he stalled.

"Sure," I agreed, "but you can get them fixed up afterward. That's what you're here for. Contra Costa county wants her—maybe to try her for murder. That's all the excuse we need to get into the joint. We go there for her. If we happen to run into anything else—well and good."

Pat finished buttoning his vest.

"Oh, all right!" he said sourly. "Have it your way. But if you get me smashed for searching a house without authority, you'll have to give me a job with your law-breaking agency."

"I will." I turned to Foley. "You'll have to stay outside, Dick. Keep your eye on the getaway. Don't bother anybody else, but if the Banbrock girl gets out, stay behind her."

"I expected it," Dick howled. "Any time there's any fun I can count on being stuck off somewhere on a street corner!"

VIII

Pat Reddy and I went straight up the bush-hidden path to the yellow house's front door, and rang the bell.

A big black man in a red fez, red silk jacket over red-striped silk shirt, red zouave pants and red slippers, opened the door. He filled the opening, framed in the black of the hall behind him.

"Is Mr. Maxwell home?" I asked.

The black man shook his head and said words in a language I don't know.

"Mr. Elwood, then?"

Another shaking of the head. More strange language.

"Let's see whoever is home then," I insisted.

Out of the jumble of words that meant nothing to me, I picked three in garbled English, which I thought were "master," "not," and "home."

The door began to close. I put a foot against it.

Pat flashed his buzzer.

Though the black man had poor English, he had knowledge of police badges.

One of his feet stamped on the floor behind him. A gong boomed deafeningly in the rear of the house.

The black man bent his weight to the door.

My weight on the foot that blocked the door, I leaned sidewise, swaying to the negro.

Slamming from the hip, I put my fist in the middle of him.

Reddy hit the door and we went into the hall.

"'Fore God, Fat Shorty," the black man gasped in good black Virginian, "you done hurt me!"

Reddy and I went by him, down the hall whose bounds were lost in darkness.

The bottom of a flight of steps stopped my feet.

A gun went off upstairs. It seemed to point at us. We didn't get the bullets.

A babel of voices—women screaming, men shouting— came and went upstairs; came and went as if a door was being opened and shut.

"Up, my boy!" Reddy yelped in my ear.

We went up the stairs. We didn't find the man who had shot at us.

At the head of the stairs, a door was locked. Reddy's bulk forced it.

We came into a bluish light. A large room, all purple and gold. Confusion of overturned furniture and rumpled rugs. A gray slipper lay near a far door. A green silk gown was in the center of the floor. No person was there.

I raced Pat to the curtained door beyond the slipper. The door was not locked. Reddy yanked it wide.

A room with three girls and a man crouching in a corner, fear in their faces. Neither of them was Myra Banbrock, or Raymond Elwood, or anyone we knew.

Our glances went away from them after the first quick look. The open door across the room grabbed our attention.

The door gave to a small room.

The room was chaos.

A small room, packed and tangled with bodies. Live bodies, seething, writhing. The room was a funnel into which men and women had been poured. They boiled noisily toward the one small window that was the funnel's outlet. Men and women, youths and girls, screaming, struggling, squirming, fighting. Some had no clothes.

"We'll get through and block the window!" Pat yelled in my ear.

"Like hell—" I began, but he was gone ahead into the confusion.

I went after him.

I didn't mean to block the window. I meant to save Pat from his foolishness. No five men could have fought through that boiling turmoil of maniacs. No ten men could have turned them from the window.

Pat—big as he is—was down when I got to him. A half dressed girl—a child—was driving at his face with sharp highheels. Hands, feet, were tearing him apart.

I cleared him with a play of gun-barrel on shins and wrists—dragged him back.

"Myra's not there!" I yelled into his ear as I helped him up. "Elwood's not there!"

I wasn't sure, but I hadn't seen them, and I doubted that they would be in this mess. These savages, boiling again to the window, with no attention for us, whoever they were, weren't insiders. They were the mob, and the principals shouldn't be among them.

"We'll try the other rooms," I yelled again. "We don't want these."

Pat rubbed the back of his hand across his torn face and laughed.

"It's a cinch I don't want 'em any more," he said.

We went back to the head of the stairs the way we had come. We saw no one. The man and girls who had been in the next room were gone.

At the head of the stairs we paused. There was no noise behind us except the now fainter babel of the lunatics fighting for their exit.

A door shut sharply downstairs.

A body came out of nowhere, hit my back, flattened me to the landing.

The feel of silk was on my cheek. A brawny hand was fumbling at my throat.

I bent my wrist until my gun, upside down, lay against my cheek. Praying for my ear, I squeezed.

My cheek took fire. My head was a roaring thing, about to burst.

The silk slid away.

Pat hauled me upright.

We started down the stairs.

Swish!

A thing came past my face, stirring my bared hair.

A thousand pieces of glass, china, plaster, exploded upward at my feet.

I tilted head and gun together.

A negro's red-silk arms were still spread over the balustrade above.

I sent him two bullets. Pat sent him two.

The negro teetered over the rail.

He came down on us, arms outflung—a dead man's swan-dive.

We scurried down the stairs from under him.

He shook the house when he landed, but we weren't watching him then.

The smooth sleek head of Raymond Elwood took our attention.

In the light from above, it showed for a furtive split-second around the newel-post at the foot of the stairs. Showed and vanished.

Pat Reddy, closer to the rail than I, went over it in a one-hand vault down into the blackness below.

I made the foot of the stairs in two jumps, jerked myself around with a hand on the newel, and plunged into the suddenly noisy dark of the hall.

A wall I couldn't see hit me. Caroming off the opposite wall, I spun into a room whose curtained grayness was the light of day after the hall.

IX

Pat Reddy stood with one hand on a chair-back, holding his belly with the other. His face was mouse-colored under its blood. His eyes were glass agonies. He had the look of a man who had been kicked.

The grin he tried failed. He nodded toward the rear of the house. I went back.

In a little passageway I found Raymond Elwood.

He was sobbing and pulling frantically at a locked door. His face was the hard white of utter terror.

I measured the distance between us.

He turned as I jumped.

I put everything I had in the downswing of my gun-barrel—

A ton of meat and bone crashed into my back.

I went over against the wall, breathless, giddy, sick.

Red-silk arms that ended in brown hands locked around me.

I wondered if there was a whole regiment of these gaudy negroes—or if I was colliding with the same one over and over.

This one didn't let me do much thinking.

He was big. He was strong. He didn't mean any good.

My gun-arm was flat at my side, straight down. I tried a shot at one of the negro's feet. Missed. Tried again. He moved his feet. I wriggled around, half facing him.

Elwood piled on my other side.

The negro bent me backward, folding my spine on itself like an accordion.

I fought to hold my knees stiff. Too much weight was hanging on me. My knees sagged. My body curved back.

Pat Reddy, swaying in the doorway, shone over the negro's shoulder like the Angel Gabriel.

Gray pain was in Pat's face, but his eyes were clear. His right hand held a gun. His left was getting a blackjack out of his hip pocket.

He swung the sap down on the negro's shaven skull.

The black man wheeled away from me, shaking his head.

Pat hit him once more before the negro closed with him—hit him full in the face, but couldn't beat him off.

Twisting my freed gun-hand up, I drilled Elwood neatly through the chest, and let him slide down me to the floor.

The negro had Pat against the wall, bothering him a lot. His broad red back was a target.

But I had used five of the six bullets in my gun. I had more in my pocket, but reloading takes time.

I stepped out of Elwood's feeble hands, and went to work with the flat of my gun on the negro. There was a roll of fat where his skull and neck fit together. The third time I hit it, he flopped, taking Pat with him.

I rolled him off. The blond police detective—not very blond now—got up.

At the other end of the passageway, an open door showed an empty kitchen.

Pat and I went to the door that Elwood had been playing with. It was a solid piece of carpentering, and neatly fastened.

Yoking ourselves together, we began to beat the door with our combined three hundred and seventy or eighty pounds.

It shook, but held. We hit it again. Wood we couldn't see tore.

Again.

The door popped away from us. We went through—down a flight of steps—rolling, snowballing down—until a cement floor stopped us.

Pat came back to life first.

"You're a hell of an acrobat," he said. "Get off my neck!"

I stood up. He stood up. We seemed to be dividing the evening between falling on the floor and getting up from the floor.

A light-switch was at my shoulder. I turned it on.

If I looked anything like Pat, we were a fine pair of nightmares. He was all raw meat and dirt, with not enough clothes left to hide much of either.

I didn't like his looks, so I looked around the basement in which we stood. To the rear was a furnace, coal-bins and a woodpile. To the front was a hallway and rooms, after the manner of the upstairs.

The first door we tried was locked, but not strongly. We smashed through it into a photographer's dark-room.

The second door was unlocked, and put us in a chemical laboratory: retorts, tubes, burners and a small still. There was a little round iron stove in the middle of the room. No one was there.

We went out into the hallway and to the third door, not so cheerfully. This cellar looked like a bloomer. We were wasting our time here, when we should have stayed upstairs. I tried the door.

It was firm beyond trembling.

We smacked it with our weight, together, experimentally. It didn't shake.

"Wait."

Pat went to the woodpile in the rear and came back with an axe.

He swung the axe against the door, flaking out a hunk of wood. Silvery points of light sparkled in the hole. The other side of the door was an iron or steel plate.

Pat put the axe down and leaned on the helve.

"You write the next prescription," he said.

I didn't have anything to suggest, except:

"I'll camp here. You beat it upstairs, and see if any of your coppers have shown up. This is a God-forsaken hole, but somebody may have sent in an alarm. See if you can find another way into this room—a window, maybe—or man-power enough to get us in through this door."

Pat turned toward the steps.

A sound stopped him—the clicking of bolts on the other side of the iron-lined door.

A jump put Pat on one side of the frame. A step put me on the other.

Slowly the door moved in. Too slowly.

I kicked it open.

Pat and I went into the room on top of my kick.

His shoulder hit the woman. I managed to catch her before she fell.

Pat took her gun. I steadied her back on her feet.

Her face was a pale blank square.

She was Myra Banbrock, but she now had none of the masculinity that had been in her photographs and description.

Steadying her with one arm—which also served to block her arms—I looked around the room.

A small cube of a room whose walls were brown-painted metal. On the floor lay a queer little dead man.

A little man in tight-fitting black velvet and silk. Black velvet blouse and breeches, black silk stockings and skull cap, black patent leather pumps. His face was small and old and bony, but smooth as stone, without line or wrinkle.

A hole was in his blouse, where it fit high under his chin. The hole bled very slowly. The floor around him showed it had been bleeding faster a little while ago.

Beyond him, a safe was open. Papers were on the floor in front of it, as if the safe had been tilted to spill them out.

The girl moved against my arm.

"You killed him?" I asked.

"Yes," too faint to have been heard a yard away.

"Why?"

She shook her short brown hair out of her eyes with a tired jerk of her head.

"Does it make any difference?" she asked. "I did kill him."

"It might make a difference," I told her, taking my arm away, and going over to shut the door. People talk more freely in a room with a closed door. "I happen to be in your father's employ. Mr. Reddy is a police detective. Of course, neither of us can smash any laws, but if you'll tell us what's what, maybe we can help you."

"My father's employ?" she questioned.

"Yes. When you and your sister disappeared, he engaged me to find you. We found your sister, and—"

Life came into her face and eyes and voice.

"I didn't kill Ruth!" she cried. "The papers lied! I didn't kill her! I didn't know she had the revolver. I didn't know it! We were going away to hide from—from everything. We stopped in the woods to burn the—those things. That's the first time I knew she had the revolver. We had talked about suicide at first, but I had persuaded her—thought I had persuaded her—not to. I tried to take the revolver away from her, but I couldn't. She shot herself while I was trying to get it away. I tried to stop her. I didn't kill her!"

This was getting somewhere.

"And then?" I encouraged her.

"And then I went to Sacramento and left the car there, and came back to San Francisco. Ruth told me she had written Raymond Elwood a letter. She told me that before I persuaded her not to kill herself—the first time. I tried to get the letter from Raymond. She had written him she was going to kill herself. I tried to get the letter, but Raymond said he had given it to Hador.

"So I came here this evening to get it. I had just found it when there was a lot of noise upstairs. Then Hador came in and found me. He bolted the door. And—and I shot him with the revolver that was in the safe. I—I shot him when he turned around, before he could say anything. It had to be that way, or I couldn't."

"You mean you shot him without being threatened or attacked by him?" Pat asked.

"Yes. I was afraid of him, afraid to let him speak. I hated him! I couldn't help it. It had to be that way. If he had talked I couldn't have shot him. He—he wouldn't have let me!"

"Who was this Hador?" I asked.

She looked away from Pat and me, at the walls, at the ceiling, at the queer little dead man on the floor.

x

"He was a——" She cleared her throat, and started again, staring down at her feet. "Raymond Elwood brought us here the first time. We thought it was funny. But Hador was a devil. He told you things and you believed them. You couldn't help it. He told you *everything* and you believed it. Perhaps we were drugged. There was always a warm bluish wine. It must have been drugged. We couldn't have done those things if it hadn't. Nobody would— He called himself a priest—a priest of Alzoa. He taught a freeing of the spirit from the flesh by—"

Her voice broke huskily. She shuddered.

"It was horrible!" she went on presently in the silence Pat and I had left for her. "But you believed him. That is the whole thing. You can't understand it unless you understand that. The things he taught could not be so. But he said they were, and you *believed* they were. Or maybe—I don't know—maybe you pretended you believed them, because you were crazy and drugs were in your blood. We came back again and again, for weeks, months, before the disgust that had to come drove us away.

"We stopped coming, Ruth and I—and Irma. And then we found out what he was. He demanded money, more money than we had been paying while we believed—or pretended belief—in his cult. We couldn't give him the money he demanded. I told him we wouldn't. He sent us photographs—of us—taken during the—the times here. They were—*pictures—you—couldn't—explain*. And they were true! We knew them true! What could we do? He said he would send copies to our father, every friend, everyone we knew—unless we paid.

"What could we do—except pay? We got the money somehow. We gave him money—more—more—more. And then we had no more—could get no more. We didn't know what to do! There was nothing to do, except— Ruth and Irma wanted to kill themselves. I thought of that, too. But I persuaded Ruth not to. I said we'd go away. I'd take her away—keep her safe. And then—then—this!"

She stopped talking, went on staring at her feet.

I looked again at the little dead man on the floor, weird in his black cap and clothes. No more blood came from his throat.

It wasn't hard to put the pieces together. This dead Hador, self-ordained priest of something or other, staging orgies under the alias of religious ceremonies. Elwood, his confederate, bringing women of family and wealth to him. A room lighted for photography, with a concealed camera. Contributions from his converts so long as they were faithful to the cult. Blackmail—with the help of the photographs—afterward.

I looked from Hador to Pat Reddy. He was scowling at the dead man. No sound came from outside the room.

"You have the letter your sister wrote Elwood?" I asked the girl.

Her hand flashed to her bosom, and crinkled paper there. "Yes."

"It says plainly she meant to kill herself?"

"Yes."

"That ought to square her with Contra Costa county," I said to Pat.

He nodded his battered head.

"It ought to," he agreed. "It's not likely that they could prove murder on her even without that letter. With it, they'll not take her into court. That's a safe bet. Another is that she won't have any trouble over this shooting. She'll come out of court free, and thanked in the bargain."

Myra Banbrock flinched away from Pat as if he had hit her in the face.

I was her father's hired man just now. I saw her side of the affair.

I lit a cigarette and studied what I could see of Pat's face through blood and grime. Pat is a right guy.

"Listen, Pat," I wheedled him, though with a voice that was as if I were not trying to wheedle him at all. "Miss Banbrock can go into court and come out free and thanked, as you say. But to do it, she's got to use everything she knows. She's got to have all the evidence there is. She's got to have all those photographs Hador took—or all we can find of them.

"Some of those pictures have sent women to suicide, Pat—at least two that we know. If Miss Banbrock goes into court, we've got to make the photographs of God knows how many other women public property. We've got to advertise things that will put Miss Banbrock—and you can't say how many other women and girls—in a position that at least two women have killed themselves to escape."

Pat scowled at me and rubbed his dirty chin with a dirtier thumb.

I took a deep breath and made my play.

"Pat, you and I came here to question Raymond Elwood, having traced him here. Maybe we suspected him of being tied up with the mob that knocked over the St. Louis bank last month. Maybe we suspected him of handling the stuff that was taken from the mail cars in that stick-up near Denver week before last. Anyway, we were after him, knowing that he had a lot of money that came from nowhere, and a real estate office that did no real estate business.

"We came here to question him in connection with one of these jobs I've mentioned. We were jumped by a couple of the shines upstairs when they found we were sleuths. The rest of it grew out of that. This religious cult business was just something we ran into, and didn't interest us especially. So far as we knew, all these folks jumped us just through friendship for the man we were trying to question. Hador was one of them, and, tussling with you, you shot him with his own gun, which, of course, is the one Miss Banbrock found in the safe."

Reddy didn't seem to like my suggestion at all. The eyes with which he regarded me were decidedly sour.

"You're goofy," he accused me. "What'll that get anybody? That won't keep Miss Banbrock out of it. She's here, isn't she, and the rest of it will come out like thread off a spool."

"But Miss Banbrock *wasn't* here," I explained. "Maybe the upstairs is full of coppers by now. Maybe not. Anyway, you're going to take Miss Banbrock out of here and turn her over to Dick Foley, who will take her home. She's got nothing to do with this party. Tomorrow she, and her father's lawyer, and I, will all go up to Martinez and make a deal with the prosecuting attorney of Contra Costa county. We'll show him how Ruth killed herself. If somebody happens to connect the Elwood who I hope is dead upstairs with the Elwood who knew the girls and Mrs. Correll, what of it? If we keep out of court—as we'll do by convincing the Contra Costa people they can't possibly convict her of her sister's murder—we'll keep out of the newspapers—and out of trouble."

Pat hung fire, thumb still to chin.

"Remember," I urged him, "it's not only Miss Banbrock we're doing this for. It's a couple of dead ones, and a flock of live ones, who certainly got mixed up with Hador of their own accords, but who don't stop being human beings on that account."

Pat shook his head stubbornly.

"I'm sorry," I told the girl with faked hopelessness. "I've done all I can, but it's a lot to ask of Reddy. I don't know that I blame him for being afraid to take a chance on—"

Pat is Irish.

"Don't be so damned quick to fly off," he snapped at me, cutting short my hypocrisy. "But why do I have to be the one that shot this Hador? Why not you?"

I had him!

"Because," I explained, "you're a bull and I'm not. There'll be less chance of a slip-up if he was shot by a bona fide, star-wearing, flat-footed officer of the peace. I killed most of those birds upstairs. You ought to do something to show you were here."

That was only part of the truth. My idea was that if Pat took the credit, he couldn't very well ease himself out afterward, no matter what happened. Pat's a right guy, and I'd trust him anywhere—but you can trust a man just as easily if you have him sewed up.

Pat grumbled and shook his head, but:

"I'm ruining myself, I don't doubt," he growled, "but I'll do it, this once.'

"Attaboy!" I went over to pick up the girl's hat from the corner in which it lay. "I'll wait here until you come back from turning her over to Dick." I gave the girl her hat and orders together. "You go to your home with the man Reddy turns you over to. Stay there until I come, which will be as soon as I can make it. Don't tell anybody anything, except that I told you to keep quiet. That includes your father. Tell him I told you not to tell him even where you saw me. Got it?"

"Yes, and I—"

Gratitude is nice to think about afterward, but it takes time when there's work to be done.

"Get going, Pat!"

They went.

XI

As soon as I was alone with the dead man I stepped over him and knelt in front of the safe, pushing letters and papers away, hunting for photographs. None was in sight. One compartment of the safe was locked.

I frisked the corpse. No key. The locked compartment wasn't very strong, but neither am I the best safe-burglar in the West. It took me a while to get into it.

What I wanted was there. A thick sheaf of negatives. A stack of prints—half a hundred of them.

I started to run through them, hunting for the Banbrock girls' pictures. I wanted to have them pocketed before Pat came back. I didn't know how much farther he would let me go.

Luck was against me—and the time I had wasted getting into the compartment. He was back before I had got past the sixth print in the stack. Those six had been—pretty bad.

"Well, that's done," Pat growled at me as he came into the room. "Dick's got her. Elwood is dead, and so is the only one of the negroes I saw upstairs. Everybody else seems to have beat it. No bulls have shown—so I put in a call for a wagonful."

I stood up, holding the sheaf of negatives in one hand, the prints in the other.

"What's all that?" he asked.

I went after him again.

"Photographs. You've just done me a big favor, Pat, and I'm not hoggish enough to ask another. But I'm going to put something in front of you, Pat. I'll give you the lay, and you can name it.

"These."—I waved the pictures at him—"are Hador's meal-tickets—the photos he was either collecting on or planning to collect on. They're photographs of people, Pat, mostly women and girls, and some of them are pretty rotten.

"If tomorrow's papers say that a flock of photos were found in this house after the fireworks, there's going to be a fat suicide-list in the next day's papers, and a fatter list of disappearances. If the papers say nothing about the photos, the lists may be a little smaller, but not much. Some of the people whose pictures are here know they are here. They will expect the police to come hunting for them. We know this much about the photographs—two women have killed themselves to get away from them. This is an armful of stuff that can dynamite a lot of people, Pat, and a lot of families—no matter which of those two ways the papers read.

"But, suppose, Pat, the papers say that just before you shot Hador he succeeded in burning a lot of pictures and papers, burning them beyond recognition. Isn't it likely, then, that there won't be any suicides? That some of the disappearances of recent months may clear themselves up? There she is, Pat—you name it."

Looking back, it seems to me I had come a lot nearer being eloquent than ever before in my life.

But Pat didn't applaud.

He cursed me. He cursed me thoroughly, bitterly, and with an amount of feeling that told me I had won another point in my little game. He called me more things than I ever listened to before from a man who was built of meat and bone, and who therefore could be smacked.

When he was through, we carried the papers and photographs and a small book of addresses we found in the safe into the next room, and fed them to the little round iron stove there. The last of them was ash before we heard the police overhead.

"That's absolutely all!" Pat declared when we got up from our work. "Don't ever ask me to do anything else for you if you live to be a thousand."

"That's absolutely all," I echoed.

I like Pat. He is a right guy. The sixth photograph in the stack had been of his wife—the coffee importer's reckless, hot-eyed daughter.

Dead Yellow Women

SHE WAS sitting straight and stiff in one of the Old Man's chairs when he called me into his office—a tall girl of perhaps twenty-four, broad-shouldered, deep-bosomed, in mannish grey clothes. That she was Oriental showed only in the black shine of her bobbed hair, in the pale yellow of her unpowdered skin, and in the fold of her upper lids at the outer eye-corners, half hidden by the dark rims of her spectacles. But there was no slant to her eyes, her nose was almost aquiline, and she had more chin than Mongolians usually have. She was modern Chinese-American from the flat heels of her tan shoes to the crown of her untrimmed felt hat.

I knew her before the Old Man introduced me. The San Francisco papers had been full of her affairs for a couple of days. They had printed photographs and diagrams, interviews, editorials, and more or less expert opinions from various sources. They had gone back to 1912 to remember the stubborn fight of the local Chinese—mostly from Fokien and Kwangtung, where democratic ideas and hatred of Manchus go together—to have her father kept out of the United States, to which he had scooted when the Manchu rule flopped. The papers had recalled the excitement in Chinatown when Shan Fang was allowed to land—insulting placards had been hung in the streets, an unpleasant reception had been planned.

But Shan Fang had fooled the Cantonese. Chinatown had never seen him. He had taken his daughter and his gold—presumably the accumulated profits of a life-time of provincial misrule—down to San Mateo County, where he had built what the papers described as a palace on the edge of the Pacific. There he had lived and died in a manner suitable to a *Ta Jen* and a millionaire.

So much for the father. For the daughter—this young woman who was coolly studying me as I sat down across the table from her: she had been ten-year-old Ai Ho, a very Chinese little girl, when her father had brought her to California. All that was Oriental of her now were the features I have mentioned and the money her father had left her. Her name, translated into English, had become Water Lily, and then, by another step, Lillian. It was as Lillian Shan that she had attended an eastern university, acquired several degrees, won a tennis championship of some sort in 1919, and published a book on the nature and significance of fetishes, whatever all that is or are.

Since her father's death, in 1921, she had lived with her four Chinese servants in the house on the shore, where she had written her first book and was now at work on another. A couple of weeks ago, she had found herself stumped, so she said—had run into a blind alley. There was, she said, a certain old cabalistic manuscript in the Arsenal Library in Paris that she believed would solve her troubles for her. So she had packed some clothes and, accompanied by her maid, a Chinese woman named Wang Ma, had taken a train for New York, leaving the three other servants to take care of the house during her absence. The decision to go to France for a look at the manuscript had been formed one morning—she was on the train before dark.

On the train between Chicago and New York, the key to the problem that had puzzled her suddenly popped into her head. Without pausing even for a night's rest in New York, she had turned around and headed back for San Francisco. At the ferry here she had tried to telephone her chauffeur to bring a car for her. No answer. A taxicab had carried her and her maid to her house. She rang the door-bell to no effect.

When her key was in the lock the door had been suddenly opened by a young Chinese man—a stranger to her. He had refused her admittance until she told him who she was. He mumbled an unintelligible explanation as she and the maid went into the hall.

Both of them were neatly bundled up in some curtains.

Two hours later Lillian Shan got herself loose—in a linen closet on the second floor. Switching on the light, she started to untie the maid. She stopped. Wang Ma was dead. The rope around her neck had been drawn too tight.

Lillian Shan went out into the empty house and telephoned the sheriff's office in Redwood City.

Two deputy sheriffs had come to the house, had listened to her story, had poked around, and had found another Chinese body—another strangled woman—buried in the cellar. Apparently she had been dead a week or a week and a half; the dampness of the ground made more positive dating impossible. Lillian Shan identified her as another of her servants—Wan Lan, the cook.

The other servants—Hoo Lun and Yin Hung—had vanished. Of the several hundred thousand dollars' worth of furnishings old Shan Fang had put into the house during his life, not a nickel's worth had been removed. There were no signs of a struggle. Everything was in order. The closest neighboring house was nearly half a mile away. The neighbors had seen nothing, knew nothing.

That's the story the newspapers had hung headlines over, and that's the story this girl, sitting very erect in her chair, speaking with businesslike briskness, shaping each word as exactly as if it were printed in black type, told the Old Man and me.

"I am not at all satisfied with the effort the San Mateo County authorities have made to apprehend the murderer or murderers," she wound up. "I wish to engage your agency."

The Old Man tapped the table with the point of his inevitable long yellow pencil and nodded at me.

"Have you any idea of your own on the murders, Miss Shan?" I asked.

"I have not."

"What do you know about the servants—the missing ones as well as the dead?"

"I really know little or nothing about them." She didn't seem very interested. "Wang Ma was the most recent of them to come to the house, and she has been with me for nearly seven years. My father employed them, and I suppose he knew something about them."

"Don't you know where they came from? Whether they have relatives? Whether they have friends? What they did when they weren't working?"

"No," she said. "I did not pry into their lives."

"The two who disappeared—what do they look like?"

"Hoo Lun is an old man, quite white-haired and thin and stooped. He did the housework. Yin Hung, who was my chauffeur and gardener, is younger, about thirty years old, I think. He is quite short, even for a Cantonese, but sturdy. His nose has been broken at some time and not set properly. It is very flat, with a pronounced bend in the bridge."

"Do you think this pair, or either of them, could have killed the women?"

"I do not think they did."

"The young Chinese—the stranger who let you in the house—what did he look like?"

"He was quite slender, and not more than twenty or twenty-one years old, with large gold fillings in his front teeth. I think he was quite dark."

"Will you tell me exactly why you are dissatisfied with what the sheriff is doing, Miss Shan?"

"In the first place, I am not sure they are competent. The ones I saw certainly did not impress me with their brilliance."

"And in the second place?"

"Really," she asked coldly, "is it necessary to go into all my mental processes?"

"It is."

She looked at the Old Man, who smiled at her with his polite, meaningless smile—a mask through which you can read nothing.

For a moment she hung fire. Then: "I don't think they are looking in very likely places. They seem to spend the greater part of their time in the vicinity of the house. It is absurd to think the murderers are going to return."

I turned that over in my mind.

"Miss Shan," I asked, "don't you think they suspect you?"

Her dark eyes burned through her glasses at me and, if possible, she made herself more rigidly straight in her chair.

"Preposterous!"

"That isn't the point," I insisted. "Do they?"

"I am not able to penetrate the police mind," she came back. "Do *you*?"

"I don't know anything about this job but what I've read and what you've just told me. I need more foundation than that to suspect anybody. But I can understand why the sheriff's office would be a little doubtful. You left in a hurry. They've got your word for why you went and why you came back, and your word is all. The woman found in the cellar could have been killed just before you left as well as just after. Wang Ma, who could have told things, is dead. The other servants are missing. Nothing was stolen. That's plenty to make the sheriff think about you!"

"Do you suspect me?" she asked again.

"No," I said truthfully. "But that proves nothing."

She spoke to the Old Man, with a chin-tilting motion, as if she were talking over my head.

"Do you wish to undertake this work for me?"

"We shall be very glad to do what we can," he said, and then to me, after they had talked terms and while she was writing a check, "you handle it. Use what men you need."

"I want to go out to the house first and look the place over," I said.

Lillian Shan was putting away her check-book.

"Very well. I am returning home now. I will drive you down."

It was a restful ride. Neither the girl nor I wasted energy on conversation. My client and I didn't seem to like each other very much. She drove well.

II

The Shan house was a big brownstone affair, set among sodded lawns. The place was hedged shoulder-high on three sides. The fourth boundary was the ocean, where it came in to make a notch in the shore-line between two small rocky points.

The house was full of hangings, rugs, pictures, and so on— a mixture of things American, European and Asiatic. I didn't spend much time inside. After a look at the linen-closet, at the still open cellar grave, and at the pale, thick-featured Danish woman who was taking care of the house until Lillian Shan could get a new corps of servants, I went outdoors again. I poked around the lawns for a few minutes, stuck my head in the garage, where two cars, besides the one in which we had come from town, stood, and then went off to waste the rest of the afternoon talking to the girl's neighbors. None of them knew anything. Since we were on opposite sides of the game, I didn't hunt up the sheriff's men.

By twilight I was back in the city, going into the apartment building in which I lived during my first year in San Francisco. I found the lad I wanted in his cubby-hole room, getting his small body into a cerise silk shirt that was something to look at. Cipriano was the bright-faced Filipino boy who looked after the building's front door in the daytime. At night, like all the Filipinos in San Francisco, he could be found down on Kearny Street, just below Chinatown, except when he was in a Chinese gambling-house passing his money over to the yellow brothers.

I had once, half-joking, promised to give the lad a fling at gum-shoeing if the opportunity ever came. I thought I could use him now.

"Come in, sir!"

He was dragging a chair out of a corner for me, bowing and smiling. Whatever else the Spaniards do for the people they rule, they make them polite.

"What's doing in Chinatown these days?" I asked as he went on with his dressing.

He gave me a white-toothed smile.

"I take eleven bucks out of bean-game last night."

"And you're getting ready to take it back tonight?"

"Not all of 'em, sir! Five bucks I spend for this shirt."

"That's the stuff," I applauded his wisdom in investing part of his fan-tan profits. "What else is doing down there?"

"Nothing unusual, sir. You want to find something?"

"Yeah. Hear any talk about the killings down the country last week? The two Chinese women?"

"No, sir. Chinaboy don't talk much about things like that. Not like us Americans. I read about those things in newspapers, but I have not heard."

"Many strangers in Chinatown nowadays?"

"All the time there's strangers, sir. But I guess maybe some new Chinaboys are there. Maybe not, though."

"How would you like to do a little work for me?"

"Yes, sir! Yes, sir! Yes, sir!" He said it oftener than that, but that will give you the idea. While he was saying it he was down on his knees, dragging a valise from under the bed. Out of the valise he took a pair of brass knuckles and a shiny revolver.

"Here! I want some information. I don't want you to knock anybody off for me."

"I don't knock 'em," he assured me, stuffing his weapons in his hip pockets. "Just carry these—maybe I need 'em."

I let it go at that. If he wanted to make himself bow-legged carrying a ton of iron it was all right with me.

"Here's what I want. Two of the servants ducked out of the house down there." I described Yin Hung and Hoo Lun. "I want to find them. I want to find what anybody in Chinatown knows about the killings. I want to find who the dead women's friends and relatives are, where they came from, and the same thing for the two men. I want to know about those strange Chinese—where they hang out, where they sleep, what they're up to.

"Now, don't try to get all this in a night. You'll be doing fine if you get any of it in a week. Here's twenty dollars. Five of it is your night's pay. You can use the other to carry you around. Don't be foolish and poke your nose into a lot of grief. Take it easy and see what you can turn up for me. I'll drop in tomorrow."

From the Filipino's room I went to the office. Everybody except Fiske, the night man, was gone, but Fiske thought the Old Man would drop in for a few minutes later in the night.

I smoked, pretended to listen to Fiske's report on all the jokes that were at the Orpheum that week, and grouched over my job. I was too well known to get anything on the quiet in Chinatown. I wasn't sure Cipriano was going to be much help. I needed somebody who was in right down there.

This line of thinking brought me around to "Dummy" Uhl. Uhl was a dummerer who had lost his store. Five years before, he had been sitting on the world. Any day on which his sad face, his package of pins, and his *I am deaf and dumb* sign didn't take twenty dollars out of the office buildings along his route was a rotten day. His big card was his ability to play the statue when skeptical people yelled or made sudden noises behind him. When the Dummy was right, a gun going off beside his ear wouldn't make him twitch an eye-lid. But too much heroin broke his nerves until a whisper was enough to make him jump. He put away his pins and his sign—another man whose social life had ruined him.

Since then Dummy had become an errand boy for whoever would stake him to the price of his necessary nose-candy. He slept somewhere in Chinatown, and he didn't care especially how he played the game. I had used him to get me some information on a window-smashing six months before. I decided to try him again.

I called "Loop" Pigatti's place—a dive down on Pacific Street, where Chinatown fringes into the Latin Quarter. Loop is a tough citizen, who runs a tough hole, and who minds his own business, which is making his dive show a profit. Everybody looks alike to Loop. Whether you're a yegg, stool-pigeon, detective, or settlement worker, you get an even break out of Loop and nothing else. But you can be sure that, unless it's something that might hurt his business, anything you tell Loop will get no further. And anything he tells you is more than likely to be right.

He answered the phone himself.

"Can you get hold of Dummy Uhl for me?" I asked after I had told him who I was.

"Maybe."

"Thanks. I'd like to see him tonight."

"You got nothin' on him?"

"No, Loop, and I don't expect to. I want him to get something for me."

"All right. Where d'you want him?"

"Send him up to my joint. I'll wait there for him."

"If he'll come," Loop promised and hung up.

I left word with Fiske to have the Old Man call me up when he came in, and then I went up to my rooms to wait for my informant.

He came in a little after ten—a short, stocky, pasty-faced man of forty or so, with mouse-colored hair streaked with yellow-white.

"Loop says y'got sumpin' f'r me."

"Yes," I said, waving him to a chair, and closing the door. "I'm buying news."

He fumbled with his hat, started to spit on the floor, changed his mind, licked his lips, and looked up at me.

"What kind o' news? I don't know nothin'."

I was puzzled. The Dummy's yellowish eyes should have showed the pin-point pupils of the heroin addict. They didn't. The pupils were normal. That didn't mean he was off the stuff—he had put cocaine into them to distend them to normal. The puzzle was—why? He wasn't usually particular enough about his appearance to go to that trouble.

"Did you hear about the Chinese killings down the shore last week?" I asked him.

"No."

"Well," I said, paying no attention to the denial, "I'm hunting for the pair of yellow men who ducked out—Hoo Lun and Yin Hung. Know anything about them?"

"No."

"It's worth a couple of hundred dollars to you to find either of them for me. It's worth another couple hundred to find out about the killings for me. It's worth another to find the slim Chinese youngster with gold teeth who opened the door for the Shan girl and her maid."

"I don't know nothin' about them things," he said.

But he said it automatically while his mind was busy counting up the hundreds I had dangled before him. I suppose his dope-addled brains made the total somewhere in the thousands. He jumped up.

"I'll see what I c'n do. S'pose you slip me a hundred now, on account."

I didn't see that.

"You get it when you deliver."

We had to argue that point, but finally he went off grumbling and growling to get me my news.

I went back to the office. The Old Man hadn't come in yet. It was nearly midnight when he arrived.

"I'm using Dummy Uhl again," I told him, "and I've put a Filipino boy down there too. I've got another scheme, but I don't know anybody to handle it. I think if we offered the missing chauffeur and house-man jobs in some out-of-the-way place up the country, perhaps they'd fall for it. Do you know anybody who could pull it for us?"

"Exactly what have you in mind?"

"It must be somebody who has a house out in the country,

the farther the better, the more secluded the better. They would phone one of the Chinese employment offices that they needed three servants—cook, house-man, and chauffeur. We throw in the cook for good measure, to cover the game. It's got to be air-tight on the other end, and, if we're going to catch our fish, we have to give 'em time to investigate. So whoever does it must have some servants, and must put up a bluff—I mean in his own neighborhood—that they are leaving, and the servants must be in on it. And we've got to wait a couple of days, so our friends here will have time to investigate. I think we'd better use Fong Yick's employment agency, on Washington Street.

"Whoever does it could phone Fong Yick tomorrow morning, and say he'd be in Thursday morning to look the applicants over. This is Monday—that'll be long enough. Our helper gets at the employment office at ten Thursday morning. Miss Shan and I arrive in a taxicab ten minutes later, when he'll be in the middle of questioning the applicants. I'll slide out of the taxi into Fong Yick's, grab anybody that looks like one of our missing servants. Miss Shan will come in a minute or two behind me and check me up—so there won't be any false-arrest mixups."

The Old Man nodded approval.

"Very well," he said. "I think I can arrange it. I will let you know tomorrow."

I went home to bed. Thus ended the first day.

III

At nine the next morning, Tuesday, I was talking to Cipriano in the lobby of the apartment building that employs him. His eyes were black drops of ink in white saucers. He thought he had got something.

"Yes, sir! Strange Chinaboys are in town, some of them. They sleep in a house on Waverly Place—on the western side, four houses from the house of Jair Quon, where I sometimes play dice. And there is more—I talk to a white man who knows they are hatchet-men from Portland and Eureka and Sacramento. They are Hip Sing men—a tong war starts—pretty soon, maybe."

"Do these birds look like gunmen to you?"

Cipriano scratched his head.

"No, sir, maybe not. But a fellow can shoot sometimes if he don't look like it. This man tells me they are Hip Sing men."

"Who was this white man?"

"I don't know the name, but he lives there. A short man— snow-bird."

"Grey hair, yellowish eyes?"

"Yes, sir."

That, as likely as not, would be Dummy Uhl. One of my men was stringing the other. The tong stuff hadn't sounded right to me anyhow. Once in a while they mix things, but usually they are blamed for somebody else's crimes. Most wholesale killings in Chinatown are the result of family or clan feuds—such as the ones the "Four Brothers" used to stage.

"This house where you think the strangers are living— know anything about it?"

"No, sir. But maybe you could go through there to the house of Chang Li Ching on other street—Spofford Alley."

"So? And who is this Chang Li Ching?"

"I don't know, sir. But he is there. Nobody sees him, but all Chinaboys say he is great man."

"So? And his house is in Spofford Alley?"

"Yes, sir, a house with red door and red steps. You find it easy, but better not fool with Chang Li Ching."

I didn't know whether that was advice or just a general remark.

"A big gun, huh?" I probed.

But my Filipino didn't really know anything about this Chang Li Ching. He was basing his opinion of the Chinese's greatness on the attitude of his fellow countrymen when they mentioned him.

"Learn anything about the two Chinese men?" I asked after I had fixed this point.

"No, sir, but I will—you bet!"

I praised him for what he had done, told him to try it again that night, and went back to my rooms to wait for Dummy Uhl, who had promised to come there at ten-thirty. It was not quite ten when I got there, so I used some of my spare time to call up the office. The Old Man said Dick Foley—our shadow ace—was idle, so I borrowed him. Then I fixed my gun and sat down to wait for my stool-pigeon.

He rang the bell at eleven o'clock. He came in frowning tremendously.

"I don't know what t' hell to make of it, kid," he spoke importantly over the cigarette he was rolling. "There's sumpin' makin' down there, an' that's a fact. Things ain't been anyways quiet since the Japs began buyin' stores in the Chink streets, an' maybe that's got sumpin' to do with it. But there ain't no strange Chinks in town—not a damn one! I got a hunch your men have gone down to L. A., but I expec' t' know f'r certain tonight. I got a Chink ribbed up t' get the dope; 'f I was you, I'd put a watch on the boats at San Pedro. Maybe those fellas'll swap papers wit' a coupla Chink sailors that'd like t' stay here."

"And there are no strangers in town?"

"Not any."

"Dummy," I said bitterly, "you're a liar, and you're a boob, and I've been playing you for a sucker. You were in on that killing, and so were your friends, and I'm going to throw you in the can, and your friends on top of you!"

I put my gun in sight, close to his scared-grey face.

"Keep yourself still while I do my phoning!"

Reaching for the telephone with my free hand, I kept one eye on the Dummy.

It wasn't enough. My gun was too close to him.

He yanked it out of my hand. I jumped for him.

The gun turned in his fingers. I grabbed it—too late. It went off, its muzzle less than a foot from where I'm thickest. Fire stung my body.

Clutching the gun with both hands I folded down to the floor. Dummy went away from there, leaving the door open behind him.

One hand on my burning belly, I crossed to the window and waved an arm at Dick Foley, stalling on a corner down the street. Then I went to the bathroom and looked to my wound. A blank cartridge does hurt if you catch it close up!

My vest and shirt and union suit were ruined, and I had a nasty scorch on my body. I greased it, taped a cushion over it, changed my clothes, loaded the gun again, and went down to the office to wait for word from Dick. The first trick in the game looked like mine. Heroin or no heroin, Dummy Uhl would not have jumped me if my guess—based on the trouble he was taking to make his eyes look right and the lie he had sprung on me about there being no strangers in Chinatown—hadn't hit close to the mark.

Dick wasn't long in joining me.

"Good pickings!" he said when he came in. The little Canadian talks like a thrifty man's telegram. "Beat it for phone. Called Hotel Irvington. Booth—couldn't get anything but number. Ought to be enough. Then Chinatown. Dived in cellar west side Waverly Place. Couldn't stick close enough to spot place. Afraid to take chance hanging around. How do you like it?"

"I like it all right. Let's look up 'The Whistler's' record."

A file clerk got it for us—a bulky envelope the size of a brief case, crammed with memoranda, clippings and letters. The gentleman's biography, as we had it, ran like this:

Neil Conyers, alias The Whistler, was born in Philadelphia—out on Whiskey Hill—in 1883. In '94, at the age of eleven, he was picked up by the Washington police. He had gone there to join Coxey's Army. They sent him home. In '98 he was arrested in his home town for stabbing another lad in a row over an election-night bonfire. This time he was released in his parents' custody. In 1901 the Philadelphia police grabbed him again, charging him with being the head of the first organized automobile-stealing ring. He was released without trial, for lack of evidence. But the district attorney lost his job in the resultant scandal. In 1908 Conyers appeared on the Pacific Coast—at Seattle, Portland, San Francisco, and Los Angeles—in company with a con-man known as "Duster" Hughes. Hughes was shot and killed the following year by a man whom he'd swindled in a fake airplane manufacturing deal. Conyers was arrested on the same deal. Two juries disagreed and he was turned loose. In 1910 the Post Office Department's famous raid on get-rich-quick promoters caught him. Again there wasn't enough evidence against him to put him away. In 1915 the law scored on him for the first time. He went to San Quentin for buncoing some visitors to the Panama-Pacific International Exposition. He stayed there for three years. In 1919 he and a Jap named Hasegawa nicked the Japanese colony of Seattle for $20,000, Conyers posing as an American who had held a commission in the Japanese army during that late war. He had a counterfeit medal of the Order of the Rising Sun which the emperor was supposed to have pinned on him. When the game fell through, Hasegawa's family made good the $20,000—Conyers got out of it with a good profit and not even any disagreeable publicity. The thing had been hushed. He returned to San Francisco after that, bought the Hotel Irvington, and had been living there now for five years without anybody being able to add another word to his criminal record. He was up to something, but nobody could learn what. There wasn't a chance in the world of getting a detective into his hotel as a guest. Apparently the joint was always without vacant rooms. It was as exclusive as the Pacific-Union Club.

This, then, was the proprietor of the hotel Dummy Uhl had got on the phone before diving into his hole in Chinatown.

I had never seen Conyers. Neither had Dick. There were a couple of photographs in his envelope. One was the profile and full-face photograph of the local police, taken when he had been picked up on the charge that led him to San Quentin. The other was a group picture: all rung up in evening clothes, with the phoney Japanese medal on his chest, he stood among half a dozen of the Seattle Japs he had trimmed—a flashlight picture taken while he was leading them to the slaughter.

These pictures showed him to be a big bird, fleshy, pompous-looking, with a heavy, square chin and shrewd eyes.

"Think you could pick him up?" I asked Dick.

"Sure."

"Suppose you go up there and see if you can get a room or apartment somewhere in the neighborhood—one you can watch the hotel from. Maybe you'll get a chance to tail him around now and then."

I put the pictures in my pocket, in case they'd come in handy, dumped the rest of the stuff back in its envelope, and went into the Old Man's office.

"I arranged that employment office stratagem," he said. "A Frank Paul, who has a ranch out beyond Martinez, will be in

Fong Yick's establishment at ten Thursday morning, carrying out his part."

"That's fine! I'm going calling in Chinatown now. If you don't hear from me for a couple of days, will you ask the street-cleaners to watch what they're sweeping up?"

He said he would.

IV

San Francisco's Chinatown jumps out of the shopping district at California Street and runs north to the Latin Quarter—a strip two blocks wide by six long. Before the fire nearly twenty-five thousand Chinese lived in those dozen blocks. I don't suppose the population is a third of that now.

Grant Avenue, the main street and spine of this strip, is for most of its length a street of gaudy shops catering to the tourist trade and flashy chop-suey houses, where the racket of American jazz orchestras drowns the occasional squeak of a Chinese flute. Farther out, there isn't so much paint and gilt, and you can catch the proper Chinese smell of spices and vinegar and dried things. If you leave the main thoroughfares and show places and start poking around in alleys and dark corners, and nothing happens to you, the chances are you'll find some interesting things—though you won't like some of them.

However, I wasn't poking around as I turned off Grant Avenue at Clay Street, and went up to Spofford Alley, hunting for the house with red steps and red door, which Cipriano had said was Chang Li Ching's. I did pause for a few seconds to look up Waverly Place when I passed it. The Filipino had told me the strange Chinese were living there, and that he thought their house might lead through to Chang Li Ching's; and Dick Foley had shadowed Dummy Uhl there.

But I couldn't guess which was the important house. Four doors from Jair Quon's gambling house, Cipriano had said, but I didn't know where Jair Quon's was. Waverly Place was a picture of peace and quiet just now. A fat Chinese was stacking crates of green vegetables in front of a grocery. Half a dozen small yellow boys were playing at marbles in the middle of the street. On the other side, a blond young man in tweeds was climbing the six steps from a cellar to the street, a painted Chinese woman's face showing for an instant before she closed the door behind him. Up the street a truck was unloading rolls of paper in front of one of the Chinese newspaper plants. A shabby guide was bringing four sightseers out of the Temple of the Queen of Heaven—a joss house over the Sue Hing headquarters.

I went on up to Spofford Alley and found my house with no difficulty at all. It was a shabby building with steps and door the color of dried blood, its windows solidly shuttered with thick, tight-nailed planking. What made it stand out from its neighbors was that its ground floor wasn't a shop or place of business. Purely residential buildings are rare in Chinatown: almost always the street floor is given to business, with the living quarters in cellar or upper stories.

I went up the three steps and tapped the red door with my knuckles.

Nothing happened.

I hit it again, harder. Still nothing. I tried it again, and this time was rewarded by the sounds of scraping and clicking inside.

At least two minutes of this scraping and clicking, and the door swung open—a bare four inches.

One slanting eye and a slice of wrinkled brown face looked out of the crack at me, above the heavy chain that held the door.

"Whata wan'?"

"I want to see Chang Li Ching."

"No savvy. Maybe closs stleet."

"Bunk! You fix your little door and run back and tell Chang Li Ching I want to see him."

"No can do! No savvy Chang."

"You tell him I'm here," I said, turning my back on the door. I sat down on the top step, and added, without looking around, "I'll wait."

While I got my cigarettes out there was silence behind me. Then the door closed softly and the scraping and clicking broke out behind it. I smoked a cigarette and another and let time go by, trying to look like I had all the patience there was.

I hoped this yellow man wasn't going to make a chump of me by letting me sit there until I got tired of it.

Chinese passed up and down the alley, scuffling along in American shoes that can never be made to fit them. Some of them looked curiously at me, some gave me no attention at all. An hour went to waste, and a few minutes, and then the familiar scraping and clicking disturbed the door.

The chain rattled as the door swung open. I wouldn't turn my head.

"Go 'way! No catch 'em Chang!"

I said nothing. If he wasn't going to let me in he would have let me sit there without further attention.

A pause.

"Whata wan'?"

"I want to see Chang Li Ching," I said without looking around.

Another pause, ended by the banging of the chain against the door-frame.

"All light."

I chucked my cigarette into the street, got up and stepped into the house. In the dimness I could make out a few pieces of cheap and battered furniture. I had to wait while the Chinese put four arm-thick bars across the door and pad-locked them there. Then he nodded at me and scuffled across the floor, a small, bent man with hairless yellow head and a neck like a piece of rope.

Out of this room, he led me into another, darker still, into a hallway, and down a flight of rickety steps. The odors of musty clothing and damp earth were strong. We walked through the dark across a dirt floor for a while, turned to the left, and cement was under my feet. We turned twice more in the dark, and then climbed a flight of unplaned wooden steps into a hall that was fairly light with the glow from shaded electric lights.

In this hall my guide unlocked a door, and we crossed a room where cones of incense burned, and where, in the light of an oil lamp, little red tables with cups of tea stood in front of wooden panels, marked with Chinese characters in gold paint, which hung on the walls. A door on the opposite side of this room let us into pitch blackness, where I had to hold the tail of my guide's loose made-to-order blue coat.

So far he hadn't once looked back at me since our tour began, and neither of us had said anything. This running upstairs and downstairs, turning to the right and turning to the left, seemed harmless enough. If he got any fun out of confusing me, he was welcome. I was confused enough now, so far as the directions were concerned. I hadn't the least idea where I might be. But that didn't disturb me so much. If I was going to be cut down, a knowledge of my geographical position wouldn't make it any more pleasant. If I was going to come out all right, one place was still as good as another.

We did a lot more of the winding around, we did some stair-climbing and some stair-descending, and the rest of the foolishness. I figured I'd been indoors nearly half an hour by now, and I had seen nobody but my guide.

Then I saw something else.

We were going down a long, narrow hall that had brown-painted doors close together on either side. All these doors were closed—secretive-looking in the dim light. Abreast of one of them, a glint of dull metal caught my eye—a dark ring in the door's center.

I went to the floor.

Going down as if I'd been knocked, I missed the flash. But I heard the roar, smelled the powder.

My guide spun around, twisting out of one slipper. In each of his hands was an automatic as big as a coal scuttle. Even while trying to get my own gun out I wondered how so puny a man could have concealed so much machinery on him.

The big guns in the little man's hands flamed at me. Chinese-fashion, he was emptying them—crash! crash! crash!

I thought he was missing me until I had my finger tight on my trigger. Then I woke up in time to hold my fire.

He wasn't shooting at me. He was pouring metal into the door behind me—the door from which I had been shot at.

I rolled away from it, across the hall.

The scrawny little man stepped closer and finished his bombardment. His slugs shredded the wood as if it had been paper. His guns clicked empty.

The door swung open, pushed by the wreck of a man who was trying to hold himself up by clinging to the sliding panel in the door's center.

Dummy Uhl—all the middle of him gone—slid down to the floor and made more of a puddle than a pile there.

The hall filled with yellow men, black guns sticking out like briars in a blackberry patch.

I got up. My guide dropped his guns to his side and sang out a guttural solo. Chinese began to disappear through various doors, except four who began gathering up what twenty bullets had left of Dummy Uhl.

The stringy old boy tucked his empty guns away and came down the hall to me, one hand held out toward my gun.

"You give 'em," he said politely.

I gave 'em. He could have had my pants.

My gun stowed away in his shirt-bosom, he looked casually at what the four Chinese were carrying away, and then at me.

"No like 'em fella, huh?" he asked.

"Not so much," I admitted.

"All light. I take you."

Our two-man parade got under way again. The ring-around-the-rosy game went on for another flight of stairs and some right and left turns, and then my guide stopped before a door and scratched it with his finger-nails.

v

The door was opened by another Chinese. But this one was none of your Cantonese runts. He was a big meat-eating wrestler—bull-throated, mountain-shouldered, gorilla-armed, leather-skinned. The god that made him had plenty of material, and gave it time to harden.

Holding back the curtain that covered the door, he stepped to one side. I went in, and found his twin standing on the other side of the door.

The room was large and cubical, its doors and windows—if any—hidden behind velvet hangings of green and blue and silver. In a big black chair, elaborately carved, behind an inlaid black table, sat an old Chinese man. His face was round and plump and shrewd, with a straggle of thin white whiskers on his chin. A dark, close-fitting cap was on his head; a purple robe, tight around his neck, showed its sable lining at the bottom, where it had fallen back in a fold over his blue satin trousers.

He did not get up from his chair, but smiled mildly over his whiskers and bent his head almost to the tea things on the table.

"It was only the inability to believe that one of your excellency's heaven-born splendor would waste his costly time on so mean a clod that kept the least of your slaves from running down to prostrate himself at your noble feet as soon as he heard the Father of Detectives was at his unworthy door."

That came out smoothly in English that was a lot clearer than my own. I kept my face straight, waiting.

"If the Terror of Evildoers will honor one of my deplorable chairs by resting his divine body on it, I can assure him the chair shall be burned afterward, so no lesser being may use it. Or will the Prince of Thief-catchers permit me to send a servant to his palace for a chair worthy of him?"

I went slowly to a chair, trying to arrange words in my mind. This old joker was spoofing me with an exaggeration— a burlesque—of the well-known Chinese politeness. I'm not hard to get along with: I'll play anybody's game up to a certain point.

"It's only because I'm weak-kneed with awe of the mighty Chang Li Ching that I dare to sit down," I explained, letting myself down on the chair, and turning my head to notice that the giants who had stood beside the door were gone.

I had a hunch they had gone no farther than the other side of the velvet hangings that hid the door.

"If it were not that the King of Finders-out"—he was at it again—"knows everything, I should marvel that he had heard my lowly name."

"Heard it? Who hasn't?" I kidded back. "Isn't the word *change*, in English, derived from Chang? Change, meaning alter, is what happens to the wisest man's opinions after he has heard the wisdom of Chang Li Ching!" I tried to get away from this vaudeville stuff, which was a strain on my head. "Thanks for having your man save my life back there in the passage."

He spreads his hands out over the table.

"It was only because I feared the Emperor of Hawkshaws would find the odor of such low blood distasteful to his elegant nostrils that the foul one who disturbed your excellency was struck down quickly. If I have erred, and you would have chosen that he be cut to pieces inch by inch, I can only offer to torture one of my sons in his place."

"Let the boy live," I said carelessly, and turned to business. "I wouldn't have bothered you except that I am so ignorant that only the help of your great wisdom could ever bring me up to normal."

"Does one ask the way of a blind man?" the old duffer asked, cocking his head to one side. "Can a star, however willing, help the moon? If it pleases the Grandfather of Bloodhounds to flatter Chang Li Ching into thinking he can add to the great one's knowledge, who is Chang to thwart his master by refusing to make himself ridiculous?"

I took that to mean he was willing to listen to my questions.

"What I'd like to know is, who killed Lillian Shan's servants, Wang Ma and Wan Lan?"

He played with a thin strand of his white beard, twisting it in a pale, small finger.

"Does the stag-hunter look at the hare?" he wanted to know. "And when so mighty a hunter pretends to concern himself with the death of servants, can Chang think anything except that it pleases the great one to conceal his real object? Yet it may be, because the dead were servants and not girdle-wearers, that the Lord of Snares thought the lowly Chang Li Ching, insignificant one of the Hundred Names, might have knowledge of them. Do not rats know the way of rats?"

He kept this stuff up for some minutes, while I sat and listened and studied his round, shrewd yellow mask of a face, and hoped that something clear would come of it all. Nothing did.

"My ignorance is even greater than I had arrogantly supposed," he brought his speech to an end. "This simple question you put is beyond the power of my muddled mind. I do not know who killed Wang Ma and Wan Lan."

I grinned at him, and put another question:

"Where can I find Hoo Lun and Yin Hung?"

"Again I must grovel in my ignorance," he murmured, "only consoling myself with the thought that the Master of Mysteries knows the answers to his questions, and is pleased to conceal his infallibly accomplished purpose from Chang."

And that was as far as I got.

There were more crazy compliments, more bowing and scraping, more assurances of eternal reverence and love, and then I was following my rope-necked guide through winding, dark halls, across dim rooms, and up and down rickety stairs again.

At the street door—after he had taken down the bars—he slid my gun out of his shirt and handed it to me. I squelched the impulse to look at it then and there to see if anything had been done to it. Instead I stuck it in my pocket and stepped through the door.

"Thanks for the killing upstairs," I said.

The Chinese grunted, bowed, and closed the door.

I went up to Stockton Street, and turned toward the office, walking along slowly, punishing my brains.

First, there was Dummy Uhl's death to think over. Had it been arranged before-hand: to punish him for bungling that morning and, at the same time, to impress me? And how? And why? Or was it supposed to put me under obligations to the Chinese? And, if so, why? Or was it just one of those complicated tricks the Chinese like? I put the subject away and pointed my thoughts at the little plump yellow man in the purple robe.

I liked him. He had humor, brains, nerve, everything. To jam him in a cell would be a trick you'd want to write home about. He was my idea of a man worth working against.

But I didn't kid myself into thinking I had anything on him. Dummy Uhl had given me a connection between The Whistler's Hotel Irvington and Chang Li Ching. Dummy Uhl had gone into action when I accused him of being mixed up in the Shan killings. That much I had—and that was all, except that Chang had said nothing to show he wasn't interested in the Shan troubles.

In this light, the chances were that Dummy's death had not been a planned performance. It was more likely that he had seen me coming, had tried to wipe me out, and had been knocked off by my guide because he was interfering with the audience Chang had granted me. Dummy couldn't have had a very valuable life in the Chinese's eye—or in anybody else's.

I wasn't at all dissatisfied with the day's work so far. I hadn't done anything brilliant, but I had got a look at my destination, or thought I had. If I was butting my head against a stone wall, I at least knew where the wall was and had seen the man who owned it.

In the office, a message from Dick Foley was waiting for me. He had rented a front apartment up the street from the Irvington and had put in a couple of hours trailing The Whistler.

The Whistler had spent half an hour in "Big Fat" Thomson's place on Market Street, talking to the proprietor and some of the sure-thing gamblers who congregate there. Then he had taxi-cabbed out to an apartment house on O'Farrell Street—the Glenway—where he had rung one of the bells. Getting no answer, he had let himself into the building with a key. An hour later he had come out and returned to his hotel. Dick hadn't been able to determine which bell he had rung, or which apartment he had visited.

I got Lillian Shan on the telephone.

"Will you be in this evening?" I asked. "I've something I want to go into with you, and I can't give it to you over the wire."

"I will be at home until seven-thirty."

"All right, I'll be down."

It was seven-fifteen when the car I had hired put me down at her front door. She opened the door for me. The Danish woman who was filling in until new servants were employed stayed there only in the daytime, returning to her own home—a mile back from the shore—at night.

The evening gown Lillian Shan wore was severe enough, but it suggested that if she would throw away her glasses and do something for herself, she might not be so unfeminine looking after all. She took me upstairs, to the library, where a clean-cut lad of twenty-something in evening clothes got up from a chair as we came in—a well-set-up boy with fair hair and skin.

His name, I learned when we were introduced, was Garthorne. The girl seemed willing enough to hold our conference in his presence. I wasn't. After I had done everything but insist point-blank on seeing her alone, she excused herself—calling him Jack—and took me out into another room.

By then I was a bit impatient.

"Who's that?" I demanded.

She put her eyebrows up for me.

"Mr. John Garthorne," she said.

"How well do you know him?"

"May I ask why you are so interested?"

"You may. Mr. John Garthorne is all wrong, I think."

"Wrong?"

I had another idea.

"Where does he live?"

She gave me an O'Farrell Street number.

"The Glenway Apartments?"

"I think so." She was looking at me without any affectation at all. "Will you please explain?"

"One more question and I will. Do you know a Chinese named Chang Li Ching?"

"No."

"All right. I'll tell you about Garthorne. So far I've run into two angles on this trouble of yours. One of them has to do with this Chang Li Ching in Chinatown, and one with an ex-convict named Conyers. This John Garthorne was in Chinatown today. I saw him coming out of a cellar that probably connects with Chang Li Ching's house. The ex-convict Conyers visited the building where Garthorne lives, early this afternoon."

Her mouth popped open and then shut.

"That is absurd!" she snapped. "I have known Mr. Garthorne for some time, and——"

"Exactly how long?"

"A long—several months."

"Where'd you meet him?"

"Through a girl I knew at college."

"What does he do for a living?"

She stood stiff and silent.

"Listen, Miss Shan," I said. "Garthorne may be all right, but I've got to look him up. If he's in the clear there'll be no harm done. I want to know what you know about him."

I got it, little by little. He was, or she thought he was, the youngest son of a prominent Richmond, Virginia, family, in disgrace just now because of some sort of boyish prank. He had come to San Francisco four months ago, to wait until his father's anger cooled. Meanwhile his mother kept him in money, leaving him without the necessity of toiling during his exile. He had brought a letter of introduction from one of Lillian Shan's schoolmates. Lillian Shan had, I gathered, a lot of liking for him.

"You're going out with him tonight?" I asked when I had got this.

"Yes."

"In his car or yours?"

She frowned, but she answered my question.

"In his. We are going to drive down to Half Moon for dinner."

"I'll need a key, then, because I am coming back here after you have gone."

"You're what?"

"I'm coming back here. I'll ask you not to say anything about my more or less unworthy suspicions to him, but my honest opinion is that he's drawing you away for the evening. So if the engine breaks down on the way back, just pretend you see nothing unusual in it."

That worried her, but she wouldn't admit I might be right. I got the key, though, and then I told her of my employment agency scheme that needed her assistance, and she promised to be at the office at half past nine Thursday morning.

I didn't see Garthorne again before I left the house.

VI

In my hired car again, I had the driver take me to the nearest village, where I bought a plug of chewing tobacco, a flash-light, and a box of cartridges at the general store. My gun is a .38 Special, but I had to take the shorter, weaker cartridges, because the storekeeper didn't keep the specials in stock.

My purchases in my pocket, we started back toward the Shan house again. Two bends in the road this side of it, I stopped the car, paid the chauffeur, and sent him on his way, finishing the trip afoot.

The house was dark all around.

Letting myself in as quietly as possible, and going easy with the flashlight, I gave the interior a combing from cellar to roof. I was the only occupant. In the kitchen, I looted the ice-box for a bite or two, which I washed down with milk. I could have used some coffee, but coffee is too fragrant.

The luncheon done, I made myself comfortable on a chair in the passageway between the kitchen and the rest of the house. On one side of the passageway, steps led down to the basement. On the other, steps led upstairs. With every door in the house except the outer ones open, the passageway was the center of things so far as hearing noises was concerned.

An hour went by—quietly except for the passing of cars on the road a hundred yards away and the washing of the Pacific down in the little cove. I chewed on my plug of tobacco—a substitute for cigarettes—and tried to count up the hours of my life I'd spent like this, sitting or standing around waiting for something to happen.

The telephone rang.

I let it ring. It might be Lillian Shan needing help, but I couldn't take a chance. It was too likely to be some egg trying to find out if anybody was in the house.

Another half hour went by with a breeze springing up from the ocean, rustling trees outside.

A noise came that was neither wind nor surf nor passing car.

Something clicked somewhere.

It was at a window, but I didn't know which. I got rid of my chew, got gun and flashlight out.

It sounded again, harshly.

Somebody was giving a window a strong play—too strong. The catch rattled, and something clicked against the pane. It was a stall. Whoever he was, he could have smashed the glass with less noise than he was making.

I stood up, but I didn't leave the passageway. The window noise was a fake to draw the attention of anyone who might be in the house. I turned my back on it, trying to see into the kitchen.

The kitchen was too black to see anything.

I saw nothing there. I heard nothing there.

Damp air blew on me from the kitchen.

That was something to worry about. I had company, and he was slicker than I. He could open doors or windows under my nose. That wasn't so good.

Weight on rubber heels, I backed away from my chair until the frame of the cellar door touched my shoulder. I wasn't sure I was going to like this party. I like an even break or better, and this didn't look like one.

So when a thin line of light danced out of the kitchen to hit the chair in the passageway, I was three steps cellar-ward, my back flat against the stair-wall.

The light fixed itself on the chair for a couple of seconds, and then began to dart around the passageway, through it into the room beyond. I could see nothing but the light.

Fresh sounds came to me—the purr of automobile engines close to the house on the road side, the soft padding of feet on the back porch, on the kitchen linoleum, quite a few feet. An odor came to me—an unmistakable odor—the smell of unwashed Chinese.

Then I lost track of these things. I had plenty to occupy me close up.

The proprietor of the flashlight was at the head of the cellar steps. I had ruined my eyes watching the light: I couldn't see him.

The first thin ray he sent downstairs missed me by an inch—which gave me time to make a map there in the dark. If he was of medium size, holding the light in his left hand, a gun in his right, and exposing as little of himself as possible— his noodle should have been a foot and a half above the beginning of the light-beam, the same distance behind it, six inches to the left—my left.

The light swung sideways and hit one of my legs.

I swung the barrel of my gun at the point I had marked X in the night.

His gun-fire cooked my cheek. One of his arms tried to take me with him. I twisted away and let him dive alone into the cellar, showing me a flash of gold teeth as he went past.

The house was full of "Ah yahs" and pattering feet.

I had to move—or I'd be pushed.

Downstairs might be a trap. I went up to the passageway again.

The passageway was solid and alive with stinking bodies. Hands and teeth began to take my clothes away from me. I knew damned well I had declared myself in on something!

I was one of a struggling, tearing, grunting and groaning mob of invisibles. An eddy of them swept me toward the kitchen. Hitting, kicking, butting, I went along.

A high-pitched voice was screaming Chinese orders.

My shoulder scraped the door-frame as I was carried into the kitchen, fighting as best I could against enemies I couldn't see, afraid to use the gun I still gripped.

I was only one part of the mad scramble. The flash of my gun might have made me the center of it. These lunatics were fighting panic now: I didn't want to show them something tangible to tear apart.

I went along with them, cracking everything that got in my way, and being cracked back. A bucket got between my feet.

I crashed down, upsetting my neighbors, rolled over a body, felt a foot on my face, squirmed from under it, and came to rest in a corner, still tangled up with the galvanized bucket.

Thank God for that bucket!

I wanted these people to go away. I didn't care who or what they were. If they'd depart in peace I'd forgive their sins.

I put my gun inside the bucket and squeezed the trigger. I got the worst of the racket, but there was enough to go around. It sounded like a crump going off.

I cut loose in the bucket again, and had another idea. Two fingers of my left hand in my mouth, I whistled as shrill as I could while I emptied the gun.

It was a sweet racket!

When my gun had run out of bullets and my lungs out of air, I was alone. I was glad to be alone. I knew why men go off and live in caves by themselves. And I didn't blame them!

Sitting there alone in the dark, I reloaded my gun.

On hands and knees I found my way to the open kitchen door, and peeped out into the blackness that told me nothing. The surf made guzzling sounds in the cove. From the other side of the house came the noise of cars. I hoped it was my friends going away.

I shut the door, locked it, and turned on the kitchen light. The place wasn't as badly upset as I had expected. Some pans and dishes were down and a chair had been broken, and the place smelled of unwashed bodies. But that was all—except a blue cotton sleeve in the middle of the floor, a straw sandal near the passageway door, and a handful of short black hairs, a bit blood-smeared, beside the sandal.

In the cellar I did not find the man I had sent down there. An open door showed how he had left me. His flashlight was there, and my own, and some of his blood.

Upstairs again, I went through the front of the house. The front door was open. Rugs had been rumpled. A blue vase was broken on the floor. A table was pushed out of place, and a couple of chairs had been upset. I found an old and greasy brown felt hat that had neither sweat-band nor hat-band. I found a grimy photograph of President Coolidge—apparently cut from a Chinese newspaper—and six wheat-straw cigarette papers.

I found nothing upstairs to show that any of my guests had gone up there.

It was half past two in the morning when I heard a car drive up to the front door. I peeped out of Lillian Shan's bedroom window, on the second floor. She was saying goodnight to Jack Garthorne.

I went back to the library to wait for her.

"Nothing happened?" were her first words, and they sounded more like a prayer than anything else.

"It did," I told her, "and I suppose you had your breakdown."

For a moment I thought she was going to lie to me, but she nodded, and dropped into a chair, not as erect as usual.

"I had a lot of company," I said, "but I can't say I found out much about them. The fact is, I bit off more than I could chew, and had to be satisfied with chasing them out."

"You didn't call the sheriff's office?" There was something strange about the tone in which she put the question.

"No—I don't want Garthorne arrested yet."

That shook the dejection out of her. She was up, tall and straight in front of me, and cold.

"I'd rather not go into that again," she said.

That was all right with me, but:

"You didn't say anything to him, I hope."

"Say anything to him?" She seemed amazed. "Do you think I would insult him by repeating your guesses—your absurd guesses?"

"That's fine," I applauded her silence if not her opinion of my theories. "Now, I'm going to stay here tonight. There isn't a chance in a hundred of anything happening, but I'll play it safe."

She didn't seem very enthusiastic about that, but she finally went off to bed.

Nothing happened between then and sun-up, of course. I left the house as soon as daylight came and gave the grounds the once over. Footprints were all over the place, from water's edge to driveway. Along the driveway some of the sod was cut where machines had been turned carelessly.

Borrowing one of the cars from the garage, I was back in San Francisco before the morning was far gone.

In the office, I asked the Old Man to put an operative behind Jack Garthorne; to have the old hat, flashlight, sandal and the rest of my souvenirs put under the microscope and searched for finger prints, foot prints, tooth-prints or what have you; and to have our Richmond branch look up the Garthornes. Then I went up to see my Filipino assistant.

He was gloomy.

"What's the matter?" I asked. "Somebody knock you over?"

"Oh, no, sir!" he protested. "But maybe I am not so good a detective. I try to follow one fella, and he turns a corner and he is gone."

"Who was he, and what was he up to?"

"I do not know, sir. There is four automobiles with men getting out of them into that cellar of which I tell you the strange Chinese live. After they are gone in, one man comes out. He wears his hat down over bandage on his upper face, and he walks away rapidly. I try to follow him, but he turns that corner, and where is he?"

"What time did all this happen?"

"Twelve o'clock, maybe."

"Could it have been later than that, or earlier?"

"Yes, sir."

My visitors, no doubt, and the man Cipriano had tried to shadow could have been the one I swatted. The Filipino hadn't thought to get the license numbers of the automobiles. He didn't know whether they had been driven by white men or Chinese, or even what make cars they were.

"You've done fine," I assured him. "Try it again tonight. Take it easy, and you'll get there."

From him I went to a telephone and called the Hall of Justice. Dummy Uhl's death had not been reported, I learned.

Twenty minutes later I was skinning my knuckles on Chang Li Ching's front door.

VII

The little old Chinese with the rope neck didn't open for me this time. Instead, a young Chinese with a smallpox-pitted face and a wide grin.

"You wanna see Chang Li Ching," he said before I could speak, and stepped back for me to enter.

I went in and waited while he replaced all the bars and locks. We went to Chang by a shorter route than before, but it was still far from direct. For a while I amused myself trying to map the route in my head as he went along, but it was too complicated, so I gave it up.

The velvet-hung room was empty when my guide showed me in, bowed, grinned, and left me. I sat down in a chair near the table and waited.

Chang Li Ching didn't put on the theatricals for me by materializing silently, or anything of the sort. I heard his soft slippers on the floor before he parted the hangings and came in. He was alone, his white whiskers ruffled in a smile that was grandfatherly.

"The Scatterer of Hordes honors my poor residence again," he greeted me, and went on at great length with the same sort of nonsense that I'd had to listen to on my first visit.

The Scatterer of Hordes part was cool enough—if it was a reference to last night's doings.

"Not knowing who he was until too late, I beaned one of your servants last night," I said when he had run out of flowers for the time. "I know there's nothing I can do to square myself for such a terrible act, but I hope you'll let me cut my throat and bleed to death in one of your garbage cans as a sort of apology."

A little sighing noise that could have been a smothered chuckle disturbed the old man's lips, and the purple cap twitched on his round head.

"The Disperser of Marauders knows all things," he murmured blandly, "even to the value of noise in driving away demons. If he says the man he struck was Chang Li Ching's servant, who is Chang to deny it?"

I tried him with my other barrel.

"I don't know much—not even why the police haven't yet heard of the death of the man who was killed here yesterday."

One of his hands made little curls in his white beard.

"I had not heard of the death," he said.

I could guess what was coming, but I wanted to take a look at it.

"You might ask the man who brought me here yesterday," I suggested.

Chang Li Ching picked up a little padded stick from the table and struck a tasseled gong that hung at his shoulder. Across the room the hangings parted to admit the pock-marked Chinese who had brought me in.

"Did death honor our hovel yesterday?" Chang asked in English.

"No, *Ta Jen*," the pock-marked one said.

"It was the nobleman who guided me here yesterday," I explained, "not this son of an emperor."

Chang imitated surprise.

"Who welcomed the King of Spies yesterday?" he asked the man at the door.

"I bring 'em, *Ta Jen*."

I grinned at the pock-marked man, he grinned back, and Chang smiled benevolently.

"An excellent jest," he said.

It was.

The pock-marked man bowed and started to duck back through the hangings. Loose shoes rattled on the boards behind him. He spun around. One of the big wrestlers I had seen the previous day loomed above him. The wrestler's eyes were bright with excitement, and grunted Chinese syllables poured out of his mouth. The pock-marked one talked back. Chang Li Ching silenced them with a sharp command. All this was in Chinese—out of my reach.

"Will the Grand Duke of Manhunters permit his servant to depart for a moment to attend to his distressing domestic affairs?"

"Sure."

Chang bowed with his hands together, and spoke to the wrestler.

"You will remain here to see that the great one is not disturbed and that any wishes he expresses are gratified."

The wrestler bowed and stood aside for Chang to pass through the door with the pock-marked man. The hangings swung over the door behind them.

I didn't waste any language on the man at the door, but got a cigarette going and waited for Chang to come back. The cigarette was half gone when a shot sounded in the building, not far away.

The giant at the door scowled.

Another shot sounded, and running feet thumped in the hall. The pock-marked man's face came through the hangings. He poured grunts at the wrestler. The wrestler scowled at me and protested. The other insisted.

The wrestler scowled at me again, rumbled, "You wait," and was gone with the other.

I finished my cigarette to the tune of muffled struggle-sounds that seemed to come from the floor below. There were two more shots, far apart. Feet ran past the door of the room I was in. Perhaps ten minutes had gone since I had been left alone.

I found I wasn't alone.

Across the room from the door, the hangings that covered the wall were disturbed. The blue, green and silver velvet bulged out an inch and settled back in place.

The disturbance happened the second time perhaps ten feet farther along the wall. No movement for a while, and then a tremor in the far corner.

Somebody was creeping along between hangings and wall.

I let them creep, still slumping in my chair with idle hands. If the bulge meant trouble, action on my part would only bring it that much quicker.

I traced the disturbance down the length of that wall and halfway across the other, to where I knew the door was. Then I lost it for some time. I had just decided that the creeper had gone through the door when the curtains opened and the creeper stepped out.

She wasn't four and a half feet high—a living ornament from somebody's shelf. Her face was a tiny oval of painted beauty, its perfection emphasized by the lacquer-black hair that was flat and glossy around her temples. Gold earrings swung beside her smooth cheeks, a jade butterfly was in her hair. A lavender jacket, glittering with white stones, covered her from under her chin to her knees. Lavender stockings showed under her short lavender trousers, and her bound-small feet were in slippers of the same color, shaped like kittens, with yellow stones for eyes and aigrettes for whiskers.

The point of all this our-young-ladies'-fashion stuff is that she was impossibly dainty. But there she was—neither a carving nor a painting, but a living small woman with fear in her black eyes and nervous, tiny fingers worrying the silk at her bosom.

Twice as she came toward me—hurrying with the awkward, quick step of the foot-bound Chinese woman—her head twisted around for a look at the hangings over the door.

I was on my feet by now, going to meet her.

Her English wasn't much. Most of what she babbled at me I missed, though I thought "yung hel-lup" might have been meant for "You help?"

I nodded, catching her under the elbows as she stumbled against me.

She gave me some more language that didn't make the situation any clearer—unless "sul-lay-vee gull" meant slave-girl and "tak-ka wah" meant take away.

"You want me to get you out of here?" I asked.

Her head, close under my chin, went up and down, and her red flower of a mouth shaped a smile that made all the other smiles I could remember look like leers.

She did some more talking. I got nothing out of it. Taking one of her elbows out of my hand, she pushed up her sleeve, baring a forearm that an artist had spent a life-time carving out of ivory. On it were five finger-shaped bruises ending in cuts where the nails had punctured the flesh.

She let the sleeve fall over it again, and gave me more words. They didn't mean anything to me, but they tinkled prettily.

"All right," I said, sliding my gun out. "If you want to go, we'll go."

Both her hands went to the gun, pushing it down, and she talked excitedly into my face, winding up with a flicking of one hand across her collar—a pantomime of a throat being cut.

I shook my head from side to side and urged her toward the door.

She balked, fright large in her eyes.

One of her hands went to my watch-pocket. I let her take the watch out.

She put the tiny tip of one pointed finger over the twelve and then circled the dial three times. I thought I got that. Thirty-six hours from noon would be midnight of the following night—Thursday.

"Yes," I said.

She shot a look at the door and led me to the table where the tea things were. With a finger dipped in cold tea she began to draw on the table's inlaid top. Two parallel lines I took for a street. Another pair crossed them. The third pair crossed the second and paralleled the first.

"Waverly Place?" I guessed.

Her face bobbed up and down, delightedly.

On what I took for the east side of Waverly Place she drew a square—perhaps a house. In the square she set what could have been a rose. I frowned at that. She erased the rose and in its place put a crooked circle, adding dots. I thought I had it. The rose had been a cabbage. This thing was a potato. The square represented the grocery store I had noticed on Waverly Place. I nodded.

Her finger crossed the street and put a square on the other side, and her face turned up to mine, begging me to understand her.

"The house across the street from the grocer's," I said slowly, and then, as she tapped my watch-pocket, I added, "at midnight tomorrow."

I don't know how much of it she caught, but she nodded her little head until her earrings were swinging like crazy pendulums.

With a quick diving motion, she caught my right hand, kissed it, and with a tottering, hoppy run vanished behind the velvet curtains.

I used my handkerchief to wipe the map off the table and was smoking in my chair when Chang Li Ching returned some twenty minutes later.

I left shortly after that, as soon as we had traded a few dizzy compliments. The pock-marked man ushered me out.

At the office there was nothing new for me. Foley hadn't been able to shadow The Whistler the night before.

I went home for the sleep I had not got last night.

VIII

At ten minutes after ten the next morning Lillian Shan and I arrived at the front door of Fong Yick's employment agency on Washington Street.

"Give me just two minutes," I told her as I climbed out. "Then come in."

"Better keep your steam up," I suggested to the driver. "We might have to slide away in a hurry."

In Fong Yick's, a lanky, grey-haired man whom I thought was the Old Man's Frank Paul was talking around a chewed cigar to half a dozen Chinese. Across the battered counter a fat Chinese was watching them boredly through immense steel-rimmed spectacles.

I looked at the half-dozen. The third from me had a crooked nose—a short, squat man.

I pushed aside the others and reached for him.

I don't know what the stuff he tried on me was—jiu jitsu,

maybe, or its Chinese equivalent. Anyhow, he crouched and moved his stiffly open hands trickily.

I took hold of him here and there, and presently had him by the nape of his neck, with one of his arms bent up behind him.

Another Chinese piled on my back. The lean, grey-haired man did something to his face, and the Chinese went over in a corner and stayed there.

That was the situation when Lillian Shan came in.

I shook the flat-nosed boy at her.

"Yin Hung!" she exclaimed.

"Hoo Lun isn't one of the others?" I asked, pointing to the spectators.

She shook her head emphatically, and began jabbering Chinese at my prisoner. He jabbered back, meeting her gaze.

"What are you going to do with him?" she asked me in a voice that wasn't quite right.

"Turn him over to the police to hold for the San Mateo sheriff. Can you get anything out of him?"

"No."

I began to push him toward the door. The steel-spectacled Chinese blocked the way, one hand behind him.

"No can do," he said.

I slammed Yin Hung into him. He went back against the wall.

"Get out!" I yelled at the girl.

The grey-haired man stopped two Chinese who dashed for the door, sent them the other way— back hard against the wall.

We left the place.

There was no excitement in the street. We climbed into the taxicab and drove the block and a half to the Hall of Justice, where I yanked my prisoner out. The rancher Paul said he wouldn't go in, that he had enjoyed the party, but now had some of his own business to look after. He went on up Kearney Street afoot.

Half-out of the taxicab, Lillian Shan changed her mind.

"Unless it's necessary," she said, "I'd rather not go in either. I'll wait here for you."

"Righto," and I pushed my captive across the sidewalk and up the steps.

Inside, an interesting situation developed.

The San Francisco police weren't especially interested in Yin Hung, though willing enough, of course, to hold him for the sheriff of San Mateo County.

Yin Hung pretended he didn't know any English, and I was curious to know what sort of story he had to tell, so I hunted around in the detectives' assembly room until I found Bill Thode of the Chinatown detail, who talks the language some.

He and Yin Hung jabbered at each other for some time.

Then Bill looked at me, laughed, bit off the end of a cigar, and leaned back in his chair.

"According to the way he tells it," Bill said, "that Wan Lan woman and Lillian Shan had a row. The next day Wan Lan's not anywheres around. The Shan girl and Wang Ma, her maid, say Wan Lan has left, but Hoo Lun tells this fellow he saw Wang Ma burning some of Wan Lan's clothes.

"So Hoo Lun and this fellow think something's wrong, and the next day they're damned sure of it, because this fellow misses a spade from his garden tools. He finds it again that night, and it's still wet with damp dirt, and he says no dirt was dug up anywheres around the place—not outside of the house anyways. So him and Hoo Lun put their heads together, didn't like the result, and decided they'd better dust out before they went wherever Wan Lan had gone. That's the message."

"Where is Hoo Lun now?"

"He says he don't know."

"So Lillian Shan and Wang Ma were still in the house when this pair left?" I asked. "They hadn't started for the East yet?"

"So he says."

"Has he got any idea why Wan Lan was killed?"

"Not that I've been able to get out of him."

"Thanks, Bill! You'll notify the sheriff that you're holding him?"

"Sure."

Of course Lillian Shan and the taxicab were gone when I came out of the Hall of Justice door.

I went back into the lobby and used one of the booths to phone the office. Still no report from Dick Foley—nothing of any value—and none from the operative who was trying to shadow Jack Garthorne. A wire had come from the Richmond branch. It was to the effect that the Garthornes were a wealthy and well-known local family, that young Jack was usually in trouble, that he had slugged a Prohibition agent during a cafe raid a few months ago, that his father had taken him out of his will and chased him from the house, but that his mother was believed to be sending him money.

That fit in with what the girl had told me.

A street car carried me to the garage where I had stuck the roadster I had borrowed from the girl's garage the previous morning. I drove around to Cipriano's apartment building. He had no news of any importance for me. He had spent the night hanging around Chinatown, but had picked up nothing.

I was a little inclined toward grouchiness as I turned the roadster west, driving out through Golden Gate Park to the Ocean Boulevard. The job wasn't getting along as snappily as I wanted it to.

I let the roadster slide down the boulevard at a good clip, and the salt air blew some of my kinks away.

A bony-faced man with pinkish mustache opened the door when I rang Lillian Shan's bell. I knew him—Tucker, a deputy sheriff.

"Hullo," he said. "What d'you want?"

"I'm hunting for her too."

"Keep on hunting," he grinned. "Don't let me stop you."

"Not here, huh?"

"Nope. The Swede woman that works for her says she was in and out half an hour before I got here, and I've been here about ten minutes now."

"Got a warrant for her?" I asked.

"You bet you! Her chauffeur squawked."

"Yes, I heard him," I said. "I'm the bright boy who gathered him in."

I spent five or ten minutes more talking to Tucker and then climbed in the roadster again.

"Will you give the agency a ring when you nab her?" I asked as I closed the door.

"You bet you."

I pointed the roadster at San Francisco again.

Just outside of Daly City a taxicab passed me, going south. Jack Garthorne's face looked through the window.

I snapped on the brakes and waved my arm. The taxicab turned and came back to me. Garthorne opened the door, but did not get out.

I got down into the road and went over to him.

"There's a deputy sheriff waiting in Miss Shan's house, if that's where you're headed."

His blue eyes jumped wide, and then narrowed as he looked suspiciously at me.

"Let's go over to the side of the road and have a little talk," I invited.

He got out of the taxicab and we crossed to a couple of comfortable-looking boulders on the other side.

"Where is Lil—Miss Shan?" he asked.

"Ask The Whistler," I suggested.

This blond kid wasn't so good. It took him a long time to get his gun out. I let him go through with it.

"What do you mean?" he demanded.

I hadn't meant anything. I had just wanted to see how the remark would hit him. I kept quiet.

"Has The Whistler got her?"

"I don't think so," I admitted, though I hated to do it. "But the point is that she has had to go in hiding to keep from being hanged for the murders The Whistler framed."

"Hanged?"

"Uh-huh. The deputy waiting in her house has a warrant for her—for murder."

He put away his gun and made gurgling noises in his throat.

"I'll go there! I'll tell everything I know!"

He started for his taxicab.

"Wait!" I called. "Maybe you'd better tell me what you know first. I'm working for her, you know."

He spun around and came back.

"Yes, that's right. You'll know what to do."

"Now what do you really know, if anything?" I asked when he was standing in front of me.

"I know the whole thing!" he cried. "About the deaths and the booze and——"

"Easy! Easy! There's no use wasting all that knowledge on the chauffeur."

He quieted down, and I began to pump him. I spent nearly an hour getting all of it.

IX

The history of his young life, as he told it to me, began with his departure from home after falling into disgrace through slugging the Prohi. He had come to San Francisco to wait until his father cooled off. Meanwhile his mother kept him in funds, but she didn't send him all the money a young fellow in a wild city could use.

That was the situation when he ran into The Whistler, who suggested that a chap with Garthorne's front could pick up some easy money in the rum-running game if he did what he was told to do. Garthorne was willing enough. He didn't like Prohibition—it had caused most of his troubles. Rum-running sounded romantic to him—shots in the dark, signal lights off the starboard bow, and so on.

The Whistler, it seemed, had boats and booze and waiting customers, but his landing arrangements were out of whack. He had his eye on a little cove down the shore line that was an ideal spot to land hooch. It was neither too close nor too far from San Francisco. It was sheltered on either side by rocky points, and screened from the road by a large house and high hedges. Given the use of that house, his troubles would be over. He could land his hooch in the cove, run it into the house, repack it innocently there, put it through the front door into his automobiles, and shoot it to the thirsty city.

The house, he told Garthorne, belonged to a Chinese girl named Lillian Shan, who would neither sell nor rent it. Garthorne was to make her acquaintance—The Whistler was already supplied with a letter of introduction written by a former classmate of the girl's, a classmate who had fallen a lot since university days—and try to work himself in with her to a degree of intimacy that would permit him to make her an offer for the use of the house. That is, he was to find out if she was the sort of person who could be approached with a more or less frank offer of a share in the profits of The Whistler's game.

Garthorne had gone through with his part, or the first of it, and had become fairly intimate with the girl, when she suddenly left for the East, sending him a note saying she would be gone several months. That was fine for the rum-runners. Garthorne, calling at the house, the next day, had learned that Wang Ma had gone with her mistress, and that the three other servants had been left in charge of the house.

That was all Garthorne knew firsthand. He had not taken part in the landing of the booze, though he would have liked to. But The Whistler had ordered him to stay away, so that he could continue his original part when the girl returned.

The Whistler told Garthorne he had bought the help of the three Chinese servants, but that the woman, Wan Lan, had been killed by the two men in a fight over their shares of the money. Booze had been run through the house once during Lillian Shan's absence. Her unexpected return gummed things. The house still held some of the booze. They had to grab her and Wang Ma and stick them in a closet until they got the stuff away. The strangling of Wang Ma had been accidental—a rope tied too tight.

The worst complication, however, was that another cargo was scheduled to land in the cove the following Tuesday night, and there was no way of getting word out to the boat that the place was closed. The Whistler sent for our hero and ordered him to get the girl out of the way and keep her out of the way until at least two o'clock Wednesday morning.

Garthorne had invited her to drive down to Half Moon with him for dinner that night. She had accepted. He had faked engine trouble, and had kept her away from the house until two-thirty, and The Whistler had told him later that everything had gone through without a hitch.

After this I had to guess at what Garthorne was driving at—he stuttered and stammered and let his ideas rattle looser than ever. I think it added up to this: he hadn't thought much about the ethics of his play with the girl. She had no attraction for him—too severe and serious to seem really feminine. And he had not pretended—hadn't carried on what could possibly be called a flirtation with her. Then he suddenly woke up to the fact that she wasn't as indifferent as he. That had been a shock to him—one he couldn't stand. He had seen things straight for the first time. He had thought of it before as simply a wit-matching game. Affection made it different—even though the affection was all on one side.

"I told The Whistler I was through this afternoon," he finished.

"How did he like it?"

"Not a lot. In fact, I had to hit him."

"So? And what were you planning to do next?"

"I was going to see Miss Shan, tell her the truth, and then—then I thought I'd better lay low."

"I think you'd better. The Whistler might not like being hit."

"I won't hide now! I'll go give myself up and tell the truth."

"Forget it!" I advised him. "That's no good. You don't know enough to help her."

That wasn't exactly the truth, because he did know that the chauffeur and Hoo Lun had still been in the house the day after her departure for the East. But I didn't want him to get out of the game yet.

"If I were you," I went on, "I'd pick out a quiet hiding place and stay there until I can get word to you. Know a good place?"

"Yes," slowly. "I have a—a friend who will hide me—down near—near the Latin Quarter."

"Near the Latin Quarter?" That could be Chinatown. I did some sharp shooting. "Waverly Place?"

He jumped.

"How did you know?"

"I'm a detective. I know everything. Ever hear of Chang Li Ching?"

"No."

I tried to keep from laughing into his puzzled face.

The first time I had seen this cut-up he was leaving a house in Waverly Place, with a Chinese woman's face showing dimly in the doorway behind him. The house had been across the street from a grocery. The Chinese girl with whom I had talked at Chang's had given me a slave-girl yarn and an invitation to that same house. Big-hearted Jack here had fallen for the same game, but he didn't know that the girl had anything to do with Chang Li Ching, didn't know that Chang existed, didn't know Chang and The Whistler were playmates. Now Jack is in trouble, and he's going to the girl to hide!

I didn't dislike this angle of the game. He was walking into a trap, but that was nothing to me—or, rather, I hoped it was going to help me.

"What's your friend's name?" I asked.

He hesitated.

"What is the name of the tiny woman whose door is across the street from the grocery?" I made myself plain.

"Hsiu Hsiu."

"All right," I encouraged him in his foolishness. "You go there. That's an excellent hiding place. Now if I want to get a Chinese boy to you with a message, how will he find you?"

"There's a flight of steps to the left as you go in. He'll have to skip the second and third steps, because they are fitted with some sort of alarm. So is the handrail. On the second floor you turn to the left again. The hall is dark. The second door to the right—on the right-hand side of the hall—lets you into a room. On the other side of the room is a closet, with a door hidden behind old clothes. There are usually people in the room the door opens into, so he'll have to wait for a chance to get through it. This room has a little balcony outside, that you can get to from either of the windows. The balcony's sides are solid, so if you crouch low you can't be seen from the street or from other houses. At the other end of the balcony there are two loose floor boards. You slide down under them into a little room between walls. The trap-door there will let you down into another just like it where I'll probably be. There's another way out of the bottom room, down a flight of steps, but I've never been that way."

A fine mess! It sounded like a child's game. But even with all this frosting on the cake our young chump hadn't tumbled. He took it seriously.

"So that's how it's done!" I said. "You'd better get there as soon as you can, and stay there until my messenger gets to you. You'll know him by the cast in one of his eyes, and maybe I'd better give him a password. Haphazard—that'll be the word. The street door—is it locked?"

"No. I've never found it locked. There are forty or fifty Chinamen—or perhaps a hundred—living in that building, so I don't suppose the door is ever locked."

"Good. Beat it now."

X

At 10:15 that night I was pushing open the door opposite the grocery in Waverly Place—an hour and three-quarters early for my date with Hsiu Hsiu. At 9:55 Dick Foley had phoned that The Whistler had gone into the red-painted door on Spofford Alley.

I found the interior dark, and closed the door softly, concentrating on the childish directions Garthorne had given me. That I knew they were silly didn't help me, since I didn't know any other route.

The stairs gave me some trouble, but I got over the second and third without touching the handrail, and went on up. I found the second door in the hall, the closet in the room behind it, and the door in the closet. Light came through the cracks around it. Listening, I heard nothing.

I pushed the door open—the room was empty. A smoking oil lamp stunk there. The nearest window made no sound as I raised it. That was inartistic—a squeak would have impressed Garthorne with his danger.

I crouched low on the balcony, in accordance with instructions, and found the loose floorboards that opened up a black hole. Feet first, I went down in, slanting at an angle that made descent easy. It seemed to be a sort of slot cut diagonally through the wall. It was stuffy, and I don't like narrow holes. I went down swiftly, coming into a small room, long and narrow, as if placed inside a thick wall.

No light was there. My flashlight showed a room perhaps eighteen feet long by four wide, furnished with table, couch and two chairs. I looked under the one rug on the floor. The trapdoor was there—a crude affair that didn't pretend it was part of the floor.

Flat on my belly, I put an ear to the trapdoor. No sound.
I raised it a couple of inches. Darkness and a faint murmuring of voices. I pushed the trapdoor wide, let it down easily
on the floor and stuck head and shoulders into the opening,
discovering then that it was a double arrangement. Another
door was below, fitting no doubt in the ceiling of the room
below.

Cautiously I let myself down on it. It gave under my foot.
I could have pulled myself up again, but since I had disturbed
it I chose to keep going.

I put both feet on it. It swung down. I dropped into light.
The door snapped up over my head. I grabbed Hsiu Hsiu and
clapped a hand over her tiny mouth in time to keep her quiet.

"Hello," I said to the startled Garthorne; "this is my boy's
evening off, so I came myself."

"Hello," he gasped.

This room, I saw, was a duplicate of the one from which I
had dropped, another cupboard between walls, though this
one had an unpainted wooden door at one end.

I handed Hsiu Hsiu to Garthorne.

"Keep her quiet," I ordered, "while——"

The clicking of the door's latch silenced me. I jumped to
the wall on the hinged side of the door just as it swung
open—the opener hidden from me by the door.

The door opened wide, but not much wider than Jack
Garthorne's blue eyes, nor than this mouth. I let the door go
back against the wall and stepped out behind my balanced
gun.

The queen of something stood there!

She was a tall woman, straight-bodied and proud. A butterfly-
shaped headdress decked with the loot of a dozen jewelry
stores exaggerated her height. Her gown was amethyst fili-
greed with gold above, a living rainbow below. The clothes
were nothing!

She was—maybe I can make it clear this way. Hsiu Hsiu
was as perfect a bit of feminine beauty as could be imagined.
She was perfect! Then comes this queen of something—and
Hsiu Hsiu's beauty went away. She was a candle in the sun.
She was still pretty—prettier than the woman in the doorway,
if it came to that—but you didn't pay any attention to her.

Hsiu Hsiu was a pretty girl: this royal woman in the doorway was—I don't know the words.

"My God!" Garthorne was whispering harshly. "I never knew it!"

"What are you doing here?" I challenged the woman.

She didn't hear me. She was looking at Hsiu Hsiu as a tigress might look at an alley cat. Hsiu Hsiu was looking at her as an alley cat might look at a tigress. Sweat was on Garthorne's face and his mouth was the mouth of a sick man.

"What are you doing here?" I repeated, stepping closer to Lillian Shan.

"I am here where I belong," she said slowly, not taking her eyes from the slave-girl. "I have come back to my people."

That was a lot of bunk. I turned to the goggling Garthorne.

"Take Hsiu Hsiu to the upper room, and keep her quiet, if you have to strangle her. I want to talk to Miss Shan."

Still dazed, he pushed the table under the trapdoor, climbed up on it, hoisted himself through the ceiling, and reached down. Hsiu Hsiu kicked and scratched, but I heaved her up to him. Then I closed the door through which Lillian Shan had come, and faced her.

"How did you get here?" I demanded.

"I went home after I left you, knowing what Yin Hung would say, because he had told me in the employment office, and when I got home— When I got home I decided to come here where I belong."

"Nonsense!" I corrected her. "When you got home you found a message there from Chang Li Ching, asking you—ordering you to come here."

She looked at me, saying nothing.

"What did Chang want?"

"He thought perhaps he could help me," she said, "and so I stayed here."

More nonsense.

"Chang told you Garthorne was in danger—had split with The Whistler."

"The Whistler?"

"You made a bargain with Chang," I accused her, paying no attention to her question. The chances were she didn't know The Whistler by that name.

She shook her head, jiggling the ornaments on her head-dress.

"There was no bargain," she said, holding my gaze too steadily.

I didn't believe her. I said so.

"You gave Chang your house—or the use of it—in exchange for his promise that"—the boob were the first words I thought of, but I changed them—"Garthorne would be saved from The Whistler, and that you would be saved from the law."

She drew herself up.

"I did," she said calmly.

I caught myself weakening. This woman who looked like the queen of something wasn't easy to handle the way I wanted to handle her. I made myself remember that I knew her when she was homely as hell in mannish clothes.

"You ought to be spanked!" I growled at her. "Haven't you had enough trouble without mixing yourself now with a flock of highbinders? Did you see The Whistler?"

"There was a man up there," she said. "I don't know his name."

I hunted through my pocket and found the picture of him taken when he was sent to San Quentin.

"That is he," she told me when I showed it to her.

"A fine partner you picked," I raged. "What do you think his word on anything is worth?"

"I did not take his word for anything. I took Chang Li Ching's word."

"That's just as bad. They're mates. What was your bargain?"

She balked again, straight, stiff-necked and level-eyed. Because she was getting away from me with this Manchu princess stuff I got peevish.

"Don't be a chump all your life!" I pleaded. "You think you made a deal. They took you in! What do you think they're using your house for?"

She tried to look me down. I tried another angle of attack.

"Here, you don't mind who you make bargains with. Make one with me. I'm still one prison sentence ahead of The Whistler, so if his word is any good at all, mine ought to be highly valuable. You tell me what the deal was. If it's half-way decent, I'll promise you to crawl out of here and forget it. If you don't tell me, I'm going to empty a gun out of the first window I can find. And you'd be surprised how many cops a shot will draw in this part of town, and how fast it'll draw them."

The threat took some of the color out of her face.

"If I tell, you will promise to do nothing?"

"You missed part of it," I reminded her. "If I think the deal is half-way on the level I'll keep quiet."

She bit her lips and let her fingers twist together, and then it came.

"Chang Li Ching is one of the leaders of the anti-Japanese movement in China. Since the death of Sun Wen—or Sun Yat-Sen, as he is called in the south of China and here—the Japanese have increased their hold on the Chinese government until it is greater than it ever was. It is Sun Wen's work that Chang Li Ching and his friends are carrying on.

"With their own government against them, their immediate necessity is to arm enough patriots to resist Japanese aggression when the time comes. That is what my house is used for. Rifles and ammunition are loaded into boats there and sent out to ships lying far offshore. This man you call The Whistler is the owner of the ships that carry the arms to China."

"And the death of the servants?" I asked.

"Wan Lan was a spy for the Chinese government—for the Japanese. Wang Ma's death was an accident, I think, though she, too, was suspected of being a spy. To a patriot, the death of traitors is a necessary thing, you can understand that? Your people are like that too when your country is in danger."

"Garthorne told me a rum-running story," I said. "How about it?"

"He believed it," she said, smiling softly at the trapdoor through which he had gone. "They told him that, because they did not know him well enough to trust him. That is why they would not let him help in the loading."

One of her hands came out to rest on my arm.

"You will go away and keep silent?" she pleaded. "These things are against the law of your country, but would you not break another country's laws to save your own country's life? Have not four hundred million people the right to fight an alien race that would exploit them? Since the day of Taou-kwang my country has been the plaything of more aggressive nations. Is any price too great for patriotic Chinese to pay to end that period of dishonor? You will not put yourself in the way of my people's liberty?"

"I hope they win," I said, "but you've been tricked. The only guns that have gone through your house have gone through in pockets! It would take a year to get a shipload through there. Maybe Chang is running guns to China. It's likely. But they don't go through your place.

"The night I was there coolies went through—coming in, not going out. They came from the beach, and they left in machines. Maybe The Whistler is running the guns over for Chang and bringing coolies back. He can get anything from a thousand dollars up for each one he lands. That's about the how of it. He runs the guns over for Chang, and brings his own stuff—coolies and no doubt some opium—back, getting his big profit on the return trip. There wouldn't be enough money in the guns to interest him.

"The guns would be loaded at a pier, all regular, masquerading as something else. Your house is used for the return. Chang may or may not be tied up with the coolie and opium game, but it's a cinch he'll let The Whistler do whatever he likes if only The Whistler will run his guns across. So, you see, you have been gypped!"

"But——"

"But nothing! You're helping Chang by taking part in the coolie traffic. And, my guess is, your servants were killed, not because they were spies, but because they wouldn't sell you out."

She was white-faced and unsteady on her feet. I didn't let her recover.

"Do you think Chang trusts The Whistler? Did they seem friendly?"

I knew he couldn't trust him, but I wanted something specific.

"No-o-o," she said slowly. "There was some talk about a missing boat."

That was good.

"They still together?"

"Yes."

"How do I get there?"

"Down these steps, across the cellar—straight across—and up two flights of steps on the other side. They were in a room to the right of the second-floor landing."

Thank God I had a direct set of instructions for once!

I jumped up on the table and rapped on the ceiling.

"Come on down, Garthorne, and bring your chaperon."

"Don't either of you budge out of here until I'm back," I told the boob and Lillian Shan when we were all together again. "I'm going to take Hsiu Hsiu with me. Come on, sister, I want you to talk to any bad men I meet. We go to see Chang Li Ching, you understand?" I made faces. "One yell out of you, and—" I put my fingers around her collar and pressed them lightly.

She giggled, which spoiled the effect a little.

"To Chang," I ordered, and, holding her by one shoulder, urged her toward the door.

We went down into the dark cellar, across it, found the other stairs, and started to climb them. Our progress was slow. The girl's bound feet weren't made for fast walking.

A dim light burned on the first floor, where we had to turn to go up to the second floor. We had just made the turn when footsteps sounded behind us.

I lifted the girl up two steps, out of the light, and crouched beside her, holding her still. Four Chinese in wrinkled street clothes came down the first-floor hall, passed our stairs without a glance, and started on.

Hsiu Hsiu opened her red flower of a mouth and let out a squeal that could have been heard over in Oakland.

I cursed, turned her loose, and started up the steps. The four Chinese came after me. On the landing ahead one of Chang's big wrestlers appeared—a foot of thin steel in his paw. I looked back.

Hsiu Hsiu sat on the bottom step, her head over her shoulder, experimenting with different sorts of yells and screams, enjoyment all over her laughing doll's face. One of the climbing yellow men was loosening an automatic.

My legs pushed me on up toward the man-eater at the head of the steps.

When he crouched close above me I let him have it.

My bullet cut the gullet out of him.

I patted his face with my gun as he tumbled down past me.

A hand caught one of my ankles.

Clinging to the railing, I drove my other foot back. Something stopped my foot. Nothing stopped me.

A bullet flaked some of the ceiling down as I made the head of the stairs and jumped for the door to the right.

Pulling it open, I plunged in.

The other of the big man-eaters caught me—caught my plunging hundred and eighty-some pounds as a boy would catch a rubber ball.

Across the room, Chang Li Ching ran plump fingers through his thin whiskers and smiled at me. Beside him, a man I knew for The Whistler started up from his chair, his beefy face twitching.

"The Prince of Hunters is welcome," Chang said, and added something in Chinese to the man-eater who held me.

The man-eater set me down on my feet, and turned to shut the door on my pursuers.

The Whistler sat down again, his red-veined eyes shifty on me, his bloated face empty of enjoyment.

I tucked my gun inside my clothes before I started across the room toward Chang. And crossing the room, I noticed something.

Behind The Whistler's chair the velvet hangings bulged just the least bit, not enough to have been noticed by anyone who hadn't seen them bulge before. So Chang didn't trust his confederate at all!

"I have something I want you to see," I told the old Chinese when I was standing in front of him, or, rather, in front of the table that was in front of him.

"That eye is privileged indeed which may gaze on anything brought by the Father of Avengers."

"I have heard," I said, as I put my hand in my pocket, "that all that starts for China doesn't get there."

The Whistler jumped up from his chair again, his mouth a snarl, his face a dirty pink. Chang Li Ching looked at him, and he sat down again.

I brought out the photograph of The Whistler standing in a group of Japs, the medal of the Order of the Rising Sun on his chest. Hoping Chang had not heard of the swindle and would not know the medal for a counterfeit, I dropped the photograph on the table.

The Whistler craned his neck, but could not see the picture.

Chang Li Ching looked at it for a long moment over his clasped hands, his old eyes shrewd and kindly, his face gentle. No muscle in his face moved. Nothing changed in his eyes.

The nails of his right hand slowly cut a red gash across the back of the clasped left hand.

"It is true," he said softly, "that one acquires wisdom in the company of the wise."

He unclasped his hands, picked up the photograph, and held it out to the beefy man. The Whistler seized it. His face drained grey, his eyes bulged out.

"Why, that's—" he began, and stopped, let the photograph drop to his lap, and slumped down in an attitude of defeat.

That puzzled me. I had expected to argue with him, to convince Chang that the medal was not the fake it was.

"You may have what you wish in payment for this," Chang Li Ching was saying to me.

"I want Lillian Shan and Garthorne cleared, and I want your fat friend here, and I want anybody else who was in on the killings."

Chang's eyes closed for a moment—the first sign of weariness I had seen on his round face.

"You may have them," he said.

"The bargain you made with Miss Shan is all off, of course," I pointed out. "I may need a little evidence to make sure I can hang this baby," nodding at The Whistler.

Chang smiled dreamily.

"That, I am regretful, is not possible."

"Why—?" I began, and stopped.

There was no bulge in the velvet curtain behind The Whistler now, I saw. One of the chair legs glistened in the light. A red pool spread on the floor under him. I didn't have to see his back to know he was beyond hanging.

"That's different," I said, kicking a chair over to the table. "Now we'll talk business."

I sat down and we went into conference.

XI

Two days later everything was cleared up to the satisfaction of police, press and public. The Whistler had been found in a dark street, hours dead from a cut in his back, killed in a bootlegging war, I heard. Hoo Lun was found. The gold-toothed Chinese who had opened the door for Lillian Shan was found. Five others were found. These seven, with Yin Hung, the chauffeur, eventually drew a life sentence apiece. They were The Whistler's men, and Chang sacrificed them without batting an eye. They had as little proof of Chang's complicity as I had, so they couldn't hit back, even if they knew that Chang had given me most of my evidence against them.

Nobody but the girl, Chang and I knew anything about Garthorne's part, so he was out, with liberty to spend most of his time at the girl's house.

I had no proof that I could tie on Chang, couldn't get any. Regardless of his patriotism, I'd have given my right eye to put the old boy away. That would have been something to write home about. But there hadn't been a chance of nailing him, so I had had to be content with making a bargain whereby he turned everything over to me except himself and his friends.

I don't know what happened to Hsiu Hsiu, the squealing slave-girl. She deserved to come through all right. I might have gone back to Chang's to ask about her, but I stayed away. Chang had learned that the medal in the photo was a trick one. I had a note from him:

Greetings and Great Love to the Unveiler of
    Secrets:
    One whose patriotic fervor and inherent stupid-
ity combined to blind him, so that he broke a

valuable tool, trusts that the fortunes of worldly traffic will not again ever place his feeble wits in opposition to the irresistible will and dazzling intellect of the Emperor of Untanglers.

You can take that any way you like. But I know the man who wrote it, and I don't mind admitting that I've stopped eating in Chinese restaurants, and that if I never have to visit Chinatown again it'll be soon enough.

The Gutting of Couffignal

WEDGE-SHAPED Couffignal is not a large island, and not far from the mainland, to which it is linked by a wooden bridge. Its western shore is a high, straight cliff that jumps abruptly up out of San Pablo Bay. From the top of this cliff the island slopes eastward, down to a smooth pebble beach that runs into the water again, where there are piers and a clubhouse and moored pleasure boats.

Couffignal's main street, paralleling the beach, has the usual bank, hotel, moving-picture theater, and stores. But it differs from most main streets of its size in that it is more carefully arranged and preserved. There are trees and hedges and strips of lawn on it, and no glaring signs. The buildings seem to belong beside one another, as if they had been designed by the same architect, and in the stores you will find goods of a quality to match the best city stores.

The intersecting streets—running between rows of neat cottages near the foot of the slope—become winding hedged roads as they climb toward the cliff. The higher these roads get, the farther apart and larger are the houses they lead to. The occupants of these higher houses are the owners and rulers of the island. Most of them are well-fed old gentlemen who, the profits they took from the world with both hands in their younger days now stowed away at safe percentages, have bought into the island colony so they may spend what is left of their lives nursing their livers and improving their golf among their kind. They admit to the island only as many storekeepers, working-people, and similar riffraff as are needed to keep them comfortably served.

That is Couffignal.

It was some time after midnight. I was sitting in a second-story room in Couffignal's largest house, surrounded by wedding presents whose value would add up to something between fifty and a hundred thousand dollars.

Of all the work that comes to a private detective (except divorce work, which the Continental Detective Agency doesn't handle) I like weddings as little as any. Usually I manage to avoid them, but this time I hadn't been able to. Dick Foley, who had been slated for the job, had been handed a black eye by an unfriendly pickpocket the day before. That let Dick out and me in. I had come up to Couffignal—a two-hour ride from San Francisco by ferry and auto stage—that morning, and would return the next.

This had been neither better nor worse than the usual wedding detail. The ceremony had been performed in a little stone church down the hill. Then the house had begun to fill with reception guests. They had kept it filled to overflowing until some time after the bride and groom had sneaked off to their eastern train.

The world had been well represented. There had been an admiral and an earl or two from England; an ex-president of a South American country; a Danish baron; a tall young Russian princess surrounded by lesser titles, including a fat, bald, jovial and black-bearded Russian general who had talked to me for a solid hour about prize fights, in which he had a lot of interest, but not so much knowledge as was possible; an ambassador from one of the Central European countries; a justice of the Supreme Court; and a mob of people whose prominence and near-prominence didn't carry labels.

In theory, a detective guarding wedding presents is supposed to make himself indistinguishable from the other guests. In practice, it never works out that way. He has to spend most of his time within sight of the booty, so he's easily spotted. Besides that, eight or ten people I recognized among the guests were clients or former clients of the Agency, and so knew me. However, being known doesn't make so much difference as you might think, and everything had gone off smoothly.

A couple of the groom's friends, warmed by wine and the necessity of maintaining their reputations as cut-ups, had tried to smuggle some of the gifts out of the room where they were displayed and hide them in the piano. But I had been expecting that familiar trick, and blocked it before it had gone far enough to embarrass anybody.

Shortly after dark a wind smelling of rain began to pile storm clouds up over the bay. Those guests who lived at a distance, especially those who had water to cross, hurried off for their homes. Those who lived on the island stayed until the first raindrops began to patter down. Then they left.

The Hendrixson house quieted down. Musicians and extra servants left. The weary house servants began to disappear in the direction of their bedrooms. I found some sandwiches, a couple of books and a comfortable armchair, and took them up to the room where the presents were now hidden under grey-white sheeting.

Keith Hendrixson, the bride's grandfather—she was an orphan—put his head in at the door.

"Have you everything you need for your comfort?" he asked.

"Yes, thanks."

He said good night and went off to bed—a tall old man, slim as a boy.

The wind and the rain were hard at it when I went downstairs to give the lower windows and doors the up-and-down. Everything on the first floor was tight and secure, everything in the cellar. I went upstairs again.

Pulling my chair over by a floor lamp, I put sandwiches, books, ash-tray, gun and flashlight on a small table beside it. Then I switched off the other lights, set fire to a Fatima, sat down, wriggled my spine comfortably into the chair's padding, picked up one of the books, and prepared to make a night of it.

The book was called *The Lord of the Sea*, and had to do with a strong, tough and violent fellow named Hogarth, whose modest plan was to hold the world in one hand. There were plots and counterplots, kidnappings, murders, prison-breakings, forgeries and burglaries, diamonds large as hats and floating forts larger than Couffignal. It sounds dizzy here, but in the book it was as real as a dime.

Hogarth was still going strong when the lights went out.

II

In the dark, I got rid of the glowing end of my cigarette by grinding it in one of the sandwiches. Putting the book down, I picked up gun and flashlight, and moved away from the chair.

Listening for noises was no good. The storm was making hundreds of them. What I needed to know was why the lights had gone off. All the other lights in the house had been turned off some time ago. So the darkness of the hall told me nothing.

I waited. My job was to watch the presents. Nobody had touched them yet. There was nothing to get excited about.

Minutes went by, perhaps ten of them.

The floor swayed under my feet. The windows rattled with a violence beyond the strength of the storm. The dull boom of a heavy explosion blotted out the sounds of wind and falling water. The blast was not close at hand, but not far enough away to be off the island.

Crossing to the window, peering through the wet glass, I could see nothing. I should have seen a few misty lights far down the hill. Not being able to see them settled one point. The lights had gone out all over Couffignal, not only in the Hendrixson house.

That was better. The storm could have put the lighting system out of whack, could have been responsible for the explosion—maybe.

Staring through the black window, I had an impression of great excitement down the hill, of movement in the night. But all was too far away for me to have seen or heard even had there been lights, and all too vague to say what was moving. The impression was strong but worthless. It didn't lead anywhere. I told myself I was getting feeble-minded, and turned away from the window.

Another blast spun me back to it. This explosion sounded nearer than the first, maybe because it was stronger. Peering through the glass again, I still saw nothing. And still had the impression of things that were big moving down there.

Bare feet pattered in the hall. A voice was anxiously calling my name. Turning from the window again, I pocketed my gun and snapped on the flashlight. Keith Hendrixson, in pajamas and bathrobe, looking thinner and older than anybody could be, came into the room.

"Is it—"

"I don't think it's an earthquake," I said, since that is the first calamity your Californian thinks of. "The lights went off a little while ago. There have been a couple of explosions down the hill since the—"

I stopped. Three shots, close together, had sounded. Rifle-shots, but of the sort that only the heaviest of rifles could make. Then, sharp and small in the storm, came the report of a far-away pistol.

"What is it?" Hendrixson demanded.

"Shooting."

More feet were pattering in the halls, some bare, some shod. Excited voices whispered questions and exclamations. The butler, a solemn, solid block of a man, partly dressed, and carrying a lighted five-pronged candlestick, came in.

"Very good, Brophy," Hendrixson said as the butler put the candlestick on the table beside my sandwiches. "Will you try to learn what is the matter?"

"I have tried, sir. The telephone seems to be out of order, sir. Shall I send Oliver down to the village?"

"No-o. I don't suppose it's that serious. Do you think it is anything serious?" he asked me.

I said I didn't think so, but I was paying more attention to the outside than to him. I had heard a thin screaming that could have come from a distant woman, and a volley of small-arms shots. The racket of the storm muffled these shots, but when the heavier firing we had heard before broke out again, it was clear enough.

To have opened the window would have been to let in gallons of water without helping us to hear much clearer. I stood with an ear tilted to the pane, trying to arrive at some idea of what was happening outside.

Another sound took my attention from the window—the ringing of the doorbell. It rang loudly and persistently.

Hendrixson looked at me. I nodded.

"See who it is, Brophy," he said.

The butler went solemnly away, and came back even more solemnly.

"Princess Zhukovski," he announced.

She came running into the room—the tall Russian girl I had seen at the reception. Her eyes were wide and dark with excitement. Her face was very white and wet. Water ran in streams down her blue waterproof cape, the hood of which covered her dark hair.

"Oh, Mr. Hendrixson!" She had caught one of his hands in both of hers. Her voice, with nothing foreign in its accents, was the voice of one who is excited over a delightful surprise. "The bank is being robbed, and the—what do you call him?—marshal of police has been killed!"

"What's that?" the old man exclaimed, jumping awkwardly, because water from her cape had dripped down on one of his bare feet. "Weegan killed? And the bank robbed?"

"Yes! Isn't it terrible?" She said it as if she were saying wonderful. "When the first explosion woke us, the general sent Ignati down to find out what was the matter, and he got down there just in time to see the bank blown up. Listen!"

We listened, and heard a wild outbreak of mixed gun-fire.

"That will be the general arriving!" she said. "He'll enjoy himself most wonderfully. As soon as Ignati returned with the news, the general armed every male in the household from Aleksandr Sergyeevich to Ivan the cook, and led them out happier than he's been since he took his division to East Prussia in 1914."

"And the duchess?" Hendrixson asked.

"He left her at home with me, of course, and I furtively crept out and away from her while she was trying for the first time in her life to put water in a samovar. This is not the night for one to stay at home!"

"H-m-m," Hendrixson said, his mind obviously not on her words. "And the bank!"

He looked at me. I said nothing. The racket of another volley came to us.

"Could you do anything down there?" he asked.

"Maybe, but—" I nodded at the presents under their covers.

"Oh, those!" the old man said. "I'm as much interested in the bank as in them; and, besides, we will be here."

"All right!" I was willing enough to carry my curiosity down the hill. "I'll go down. You'd better have the butler stay in here, and plant the chauffeur inside the front door. Better give them guns if you have any. Is there a raincoat I can borrow? I brought only a light overcoat with me."

Brophy found a yellow slicker that fit me. I put it on, stowed gun and flashlight conveniently under it, and found my hat while Brophy was getting and loading an automatic pistol for himself and a rifle for Oliver, the mulatto chauffeur.

Hendrixson and the princess followed me downstairs. At the door I found she wasn't exactly following me—she was going with me.

"But, Sonya!" the old man protested.

"I'm not going to be foolish, though I'd like to," she promised him. "But I'm going back to my Irinia Androvana, who will perhaps have the samovar watered by now."

"That's a sensible girl!" Hendrixson said, and let us out into the rain and the wind.

It wasn't weather to talk in. In silence we turned downhill between two rows of hedging, with the storm driving at our backs. At the first break in the hedge I stopped, nodding toward the black blot a house made.

"That is your—"

Her laugh cut me short. She caught my arm and began to urge me down the road again.

"I only told Mr. Hendrixson that so he would not worry," she explained. "You do not think I am not going down to see the sights."

III

She was tall. I am short and thick. I had to look up to see her face—to see as much of it as the rain-grey night would let me see.

"You'll be soaked to the hide, running around in this rain," I objected.

"What of that? I am dressed for it."

She raised a foot to show me a heavy waterproof boot and a woolen-stockinged leg.

"There's no telling what we'll run into down there, and I've got work to do," I insisted. "I can't be looking out for you."

"I can look out for myself."

She pushed her cape aside to show me a square automatic pistol in one hand.

"You'll be in my way."

"I will not," she retorted. "You'll probably find I can help you. I'm as strong as you, and quicker, and I can shoot."

The reports of scattered shooting had punctuated our argument, but now the sound of heavier firing silenced the dozen objections to her company that I could still think of. After all, I could slip away from her in the dark if she became too much of a nuisance.

"Have it your own way," I growled, "but don't expect anything from me."

"You're so kind," she murmured as we got under way again, hurrying now, with the wind at our backs speeding us along.

Occasionally dark figures moved on the road ahead of us, but too far away to be recognizable. Presently a man passed us, running uphill—a tall man whose nightshirt hung out of his trousers, down below his coat, identifying him as a resident.

"They've finished the bank and are at Medcraft's!" he yelled as he went by.

"Medcraft is the jeweler," the girl informed me.

The sloping under our feet grew less sharp. The houses—dark but with faces vaguely visible here and there at windows—came closer together. Below, the flash of a gun could be seen now and then—orange streaks in the rain.

Our road put us into the lower end of the main street just as a staccato rat-ta-tat broke out.

I pushed the girl into the nearest doorway, and jumped in after her.

Bullets ripped through walls with the sound of hail tapping on leaves.

That was the thing I had taken for an exceptionally heavy rifle—a machine gun.

The girl had fallen back in a corner, all tangled up with something. I helped her up. The something was a boy of seventeen or so, with one leg and a crutch.

"It's the boy who delivers papers," Princess Zhukovski said, "and you've hurt him with your clumsiness."

The boy shook his head, grinning as he got up.

"No'm, I ain't hurt none, but you kind of scared me, jumping on me like that."

She had to stop and explain that she hadn't jumped on him, that she had been pushed into him by me, and that she was sorry and so was I.

"What's happening?" I asked the newsboy when I could get a word in.

"Everything," he boasted, as if some of the credit were his. "There must be a hundred of them, and they've blowed the bank wide open, and now some of 'em is in Medcraft's, and I guess they'll blow that up, too. And they killed Tom Weegan. They got a machine gun on a car in the middle of the street. That's it shooting now."

"Where's everybody—all the merry villagers?"

"Most of 'em are up behind the Hall. They can't do nothing, though, because the machine gun won't let 'em get near enough to see what they're shooting at, and that smart Bill Vincent told me to clear out, 'cause I've only got one leg, as if I couldn't shoot as good as the next one, if I only had something to shoot with!"

"That wasn't right of them," I sympathized. "But you can do something for me. You can stick here and keep your eye on this end of the street, so I'll know if they leave in this direction."

"You're not just saying that so I'll stay here out of the way, are you?"

"No," I lied. "I need somebody to watch. I was going to leave the princess here, but you'll do better."

"Yes," she backed me up, catching the idea. "This gentleman is a detective, and if you do what he asks you'll be helping more than if you were up with the others."

The machine gun was still firing, but not in our direction now.

"I'm going across the street," I told the girl. "If you—"

"Aren't you going to join the others?"

"No. If I can get around behind the bandits while they're busy with the others, maybe I can turn a trick."

"Watch sharp now!" I ordered the boy, and the princess and I made a dash for the opposite sidewalk.

We reached it without drawing lead, sidled along a building for a few yards, and turned into an alley. From the alley's other end came the smell and wash and the dull blackness of the bay.

While we moved down this alley I composed a scheme by which I hoped to get rid of my companion, sending her off on a safe wild-goose chase. But I didn't get a chance to try it out.

The big figure of a man loomed ahead of us.

Stepping in front of the girl, I went on toward him. Under my slicker I held my gun on the middle of him.

He stood still. He was larger than he had looked at first. A big, slope-shouldered, barrel-bodied husky. His hands were empty. I spotted the flashlight on his face for a split second. A flat-cheeked, thick-featured face, with high cheek-bones and a lot of ruggedness in it.

"Ignati!" the girl exclaimed over my shoulder.

He began to talk what I suppose was Russian to the girl. She laughed and replied. He shook his big head stubbornly, insisting on something. She stamped her foot and spoke sharply. He shook his head again and addressed me.

"General Pleshskev, he tell me bring Princess Sonya to home."

His English was almost as hard to understand as his Russian. His tone puzzled me. It was as if he was explaining some absolutely necessary thing that he didn't want to be blamed for, but that nevertheless he was going to do.

While the girl was speaking to him again, I guessed the answer. This big Ignati had been sent out by the general to bring the girl home, and he was going to obey his orders if he had to carry her. He was trying to avoid trouble with me by explaining the situation.

"Take her," I said, stepping aside.

The girl scowled at me, laughed.

"Very well, Ignati," she said in English, "I shall go home," and she turned on her heel and went back up the alley, the big man close behind her.

Glad to be alone, I wasted no time in moving in the opposite direction until the pebbles of the beach were under my feet. The pebbles ground harshly under my heels. I moved back to more silent ground and began to work my way as swiftly as I could up the shore toward the center of action.

The machine gun barked on. Smaller guns snapped. Three concussions, close together—bombs, hand grenades, my ears and my memory told me.

The stormy sky glared pink over a roof ahead of me and to the left. The boom of the blast beat my ear-drums. Fragments I couldn't see fell around me. That, I thought, would be the jeweler's safe blowing apart.

I crept on up the shore line. The machine gun went silent. Lighter guns snapped, snapped, snapped. Another grenade went off. A man's voice shrieked pure terror.

Risking the crunch of pebbles, I turned down to the water's edge again. I had seen no dark shape on the water that could have been a boat. There had been boats moored along this beach in the afternoon. With my feet in the water of the bay I still saw no boat. The storm could have scattered them, but I didn't think it had. The island's western height shielded this shore. The wind was strong here, but not violent.

My feet sometimes on the edge of the pebbles, sometimes in the water, I went on up the shore line. Now I saw a boat. A gently bobbing black shape ahead. No light was on it. Nothing I could see moved on it. It was the only boat on that shore. That made it important.

Foot by foot, I approached.

A shadow moved between me and the dark rear of a building. I froze. The shadow, man-size, moved again, in the direction from which I was coming.

Waiting, I didn't know how nearly invisible, or how plain, I might be against my background. I couldn't risk giving myself away by trying to improve my position.

Twenty feet from me the shadow suddenly stopped.

I was seen. My gun was on the shadow.

"Come on," I called softly. "Keep coming. Let's see who you are."

The shadow hesitated, left the shelter of the building, drew nearer. I couldn't risk the flashlight. I made out dimly a handsome face, boyishly reckless, one cheek dark-stained.

"Oh, how d'you do?" the face's owner said in a musical baritone voice. "You were at the reception this afternoon."

"Yes."

"Have you seen Princess Zhukovski? You know her?"

"She went home with Ignati ten minutes or so ago."

"Excellent!" He wiped his stained cheek with a stained handkerchief, and turned to look at the boat. "That's Hendrixson's boat," he whispered. "They've got it and they've cast the others off."

"That would mean they are going to leave by water."

"Yes," he agreed, "unless— Shall we have a try at it?"

"You mean jump it?"

"Why not?" he asked. "There can't be very many aboard. God knows there are enough of them ashore. You're armed. I've a pistol."

"We'll size it up first," I decided, "so we'll know what we're jumping."

"That is wisdom," he said, and led the way back to the shelter of the buildings.

Hugging the rear walls of the buildings, we stole toward the boat.

The boat grew clearer in the night. A craft perhaps forty-five feet long, its stern to the shore, rising and falling beside a small pier. Across the stern something protruded. Something I couldn't quite make out. Leather soles scuffled now and then on the wooden deck. Presently a dark head and shoulders showed over the puzzling thing in the stern.

The Russian lad's eyes were better than mine.

"Masked," he breathed in my ear. "Something like a stocking over his head and face."

The masked man was motionless where he stood. We were motionless where we stood.

"Could you hit him from here?" the lad asked.

"Maybe, but night and rain aren't a good combination for sharpshooting. Our best bet is to sneak as close as we can, and start shooting when he spots us."

"That is wisdom," he agreed.

Discovery came with our first step forward. The man in the boat grunted. The lad at my side jumped forward. I recognized the thing in the boat's stern just in time to throw out a leg and trip the young Russian. He tumbled down, all sprawled out on the pebbles. I dropped behind him.

The machine gun in the boat's stern poured metal over our heads.

IV

"No good rushing that!" I said. "Roll out of it!"

I set the example by revolving toward the back of the building we had just left.

The man at the gun sprinkled the beach, but sprinkled it at random, his eyes no doubt spoiled for night-seeing by the flash of his gun.

Around the corner of the building, we sat up.

"You saved my life by tripping me," the lad said coolly.

"Yes. I wonder if they've moved the machine gun from the street, or if—"

The answer to that came immediately. The machine gun in the street mingled its vicious voice with the drumming of the one in the boat.

"A pair of them!" I complained. "Know anything about the layout?"

"I don't think there are more than ten or twelve of them," he said, "although it is not easy to count in the dark. The few I have seen are completely masked—like the man in the boat. They seem to have disconnected the telephone and light lines first and then to have destroyed the bridge. We attacked them while they were looting the bank, but in front they had a machine gun mounted in an automobile, and we were not equipped to combat on equal terms."

"Where are the islanders now?"

"Scattered, and most of them in hiding, I fancy, unless General Pleshskev has succeeded in rallying them again."

I frowned and beat my brains together. You can't fight machine guns and hand grenades with peaceful villagers and retired capitalists. No matter how well led and armed they are, you can't do anything with them. For that matter, how could anybody do much against a game of that toughness?

"Suppose you stick here and keep your eye on the boat," I suggested. "I'll scout around and see what's doing further up, and if I can get a few good men together, I'll try to jump the boat again, probably from the other side. But we can't count on that. The get-away will be by boat. We can count on that, and try to block it. If you lie down you can watch the boat around the corner of the building without making much of a target of yourself. I wouldn't do anything to attract attention until the break for the boat comes. Then you can do all the shooting you want."

"Excellent!" he said. "You'll probably find most of the islanders up behind the church. You can get to it by going straight up the hill until you come to an iron fence, and then follow that to the right."

"Right."

I moved off in the direction he had indicated.

At the main street I stopped to look around before venturing across. Everything was quiet there. The only man I could see was spread out face-down on the sidewalk near me.

On hands and knees I crawled to his side. He was dead. I didn't stop to examine him further, but sprang up and streaked for the other side of the street.

Nothing tried to stop me. In a doorway, flat against a wall, I peeped out. The wind had stopped. The rain was no longer a driving deluge, but a steady down-pouring of small drops. Couffignal's main street, to my senses, was a deserted street.

I wondered if the retreat to the boat had already started. On the sidewalk, walking swiftly toward the bank, I heard the answer to that guess.

High up on the slope, almost up to the edge of the cliff, by the sound, a machine gun began to hurl out its stream of bullets.

Mixed with the racket of the machine gun were the sounds of smaller arms, and a grenade or two.

At the first crossing, I left the main street and began to run up the hill. Men were running toward me. Two of them passed, paying no attention to my shouted, "What's up now?"

The third man stopped because I grabbed him—a fat man whose breath bubbled, and whose face was fish-belly white.

"They've moved the car with the machine gun on it up behind us," he gasped when I had shouted my question into his ear again.

"What are you doing without a gun?" I asked.

"I—I dropped it."

"Where's General Pleshskev?"

"Back there somewhere. He's trying to capture the car, but he'll never do it. It's suicide! Why don't help come?"

Other men had passed us, running downhill, as we talked. I let the white-faced man go, and stopped four men who weren't running so fast as the others.

"What's happening now?" I questioned them.

"They's going through the houses up the hill," a sharp-featured man with a small mustache and a rifle said.

"Has anybody got word off the island yet?" I asked.

"Can't," another informed me. "They blew up the bridge first thing."

"Can't anybody swim?"

"Not in that wind. Young Catlan tried it and was lucky to get out again with a couple of broken ribs."

"The wind's gone down," I pointed out.

The sharp-featured man gave his rifle to one of the others and took off his coat.

"I'll try it," he promised.

"Good! Wake up the whole country, and get word through to the San Francisco police boat and to the Mare Island Navy Yard. They'll lend a hand if you tell 'em the bandits have machine guns. Tell 'em the bandits have an armed boat waiting to leave in. It's Hendrixson's."

The volunteer swimmer left.

"A boat?" two of the men asked together.

"Yes. With a machine gun on it. If we're going to do anything, it'll have to be now, while we're between them and their get-away. Get every man and every gun you can find down there. Tackle the boat from the roofs if you can. When the bandits' car comes down there, pour it into it. You'll do better from the buildings than from the street."

The three men went on downhill. I went uphill, toward the crackling of firearms ahead. The machine gun was working irregularly. It would pour out its rat-tat-tat for a second or so, and then stop for a couple of seconds. The answering fire was thin, ragged.

I met more men, learned from them that the general, with less than a dozen men, was still fighting the car. I repeated the advice I had given the other men. My informants went down to join them. I went on up.

A hundred yards farther along, what was left of the general's dozen broke out of the night, around and past me, flying downhill, with bullets hailing after them.

The road was no place for mortal man. I stumbled over two bodies, scratched myself in a dozen places getting over a hedge. On soft, wet sod I continued my uphill journey.

The machine gun on the hill stopped its clattering. The one in the boat was still at work.

The one ahead opened again, firing too high for anything near at hand to be its target. It was helping its fellow below, spraying the main street.

Before I could get closer it had stopped. I heard the car's motor racing. The car moved toward me.

Rolling into the hedge, I lay there, straining my eyes through the spaces between the stems. I had six bullets in a gun that hadn't yet been fired on this night that had seen tons of powder burned.

When I saw wheels on the lighter face of the road, I emptied my gun, holding it low.

The car went on.

I sprang out of my hiding-place.

The car was suddenly gone from the empty road.

There was a grinding sound. A crash. The noise of metal folding on itself. The tinkle of glass.

I raced toward those sounds.

V

Out of a black pile where an engine sputtered, a black figure leaped—to dash off across the soggy lawn. I cut after it, hoping that the others in the wreck were down for keeps.

I was less than fifteen feet behind the fleeing man when he cleared a hedge. I'm no sprinter, but neither was he. The wet grass made slippery going.

He stumbled while I was vaulting the hedge. When we straightened out again I was not more than ten feet behind him.

Once I clicked my gun at him, forgetting I had emptied it. Six cartridges were wrapped in a piece of paper in my vest pocket, but this was no time for loading.

I was tempted to chuck the empty gun at his head. But that was too chancy.

A building loomed ahead. My fugitive bore off to the right, to clear the corner.

To the left a heavy shotgun went off.

The running man disappeared around the house-corner.

"Sweet God!" General Pleshskev's mellow voice complained. "That with a shotgun I should miss all of a man at the distance!"

"Go round the other way!" I yelled, plunging around the corner after my quarry.

His feet thudded ahead. I could not see him. The general puffed around from the other side of the house.

"You have him?"

"No."

In front of us was a stone-faced bank, on top of which ran a path. On either side of us was a high and solid hedge.

"But, my friend," the general protested. "How could he have—?"

A pale triangle showed on the path above—a triangle that could have been a bit of shirt showing above the opening of a vest.

"Stay here and talk!" I whispered to the general, and crept forward.

"It must be that he has gone the other way," the general carried out my instructions, rambling on as if I were standing beside him, "because if he had come my way I should have seen him, and if he had raised himself over either of the hedges or the embankment, one of us would surely have seen him against . . ."

He talked on and on while I gained the shelter of the bank on which the path sat, while I found places for my toes in the rough stone facing.

The man on the road, trying to make himself small with his back in a bush, was looking at the talking general. He saw me when I had my feet on the path.

He jumped, and one hand went up.

I jumped, with both hands out.

A stone, turning under my foot, threw me sidewise, twisting my ankle, but saving my head from the bullet he sent at it.

My outflung left arm caught his legs as I spilled down. He came over on top of me. I kicked him once, caught his gun-arm, and had just decided to bite it when the general puffed up over the edge of the path and prodded the man off me with the muzzle of the shotgun.

When it came my turn to stand up, I found it not so good. My twisted ankle didn't like to support its share of my hundred-and-eighty-some pounds. Putting most of my weight on the other leg, I turned my flashlight on the prisoner.

"Hello, Flippo!" I exclaimed.

"Hello!" he said without joy in the recognition.

He was a roly-poly Italian youth of twenty-three or -four. I had helped send him to San Quentin four years ago for his part in a payroll stick-up. He had been out on parole for several months now.

"The prison board isn't going to like this," I told him.

"You got me wrong," he pleaded. "I ain't been doing a thing. I was up here to see some friends. And when this thing busted loose I had to hide, because I got a record, and if I'm picked up I'll be railroaded for it. And now you got me, and you think I'm in on it!"

"You're a mind reader," I assured him, and asked the general: "Where can we pack this bird away for a while, under lock and key?"

"In my house there is a lumber-room with a strong door and not a window."

"That'll do it. March, Flippo!"

General Pleshskev collared the youth, while I limped along behind them, examining Flippo's gun, which was loaded except for the one shot he had fired at me, and reloading my own.

We had caught our prisoner on the Russian's grounds, so we didn't have far to go.

The general knocked on the door and called out something in his language. Bolts clicked and grated, and the door was swung open by a heavily mustached Russian servant. Behind him the princess and a stalwart older woman stood.

We went in while the general was telling his household about the capture, and took the captive up to the lumber-room. I frisked him for his pocket-knife and matches—he had nothing else that could help him get out—locked him in and braced the door solidly with a length of board. Then we went downstairs again.

"You are injured!" the princess, seeing me limp across the floor, cried.

"Only a twisted ankle," I said. "But it does bother me some. Is there any adhesive tape around?"

"Yes," and she spoke to the mustached servant, who went out of the room and presently returned, carrying rolls of gauze and tape and a basin of steaming water.

"If you'll sit down," the princess said, taking these things from the servant.

But I shook my head and reached for the adhesive tape.

"I want cold water, because I've got to go out in the wet again. If you'll show me the bathroom, I can fix myself up in no time."

We had to argue about that, but I finally got to the bathroom, where I ran cold water on my foot and ankle, and strapped it with adhesive tape, as tight as I could without stopping the circulation altogether. Getting my wet shoe on again was a job, but when I was through I had two firm legs under me, even if one of them did hurt some.

When I rejoined the others I noticed that the sound of firing no longer came up the hill, and that the patter of rain was lighter, and a grey streak of coming daylight showed under a drawn blind.

I was buttoning my slicker when the knocker rang on the front door. Russian words came through, and the young Russian I had met on the beach came in.

"Aleksandr, you're—" the stalwart older woman screamed when she saw the blood on his cheek, and fainted.

He paid no attention to her at all, as if he was used to having her faint.

"They've gone in the boat," he told me while the girl and two men servants gathered up the woman and laid her on an ottoman.

"How many?" I asked.

"I counted ten, and I don't think I missed more than one or two, if any."

"The men I sent down there couldn't stop them?"

He shrugged.

"What would you? It takes a strong stomach to face a machine gun. Your men had been cleared out of the buildings almost before they arrived."

The woman who had fainted had revived by now and was pouring anxious questions in Russian at the lad. The princess was getting into her blue cape. The woman stopped questioning the lad and asked her something.

"It's all over," the princess said. "I am going to view the ruins."

That suggestion appealed to everybody. Five minutes later all of us, including the servants, were on our way downhill. Behind us, around us, in front of us, were other people going downhill, hurrying along in the drizzle that was very gentle now, their faces tired and excited in the bleak morning light.

Halfway down, a woman ran out of a cross-path and began to tell me something. I recognized her as one of Hendrixson's maids.

I caught some of her words.

"Presents gone. . . . Mr. Brophy murdered. . . . Oliver. . . ."

VI

"I'll be down later," I told the others, and set out after the maid.

She was running back to the Hendrixson house. I couldn't run, couldn't even walk fast. She and Hendrixson and more of his servants were standing on the front porch when I arrived.

"They killed Oliver and Brophy," the old man said.

"How?"

"We were in the back of the house, the rear second story, watching the flashes of the shooting down in the village. Oliver was down here, just inside the front door, and Brophy in the room with the presents. We heard a shot in there, and immediately a man appeared in the doorway of our room, threatening us with two pistols, making us stay there for perhaps ten minutes. Then he shut and locked the door and went away. We broke the door down—and found Brophy and Oliver dead."

"Let's look at them."

The chauffeur was just inside the front door. He lay on his back, with his brown throat cut straight across the front, almost back to the vertebrae. His rifle was under him. I pulled it out and examined it. It had not been fired.

Upstairs, the butler Brophy was huddled against a leg of one of the tables on which the presents had been spread. His gun was gone. I turned him over, straightened him out, and found a bullet-hole in his chest. Around the hole his coat was charred in a large area.

Most of the presents were still here. But the most valuable pieces were gone. The others were in disorder, lying around any which way, their covers pulled off.

"What did the one you saw look like?" I asked.

"I didn't see him very well," Hendrixson said. "There was no light in our room. He was simply a dark figure against the candle burning in the hall. A large man in a black rubber raincoat, with some sort of black mask that covered his whole head and face, with small eyeholes."

"No hat?"

"No, just the mask over his entire face and head."

As we went downstairs again I gave Hendrixson a brief account of what I had seen and heard and done since I had left him. There wasn't enough of it to make a long tale.

"Do you think you can get information about the others from the one you caught?" he asked, as I prepared to go out.

"No. But I expect to bag them just the same."

Couffignal's main street was jammed with people when I limped into it again. A detachment of Marines from Mare Island was there, and men from a San Francisco police boat. Excited citizens in all degrees of partial nakedness boiled around them. A hundred voices were talking at once, recounting their personal adventures and braveries and losses and what they had seen. Such words as machine gun, bomb, bandit, car, shot, dynamite, and killed sounded again and again, in every variety of voice and tone.

The bank had been completely wrecked by the charge that had blown the vault. The jewelry store was another ruin. A grocer's across the street was serving as a field hospital. Two doctors were toiling there, patching up damaged villagers.

I recognized a familiar face under a uniform cap—Sergeant Roche of the harbor police—and pushed through the crowd to him.

"Just get here?" he asked as we shook hands. "Or were you in on it?"

"In on it."

"What do you know?"

"Everything."

"Who ever heard of a private detective that didn't," he joshed as I led him out of the mob.

"Did you people run into an empty boat out in the bay?" I asked when we were away from audiences.

"Empty boats have been floating around the bay all night," he said.

I hadn't thought of that.

"Where's your boat now?" I asked him.

"Out trying to pick up the bandits. I stayed with a couple of men to lend a hand here."

"You're in luck," I told him. "Now sneak a look across the street. See the stout old boy with the black whiskers? Standing in front of the druggist's."

General Pleshskev stood there, with the woman who had fainted, the young Russian whose bloody cheek had made her faint, and a pale, plump man of forty-something who had been with them at the reception. A little to one side stood big Ignati, the two men-servants I had seen at the house, and another who was obviously one of them. They were chatting together and watching the excited antics of a red faced property-owner who was telling a curt lieutenant of Marines that it was his own personal private automobile that the bandits had stolen to mount their machine gun on, and what he thought should be done about it.

"Yes," said Roche, "I see your fellow with the whiskers."

"Well, he's your meat. The woman and two men with him are also your meat. And those four Russians standing to the left are some more of it. There's another missing, but I'll take care of that one. Pass the word to the lieutenant, and you can round up those babies without giving them a chance to fight back. They think they're safe as angels."

"Sure, are you?" the sergeant asked.

"Don't be silly!" I growled, as if I had never made a mistake in my life.

I had been standing on my one good prop. When I put my weight on the other to turn away from the sergeant, it stung me all the way to the hip. I pushed my back teeth together and began to work painfully through the crowd to the other side of the street.

The princess didn't seem to be among those present. My idea was that, next to the general, she was the most important member of the push. If she was at their house, and not yet suspicious, I figured I could get close enough to yank her in without a riot.

Walking was hell. My temperature rose. Sweat rolled out on me.

"Mister, they didn't none of 'em come down that way."

The one-legged newsboy was standing at my elbow. I greeted him as if he were my pay-check.

"Come on with me," I said, taking his arm. "You did fine down there, and now I want you to do something else for me."

Half a block from the main street I led him up on the porch of a small yellow cottage. The front door stood open, left that way when the occupants ran down to welcome police and Marines, no doubt. Just inside the door, beside a hall rack, was a wicker porch chair. I committed unlawful entry to the extent of dragging that chair out on the porch.

"Sit down, son," I urged the boy.

He sat, looking up at me with puzzled freckled face. I took a firm grip on his crutch and pulled it out of his hand.

"Here's five bucks for rental," I said, "and if I lose it I'll buy you one of ivory and gold."

And I put the crutch under my arm and began to propel myself up the hill.

It was my first experience with a crutch. I didn't break any records. But it was a lot better than tottering along on an unassisted bum ankle.

The hill was longer and steeper than some mountains I've seen, but the gravel walk to the Russians' house was finally under my feet.

I was still some dozen feet from the porch when Princess Zhukovski opened the door.

VII

"Oh!" she exclaimed, and then, recovering from her surprise, "your ankle is worse!"

She ran down the steps to help me climb them. As she came I noticed that something heavy was sagging and swinging in the right-hand pocket of her grey flannel jacket.

With one hand under my elbow, the other arm across my back, she helped me up the steps and across the porch. That assured me she didn't think I had tumbled to the game. If she had, she wouldn't have trusted herself within reach of my hands. Why, I wondered, had she come back to the house after starting downhill with the others?

While I was wondering we went into the house, where she planted me in a large and soft leather chair.

"You must certainly be starving after your strenuous night," she said. "I will see if——"

"No, sit down." I nodded at a chair facing mine. "I want to talk to you."

She sat down, clasping her slender white hands in her lap. In neither face nor pose was there any sign of nervousness, not even of curiosity. And that was overdoing it.

"Where have you cached the plunder?" I asked.

The whiteness of her face was nothing to go by. It had been white as marble since I had first seen her. The darkness of her eyes was as natural. Nothing happened to her other features. Her voice was smoothly cool.

"I am sorry," she said. "The question doesn't convey any-thing to me."

"Here's the point," I explained. "I'm charging you with complicity in the gutting of Couffignal, and in the murders that went with it. And I'm asking you where the loot has been hidden."

Slowly she stood up, raised her chin, and looked at least a mile down at me.

"How dare you? How dare you speak so to me, a Zhukovski!"

"I don't care if you're one of the Smith Brothers!" Leaning forward, I had pushed my twisted ankle against a leg of the chair, and the resulting agony didn't improve my disposition. "For the purpose of this talk you are a thief and a murderer."

Her strong slender body became the body of a lean crouching animal. Her white face became the face of an enraged animal. One hand—claw now—swept to the heavy pocket of her jacket.

Then, before I could have batted an eye—though my life seemed to depend on my not batting it—the wild animal had vanished. Out of it—and now I know where the writers of the old fairy stories got their ideas—rose the princess again, cool and straight and tall.

She sat down, crossed her ankles, put an elbow on an arm of her chair, propped her chin on the back of that hand, and looked curiously into my face.

"However," she murmured, "did you chance to arrive at so strange and fanciful a theory?"

"It wasn't chance, and it's neither strange nor fanciful," I said. "Maybe it'll save time and trouble if I show you part of the score against you. Then you'll know how you stand and won't waste your brains pleading innocence."

"I should be grateful," she smiled, "very!"

I tucked my crutch in between one knee and the arm of my chair, so my hands would be free to check off my points on my fingers.

"First—whoever planned the job knew the island—not fairly well, but every inch of it. There's no need to argue about that. Second—the car on which the machine gun was mounted was local property, stolen from the owner here. So was the boat in which the bandits were supposed to have escaped. Bandits from the outside would have needed a car or a boat to bring their machine guns, explosives, and grenades here and there doesn't seem to be any reason why they shouldn't have used that car or boat instead of stealing a fresh one. Third—there wasn't the least hint of the professional bandit touch on this job. If you ask me, it was a military job from beginning to end. And the worst safe-burglar in the world could have got into both the bank vault and the jeweler's safe without wrecking the buildings. Fourth—bandits from the outside wouldn't have destroyed the bridge. They might have blocked it, but they wouldn't have destroyed it. They'd have saved it in case they had to make their get-away in that direction. Fifth—bandits figuring on a get-away by boat would have cut the job short, wouldn't have spread it over the whole night. Enough racket was made here to wake up California all the way from Sacramento to Los Angeles. What you people did was to send one man out in the boat, shooting, and he didn't go far. As soon as he was at a safe distance, he went overboard, and swam back to the island. Big Ignati could have done it without turning a hair."

That exhausted my right hand. I switched over, counting on my left.

"Sixth—I met one of your party, the lad, down on the beach, and he was coming from the boat. He suggested that we jump it. We were shot at, but the man behind the gun was playing with us. He could have wiped us out in a second if he had been in earnest, but he shot over our heads. Seventh—that same lad is the only man on the island, so far as I know, who saw the departing bandits. Eighth—all of your people that I ran into were especially nice to me, the general even spending an hour talking to me at the reception this afternoon. That's a distinctive amateur crook trait. Ninth—after the machine gun car had been wrecked I chased its occupant. I lost him around this house. The Italian boy I picked up wasn't him. He couldn't have climbed up on the path without my seeing him. But he could have run around to the general's side of the house and vanished indoors there. The general liked him, and would have helped him. I know that, because the general performed a downright miracle by missing him at some six feet with a shotgun. Tenth—you called at Hendrixson's house for no other purpose than to get me away from there."

That finished the left hand. I went back to the right.

"Eleventh—Hendrixson's two servants were killed by someone they knew and trusted. Both were killed at close quarters and without firing a shot. I'd say you got Oliver to let you into the house, and were talking to him when one of your men cut his throat from behind. Then you went upstairs and probably shot the unsuspecting Brophy yourself. He wouldn't have been on his guard against you. Twelfth—but that ought to be enough, and I'm getting a sore throat from listing them."

She took her chin off her hand, took a fat white cigarette out of a thin black case, and held it in her mouth while I put a match to the end of it. She took a long pull at it—a draw that accounted for a third of its length—and blew the smoke down at her knees.

"That would be enough," she said when all these things had been done, "if it were not that you yourself know it was impossible for us to have been so engaged. Did you not see us—did not everyone see us—time and time again?"

"That's easy!" I argued. "With a couple of machine guns, a trunkful of grenades, knowing the island from top to bottom, in the darkness and in a storm, against bewildered civilians— it was duck soup. There are nine of you that I know of, including two women. Any five of you could have carried on the work, once it was started, while the others took turns appearing here and there, establishing alibis. And that is what you did. You took turns slipping out to alibi yourselves. Everywhere I went I ran into one of you. And the general! That whiskered old joker running around leading the simple citizens to battle! I'll bet he led 'em plenty! They're lucky there are any of 'em alive this morning!"

She finished her cigarette with another inhalation, dropped the stub on the rug, ground out the light with one foot, sighed wearily, put her hands on her hips, and asked:

"And now what?"

"Now I want to know where you have stowed the plunder."

The readiness of her answer surprised me.

"Under the garage, in a cellar we dug secretly there some months ago."

I didn't believe that, of course, but it turned out to be the truth.

I didn't have anything else to say. When I fumbled with my borrowed crutch, preparing to get up, she raised a hand and spoke gently:

"Wait a moment, please. I have something to suggest."

Half standing, I leaned toward her, stretching out one hand until it was close to her side.

"I want the gun," I said.

She nodded, and sat still while I plucked it from her pocket, put it in one of my own, and sat down again.

VIII

"You said a little while ago that you didn't care who I was," she began immediately. "But I want you to know. There are so many of us Russians who once were somebodies and who now are nobodies that I won't bore you with the repetition of a tale the world has grown tired of hearing. But you must remember that this weary tale is real to us who are its subjects. However, we fled from Russia with what we could carry of our property, which fortunately was enough to keep us in bearable comfort for a few years.

"In London we opened a Russian restaurant, but London was suddenly full of Russian restaurants, and ours became, instead of a means of livelihood, a source of loss. We tried teaching music and languages, and so on. In short, we hit on all the means of earning our living that other Russian exiles hit upon, and so always found ourselves in overcrowded, and thus unprofitable, fields. But what else did we know—could we do?

"I promised not to bore you. Well, always our capital shrank, and always the day approached on which we should be shabby and hungry, the day when we should become familiar to readers of your Sunday papers—charwomen who had been princesses, dukes who now were butlers. There was no place for us in the world. Outcasts easily become outlaws. Why not? Could it be said that we owed the world any fealty? Had not the world sat idly by and seen us despoiled of place and property and country?

"We planned it before we had heard of Couffignal. We could find a small settlement of the wealthy, sufficiently isolated, and, after establishing ourselves there, we would plunder it. Couffignal, when we found it, seemed to be the ideal place. We leased this house for six months, having just enough capital remaining to do that and to live properly here while our plans matured. Here we spent four months establishing ourselves, collecting our arms and our explosives, mapping our offensive, waiting for a favorable night. Last night seemed to be that night, and we had provided, we thought, against every eventuality. But we had not, of course, provided against your presence and your genius. They were simply others of the unforeseen misfortunes to which we seem eternally condemned."

She stopped, and fell to studying me with mournful large eyes that made me feel like fidgeting.

"It's no good calling me a genius," I objected. "The truth is you people botched your job from beginning to end. Your general would get a big laugh out of a man without military training who tried to lead an army. But here are you people with absolutely no criminal experience trying to swing a trick that needed the highest sort of criminal skill. Look at how you all played around with me! Amateur stuff! A professional crook with any intelligence would have either let me alone or knocked me off. No wonder you flopped! As for the rest of it—your troubles—I can't do anything about them."

"Why?" very softly. "Why can't you?"

"Why should I?" I made it blunt.

"No one else knows what you know." She bent forward to put a white hand on my knee. "There is wealth in that cellar beneath the garage. You may have whatever you ask."

I shook my head.

"You aren't a fool!" she protested. "You know——"

"Let me straighten this out for you," I interrupted. "We'll disregard whatever honesty I happen to have, sense of loyalty to employers, and so on. You might doubt them, so we'll throw them out. Now I'm a detective because I happen to like the work. It pays me a fair salary, but I could find other jobs that would pay more. Even a hundred dollars more a month would be twelve hundred a year. Say twenty-five or thirty thousand dollars in the years between now and my sixtieth birthday.

"Now I pass up that twenty-five or thirty thousand of honest gain because I like being a detective, like the work. And liking work makes you want to do it as well as you can. Otherwise there'd be no sense to it. That's the fix I am in. I don't know anything else, don't enjoy anything else, don't want to know or enjoy anything else. You can't weigh that against any sum of money. Money is good stuff. I haven't anything against it. But in the past eighteen years I've been getting my fun out of chasing crooks and tackling puzzles, my satisfaction out of catching crooks and solving riddles. It's the only kind of sport I know anything about, and I can't imagine a pleasanter future than twenty-some years more of it. I'm not going to blow that up!"

She shook her head slowly, lowering it, so that now her dark eyes looked up at me under the thin arcs of her brows.

"You speak only of money," she said. "I said you may have whatever you ask."

That was out. I don't know where these women get their ideas.

"You're still all twisted up," I said brusquely, standing now and adjusting my borrowed crutch. "You think I'm a man and you're a woman. That's wrong. I'm a manhunter and you're something that has been running in front of me. There's nothing human about it. You might just as well expect a hound to play tiddly-winks with the fox he's caught. We're wasting time anyway. I've been thinking the police or Marines might come up here and save me a walk. You've been waiting for your mob to come back and grab me. I could have told you they were being arrested when I left them."

That shook her. She had stood up. Now she fell back a step, putting a hand behind her for steadiness, on her chair. An exclamation I didn't understand popped out of her mouth. Russian, I thought, but the next moment I knew it had been Italian.

"Put your hands up."

It was Flippo's husky voice. Flippo stood in the doorway, holding an automatic.

IX

I raised my hands as high as I could without dropping my supporting crutch, meanwhile cursing myself for having been too careless, or too vain, to keep a gun in my hand while I talked to the girl.

So this was why she had come back to the house. If she freed the Italian, she had thought, we would have no reason for suspecting that he hadn't been in on the robbery, and so we would look for the bandits among his friends. A prisoner, of course, he might have persuaded us of his innocence. She had given him the gun so he could either shoot his way clear, or, what would help her as much, get himself killed trying.

While I was arranging these thoughts in my head, Flippo had come up behind me. His empty hand passed over my body, taking away my own gun, his, and the one I had taken from the girl.

"A bargain, Flippo," I said when he had moved away from me, a little to one side, where he made one corner of a triangle whose other corners were the girl and I. "You're out on parole, with some years still to be served. I picked you up with a gun on you. That's plenty to send you back to the big house. I know you weren't in on this job. My idea is that you were up here on a smaller one of your own, but I can't prove that and don't want to. Walk out of here, alone and neutral, and I'll forget I saw you."

Little thoughtful lines grooved the boy's round, dark face.

The princess took a step toward him.

"You heard the offer I just now made him?" she asked. "Well, I make that offer to you, if you will kill him."

The thoughtful lines in the boy's face deepened.

"There's your choice, Flippo," I summed up for him. "All I can give you is freedom from San Quentin. The princess can give you a fat cut of the profits in a busted caper, with a good chance to get yourself hanged."

The girl, remembering her advantage over me, went at him hot and heavy in Italian, a language in which I know only four words. Two of them are profane and the other two obscene. I said all four.

The boy was weakening. If he had been ten years older, he'd have taken my offer and thanked me for it. But he was young and she—now that I thought of it—was beautiful. The answer wasn't hard to guess.

"But not to bump him off," he said to her, in English, for my benefit. "We'll lock him up in there where I was at."

I suspected Flippo hadn't any great prejudice against murder. It was just that he thought this one unnecessary, unless he was kidding me to make the killing easier.

The girl wasn't satisfied with his suggestion. She poured more hot Italian at him. Her game looked sure-fire, but it had a flaw. She couldn't persuade him that his chances of getting any of the loot away were good. She had to depend on her charms to swing him. And that meant she had to hold his eye.

He wasn't far from me.

She came close to him. She was singing, chanting, crooning Italian syllables into his round face.

She had him.

He shrugged. His whole face said yes. He turned—

I knocked him on the noodle with my borrowed crutch.

The crutch splintered apart. Flippo's knees bent. He stretched up to his full height. He fell on his face on the floor. He lay there, dead-still, except for a thin worm of blood that crawled out of his hair to the rug.

A step, a tumble, a foot or so of hand-and-knee scrambling put me within reach of Flippo's gun.

The girl, jumping out of my path, was half-way to the door when I sat up with the gun in my hand.

"Stop!" I ordered.

"I shan't," she said, but she did, for the time at least. "I am going out."

"You are going out when I take you."

She laughed, a pleasant laugh, low and confident.

"I'm going out before that," she insisted good-naturedly.

I shook my head.

"How do you purpose stopping me?" she asked.

"I don't think I'll have to," I told her. "You've got too much sense to try to run while I'm holding a gun on you."

She laughed again, an amused ripple.

"I've got too much sense to stay," she corrected me. "Your crutch is broken, and you're lame. You can't catch me by running after me, then. You pretend you'll shoot me, but I don't believe you. You'd shoot me if I attacked you, of course, but I shan't do that. I shall simply walk out, and you know you won't shoot me for that. You'll wish you could, but you won't. You'll see."

Her face turned over her shoulder, her dark eyes twinkling at me, she took a step toward the door.

"Better not count on that!" I threatened.

For answer to that she gave me a cooing laugh. And took another step.

"Stop, you idiot!" I bawled at her.

Her face laughed over her shoulder at me. She walked without haste to the door, her short skirt of grey flannel shaping itself to the calf of each grey wool-stockinged leg as its mate stepped forward.

Sweat greased the gun in my hand.

When her right foot was on the doorsill, a little chuckling sound came from her throat.

"Adieu!" she said softly.

And I put a bullet in the calf of her left leg.

She sat down—plump! Utter surprise stretched her white face. It was too soon for pain.

I had never shot a woman before. I felt queer about it.

"You ought to have known I'd do it!" My voice sounded harsh and savage and like a stranger's in my ears. "Didn't I steal a crutch from a cripple?"

The Assistant Murderer

I

The Man in Gray

GOLD on the door, edged with black, said *Alexander Rush, Private Detective*. Inside, an ugly man sat tilted back in a chair, his feet on a yellow desk.

The office was in no way lovely. Its furnishings were few and old with the shabby age of second-handom. A shredding square of dun carpet covered the floor. On one buff wall hung a framed certificate that licensed Alexander Rush to pursue the calling of private detective in the city of Baltimore in accordance with certain red-numbered regulations. A map of the city hung on another wall. Beneath the map a frail bookcase, small as it was, gaped emptily around its contents: a yellowish railway guide, a smaller hotel directory, and street and telephone directories for Baltimore, Washington and Philadelphia. An insecure oaken clothes-tree held up a black derby and a black overcoat beside a white sink in one corner. The four chairs in the room were unrelated to one another in everything except age. The desk's scarred top held, in addition to the proprietor's feet, a telephone, a black-clotted inkwell, a disarray of papers having generally to do with criminals who had escaped from one prison or another, and a grayed ashtray that held as much ash and as many black cigar stumps as a tray of its size could expect to hold.

An ugly office—the proprietor was uglier.

His head was squatly pear-shaped. Excessively heavy, wide, blunt at the jaw, it narrowed as it rose to the close-cropped, erect grizzled hair that sprouted above a low, slanting forehead. His complexion was of a rich darkish red, his skin tough in texture and rounded over thick cushions of fat. These fundamental inelegancies were by no means all his ugliness. Things had been done to his features.

One way you looked at his nose, you said it was crooked. Another way, you said it could not be crooked; it had no shape at all. Whatever your opinion of its form, you could not deny its color. Veins had been broken to pencil its already florid surface with brilliant red stars and curls and puzzling scrawls that looked as if they must have some secret meanings. His lips were thick, tough-skinned. Between them showed the brassy glint of two solid rows of gold teeth, the lower row lapping the upper, so undershot was the bulging jaw. His eyes—small, deep-set and pale blue of iris—were bloodshot to a degree that made you think he had a heavy cold. His ears accounted for some of his earlier years: they were the thickened, twisted cauliflower ears of the pugilist.

A man of forty-something, ugly, sitting tilted back in his chair, feet on desk.

The gilt-labeled door opened and another man came into the office. Perhaps ten years younger than the man at the desk, he was, roughly speaking, everything that one was not. Fairly tall, slender, fair-skinned, brown-eyed, he would have been as little likely to catch your eye in a gambling house as in an art gallery. His clothes—suit and hat were gray—were fresh and properly pressed, and even fashionable in that inconspicuous manner which is one sort of taste. His face was likewise unobtrusive, which was surprising when you considered how narrowly it missed handsomeness through the least meagerness of mouth—a mark of the too cautious man.

Two steps into the office he hesitated, brown eyes glancing from shabby furnishings to ill-visaged proprietor. So much ugliness seemed to disconcert the man in gray. An apologetic smile began on his lips, as if he were about to murmur, "I beg your pardon, I'm in the wrong office."

But when he finally spoke it was otherwise. He took another step forward, asking uncertainly:

"You are Mr. Rush?"

"Yeah." The detective's voice was hoarse with a choking harshness that seemed to corroborate the heavy-cold testimony of his eyes. He put his feet down on the floor and jerked a fat, red hand at a chair. "Sit down, sir."

The man in gray sat down, tentatively upright on the chair's front edge.

"Now what can I do for you?" Alec Rush croaked amiably.

"I want—I wish—I would like—" and further than that the man in gray said nothing.

"Maybe you'd better just tell me what's wrong," the detective suggested. "Then I'll know what you want of me," and he smiled.

There was kindliness in Alec Rush's smile, and it was not easily resisted. True, his smile was a horrible grimace out of a nightmare, but that was its charm. When your gentle-countenanced man smiles there is small gain: his smile expresses little more than his reposed face. But when Alec Rush distorted his ogre's mask so that jovial friendliness peeped incongruously from his savage red eyes, from his brutal metal-studded mouth—then that was a heartening, a winning thing.

"Yes, I daresay that would be better." The man in gray sat back in his chair, more comfortably, less transiently. "Yesterday on Fayette Street, I met a—a young woman I know. I hadn't—we hadn't met for several months. That isn't really pertinent, however. But after we separated—we had talked for a few minutes—I saw a man. That is, he came out of a doorway and went down the street in the same direction she had taken, and I got the idea he was following her. She turned into Liberty Street and he did likewise. Countless people walk along that same route, and the idea that he was following her seemed fantastic, so much so that I dismissed it and went on about my business.

"But I couldn't get the notion out of my head. It seemed to me there had been something peculiarly intent in his carriage, and no matter how much I told myself the notion was absurd, it persisted in worrying me. So last night, having nothing especial to do, I drove out to the neighborhood of—of the young woman's house. And I saw the same man again. He was standing on a corner two blocks from her house. It was the same man—I'm certain of it. I tried to watch him, but while I was finding a place for my car he disappeared and I did not see him again. Those are the circumstances. Now will you look into it, learn if he is actually following her, and why?"

"Sure," the detective agreed hoarsely, "but didn't you say anything to the lady or to any of her family?"

The man in gray fidgeted in his chair and looked at the stringy dun carpet.

"No, I didn't. I didn't want to disturb her, frighten her, and still don't. After all, it may be no more than a meaningless coincidence, and—and—well—I don't— That's impossible! What I had in mind was for you to find out what is wrong, if anything, and remedy it without my appearing in the matter at all."

"Maybe, but, mind you, I'm not saying I will. I'd want to know more first."

"More? You mean more——"

"More about you and her."

"But there is nothing about us!" the man in gray protested. "It is exactly as I have told you. I might add that the young woman is—is married, and that until yesterday I had not seen her since her marriage."

"Then your interest in her is—?" The detective let the husky interrogation hang incompleted in the air.

"Of friendship—past friendship."

"Yeah. Now who is this young woman?"

The man in gray fidgeted again.

"See here, Rush," he said, coloring, "I'm perfectly willing to tell you, and shall, of course, but I don't want to tell you unless you are going to handle this thing for me. I mean I don't want to be bringing her name into it if—if you aren't. Will you?"

Alec Rush scratched his grizzled head with a stubby forefinger.

"I don't know," he growled. "That's what I'm trying to find out. I can't take hold of a job that might be anything. I've got to know that you're on the up-and-up."

II
Two Names

Puzzlement disturbed the clarity of the younger man's brown eyes. "But I didn't think you'd be——" He broke off and looked away from the ugly man.

"Of course you didn't." A chuckle rasped in the detective's burly throat, the chuckle of a man touched in a once sore spot that is no longer tender. He raised a big hand to arrest his prospective client in the act of rising from his chair. "What you did, on a guess, was to go to one of the big agencies and tell 'em your story. They wouldn't touch it unless you cleared up the fishy points. Then you ran across my name, remembered I was chucked out of the department a couple of years ago. 'There's my man,' you said to yourself, 'a baby who won't be so choicy!' "

The man in gray protested with head and gesture and voice that this was not so. But his eyes were sheepish.

Alec Rush laughed harshly again and said, "No matter. I ain't sensitive about it. I can talk about politics, and being made the goat, and all that, but the records show the Board of Police Commissioners gave me the air for a list of crimes that would stretch from here to Canton Hollow. All right, sir! I'll take your job. It sounds phony, but maybe it ain't. It'll cost you fifteen a day and expenses."

"I can see that it sounds peculiar," the younger man assured the detective, "but you'll find that it's quite all right. You'll want a retainer, of course."

"Yes, say fifty."

The man in gray took five new ten-dollar bills from a pigskin billfold and put them on the desk. With a thick pen Alec Rush began to make muddy ink-marks on a receipt blank.

"Your name?" he asked.

"I would rather not. I'm not to appear in it, you know. My name would not be of importance, would it?"

Alec Rush put down his pen and frowned at his client.

"Now! Now!" he grumbled good-naturedly. "How am I going to do business with a man like you?"

The man in gray was sorry, even apologetic, but he was stubborn in his reticence. He would not give his name. Alec Rush growled and complained, but pocketed the five ten-dollar bills.

"It's in your favor, maybe," the detective admitted as he surrendered, "though it ain't to your credit. But if you were off-color I guess you'd have sense enough to fake a name. Now this young woman—who is she?"

"Mrs. Hubert Landow."

"Well, well, we've got a name at last! And where does Mrs. Landow live?"

"On Charles-Street Avenue," the man in gray said, and gave a number.

"Her description?"

"She is twenty-two or -three years old, rather tall, slender in an athletic way, with auburn hair, blue eyes and very white skin."

"And her husband? You know him?"

"I have seen him. He is about my age—thirty—but larger than I, a tall, broad-shouldered man of the clean-cut blond type."

"And your mystery man? What does he look like?"

"He's quite young, not more than twenty-two at the most, and not very large—medium size, perhaps, or a little under. He's very dark, with high cheek-bones and a large nose. High, straight shoulders, too, but not broad. He walks with small, almost mincing, steps."

"Clothes?"

"He was wearing a brown suit and a tan cap when I saw him on Fayette Street yesterday afternoon. I suppose he wore the same last night, but I'm not positive."

"I suppose you'll drop in here for my reports," the detective wound up, "since I won't know where to send them to you?"

"Yes." The man in gray stood up and held out his hand. "I'm very grateful to you for undertaking this, Mr. Rush."

Alec Rush said that was all right. They shook hands, and the man in gray went out.

The ugly man waited until his client had had time to turn off into the corridor that led to the elevators. Then the detective said, "Now, Mr. Man!" got up from his chair, took his hat from the clothes-tree in the corner, locked his office door behind him, and ran down the back stairs.

He ran with the deceptive heavy agility of a bear. There was something bear-like, too, in the looseness with which his blue suit hung on his stout body, and in the set of his heavy shoulders—sloping, limber-jointed shoulders whose droop concealed much of their bulk.

He gained the ground floor in time to see the gray back of his client issuing into the street. In his wake Alec Rush sauntered. Two blocks, a turn to the left, another block and a turn to the right. The man in gray went into the office of a trust company that occupied the ground floor of a large office building.

The rest was the mere turning of a hand. Half a dollar to a porter: the man in gray was Ralph Millar, assistant cashier.

Darkness was settling in Charles-Street Avenue when Alec Rush, in a modest black coupé, drove past the address Ralph Millar had given him. The house was large in the dusk, spaced from its fellows as from the paving by moderate expanses of fenced lawn.

Alec Rush drove on, turned to the left at the first crossing, again to the left at the next, and at the next. For half an hour he guided his car along a many-angled turning and returning route until, when finally he stopped beside the curb at some distance from, but within sight of, the Landow house, he had driven through every piece of thoroughfare in the vicinity of that house.

He had not seen Millar's dark, high-shouldered young man.

Lights burned brightly in Charles-Street Avenue, and the night traffic began to purr southward into the city. Alec Rush's heavy body slumped against the wheel of his coupé while he filled its interior with pungent fog from a black cigar, and held patient, bloodshot eyes on what he could see of the Landow residence.

Three-quarters of an hour passed, and there was motion in the house. A limousine left the garage in the rear for the front door. A man and a woman, faintly distinguishable at that distance, left the house for the limousine. The limousine moved out into the cityward current. The third car behind it was Alec Rush's modest coupé.

III
The Man in the Doorway

Except for a perilous moment at North Avenue, when the interfering cross-stream of traffic threatened to separate him from his quarry, Alec Rush followed the limousine without difficulty. In front of a Howard Street theatre it discharged its freight: a youngish man and a young woman, both tall, evening-clad, and assuringly in agreement with the descriptions the detective had got from his client.

The Landows went into the already dark theatre while Alec Rush was buying his ticket. In the light of the first intermission he discovered them again. Leaving his seat for the rear of the auditorium, he found an angle from which he could study them for the remaining five minutes of illumination.

Hubert Landow's head was rather small for his stature, and the blond hair with which it was covered threatened each moment to escape from its imposed smoothness into crisp curls. His face, healthily ruddy, was handsome in a muscular, very masculine way, not indicative of any great mental nimbleness. His wife had that beauty which needs no cataloguing. However, her hair was auburn, her eyes blue, her skin white, and she looked a year or two older than the maximum twenty-three Millar had allowed her.

While the intermission lasted Hubert Landow talked to his wife eagerly, and his bright eyes were the eyes of a lover. Alec Rush could not see Mrs. Landow's eyes. He saw her replying now and again to her husband's words. Her profile showed no answering eagerness. She did not show she was bored.

Midway the last act, Alec Rush left the theatre to maneuver his coupé into a handy position from which to cover the Landows' departure. But their limousine did not pick them up when they left the theatre. They turned down Howard Street afoot, going to a rather garish second-class restaurant, where an abbreviated orchestra succeeded by main strength in concealing its smallness from the ear.

His coupé conveniently parked, Alec Rush found a table from which he could watch his subjects without being himself noticeable. Husband still wooed wife with incessant, eager talking. Wife was listless, polite, unkindled. Neither more than touched the food before them. They danced once, the woman's face as little touched by immediate interest as when she listened to her husband's words. A beautiful face, but empty.

The minute hand of Alec Rush's nickel-plated watch had scarcely begun its last climb of the day from where VI is inferred to XII when the Landows left the restaurant. The limousine—against its side a young Norfolk-jacketed Negro smoking—was two doors away. It bore them back to their house. The detective, having seen them into the house, having seen the limousine into the garage, drove his coupé again around and around through the neighboring thoroughfares. And saw nothing of Millar's dark young man.

Then Alec Rush went home and to bed.

At eight o'clock the next morning ugly man and modest coupé were stationary in Charles-Street Avenue again. Male Charles-Street Avenue went with the sun on its left toward its offices. As the morning aged and the shadows grew shorter and thicker, so, generally, did the individuals who composed this morning procession. Eight-o'clock was frequently young and slender and brisk, Eight-thirty less so, Nine still less, and rear-guard Ten-o'clock was preponderantly neither young nor slender, and more often sluggish than brisk.

Into this rear guard, though physically he belonged to no later period than eight-thirty, a blue roadster carried Hubert Landow. His broad shoulders were blue-coated, his blond hair gray-capped, and he was alone in the roadster. With a glance around to make sure Millar's dark young man was not in sight, Alec Rush turned his coupé in the blue car's wake.

They rode swiftly into the city, down into its financial center, where Hubert Landow deserted his roadster before a Redwood Street stock-broker's office. The morning had become noon before Landow was in the street again, turning his roadster northward.

When shadowed and shadower came to rest again they were in Mount Royal Avenue. Landow got out of his car and strode briskly into a large apartment building. A block distant, Alec Rush lighted a black cigar and sat still in his coupé. Half an hour passed. Alec Rush turned his head and sank his gold teeth deep into his cigar.

Scarcely twenty feet behind the coupé, in the doorway of a garage, a dark young man with high cheek-bones, high, straight shoulders, loitered. His nose was large. His suit was brown, as were the eyes with which he seemed to pay no especial attention to anything through the thin blue drift of smoke from the tip of a drooping cigarette.

Alec Rush took his cigar from his mouth to examine it, took a knife from his pocket to trim the bitten end, restored cigar to mouth and knife to pocket, and thereafter was as indifferent to all Mount Royal Avenue as the dark youth behind him. The one drowsed in his doorway. The other dozed in his car. And the afternoon crawled past one o'clock, past one-thirty.

Hubert Landow came out of the apartment building, vanished swiftly in his blue roadster. His going stirred neither of the motionless men, scarcely their eyes. Not until another fifteen minutes had gone did either of them move.

Then the dark youth left his doorway. He moved without haste, up the street, with short, almost mincing, steps. The back of Alec Rush's black-derbied head was to the youth when he passed the coupé, which may have been chance, for none could have said that the ugly man had so much as glanced at the other since his first sight of him. The dark young man let his eyes rest on the detective's back without interest as he passed. He went on up the street toward the apartment building Landow had visited, up its steps and out of sight into it.

When the dark young man had disappeared, Alec Rush threw away his cigar, stretched, yawned, and awakened the coupé's engine. Four blocks and two turnings from Mount Royal Avenue, he got out of the automobile, leaving it locked and empty in front of a gray stone church. He walked back to Mount Royal Avenue, to halt on a corner two blocks above his earlier position.

He had another half-hour of waiting before the dark young man appeared. Alec Rush was buying a cigar in a glass-fronted cigar store when the other passed. The young man boarded a street car at North Avenue and found a seat. The detective boarded the same car at the next corner and stood on the rear platform. Warned by an indicative forward hitching of the young man's shoulders and head, Alec Rush was the first passenger off the car at Madison Avenue, and the first aboard a southbound car there. And again, he was off first at Franklin Street.

The dark youth went straight to a rooming-house in this street, while the detective came to rest beside the window of a corner drug store specializing in theatrical make-up. There he loafed until half-past three. When the dark young man came into the street again it was to walk—Alec Rush behind him—to Eutaw Street, board a car, and ride to Camden Station.

There, in the waiting-room, the dark young man met a young woman who frowned and asked:

"Where in the hell have you been at?"

IV
The Man in the Picture

Passing them, the detective heard the petulant greeting, but the young man's reply was pitched too low for him to catch, nor did he hear anything else the young woman said. They talked for perhaps ten minutes, standing together in a deserted end of the waiting-room, so that Alec Rush could not have approached them without making himself conspicuous.

The young woman seemed to be impatient, urgent. The young man seemed to explain, to reassure. Now and then he gestured with the ugly, deft hands of a skilled mechanic. His companion became more agreeable. She was short, square, as if carved economically from a cube. Consistently, her nose also was short and her chin square. She had, on the whole, now that her earlier displeasure was passing, a merry face, a pert, pugnacious, rich-blooded face that advertised inexhaustible vitality. That advertisement was in every feature, from the live ends of her cut brown hair to the earth-gripping pose of her feet on the cement flooring. Her clothes were dark, quiet, expensive, but none too gracefully worn, hanging just the least bit bunchily here and there on her sturdy body.

Nodding vigorously several times, the young man at length tapped his cap-visor with two careless fingers and went out into the street. Alec Rush let him depart unshadowed. But when, walking slowly out to the iron train-shed gates, along them to the baggage window, thence to the street door, the young woman passed out of the station, the ugly man was behind her. He was still behind her when she joined the four o'clock shopping crowd at Lexington Street.

The young woman shopped with the whole-hearted air of one with nothing else on her mind. In the second department store she visited, Alec Rush left her looking at a display of laces while he moved as swiftly and directly as intervening shoppers would permit toward a tall, thick-shouldered, gray-haired woman in black, who seemed to be waiting for someone near the foot of a flight of stairs.

"Hello, Alec!" she said when he touched her arm, and her humorous eyes actually looked with pleasure at his uncouth face. "What are you doing in my territory?"

"Got a booster for you," he mumbled. "The chunky girl in blue at the lace counter. Make her?"

The store detective looked and nodded.

"Yes. Thanks, Alec. You're sure she's boosting, of course?"

"Now, Minnie!" he complained, his rasping voice throttled down to a metallic growl. "Would I be giving you a bum rumble? She went south with a couple of silk pieces, and it's more than likely she's got herself some lace by now."

"Um-hmm," said Minnie. "Well, when she sticks her foot on the sidewalk, I'll be with her."

Alec Rush put his hand on the store detective's arm again.

"I want a line on her," he said. "What do you say we tail her around and see what she's up to before we knock her over?"

"If it doesn't take all day," the woman agreed. And when the chunky girl in blue presently left the lace counter and the store, the detectives followed, into another store, ranging too far behind her to see any thieving she might have done, content to keep her under surveillance. From this last store their prey went down to where Pratt Street was dingiest, into a dingy three-story house of furnished flats.

Two blocks away a policeman was turning a corner.

"Take a plant on the joint while I get the copper," Alec Rush ordered.

When he returned with the policeman the store detective was waiting in the vestibule.

"Second floor," she said.

Behind her the house's street door stood open to show a dark hallway and the foot of a tattered-carpeted flight of steps. Into this dismal hallway appeared a slovenly thin woman in rumpled gray cotton, saying whiningly as she came forward, "What do you want? I keep a respectable house, I'll have you understand, and I——"

"Chunky, dark-eyed girl living here," Alec Rush croaked. "Second floor. Take us up."

The woman's scrawny face sprang into startled lines, faded eyes wide, as if mistaking the harshness of the detective's voice for the harshness of great emotion.

"Why—why—" she stammered, and then remembered the first principle of shady rooming-house management—never to stand in the way of the police. "I'll take you up," she agreed, and, hitching her wrinkled skirt in one hand, led the way up the stairs.

Her sharp fingers tapped on a door near the head of the stairs.

"Who's that?" a casually curt feminine voice asked.

"Landlady."

The chunky girl in blue, without her hat now, opened the door. Alec Rush moved a big foot forward to hold it open, while the landlady said, "This is her," the policeman said, "You'll have to come along," and Minnie said, "Dearie, we want to come in and talk to you."

"My God!" exclaimed the girl. "There'd be just as much sense to it if you'd all jumped out at me and yelled 'Boo!' "

"This ain't any way," Alec Rush rasped, moving forward, grinning his hideous friendly grin. "Let's go in where we can talk it over."

Merely by moving his loose-jointed bulk a step this way, a half-step that, turning his ugly face on this one and that one, he herded the little group as he wished, sending the landlady discontentedly away, marshaling the others into the girl's rooms.

"Remember, I got no idea what this is all about," said the girl when they were in her living-room, a narrow room where blue fought with red without ever compromising on purple. "I'm easy to get along with, and if you think this is a nice place to talk about whatever you want to talk about, go ahead! But if you're counting on me talking, too, you'd better smart me up."

"Boosting, dearie," Minnie said, leaning forward to pat the girl's arm. "I'm at Goodbody's."

"You think I've been shoplifting? Is that the idea?"

"Yeah. Exactly. Uh-huh. That's what." Alec Rush left her no doubt on the point.

The girl narrowed her eyes, puckered her red mouth, squinted sidewise at the ugly man.

"It's all right with me," she announced, "so long as Goodbody's hanging the rap on me—somebody I can sue for a million when it flops. I've got nothing to say. Take me for my ride."

"You'll get your ride, sister," the ugly man rasped good-naturedly. "Nobody's going to beat you out of it. But do you mind if I look around your place a little first?"

"Got anything with a judge's name on it that says you can?"

"No."

"Then you don't get a peep!"

Alec Rush chuckled, thrust his hands into his trouser pockets, and began to wander through the rooms, of which there were three. Presently he came out of the bedroom carrying a photograph in a silver frame.

"Who's this?" he asked the girl.

"Try and find out!"

"I am trying," he lied.

"You big bum!" said she. "You couldn't find water in the ocean!"

Alec Rush laughed with coarse heartiness. He could afford to. The photograph in his hand was of Hubert Landow.

v

The Overpaid Assassin

Twilight was around the gray stone church when the owner of the deserted coupé returned to it. The chunky girl—Polly Vanness was the name she had given—had been booked and lodged in a cell in the Southwestern Police Station. Quantities of stolen goods had been found in her flat. Her harvest of that afternoon was still on her person when Minnie and a police matron searched her. She had refused to talk. The detective had said nothing to her about his knowledge of the photograph's subject, or of her meeting in the railroad station with the dark young man. Nothing found in her rooms threw any light on either of these things.

Having eaten his evening meal before coming back to his car, Alec Rush now drove out to Charles-Street Avenue.

Lights glowed normally in the Landow house when he passed it. A little beyond it he turned his coupé so that it pointed toward the city, and brought it to rest in a tree-darkened curbside spot within sight of the house.

The night went along and no one left or entered the Landow house.

Finger nails clicked on the coupé's glass door.

A man stood there. Nothing could be said of him in the darkness except that he was not large, and that to have escaped the detective's notice until now he must have stealthily stalked the car from the rear.

Alec Rush put out a hand and the door swung open.

"Got a match?" the man asked.

The detective hesitated, said, "Yeah," and held out a box.

A match scraped and flared into a dark young face: large nose, high cheekbones: the young man Alec Rush had shadowed that afternoon.

But recognition, when it was voiced, was voiced by the dark young man.

"I thought it was you," he said simply as he applied the flaming match to his cigarette. "Maybe you don't know me, but I knew you when you were on the force."

The ex-detective-sergeant gave no meaning at all to a husky "Yeah."

"I thought it was you in the heap on Mount Royal this afternoon, but I couldn't make sure," the young man continued, entering the coupé, sitting beside the detective, closing the door. "Scuttle Zeipp's me. I ain't as well known as Napoleon, so if you've never heard of me there's no hard feelings."

"Yeah."

"That's the stuff! When you once think up a good answer, stick to it." Scuttle Zeipp's face was a sudden bronze mask in the glow of his cigarette. "The same answer'll do for my next question. You're interested in these here Landows? Yeah," he added in hoarse mimicry of the detective's voice.

Another inhalation lighted his face, and his words came smokily out as the glow faded.

"You ought to want to know what I'm doing hanging around 'em. I ain't tight. I'll tell you. I've been slipped half a grand to bump off the girl—twice. How do you like that?"

"I hear you," said Alec Rush. "But anybody can talk that knows the words."

"Talk? Sure it's talk," Zeipp admitted cheerfully. "But so's it talk when the judge says 'hanged by the neck until dead and may God have mercy on your soul!' Lots of things are talk, but that don't always keep 'em from being real."

"Yeah?"

"Yeah, brother, yeah! Now listen to this: it's one for the cuff. A certain party comes to me a couple of days ago with a knock-down from a party that knows me. See? This certain party asks me what I want to bump off a broad. I thought a grand would be right, and said so. Too stiff. We come together on five hundred. I got two-fifty down and get the rest when the Landow twist is cold. Not so bad for a soft trick— a slug through the side of a car—huh?"

"Well, what are you waiting for?" the detective asked. "You want to make it a fancy caper—kill her on her birthday or a legal holiday?"

Scuttle Zeipp smacked his lips and poked the detective's chest with a finger in the dark.

"Not any, brother! I'm thinking way ahead of you! Listen to this: I pocket my two-fifty advance and come up here to give the ground a good casing, not wanting to lam into anything I didn't know was here. While I'm poking around, I run into another party that's poking around. This second party gives me a tumble, I talk smart, and bingo! First thing you know she's propositioning me. What do you guess? She wants to know what I want to bump off a broad! Is it the same one *she* wants stopped? I hope to tell you it is!

"I ain't so silly! I get my hands on another two hundred and fifty berries, with that much more coming when I put over the fast one. Now do you think I'm going to do anything to that Landow baby? You're dumb if you do. She's my meal ticket. If she lives till I pop her, she'll be older than either you or the bay. I've got five hundred out of her so far. What's the matter with sticking around and waiting for more customers that don't like her? If two of 'em want to buy her out of the world, why not more? The answer is, 'Yeah!' And on top of that, here you are snooping around her. Now there it is, brother, for you to look at and taste and smell."

Silence held for several minutes, in the darkness of the coupé's interior, and then the detective's harsh voice put a skeptical question:

"And who are these certain parties that want her out of the way?"

"Be yourself!" Scuttle Zeipp admonished him. "I'm laying down on 'em, right enough, but I ain't feeding 'em to you."

"What are you giving me all this for then?"

"What for? Because you're in on the lay somewhere. Crossing each other, neither of us can make a thin dimmer. If we don't hook up we'll just ruin the racket for each other. I've already made half a grand off this Landow. That's mine, but there's more to be picked up by a couple of men that know what they're doing. All right. I'm offering to throw in with you on a two-way cut of whatever else we can get. But my parties are out! I don't mind throwing them down, but I ain't rat enough to put the finger on them for you."

Alec Rush grunted and croaked another dubious inquiry.

"How come you trust me so much, Scuttle?"

The hired killer laughed knowingly.

"Why not? You're a right guy. You can see a profit when it's showed to you. They didn't chuck you off the force for forgetting to hang up your stocking. Besides, suppose you want to double-cross me, what can you do? You can't prove anything. I told you I didn't mean the woman any harm. I ain't even packing a gun. But all that's the bunk. You're a wise head. You know what's what. Me and you, Alec, we can get plenty!"

Silence again, until the detective spoke slowly, thoughtfully.

"The first thing would be to get a line on the reasons your parties want the girl put out. Got anything on that?"

"Not a whisper."

"Both of 'em women, I take it."

Scuttle Zeipp hesitated.

"Yes," he admitted. "But don't be asking me anything about 'em. In the first place, I don't know anything, and in the second, I wouldn't tip their mitts if I did."

"Yeah," the detective croaked, as if he quite understood his companion's perverted idea of loyalty. "Now if they're women, the chances are the racket hangs on a man. What do you think of Landow? He's a pretty lad."

Scuttle Zeipp leaned over to put his finger against the detective's chest again.

"You've got it, Alec! That could be it, damned if it couldn't!"

"Yeah," Alec Rush agreed, fumbling with the levers of his car. "We'll get away from here and stay away until I look into him."

At Franklin Street, half a block from the rooming-house into which he had shadowed the young man that afternoon, the detective stopped his coupé.

"You want to drop out here?" he asked.

Scuttle Zeipp looked sidewise, speculatively, into the elder man's ugly face.

"It'll do," the young man said, "but you're a damned good guesser, just the same." He stopped with a hand on the door. "It's a go, is it, Alec? Fifty-fifty?"

"I wouldn't say so," Alec Rush grinned at him with hideous good-nature. "You're not a bad lad, Scuttle, and if there's any gravy you'll get yours, but don't count on me mobbing up with you."

Zeipp's eyes jerked to slits, his lips snarled back from yellow teeth that were set edge to edge.

"You sell me out, you damned gorilla, and I'll—" He laughed the threat out of being, his dark face young and careless again. "Have it your own way, Alec. I didn't make no mistake when I throwed in with you. What you say goes."

"Yeah," the ugly man agreed. "Lay off that joint out there until I tell you. Maybe you'd better drop in to see me tomorrow. The phone book'll tell you where my office is. So long, kid."

"So long, Alec."

VI

Cathedral Street

In the morning Alec Rush set about investigating Hubert Landow. First he went to the City Hall, where he examined the gray books in which marriage licenses are indexed. Hubert Britman Landow and Sara Falsoner had been married six months before, he learned.

The bride's maiden name thickened the red in the detective's bloodshot eyes. Air hissed sharply from his flattened nostrils. "Yeah! Yeah!" he said to himself, so raspingly that a lawyer's skinny clerk, fiddling with other records at his elbow, looked frightenedly at him and edged a little away.

From the City Hall, Alec Rush carried the bride's name to two newspaper offices, where, after studying the files, he bought an armful of six-months-old papers. He took the papers to his office, spread them on his desk, and attacked them with a pair of shears. When the last one had been cut and thrown aside, there remained on his desk a thick sheaf of clippings.

Arranging his clippings in chronological order, Alec Rush lighted a black cigar, put his elbows on the desk, his ugly head between his palms, and began to read a story with which newspaper-reading Baltimore had been familiar half a year before.

Purged of irrelevancies and earlier digressions, the story was essentially this:

Jerome Falsoner, aged forty-five, was a bachelor who lived alone in a flat in Cathedral Street, on an income more than sufficient for his comfort. He was a tall man, but of delicate physique, the result, it may have been, of excessive indulgence in pleasure on a constitution none too strong in the beginning. He was well known, at least by sight, to all night-living Baltimoreans, and to those who frequented race-track, gambling-house, and the furtive cockpits that now and then materialize for a few brief hours in the forty miles of country that lie between Baltimore and Washington.

One Fanny Kidd, coming as was her custom at ten o'clock one morning to "do" Jerome Falsoner's rooms, found him lying on his back in his living-room, staring with dead eyes at a spot on the ceiling, a bright spot that was reflected sunlight— reflected from the metal hilt of his paper-knife, which protruded from his chest.

Police investigation established four facts:

First, Jerome Falsoner had been dead for fourteen hours when Fanny Kidd found him, which placed his murder at about eight o'clock the previous evening.

Second, the last persons known to have seen him alive were a woman named Madeline Boudin, with whom he had been intimate, and three of her friends. They had seen him, alive, at some time between seven-thirty and eight o'clock, or less than half an hour before his death. They had been driving down to a cottage on the Severn River, and Madeline Boudin had told the others she wanted to see Falsoner before she went. The others had remained in their car while she rang the bell. Jerome Falsoner opened the street door and she went in. Ten minutes later she came out and rejoined her friends. Jerome Falsoner came to the door with her, waving a hand at one of the men in the car—a Frederick Stoner, who knew Falsoner slightly, and who was connected with the district attorney's office. Two women, talking on the steps of a house across the street, had also seen Falsoner, and had seen Madeline Boudin and her friends drive away.

Third, Jerome Falsoner's heir and only near relative was his niece, Sara Falsoner, who, by some vagary of chance, was marrying Hubert Landow at the very hour that Fanny Kidd was finding her employer's dead body. Niece and uncle had seldom seen one another. The niece—for police suspicion settled on her for a short space—was definitely proved to have been at home, in her apartment in Carey Street, from six o'clock the evening of the murder until eight-thirty the next morning. Her husband, her fiancé then, had been there with her from six until eleven that evening. Prior to her marriage, the girl had been employed as stenographer by the same trust company that employed Ralph Millar.

Fourth, Jerome Falsoner, who had not the most even of dispositions, had quarreled with an Icelander named Einer Jokumsson in a gambling-house two days before he was murdered. Jokumsson had threatened him. Jokumsson—a short, heavily built man, dark-haired, dark-eyed—had vanished from his hotel, leaving his bags there, the day the body was found, and had not been seen since.

The last of these clippings carefully read, Alec Rush rocked back in his chair and made a thoughtful monster's face at the ceiling. Presently he leaned forward again to look into the telephone directory, and to call the number of Ralph Millar's trust company. But when he got his number he changed his mind.

"Never mind," he said into the instrument, and, called a number that was Goodbody's. Minnie, when she came to the telephone, told him that Polly Vanness had been identified as one Polly Bangs, arrested in Milwaukee two years ago for shoplifting, and given a two-year sentence. Minnie also said that Polly Bangs had been released on bail early that morning.

Alec Rush pushed back the telephone and looked through his clippings again until he found the address of Madeline Boudin, the woman who had visited Falsoner so soon before his death. It was a Madison Avenue number. Thither his coupé carried the detective.

No, Miss Boudin did not live there. Yes, she had lived there, but had moved four months ago. Perhaps Mrs. Blender, on the third floor, would know where she lived now. Mrs. Blender did not know. She knew Miss Boudin had moved to an apartment-house in Garrison Avenue, but did not think she was living there now. At the Garrison Avenue house: Miss Boudin had moved away a month and a half ago—somewhere in Mount Royal Avenue, perhaps. The number was not known.

The coupé carried its ugly owner to Mount Royal Avenue, to the apartment building he had seen first Hubert Landow and then Scuttle Zeipp visit the previous day. At the manager's office he made inquiries about a Walter Boyden, who was thought to live there. Walter Boyden was not known to the manager. There was a Miss Boudin in 604, but her name was B-o-u-d-i-n, and she lived alone.

Alec Rush left the building and got in his car again. He screwed up his savage red eyes, nodded his head in a satisfied way, and with one finger described a small circle in the air. Then he returned to his office.

Calling the trust company's number again, he gave Ralph Millar's name, and presently was speaking to the assistant cashier.

"This is Rush. Can you come up to the office right away?"

"What's that? Certainly. But how—how—? Yes, I'll be up in a minute."

None of the surprise that had been in Millar's telephoned voice was apparent when he reached the detective's office. He asked no questions concerning the detective's knowledge of his identity. In brown today, he was as neatly inconspicuous as he had been yesterday in gray.

"Come in," the ugly man welcomed him. "Sit down. I've got to have some more facts, Mr. Millar."

Millar's thin mouth tightened and his brows drew together with obstinate reticence.

"I thought we settled that point, Rush. I told you——"

Alec Rush frowned at his client with jovial, though frightful exasperation.

"I know what you told me," he interrupted. "But that was then and this is now. The thing's coming unwound on me, and I can see just enough to get myself tangled up if I don't watch Harvey. I found your mysterious man, talked to him. He was following Mrs. Landow, right enough. According to the way he tells it, he's been hired to kill her."

Millar leaped from his chair to lean over the yellow desk, his face close to the detective's.

"My God, Rush, what are you saying? To kill her?"

"Now, now! Take it easy. He's not going to kill her. I don't think he ever meant to. But he claims he was hired to do it."

"You've arrested him? You've found the man who hired him?"

The detective squinted up his bloodshot eyes and studied the younger man's passionate face.

"As a matter of fact," he croaked calmly when he had finished his examination, "I haven't done either of those things. She's in no danger just now. Maybe the lad was stringing me, maybe he wasn't, but either way he wouldn't have spilled it to me if he meant to do anything. And when it comes right down to it, Mr. Millar, do you want him arrested?"

"Yes! That is——" Millar stepped back from the desk, sagged limply down on the chair again, and put shaking hands over his face. "My God, Rush, I don't know!" he gasped.

VII
Millar Talks

"Exactly," said Alec Rush. "Now here it is. Mrs. Landow was Jerome Falsoner's niece and heir. She worked for your trust company. She married Landow the morning her uncle was found dead. Yesterday Landow visited the building where

Madeline Boudin lives. She was the last person known to have been in Falsoner's rooms before he was killed. But her alibi seems to be as air-tight as the Landows'. The man who claims he was hired to kill Mrs. Landow also visited Madeline Boudin's building yesterday. I saw him go in. I saw him meet another woman. A shoplifter, the second one. In her rooms I found a photograph of Hubert Landow. Your dark man claims he was hired twice to kill Mrs. Landow by two women, neither knowing the other had hired him. He won't tell me who they are, but he doesn't have to."

The hoarse voice stopped and Alec Rush waited for Millar to speak. But Millar was for the time without a voice. His eyes were wide and despairingly empty. Alec Rush raised one big hand, folded it into a fist that was almost perfectly spherical, and thumped his desk softly.

"There it is, Mr. Millar," he rasped. "A pretty tangle. If you'll tell me what you know, we'll get it straightened out, never fear. If you don't—I'm out!"

Now Millar found words, however jumbled.

"You couldn't, Rush! You can't desert me—us—her! It's not— You're not——"

But Alec Rush shook his ugly pear-shaped head with slow emphasis.

"There's murder in this and the Lord knows what all. I've got no liking for a blindfolded game. How do I know what you're up to? You can tell me what you know—everything—or you can find yourself another detective. That's flat."

Ralph Millar's fingers picked at each other, his teeth pulled at his lips, his harassed eyes pleaded with the detective.

"You can't, Rush," he begged. "She's still in danger. Even if you are right about that man not attacking her, she's not safe. The women who hired him can hire another. You've got to protect her, Rush."

"Yeah? Then you've got to talk."

"I've got to—? Yes, I'll talk, Rush. I'll tell you anything you ask. But there's really nothing—or almost nothing—I know beyond what you've already learned."

"She worked for your trust company?"

"Yes, in my department."

"Left there to be married?"

"Yes. That is— No, Rush, the truth is she was discharged. It was an outrage, but——"

"When was this?"

"It was the day before the—before she was married."

"Tell me about it."

"She had— I'll have to explain her situation to you first, Rush. She is an orphan. Her father, Ben Falsoner, had been wild in his youth—and perhaps not only in his youth—as I believe all the Falsoners have been. However, he had quarreled with his father—old Howard Falsoner—and the old man had cut him out of the will. But not altogether out. The old man hoped Ben would mend his ways, and he didn't mean to leave him with nothing in that event. Unfortunately he trusted it to his other son, Jerome.

"Old Howard Falsoner left a will whereby the income from his estate was to go to Jerome during Jerome's life. Jerome was to provide for his brother Ben as he saw fit. That is, he had an absolutely free hand. He could divide the income equally with his brother, or he could give him a pittance, or he could give him nothing, as Ben's conduct deserved. On Jerome's death the estate was to be divided equally among the old man's grandchildren.

"In theory, that was a fairly sensible arrangement, but not in practice—not in Jerome Falsoner's hands. You didn't know him? Well, he was the last man you'd ever trust with a thing of that sort. He exercised his power to the utmost. Ben Falsoner never got a cent from him. Three years ago Ben died, and so the girl, his only daughter, stepped into his position in relation to her grandfather's money. Her mother was already dead. Jerome Falsoner never paid her a cent.

"That was her situation when she came to the trust company two years ago. It wasn't a happy one. She had at least a touch of the Falsoner recklessness and extravagance. There she was: heiress to some two million dollars—for Jerome had never married and she was the only grandchild—but without any present income at all, except her salary, which was by no means a large one.

"She got in debt. I suppose she tried to economize at times, but there was always that two million dollars ahead to make scrimping doubly distasteful. Finally, the trust company officials heard of her indebtedness. A collector or two came to the office, in fact. Since she was employed in my department, I had the disagreeable duty of warning her. She promised to pay her debts and contract no more, and I suppose she did try, but she wasn't very successful. Our officials are old-fashioned, ultra-conservative. I did everything I could to save her, but it was no good. They simply would not have an employee who was heels over head in debt."

Millar paused a moment, looked miserably at the floor, and went on:

"I had the disagreeable task of telling her her services were no longer needed. I tried to— It was awfully unpleasant. That was the day before she married Landow. It—" he paused and, as if he could think of nothing else to say, repeated, "Yes, it was the day before she married Landow," and fell to staring miserably at the floor again.

Alec Rush, who had sat as still through the recital of this history as a carven monster on an old church, now leaned over his desk and put a husky question:

"And who is this Hubert Landow? What is he?"

Ralph Millar shook his downcast head.

"I don't know him. I've seen him. I know nothing of him."

"Mrs. Landow ever speak of him? I mean when she was in the trust company?"

"It's likely, but I don't remember."

"So you didn't know what to make of it when you heard she'd married him?"

The younger man looked up with frightened brown eyes.

"What are you getting at, Rush? You don't think— Yes, as you say, I was surprised. What are you getting at?"

"The marriage license," the detective said, ignoring his client's repeated question, "was issued to Landow four days before the wedding-day, four days before Jerome Falsoner's body was found."

Millar chewed a finger nail and shook his head hopelessly.

"I don't know what you're getting at," he mumbled around the finger. "The whole thing is bewildering."

"Isn't it a fact, Mr. Millar," the detective's voice filled the office with hoarse insistence, "that you were on more friendly terms with Sara Falsoner than with anyone else in the trust company?"

The younger man raised his head and looked Alec Rush in the eye—held his gaze with brown eyes that were doggedly level.

"Your fact is," he said quietly, "that I asked Sara Falsoner to marry me the day she left."

"Yeah. And she——?"

"And she—I suppose it was my fault. I was clumsy, crude, whatever you like. God knows what she thought—that I was asking her to marry me out of pity, that I was trying to force her into marriage by discharging her when I knew she was over her head in debt! She might have thought anything. Anyhow, it was—it was disagreeable."

"You mean she not only refused you, but was—well—disagreeable about it?"

"I do mean that."

Alec Rush sat back in his chair and brought fresh grotesqueries into his face by twisting his thick mouth crookedly up at one corner. His red eyes were evilly reflective on the ceiling.

"The only thing for it," he decided, "is to go to Landow and give him what we've got."

"But are you sure he——?" Millar objected indefinitely.

"Unless he's one whale of an actor, he's a lot in love with his wife," the detective said with certainty. "That's enough to justify taking the story to him."

Millar was not convinced.

"You're sure it would be wisest?"

"Yeah. We've got to go to one of three people with the tale—him, her, or the police. I think he's the best bet, but take your choice."

The younger man nodded reluctantly.

"All right. But you don't have to bring me into it, do you?" with quick alarm. "You can handle it so I won't be involved. You understand what I mean? She's his wife, and it would be——"

"Sure," Alec Rush promised, "I'll keep you covered up."

VIII
Sara Talks

Hubert Landow, twisting the detective's card in his fingers, received Alec Rush in a somewhat luxuriously furnished room in the second story of the Charles-Street Avenue house. He was standing—tall, blond, boyishly handsome—in the middle of the floor, facing the door, when the detective—fat, grizzled, battered and ugly—was shown in.

"You wish to see me? Here, sit down."

Hubert Landow's manner was neither restrained nor hearty. It was precisely the manner that might be expected of a young man receiving an unexpected call from so savage-visaged a detective.

"Yeah," said Alec Rush as they sat in facing chairs. "I've got something to tell you. It won't take much time, but it's kind of wild. It might be a surprise to you, and it might not. But it's on the level. I don't want you to think I'm kidding you."

Hubert Landow bent forward, his face all interest.

"I won't," he promised. "Go on."

"A couple of days ago I got a line on a man who might be tied up in a job I'm interested in. He's a crook. Trailing him around, I discovered he was interested in your affairs, and your wife's. He's shadowed you and he's shadowed her. He was loafing down the street from a Mount Royal Avenue apartment that you went in yesterday, and he went in there later himself."

"But what the devil is he up to?" Landow exclaimed. "You think he's——"

"Wait," the ugly man advised. "Wait until you've heard it all, and then you can tell me what you make of it. He came out of there and went to Camden Station, where he met a young woman. They talked a bit, and later in the afternoon she was picked up in a department store—shoplifting. Her name is Polly Bangs, and she's done a hitch in Wisconsin for the same racket. Your photograph was on her dresser."

"My photograph?"

Alec Rush nodded placidly up into the face of the young man who was now standing.

"Yours. You know this Polly Bangs? A chunky, square-built girl of twenty-six or so, with brown hair and eyes—saucy looking?"

Hubert Landow's face was a puzzled blank.

"No! What the devil could she be doing with my picture?" he demanded. "Are you sure it was mine?"

"Not dead sure, maybe, but sure enough to need proof that it wasn't. Maybe she's somebody you've forgotten, or maybe she ran across the picture somewhere and kept it because she liked it."

"Nonsense!" The blond man squirmed at this tribute to his face, and blushed a vivid red beside which Alec Rush's complexion was almost colorless. "There must be some sensible reason. She has been arrested, you say?"

"Yeah, but she's out on bail now. But let me get along with my story. Last night this thug I've told you about and I had a talk. He claims he has been hired to kill your wife."

Hubert Landow, who had returned to his chair, now jerked in it so that its joints creaked strainingly. His face, crimson a second ago, drained paper-white. Another sound than the chair's creaking was faint in the room: the least of muffled gasps. The blond young man did not seem to hear it, but Alec Rush's bloodshot eyes flicked sidewise for an instant to focus fleetingly on a closed door across the room.

Landow was out of his chair again, leaning down to the detective, his fingers digging into the ugly man's loose muscular shoulders.

"This is horrible!" he was crying. "We've got to—"

The door at which the detective had looked a moment ago opened. A beautiful tall girl came through—Sara Landow. Her hair rumpled, was an auburn cloud around her white face. Her eyes were dead things. She walked slowly toward the men, her body inclined a little forward, as if against a strong wind.

"It's no use, Hubert." Her voice was dead as her eyes. "We may as well face it. It's Madeline Boudin. She has found out that I killed my uncle."

"Hush, darling, hush!" Landow caught his wife in his arms and tried to soothe her with a caressing hand on her shoulder. "You don't know what you're saying."

"Oh, but I do." She shrugged herself listlessly out of his arms and sat in the chair Alec Rush had just vacated. "It's Madeline Boudin, you know it is. She knows I killed Uncle Jerome."

Landow whirled to the detective, both hands going out to grip the ugly man's arm.

"You won't listen to what she's saying, Rush?" he pleaded. "She hasn't been well. She doesn't know what she's saying."

Sara Landow laughed with weary bitterness.

"Haven't been well?" she said. "No, I haven't been well, not since I killed him. How could I be well after that? You are a detective." Her eyes lifted their emptiness to Alec Rush. "Arrest me. I killed Jerome Falsoner."

Alec Rush, standing arms akimbo, legs apart, scowled at her, saying nothing.

"You can't, Rush!" Landow was tugging at the detective's arm again. "You can't, man. It's ridiculous! You—"

"Where does this Madeline Boudin fit in?" Alec Rush's harsh voice demanded. "I know she was chummy with Jerome, but why should she want your wife killed?"

Landow hesitated, shifting his feet, and when he replied it was reluctantly.

"She was Jerome's mistress, had a child by him. My wife, when she learned of it, insisted on making her a settlement out of the estate. It was in connection with that that I went to see her yesterday."

"Yeah. Now to get back to Jerome: you and your wife were supposed to be in her apartment at the time he was killed, if I remember right?"

Sara Landow sighed with spiritless impatience.

"Must there be all this discussion?" she asked in a small, tired voice. "I killed him. No one else killed him. No one else was there when I killed him. I stabbed him with the paper-knife when he attacked me, and he said, 'Don't! Don't!' and began to cry, down on his knees, and I ran out."

Alec Rush looked from the girl to the man. Landow's face was wet with perspiration, his hands were white fists, and something quivered in his chest. When he spoke his voice was as hoarse as the detective's, if not so loud.

"Sara, will you wait here until I come back? I'm going out for a little while, possibly an hour. You'll wait here and not do anything until I return?"

"Yes," the girl said, neither curiosity nor interest in her voice. "But it's no use, Hubert. I should have told you in the beginning. It's no use."

"Just wait for me, Sara," he pleaded, and then bent his head to the detective's deformed ear. "Stay with her, Rush, for God's sake!" he whispered, and went swiftly out of the room.

The front door banged shut. An automobile purred away from the house. Alec Rush spoke to the girl.

"Where's the phone?"

"In the next room," she said, without looking up from the handkerchief her fingers were measuring.

The detective crossed to the door through which she had entered the room, found that it opened into a library, where a telephone stood in a corner. On the other side of the room a clock indicated three-thirty-five. The detective went to the telephone and called Ralph Millar's office, asked for Millar, and told him:

"This is Rush. I'm at the Landow's. Come up right away."

"But I can't, Rush. Can't you understand my—"

"Can't hell!" croaked Alec Rush. "Get here quick!"

IX
The Shadow

The young woman with dead eyes, still playing with the hem of her handkerchief, did not look up when the ugly man returned to the room. Neither of them spoke. Alec Rush, standing with his back to a window, twice took out his watch to glare savagely at it.

The faint tingling of the doorbell came from below. The detective went across to the hall door and down the front stairs, moving with heavy swiftness. Ralph Millar, his face a field in which fear and embarrassment fought, stood in the vestibule, stammering something unintelligible to the maid who had opened the door. Alec Rush put the girl brusquely aside, brought Millar in, guided him upstairs.

"She says she killed Jerome," he muttered into his client's ear as they mounted.

Ralph Millar's face went dreadfully white, but there was no surprise in it.

"You knew she killed him?" Alec Rush growled.

Millar tried twice to speak and made no sound. They were on the second-floor landing before the words came.

"I saw her on the street that night, going toward his flat!"

Alec Rush snorted viciously and turned the younger man toward the room where Sara Landow sat.

"Landow's out," he whispered hurriedly. "I'm going out. Stay with her. She's shot to hell—likely to do anything if she's left alone. If Landow gets back before I do, tell him to wait for me."

Before Millar could voice the confusion in his face they were across the sill and into the room. Sara Landow raised her head. Her body was lifted from the chair as if by an invisible power. She came up tall and erect on her feet. Millar stood just inside the door. They looked eye into eye, posed each as if in the grip of a force pushing them together, another holding them apart.

Alec Rush hurried clumsily and silently down to the street.

In Mount Royal Avenue, Alec Rush saw the blue roadster at once. It was standing empty before the apartment building in which Madeline Boudin lived. The detective drove past it and turned his coupé in to the curb three blocks below. He had barely come to rest there when Landow ran out of the apartment building, jumped into his car, and drove off. He drove to a Charles Street hotel. Behind him went the detective.

In the hotel, Landow walked straight to the writing room. For half an hour he sat there, bending over a desk, covering sheet after sheet of paper with rapidly written words, while the detective sat behind a newspaper in a secluded angle of the lobby, watching the writing-room exit. Landow came out of the room stuffing a thick envelope in his pocket, left the hotel, got into his machine, and drove to the office of a messenger service company in St. Paul Street.

He remained in this office for five minutes. When he came out he ignored his roadster at the curb, walking instead to

Calvert Street, where he boarded a northbound street-car. Alec Rush's coupé rolled along behind the car. At Union Station, Landow left the street-car and went to the ticket window. He had just asked for a one-way ticket to Philadelphia when Alec Rush tapped him on the shoulder.

Hubert Landow turned slowly, the money for his ticket still in his hand. Recognition brought no expression to his handsome face.

"Yes," he said coolly, "what is it?"

Alec Rush nodded his ugly head at the ticket-window, at the money in Landow's hand.

"This is nothing for you to be doing," he growled.

"Here you are," the ticket-seller said through his grille. Neither of the men in front paid any attention to him. A large woman in pink, red and violet, jostling Landow, stepped on his foot and pushed past him to the window. Landow stepped back, the detective following.

"You shouldn't have left Sara alone," said Landow. "She's—"

"She's not alone. I got somebody to stay with her."

"Not—?"

"Not the police, if that's what you're thinking."

Landow began to pace slowly down the long concourse, the detective keeping step with him. The blond man stopped and looked sharply into the other's face.

"Is it that fellow Millar who's with her?" he demanded.

"Yeah."

"Is he the man you're working for, Rush?"

"Yeah."

Landow resumed his walking. When they had reached the northern extremity of the concourse, he spoke again.

"What does he want, this Millar?"

Alec Rush shrugged his thick, limber shoulders and said nothing.

"Well, what do you want?" the young man asked with some heat, facing the detective squarely now.

"I don't want you going out of town."

Landow pondered that, scowling.

"Suppose I insist on going," he asked, "how will you stop me?"

"Accomplice after the fact in Jerome's murder would be a charge I could hold you on."

Silence again, until broken by Landow.

"Look here, Rush. You're working for Millar. He's out at my house. I've just sent a letter out to Sara by messenger. Give them time to read it, and then phone Millar there. Ask him if he wants me held or not."

Alec Rush shook his head decidedly.

"No good," he rasped. "Millar's too rattle-brained for me to take his word for anything like that over the phone. We'll go back there and have a talk all around."

Now it was Landow who balked.

"No," he snapped. "I won't!" He looked with cool calculation at the detective's ugly face. "Can I buy you, Rush?"

"No, Landow. Don't let my looks and my record kid you."

"I thought not." Landow looked at the roof and at his feet, and he blew his breath out sharply. "We can't talk here. Let's find a quiet place."

"The heap's outside," Alec Rush said, "and we can sit in that."

X
Bangs

Seated in Alec Rush's coupé, Hubert Landow lighted a cigarette, the detective one of his black cigars.

"That Polly Bangs you were talking about, Rush," the blond man said without preamble, "is my wife. My name is Henry Bangs. You won't find my fingerprints anywhere. When Polly was picked up in Milwaukee a couple of years ago and sent over, I came east and fell in with Madeline Boudin. We made a good team. She had brains in chunks, and if I've got somebody to do my thinking for me, I'm a pretty good worker myself."

He smiled at the detective, pointing at his own face with his cigarette. While Alec Rush watched, a tide of crimson surged into the blond man's face until it was rosy as a blushing schoolgirl's. He laughed again and the blush began to fade.

"That's my best trick," he went on. "Easy if you have the gift and keep in practice: fill your lungs, try to force the air out while keeping it shut off at the larynx. It's a gold mine for a grifter! You'd be surprised how people will trust me after I've turned on a blush or two for 'em. So Madeline and I were in the money. She had brains, nerve and a good front. I have everything but brains. We turned a couple of tricks—one con and one blackmail—and then she ran into Jerome Falsoner. We were going to give him the squeeze at first. But when Madeline found out that Sara was his heiress, that she was in debt, and that she and her uncle were on the outs, we ditched that racket and cooked a juicier one. Madeline found somebody to introduce me to Sara. I made myself agreeable, playing the boob—the shy but worshipful young man.

"Madeline had brains, as I've said. She used 'em all this time. I hung around Sara, sending her candy, books, flowers, taking her to shows and dinner. The books and shows were part of Madeline's work. Two of the books mentioned the fact that a husband can't be made to testify against his wife in court, nor wife against husband. One of the plays touched the same thing. That was planting the seeds. We planted another with my blushing and mumbling—persuaded Sara, or rather let her discover for herself, that I was the clumsiest liar in the world.

"The planting done, we began to push the game along. Madeline kept on good terms with Jerome. Sara was getting deeper in debt. We helped her in still deeper. We had a burglar clean out her apartment one night—Ruby Sweeger, maybe you know him. He's in stir now for another caper. He got what money she had and most of the things she could have hocked in a pinch. Then we stirred up some of the people she owed, sent them anonymous letters warning them not to count too much on her being Jerome's heir. Foolish letters, but they did the trick. A couple of her creditors sent collectors to the trust company.

"Jerome got his income from the estate quarterly. Madeline knew the dates, and Sara knew them. The day before the next one, Madeline got busy on Sara's creditors again. I don't know what she told them this time, but it was enough. They descended on the trust company in a flock, with the result that the next day Sara was given two weeks' pay and discharged. When she came out I met her—by chance—yes, I'd been watching for her since morning. I took her for a drive and got her back to her apartment at six o'clock. There we found more frantic creditors waiting to pounce on her. I chased them out, played the big-hearted boy, making embarrassed offers of all sorts of help. She refused them, of course, and I could see decision coming into her face. She knew this was the day on which Jerome got his quarterly check. She determined to go see him, to demand that he pay her debts at least. She didn't tell me where she was going, but I could see it plain enough, since I was looking for it.

"I left her and waited across the street from her apartment, in Franklin Square, until I saw her come out. Then I found a telephone, called up Madeline, and told her Sara was on her way to her uncle's flat."

Landow's cigarette scorched his fingers. He dropped it, crushed it under his foot, lighted another.

"This is a long-winded story, Rush," he apologized, "but it'll soon be over now."

"Keep talking, son," said Alec Rush.

"There were some people in Madeline's place when I phoned her—people trying to persuade her to go down the country on a party. She agreed now. They would give her an even better alibi than the one she had cooked up. She told them she had to see Jerome before she left, and they drove her over to his place and waited in their car while she went in with him.

"She had a pint bottle of cognac with her, all doped and ready. She poured out a drink of it for Jerome, telling him of the new bootlegger she had found who had a dozen or more cases of this cognac to sell at a reasonable price. The cognac was good enough and the price low enough to make Jerome think she had dropped in to let him in on something good. He gave her an order to pass on to the bootlegger. Making sure his steel paper-knife was in full view on the table, Madeline rejoined her friends, taking Jerome as far as the door so they would see he was still alive, and drove off.

"Now I don't know what Madeline had put in that cognac. If she told me, I've forgotten. It was a powerful drug—not a poison, you understand, but an excitant. You'll see what I mean when you hear the rest. Sara must have reached her uncle's flat ten or fifteen minutes after Madeline's departure. Her uncle's face, she says, was red, inflamed, when he opened the door for her. But he was a frail man, while she was strong, and she wasn't afraid of the devil himself, for that matter. She went in and demanded that he settle her debts, even if he didn't choose to make her an allowance out of his income.

"They were both Falsoners, and the argument must have grown hot. Also the drug was working on Jerome, and he had no will with which to fight it. He attacked her. The paper-knife was on the table, as Madeline had seen. He was a maniac. Sara was not one of your corner-huddling, screaming girls. She grabbed the paper-knife and let him have it. When he fell, she turned and ran.

"Having followed her as soon as I'd finished telephoning to Madeline, I was standing on Jerome's front steps when she dashed out. I stopped her and she told me she'd killed her uncle. I made her wait there while I went in, to see if he was really dead. Then I took her home, explaining my presence at Jerome's door by saying, in my boobish, awkward way, that I had been afraid she might do something reckless and had thought it best to keep an eye on her.

"Back in her apartment, she was all for giving herself up to the police. I pointed out the danger in that, arguing that, in debt, admittedly going to her uncle for money, being his heiress, she would most certainly be convicted of having murdered him so she would get the money. Her story of his attack, I persuaded her, would be laughed at as a flimsy yarn. Dazed, she wasn't hard to convince. The next step was easy. The police would investigate her, even if they didn't especially suspect her. I was, so far as we knew, the only person whose testimony could convict her. I was loyal enough, but wasn't I the clumsiest liar in the world? Didn't the mildest lie make me blush like an auctioneer's flag? The way around that difficulty lay in what two of the books I had given her, and one of the plays we had seen, had shown: if I was her husband I couldn't be made to testify against her. We were married the next morning, on a license I had been carrying for nearly a week.

"Well, there we were. I was married to her. She had a couple of millions coming when her uncle's affairs were straightened out. She couldn't possibly, it seemed, escape arrest and conviction. Even if no one had seen her entering or leaving her uncle's flat, everything still pointed to her guilt, and the foolish course I had persuaded her to follow would simply ruin her chance of pleading self-defense. If they hanged her, the two million would come to me. If she got a long term in prison, I'd have the handling of the money at least."

Landow dropped and crushed his second cigarette and stared for a moment straight ahead into distance.

"Do you believe in God, or Providence, or Fate, or any of that, Rush?" he asked. "Well, some believe in one thing and some in another, but listen. Sara was never arrested, never even really suspected. It seems there was some sort of Finn or Swede who had had a run-in with Jerome and threatened him. I suppose he couldn't account for his whereabouts the night of the killing, so he went into hiding when he heard of Jerome's murder. The police suspicion settled on him. They looked Sara up, of course, but not very thoroughly. No one seems to have seen her in the street, and the people in her apartment house, having seen her come in at six o'clock with me, and not having seen her—or not remembering if they did—go out or in again, told the police she had been in all evening. The police were too much interested in the missing Finn, or whatever he was, to look any further into Sara's affairs.

"So there we were again. I was married into the money, but I wasn't fixed so I could hand Madeline her cut. Madeline said we'd let things run along as they were until the estate was settled up, and then we could tip Sara off to the police. But by the time the money was settled up there was another hitch. This one was my doing. I—I—well, I wanted to go on just as we were. Conscience had nothing to do with it, you understand? It was simply that—well—that living on with Sara was the only thing I wanted. I wasn't even sorry for what I'd done, because if it hadn't been for that I would never have had her.

"I don't know whether I can make this clear to you, Rush, but even now I don't regret any of it. If it could have been different—but it couldn't. It had to be this way or none. And I've had those six months. I can see that I've been a chump. Sara was never for me. I got her by a crime and a trick, and while I held on to a silly hope that some day she'd—she'd look at me as I did at her, I knew in my heart all the time it was no use. There had been a man—your Millar. She's free now that it's out about my being married to Polly, and I hope she—I hope— Well, Madeline began to howl for action. I told Sara that Madeline had had a child by Jerome, and Sara agreed to settle some money on her. But that didn't satisfy Madeline. It wasn't sentiment with her. I mean, it wasn't any feeling for me, it was just the money. She wanted every cent she could get, and she couldn't get enough to satisfy her in a settlement of the kind Sara wanted to make.

"With Polly, it was that too, but maybe a little more. She's fond of me, I think. I don't know how she traced me here after she got out of the Wisconsin big house, but I can see how she figured things. I was married to a wealthy woman. If the woman died—shot by a bandit in a hold-up attempt—then I'd have money, and Polly would have both me and money. I haven't seen her, wouldn't know she was in Baltimore if you hadn't told me, but that's the way it would work out in her mind. The killing idea would have occurred just as easily to Madeline. I had told her I wouldn't stand for pushing the game through on Sara. Madeline knew that if she went ahead on her own hook and hung the Falsoner murder on Sara I'd blow up the whole racket. But if Sara died, then I'd have the money and Madeline would draw her cut. So that was it.

"I didn't know that until you told me, Rush. I don't give a damn for your opinion of me, but it's God's truth that I didn't know that either Polly or Madeline was trying to have Sara killed. Well, that's about all. Were you shadowing me when I went to the hotel?"

"Yeah."

"I thought so. That letter I wrote and sent home told just about what I've told you, spilled the whole story. I was going to run for it, leaving Sara in the clear. She's clear, all right, but now I'll have to face it. But I don't want to see her again, Rush."

"I wouldn't think you would," the detective agreed. "Not after making a killer of her."

"But I didn't," Landow protested. "She isn't. I forgot to tell you that, but I put it in the letter. Jerome Falsoner was not dead, not even dying, when I went past her into the flat. The knife was too high in his chest. I killed him, driving the knife into the same wound again, but downward. That's what I went in for, to make sure he was finished!"

Alec Rush screwed up his savage bloodshot eyes, looked long into the confessed murderer's face.

"That's a lie," he croaked at last, "but a decent one. Are you sure you want to stick to it? The truth will be enough to clear the girl, and maybe won't swing you."

"What difference does it make?" the younger man asked. "I'm a gone baby anyhow. And I might as well put Sara in the clear with herself as well as with the law. I'm caught to rights and another rap won't hurt. I told you Madeline had brains. I was afraid of them. She'd have had something up her sleeve to spring on us—to ruin Sara with. She could out-smart me without trying. I couldn't take any chances."

He laughed into Alec Rush's ugly face and, with a somewhat theatrical gesture, jerked one cuff an inch or two out of his coat-sleeve. The cuff was still damp with a maroon stain.

"I killed Madeline an hour ago," said Henry Bangs, alias Hubert Landow.

Creeping Siamese

STANDING beside the cashier's desk in the front office of the Continental Detective Agency's San Francisco branch, I was watching Porter check up my expense account when the man came in. He was a tall man, raw-boned, hard-faced. Grey clothes bagged loosely from his wide shoulders. In the late afternoon sunlight that came through partially drawn blinds, his skin showed the color of new tan shoes.

He opened the door briskly, and then hesitated, standing in the doorway, holding the door open, turning the knob back and forth with one bony hand. There was no indecision in his face. It was ugly and grim, and its expression was the expression of a man who is remembering something disagreeable.

Tommy Howd, our freckled and snub-nosed office boy, got up from his desk and went to the rail that divided the office.

"Do you—?" Tommy began, and jumped back.

The man had let go the doorknob. He crossed his long arms over his chest, each hand gripping a shoulder. His mouth stretched wide in a yawn that had nothing to do with relaxation. His mouth clicked shut. His lips snarled back from clenched yellow teeth.

"Hell!" he grunted, full of disgust, and pitched down on the floor.

I heaved myself over the rail, stepped across his body, and went out into the corridor.

Four doors away, Agnes Braden, a plump woman of thirty-something who runs a public stenographic establishment, was going into her office.

"Miss Braden!" I called, and she turned, waiting for me to come up. "Did you see the man who just came in our office?"

"Yes." Curiosity put lights in her green eyes. "A tall man who came up in the elevator with me. Why?"

"Was he alone?"

"Yes. That is, he and I were the only ones who got off at this floor. Why?"

"Did you see anybody close to him?"

"No, though I didn't notice him in the elevator. Why?"

"Did he act funny?"

"Not that I noticed. Why?"

"Thanks. I'll drop in and tell you about it later."

I made a circuit of the corridors on our floor, finding nothing.

The raw-boned man was still on the floor when I returned to the office, but he had been turned over on his back. He was as dead as I had thought. The Old Man, who had been examining him, straightened up as I came in. Porter was at the telephone, trying to get the police. Tommy Howd's eyes were blue half-dollars in a white face.

"Nothing in the corridors," I told the Old Man. "He came up in the elevator with Agnes Braden. She says he was alone, and she saw nobody close to him."

"Quite so." The Old Man's voice and smile were as pleasantly polite as if the corpse at his feet had been a part of the pattern in the carpet. Fifty years of sleuthing have left him with no more emotion than a pawnbroker. "He seems to have been stabbed in the left breast, a rather large wound that was staunched with this piece of silk"—one of his feet poked at a rumpled ball of red cloth on the floor—"which seems to be a sarong."

Today is never Tuesday to the Old Man: it *seems* to be Tuesday.

"On his person," he went on, "I have found some nine hundred dollars in bills of various denominations, and some silver; a gold watch and a pocket knife of English manufacture; a Japanese silver coin, 50 *sen*; tobacco, pipe and matches; a Southern Pacific timetable; two handkerchiefs without laundry marks; a pencil and several sheets of blank paper; four two-cent stamps; and a key labeled *Hotel Montgomery, Room 540*.

"His clothes seem to be new. No doubt we shall learn something from them when we make a more thorough examination, which I do not care to make until the police come. Meanwhile, you had better go to the Montgomery and see what you can learn there."

In the Hotel Montgomery's lobby the first man I ran into was the one I wanted: Pederson, the house copper, a blond-mustached ex-bartender who doesn't know any more about gum-shoeing than I do about saxaphones, but who does know people and how to handle them, which is what his job calls for.

"Hullo!" he greeted me. "What's the score?"

"Six to one, Seattle, end of the fourth. Who's in 540, Pete?"

"They're not playing in Seattle, you chump! Portland! A man that hasn't got enough civic spirit to know where his team—"

"Stop it, Pete! I've got no time to be fooling with your childish pastimes. A man just dropped dead in our joint with one of your room-keys in his pocket—540."

Civic spirit went blooey in Pederson's face.

"540?" He stared at the ceiling. "That would be that fellow Rounds. Dropped dead, you say?"

"Dead. Tumbled down in the middle of the floor with a knife-cut in him. Who is this Rounds?"

"I couldn't tell you much off-hand. A big bony man with leathery skin. I wouldn't have noticed him excepting he was such a sour looking body."

"That's the bird. Let's look him up."

At the desk we learned that the man had arrived the day before, registering as H. R. Rounds, New York, and telling the clerk he expects to leave within three days. There was no record of mail or telephone calls for him. Nobody knew when he had gone out, since he had not left his key at the desk. Neither elevator boys nor bell-hops could tell us anything.

His room didn't add much to our knowledge. His baggage consisted of one pigskin bag, battered and scarred, and covered with the marks of labels that had been scraped off. It was locked, but traveling bags locks don't amount to much. This one held us up about five minutes.

Rounds' clothes—some in the bag, some in the closet— were neither many nor expensive, but they were all new. The washable stuff was without laundry marks. Everything was of popular makes, widely advertised brands that could be bought in any city in the country. There wasn't a piece of paper with anything written on it. There wasn't an identifying tag. There wasn't anything in the room to tell where Rounds had come from or why.

Pederson was peevish about it.

"I guess if he hadn't got killed he'd of beat us out of a week's bill! These guys that don't carry anything to identify 'em, and that don't leave their keys at the desk when they go out, ain't to be trusted too much!"

We had just finished our search when a bell-hop brought Detective Sergeant O'Gar, of the police department Homicide Detail, into the room.

"Been down to the Agency?" I asked him.

"Yeah, just came from there."

"What's new?"

O'Gar pushed back his wide-brimmed black village-constable's hat and scratched his bullet head.

"Not a heap. The doc says he was opened with a blade at least six inches long by a couple wide, and that he couldn't of lived two hours after he got the blade—most likely not more'n one. We didn't find any news on him. What've you got here?"

"His name is Rounds. He registered here yesterday from New York. His stuff is new, and there's nothing on any of it to tell us anything except that he didn't want to leave a trail. No letters, no memoranda, nothing. No blood, no signs of a row, in the room."

O'Gar turned to Pederson.

"Any brown men been around the hotel? Hindus or the like?"

"Not that I saw," the house copper said. "I'll find out for you."

"Then the red silk was a sarong?" I asked.

"And an expensive one," the detective sergeant said. "I saw a lot of 'em the four years I was soldiering on the islands, but I never saw as good a one as that."

"Who wears them?"

"Men and women in the Philippines, Borneo, Java, Sumatra, Malay Peninsula, parts of India."

"Is it your idea that whoever did the carving advertised himself by running around in the streets in a red petticoat?"

"Don't try to be funny!" he growled at me. "They're often enough twisted or folded up into sashes or girdles. And how do I know he was knifed in the street? For that matter, how do I know he wasn't cut down in your joint?"

"We always bury our victims without saying anything about 'em. Let's go down and give Pete a hand in the search for your brown men."

That angle was empty. Any brown men who had snooped around the hotel had been too good at it to be caught.

I telephoned the Old Man, telling him what I had learned—which didn't cost me much breath—and O'Gar and I spent the rest of the evening sharp-shooting around without ever getting on the target once. We questioned taxicab drivers, questioned the three Roundses listed in the telephone book, and our ignorance was as complete when we were through as when we started.

The morning papers, on the streets at a little after eight o'clock that evening, had the story as we knew it.

At eleven o'clock O'Gar and I called it a night, separating in the direction of our respective beds.

We didn't stay apart long.

II

I opened my eyes sitting on the side of my bed in the dim light of a moon that was just coming up, with the ringing telephone in my hand.

O'Gar's voice: "1856 Broadway! On the hump!"

"1856 Broadway," I repeated, and he hung up.

I finished waking up while I phoned for a taxicab, and then wrestled my clothes on. My watch told me it was 12:55 A.M. as I went downstairs. I hadn't been fifteen minutes in bed.

1856 Broadway was a three-story house set behind a pocket-size lawn in a row of like houses behind like lawns. The others were dark. 1856 shed light from every window, and from the open front door. A policeman stood in the vestibule.

"Hello, Mac! O'Gar here?"

"Just went in."

I walked into a brown and buff reception hall, and saw the detective sergeant going up the wide stairs.

"What's up?" I asked as I joined him.

"Don't know."

On the second floor we turned to the left, going into a library or sitting room that stretched across the front of the house.

A man in pajamas and bathrobe sat on a davenport there, with one bared leg stretched out on a chair in front of him. I recognized him when he nodded to me: Austin Richter, owner of a Market Street moving picture theater. He was a round-faced man of forty five or so, partly bald, for whom the Agency had done some work a year or so before in connection with a ticket-seller who had departed without turning in the day's receipts.

In front of Richter a thin white-haired man with doctor written all over him stood looking at Richter's leg, which was wrapped in a bandage just below the knee. Beside the doctor, a tall woman in a fur-trimmed dressing-gown stood, a roll of gauze and a pair of scissors in her hands. A husky police corporal was writing in a notebook at a long narrow table, a thick hickory walking stick laying on the bright blue table cover at his elbow.

All of them looked around at us as we came into the room. The corporal got up and came over to us.

"I knew you were handling the Rounds job, sergeant, so I thought I'd best get word to you as soon as I heard they was brown men mixed up in this."

"Good work, Flynn," O'Gar said. "What happened here?"

"Burglary, or maybe only attempted burglary. They was four of them—crashed the kitchen door."

Richter was sitting up very straight, and his blue eyes were suddenly excited, as were the brown eyes of the woman.

"I beg your pardon," he said, "but is there—you mentioned brown men in connection with another affair—is there another?"

O'Gar looked at me.

"You haven't seen the morning papers?" I asked the theatre owner.

"No."

"Well, a man came into the Continental office late this afternoon, with a stab in his chest, and died there. Pressed against the wound, as if to stop the bleeding, was a sarong, which is where we got the brown men idea."

"His name?"

"Rounds, H. R. Rounds."

The name brought no recognition into Richter's eyes.

"A tall man, thin, with dark skin?" he asked. "In a grey suit?"

"All of that."

Richter twisted around to look at the woman.

"Molloy!" he exclaimed.

"Molloy!" she exclaimed.

"So you know him?"

Their faces came back toward me.

"Yes. He was here this afternoon. He left—"

Richter stopped, to turn to the woman again, questioningly.

"Yes, Austin," she said, putting gauze and scissors on the table, and sitting down beside him on the davenport. "Tell them."

He patted her hand and looked up at me again with the expression of a man who has seen a nice spot on which to lay down a heavy load.

"Sit down. It isn't a long story, but sit down."

We found ourselves chairs.

"Molloy—Sam Molloy—that is his name, or the name I have always known him by. He came here this afternoon. He'd either called up the theater or gone there, and they had told him I was home. I hadn't seen him for three years. We could see—both my wife and I—that there was something the matter with him when he came in.

"When I asked him, he said he'd been stabbed, by a Siamese, on his way here. He didn't seem to think the wound amounted to much, or pretended he didn't. He wouldn't let us fix it for him, or look at it. He said he'd go to a doctor after he left, after he'd got rid of the thing. That was what he had come to me for. He wanted me to hide it, to take care of it until he came for it again.

"He didn't talk much. He was in a hurry, and suffering. I didn't ask him any questions. I couldn't refuse him anything. I couldn't question him even though he as good as told us that it was illegal as well as dangerous. He saved our lives once—more than my wife's life—down in Mexico, where we first knew him. That was in 1916. We were caught down there during the Villa troubles. Molloy was running guns over the border, and he had enough influence with the bandits to have us released when it looked as if we were done for.

"So this time, when he wanted me to do something for him, I couldn't ask him about it. I said, 'Yes,' and he gave me the package. It wasn't a large package: about the size of—well—a loaf of bread, perhaps, but quite heavy for its size. It was wrapped in brown paper. We unwrapped it after he had gone, that is, we took the paper off. But the inner wrapping was of canvas, tied with silk cord, and sealed, so we didn't open that. We put it upstairs in the pack room, under a pile of old magazines.

"Then, at about a quarter to twelve tonight—I had only been in bed a few minutes, and hadn't gone to sleep yet—I heard a noise in here. I don't own a gun, and there's nothing you could properly call a weapon in the house, but that walking stick"—indicating the hickory stick on the table—"was in a closet in our bedroom. So I got that and came in here to see what the noise was.

"Right outside the bedroom door I ran into a man. I could see him better than he could see me, because this door was open and he showed against the window. He was between me and it, and the moonlight showed him fairly clear. I hit him with the stick, but didn't knock him down. He turned and ran in here. Foolishly, not thinking that he might not be alone, I ran after him. Another man shot me in the leg just as I came through the door.

"I fell, of course. While I was getting up, two of them came in with my wife between them. There were four of them. They were medium-sized men, brown-skinned, but not so dark. I took it for granted that they were Siamese, because Molloy had spoken of Siamese. They turned on the lights here, and one of them, who seemed to be the leader, asked me:

" 'Where is it?'

"His accent was pretty bad, but you could understand his words good enough. Of course I knew they were after what Molloy had left, but I pretended I didn't. They told me, or rather the leader did, that he knew it had been left here, but they called Molloy by another name—Dawson. I said I didn't know any Dawson, and nothing had been left here, and I tried to get them to tell me what they expected to find. They wouldn't though—they just called it '*it.*'

"They talked among themselves, but of course I couldn't make out a word of what they were saying, and then three of them went out, leaving one here to guard us. He had a Luger pistol. We could hear the others moving around the house. The search must have lasted an hour. Then the one I took for the leader came in, and said something to our guard. Both of them looked quite elated.

" 'It is not wise if you will leave this room for many minutes,' the leader said to me, and they left us—both of them—closing the door behind them.

"I knew they were going, but I couldn't walk on this leg. From what the doctor says, I'll be lucky if I walk on it inside of a couple of months. I didn't want my wife to go out, and perhaps run into one of them before they'd got away, but she insisted on going. She found they'd gone, and she phoned the police, and then ran up to the pack room and found Molloy's package was gone."

"And this Molloy didn't give you any hint at all as to what was in the package?" O'Gar asked when Richter had finished.

"Not a word, except that it was something the Siamese were after."

"Did he know the Siamese who stabbed him?" I asked.

"I think so," Richter said slowly, "though I am not sure he said he did."

"Do you remember his words?"

"Not exactly, I'm afraid."

"I think I remember them," Mrs. Richter said. "My husband, Mr. Richter, asked him, 'What's the matter, Molloy? Are you hurt, or sick?'

"Molloy gave a little laugh, putting a hand on his chest, and said, 'Nothing much. I run into a Siamese who was looking for me on my way here, and got careless and let him scratch me. But I kept my little bundle!' And he laughed again, and patted the package."

"Did he say anything else about the Siamese?"

"Not directly," she replied, "though he did tell us to watch out for any Asiatics we saw around the neighborhood. He said he wouldn't leave the package if he thought it would make trouble for us, but that there was always a chance that something would go wrong, and we'd better be careful. And he told my husband"—nodding at Richter—"that the Siamese had been dogging him for months, but now that he had a safe place for the package he was going to 'take them for a walk and forget to bring them back.' That was the way he put it."

"How much do you know about Molloy?"

"Not a great deal, I'm afraid," Richter took up the answering again. "He liked to talk about the places he had been and the things he had seen, but you couldn't get a word out of him about his own affairs. We met him first in Mexico, as I have told you, in 1916. After he saved us down there and got us away, we didn't see him again for nearly four years. He rang the bell one night, and came in for an hour or two. He was on his way to China, he said, and had a lot of business to attend to before he left the next day.

"Some months later I had a letter from him, from the Queen's Hotel in Kandy, asking me to send him a list of the importers and exporters in San Francisco. He wrote me a letter thanking me for the list, and I didn't hear from him again until he came to San Francisco for a week, about a year later. That was in 1921, I think.

"He was here for another week about a year after that, telling us that he had been in Brazil, but, as usual, not saying what he had been doing there. Some months later I had a letter from him, from Chicago, saying he would be here the following week. However, he didn't come. Instead, some time later, he wrote from Vladivostok, saying he hadn't been able to make it. Today was the first we'd heard of him since then."

"Where's his home? His people?"

"He always says he has neither. I've an idea he was born in England, though I don't know that he ever said so, or what made me think so."

"Got any more questions?" I asked O'Gar.

"No. Let's give the place the eye, and see if the Siamese left any leads behind 'em."

The eye we gave the house was thorough. We didn't split the territory between us, but went over everything together— everything from roof to cellar—every nook, drawer, corner.

The cellar did most for us: it was there, in the cold furnace, that we found the handful of black buttons and the fire-darkened garter clasps. But the upper floors hadn't been altogether worthless: in one room we had found the crumpled sales slip of an Oakland store, marked *1 table cover*; and in another room we had found no garters.

"Of course it's none of my business," I told Richter when O'Gar and I joined the others again, "but I think maybe if you plead self-defense you might get away with it."

He tried to jump up from the davenport, but his shot leg failed him.

The woman got up slowly.

"And maybe that would leave an out for you," O'Gar told her. "Why don't you try to persuade him?"

"Or maybe it would be better if you plead the self-defense," I suggested to her. "You could say that Richter ran to your help when your husband grabbed you, that your husband shot him and was turning his gun on you when you stabbed him. That would sound smooth enough."

"My husband?"

"Uh-huh, Mrs. Rounds-Molloy-Dawson. Your late husband, anyway."

Richter got his mouth far enough closed to get words out of it.

"What is the meaning of this damned nonsense?" he demanded.

"Them's harsh words to come from a fellow like you," O'Gar growled at him. "If this is nonsense, what do you make of that yarn you told us about creeping Siamese and mysterious bundles, and God knows what all?"

"Don't be too hard on him," I told O'Gar. "Being around movies all the time has poisoned his idea of what sounds plausible. If it hadn't, he'd have known better than to see a Siamese in the moonlight at 11:45, when the moon was just coming up at somewhere around 12:45, when you phoned me."

Richter stood up on his one good leg.

The husky police corporal stepped close to him.

"Hadn't I better frisk him, sergeant?"

O'Gar shook his bullet head.

"Waste of time. He's got nothing on him. They cleaned the

place of weapons. The chances are the lady dropped them in the bay when she rode over to Oakland to get a table cover to take the place of the sarong her husband carried away with him."

That shook the pair of them. Richter pretended he hadn't gulped, and the woman had a fight of it before she could make her eyes stay still on mine.

O'Gar struck while the iron was hot by bringing the buttons and garters clasps we had salvaged out of his pocket, and letting them trickle from one hand to another. That used up the last bit of the facts we had.

I threw a lie at them.

"Never me to knock the press, but you don't want to put too much confidence in what the papers say. For instance, a fellow might say a few pregnant words before he died, and the papers might say he didn't. A thing like that would confuse things."

The woman reared up her head and looked at O'Gar.

"May I speak to Austin alone?" she asked. "I don't mean out of your sight."

The detective sergeant scratched his head and looked at me. This letting your victims go into conference is always a ticklish business: they may decide to come clean, and then again, they may frame up a new out. On the other hand, if you don't let them, the chances are they get stubborn on you, and you can't get anything out of them. One way was as risky as another. I grinned at O'Gar and refused to make a suggestion. He could decide for himself, and, if he was wrong, I'd have him to dump the blame on. He scowled at me, and then nodded to the woman.

"You can go over into that corner and whisper together for a couple of minutes," he said, "but no foolishness."

She gave Richter the hickory stick, took his other arm, helped him hobble to a far corner, pulled a chair over there for him. He sat with his back to us. She stood behind him, leaning over his shoulder, so that both their faces were hidden from us.

O'Gar came closer to me.

"What do you think?" he muttered.

"I think they'll come through."

"That shot of yours about being Molloy's wife hit center. I missed that one. How'd you make it?"

"When she was telling us what Molloy had said about the Siamese she took pains both times she said 'my husband' to show that she meant Richter."

"So? Well—"

The whispering in the far corner had been getting louder, so that the s's had become sharp hisses. Now a clear emphatic sentence came from Richter's mouth.

"I'll be damned if I will!"

Both of them looked furtively over their shoulders, and they lowered their voices again, but not for long. The woman was apparently trying to persuade him to do something. He kept shaking his head. He put a hand on her arm. She pushed it away, and kept on whispering.

He said aloud, deliberately:

"Go ahead, if you want to be a fool. It's your neck. I didn't put the knife in him."

She jumped away from him, her eyes black blazes in a white face. O'Gar and I moved softly toward them.

"You rat!" she spat at Richter, and spun to face us.

"I killed him!" she cried. "This thing in the chair tried to and—"

Richter swung the hickory stick.

I jumped for it—missed—crashed into the back of his chair. Hickory stick, Richter, chair, and I sprawled together on the floor. The corporal helped me up. He and I picked Richter up and put him on the davenport again.

The woman's story poured out of her angry mouth:

"His name wasn't Molloy. It was Lange, Sam Lange. I married him in Providence in 1913 and went to China with him—to Canton, where he had a position with a steamship line. We didn't stay there long, because he got into some trouble through being mixed up in the revolution that year. After that we drifted around, mostly around Asia.

"We met this thing"—she pointed at the now sullenly quiet Richter—"in Singapore, in 1919, I think—right after the World War was over. His name is Holley, and Scotland Yard can tell you something about him. He had a proposition. He knew of a gem-bed in upper Burma, one of many that were hidden from the British when they took the country. He knew the natives who were working it, knew where they were hiding their gems.

"My husband went in with him, with two other men that were killed. They looted the natives' cache, and got away with a whole sackful of sapphires, topazes and even a few rubies. The two other men were killed by the natives and my husband was badly wounded.

"We didn't think he could live. We were hiding in a hut near the Yunnan border. Holley persuaded me to take the gems and run away with them. It looked as if Sam was done for, and if we stayed there long we'd be caught. I can't say that I was crazy about Sam anyway; he wasn't the kind you would be, after living with him for a while.

"So Holley and I took it and lit out. We had to use a lot of the stones to buy our way through Yunnan and Kwangsi and Kwangtung, but we made it. We got to San Francisco with enough to buy this house and the movie theater, and we've been here since. We've been honest since we came here, but I don't suppose that means anything. We had enough money to keep us comfortable.

"Today Sam showed up. We hadn't heard of him since we left him on his back in Burma. He said he'd been caught and jailed for three years. Then he'd got away, and had spent the other three hunting for us. He was that kind. He didn't want me back, but he did want money. He wanted everything we had. Holley lost his nerve. Instead of bargaining with Sam, he lost his head and tried to shoot him.

"Sam took his gun away from him and shot him in the leg. In the scuffle Sam had dropped a knife—a kris, I think. I picked it up, but he grabbed me just as I got it. I don't know how it happened. All I saw was Sam staggering back, holding his chest with both hands—and the kris shining red in my hand.

"Sam had dropped his gun. Holley got it and was all for shooting Sam, but I wouldn't let him. It happened in this room. I don't remember whether I gave Sam the sarong we used for a cover on the table or not. Anyway, he tried to stop the blood with it. He went away then, while I kept Holley from shooting him.

"I knew Sam wouldn't go to the police, but I didn't know

what he'd do. And I knew he was hurt bad. If he dropped dead somewhere, the chances are he'd be traced here. I watched from a window as he went down the street, and nobody seemed to pay any attention to him, but he looked so conspicuously wounded to me that I thought everybody would be sure to remember him if it got into the papers that he had been found dead somewhere.

"Holley was even more scared than I. We couldn't run away, because he had a shot leg. So we made up that Siamese story, and I went over to Oakland, and bought the table cover to take the place of the sarong. We had some guns and even a few oriental knives and swords here. I wrapped them up in paper, breaking the swords, and dropped them off the ferry when I went to Oakland.

"When the morning papers came out we read what had happened, and then we went ahead with what we had planned. We burned the suit Holley had worn when he was shot, and his garters—because the pants had a bullet-hole in them, and the bullet had cut one garter. We fixed a hole in his pajama-leg, unbandaged his leg,—I had fixed it as well as I could,—and washed away the clotted blood until it began to bleed again. Then I gave the alarm."

She raised both hands in a gesture of finality and made a clucking sound with her tongue.

"And there you are," she said.

"You got anything to say?" I asked Holley, who was staring at his bandaged leg.

"To my lawyer," he said without looking up.

O'Gar spoke to the corporal.

"The wagon, Flynn."

Ten minutes later we were in the street, helping Holley and the woman into a police car.

Around the corner on the other side of the street came three brown-skinned men, apparently Malay sailors. The one in the middle seemed to be drunk, and the other two were supporting him. One of them had a package that could have held a bottle under his arm.

O'Gar looked from them to me and laughed.

"We wouldn't be doing a thing to those babies right now if we had fallen for that yarn, would we?" he whispered.

"Shut up, you, you big heap!" I growled back, nodding at Holley, who was in the car by now. "If that bird sees them he'll identify 'em as his Siamese, and God knows what a jury would make of it!"

We made the puzzled driver twist the car six blocks out of his way to be sure we'd miss the brown men. It was worth it, because nothing interfered with the twenty years apiece that Holley and Mrs. Lange drew.

The Big Knock-Over

I FOUND Paddy the Mex in Jean Larrouy's dive. Paddy—an amiable con man who looked like the King of Spain—showed me his big white teeth in a smile, pushed a chair out for me with one foot, and told the girl who shared his table:

"Nellie, meet the biggest-hearted dick in San Francisco. This little fat guy will do anything for anybody, if only he can send 'em over for life in the end." He turned to me, waving his cigar at the girl: "Nellie Wade, and you can't get anything on her. She don't have to work—her old man's a bootlegger."

She was a slim girl in blue—white skin, long green eyes, short chestnut hair. Her sullen face livened into beauty when she put a hand across the table to me, and we both laughed at Paddy.

"Five years?" she asked.

"Six," I corrected.

"Damn!" said Paddy, grinning and hailing a waiter. "Some day I'm going to fool a sleuth."

So far he had fooled all of them—he had never slept in a hoosegow.

I looked at the girl again. Six years before, this Angel Grace Cardigan had buncoed half a dozen Philadelphia boys out of plenty. Dan Morey and I had nailed her, but none of her victims would go to the bat against her, so she had been turned loose. She was a kid of nineteen then, but already a smooth grifter.

In the middle of the floor one of Larrouy's girls began to sing *Tell Me What You Want and I'll Tell You What You Get.* Paddy the Mex tipped a gin-bottle over the glasses of gingerale the waiter had brought. We drank and I gave Paddy a piece of paper with a name and address penciled on it.

"Itchy Maker asked me to slip you that," I explained. "I saw him in the Folsom big house yesterday. It's his mother, he says, and he wants you to look her up and see if she wants anything. What he means, I suppose, is that you're to give her his cut from the last trick you and he turned."

538

"You hurt my feelings," Paddy said, pocketing the paper and bringing out the gin again.

I downed the second gin-gingerale and gathered in my feet, preparing to rise and trot along home. At that moment four of Larrouy's clients came in from the street. Recognition of one of them kept me in my chair. He was tall and slender and all dolled up in what the well-dressed man should wear. Sharp-eyed, sharp-faced, with lips thin as knife-edges under a small pointed mustache—Bluepoint Vance. I wondered what he was doing three thousand miles away from his New York hunting-grounds.

While I wondered I put the back of my head to him, pretending interest in the singer, who was now giving the customers *I Want to Be a Bum*. Beyond her, back in a corner, I spotted another familiar face that belonged in another city—Happy Jim Hacker, round and rosy Detroit gunman, twice sentenced to death and twice pardoned.

When I faced front again, Bluepoint Vance and his three companions had come to rest two tables away. His back was to us. I sized up his playmates.

Facing Vance sat a wide-shouldered young giant with red hair, blue eyes and a ruddy face that was good-looking in a tough, savage way. On his left was a shifty-eyed dark girl in a floppy hat. She was talking to Vance. The red-haired giant's attention was all taken by the fourth member of the party, on his right. She deserved it.

She was neither tall nor short, thin nor plump. She wore a black Russian tunic affair, green-trimmed and hung with silver dinguses. A black fur coat was spread over the chair behind her. She was probably twenty. Her eyes were blue, her mouth red, her teeth white, the hair-ends showing under her black-green-and-silver turban were brown, and she had a nose. Without getting steamed up over the details, she was nice. I said so. Paddy the Mex agreed with a "That's what," and Angel Grace suggested that I go over and tell Red O'Leary I thought her nice.

"Red O'Leary the big bird?" I asked, sliding down in my seat so I could stretch a foot under the table between Paddy and Angel Grace. "Who's his nice girl friend?"

"Nancy Regan, and the other one's Sylvia Yount."

"And the slicker with his back to us?" I probed.

Paddy's foot, hunting the girl's under the table, bumped mine.

"Don't kick me, Paddy," I pleaded. "I'll be good. Anyway, I'm not going to stay here to be bruised. I'm going home."

I swapped so-longs with them and moved toward the street, keeping my back to Bluepoint Vance.

At the door I had to step aside to let two men come in. Both knew me, but neither gave me a tumble—Sheeny Holmes (not the old-timer who staged the Moose Jaw looting back in the buggy-riding days) and Denny Burke, Baltimore's King of Frog Island. A good pair—neither of them would think of taking a life unless assured of profit and political protection.

Outside, I turned down toward Kearny Street, strolling along, thinking that Larrouy's joint had been full of crooks this one night, and that there seemed to be more than a sprinkling of prominent visitors in our midst. A shadow in a doorway interrupted my brain-work.

The shadow said, "Ps-s-s-s! Ps-s-s-s!"

Stopping, I examined the shadow until I saw it was Beno, a hophead newsie who had given me a tip now and then in the past—some good, some phoney.

"I'm sleepy," I growled as I joined Beno and his arm-load of newspapers in the doorway, "and I've heard the story about the Mormon who stuttered, so if that's what's on your mind, say so, and I'll keep going."

"I don't know nothin' about no Mormons," he protested, "but I know somethin' else."

"Well?"

"'S all right for you to say 'Well,' but what I want to know is, what am I gonna get out of it?"

"Flop in the nice doorway and go shut-eye," I advised him, moving toward the street again. "You'll be all right when you wake up."

"Hey! Listen, I got somethin' for you. Hones' to Gawd!"

"Well?"

"Listen!" He came close, whispering. "There's a caper rigged for the Seaman's National. I don't know what's the racket, but it's real. Hones' to Gawd! I ain't stringin' you. I can't give you no monickers. You know I would if I knowed 'em. Hones' to Gawd! Gimme ten bucks. It's worth that to you, ain't it? This is straight dope—hones' to Gawd!"

"Yeah, straight from the nose-candy!"

"No! Hones' to Gawd! I—"

"What *is* the caper, then?"

"I don't know. All I got was that the Seaman's is gonna be nicked, Hones' to—"

"Where'd you get it?"

Beno shook his head. I put a silver dollar in his hand.

"Get another shot and think up the rest of it," I told him, "and if it's amusing enough I'll give you the other nine bucks."

I walked on down to the corner, screwing up my forehead over Beno's tale. By itself, it sounded like what it probably was—a yarn designed to get a dollar out of a trusting gumshoe. But it wasn't altogether by itself. Larrouy's—just one drum in a city that had a number—had been heavy with grifters who were threats against life and property. It was worth a look-see, especially since the insurance company covering the Seaman's National Bank was a Continental Detective Agency client.

Around the corner, twenty feet or so along Kearny Street, I stopped.

From the street I had just quit came two bangs—the reports of a heavy pistol. I went back the way I had come. As I rounded the corner I saw men gathering in a group up the street. A young Armenian—a dapper boy of nineteen or twenty—passed me, going the other way, sauntering along, hands in pockets, softly whistling *Broken-hearted Sue.*

I joined the group—now becoming a crowd—around Beno. Beno was dead, blood from two holes in his chest staining the crumpled newspapers under him.

I went up to Larrouy's and looked in. Red O'Leary, Bluepoint Vance, Nancy Regan, Sylvia Yount, Paddy the Mex, Angel Grace, Denny Burke, Sheeny Holmes, Happy Jim Hacker—not one of them was there.

Returning to Beno's vicinity, I loitered with my back to a wall while the police arrived, asked questions, learned nothing, found no witnesses, and departed, taking what was left of the newsie with them.

I went home and to bed.

II

In the morning I spent on hour in the Agency file-room, digging through the gallery and records. We didn't have anything on Red O'Leary, Denny Burke, Nancy Regan, Sylvia Yount, and only some guesses on Paddy the Mex. Nor were there any open jobs definitely chalked against Angel Grace, Bluepoint Vance, Sheeny Holmes and Happy Jim Hacker, but their photos were there. At ten o'clock—bank opening time—I set out for the Seaman's National, carrying these photos and Beno's tip.

The Continental Detective Agency's San Francisco office is located in a Market Street office building. The Seaman's National Bank occupies the ground floor of a tall gray building in Montgomery Street, San Francisco's financial center. Ordinarily, since I don't like even seven blocks of unnecessary walking, I would have taken a street car. But there was some sort of traffic jam on Market Street, so I set out afoot, turning off along Grant Avenue.

A few blocks of walking, and I began to see that something was wrong with the part of town I was heading for. Noises for one thing—roaring, rattling, explosive noises. At Sutter Street a man passed me, holding his face with both hands and groaning as he tried to push a dislocated jaw back in place. His cheek was scraped red.

I went down Sutter Street. Traffic was in a tangle that reached to Montgomery Street. Excited, bare-headed men were running around. The explosive noises were clearer. An automobile full of policemen went down past me, going as fast as traffic would let it. An ambulance came up the street, clanging its gong, taking to the sidewalks where the traffic tangle was worst.

I crossed Kearny Street on the trot. Down the other side of the street two patrolmen were running. One had his gun out. The explosive noises were a drumming chorus ahead.

Rounding into Montgomery Street, I found few sightseers ahead of me. The middle of the street was filled with trucks, touring cars, taxis—deserted there. Up in the next block—between Bush and Pine Streets—hell was on a holiday.

The holiday spirit was gayest in the middle of the block, where the Seaman's National Bank and the Golden Gate Trust Company faced each other across the street.

For the next six hours I was busier than a flea on a fat woman.

III

Late that afternoon I took a recess from bloodhounding and went up to the office for a pow-wow with the Old Man. He was leaning back in his chair, staring out the window, tapping on his desk with the customary long yellow pencil.

A tall, plump man in his seventies, this boss of mine, with a white-mustached, baby-pink grandfatherly face, mild blue eyes behind rimless spectacles, and no more warmth in him than a hangman's rope. Fifty years of crook-hunting for the Continental had emptied him of everything except brains and a soft-spoken, gently smiling shell of politeness that was the same whether things went good or bad—and meant as little at one time as another. We who worked under him were proud of his cold-bloodedness. We used to boast that he could spit icicles in July, and we called him Pontius Pilate among ourselves, because he smiled politely when he sent us out to be crucified on suicidal jobs.

He turned from the window as I came in, nodded me to a chair, and smoothed his mustache with the pencil. On his desk the afternoon papers screamed the news of the Seaman's National Bank and Golden Gate Trust Company double-looting in five colors.

"What is the situation?" he asked, as one would ask about the weather.

"The situation is a pip," I told him. "There were a hundred and fifty crooks in the push if there was one. I saw a hundred myself—or think I did—and there were slews of them that I didn't see—planted where they could jump out and bite when fresh teeth were needed. They bit, too. They bushwacked the police and made a merry wreck out of 'em—going and coming. They hit the two banks at ten sharp—took over the whole block—chased away the reasonable people—dropped the others. The actual looting was duck soup to a mob of that size. Twenty or thirty of 'em to each of the banks while the others held the street. Nothing to it but wrap up the spoils and take 'em home.

"There's a highly indignant business men's meeting down there now—wild-eyed stockbrokers up on their hind legs yelling for the chief of police's heart's blood. The police didn't do any miracles, that's a cinch, but no police department is equipped to handle a trick of that size—no matter how well they think they are. The whole thing lasted less than twenty minutes. There were, say, a hundred and fifty thugs in on it, loaded for bear, every play mapped to the inch. How are you going to get enough coppers down there, size up the racket, plan your battle, and put it over in that little time? It's easy enough to say the police should look ahead—should have a dose for every emergency—but these same birds who are yelling, 'Rotten,' down there now would be the first to squawk, 'Robbery,' if their taxes were boosted a couple of cents to buy more policemen and equipment.

"But the police fell down—there's no question about that—and there will be a lot of beefy necks feel the ax. The armored cars were no good, the grenading was about fifty-fifty, since the bandits knew how to play that game, too. But the real disgrace of the party was the police machine-guns. The bankers and brokers are saying they were fixed. Whether they were deliberately tampered with, or were only carelessly taken care of, is anybody's guess, but only one of the damned things would shoot, and it not very well.

"The getaway was north on Montgomery to Columbus. Along Columbus the parade melted, a few cars at a time, into side streets. The police ran into an ambush between Washington and Jackson, and by the time they had shot their way through it the bandit cars had scattered all over the city. A lot of 'em have been picked up since then—empty.

"All the returns aren't in yet, but right now the score stands something like this: The haul will run God only knows how far into the millions—easily the richest pickings ever got with civilian guns. Sixteen coppers were knocked off, and three times that many wounded. Twelve innocent spectators, bank clerks, and the like, were killed and about as many banged around. There are two bandits and five shot-ups who might be either thugs or spectators that got too close. The bandits lost seven dead that we know of and thirty-one prisoners, most of them bleeding somewhere.

"One of the dead was Fat Boy Clarke. Remember him? He shot his way out of a Des Moines courtroom three or four years ago. Well, in his pocket we found a piece of paper, a map of Montgomery Street between Pine and Bush, the block of the looting. On the back of the map were typed instructions, telling him exactly what to do and when to do it. An X on the map showed him where he was to park the car in which he arrived with his seven men, and there was a circle where he was to stand with them, keeping an eye on things in general and on the windows and roofs of the buildings across the street in particular. Figures 1, 2, 3, 4, 5, 6, 7, 8 on the map marked doorways, steps, a deep window, and so on, that were to be used for shelter if shots had to be traded with those windows and roofs. Clarke was to pay no attention to the Bush Street end of the block, but if the police charged the Pine Street end he was to move his men up there, distributing them among points marked a, b, c, d, e, f, g, and h. (His body was found on the spot marked a.) Every five minutes during the looting he was to send a man to an automobile standing in the street at a point marked on the map with a star, to see if there were any new instructions. He was to tell his men that if he were shot down one of them must report to the car, and a new leader would be given them. When the signal for the getaway was given, he was to send one of his men to the car in which he had come. If it was still in commission, this man was to drive it, not passing the car ahead of him. If it was out of whack, the man was to report to the star-marked car for instructions how to get a new one. I suppose they counted on finding enough parked cars to take care of this end. While Clarke waited for his car he and his men were to throw as much lead as possible at every target in their district, and none of them was to board the car until it came abreast of them. Then they were to drive out Montgomery to Columbus to—blank.

"Get that?" I asked. "Here are a hundred and fifty gunmen, split into groups under group-leaders, with maps and schedules showing what each man is to do, showing the fire-plug he's to kneel behind, the brick he's to stand on, where he's to spit—everything but the name and address of the policeman he's to shoot! It's just as well Beno couldn't give me the details—I'd have written it off as a hop-head's dream!"

"Very interesting," the Old Man said, smiling blandly.

"The Fat Boy's was the only timetable we found," I went on with my history. "I saw a few friends among the killed and caught, and the police are still identifying others. Some are local talent, but most of 'em seem to be imported stock. Detroit, Chi, New York, St. Louis, Denver, Portland, L.A., Philly, Baltimore—all seem to have sent delegates. As soon as the police get through identifying them I'll make out a list.

"Of those who weren't caught, Bluepoint Vance seems to be the main squeeze. He was in the car that directed operations. I don't know who else was there with him. The Shivering Kid was in on the festivities, and I think Alphabet Shorty McCoy, though I didn't get a good look at him. Sergeant Bender told me he spotted Toots Salda and Darby M'Laughlin in the push, and Morgan saw the Did-and-Dat Kid. That's a good cross-section of the layout—gunmen, swindlers, hijackers from all over Rand-McNally.

"The Hall of Justice has been a slaughter-house all afternoon. The police haven't killed any of their guests—none that I know of—but they're sure-God making believers out of them. Newspaper writers who like to sob over what they call the third degree should be down there now. After being knocked around a bit, some of the guests have talked. But the hell of it is they don't know a whole lot. They know some names—Denny Burke, Toby the Lugs, Old Pete Best, Fat Boy Clarke and Paddy the Mex were named—and that helps some, but all the smacking power in the police force arm can't bring out anything else.

"The racket seems to have been organized like this: Denny Burke, for instance, is known as a shifty worker in Baltimore. Well, Denny talks to eight or ten likely boys, one at a time. 'How'd you like to pick up a piece of change out on the Coast?' he asks them. 'Doing what?' the candidate wants to know. 'Doing what you're told,' the King of Frog Island says. 'You know me. I'm telling you this is the fattest picking ever rigged, a kick in the pants to go through—air-tight. Every-body in on it will come home lousy with cush—and they'll all come home if they don't dog it. That's all I'm spilling. If you don't like it—forget it.'

"And these birds did know Denny, and if he said the job was good that was enough for them. So they put in with him. He told them nothing. He saw that they had guns, gave 'em each a ticket to San Francisco and twenty bucks, and told them where to meet him here. Last night he collected them and told them they went to work this morning. By that time they had moved around the town enough to see that it was bubbling over with visiting talent, including such moguls as Toots Salda, Bluepoint Vance and the Shivering Kid. So this morning they went forth eagerly with the King of Frog Island at their head to do their stuff.

"The other talkers tell varieties of the same tale. The po-lice found room in their crowded jail to stick in a few stool-pigeons. Since few of the bandits knew very many of the others, the stools had an easy time of it, but the only thing they could add to what we've got is that the prisoners are looking for a wholesale delivery tonight. They seem to think their mob will crash the prison and turn 'em loose. That's probably a lot of chewing-gum, but anyway this time the po-lice will be ready.

"That's the situation as it stands now. The police are sweeping the streets, picking up everybody who needs a shave or can't show a certificate of attendance signed by his parson, with special attention to outward bound trains, boats and automobiles. I sent Jack Counihan and Dick Foley down North Beach way to play the joints and see if they can pick up anything."

"Do you think Bluepoint Vance was the actual directing in-telligence in this robbery?" the Old Man asked.

"I hope so—we know him."

The Old Man turned his chair so his mild eyes could stare out the window again, and he tapped his desk reflectively with the pencil.

"I'm afraid not," he said in a gently apologetic tone. "Vance is a shrewd, resourceful and determined criminal, but his weakness is one common to his type. His abilities are all for present action and not for planning ahead. He has executed some large operations, but I've always thought I saw in them some other mind at work behind him."

I couldn't quarrel with that. If the Old Man said something was so, then it probably was, because he was one of these cautious babies who'll look out of the window at a cloudburst and say, "It seems to be raining," on the off-chance that somebody's pouring water off the roof.

"And who is this arch-gonnif?" I asked.

"You'll probably know that before I do," he said, smiling benignantly.

IV

I went back to the Hall and helped boil more prisoners in oil until around eight o'clock, when my appetite reminded me I hadn't eaten since breakfast. I attended to that, and then turned down toward Larrouy's, ambling along leisurely, so the exercise wouldn't interfere with my digestion. I spent three-quarters of an hour in Larrouy's, and didn't see anybody who interested me especially. A few gents I knew were present, but they weren't anxious to associate with me—it's not always healthy in criminal circles to be seen wagging your chin with a sleuth right after a job has been turned.

Not getting anything there, I moved up the street to Wop Healy's—another hole. My reception was the same here—I was given a table and let alone. Healy's orchestra was giving *Don't You Cheat*, all they had, while those customers who felt athletic were romping it out on the dance-floor. One of the dancers was Jack Counihan, his arms full of a big olive-skinned girl with a pleasant, thick-featured, stupid face.

Jack was a tall, slender lad of twenty-three or four who had drifted into the Continental's employ a few months before. It was the first job he'd ever had, and he wouldn't have had it if his father hadn't insisted that if sonny wanted to keep his fingers in the family till he'd have to get over the notion that squeezing through a college graduation was enough work for one lifetime. So Jack came to the Agency. He thought gumshoeing would be fun. In spite of the fact that he'd rather catch the wrong man than wear the wrong necktie, he was a promising young thief-catcher. A likable youngster, well-muscled for all his slimness, smooth-haired, with a gentleman's face and a gentleman's manner, nervy, quick with head and hands, full of the don't-give-a-damn gaiety that belonged to his youthfulness. He was jingle-brained, of course, and needed holding, but I would rather work with him than with a lot of old-timers I knew.

Half an hour passed with nothing to interest me.

Then a boy came into Healy's from the street—a small kid, gaudily dressed, very pressed in the pants-legs, very shiny in the shoes, with an impudent sallow face of pronounced cast. This was the boy I had seen sauntering down Broadway a moment after Beno had been rubbed out.

Leaning back in my chair so that a woman's wide-hatted head was between us, I watched the young Armenian wind between tables to one in a far corner, where three men sat. He spoke to them—off-hand—perhaps a dozen words—and moved away to another table where a snub-nosed, black-haired man sat alone. The boy dropped into the chair facing snub-nose, spoke a few words, sneered at snub-nose's questions, and ordered a drink. When his glass was empty he crossed the room to speak to a lean, buzzard-faced man, and then went out of Healy's.

I followed him out, passing the table where Jack sat with the girl, catching his eye. Outside, I saw the young Armenian half a block away. Jack Counihan caught up with me, passed me. With a Fatima in my mouth I called to him:

"Got a match, brother?"

While I lighted my cigarette with a match from the box he gave me I spoke behind my hands:

"The goose in the glad rags—tail him. I'll string behind you. I don't know him, but if he blipped Beno off for talking to me last night, he knows me. On his heels!"

Jack pocketed his matches and went after the boy. I gave Jack a lead and then followed him. And then an interesting thing happened.

The street was fairly well filled with people, mostly men, some walking, some loafing on corners and in front of soft-drink parlors. As the young Armenian reached the corner of an alley where there was a light, two men came up and spoke to him, moving a little apart so that he was between them. The boy would have kept walking apparently paying no attention to them, but one checked him by stretching an arm out in front of him. The other man took his right hand out of his pocket and flourished it in the boy's face so that the nickel-plated knuckles on it twinkled in the light. The boy ducked swiftly under threatening hand and outstretched arm, and went on across the alley, walking, and not even looking over his shoulder at the two men who were now closing on his back.

Just before they reached him another reached them—a broad-backed, long-armed, ape-built man I had not seen before. His gorilla's paws went out together. Each caught a man. By the napes of their necks he yanked them away from the boy's back, shook them till their hats fell off, smacked their skulls together with a crack that was like a broom-handle breaking, and dragged their rag-limp bodies out of sight up the alley. While this was happening the boy walked jauntily down the street, without a backward glance.

When the skull-cracker came out of the alley I saw his face in the light—a dark-skinned, heavily-lined face, broad and flat, with jaw-muscles bulging like abscesses under his ears. He spit, hitched his pants, and swaggered down the street after the boy.

The boy went into Larrouy's. The skull-cracker followed him in. The boy came out, and in his rear—perhaps twenty feet behind—the skull-cracker rolled. Jack had tailed them into Larrouy's while I had held up the outside.

"Still carrying messages?" I asked.

"Yes. He spoke to five men in there. He's got plenty of body-guard, hasn't he?"

"Yeah," I agreed. "And you be damned careful you don't get between them. If they split, I'll shadow the skull-cracker, you keep the goose."

We separated and moved after our game. They took us to all the hangouts in San Francisco, to cabarets, grease-joints, pool-rooms, saloons, flop-houses, hook-shops, gambling-joints and what have you. Everywhere the kid found men to speak his dozen words to, and between calls, he found them on street-corners.

I would have liked to get behind some of these birds, but I didn't want to leave Jack alone with the boy and his body-guard—they seemed to mean too much. And I couldn't stick Jack on one of the others, because it wasn't safe for me to hang too close to the Armenian boy. So we played the game as we had started it, shadowing our pair from hole to hole, while night got on toward morning.

It was a few minutes past midnight when they came out of a small hotel up on Kearny Street, and for the first time since we had seen them they walked together, side by side, up to Green Street, where they turned east along the side of Telegraph Hill. Half a block of this, and they climbed the front steps of a ramshackle furnished-room house and disappeared inside. I joined Jack Counihan on the corner where he had stopped.

"The greetings have all been delivered," I guessed, "or he wouldn't have called in his bodyguard. If there's nothing stirring within the next half hour I'm going to beat it. You'll have to take a plant on the joint till morning."

Twenty minutes later the skull-cracker came out of the house and walked down the street.

"I'll take him," I said. "You stick to the other baby."

The skull-cracker took ten or twelve steps from the house and stopped. He looked back at the house, raising his face to look at the upper stories. Then Jack and I could hear what had stopped him. Up in the house a man was screaming. It wasn't much of a scream in volume. Even now, when it had increased in strength, it barely reached our ears. But in it—in that one wailing voice—everything that fears death seemed to cry out its fear. I heard Jack's teeth click. I've got horny skin all over what's left of my soul, but just the same my forehead twitched. The scream was so damned weak for what it said.

The skull-cracker moved. Five gliding strides carried him back to the house. He didn't touch one of the six or seven front steps. He went from pavement to vestibule in a spring no monkey could have beaten for swiftness, ease or silence. One minute, two minutes, three minutes, and the screaming stopped. Three more minutes and the skull-cracker was leaving the house again. He paused on the sidewalk to spit and hitch his pants. Then he swaggered off down the street.

"He's your meat, Jack," I said. "I'm going to call on the boy. He won't recognize me now."

V

The street-door of the rooming-house was not only unlocked but wide open. I went through it into a hallway, where a dim light burning upstairs outlined a flight of steps. I climbed them and turned toward the front of the house. The scream had come from the front—either this floor or the third. There was a fair likelihood of the skull-cracker having left the room-door unlocked, just as he had not paused to close the street-door.

I had no luck on the second floor, but the third knob I cautiously tried on the third floor turned in my hand and let its door edge back from the frame. In front of this crack I waited a moment, listening to nothing but a throbbing snore somewhere far down the hallway. I put a palm against the door and eased it open another foot. No sound. The room was black as an honest politician's prospects. I slid my hand across the frame, across a few inches of wall-paper, found a light button, pressed it. Two globes in the center of the room threw their weak yellow light on the shabby room and on the young Armenian who lay dead across the bed.

I went into the room, closed the door and stepped over to the bed. The boy's eyes were wide and bulging. One of his temples was bruised. His throat gaped with a red slit that ran actually from ear to ear. Around the slit, in the few spots not washed red, his thin neck showed dark bruises. The skull-cracker had dropped the boy with a poke in the temple and had choked him until he thought him dead. But the kid had revived enough to scream—not enough to keep from screaming. The skull-cracker had returned to finish the job with a knife. Three streaks on the bed-clothes showed where the knife had been cleaned.

The lining of the boy's pockets stuck out. The skull-cracker had turned them out. I went through his clothes, but with no better luck than I expected—the killer had taken everything. The room gave me nothing—a few clothes, but not a thing out of which information could be squeezed.

My prying done, I stood in the center of the floor scratching my chin and considering. In the hall a floor-board creaked. Three backward steps on my rubber heels put me in the musty closet, dragging the door all but half an inch shut behind me.

Knuckles rattled on the room door as I slid my gun off my hip. The knuckles rattled again and a feminine voice said, "Kid, oh, Kid!" Neither knuckles nor voice was loud. The lock clicked as the knob was turned. The door opened and framed the shifty-eyed girl who had been called Sylvia Yount by Angel Grace.

Her eyes lost their shiftiness for surprise when they settled on the boy.

"Holy hell!" she gasped, and was gone.

I was half out of the closet when I heard her tip toeing back. In my hole again, I waited, my eye to the crack. She came in swiftly, closed the door silently, and went to lean over the dead boy. Her hands moved over him, exploring the pockets whose linings I had put back in place.

"Damn such luck!" she said aloud when the unprofitable frisking was over, and went out of the house.

I gave her time to reach the sidewalk. She was headed toward Kearny Street when I left the house. I shadowed her down Kearny to Broadway, up Broadway to Larrouy's. Larrouy's was busy, especially near the door, with customers going and coming. I was within five feet of the girl when she stopped a waiter and asked, in a whisper that was excited enough to carry, "Is Red here?"

The waiter shook his head.

"Ain't been in tonight."

The girl went out of the dive, hurrying along on clicking heels to a hotel in Stockton Street.

While I looked through the glass front, she went to the desk and spoke to the clerk. He shook his head. She spoke again and he gave her paper and envelope, on which she scribbled with the pen beside the register. Before I had to leave for a safer position from which to cover her exit, I saw which pigeon-hole the note went into.

From the hotel the girl went by street-car to Market and Powell Streets, and then walked up Powell to O'Farrell, where a fat-faced young man in gray overcoat and gray hat left the curb to link arms with her and lead her to a taxi stand up O'Farrell Street. I let them go, making a note of the taxi number—the fat-faced man looked more like a customer than a pal.

It was a little shy of two in the morning when I turned back into Market Street and went up to the office. Fiske, who holds down the Agency at night, said Jack Counihan had not reported, nothing else had come in. I told him to rouse me an operative, and in ten or fifteen minutes he succeeded in getting Mickey Linehan out of bed and on the wire.

"Listen, Mickey," I said, "I've got the nicest corner picked out for you to stand on the rest of the night. So pin on your diapers and toddle down there, will you?"

In between his grumbling and cursing I gave him the name and number of the Stockton Street hotel, described Red O'Leary, and told him which pigeon-hole the note had been put in.

"It mightn't be Red's home, but the chance is worth covering," I wound up. "If you pick him up, try not to lose him before I can get somebody down there to take him off your hands."

I hung up during the outburst of profanity this insult brought.

The Hall of Justice was busy when I reached it, though nobody had tried to shake the upstairs prison loose yet. Fresh lots of suspicious characters were being brought in every few minutes. Policemen in and out of uniform were everywhere. The detective bureau was a bee-hive.

Trading information with the police detectives, I told them about the Armenian boy. We were making up a party to visit the remains when the captain's door opened and Lieutenant Duff came into the assembly room.

"*Allez! Oop!*" he said, pointing a thick finger at O'Gar, Tully, Reeder, Hunt and me. "There's a thing worth looking at in Fillmore."

We followed him out to an automobile.

VI

A gray frame house in Fillmore Street was our destination. A lot of people stood in the street looking at the house. A police-wagon stood in front of it, and police uniforms were indoors and out.

A red-mustached corporal saluted Duff and led us into the house, explaining as we went, "'Twas the neighbors give us the rumble, complaining of the fighting, and when we got here, faith, there weren't no fight left in nobody."

All the house held was fourteen dead men.

Eleven of them had been poisoned—over-doses of knock-out drops in their booze, the doctors said. The other three had been shot, at intervals along the hall. From the looks of the remains, they had drunk a toast—a loaded one—and those who hadn't drunk, whether because of temperance or suspicious natures, had been gunned as they tried to get away.

The identity of the bodies gave us an idea of what their toast had been. They were all thieves—they had drunk their poison to the day's looting.

We didn't know all the dead men then, but all of us knew some of them, and the records told us who the others were later. The completed list read like *Who's Who in Crookdom*.

There was the Dis-and-Dat Kid, who had crushed out of Leavenworth only two months before; Sheeny Holmes; Snohomish Whitey, supposed to have died a hero in France in 1919; L.A. Slim, from Denver, sockless and underwearless as usual, with a thousand-dollar bill sewed in each shoulder of his coat; Spider Girrucci wearing a steel-mesh vest under his shirt and a scar from crown to chin where his brother had carved him years ago; Old Pete Best, once a congressman; Nigger Vojan, who once won $175,000 in a Chicago crap-game— *Abacadbra* tattooed on him in three places; Alphabet Shorty McCoy; Tom Brooks, Alphabet Shorty's brother-in-law, who invented the Richmond *razzle-dazzle*, and bought three hotels with the profits; Red Cudahy, who stuck up a Union Pacific train in 1924; Denny Burke; Bull McGonickle, still pale from fifteen years in Joliet; Toby the Lugs, Bull's running-mate, who used to brag about picking President Wilson's pocket in a Washington vaudeville theater; and Paddy the Mex.

Duff looked them over and whistled.

"A few more tricks like this," he said, "and we'll all be out of jobs. There won't be any grifters left to protect the tax-payers from."

"I'm glad you like it," I told him. "Me—I'd hate like hell to be a San Francisco copper the next few days."

"Why especially?"

"Look at this—one grand piece of double-crossing. This village of ours is full of mean lads who are waiting right now for these stiffs to bring 'em their cut of the stick-up. What do you think's going to happen when the word gets out that there's not going to be any gravy for the mob? There are going to be a hundred and more stranded thugs busy raising getaway dough. There'll be three burglaries to a block and a stick-up to every corner until the carfare's raised. God bless you, my son, you're going to sweat for your wages!"

Duff shrugged his thick shoulders and stepped over bodies to get to the telephone. When he was through I called the Agency.

"Jack Counihan called a couple of minutes ago," Fiske told me, and gave me an Army Street address. "He says he put his man in there, with company."

I phoned for a taxi, and then told Duff, "I'm going to run out for a while. I'll give you a ring here if there's anything to the angle, or if there isn't. You'll wait?"

"If you're not too long."

I got rid of my taxicab two blocks from the address Fiske had given me, and walked down Army Street to find Jack Counihan planted on a dark corner.

"I got a bad break," was what he welcomed me with. "While I was phoning from the lunch-room up the street some of my people ran out on me."

"Yeah? What's the dope?"

"Well, after that apey chap left the Green Street house he trolleyed to a house in Fillmore Street, and——"

"What number?"

The number Jack gave was that of the death-house I had just left.

"In the next ten or fifteen minutes just about that many other chaps went into the same house. Most of them came afoot, singly or in pairs. Then two cars came up together, with nine men in them—I counted them. They went into the house, leaving their machines in front. A taxi came past a little later, and I stopped it, in case my chap should motor away.

"Nothing happened for at least half an hour after the nine chaps went in. Then everybody in the house seemed to become demonstrative—there was a quantity of yelling and shooting. It lasted long enough to awaken the whole neighborhood. When it stopped, ten men—I counted them—ran out of the house, got into the two cars, and drove away. My man was one of them.

"My faithful taxi and I cried *Yoicks* after them, and they brought us here, going into that house down the street in front of which one of their motors still stands. After half an hour or so I thought I'd better report, so, leaving my taxi around the corner—where it's still running up expenses—I went up to yon all-night caravansary and phoned Fiske. And when I came back, one of the cars was gone—and I, woe is me!—don't know who went with it. Am I rotten?"

"Sure! You should have taken their cars along to the phone with you. Watch the one that's left while I collect a strong-arm squad."

I went up to the lunch-room and phoned Duff, telling him where I was, and:

"If you bring your gang along maybe there'll be profit in it. A couple of carloads of folks who were in Fillmore Street and didn't stay there came here, and part of 'em may still be here, if you make it sudden."

Duff brought his four detectives and a dozen uniformed men with him. We hit the house front and back. No time was wasted ringing the bell. We simply tore down the doors and went in. Everything inside was black until flashlights lit it up. There was no resistance. Ordinarily the six men we found in there would have damned near ruined us in spite of our outnumbering them. But they were too dead for that.

We looked at one another sort of open-mouthed.

"This is getting monotonous," Duff complained, biting off a hunk of tobacco. "Everybody's work is pretty much the same thing over and over, but I'm tired of walking into roomfuls of butchered crooks."

The catalog here had fewer names than the other, but they were bigger names. The Shivering Kid was here—nobody would collect all the reward money piled up on him now; Darby M'Laughlin, his horn-rimmed glasses crooked on his nose, ten thousand dollars' worth of diamonds on fingers and tie; Happy Jim Hacker; Donkey Marr, the last of the bow-legged Marrs, killers all, father and five sons; Toots Salda, the strongest man in crookdom, who had once picked up and run away with two Savannah coppers to whom he was hand-cuffed; and Rumdum Smith, who killed Lefty Read in Chi in 1916—a rosary wrapped around his left wrist.

No gentlemanly poisoning here—these boys had been mowed down with a 30-30 rifle fitted with a clumsy but effective home-made silencer. The rifle lay on the kitchen table. A door connected the kitchen with the dining-room. Directly opposite that door, double doors—wide open—opened into the room in which the dead thieves lay. They were all close to the front wall, lying as if they had been lined up against the wall to be knocked off.

The gray-papered wall was spattered with blood, punctured with holes where a couple of bullets had gone all the way through. Jack Counihan's young eyes picked out a stain on the paper that wasn't accidental. It was close to the floor, beside the Shivering Kid, and the Kid's right hand was stained with blood. He had written on the wall before he died—with fingers dipped in his own and Toots Salda's blood. The letters in the words showed breaks and gaps where his fingers had run dry, and the letters were crooked and straggly, because he must have written them in the dark.

By filling in the gaps, allowing for the kinks, and guessing where there weren't any indications to guide us, we got two words: *Big Flora*.

"They don't mean anything to me," Duff said, "but it's a name and most of the names we have belong to dead men now, so it's time we were adding to our list."

"What do you make of it?" asked bullet-headed O'Gar, detective-sergeant in the Homicide Detail, looking at the bodies. "Their pals got the drop on them, lined them against the wall, and the sharpshooter in the kitchen shot 'em down—bing-bing-bing-bing-bing-bing?"

"It reads that way," the rest of us agreed.

"Ten of 'em came here from Fillmore Street," I said. "Six stayed here. Four went to another house—where part of 'em are now cutting down the other part. All that's necessary is to trail the corpses from house to house until there's only one man left—and he's bound to play it through by croaking himself, leaving the loot to be recovered in the original packages. I hope you folks don't have to stay up all night to find the remains of that last thug. Come on, Jack, let's go home for some sleep."

VII

It was exactly 5 a.m. when I separated the sheets and crawled into my bed. I was asleep before the last draw of smoke from my good-night Fatima was out of my lungs. The telephone woke me at 5:15.

Fiske was talking: "Mickey Linehan just phoned that your Red O'Leary came home to roost half an hour ago."

"Have him booked," I said, and was asleep again by 5:17.

With the help of the alarm clock I rolled out of bed at nine, breakfasted, and went down to the detective bureau to see how the police had made out with the red-head. Not so good.

"He's got us stopped," the captain told me. "He's got alibis for the time of the looting and for last night's doings. And we can't even vag the son-of-a-gun. He's got means of support. He's salesman for Humperdickel's Universal Encyclopædiac Dictionary of Useful and Valuable Knowledge, or something like it. He started peddling these pamphlets the day before the knock-over, and at the time it was happening he was ringing doorbells and asking folks to buy his durned books. Anyway, he's got three witnesses that say so. Last night he was in a hotel from eleven to four-thirty this morning, playing cards, and he's got witnesses. We didn't find a durned thing on him or in his room."

I borrowed the captain's phone to call Jack Counihan's house.

"Could you identify any of the men you saw in the cars last night?" I asked when he had been stirred out of bed.

"No. It was dark and they moved too fast. I could barely make sure of my chap."

"Can't, huh?" the captain said. "Well, I can hold him twenty-four hours without laying charges, and I'll do that, but I'll have to spring him then unless you can dig up something."

"Suppose you turn him loose now," I suggested after thinking through my cigarette for a few minutes. "He's got himself all alibied up, so there's no reason why he should hide out on us. We'll let him alone all day—give him time to make sure he isn't being tailed—and then we'll get behind him tonight and stay behind him. Any dope on Big Flora?"

"No. That kid that was killed in Green Street was Bernie Bernheimer, alias the Motsa Kid. I guess he was a dip—he ran with dips—but he wasn't very—"

The buzz of the phone interrupted him. He said, "Hello, yes," and "Just a minute," into the instrument, and slid it across the desk to me.

A feminine voice: "This is Grace Cardigan. I called your Agency and they told me where to get you. I've got to see you. Can you meet me now?"

"Where are you?"

"In the telephone station on Powell Street."

"I'll be there in fifteen minutes," I said.

Calling the Agency, I got hold of Dick Foley and asked him to meet me at Ellis and Market right away. Then I gave the captain back his phone, said "See you later," and went uptown to keep my dates.

Dick Foley was on his corner when I got there. He was a swarthy little Canadian who stood nearly five feet in his high-heeled shoes, weighed a hundred pounds minus, talked like a Scotchman's telegram, and could have shadowed a drop of salt water from the Golden Gate to Hongkong without ever losing sight of it.

"You know Angel Grace Cardigan?" I asked him.

He saved a word by shaking his head, no.

"I'm going to meet her in the telephone station. When I'm through, stay behind her. She's smart, and she'll be looking for you, so it won't be duck soup, but do what you can."

Dick's mouth went down at the corners and one of his rare long-winded streaks hit him.

"Harder they look, easier they are," he said.

He trailed along behind me while I went up to the station. Angel Grace was standing in the doorway. Her face was more sullen than I had ever seen it, and therefore less beautiful—except her green eyes, which held too much fire for sullenness. A rolled newspaper was in one of her hands. She neither spoke, smiled nor nodded.

"We'll go to Charley's, where we can talk," I said, guiding her down past Dick Foley.

Not a murmur did I get out of her until we were seated cross-table in the restaurant booth, and the waiter had gone off with our orders. Then she spread the newspaper out on the table with shaking hands.

"Is this on the level?" she demanded.

I looked at the story her shaking finger tapped—an account of the Fillmore and Army Street findings, but a cagey account. A glance showed that no names had been given, that the police had censored the story quite a bit. While I pretended to read I wondered whether it would be to my advantage to tell the girl the story was a fake. But I couldn't see any clear profit in that, so I saved my soul a lie.

"Practically straight," I admitted.

"You were there?"

She had pushed the paper aside to the floor and was leaning over the table.

"With the police."

"Was—?" Her voice broke huskily. Her white fingers wadded the tablecloth in two little bunches half-way between us. She cleared her throat. "Who was—?" was as far as she got this time.

A pause. I waited. Her eyes went down, but not before I had seen water dulling the fire in them. During the pause the waiter came in, put our food down, went away.

"You know what I want to ask," she said presently, her voice low, choked. "Was he? Was he? For God's sake tell me!"

I weighed them—truth against lie, lie against truth. Once more truth triumphed.

"Paddy the Mex was shot—killed—in the Fillmore Street house," I said.

The pupils of her eyes shrank to pinpoints—spread again until they almost covered the green irises. She made no sound. Her face was empty. She picked up a fork and lifted a forkful of salad to her mouth—another. Reaching across the table, I took the fork out of her hand.

"You're only spilling it on your clothes," I growled. "You can't eat without opening your mouth to put the food in."

She put her hands across the table, reaching for mine, trembling, holding my hand with fingers that twitched so that the nails scratched me.

"You're not lying to me?" she half sobbed, half chattered. "You're on the square! You were white to me that time in Philly! Paddy always said you were one white dick! You're not tricking me?"

"Straight up," I assured her. "Paddy meant a lot to you?"

She nodded dully, pulling herself together, sinking back in a sort of stupor.

"The way's open to even up for him," I suggested.

"You mean—?"

"Talk."

She stared at me blankly for a long while, as if she was trying to get some meaning out of what I had said. I read the answer in her eyes before she put it in words.

"I wish to God I could! But I'm Paper-box-John Cardigan's daughter. It isn't in me to turn anybody up. You're on the wrong side. I can't go over. I wish I could. But there's too much Cardigan in me. I'll be hoping every minute that you nail them, and nail them dead right, but—"

"Your sentiments are noble, or words to that effect," I sneered at her. "Who do you think you are—Joan of Arc? Would your brother Frank be in stir now if his partner, Johnny the Plumber, hadn't put the finger on him for the Great Falls bulls? Come to life, dearie! You're a thief among thieves, and those who don't double-cross get crossed. Who rubbed your Paddy the Mex out? Pals! But you mustn't slap back at 'em because it wouldn't be clubby. My God!"

My speech only thickened the sullenness in her face.

"I'm going to slap back," she said, "but I can't, can't split. I can't, I tell you. If you were a gun, I'd— Anyway, what help I get will be on my side of the game. Let it go at that, won't you? I know how you feel about it, but— Will you tell me who besides—who else was—was found in those houses?"

"Oh, sure!" I snarled. "I'll tell you everything. I'll let you pump me dry. But you mustn't give me any hints, because it might not be in keeping with the ethics of your highly honorable profession!"

Being a woman, she ignored all this, repeating, "Who else?"

"Nothing stirring. But I will do this—I'll tell you a couple who weren't there—Big Flora and Red O'Leary."

Her dopiness was gone. She studied my face with green eyes that were dark and savage.

"Was Bluepoint Vance?" she demanded.

"What do you guess?" I replied.

She studied my face for a moment longer and then stood up.

"Thanks for what you've told me," she said, "and for meeting me like this. I do hope you win."

She went out to be shadowed by Dick Foley. I ate my lunch.

VIII

At four o'clock that afternoon Jack Counihan and I brought our hired automobile to rest within sight of the front door of the Stockton Street hotel.

"He cleared himself with the police, so there's no reason why he should have moved, maybe," I told Jack, "and I'd rather not monkey with the hotel people, not knowing them. If he doesn't show by late we'll have to go up against them then."

We settled down to cigarettes, guesses on who'd be the next heavyweight champion and when, the possibilities of Prohibition being either abolished or practiced, where to get good gin and what to do with it, the injustice of the new Agency ruling that for purposes of expense accounts Oakland was not to be considered out of town, and similar exciting topics, which carried us from four o'clock to ten minutes past nine.

At 9:10 Red O'Leary came out of the hotel.

"God is good," said Jack as he jumped out of the machine to do the footwork while I stirred the motor.

The fire-topped giant didn't take us far. Larrouy's front door gobbled him. By the time I had parked the car and gone into the dive, both O'Leary and Jack had found seats. Jack's table was on the edge of the dance-floor. O'Leary's was on the other side of the establishment, against the wall, near a corner. A fat blond couple were leaving the table back in that corner when I came in, so I persuaded the waiter who was guiding me to a table to make it that one.

O'Leary's face was three-quarters turned away from me. He was watching the front door, watching it with an earnestness that turned suddenly to happiness when a girl appeared there. She was the girl Angel Grace had called Nancy Regan. I have already said she was nice. Well, she was. And the cocky little blue hat that hid all her hair didn't handicap her niceness any tonight.

The red-head scrambled to his feet and pushed a waiter and a couple of customers out of his way as he went to meet her. As reward for his eagerness he got some profanity that he didn't seem to hear and a blue-eyed, white-toothed smile that was—well—nice. He brought her back to his table and put her in a chair facing me, while he sat very much facing her.

His voice was a baritone rumble out of which my snooping ears could pick no words. He seemed to be telling her a lot, and she listened as if she liked it.

"But, Reddy, dear, you shouldn't," she said once. Her voice—I know other words, but we'll stick to this one—was nice. Outside of the music in it, it had quality. Whoever this gunman's moll was, she either had had a good start in life or had learned her stuff well. Now and then, when the orchestra came up for air, I would catch a few words, but they didn't tell me anything except that neither she nor her rowdy play-mate had anything against the other.

The joint had been nearly empty when she came in. By ten o'clock it was fairly crowded, and ten o'clock is early for Larrouy's customers. I began to pay less attention to Red's girl—even if she was nice—and more to my other neighbors. It struck me that there weren't many women in sight. Checking up on that, I found damned few women in proportion to the men. Men—rat-faced men, hatchet-faced men, square-jawed men, slack-chinned men, pale men, ruddy men, dark men, bull-necked men, scrawny men, funny-looking men, tough-looking men, ordinary men—sitting two to a

table, four to a table, more coming in—and damned few
women.

These men talked to one another, as if they weren't much
interested in what they were saying. They looked casually
around the joint, with eyes that were blankest when they
came to O'Leary. And always those casual—bored—glances
did rest on O'Leary for a second or two.

I returned my attention to O'Leary and Nancy Regan. He
was sitting a little more erect in his chair than he had been, but
it was an easy, supple erectness, and though his shoulders had
hunched a bit, there was no stiffness in them. She said something to him. He laughed, turning his face toward the center
of the room, so that he seemed to be laughing not only at what
she had said, but also at these men who sat around him, waiting. It was a hearty laugh, young and careless.

The girl looked surprised for a moment, as if something in
the laugh puzzled her, then she went on with whatever she
was telling him. She didn't know she was sitting on dynamite,
I decided. O'Leary knew. Every inch of him, every gesture,
said, "I'm big, strong, young, tough and red-headed. When
you boys want to do your stuff I'll be here."

Time slid by. Few couples danced. Jean Larrouy went
around with dark worry in his round face. His joint was full
of customers, but he would rather have had it empty.

By eleven o'clock I stood up and beckoned to Jack
Counihan. He came over, we shook hands, exchanged *How's
everythings* and *Getting muches*, and he sat at my table.

"What is happening?" he asked under cover of the orchestra's din. "I can't see anything, but there is something in the
air. Or am I being hysterical?"

"You will be presently. The wolves are gathering, and Red
O'Leary's the lamb. You could pick a tenderer one if you had
a free hand, maybe. But these bimbos once helped pluck a
bank, and when pay-day came there wasn't anything in their
envelopes, not even any envelopes. The word got out that
maybe Red knew how-come. Hence this. They're waiting
now—maybe for somebody—maybe till they get enough
hooch in them."

"And we sit here because it's the nearest table to the target
for all these fellows' bullets when the blooming lid blows

off?" Jack inquired. "Let's move over to Red's table. It's still nearer, and I rather like the appearance of the girl with him."

"Don't be impatient, you'll have your fun," I promised him. "There's no sense in having this O'Leary killed. If they bargain with him in a gentlemanly way, we'll lay off. But if they start heaving things at him, you and I are going to pry him and his girl friend loose."

"Well spoken, my hearty!" He grinned, whitening around the mouth. "Are there any details, or do we just simply and unostentatiously pry 'em loose?"

"See the door behind me, to the right? When the pop-off comes, I'm going back there and open it up. You hold the line midway between. When I yelp, you give Red whatever help he needs to get back there."

"Aye, aye!" He looked around the room at the assembled plug-uglies, moistened his lips, and looked at the hand holding his cigarette, a quivering hand. "I hope you won't think I'm in a funk," he said. "But I'm not an antique murderer like you. I get a reaction out of this prospective slaughtering."

"Reaction, my eye," I said. "You're scared stiff. But no nonsense, mind! If you try to make a vaudeville act out of it I'll ruin whatever these guerrillas leave of you. You do what you're told, and nothing else. If you get any bright ideas, save 'em to tell me about afterward."

"Oh, my conduct will be most exemplary!" he assured me.

IX

It was nearly midnight when what the wolves waited for came. The last pretense of indifference went out of faces that had been gradually taking on tenseness. Chairs and feet scraped as men pushed themselves back a little from their tables. Muscles flexed bodies into readiness for action. Tongues licked lips and eyes looked eagerly at the front door.

Bluepoint Vance was coming into the room. He came alone, nodding to acquaintances on this side and that, carrying his tall body gracefully, easily, in its well-cut clothing. His sharp-featured face was smilingly self-confident. He came without haste and without delay to Red O'Leary's table. I couldn't see Red's face, but muscles thickened the back of his neck. The girl smiled cordially at Vance and gave him her hand. It was naturally done. She didn't know anything.

Vance turned his smile from Nancy Regan to the red-haired giant a smile that was a trifle cat-to-mousey.

"How's everything, Red?" he asked.

"Everything suits me," bluntly.

The orchestra had stopped playing. Larrouy, standing by the street door, was mopping his forehead with a handkerchief. At the table to my right, a barrel-chested, broken-nosed bruiser in a widely striped suit was breathing heavily between his gold teeth, his watery gray eyes bulging at O'Leary, Vance and Nancy. He was in no way conspicuous there were too many others holding the same pose.

Bluepoint Vance turned his head, called to a waiter: "Bring me a chair."

The chair was brought and put at the unoccupied side of the table, facing the wall. Vance sat down, slumping back in the chair, leaning indolently toward Red, his left arm hooked over the chair-back, his right hand holding a cigarette.

"Well, Red," he said when he was thus installed, "have you got any news for me?"

His voice was suave, but loud enough for those at nearby tables to hear.

"Not a word." O'Leary's voice made no pretense of friendliness, nor of caution.

"What, no spinach?" Vance's thin-lipped smile spread, and his dark eyes had a mirthful but not pleasant glitter. "Nobody gave you anything to give me?"

"No," said O'Leary, emphatically.

"My goodness!" said Vance, the smile in his eyes and mouth deepening, and getting still less pleasant. "That's ingratitude! Will you help me collect, Red?"

"No."

I was disgusted with this red-head—half-minded to let him go under when the storm broke. Why couldn't he have stalled his way out—fixed up a fancy tale that Bluepoint would have had to half-way accept? But no—this O'Leary boy was so damned childishly proud of his toughness that he had to make a show of it when he should have been using his bean. If it had been only his own carcass that was due for a beating, it would have been all right. But it wasn't all right that Jack and I should have to suffer. This big chump was too valuable to lose. We'd have to get ourselves all battered up saving him from the rewards of his own pig-headedness. There was no justice in it.

"I've got a lot of money coming to me, Red." Vance spoke lazily, tauntingly. "And I need that money." He drew on his cigarette, casually blew the smoke into the red-head's face, and drawled, "Why, do you know the laundry charges twenty-six cents just for doing a pair of pajamas? I need money."

"Sleep in your underclothes," said O'Leary.

Vance laughed. Nancy Regan smiled, but in a bewildered way. She didn't seem to know what it was all about, but she couldn't help knowing that it was about something.

O'Leary leaned forward and spoke deliberately, loud enough for any to hear:

"Bluepoint, I've got nothing to give you—now or ever. And that goes for anybody else that's interested. If you or them think I owe you something—try and get it. To hell with you, Bluepoint Vance! If you don't like it—you've got friends here. Call 'em on!"

What a prime young idiot! Nothing would suit him but an ambulance—and I must be dragged along with him.

Vance grinned evilly, his eyes glittering into O'Leary's face.

"You'd like that, Red?"

O'Leary hunched his big shoulders and let them drop.

"I don't mind a fight," he said. "But I'd like to get Nancy out of it." He turned to her. "Better run along, honey, I'm going to be busy."

She started to say something, but Vance was talking to her. His words were lightly spoken, and he made no objection to her going. The substance of what he told her was that she was going to be lonely without Red. But he went intimately into the details of that loneliness.

Red O'Leary's right hand rested on the table. It went up to Vance's mouth. The hand was a fist when it got there. A wallop of that sort is awkward to deliver. The body can't give it much. It has to depend on the arm muscles, and not on the best of those. Yet Bluepoint Vance was driven out of his chair and across to the next table.

Larrouy's chairs went empty. The shindig was on.

"On your toes," I growled at Jack Counihan, and, doing my best to look like the nervous little fat man I was, I ran toward the back door, passing men who were moving not yet swiftly toward O'Leary. I must have looked the part of a scared trouble-dodger, because nobody stopped me, and I reached the door before the pack had closed on Red. The door was closed, but not locked. I wheeled with my back to it, black-jack in right hand, gun in left. Men were in front of me, but their backs were to me.

O'Leary was towering in front of his table, his tough red face full of bring-on-your-hell, his big body balanced on the balls of his feet. Between us, Jack Counihan stood, his face turned to me, his mouth twitching in a nervous grin, his eyes dancing with delight. Bluepoint Vance was on his feet again. Blood trickled from his thin lips, down his chin. His eyes were cool. They looked at Red O'Leary with the businesslike look of a logger sizing up the tree he's going to bring down. Vance's mob watched Vance.

"Red!" I bawled into the silence. "This way, Red!"

Faces spun to me—every face in the joint—millions of them.

"Come on, Red!" Jack Counihan yelped, taking a step forward, his gun out.

Bluepoint Vance's hand flashed to the V of his coat. Jack's gun snapped at him. Bluepoint had thrown himself down before the boy's trigger was yanked. The bullet went wide, but Vance's draw was gummed.

Red scooped the girl up with his left arm. A big automatic blossomed in his right fist. I didn't pay much attention to him after that. I was busy.

Larrouy's home was pregnant with weapons—guns, knives, saps, knucks, club-swung chairs and bottles, miscellaneous implements of destruction. Men brought their weapons over to mingle with me. The game was to nudge me away from my door. O'Leary would have liked it. But I was no fire-haired young rowdy. I was pushing forty, and I was twenty pounds overweight. I had the liking for ease that goes with that age and weight. Little ease I got.

A squint-eyed Portuguese slashed at my neck with a knife that spoiled my necktie. I caught him over the ear with the side of my gun before he could get away, saw the ear tear loose. A grinning kid of twenty went down for my legs—football stuff. I felt his teeth in the knee I pumped up, and felt them break. A pock-marked mulatto pushed a gun-barrel over the shoulder of the man in front of him. My blackjack crunched the arm of the man in front. He winced sidewise as the mulatto pulled the trigger—and had the side of his face blown away.

I fired twice—once when a gun was leveled within a foot of my middle, once when I discovered a man standing on a table not far off taking careful aim at my head. For the rest I trusted to my arms and legs, and saved bullets. The night was young and I had only a dozen pills—six in the gun, six in my pocket.

It was a swell bag of nails. Swing right, swing left, kick, swing right, swing left, kick. Don't hesitate, don't look for targets. God will see that there's always a mug there for your gun or blackjack to sock, a belly for your foot.

A bottle came through and found my forehead. My hat saved me some, but the crack didn't do me any good. I swayed and broke a nose where I should have smashed a skull. The room seemed stuffy, poorly ventilated. Somebody ought to tell Larrouy about it. How do you like that lead-and-leather pat on the temple, blondy? This rat on my left is getting too close. I'll draw him in by bending to the right to poke the mulatto, and then I'll lean back into him and let him have it. Not bad! But I can't keep this up all night. Where are Red and Jack? Standing off watching me?

Somebody socked me in the shoulder with something—a piano from the feel of it. A bleary-eyed Greek put his face where I couldn't miss it. Another thrown bottle took my hat and part of my scalp. Red O'Leary and Jack Counihan smashed through, dragging the girl between them.

X

While Jack put the girl through the door, Red and I cleared a little space in front of us. He was good at that. When he chucked them back they went back. I didn't dog it on him, but I did let him get all the exercise he wanted.

"All right!" Jack called.

Red and I went through the door, slammed it shut. It wouldn't hold even if locked. O'Leary sent three slugs through it to give the boys something to think about, and our retreat got under way.

We were in a narrow passageway lighted by a fairly bright light. At the other end was a closed door. Halfway down, to the right, steps led up.

"Straight ahead?" asked Jack, who was in front.

O'Leary said, "Yes." and I said, "No. Vance will have that blocked by now if the bulls haven't. Upstairs—the roof."

We reached the stairs. The door behind us burst open. The light went out. The door at the other end of the passage slammed open. No light came through either door. Vance would want light. Larrouy must have pulled the switch, trying to keep his dump from being torn to toothpicks.

Tumult boiled in the dark passage as we climbed the stairs by the touch system. Whoever had come through the back door was mixing it with those who had followed us—mixing it with blows, curses and an occasional shot. More power to them! We climbed, Jack leading, the girl next, then me, and last of all, O'Leary.

Jack was gallantly reading road-signs to the girl: "Careful of the landing, half a turn to the left now, put your right hand on the wall and—"

"Shut up!" I growled at him. "It's better to have her falling down than to have everybody in the drum fall on us."

We reached the second floor. It was black as black. There were three stories to the building.

"I've mislaid the blooming stairs," Jack complained.

We poked around in the dark, hunting for the flight that should lead up toward our roof. We didn't find it. The riot downstairs was quieting. Vance's voice was telling his push that they were mixing it with each other, asking where we had gone. Nobody seemed to know. We didn't know, either.

"Come on," I grumbled, leading the way down the dark hall toward the back of the building. "We've got to go somewhere."

There was still noise downstairs, but no more fighting. Men were talking about getting lights. I stumbled into a door at the end of the hall, pushed it open. A room with two windows through which came a pale glow from the street lights. It seemed brilliant after the hall. My little flock followed me in and we closed the door.

Red O'Leary was across the room, his noodle to an open window.

"Back street," he whispered. "No way down unless we drop."

"Anybody in sight?" I asked.

"Don't see any."

I looked around the room—bed, couple of chairs, chest of drawers, and a table.

"The table will go through the window," I said. "We'll chuck it as far as we can and hope the racket will lead 'em out there before they decide to look up here."

Red and the girl were assuring each other that each was still all in one piece. He broke away from her to help me with the table. We balanced it, swung it, let it go. It did nicely, crashing into the wall of the building opposite, dropping down into a backyard to clang and clatter on a pile of tin, or a collection of garbage cans, or something beautifully noisy. You couldn't have heard it more than a block and a half away.

We got away from the window as men bubbled out of Larrouy's back door.

The girl, unable to find any wounds on O'Leary, had turned to Jack Counihan. He had a cut cheek. She was monkeying with it and a handkerchief.

"When you finish that," Jack was telling her, "I'm going out and get one on the other side."

"I'll never finish if you keep talking—you jiggle your cheek."

"That's a swell idea," he exclaimed. "San Francisco is the second largest city in California. Sacramento is the State capital. Do you like geography? Shall I tell you about Java? I've never been there, but I drink their coffee. If—"

"Silly!" she said, laughing. "If you don't hold still I'll stop now."

"Not so good," he said. "I'll be still."

She wasn't doing anything except wiping blood off his cheek, blood that had better been let dry there. When she finished this perfectly useless surgery, she took her hand away slowly, surveying the hardly noticeable results with pride. As her hand came on a level with his mouth, Jack jerked his head forward to kiss the tip of one passing finger.

"Silly!" she said again, snatching her hand away.

"Lay off that," said Red O'Leary, "or I'll knock you off."

"Pull in your neck," said Jack Counihan.

"Reddy!" the girl cried, too late.

The O'Leary right looped out. Jack took the punch on the button, and went to sleep on the floor. The big red-head spun on the balls of his feet to loom over me.

"Got anything to say?" he asked.

I grinned down at Jack, up at Red.

"I'm ashamed of him," I said. "Letting himself be stopped by a paluka who leads with his right."

"You want to try it?"

"Reddy! Reddy!" the girl pleaded, but nobody was listening to her.

"If you'll lead with your right," I said.

"I will," he promised, and did.

I grandstanded, slipping my head out of the way, laying a forefinger on his chin.

"That could have been a knuckle," I said.

"Yes? This one is."

I managed to get under his left, taking the forearm across the back of my neck. But that about played out the acrobatics. It looked as if I would have to see what I could do to him, if any. The girl grabbed his arm and hung on.

"Reddy, darling, haven't you had enough fighting for one night? Can't you be sensible, even if you are Irish?"

I was tempted to paste the big chaw while his playmate had him tied up.

He laughed down at her, ducked his head to kiss her mouth, and grinned at me.

"There's always some other time," he said good-naturedly.

XI

"We'd better get out of here if we can," I said. "You've made too much rumpus for it to be safe."

"Don't get it up in your neck, little man," he told me. "Hold on to my coat-tails and I'll pull you out."

The big tramp. If it hadn't been for Jack and me he wouldn't have had any coat-tail by now.

We moved to the door, listened there, heard nothing.

"The stairs to the third floor must be up front," I whispered. "We'll try for them now."

We opened the door carefully. Enough light went past us into the hall to show a promise of emptiness. We crept down the hall, Red and I each holding one of the girl's hands. I hoped Jack would come out all right, but he had put himself to sleep, and I had troubles of my own.

I hadn't known that Larrouy's was large enough to have two miles of hallway. It did. It was an even mile in the darkness to the head of the stairs we had come up. We didn't pause there to listen to the voices below. At the end of the next mile O'Leary's foot found the bottom step of the flight leading up.

Just then a yell broke out at the head of the other flight.

"All up—they're up here!"

A white light beamed up on the yeller, and a brogue addressed him from below: "Come on down, ye windbag."

"The police," Nancy Regan whispered, and we hustled up our new-found steps to the third floor.

More darkness, just like that we'd left. We stood still at the top of the stairs. We didn't seem to have any company.

"The roof," I said. "We'll risk matches."

Back in a corner our feeble match-light found us a ladder nailed to the wall, leading to a trap in the ceiling. As little later as possible we were on Larrouy's roof, the trap closed behind us.

"All silk so far," said O'Leary, "and if Vance's rats and the bulls will play a couple of seconds longer—bingavast."

I led the way across the roofs. We dropped ten feet to the next building, climbed a bit to the next, and found on the other side of it a fire-escape that ran down to a narrow court with an opening into the back street.

"This ought to do it," I said, and went down.

The girl came behind me, and then Red. The court into which we dropped was empty—a narrow cement passage between buildings. The bottom of the fire-escape creaked as it hinged down under my weight, but the noise didn't stir anything. It was dark in the court, but not black.

"When we hit the street, we split," O'Leary told me, without a word of gratitude for my help—the help he didn't seem to know he had needed. "You roll your hoop, we'll roll ours."

"Uh-huh," I agreed, chasing my brains around in my skull. "I'll scout the alley first."

Carefully I picked my way down to the end of the court and risked the top of my hatless head to peep into the back street. It was quiet, but up at the corner, a quarter of a block above, two loafers seemed to be loafing attentively. They weren't coppers. I stepped out into the back street and beckoned them down. They couldn't recognize me at that distance, in that light, and there was no reason why they shouldn't think me one of Vance's crew, if they belonged to him.

As they came toward me I stepped back into the court and hissed for Red. He wasn't a boy you had to call twice to a row. He got to me just as they arrived. I took one. He took the other.

Because I wanted a disturbance, I had to work like a mule to get it. These bimbos were a couple of lollipops for fair. There wouldn't have been an ounce of fight in a ton of them. The one I had didn't know what to make of my roughing him around. He had a gun, but he managed to drop it first thing, and in the wrestling it got kicked out of reach. He hung on while I sweated ink jockeying him around into position. The darkness helped, but even at that it was no cinch to pretend he was putting up a battle while I worked him around behind O'Leary, who wasn't having any trouble at all with his man.

Finally I made it. I was behind O'Leary, who had his man pinned against the wall with one hand, preparing to sock him again with the other. I clamped my left hand on my playmate's wrist, twisted him to his knees, got my gun out, and shot O'Leary in the back, just below the right shoulder.

Red swayed, jamming his man into the wall. I beaned mine with the gun-butt.

"Did he get you, Red?" I asked, steadying him with an arm, knocking his prisoner across the noodle.

"Yeah."

"Nancy," I called.

She ran to us.

"Take his other side," I told her. "Keep on your feet, Red, and we'll make the sneak O.K."

The bullet was too freshly in him to slow him up yet, though his right arm was out of commission. We ran down the back street to the corner. We had pursuers before we made it. Curious faces looked at us in the street. A policeman a block away began to move our way. The girl helping O'Leary on one side, me on the other, we ran half a block away from the copper, to where I had left the automobile Jack and I had used. The street was active by the time I got the machinery grinding and the girl had Red stowed safely in the back seat. The copper sent a yell and a high bullet after us. We left the neighborhood.

I didn't have any special destination yet, so, after the necessary first burst of speed, I slowed up a little, went around lots of corners, and brought the bus to rest in a dark street beyond Van Ness Avenue.

Red was drooping in one corner of the back, the girl holding him up, when I screwed around in my seat to look at them.

"Where to?" I asked.

"A hospital, a doctor, something!" the girl cried. "He's dying!"

I didn't believe that. If he was, it was his own fault. If he had had enough gratitude to take me along with him as a friend I wouldn't have had to shoot him so I could go along as nurse.

"Where to, Red?" I asked him, prodding his knee with a finger.

He spoke thickly, giving me the address of the Stockton Street hotel.

"That's no good," I objected. "Everybody in town knows you bunk there, and if you go back, it's lights out for yours. Where to?"

"Hotel," he repeated.

I got up, knelt on the seat, and leaned back to work on him. He was weak. He couldn't have much resistance left.

Bulldozing a man who might after all be dying wasn't gentlemanly, but I had invested a lot of trouble in this egg, trying to get him to lead me to his friends, and I wasn't going to quit in the stretch. For a while it looked as if he wasn't weak enough yet, as if I'd have to shoot him again. But the girl sided with me, and between us we finally convinced him that his only safe bet was to go somewhere where he could hide while he got the right kind of care. We didn't actually convince him—we wore him out and he gave in because he was too weak to argue longer. He gave me an address out by Holly Park.

Hoping for the best, I pointed the machine thither.

XII

The house was a small one in a row of small houses. We took the big boy out of the car and between us to the door. He could just about make it with our help. The street was dark. No light showed from the house. I rang the bell.

Nothing happened. I rang again, and then once more.

"Who is it?" a harsh voice demanded from the inside.

"Red's been hurt," I said.

Silence for a while. Then the door opened half a foot. Through the opening a light came from the interior, enough light to show the flat face and bulging jaw-muscles of the skull-cracker who had been the Motsa Kid's guardian and executioner.

"What the hell?" he asked.

"Red was jumped. They got him," I explained, pushing the limp giant forward.

We didn't crash the gate that way. The skull-cracker held the door as it was.

"You'll wait," he said, and shut the door in our faces. His voice sounded from within, "Flora." That was all right—Red had brought us to the right place.

When he opened the door again he opened it all the way, and Nancy Regan and I took our burden into the hall. Beside the skull-cracker stood a woman in a low-cut black silk gown—Big Flora, I supposed.

She stood at least five feet ten in her high-heeled slippers. They were small slippers, and I noticed that her ringless hands were small. The rest of her wasn't. She was broad-shouldered, deep-bosomed, thick-armed, with a pink throat which, for all its smoothness, was muscled like a wrestler's. She was about my age—close to forty—with very curly and very yellow bobbed hair, very pink skin, and a handsome, brutal face. Her deep-set eyes were gray, her thick lips were well-shaped, her nose was just broad enough and curved enough to give her a look of strength, and she had chin enough to support it. From forehead to throat her pink skin was underlaid with smooth, thick, strong muscles.

This Big Flora was no toy. She had the look and the poise of a woman who could have managed the looting and the double-crossing afterward. Unless her face and body lied, she had all the strength of physique, mind and will that would be needed, and some to spare. She was made of stronger stuff than either the ape-built bruiser at her side or the red-haired giant I was holding.

"Well?" she asked, when the door had been closed behind us. Her voice was deep but not masculine—a voice that went well with her looks.

"Vance ganged him in Larrouy's. He took one in the back," I said.

"Who are you?"

"Get him to bed," I stalled. "We've got all night to talk."

She turned, snapping her fingers. A shabby little old man darted out of a door toward the rear. His brown eyes were very scary.

"Get to hell upstairs," she ordered. "Fix the bed, get hot water and towels."

The little old man scrambled up the stairs like a rheumatic rabbit.

The skull-cracker took the girl's side of Red, and he and I carried the giant up to a room where the little man was scurrying around with basins and cloth. Flora and Nancy Regan followed us. We spread the wounded man face-down on the bed and stripped him. Blood still ran from the bullet-hole. He was unconscious.

Nancy Regan went to pieces.

"He's dying! He's dying! Get a doctor! Oh, Reddy, dearest—"

"Shut up!" said Big Flora. "The damned fool ought to croak—going to Larrouy's tonight!" She caught the little man by the shoulder and threw him at the door. "Zonite and more water," she called after him. "Give me your knife, Pogy."

The ape-built man took from his pocket a spring-knife with a long blade that had been sharpened until it was narrow and thin. This is the knife, I thought, that cut the Motsa Kid's throat.

With it, Big Flora cut the bullet out of Red O'Leary's back.

The ape-built Pogy kept Nancy Regan over in a corner of the room while the operating was done. The little scared man knelt beside the bed, handing the woman what she asked for, mopping up Red's blood as it ran from the wound.

I stood beside Flora, smoking cigarettes from the pack she had given me. When she raised her head, I would transfer the cigarette from my mouth to hers. She would fill her lungs with a draw that ate half the cigarette and nod. I would take the cigarette from her mouth. She would blow out the smoke and bend to her work again. I would light another cigarette from what was left of that one, and be ready for her next smoke.

Her bare arms were blood to the elbows. Her face was damp with sweat. It was a gory mess, and it took time. But when she straightened up for the last smoke, the bullet was out of Red, the bleeding had stopped, and he was bandaged.

"Thank God that's over," I said, lighting one of my own cigarettes. "Those pills you smoke are terrible."

The little scared man was cleaning up. Nancy Regan had fainted in a chair across the room, and nobody was paying any attention to her.

"Keep your eye on this gent, Pogy," Big Flora told the skull-cracker, nodding at me, "while I wash up."

I went over to the girl, rubbed her hands, put some water on her face, and got her awake.

"The bullet's out. Red's sleeping. He'll be picking fights again within a week," I told her.

She jumped up and ran over to the bed.

Flora came in. She had washed and had changed her blood-stained black gown for a green kimono affair, which gaped here and there to show a lot of orchid-colored underthings.

"Talk," she commanded, standing in front of me. "Who, what and why?"

"I'm Percy Maguire," I said, as if this name, which I had just thought up, explained everything.

"That's the who," she said, as if my phoney alias explained nothing. "Now what's the what and why?"

The ape-built Pogy, standing on one side, looked me up and down. I'm short and lumpy. My face doesn't scare children, but it's a more or less truthful witness to a life that hasn't been overburdened with refinement and gentility. The evening's entertainment had decorated me with bruises and scratches, and had done things to what was left of my clothes.

"Percy," he echoed, showing wide-spaced yellow teeth in a grin. "My Gawd, brother, your folks must have been color-blind!"

"That's the what and why," I insisted to the woman, paying no attention to the wheeze from the zoo. "I'm Percy Maguire, and I want my hundred and fifty thousand dollars."

The muscles in her brows came down over her eyes.

"You've got a hundred and fifty thousand dollars, have you?"

I nodded up into her handsome brutal face.

"Yeah," I said. "That's what I came for."

"Oh, you haven't got them? You want them?"

"Listen, sister, I want my dough." I had to get tough if this play was to go over. "This swapping *Oh-have-yous* and *Yes-I-haves* don't get me anything but a thirst. We were in the big knock-over, see? And after that, when we find the pay-off's a bust, I said to the kid I was training with, 'Never mind, Kid, we'll get our whack. Just follow Percy.' And then Bluepoint comes to me and asks me to throw in with him, and I said, 'Sure!' and me and the kid throw in with him until we all come across Red in the dump tonight. Then I told the kid, 'These coffee-and-doughnut guns are going to rub Red out, and that won't get us anything. We'll take him away from 'em and make him steer us to where Big Flora's sitting on the jack. We ought to be good for a hundred and fifty grand apiece, now that there's damned few in on it. After we get that, if we want to bump Red off, all right. But business before pleasure, and a hundred and fifty thou is business.' So we did. We opened an out for the big boy when he didn't have any. The kid got mushy with the broad along the road and got knocked for a loop. That was all-right with me. If she was worth a hundred and fifty grand to him—fair enough. I came on with Red. I pulled the big tramp out after he stopped the slug. By rights I ought to collect the kid's dib, too—making three hundred thou for me—but give me the hundred and fifty I started out for and we'll call it even-steven."

I thought this hocus ought to stick. Of course I wasn't counting on her ever giving me any money, but if the rank and file of the mob hadn't known these people, why should these people know everybody in the mob?

Flora spoke to Pogy:

"Get that damned heap away from the front door."

I felt better when he went out. She wouldn't have sent him out to move the car if she had meant to do anything to me right away.

"Got any food in the joint?" I asked, making myself at home.

She went to the head of the steps and yelled down, "Get something for us to eat."

Red was still unconscious. Nancy Regan sat beside him, holding one of his hands. Her face was drained white. Big Flora came into the room again, looked at the invalid, put a hand on his forehead, felt his pulse.

"Come on downstairs," she said.

"I—I'd rather stay here, if I may," Nancy Regan said. Voice and eyes showed utter terror of Flora.

The big woman, saying nothing, went downstairs. I followed her to the kitchen, where the little man was working on ham and eggs at the range. The window and back door, I saw, were reinforced with heavy planking and braced with timbers nailed to the floor. The clock over the sink said 2.50 a.m.

Flora brought out a quart of liquor and poured drinks for herself and me. We sat at the table and while we waited for our food she cursed Red O'Leary and Nancy Regan, because he had got himself disabled keeping a date with her at a time when Flora needed his strength most. She cursed them individually, as a pair, and was making it a racial matter by cursing all the Irish when the little man gave us our ham and eggs.

We had finished the solids and were stirring hooch in our second cups of coffee when Pogy came back. He had news.

"There's a couple of mugs hanging around the corner that I don't much like."

"Bulls or——?" Flora asked.

"Or," he said.

Flora began to curse Red and Nancy again. But she had pretty well played that line out already. She turned to me.

"What the hell did you bring them here for?" she demanded. "Leaving a mile-wide trail behind you! Why didn't you let the lousy bum die where he got his dose?"

"I brought him here for my hundred and fifty grand. Slip it to me and I'll be on my way. You don't owe me anything else. I don't owe you anything. Give me my rhino instead of lip and I'll pull my freight."

"Like hell you will," said Pogy.

The woman looked at me under lowered brows and drank her coffee.

XIII

Fifteen minutes later the shabby little old man came running into the kitchen, saying he had heard feet on the roof. His faded brown eyes were dull as an ox's with fright, and his withered lips writhed under his straggly yellow-white mustache.

Flora profanely called him a this-and-that kind of old one-thing-and-another and chased him upstairs again. She got up from the table and pulled the green kimono tight around her big body.

"You're here," she told me, "and you'll put in with us. There's no other way. Got a rod?"

I admitted I had a gun but shook my head at the rest of it.

"This is not my wake—yet," I said. "It'll take one hundred and fifty thousand berries, spot cash, paid in the hand, to buy Percy in on it."

I wanted to know if the loot was on the premises.

Nancy Regan's tearful voice came from the stairs:

"No, no, darling! Please, please, go back to bed! You'll kill yourself, Reddy, dear!"

Red O'Leary strode into the kitchen. He was naked except for a pair of gray pants and his bandage. His eyes were feverish and happy. His dry lips were stretched in a grin. He had a gun in his left hand. His right arm hung useless. Behind him trotted Nancy. She stopped pleading and shrank behind him when she saw Big Flora.

"Ring the gong, and let's go," the half-naked red-head laughed. "Vance is in our street."

Flora went over to him, put her fingers on his wrist, held them there a couple of seconds, and nodded:

"You crazy son-of-a-gun," she said in a tone that was more like maternal pride than anything else. "You're good for a fight right now. And a damned good thing, too, because you're going to get it."

Red laughed—a triumphant laugh that boasted of his toughness—then his eyes turned to me. Laughter went out of them and a puzzled look drew them narrow.

"Hello," he said. "I dreamed about you, but I can't remember what it was. It was— Wait. I'll get it in a minute. It was— By God! I dreamed it was you that plugged me!"

Flora smiled at me, the first time I had seen her smile, and she spoke quickly:

"Take him, Pogy!"

I twisted obliquely out of my chair.

Pogy's fist took me in the temple. Staggering across the room, struggling to keep my feet, I thought of the bruise on the dead Motsa Kid's temple.

Pogy was on me when the wall bumped me upright.

I put a fist—spat!—in his flat nose. Blood squirted, but his hairy paws gripped me. I tucked my chin in, ground the top of my head into his face. The scent Big Flora used came strong to me. Her silk clothes brushed against me. With both hands full of my hair she pulled my head back, stretching my neck for Pogy. He took hold of it with his paws. I quit. He didn't throttle me any more than was necessary, but it was bad enough.

Flora frisked me for gun and blackjack.

".38 special," she named the caliber of the gun. "I dug a .38

special bullet out of you, Red." The words came faintly to me through the roaring in my ears.

The little old man's voice was chattering in the kitchen. I couldn't make out anything he said. Pogy's hands went away from me. I put my own hands to my throat. It was hell not to have any pressure at all there. The blackness went slowly away from my eyes, leaving a lot of little purple clouds that floated around and around. Presently I could sit up on the floor. I knew by that I had been lying down on it.

The purple clouds shrank until I could see past them enough to know there were only three of us in the room now. Cringing in a chair, back in a corner, was Nancy Regan. On another chair, beside the door, a black pistol in his hand, sat the scared little old man. His eyes were desperately frightened. Gun and hand shook at me. I tried to ask him to either stop shaking or move his gun away from me, but I couldn't get any words out yet.

Upstairs, guns boomed, their reports exaggerated by the smallness of the house.

The little man winced.

"Let me get out," he whispered with unexpected abruptness, "and I will give you everything. I will! Everything—if you will let me get out of this house!"

This feeble ray of light where there hadn't been a dot gave me back the use of my vocal apparatus.

"Talk turkey," I managed to say.

"I will give you those upstairs—that she-devil. I will give you the money. I will give you all—if you will let me go out. I am old. I am sick. I cannot live in prison. What have I to do with robberies? Nothing. Is it my fault that she-devil—? You have seen it here. I am a slave—I who am near the end of my life. Abuse, cursings, beatings—and those are not enough. Now I must go to prison because that she-devil is a she-devil. I am an old man who cannot live in prisons. You let me go out. You do me that kindness. I will give you that she-devil—those other devils—the money they stole. That I will do!"

Thus this panic-stricken little old man, squirming and fidgeting on his chair.

"How can I get you out?" I asked, getting up from the floor, my eye on his gun. If I could get to him while we talked. . . .

"How not? You are a friend of the police—that I know. The police are here now—waiting for daylight before they come into this house. I myself with my old eyes saw them take that Bluepoint Vance. You can take me out past your friends, the police. You do what I ask, and I will give you those devils and their moneys."

"Sounds good" I said, taking a careless step toward him. "But can I just stroll out of here when I want to?"

"No! No!" he said, paying no attention to the second step I took toward him. "But first I will give you those three devils. I will give them to you alive but without power. And their money. That I will do, and then you will take me out—and this girl here." He nodded suddenly at Nancy, whose white face, still nice in spite of its terror, was mostly wide eyes just now. "She, too, has nothing to do with those devils' crimes. She must go with me."

I wondered what this old rabbit thought he could do. I frowned exceedingly thoughtful while I took still another step toward him.

"Make no mistake," he whispered earnestly. "When that she-devil comes back into this room you will die—she will kill you certainly."

Three more steps and I would be close enough to take hold of him and his gun.

Footsteps were in the hall. Too late for a jump.

"Yes?" he hissed desperately.

I nodded a split-second before Big Flora came through the door.

XIV

She was dressed for action in a pair of blue pants that were probably Pogy's, beaded moccasins, a silk waist. A ribbon held her curly yellow hair back from her face. She had a gun in one hand, one in each hip pocket.

The one in her hand swung up.

"You're done," she told me, quite matter-of-fact.

My newly acquired confederate whined, "Wait, wait, Flora! Not here like this, please! Let me take him into the cellar."

She scowled at him, shrugging her silken shoulders.

"Make it quick," she said. "It'll be light in another half-hour."

I felt too much like crying to laugh at them. Was I supposed to think this woman would let the rabbit change her plans? I suppose I must have put some value on the old gink's help, or I wouldn't have been so disappointed when this little comedy told me it was a frame-up. But any hole they worked me into couldn't be any worse than the one I was in.

So I went ahead of the old man into the hall, opened the door he indicated, switched on the basement light, and went down the rough steps.

Close behind me he was whispering, "I'll first show you the moneys, and then I will give to you those devils. And you will not forget your promise? I and that girl shall go out through the police?"

"Oh, yes," I assured the old joker.

He came up beside me, sticking a gun-butt in my hand.

"Hide it," he hissed, and, when I had pocketed that one, gave me another, producing them with his free hand from under his coat.

Then he actually showed me the loot. It was still in the boxes and bags in which it had been carried from the banks. He insisted on opening some of them to show me the money—green bundles belted with the bank's yellow wrappers. The boxes and bags were stacked in a small brick cell that was fitted with a padlocked door, to which he had the key.

He closed the door when we were through looking, but he did not lock it, and he led me back part of the way we had come.

"That, as you see, is the money," he said. "Now for those. You will stand here, hiding behind these boxes."

A partition divided the cellar in half. It was pierced by a doorway that had no door. The place the old man told me to hide was close beside this doorway, between the partition and four packing-cases. Hiding there, I would be to the right of, and a little behind, anyone who came downstairs and walked through the cellar toward the cell that held the money. That is, I would be in that position when they went to go through the doorway in the partition.

The old man was fumbling beneath one of the boxes. He brought out an eighteen-inch length of lead pipe stuffed in a similar length of black garden hose. He gave this to me as he explained everything.

"They will come down here one at a time. When they are about to go through this door, you will know what to do with this. And then you will have them, and I will have your promise. Is it not so?"

"Oh, yes," I said, all up in the air.

He went upstairs. I crouched behind the boxes, examining the guns he had given me—and I'm damned if I could find anything wrong with them. They were loaded and they seemed to be in working order. That finishing touch completely balled me up. I didn't know whether I was in a cellar or a balloon.

When Red O'Leary, still naked except for pants and bandage, came into the cellar, I had to shake my head violently to clear it in time to bat him across the back of the noodle as his first bare foot stepped through the doorway. He sprawled down on his face.

The old man scurried down the steps, full of grins.

"Hurry! Hurry!" he panted, helping me drag the redhead back into the money cell. Then he produced two pieces of cord and tied the giant hand and foot.

"Hurry!" he panted again as he left me to run upstairs, while I went back to my hiding-place and hefted the lead-pipe, wondering if Flora had shot me and I was now enjoying the rewards of my virtue—in a heaven where I could enjoy myself forever and ever socking folks who had been rough with me down below.

The ape-built skull-cracker came down, reached the door. I cracked his skull. The little man came scurrying. We dragged Pogy to the cell, tied him up.

"Hurry!" panted the old gink, dancing up and down in his excitement. "That she-devil next—and strike hard!"

He scrambled upstairs and I could hear his feet pattering overhead.

I got rid of some of my bewilderment, making room for a little intelligence in my skull. This foolishness we were up to wasn't so. It couldn't be happening. Nothing ever worked out just that way. You didn't stand in corners and knock down people one after the other like a machine, while a scrawny little bozo up at the other end fed them to you. It was too damned silly! I had enough!

I passed up my hiding place, put down the pipe and found another spot to crouch in, under some shelves, near the steps. I hunkered down there with a gun in each fist. This game I was playing in was—it had to be—gummy around the edges. I wasn't going to stay put any longer.

Flora came down the steps. Two steps behind her the little man trotted.

Flora had a gun in each hand. Her gray eyes were everywhere. Her head was down like an animal's coming to a fight. Her nostrils quivered. Her body, coming down neither slowly nor swiftly, was balanced like a dancer's. If I live to a million I'll never forget the picture this handsome brutal woman made coming down those unplaned cellar stairs. She was a beautiful fight-bred animal going to a fight.

She saw me as I straightened.

"Drop 'em!" I said, but I knew she wouldn't.

The little man flicked a limp brown blackjack out of his sleeve and knocked her behind the ear just as she swung her left gun on me.

I jumped over and caught her before she hit the cement.

"Now, you see!" the old man said gleefully. "You have the money and you have them. And now you will get me and that girl out."

"First we'll stow this with the others," I said.

After he had helped me do that I told him to lock the cell door. He did, and I took the key with one hand, his neck with the other. He squirmed like a snake while I ran my other hand over his clothes, removing the blackjack and a gun, and finding a money-belt around his waist.

"Take it off," I ordered. "You don't carry anything out with you."

His fingers worked with the buckle, dragged the belt from under his clothes, let it fall on the floor. It was padded fat.

Still holding his neck, I took him upstairs, where the girl still sat frozen on the kitchen chair. It took a stiff hooker of whisky and a lot of words to thaw her into understanding that she was going out with the old man and that she wasn't to say a word to anybody, especially not to the police.

"Where's Reddy?" she asked when color had come back into her face—which had even at the worst never lost its niceness—and thoughts to her head.

I told her he was all right, and promised her he would be in a hospital before the morning was over. She didn't ask anything else. I shooed her upstairs for her hat and coat, went with the old man while he got his hat, and then put the pair of them in the front ground-floor room.

"Stay here till I come for you," I said, and I locked the door and pocketed the key when I went out.

XV

The front door and the front window on the ground floor had been planked and braced like the rear ones. I didn't like to risk opening them, even though it was fairly light by now. So I went upstairs, fashioned a flag of truce out of a pillow-slip and a bed-slat, hung it out a window, waited until a heavy voice said, "All right, speak your piece," and then I showed myself and told the police I'd let them in.

It took five minutes' work with a hatchet to pry the front door loose. The chief of police, the captain of detectives, and half the force were waiting on the front steps and pavement when I got the door open. I took them to the cellar and turned Big Flora, Pogy and Red O'Leary over to them, with the money. Flora and Pogy were awake, but not talking.

While the dignitaries were crowded around the spoils I went upstairs. The house was full of police sleuths. I swapped greetings with them as I went through to the room where I had left Nancy Regan and the old gink. Lieutenant Duff was trying the locked door, while O'Gar and Hunt stood behind him.

I grinned at Duff and gave him the key.

He opened the door, looked at the old man and the girl—mostly at her—and then at me. They were standing in the center of the room. The old man's faded eyes were miserably worried, the girl's blue ones darkly anxious. Anxiety didn't ruin her looks a bit.

"If that's yours I don't blame you for locking it up," O'Gar muttered in my ear.

"You can run along now," I told the two in the room. "Get all the sleep you need before you report for duty again."

They nodded and went out of the house.

"That's how your Agency evens up?" Duff said. "The she-employees make up in looks for the ugliness of the he's."

Dick Foley came into the hall.

"How's your end?" I asked.

"Finis. The Angel led me to Vance. He led here. I led the bulls here. They got him—got her."

Two shots crashed in the street.

We went to the door and saw excitement in a police car down the street. We went down there. Bluepoint Vance, handcuffs on his wrists, was writhing half on the seat, half on the floor.

"We were holding him here in the car, Houston and me," a hard-mouthed plain-clothes man explained to Duff. "He made a break, grabbed Houston's gat with both hands. I had to drill him—twice. The cap'll raise hell! He specially wanted him kept here to put up against the others. But God knows I wouldn't of shot him if it hadn't been him or Houston!"

Duff called the plain-clothesman a damned clumsy mick as they lifted Vance up on the seat. Bluepoint's tortured eyes focused on me.

"I—know—you?" he asked painfully. "Continental—New —York?"

"Yes," I said.

"Couldn't—place—you—Larrouy's—with—Red."

He stopped to cough blood.

"Got—Red?"

"Yeah," I told him. "Got Red, Flora, Pogy and the cush."

"But—not—Papa—dop—oul—os."

"Papa does what?" I asked impatiently, a shiver along my spine.

He pulled himself up on the seat.

"Papadopoulos," he repeated, with an agonizing summoning of the little strength left in him. "I tried—shoot him—saw him—walk 'way—with girl—bull—too damn quick—wish . . ."

His words ran out. He shuddered. Death wasn't a sixteenth of an inch behind his eyes. A white-coated intern tried to get past me into the car. I pushed him out of the way and leaned in, taking Vance by the shoulders. The back of my neck was ice. My stomach was empty.

"Listen, Bluepoint," I yelled in his face. "Papadopoulos? Little old man? Brains of the push?"

"Yes," Vance said, and the last live blood in him came out with the word.

I let him drop back on the seat and walked away.

Of course! How had I missed it? The little old scoundrel—if he hadn't, for all his scariness, been the works, how could he have so neatly turned the others over to me one at a time? They had been absolutely cornered. It was be killed fighting, or surrender and be hanged. They had no other way out. The police had Vance, who could and would tell them that the little buzzard was the headman—there wasn't even a chance for him beating the courts with his age, his weakness and his mask of being driven around by the others.

And there I had been—with no choice but to accept his offer. Otherwise lights out for me. I had been putty in his hands, his accomplices had been putty. He had slipped the cross over on them as they had helped him slip it over on the others—and I had sent him safely away.

Now I could turn the city upside down for him—my promise had been only to get him out of the house—but . . .

What a life!

$106,000 Blood Money

I'M Tom-Tom Carey," he said, drawling the words.

I nodded at the chair beside my desk and weighed him in while he moved to it. Tall, wide-shouldered, thick-chested, thin-bellied, he would add up to say a hundred and ninety pounds. His swarthy face was hard as a fist, but there was nothing ill-humored in it. It was the face of a man of forty-something who lived life raw and thrived on it. His blue clothes were good and he wore them well.

In the chair, he twisted brown paper around a charge of Bull Durham and finished introducing himself:

"I'm Paddy the Mex's brother."

I thought maybe he was telling the truth. Paddy had been like this fellow in coloring and manner.

"That would make your real name Carrera," I suggested.

"Yes," he was lighting his cigarette. "Alfredo Estanislao Cristobal Carrera, if you want all the details."

I asked him how to spell Estanislao, wrote the name down on a slip of paper, adding *alias Tom-Tom Carey*, rang for Tommy Howd, and told him to have the file clerk see if we had anything on it.

"While your people are opening graves I'll tell you why I'm here," the swarthy man drawled through smoke when Tommy had gone away with the paper.

"Tough—Paddy being knocked off like that," I said.

"He was too damned trusting to live long," his brother explained. "This is the kind of hombre he was—the last time I saw him was four years ago, here in San Francisco. I'd come in from an expedition down to—never mind where. Anyway I was flat. Instead of pearls all I'd got out of the trip was a bullet-crease over my hip. Paddy was dirty with fifteen thousand or so he'd just nicked somebody for. The afternoon I saw him he had a date that he was leery of toting so much money to. So he gives me the fifteen thousand to hold for him till that night."

Tom-Tom Carey blew out smoke and smiled softly past me at a memory.

"That's the kind of hombre he was," he went on. "He'd trust even his own brother. I went to Sacramento that afternoon and caught a train East. A girl in Pittsburgh helped me spend the fifteen thousand. Her name was Laurel. She liked rye whisky with milk for a chaser. I used to drink it with her till I was all curdled inside, and I've never had any appetite for *schmierkäse* since. So there's a hundred thousand dollars reward on this Papadopoulos, is there?"

"And six. The insurance companies put up a hundred thousand, the bankers' association five, and the city a thousand."

Tom-Tom Carey chucked the remains of his cigarette in the cuspidor and began to assemble another one.

"Suppose I hand him to you?" he asked. "How many ways will the money have to go?"

"None of it will stop here," I assured him. "The Continental Detective Agency doesn't touch reward money—and won't let its hired men. If any of the police are in on the pinch they'll want a share."

"But if they aren't, it's all mine?"

"If you turn him in without help, or without any help except ours."

"I'll do that." The words were casual. "So much for the arrest. Now for the conviction part. If you get him, are you sure you can nail him to the cross?"

"I ought to be, but he'll have to go up against a jury—and that means anything can happen."

The muscular brown hand holding the brown cigarette made a careless gesture.

"Then maybe I'd better get a confession out of him before I drag him in," he said off-hand.

"It would be safer that way," I agreed. "You ought to let that holster down an inch or two. It brings the gun-butt too high. The bulge shows when you sit down."

"Uh-huh. You mean the one on the left shoulder. I took it away from a fellow after I lost mine. Strap's too short. I'll get another one this afternoon."

Tommy came in with a folder labeled, *Carey, Tom-Tom, 1361-C*. It held some newspaper clippings, the oldest dated ten years back, the youngest eight months. I read them through, passing each one to the swarthy man as I finished it. Tom-

Tom Carey was written down in them as soldier of fortune, gun-runner, seal poacher, smuggler and pirate. But it was all alleged, supposed and suspected. He had been captured variously but never convicted of anything.

"They don't treat me right," he complained placidly when we were through reading. "For instance, stealing that Chinese gunboat wasn't my fault. I was forced to do it—I was the one that was double-crossed. After they'd got the stuff aboard they wouldn't pay for it. I couldn't unload it. I couldn't do anything but take gunboat and all. The insurance companies must want this Papadopoulos plenty to hang a hundred thousand on him."

"Cheap enough if it lands him," I said. "Maybe he's not all the newspapers picture him as, but he's more than a handful. He gathered a whole damned army of strong-arm men here, took over a block in the center of the financial district, looted the two biggest banks in the city, fought off the whole police department, made his getaway, ditched the army, used some of his lieutenants to bump off some more of them,—that's where your brother Paddy got his,—then, with the help of Pogy Reeve, Big Flora Brace and Red O'Leary, wiped out the rest of his lieutenants. And remember, these lieutenants weren't schoolboys—they were slick grifters like Bluepoint Vance and the Shivering Kid and Darby M'Laughlin—birds who knew their what's what."

"Uh-huh." Carey was unimpressed. "But it was a bust just the same. You got all the loot back, and he just managed to get away himself."

"A bad break for him," I explained. "Red O'Leary broke out with a complication of love and vanity. You can't chalk that against Papadopoulos. Don't get the idea he's half-smart. He's dangerous, and I don't blame the insurance companies for thinking they'll sleep better if they're sure he's not out where he can frame some more tricks against their policy-holding banks."

"Don't know much about this Papadopoulos, do you?"

"No." I told the truth. "And nobody does. The hundred thousand offer made rats out of half the crooks in the country. They're as hot after him as we—not only bcause of the reward but because of his wholesale double-crossing. And they know just as little about him as we do—that he's had his fingers in a dozen or more jobs, that he was the brains behind Bluepoint Vance's bond tricks, and that his enemies have a habit of dying young. But nobody knows where he came from, or where he lives when he's home. Don't think I'm touting him as a Napoleon or a Sunday-supplement master mind—but he's a shifty, tricky old boy. As you say, I don't know much about him—but there are lots of people I don't know much about."

Tom-Tom Carey nodded to show he understood the last part and began making his third cigarette.

"I was in Nogales when Angel Grace Cardigan got word to me that Paddy had been done in," he said. "That was nearly a month ago. She seemed to think I'd romp up here pronto—but it was no skin off my face. I let it sleep. But last week I read in a newspaper about all this reward money being posted on the hombre she blamed for Paddy's rub-out. That made it different—a hundred thousand dollars different. So I shipped up here, talked to her, and then came in to make sure there'll be nothing between me and the blood money when I put the loop on this Papadoodle."

"Angel Grace sent you to me?" I inquired.

"Uh-huh—only she don't know it. She dragged you into the story—said you were a friend of Paddy's, a good guy for a sleuth, and hungry as hell for this Papadoodle. So I thought you'd be the gent for me to see."

"When did you leave Nogales?"

"Tuesday—last week."

"That," I said, prodding my memory, "was the day after Newhall was killed across the border."

The swarthy man nodded. Nothing changed in his face.

"How far from Nogales was that?" I asked.

"He was gunned down near Oquitoa—that's somewhere around sixty miles southwest of Nogales. You interested?"

"No—except I was wondering about your leaving the place where he was killed the day after he was killed, and coming up where he had lived. Did you know him?"

"He was pointed out to me in Nogales as a San Francisco millionaire going with a party to look at some mining property in Mexico. I was figuring on maybe selling him something later, but the Mexican patriots got him before I did."

"And so you came north?"

"Uh-huh. The hubbub kind of spoiled things for me. I had a nice little business in—call it supplies—to and fro across the line. This Newhall killing turned the spotlight on that part of the country. So I thought I'd come up and collect that hundred thousand and give things a chance to settle down there. Honest, brother, I haven't killed a millionaire in weeks, if that's what's worrying you."

"That's good. Now, as I get it, you're counting on landing Papadopoulos. Angel Grace sent for you, thinking you'd run him down just to even up for Paddy's killing, but it's the money you want, so you figure on playing with me as well as the Angel. That right?"

"Check."

"You know what'll happen if she learns you're stringing along with me?"

"Uh-huh. She'll chuck a convulsion—kind of balmy on the subject of keeping clear of the police, isn't she?"

"She is—somebody told her something about honor among thieves once and she's never got over it. Her brother's doing a hitch up north now—Johnny the Plumber sold him out. Her man Paddy was mowed down by his pals. Did either of those things wake her up? Not a chance. She'd rather have Papadopoulos go free than join forces with us."

"That's all right," Tom-Tom Carey assured me. "She thinks I'm the loyal brother—Paddy couldn't have told her much about me—and I'll handle her. You having her shadowed?"

I said: "Yes—ever since she was turned loose. She was picked up the same day Flora and Pogy and Red were grabbed, but we hadn't anything on her except that she had been Paddy's lady-love, so I had her sprung. How much dope did you get out of her?"

"Descriptions of Papadoodle and Nancy Regan, and that's all. She don't know any more about them than I do. Where does this Regan girl fit in?"

"Hardly any, except that she might lead us to Papadopoulos. She was Red's girl. It was keeping a date with her that he upset the game. When Papadopoulos wriggled out he took the girl with him. I don't know why. She wasn't in on the stick-ups."

Tom-Tom Carey finished making and lighting his fifth cigarette and stood up.

"Are we teamed?" he asked as he picked up his hat.

"If you turn in Papadopoulos I'll see that you get every nickel you're entitled to," I replied. "And I'll give you a clear field—I won't handicap you with too much of an attempt to keep my eyes on your actions."

He said that was fair enough, told me he was stopping at a hotel in Ellis Street, and went away.

II

Calling the late Taylor Newhall's office on the phone, I was told that if I wanted any information about his affairs I should try his country residence, some miles south of San Francisco. I tried it. A ministerial voice that said it belonged to the butler told me that Newhall's attorney, Franklin Ellert, was the person I should see. I went over to Ellert's office.

He was a nervous, irritable old man with a lisp and eyes that stuck out with blood pressure.

"Is there any reason," I asked point-blank, "for supposing that Newhall's murder was anything more than a Mexican bandit outburst? Is it likely that he was killed purposely, and not resisting capture?"

Lawyers don't like to be questioned. This one sputtered and made faces at me and let his eyes stick out still further and, of course, didn't give me an answer.

"How? How?" he snapped disagreeably. "Exthplain your meaning, thir!"

He glared at me and then at the desk, pushing papers around with excited hands, as if he were hunting for a police whistle. I told my story—told him about Tom-Tom Carey.

Ellert sputtered some more, demanded, "What the devil do you mean?" and made a complete jumble of the papers on his desk.

"I don't mean anything," I growled back. "I'm just telling you what was said."

"Yeth! Yeth! I know!" He stopped glaring at me and his voice was less peevish. "But there ith abtholutely no reathon for thuthpecting anything of the thort. None at all, thir, none at all!"

"Maybe you're right." I turned to the door. "But I'll poke into it a little anyway."

"Wait! Wait!" He scrambled out of his chair and ran around the desk to me. "I think you are mithtaken, but if you are going to invethtigate it I would like to know what you dithcover. Perhapth you'd better charge me with your regular fee for whatever ith done, and keep me informed of your progreth. Thatithfactory?"

I said it was, came back to his desk and began to question him. There was, as the lawyer had said, nothing in Newhall's affairs to stir us up. The dead man was several times a million-aire, with most of his money in mines. He had inherited nearly half his money. There was no shady practice, no claim-jumping, no trickery in his past, no enemies. He was a widower with one daughter. She had everything she wanted while he lived, and she and her father had been very fond of one another. He had gone to Mexico with a party of mining men from New York who expected to sell him some property there. They had been attacked by bandits, had driven them off, but Newhall and a geologist named Parker had been killed during the fight.

Back in the office, I wrote a telegram to our Los Angeles branch, asking that an operative be sent to Nogales to pry into Newhall's killing and Tom-Tom Carey's affairs. The clerk to whom I gave it to be coded and sent told me the Old Man wanted to see me. I went into his office and was introduced to a short, rolly-polly man named Hook.

"Mr. Hook," the Old Man said, "is the proprietor of a restaurant in Sausalito. Last Monday he employed a waitress named Nelly Riley. She told him she had come from Los Angeles. Her description, as Mr. Hook gives it, is quite simi-lar to the description you and Counihan have given of Nancy Regan. Isn't it?" he asked the fat man.

"Absolutely. It's exactly what I read in the papers. She's five feet five inches tall, about, and medium in size, and she's got blue eyes and brown hair, and she's around twenty-one or two, and she's got looks, and the thing that counts most is she's high-hat as the devil—she don't think nothin's good enough for her. Why, when I tried to be a little sociable she told me to keep my 'dirty paws' to myself. And then I found out she didn't know hardly nothing about Los Angeles, though she claimed to have lived there two or three years. I bet you she's the girl, all right," and he went on talking about how much reward money he ought to get.

"Are you going back there now?" I asked him.

"Pretty soon. I got to stop and see about some dishes. Then I'm going back."

"This girl will be working?"

"Yes."

"Then we'll send a man over with you—one who knows Nancy Regan."

I called Jack Counihan in from the operatives' room and introduced him to Hook. They arranged to meet in half an hour at the ferry and Hook waddled out.

"This Nelly Riley won't be Nancy Regan," I said. "But we can't afford to pass up even a hundred to one chance."

I told Jack and the Old Man about Tom-Tom Carey and my visit to Ellert's office. The Old Man listened with his usual polite attentiveness. Young Counihan—only four months in the man-hunting business—listened with wide eyes.

"You'd better run along now and meet Hook," I said when I had finished, leaving the Old Man's office with Jack. "And if she should be Nancy Regan—grab her and hang on." We were out of the Old Man's hearing, so I added, "And for God's sake don't let your youthful gallantry lead you to a poke in the jaw this time. Pretend you're grown up."

The boy blushed, said, "Go to hell!" adjusted his necktie, and set off to meet Hook.

I had some reports to write. After I had finished them I put my feet on my desk, made cavities in a package of Fatimas, and thought about Tom-Tom Carey until six o'clock. Then I went down to the States for my abalone chowder and minute steak and home to change clothes before going out Sea Cliff way to sit in a poker game.

The telephone interrupted my dressing. Jack Counihan was on the other end.

"I'm in Sausalito. The girl wasn't Nancy, but I've got hold of something else. I'm not sure how to handle it. Can you come over?"

"Is it important enough to cut a poker game for?"

"Yes, it's—I think it's big." He was excited. "I wish you would come over. I really think it's a lead."

"Where are you?"

"At the ferry there. Not the Golden Gate, the other."

"All right. I'll catch the first boat."

III

An hour later I walked off the boat in Sausalito. Jack Counihan pushed through the crowd and began talking:

"Coming down here on my way back——"

"Hold it till we get out of the mob," I advised him. "It must be tremendous—the eastern point of your collar is bent."

He mechanically repaired this defect in his otherwise immaculate costuming while we walked to the street, but he was too intent on whatever was on his mind to smile.

"Up this way," he said, guiding me around a corner. "Hook's lunch-room is on the corner. You can take a look at the girl if you like. She's of the same size and complexion as Nancy Regan, but that is all. She's a tough little job who probably was fired for dropping her chewing gum in the soup the last place she worked."

"All right. That let's her out. Now what's on your mind?"

"After I saw her I started back to the ferry. A boat came in while I was still a couple of blocks away. Two men who must have come in on it came up the street. They were Greeks, rather young, tough, though ordinarily I shouldn't have paid much attention to them. But, since Papadopoulos is a Greek, we have been interested in them, of course, so I looked at these chaps. They were arguing about something as they walked, not talking loud, but scowling at one another. As they passed me the chap on the gutter side said to the other, 'I tell him it's been twenty-nine days.'

"Twenty-nine days. I counted back and it's just twenty-nine days since we started hunting for Papadopoulos. He is a Greek and these chaps were Greeks. When I had finished counting I turned around and began to follow them. They took me all the way through the town and up a hill on the fringe. They went to a little cottage—it couldn't have more than three rooms—set back in a clearing in the woods by itself. There was a 'For Sale' sign on it, and no curtains in the windows, no sign of occupancy—but on the ground behind the back door there was a wet place, as if a bucket or pan of water had been thrown out.

"I stayed in the bushes until it got a little darker. Then I went closer. I could hear people inside, but I couldn't see anything through the windows. They're boarded up. After a while the two chaps I had followed came out, saying something in a language I couldn't understand to whoever was in the cottage. The cottage door stayed open until the two men had gone out of sight down the path—so I couldn't have followed them without being seen by whoever was at the door.

"Then the door was closed and I could hear people moving around inside—or perhaps only one person—and could smell cooking, and some smoke came out of the chimney. I waited and waited and nothing more happened and I thought I had better get in touch with you."

"Sounds interesting," I agreed.

We were passing under a street light. Jack stopped me with a hand on my arm and fished something out of his overcoat pocket.

"Look!" He held it out to me. A charred piece of blue cloth. It could have been the remains of a woman's hat that had been three-quarters burned. I looked at it under the street light and then used my flashlight to examine it more closely.

"I picked it up behind the cottage while I was nosing around," Jack said, "and—"

"And Nancy Regan wore a hat of that shade the night she and Papadopoulos vanished," I finished for him. "On to the cottage."

We left the street lights behind, climbed the hill, dipped down into a little valley, turned into a winding sandy path, left that to cut across sod between trees to a dirt road, trod half a mile of that, and then Jack led the way along a narrow path that wound through a black tangle of bushes and small trees. I hoped he knew where he was going.

"Almost there," he whispered to me.

A man jumped out of the bushes and took me by the neck.

My hands were in my overcoat pockets—one holding the flashlight, the other my gun.

I pushed the muzzle of the pocketed gun toward the man—pulled the trigger.

The shot ruined seventy-five dollars' worth of overcoat for me. But it took the man away from my neck.

That was lucky. Another man was on my back.

I tried to twist away from him—didn't altogether make it—felt the edge of a knife along my spine.

That wasn't so lucky—but it was better than getting the point.

I butted back at his face—missed—kept twisting and squirming while I brought my hands out of my pockets and clawed at him.

The blade of his knife came flat against my cheek. I caught the hand that held it and let myself go—down backward—him under.

He said: "Uh!"

I rolled over, got hands and knees on the ground, was grazed by a fist, scrambled up.

Fingers dragged at my ankle.

My behavior was ungentlemanly. I kicked the fingers away—found the man's body—kicked it twice—hard.

Jack's voice whispered my name. I couldn't see him in the blackness, nor could I see the man I had shot.

"All right here," I told Jack. "How did you come out?"

"Top-hole. Is that all of it?"

"Don't know, but I'm going to risk a peek at what I've got."

Tilting my flashlight down at the man under my foot, I snapped it on. A thin blond man, his face blood-smeared, his pink-rimmed eyes jerking as he tried to play 'possum in the glare.

"Come out of it!" I ordered.

A heavy gun went off back in the bush—another, lighter one. The bullets ripped through the foliage.

I switched off the light, bent to the man on the ground, knocked him on the top of the head with my gun.

"Crouch down low," I whispered to Jack.

The smaller gun snapped again, twice. It was ahead, to the left.

I put my mouth to Jack's ear.

"We're going to that damned cottage whether anybody likes it or no. Keep low and don't do any shooting unless you can see what you're shooting at. Go ahead."

Bending as close to the ground as I could, I followed Jack up the path. The position stretched the slash in my back—a scalding pain from between my shoulders almost to my waist. I could feel blood trickling down over my hips—or thought I could.

The going was too dark for stealthiness. Things crackled under our feet, rustled against our shoulders. Our friends in the bush used their guns. Luckily, the sound of twigs breaking and leaves rustling in pitch blackness isn't the best of targets. Bullets zipped here and there, but we didn't stop any of them. Neither did we shoot back.

We halted where the end of the bush left the night a weaker gray.

"That's it," Jack said about a square shape ahead.

"On the jump," I grunted and lit out for the dark cottage.

Jack's long slim legs kept him easily at my side as we raced across the clearing.

A man-shape oozed from behind the blot of the building and his gun began to blink at us. The shots came so close together that they sounded like one long stuttering bang.

Pulling the youngster with me, I flopped, flat to the ground except where a ragged-edged empty tin-can held my face up.

From the other side of the building another gun coughed. From a tree-stem to the right, a third.

Jack and I began to burn powder back at them.

A bullet kicked my mouth full of dirt and pebbles. I spit mud and cautioned Jack:

"You're shooting too high. Hold it low and pull easy."

A hump showed in the house's dark profile. I sent a bullet at it.

A man's voice yelled: "Ow—ooh!" and then, lower but very bitter, "Oh, damn you—damn you!"

For a warm couple of seconds bullets spattered all around

us. Then there was not a sound to spoil the night's quietness.

When the silence had lasted five minutes, I got myself up on hands and knees and began to move forward, Jack following. The ground wasn't made for that sort of work. Ten feet of it was enough. We stood up and walked the rest of the way to the building.

"Wait," I whispered, and leaving Jack at one corner of the building, I circled it, seeing nobody, hearing nothing but the sounds I made.

We tried the front door. It was locked but rickety.

Bumping it open with my shoulder, I went indoors—flashlight and gun in my fists.

The shack was empty.

Nobody—no furnishings—no traces of either in the two bare rooms—nothing but bare wooden walls, bare floor, bare ceiling, with a stove-pipe connected to nothing sticking through it.

Jack and I stood in the middle of the floor, looked at the emptiness, and cursed the dump from back door to front for being empty. We hadn't quite finished when feet sounded outside, a white light beamed on the open doorway, and a cracked voice said:

"Hey! You can come out one at a time—kind of easy like!"

"Who says so?" I asked, snapping off the flashlight, moving over close to a side wall.

"A whole goldurned flock of deputy sheriffs," the voice answered.

"Couldn't you push one of 'em in and let us get a look at him?" I asked. "I've been choked and carved and shot at tonight until I haven't got much faith left in anybody's word."

A lanky, knock-kneed man with a thin leathery face appeared in the doorway. He showed me a buzzer, I fished out my credentials, and the other deputies came in. There were three of them in all.

"We were driving down the road bound for a little job near the point when we heard the shooting," the lanky one explained. "What's up?"

I told him.

"This shack's been empty a long while," he said when I had

finished. "Anybody could have camped in it easy enough. Think it was that Papadopoulos, huh? We'll kind of look around for him and his friends—especial since there's that nice reward money."

We searched the woods and found nobody. The man I had knocked down and the man I had shot were both gone.

Jack and I rode back to Sausalito with the deputies. I hunted up a doctor there and had my back bandaged. He said the cut was long but shallow. Then we returned to San Francisco and separated in the direction of our homes.

And thus ended the day's doings.

IV

Here is something that happened next morning. I didn't see it. I heard about it a little before noon and read about it in the papers that afternoon. I didn't know then that I had any personal interest in it, but later I did—so I'll put it in here where it happened.

At ten o'clock that morning, into busy Market Street, staggered a man who was naked from the top of his battered head to the soles of his blood-stained feet. From his bare chest and sides and back, little ribbons of flesh hung down, dripping blood. His left arm was broken in two places. The left side of his bald head was smashed in. An hour later he died in the emergency hospital—without having said a word to anyone, with the same vacant, distant look in his eyes.

The police easily ran back the trail of blood drops. They ended with a red smear in an alley beside a small hotel just off Market Street. In the hotel, the police found the room from which the man had jumped, fallen, or been thrown. The bed was soggy with blood. On it were torn and twisted sheets that had been knotted and used rope-wise. There was also a towel that had been used as a gag.

The evidence read that the naked man had been gagged, trussed up and worked on with a knife. The doctors said the ribbons of flesh had been cut loose, not torn or clawed. After the knife-user had gone away, the naked man had worked free of his bonds, and, probably crazed by pain, had either jumped or fallen out of the window. The fall had crushed his skull and broken his arm, but he had managed to walk a block and a half in that condition.

The hotel management said the man had been there two days. He was registered as H. F. Barrows, City. He had a black gladstone bag in which, besides clothes, shaving implements and so on, the police found a box of .38 cartridges, a black handkerchief with eye-holes cut in it, four skeleton keys, a small jimmy, and a quantity of morphine, with a needle and the rest of the kit. Elsewhere in the room they found the rest of his clothes, a .38 revolver and two quarts of liquor. They didn't find a cent.

The supposition was that Barrows had been a burglar, and that he had been tied up, tortured and robbed, probably by pals, between eight and nine that morning. Nobody knew anything about him. Nobody had seen his visitor or visitors. The room next to his on the left was unoccupied. The occupant of the room on the other side had left for his work in a furniture factory before seven o'clock.

While this was happening I was at the office, sitting forward in my chair to spare my back, reading reports, all of which told how operatives attached to various Continental Detective Agency branches had continued to fail to turn up any indications of the past, present, or future whereabouts of Papadopoulos and Nancy Regan. There was nothing novel about these reports—I had been reading similar ones for three weeks.

The Old Man and I went out to luncheon together, and I told him about the previous night's adventures in Sausalito while we ate. His grandfatherly face was as attentive as always, and his smile as politely interested, but when I was half through my story he turned his mild blue eyes from my face to his salad and he stared at his salad until I had finished talking. Then, still not looking up, he said he was sorry I had been cut. I thanked him and we ate a while.

Finally he looked at me. The mildness and courtesy he habitually wore over his cold-bloodedness were in face and eyes and voice as he said:

"This first indication that Papadopoulos is still alive came immediately after Tom-Tom Carey's arrival."

It was my turn to shift my eyes.

I looked at the roll I was breaking while I said: "Yes."

That afternoon a phone call came in from a woman out in the Mission who had seen some highly mysterious happenings and was sure they had something to do with the well-advertised bank robberies. So I went out to see her and spent most of the afternoon learning that half of her happenings were imaginary and the other half were the efforts of a jealous wife to get the low-down on her husband.

It was nearly six o'clock when I returned to the Agency. A few minutes later Dick Foley called me on the phone. His teeth were chattering until I could hardly get the words.

"C-c-canyoug-g-get-t-townt-t-tooth-ar-r-rbr-r-spittle?"

"What?" I asked, and he said the same thing again, or worse. But by this time I had guessed that he was asking me if I could get down to the Harbor Hospital.

I told him I could in ten minutes, and with the help of a taxi I did.

V

The little Canadian operative met me at the hospital door. His clothes and hair were dripping wet, but he had had a shot of whisky and his teeth had stopped chattering.

"Damned fool jumped in bay!" he barked as if it were my fault.

"Angel Grace?"

"Who else was I shadowing? Got on Oakland ferry. Moved off by self by rail. Thought she was going to throw something over. Kept eye on her. Bingo! She jumps." Dick sneezed. "I was goofy enough to jump after her. Held her up. Were fished out. In there," nodding his wet head toward the interior of the hospital.

"What happened before she took the ferry?"

"Nothing. Been in joint all day. Straight out to ferry."

"How about yesterday?"

"Apartment all day. Out at night with man. Roadhouse. Home at four. Bad break. Couldn't tail him off."

"What did he look like?"

The man Dick described was Tom-Tom Carey.

"Good," I said. "You'd better beat it home for a hot bath and some dry rags."

I went in to see the near-suicide.

She was lying on her back on a cot, staring at the ceiling. Her face was pale, but it always was, and her green eyes were no more sullen than usual. Except that her short hair was dark with dampness she didn't look as if anything out of the ordinary had happened.

"You think of the funniest things to do," I said when I was beside the bed.

She jumped and her face jerked around to me, startled. Then she recognized me and smiled—a smile that brought into her face the attractiveness that habitual sullenness kept out.

"You have to keep in practice—sneaking up on people?" she asked. "Who told you I was here?"

"Everybody knows it. Your pictures are all over the front pages of the newspapers, with your life history and what you said to the Prince of Wales."

She stopped smiling and looked steadily at me.

"I got it!" she exclaimed after a few seconds. "That runt who came in after me was one of your ops—tailing me. Wasn't he?"

"I didn't know anybody had to go in after you," I answered. "I thought you came ashore after you had finished your swim. Didn't you want to land?"

She wouldn't smile. Her eyes began to look at something horrible.

"Oh! Why didn't they let me alone?" she wailed, shuddering. "It's a rotten thing, living."

I sat down on a small chair beside the white bed and patted the lump her shoulder made in the sheets.

"What was it?" I was surprised at the fatherly tone I achieved. "What did you want to die for, Angel?"

Words that wanted to be said were shiny in her eyes, tugged at muscles in her face, shaped her lips—but that was all. The words she said came out listlessly, but with a reluctant sort of finality. They were:

"No. You're law. I'm thief. I'm staying on my side of the fence. Nobody can say—"

"All right! All right!" I surrendered. "But for God's sake don't make me listen to another of those ethical arguments. Is there anything I can do for you?"

"Thanks, no."

"There's nothing you want to tell me?"

She shook her head.

"You're all right now?"

"Yes, I was being shadowed, wasn't I? Or you wouldn't have known about it so soon."

"I'm a detective—I know everything. Be a good girl."

From the hospital I went up to the Hall of Justice, to the police detective bureau. Lieutenant Duff was holding down the captain's desk. I told him about the Angel's dive.

"Got any idea what she was up to?" he wanted to know when I had finished.

"She's too far off center to figure. I want her vagged."

"Yeah? I thought you wanted her loose so you could catch her."

"That's about played out now. I'd like to try throwing her in the can for thirty days. Big Flora is in waiting trial. The Angel knows Flora was one of the troupe that rubbed out her Paddy. Maybe Flora don't know the Angel. Let's see what will come of mixing the two babies for a month."

"Can do," Duff agreed. "This Angel's got no visible means of support, and it's a cinch she's got no business running around jumping in people's bays. I'll put the word through."

From the Hall of Justice I went up to the Ellis Street hotel at which Tom-Tom Carey had told me he was registered. He was out. I left word that I would be back in an hour, and used that hour to eat. When I returned to the hotel the tall swarthy man was sitting in the lobby. He took me up to his room and set out gin, orange juice and cigars.

"Seen Angel Grace?" I asked.

"Yes, last night. We did the dumps."

"Seen her today?"

"No."

"She jumped in the bay this afternoon."

"The hell she did." He seemed moderately surprised. "And then?"

"She was fished out. She's O.K."

The shadow in his eyes could have been some slight disappointment.

"She's a funny sort of kid," he remarked. "I wouldn't say Paddy didn't show good taste when he picked her, but she's a queer one!"

"How's the Papadopoulos hunt progressing?"

"It is. But you oughtn't have split on your word. You half-way promised you wouldn't have me shadowed."

"I'm not the big boss," I apologized. "Sometimes what I want don't fit in with what the headman wants. This shouldn't bother you much—you can shake him, can't you?"

"Uh-huh. That's what I've been doing. But it's a damned nuisance jumping in and out of taxis and back doors."

We talked and drank a few minutes longer, and then I left Carey's room and hotel, and went to a drug-store telephone booth, where I called Dick Foley's home, and gave Dick the swarthy man's description and address.

"I don't want you to tail Carey, Dick. I want you to find out who is trying to tail him—and that shadower is the bird you're to stick to. The morning will be time enough to start—get yourself dried out."

And that was the end of that day.

VI

I woke to a disagreeable rainy morning. Maybe it was the weather, maybe I'd been too frisky the day before, anyway the slit in my back was like a foot-long boil. I phoned Dr. Canova, who lived on the floor below me, and had him look at the cut before he left for his downtown office. He rebandaged it and told me to take life easy for a couple of days. It felt better after he had fooled with it, but I phoned the Agency and told the Old Man that unless something exciting broke I was going to stay on sick-call all day.

I spent the day propped up in front of the gas-log, reading, and smoking cigarettes that wouldn't burn right on account of the weather. That night I used the phone to organize a poker game, in which I got very little action one way or the other. In the end I was fifteen dollars ahead, which was just about five dollars less than enough to pay for the booze my guests had drunk on me.

My back was better the following day, and so was the day. I went down to the Agency. There was a memorandum on my desk saying Duff had phoned that Angel Grace Cardigan had been vagged—thirty days in the city prison. There was a familiar pile of reports from various branches on their operatives' inability to pick up anything on Papadopoulos and Nancy Regan. I was running through these when Dick Foley came in.

"Made him," he reported. "Thirty or thirty-two. Five, six. Hundred, thirty. Sandy hair, complexion. Blue eye. Thin face, some skin off. Rat. Lives dump in Seventh Street."

"What did he do?"

"Tailed Carey one block. Carey shook him. Hunted for Carey till two in morning. Didn't find him. Went home. Take him again?"

"Go up to his flophouse and find out who he is."

The little Canadian was gone half an hour.

"Sam Arlie," he said when he returned. "Been there six months. Supposed to be barber—when he's working—if ever."

"I've got two guesses about this Arlie," I told Dick. "The first is that he's the gink who carved me in Sausalito the other night. The second is that something's going to happen to him."

It was against Dick's rules to waste words, so he said nothing.

I called Tom-Tom Carey's hotel and got the swarthy man on the wire.

"Come over," I invited him. "I've got some news for you."

"As soon as I'm dressed and breakfasted," he promised.

"When Carey leaves here you're to go along behind him," I told Dick after I had hung up. "If Arlie connects with him now, maybe there'll be something doing. Try to see it."

Then I phoned the detective bureau and made a date with Sergeant Hunt to visit Angel Grace Cardigan's apartment. After that I busied myself with paper work until Tommy came in to announce the swarthy man from Nogales.

"The jobbie who's tailing you," I informed him when he had sat down and begun work on a cigarette, "is a barber named Arlie," and I told him where Arlie lived.

"Yes. A slim-faced, sandy lad?"

I gave him the description Dick had given me.

"That's the hombre," Tom-Tom Carey said. "Know anything else about him?"

"No."

"You had Angel Grace vagged."

It was neither an accusation nor a question, so I didn't answer it.

"It's just as well," the tall man went on. "I'd have had to send her away. She was bound to gum things with her foolishness when I got ready to swing the loop."

"That'll be soon?"

"That all depends on how it happens." He stood up, yawned and shook his wide shoulders. "But nobody would starve to death if they decided not to eat any more till I'd got him. I oughtn't have accused you of having me shadowed."

"It didn't spoil my day."

Tom-Tom Carey said, "So long," and sauntered out.

I rode down to the Hall of Justice, picked up Hunt, and we went to the Bush Street apartment house in which Angel Grace Cardigan had lived. The manager—a highly scented fat woman with a hard mouth and soft eyes—already knew her tenant was in the cooler. She willingly took us up to the girl's rooms.

The Angel wasn't a good housekeeper. Things were clean enough, but upset. The kitchen sink was full of dirty dishes. The folding bed was worse than loosely made up. Clothes and odds and ends of feminine equipment hung over everything from bathroom to kitchen.

We got rid of the landlady and raked the place over thoroughly. We came away knowing all there was to know about the girl's wardrobe, and a lot about her personal habits. But we didn't find anything pointing Papadopoulosward.

No report came in on the Carey-Arlie combination that afternoon or evening, though I expected to hear from Dick every minute.

At three o'clock in the morning my bedside phone took my ear out of the pillows. The voice that came over the wire was the Canadian op's.

"Exit Arlie," he said.

"R.I.P.?"

"Yep."

"How?"

"Lead."

"Our lad's?"

"Yep."

"Keep till morning?"

"Yep."

"See you at the office," and I went back to sleep.

VII

When I arrived at the Agency at nine o'clock, one of the clerks had just finished decoding a night letter from the Los Angeles operative who had been sent over to Nogales. It was a long telegram, and meaty.

It said that Tom-Tom Carey was well known along the border. For some six months he had been engaged in over-the-line traffic—guns going south, booze, and probably dope and immigrants, coming north. Just before leaving there the previous week he had made inquiries concerning one Hank Barrows. This Hank Barrows' description fit the H. F. Barrows who had been cut into ribbons, who had fallen out the hotel window and died.

The Los Angeles operative hadn't been able to get much of a line on Barrows, except that he hailed from San Francisco, had been on the border only a few days, and had apparently returned to San Francisco. The operative had turned up nothing new on the Newhall killing—the signs still read that he had been killed resisting capture by Mexican patriots.

Dick Foley came into my office while I was reading the news. When I had finished he gave me his contribution to the history of Tom-Tom Carey.

"Tailed him out of here. To hotel. Arlie on corner. Eight o'clock, Carey out. Garage. Hire car without driver. Back hotel. Checked out. Two bags. Out through park. Arlie after him in flivver. My boat after Arlie. Down boulevard. Off cross-road. Dark. Lonely. Arlie steps on gas. Closes in. Bang! Carey stops. Two guns going. Exit Arlie. Carey back to city.

Hotel Marquis. Registers George F. Danby, San Diego. Room 622."

"Did Tom-Tom frisk Arlie after he dropped him?"

"No. Didn't touch him."

"So? Take Mickey Linehan with you. Don't let Carey get out of your sight. I'll get somebody up to relieve you and Mickey late tonight, if I can, but he's got to be shadowed twenty-four hours a day until—" I didn't know what came after that so I stopped talking.

I took Dick's story into the Old Man's office and told it to him, winding up:

"Arlie shot first, according to Foley, so Carey gets a self-defense on it, but we're getting action at last and I don't want to do anything to slow it up. So I'd like to keep what we know about this shooting quiet for a couple of days. It won't increase our friendship any with the county sheriff if he finds out what we're doing, but I think it's worth it."

"If you wish," the Old Man agreed, reaching for his ringing phone.

He spoke into the instrument and passed it on to me. Detective-sergeant Hunt was talking:

"Flora Brace and Grace Cardigan crushed out just before daylight. The chances are they—"

I wasn't in a humor for details.

"A clean sneak?" I asked.

"Not a lead on 'em so far, but—"

"I'll get the details when I see you. Thanks," and I hung up.

"Angel Grace and Big Flora have escaped from the city prison," I passed the news on to the Old Man.

He smiled courteously, as if at something that didn't especially concern him.

"You were congratulating yourself on getting action," he murmured.

I turned my scowl to a grin, mumbled, "Well, maybe," went back to my office and telephoned Franklin Ellert. The lisping attorney said he would be glad to see me, so I went over to his office.

"And now, what progreth have you made?" he asked eagerly when I was seated beside his desk.

"Some. A man named Barrows was also in Nogales when Newhall was killed, and also came to San Francisco right after. Carey followed Barrows up here. Did you read about the man found walking the streets naked, all cut up?"

"Yeth."

"That was Barrows. Then another man comes into the game—a barber named Arlie. He was spying on Carey. Last night, in a lonely road south of here, Arlie shot at Carey. Carey killed him."

The old lawyer's eyes came out another inch.

"What road?" he gasped.

"You want the exact location?"

"Yeth!"

I pulled his phone over, called the Agency, had Dick's report read to me, gave the attorney the information he wanted.

It had an effect on him. He hopped out of his chair. Sweat was shiny along the ridges wrinkles made in his face.

"Mith Newhall ith down there alone! That plath ith only half a mile from her houth!"

I frowned and beat my brains together, but I couldn't make anything out of it.

"Suppose I put a man down there to look after her?" I suggested.

"Exthellent!" His worried face cleared until there weren't more than fifty or sixty wrinkles in it. "The would prefer to thtay there during her firth grief over her fatherth death. You will thend a capable man?"

"The Rock of Gibraltar is a leaf in the breeze beside him. Give me a note for him to take down. Andrew MacElroy is his name."

While the lawyer scribbled the note I used his phone again to call the Agency, to tell the operator to get hold of Andy and tell him I wanted him. I ate lunch before I returned to the Agency. Andy was waiting when I got there.

Andy MacElroy was a big boulder of a man—not very tall, but thick and hard of head and body. A glum, grim man with no more imagination than an adding machine. I'm not even sure he could read. But I was sure that when Andy was told to do something, he did it and nothing else. He didn't know enough not to.

I gave him the lawyer's note to Miss Newhall, told him where to go and what to do, and Miss Newhall's troubles were off my mind.

Three times that afternoon I heard from Dick Foley and Mickey Linehan. Tom-Tom Carey wasn't doing anything very exciting, though he had bought two boxes of .44 cartridges in a Market Street sporting goods establishment.

The afternoon papers carried photographs of Big Flora Brace and Angel Grace Cardigan, with a story of their escape. The story was as far from the probable facts as newspaper stories generally are. On another page was an account of the discovery of the dead barber in the lonely road. He had been shot in the head and in the chest, four times in all. The county officials' opinion was that he had been killed resisting a stick-up, and that the bandits had fled without robbing him.

At five o'clock Tommy Howd came to my door.

"That guy Carey wants to see you again," the freckle-faced boy said.

"Shoot him in."

The swarthy man sauntered in, said "Howdy," sat down, and made a brown cigarette.

"Got anything special on for tonight?" he asked when he was smoking.

"Nothing I can't put aside for something better. Giving a party?"

"Uh-huh. I had thought of it. A kind of surprise party for Papadoodle. Want to go along?"

It was my turn to say, "Uh-huh."

"I'll pick you up at eleven—Van Ness and Geary," he drawled. "But this has got to be a kind of tight party—just you and me—and him."

"No. There's one more who'll have to be in on it. I'll bring him along."

"I don't like that." Tom-Tom Carey shook his head slowly, frowning amiably over his cigarette. "You sleuths oughtn't out-number me. It ought to be one and one."

"You won't be out-numbered," I explained. "This jobbie I'm bringing won't be on my side more than yours. And it'll pay you to keep as sharp an eye on him as I do—and to see he don't get behind either of us if we can help it."

"Then what do you want to lug him along for?"

"Wheels within wheels," I grinned.

The swarthy man frowned again, less amiably now.

"The hundred and six thousand reward money—I'm not figuring on sharing that with anybody."

"Right enough," I agreed. "Nobody I bring along will declare themselves in on it."

"I'll take your word for it." He stood up. "And we've got to watch this hombre, huh?"

"If we want everything to go all right."

"Suppose he gets in the way—cuts up on us. Can we put it to him, or do we just say, 'Naughty! Naughty!'?"

"He'll have to take his own chances."

"Fair enough." His hard face was good-natured again as he moved toward the door. "Eleven o'clock at Van Ness and Geary."

VIII

I went back into the operatives' room, where Jack Counihan was slumped down in a chair reading a magazine.

"I hope you've thought up something for me to do," he greeted me. "I'm getting bed-sores from sitting around."

"Patience, son, patience—that's what you've got to learn if you're ever going to be a detective. Why when I was a child of your age, just starting in with the Agency, I was lucky—"

"Don't start that," he begged. Then his good-looking young face got earnest. "I don't see why you keep me cooped up here. I'm the only one besides you who really got a good look at Nancy Regan. I should think you would have me out hunting for her."

"I told the Old Man the same thing," I sympathized. "But he is afraid to risk something happening to you. He says in all his fifty years of gum-shoeing he's never seen such a handsome op, besides being a fashion plate and a social butterfly and the heir to millions. His idea is we ought to keep you as a sort of show piece, and not let you—"

"Go to hell!" Jack said, all red in the face.

"But I persuaded him to let me take the cotton packing off you tonight," I continued. "So meet me at Van Ness and Geary before eleven o'clock."

"Action?" He was all eagerness.

"Maybe."

"What are we going to do?"

"Bring your little pop-gun along." An idea came into my head and I worded it. "You'd better be all dressed up—evening duds."

"Dinner coat?"

"No—the limit—everything but the high hat. Now for your behavior: you're not supposed to be an op. I'm not sure just what you're supposed to be, but it doesn't make any difference. Tom-Tom Carey will be along. You act as if you were neither my friend nor his—as if you didn't trust either of us. We'll be cagey with you. If anything is asked that you don't know the answer to—you fall back on hostility. But don't crowd Carey too far. Got it?"

"I—I think so." He spoke slowly, screwing up his forehead. "I'm to act as if I was going along on the same business as you, but that outside of that we weren't friends. As if I wasn't willing to trust you. That it?"

"Very much. Watch yourself. You'll be swimming in nitro-glycerine all the way."

"What is up? Be a good chap and give me some idea."

I grinned up at him. He was a lot taller than I.

"I could," I admitted, "but I'm afraid it would scare you off. So I'd better tell you nothing. Be happy while you can. Eat a good dinner. Lots of condemned folks seem to eat hearty breakfasts of ham and eggs just before they parade out to the rope. Maybe you wouldn't want 'em for dinner, but—"

At five minutes to eleven that night Tom-Tom Carey brought a black touring car to the corner where Jack and I stood waiting in a fog that was like a damp fur coat.

"Climb in," he ordered as we came to the curb.

I opened the front door and motioned Jack in. He rang up the curtain on his little act, looking coldly at me and opening the rear door.

"I'm going to sit back here," he said bluntly.

"Not a bad idea," and I climbed in beside him.

Carey twisted around in his seat and he and Jack stared at each other for a while. I said nothing, did not introduce them. When the swarthy man had finished sizing the young-ster up, he looked from the boy's collar and tie—all of his evening clothes not hidden by his overcoat—to me, grinned, and drawled:

"Your friend's a waiter, huh?"

I laughed, because the indignation that darkened the boy's face and popped his mouth open was natural, not part of his acting. I pushed my foot against his. He closed his mouth, said nothing, looked at Tom-Tom Carey and me as if we were specimens of some lower form of animal life.

I grinned back at Carey and asked, "Are we waiting for anything?"

He said we weren't, left off staring at Jack, and put the ma-chine in motion. He drove us out through the park, down the boulevard. Traffic going our way and the other loomed out of and faded into the fog-thick night. Presently we left the city be-hind, and ran out of the fog into clear moonlight. I didn't look at any of the machines running behind us, but I knew that in one of them Dick Foley and Mickey Linehan should be riding.

Tom-Tom Carey swung our car off the boulevard, into a road that was smooth and well made, but not much traveled.

"Wasn't a man killed down along here somewhere last night?" I asked.

Carey nodded his head without turning it, and, when we had gone another quarter-mile, said: "Right here."

We rode a little slower now, and Carey turned off his lights. In the road that was half moon-silver, half shadow-gray, the machine barely crept along for perhaps a mile. We stopped in the shade of tall shrubs that darkened a spot of the road.

"All ashore that's going ashore," Tom-Tom Carey said, and got out of the car.

Jack and I followed him. Carey took off his overcoat and threw it into the machine.

"The place is just around the bend, back from the road," he told us. "Damn this moon! I was counting on fog."

I said nothing, nor did Jack. The boy's face was white and excited.

"We'll bee-line it," Carey said, leading the way across the road to a high wire fence.

He went over the fence first, then Jack, then—the sound of someone coming along the road from ahead stopped me. Signalling silence to the two men on the other side of the fence, I made myself small beside a bush. The coming steps were light, quick, feminine.

A girl came into the moonlight just ahead. She was a girl of twenty-something, neither tall nor short, thin nor plump. She was short-skirted, bare-haired, sweatered. Terror was in her white face, in the carriage of her hurrying figure— but something else was there too—more beauty than a middle-aged sleuth was used to seeing.

When she saw Carey's automobile bulking in the shadow, she stopped abruptly, with a gasp that was almost a cry.

I walked forward, saying:

"Hello, Nancy Regan."

This time the gasp was a cry.

"Oh! Oh!" Then, unless the moonlight was playing tricks, she recognized me and terror began to go away from her. She put both hands out to me, with relief in the gesture.

"Well?" A bearish grumble came from the big boulder of a man who had appeared out of the darkness behind her. "What's all this?"

"Hello, Andy," I greeted the boulder.

"Hullo," MacElroy echoed and stood still.

Andy always did what he was told to do. He had been told to take care of Miss Newhall. I looked at the girl and then at him again.

"Is this Miss Newhall?" I asked.

"Yeah," he rumbled. "I came down like you said, but she told me she didn't want me—wouldn't let me in the house. But you hadn't said anything about coming back. So I just camped outside, moseying around, keeping my eyes on things. And when I seen her shinnying out a window a little while ago, I just went on along behind her to take care of her, like you said I was to do."

Tom-Tom Carey and Jack Counihan came back into the road, crossed it to us. The swarthy man had an automatic in one hand. The girl's eyes were glued on mine. She paid no attention to the others.

"What is it all about?" I asked her.

"I don't know," she babbled, her hands holding on to mine, her face close to mine. "Yes, I'm Ann Newhall. I didn't know. I thought it was fun. And then when I found out it wasn't I couldn't get out of it."

Tom-Tom Carey grunted and stirred impatiently. Jack Counihan was staring down the road. Andy MacElroy stood stolid in the road, waiting to be told what to do next. The girl never once looked from me to any of these others.

"How did you get in with them?" I demanded. "Talk fast."

IX

I had told the girl to talk fast. She did. For twenty minutes she stood there and turned out words in a chattering stream that had no breaks except where I cut in to keep her from straying from the path I wanted her to follow. It was jumbled, almost incoherent in spots, and not always plausible, but the notion stayed with me throughout that she was trying to tell the truth—most of the time.

And not for a fraction of a second did she turn her gaze from my eyes. It was as if she was afraid to look anywhere else.

This millionaire's daughter had, two months before, been one of a party of four young people returning late at night from some sort of social affair down the coast. Somebody suggested that they stop at a roadhouse along their way—a particularly tough joint. Its toughness was its attraction, of course—toughness was more or less of a novelty to them. They got a first-hand view of it that night, for, nobody knew just how, they found themselves taking part in a row before they had been ten minutes in the dump.

The girl's escort had shamed her by showing an unreasonable amount of cowardice. He had let Red O'Leary turn him over his knee and spank him—and had done nothing about it afterward. The other youth in the party had been not much braver. The girl, insulted by this meekness, had walked across to the red-haired giant who had wrecked her escort, and she had spoken to him loud enough for everybody to hear:

"Will you please take me home?"

Red O'Leary was glad to do it. She left him a block or two from her city house. She told him her name was Nancy Regan. He probably doubted it, but he never asked her any questions, pried into her affairs. In spite of the difference in their worlds, a genuine companionship had grown up between them. She liked him. He was so gloriously a roughneck that she saw him as a romantic figure. He was in love with her, knew she was miles above him, and so she had no trouble making him behave so far as she was concerned.

They met often. He took her to all the rowdy holes in the bay district, introduced her to yeggs, gunmen, swindlers, told her wild tales of criminal adventuring. She knew he was a crook, knew he was tied up in the Seamen's National and Golden Gate Trust jobs when they broke. But she saw it all as a sort of theatrical spectacle. She didn't see it as it was.

She woke up the night they were in Larrouy's and were jumped by the crooks that Red had helped Papadopoulos and the others double-cross. But it was too late then for her to wriggle clear. She was blown along with Red to Papadopoulos' hangout after I had shot the big lad. She saw then what her romantic figures really were—what she had mixed herself with.

When Papadopoulos escaped, taking her with him, she was wide awake, cured, through forever with her dangerous trifling with outlaws. So she thought. She thought Papadopoulos was the little, scary old man he seemed to be— Flora's slave, a harmless old duffer too near the grave to have any evil in him. He had been whining and terrified. He begged her not to forsake him, pleaded with her while tears ran down his withered cheeks, begging her to hide him from Flora. She took him to her country house and let him fool around in the garden, safe from prying eyes. She had no idea that he had known who she was all along, had guided her into suggesting this arrangement.

Even when the newspapers said he had been the commander-in-chief of the thug army, when the hundred and six thousand dollar reward was offered for his arrest, she believed in his innocence. He convinced her that Flora and Red had simply put the blame for the whole thing on him so they could get off with lighter sentences. He was such a frightened old gink—who wouldn't have believed him?

Then her father's death in Mexico had come and grief had occupied her mind to the exclusion of most other things until this day, when Big Flora and another girl—probably Angel Grace Cardigan—had come to the house. She had been deathly afraid of Big Flora when she had seen her before. She was more afraid now. And she soon learned that Papadopoulos was not Flora's slave but her master. She saw the old buzzard as he really was. But that wasn't the end of her awakening.

Angel Grace had suddenly tried to kill Papadopoulos. Flora had overpowered her. Grace, defiant, had told them she was Paddy's girl. Then she had screamed at Ann Newhall:

"And you, you damned fool, don't you know they killed your father? Don't you know—?"

Big Flora's fingers, around Angel Grace's throat, stopped her words. Flora tied up the Angel and turned to the Newhall girl.

"You're in it," she said brusquely. "You're in it up to your neck. You'll play along with us, or else— Here's how it stands, dearie. The old man and I are both due to step off if we're caught. And you'll do the dance with us. I'll see to that. Do what you're told, and we'll all come through all right. Get funny, and I'll beat holy hell out of you."

The girl didn't remember much after that. She had a dim recollection of going to the door and telling Andy she didn't want his services. She did this mechanically, not even needing to be prompted by the big blonde woman who stood close behind her. Later, in the same fearful daze, she had gone out her bedroom window, down the vine-covered side of the porch, and away from the house, running along the road, not going anywhere, just escaping.

That was what I learned from the girl. She didn't tell me all of it. She told me very little of it in those words. But that is the story I got by combining her words, her manner of telling them, her facial expressions, with what I already knew, and what I could guess.

And not once while she talked had her eyes turned from mine. Not once had she shown that she knew there were other men standing in the road with us. She stared into my face with a desperate fixity, as if she was afraid not to, and her hands held mine as if she might sink through the ground if she let go.

"How about your servants?" I asked.

"There aren't any there now."

"Papadopoulos persuaded you to get rid of them?"

"Yes—several days ago."

"Then Papadopoulos, Flora and Angel Grace are alone in the house now?"

"Yes."

"They know you ducked?"

"I don't know. I don't think they do. I had been in my room some time. I don't think they suspected I'd dare do anything but what they told me."

It annoyed me to find I was staring into the girl's eyes as fixedly as she into mine, and that when I wanted to take my gaze away it wasn't easily done. I jerked my eyes away from her, took my hands away.

"The rest of it you can tell me later," I growled, and turned to give Andy MacElroy his orders. "You stay here with Miss Newhall until we get back from the house. Make yourselves comfortable in the car."

The girl put a hand on my arm.

"Am I—? Are you—?"

"We're going to turn you over to the police, yes," I assured her.

"No! No!"

"Don't be childish," I begged. "You can't run around with a mob of cutthroats, get yourself tied up in a flock of crimes, and then when you're tripped say, 'Excuse it, please,' and go free. If you tell the whole story in court—including the parts you haven't told me—the chances are you'll get off. But there's no way in God's world for you to escape arrest. Come on," I told Jack and Tom-Tom Carey. "We've got to shake it up if we want to find our folks at home."

Looking back as I climbed the fence, I saw that Andy had put the girl in the car and was getting in himself.

"Just a moment," I called to Jack and Carey, who were already starting across the field.

"Thought of something else to kill time," the swarthy man complained.

I went back across the road to the car and spoke quickly and softly to Andy:

"Dick Foley and Mickey Linehan should be hanging around the neighborhood. As soon as we're out of sight, hunt 'em up. Turn Miss Newhall over to Dick. Tell him to take her with him and beat it for a phone—rouse the sheriff. Tell Dick he's to turn the girl over to the sheriff, to hold for the San Francisco police. Tell him he's not to give her up to anybody else—not even to me. Got it?"

"Got it."

"All right. After you've told him that and have given him the girl, then you bring Mickey Linehan to the Newhall house as fast as you can make it. We'll likely need all the help we can get as soon as we can get it."

"Got you," Andy said.

X

"What are you up to?" Tom-Tom Carey asked suspiciously when I rejoined Jack and him.

"Detective business."

"I ought to have come down and turned the trick all by myself," he grumbled. "You haven't done a damned thing but waste time since we started."

"I'm not the one that's wasting it now."

He snorted and set out across the field again, Jack and I following him. At the end of the field there was another fence to be climbed. Then we came over a little wooded ridge and the Newhall house lay before us—a large white house, glistening in the moonlight, with yellow rectangulars where blinds were down over the windows of lighted rooms. The lighted rooms were on the ground floor. The upper floor was dark. Everything was quiet.

"Damn the moonlight!" Tom-Tom Carey repeated, bringing another automatic out of his clothes, so that he now had one in each hand.

Jack started to take his gun out, looked at me, saw I was letting mine rest, let his slide back in his pocket.

Tom-Tom Carey's face was a dark stone mask—slits for eyes, slit for mouth—the grim mask of a manhunter, a man-killer. He was breathing softly, his big chest moving gently. Beside him, Jack Counihan looked like an excited school-boy. His face was ghastly, his eyes all stretched out of shape, and he was breathing like a tire-pump. But his grin was genuine, for all the nervousness in it.

"We'll cross to the house on this side," I whispered. "Then one of us can take the front, one the back, and the other can wait till he sees where he's needed most. Right?"

"Right," the swarthy one agreed.

"Wait!" Jack exclaimed. "The girl came down the vines from an upper window. What's the matter with my going up that way? I'm lighter than either of you. If they haven't missed her, the window would still be open. Give me ten minutes to find the window, get through it, and get myself placed. Then when you attack I'll be there behind them. How's that?" he demanded applause.

"And what if they grab you as soon as you light?" I objected.

"Suppose they do. I can make enough racket for you to hear. You can gallop to the attack while they're busy with me. That'll be just as good."

"Blue hell!" Tom-Tom Carey barked. "What good's all that? The other way's best. One of us at the front door, one at the back, kick 'em in and go in shooting."

"If this new one works, it'll be better," I gave my opinion. "If you want to jump in the furnace, Jack, I won't stop you. I won't cheat you out of your heroics."

"No!" the swarthy man snarled. "Nothing doing!"

"Yes," I contradicted him. "We'll try it. Better take twenty minutes, Jack. That won't give you any time to waste."

He looked at his watch and I at mine, and he turned toward the house.

Tom-Tom Carey, scowling darkly, stood in his way. I cursed and got between the swarthy man and the boy. Jack went around my back and hurried away across the too-bright space between us and the house.

"Keep your feet on the ground," I told Carey. "There are a lot of things to this game you don't know anything about."

"Too damned many!" he snarled, but he let the boy go.

There was no open second-story window on our side of the building. Jack rounded the rear of the house and went out of sight.

A faint rustling sounded behind us. Carey and I spun together. His guns went up. I stretched out an arm across them, pushing them down.

"Don't have a hemorrhage," I cautioned him. "This is just another of the things you don't know about."

The rustling had stopped.

"All right," I called softly.

Mickey Linehan and Andy MacElroy came out of the tree-shadows.

Tom-Tom Carey stuck his face so close to mine that I'd have been scratched if he had forgotten to shave that day.

"You double-crossing—"

"Behave! Behave! A man of your age!" I admonished him. "None of these boys want any of your blood money."

"I don't like this gang stuff," he snarled. "We—"

"We're going to need all the help we can get," I interrupted, looking at my watch. I told the two operatives: "We're going to close in on the house now. Four of us ought to be able to wrap it up snug. You know Papadopoulos, Big Flora and Angel Grace by description. They're in there. Don't take any chances with them—Flora and Papadopoulos are dynamite. Jack Counihan is trying to ease inside now. You two look after the back of the joint. Carey and I will take the front. We'll make the play. You see that nobody leaks out on us. Forward march!"

The swarthy man and I headed for the front porch—a wide porch, grown over with vines on the side, yellowly illuminated now by the light that came through four curtained French windows.

We hadn't taken our first steps across the porch when one of these tall windows moved—opened.

The first thing I saw was Jack Counihan's back.

He was pushing the casement open with a hand and foot, not turning his head.

Beyond the boy—facing him across the brightly lighted room—stood a man and a woman. The man was old, small, scrawny, wrinkled, pitifully frightened—Papadopoulos. I saw he had shaved off his straggly white mustache. The woman was tall, full-bodied, pink-fleshed and yellow-haired—a she-athlete of forty with clear gray eyes set deep in a handsome brutal face—Big Flora Brace. They stood very still, side by side, watching the muzzle of Jack Counihan's gun.

While I stood in front of the window looking at this scene, Tom-Tom Carey, his two guns up, stepped past me, going through the tall window to the boy's side. I did not follow him into the room.

Papadopoulos' scary brown eyes darted to the swarthy man's face. Flora's gray ones moved there deliberately, and then looked past him to me.

"Hold it, everybody!" I ordered, and moved away from the window, to the side of the porch where the vines were thinnest.

Leaning out between the vines, so my face was clear in the moonlight, I looked down the side of the building. A shadow in the shadow of the garage could have been a man. I put an arm out in the moonlight and beckoned. The shadow came toward me—Mickey Linehan. Andy MacElroy's head peeped around the back of the house. I beckoned again and he followed Mickey.

I returned to the open window.

Papadopoulos and Flora—a rabbit and a lioness—stood looking at the guns of Carey and Jack. They looked again at me when I appeared, and a smile began to curve the woman's full lips.

Mickey and Andy came up and stood beside me. The woman's smile died grimly.

"Carey," I said, "you and Jack stay as is. Mickey, Andy, go in and take hold of our gifts from God."

When the two operatives stepped through the window—things happened.

Papadopoulos screamed.

Big Flora lunged against him, knocking him at the back door.

"Go! Go!" she roared.

Stumbling, staggering, he scrambled across the room.

Flora had a pair of guns—sprung suddenly into her hands. Her big body seemed to fill the room, as if by will-power she had become a giantess. She charged—straight at the guns Jack and Carey held—blotting the back door and the fleeing man from their fire.

A blur to one side was Andy MacElroy moving.

I had a hand on Jack's gun-arm.

"Don't shoot," I muttered in his ear.

Flora's guns thundered together. But she was tumbling. Andy had crashed into her. Had thrown himself at her legs as a man would throw a boulder.

When Flora tumbled, Tom-Tom Carey stopped waiting.

His first bullet was sent so close past her that it clipped her curled yellow hair. But it went past—caught Papadopoulos just as he went through the door. The bullet took him low in the back—smeared him out on the floor.

Carey fired again—again—again—into the prone body.

"It's no use," I growled. "You can't make him any deader."

He chuckled and lowered his guns.

"Four into a hundred and six." All his ill-humor, his grimness was gone. "That's twenty-six thousand, five hundred dollars each of those slugs was worth to me."

Andy and Mickey had wrestled Flora into submission and were hauling her up off the floor.

I looked from them back to the swarthy man, muttering, "It's not all over yet."

"No?" He seemed surprised. "What next?"

"Stay awake and let your conscience guide you," I replied, and turned to the Counihan youngster. "Come along Jack."

I led the way out through the window and across the porch, where I leaned against the railing. Jack followed and stood in front of me, his gun still in his hand, his face white and tired from nervous tension. Looking over his shoulder, I could see the room we had just quit. Andy and Mickey had Flora sitting between them on a sofa. Carey stood a little to one side, looking curiously at Jack and me. We were in the middle of the band of light that came through the open window. We could see inside—except that Jack's back was that way—and could be seen from there, but our talk couldn't be overheard unless we made it loud.

All that was as I wanted it.

"Now tell me about it," I ordered Jack.

XI

"Well, I found the open window," the boy began.

"I know all that part," I cut in. "You came in and told your friends—Papadopoulos and Flora—about the girl's escape, and that Carey and I were coming. You advised them to make out you had captured them single-handed. That would draw Carey and me in. With you unsuspected behind us, it would be easy for the three of you to grab the two of us. After that you could stroll down the road and tell Andy I had sent you for the girl. That was a good scheme—except that you didn't know I had Dick and Mickey up my sleeve, didn't know I wouldn't let you get behind me. But all that isn't what I want to know. I want to know why you sold us out—and what you think you're going to do now."

"Are you crazy?" His young face was bewildered, his young eyes horrified. "Or is this some—?"

"Sure, I'm crazy," I confessed. "Wasn't I crazy enough to let you lead me into that trap in Sausalito? But I wasn't too crazy to figure it out afterward. I wasn't too crazy to see that Ann Newhall was afraid to look at you. I'm not crazy enough to think you could have captured Papadopoulos and Flora unless they wanted you to. I'm crazy—but in moderation."

Jack laughed—a reckless young laugh, but too shrill. His eyes didn't laugh with mouth and voice. While he was laughing his eyes looked from me to the gun in his hand and back to me.

"Talk, Jack," I pleaded huskily, putting a hand on his shoulder. "For God's sake why did you do it?"

The boy shut his eyes, gulped, and his shoulders twitched. When his eyes opened they were hard and glittering and full of merry hell.

"The worst part of it," he said harshly, moving his shoulder from under my hand, "is that I wasn't a very good crook, was I? I didn't succeed in deluding you."

I said nothing.

"I suppose you've earned your right to the story," he went on after a little pause. His voice was consciously monotonous, as if he was deliberately keeping out of it every tone or accent that might seem to express emotion. He was too young to talk naturally. "I met Ann Newhall three weeks ago, in my own home. She had gone to school with my sisters, though I had never met her before. We knew each other at once, of course—I knew she was Nancy Regan, she knew I was a Continental operative.

"So we went off by ourselves and talked things over. Then she took me to see Papadopoulos. I liked the old boy and he liked me. He showed me how we together could accumulate unheard-of piles of wealth. So there you are. The prospect of all that money completely devastated my morals. I told him about Carey as soon as I had heard from you, and I led you into that trap, as you say. He thought it would be better if you stopped bothering us before you found the connection between Newhall and Papadopoulos.

"After that failure, he wanted me to try again, but I refused to have a hand in any more fiascos. There's nothing sillier than a murder that doesn't come off. Ann Newhall is quite innocent of everything except folly. I don't think she has the slightest suspicion that I have had any part in the dirty work beyond refraining from having everybody arrested. That, my dear Sherlock, about concludes the confession."

I had listened to the boy's story with a great show of sympathetic attentiveness. Now I scowled at him and spoke accusingly, but still not without friendliness.

"Stop spoofing! The money Papadopoulos showed you didn't buy you. You met the girl and were too soft to turn her in. But your vanity—your pride in looking at yourself as a pretty cold proposition—wouldn't let you admit it even to yourself. You had to have a hard-boiled front. So you were meat to Papadopoulos' grinder. He gave you a part you could play to yourself—a super-gentleman-crook, a master-mind, a desperate suave villain, and all that kind of romantic garbage. That's the way you went, my son. You went as far as possible beyond what was needed to save the girl from the hoose-gow—just to show the world, but chiefly yourself, that you were not acting through sentimentality, but according to your own reckless desires. There you are. Look at yourself."

Whatever he saw in himself—what I had seen or something else—his face slowly reddened, and he wouldn't look at me. He looked past me at the distant road.

I looked into the lighted room beyond him. Tom-Tom Carey had advanced to the center of the floor, where he stood watching us. I jerked a corner of my mouth at him—a warning.

"Well," the boy began again, but he didn't know what to say after that. He shuffled his feet and kept his eyes from my face.

I stood up straight and got rid of the last trace of my hypocritical sympathy.

"Give me your gun, you lousy rat!" I snarled at him.

He jumped back as if I had hit him. Craziness writhed in his face. He jerked his gun chest-high.

Tom-Tom Carey saw the gun go up. The swarthy man fired twice. Jack Counihan was dead at my feet.

Mickey Linehan fired once. Carey was down on the floor, bleeding from the temple.

I stepped over Jack's body, went into the room, knelt beside the swarthy man. He squirmed, tried to say something, died before he could get it out. I waited until my face was straight before I stood up.

Big Flora was studying me with narrowed gray eyes. I stared back at her.

"I don't get it all yet," she said slowly, "but if you—"

"Where's Angel Grace?" I interrupted.

"Tied to the kitchen table," she informed me, and went on with her thinking aloud. "You've dealt a hand that—"

"Yeah," I said sourly, "I'm another Papadopoulos."

Her big body suddenly quivered. Pain clouded her handsome brutal face. Two tears came out of her lower eye-lids.

I'm damned if she hadn't loved the old scoundrel!

XII

It was after eight in the morning when I got back to the city. I ate breakfast and then went up to the Agency, where I found the Old Man going through his morning mail.

"It's all over," I told him. "Papadopoulos knew Nancy Regan was Taylor Newhall's heiress. When he needed a hiding-place after the bank jobs flopped, he got her to take him down to the Newhall country place. He had two holds on her. She pitied him as a misused old duffer, and she was—even if innocently—an accomplice after the fact in the stick-ups.

"Pretty soon Papa Newhall had to go to Mexico on business. Papadopoulos saw a chance to make something. If Newhall was knocked off, the girl would have millions—and the old thief knew he could take them away from her. He sent Barrows down to the border to buy the murder from some Mexican bandits. Barrows put it over, but talked too much. He told a girl in Nogales that he had to go back 'to 'Frisco to collect plenty from an old Greek,' and then he'd return and buy her the world. The girl passed the news on to Tom-Tom Carey. Carey put a lot of twos together and got at least a dozen for an answer. He followed Barrows up here.

"Angel Grace was with him the morning he called on Barrows here—to find out if his 'old Greek' really was Papadopoulos, and where he could be found. Barrows was too full of morphine to listen to reason. He was so dope-deadened that even after the dark man began to reason with a knife-blade he had to whittle Barrows all up before he began to feel hurt. The carving sickened Angel Grace. She left, after vainly trying to stop Carey. And when she read in the afternoon papers what a finished job he had made of it, she tried to commit suicide, to stop the images from crawling around in her head.

"Carey got all the information Barrows had, but Barrows didn't know where Papadopoulos was hiding. Papadopoulos learned of Carey's arrival—you know how he learned. He sent Arlie to stop Carey. Carey wouldn't give the barber a chance—until the swarthy man began to suspect Papadopoulos might be at the Newhall place. He drove down there, letting Arlie follow. As soon as Arlie discovered his destination, Arlie closed in, hell-bent on stopping Carey at any cost. That was what Carey wanted. He gunned Arlie, came back to town, got hold of me, and took me down to help wind things up.

"Meanwhile, Angel Grace, in the cooler, had made friends with Big Flora. She knew Flora but Flora didn't know her. Papadopoulos had arranged a crush-out for Flora. It's always easier for two to escape than one. Flora took the Angel along, took her to Papadopoulos. The Angel went for him, but Flora knocked her for a loop.

"Flora, Angel Grace and Ann Newhall, alias Nancy Regan, are in the county jail," I wound up. "Papadopoulos, Tom-Tom Carey and Jack Counihan are dead."

I stopped talking and lighted a cigarette, taking my time, watching cigarette and match carefully throughout the operation. The Old Man picked up a letter, put it down without reading it, picked up another.

"They were killed in course of making the arrests?" His mild voice held nothing but its usual unfathomable politeness.

"Yes. Carey killed Papadopoulos. A little later he shot Jack. Mickey—not knowing—not knowing anything except that the dark man was shooting at Jack and me—we were standing apart talking—shot and killed Carey." The words twisted around my tongue, wouldn't come out straight. "Neither Mickey nor Andy know that Jack— Nobody but you and I know exactly what the thing—exactly what Jack was doing. Flora Brace and Ann Newhall did know, but if we say he was acting on orders all the time, nobody can deny it."

The Old Man nodded his grandfatherly face and smiled, but for the first time in the years I had known him I knew what he was thinking. He was thinking that if Jack had come through alive we would have had the nasty choice between letting him go free or giving the Agency a black-eye by advertising the fact that one of our operatives was a crook.

I threw away my cigarette and stood up. The Old Man stood also, and held out a hand to me.

"Thank you," he said.

I took his hand, and I understood him, but I didn't have anything I wanted to confess—even by silence.

"It happened that way," I said deliberately. "I played the cards so we would get the benefit of the breaks—but it just happened that way."

He nodded, smiling benignantly.

"I'm going to take a couple of weeks off," I said from the door.

I felt tired, washed out.

The Main Death

THE CAPTAIN told me Hacken and Begg were handling the job. I caught them leaving the detectives' assembly room. Begg was a freckled heavyweight, as friendly as a Saint Bernard puppy, but less intelligent. Lanky detective-sergeant Hacken, not so playful, carried the team's brains behind his worried hatchet face.

"In a hurry?" I inquired.

"Always in a hurry when we're quitting for the day," Begg said, his freckles climbing up his face to make room for his grin.

"What do you want?" Hacken asked.

"I want the low-down on the Main doings—if any."

"You going to work on it?"

"Yes," I said, "for Main's boss—Gungen."

"Then you can tell us something. Why'd he have the twenty thou in cash?"

"Tell you in the morning," I promised. "I haven't seen Gungen yet. Got a date with him tonight."

While we talked we had gone into the assembly room, with its school-room arrangement of desks and benches. Half a dozen police detectives were scattered among them, doing reports. We three sat around Hacken's desk and the lanky detective-sergeant talked:

"Main got home from Los Angeles at eight, Sunday night, with twenty thousand in his wallet. He'd gone down there to sell something for Gungen. You find out why he had that much in cash. He told his wife he had driven up from L.A. with a friend—no name. She went to bed around ten-thirty, leaving him reading. He had the money—two hundred hundred-dollar bills—in a brown wallet.

"So far, so good. He's in the living-room reading. She's in the bedroom sleeping. Just the two of them in the apartment. A racket wakes her. She jumps out of bed, runs into the living-room. There's Main wrestling with a couple of men. One's tall and husky. The other's little—kind of girlish built. Both have got black handkerchiefs over their mugs and caps pulled down.

636

"When Mrs. Main shows, the little one breaks away from Main and sticks her up. Puts a gun in Mrs. Main's face and tells her to behave. Main and the other guy are still scuffling. Main has got his gun in his hand, but the thug has him by the wrist, trying to twist it. He makes it pretty soon—Main drops the rod. The thug flashes his own, holding Main off while he bends down to pick up the one that fell.

"When the man stoops, Main piles on him. He manages to knock the fellow's gun out of his hand, but by that time the fellow had got the one on the floor—the one Main had dropped. They're heaped up there for a couple of seconds. Mrs. Main can't see what's happening. Then bang! Main's falling away, his vest burning where the shot had set fire to it, a bullet in his heart, his gun smoking in the masked guy's fist. Mrs. Main passes out.

"When she comes to there's nobody in the apartment but herself and her dead husband. His wallet's gone, and so is his gun. She was unconscious for about half an hour. We know that, because other people heard the shot and could give us the time—even if they didn't know where it came from.

"The Main's apartment is on the sixth floor. It's an eight-story building. Next door to it, on the corner of Eighteenth Avenue, is a two-story building grocery downstairs, grocer's flat upstairs. Behind these buildings runs a narrow back street —an alley. All right.

"Kinney—the patrolman on that beat—was walking down Eighteenth Avenue. He heard the shot. It was clear to him, because the Mains' apartment is on that side of the building—the side overlooking the grocer's—but Kinney couldn't place it right away. He wasted time scouting around up the street. By the time he got down as far as the alley in his hunting, the birds had flown. Kinney found signs of 'em though— they had dropped a gun in the alley—the gun they'd taken from Main and shot him with. But Kinney didn't see 'em— didn't see anybody who might have been them.

"Now, from a hall window of the apartment house's third floor to the roof of the grocer's building is easy going. Anybody but a cripple could make it—in or out—and the window's never locked. From the grocer's roof to the back street is almost as easy. There's a cast iron pipe, a deep window, a door with heavy hinges sticking out—a regular ladder up and down that back wall. Begg and I did it without working up a sweat. The pair could have gone in that way. We know they left that way. On the grocer's roof we found Main's wallet—empty, of course—and a handkerchief. The wallet had metal corners. The handkerchief had caught on one of 'em, and went with it when the crooks tossed it away."

"Main's handkerchief?"

"A woman's—with an E in one corner."

"Mrs. Main's?"

"Her name is Agnes," Hacken said. "We showed her the wallet, the gun, and the handkerchief. She identified the first two as her husband's, but the handkerchief was a new one on her. However, she could give us the name of the perfume on it—*Dèsir du Cœur*. And—with it for a guide—she said the smaller of the masked pair could have been a woman. She had already described him as kind of girlish built."

"Any fingerprints, or the like?" I asked.

"No. Phels went over the apartment, the window, the roof, the wallet and the gun. Not a smear."

"Mrs. Main identify 'em?"

"She says she'd know the little one. Maybe she would."

"Got anything on the who?"

"Not yet," the lanky detective-sergeant said as we moved toward the door.

In the street I left the police sleuths and set out for Bruno Gungen's home in Westwood Park.

The dealer in rare and antique jewelry was a little bit of a man and a fancy one. His dinner jacket was corset-tight around his waist, padded high and sharp at the shoulders. Hair, mustache and spade-shaped goatee were dyed black and greased until they were as shiny as his pointed pink fingernails. I wouldn't bet a cent that the color in his fifty-year-old cheeks wasn't rouge.

He came out of the depths of a leather library chair to give me a soft, warm hand that was no larger than a child's, bowing and smiling at me with his head tilted to one side.

Then he introduced me to his wife, who bowed without getting up from her seat at the table. Apparently she was a little more than a third of his age. She couldn't have been a day over nineteen, and she looked more like sixteen. She was as small as he, with a dimpled olive-skinned face, round brown eyes, a plump painted mouth and the general air of an expensive doll in a toy-store window.

Bruno Gungen explained to her at some length that I was connected with the Continental Detective Agency, and that he had employed me to help the police find Jeffrey Main's murderers and recover the stolen twenty thousand dollars.

She murmured, "Oh, yes!" in a tone that said she was not the least bit interested, and stood up, saying, "Then I'll leave you to—"

"No, no, my dear!" Her husband was waving his pink fingers at her. "I would have no secrets from you."

His ridiculous little face jerked around to me, cocked itself sidewise, and he asked, with a little giggle:

"Is not that so? That between husband and wife there should be no secrets?"

I pretended I agreed with him.

"You, I know, my dear," he addressed his wife, who had sat down again, "are as much interested in this as I, for did we not have an equal affection for dear Jeffrey? Is it not so?"

She repeated, "Oh, yes!" with the same lack of interest.

Her husband turned to me and said, "Now?" encouragingly.

"I've seen the police," I told him. "Is there anything you can add to their story? Anything new? Anything you didn't tell them?"

He whisked his face around toward his wife.

"Is there, Enid, dear?"

"I know of nothing," she replied.

He giggled and made a delighted face at me.

"That is it," he said. "We know of nothing."

"He came back to San Francisco eight o'clock Sunday night—three hours before he was killed and robbed—with twenty thousand dollars in hundred-dollar bills. What was he doing with it?"

"It was the proceeds of a sale to a customer," Bruno Gungen explained. "Mr. Nathaniel Ogilvie, of Los Angeles."

"But why cash?"

The little man's painted face screwed itself up into a shrewd leer.

"A bit of hanky-panky," he confessed complacently, "a trick of the trade, as one says. You know the genus collector? Ah, there is a study for you! Observe. I obtain a golden tiara of early Grecian workmanship, or let me be correct—purporting to be of early Grecian workmanship, purporting also to have been found in Southern Russia, near Odessa. Whether there is any truth in either of these suppositions I do not know, but certainly the tiara is a thing of beauty."

He giggled.

"Now I have a client, a Mr. Nathaniel Ogilvie, of Los Angeles, who has an appetite for curios of the sort—a very devil of a *cacoethes carpendi*. The value of these items, you will comprehend, is exactly what one can get for them—no more, little less. This tiara—now ten thousand dollars is the least I could have expected for it, if sold as one sells an ordinary article of the sort. But can one call a golden cap made long ago for some forgotten Scythian king an ordinary article of any sort? No! No! So, swaddled in cotton, intricately packed, Jeffrey carries this tiara to Los Angeles to show our Mr. Ogilvie.

"In what manner the tiara came into our hands Jeffrey will not say. But he will hint at devious intrigues, smuggling, a little of violence and lawlessness here and there, the necessity for secrecy. For your true collector, there is the bait! Nothing is anything to him except as it is difficultly come by. Jeffrey will not lie. No! *Mon Dieu*, that would be dishonest, despicable! But he will suggest much, and he will refuse, oh, so emphatically! to take a check for the tiara. No check, my dear sir! Nothing which may be traced! Cash moneys!

"Hanky-panky, as you see. But where is the harm? Mr. Ogilvie is certainly going to buy the tiara, and our little deceit simply heightens his pleasure in his purchase. He will enjoy its possession so much the more. Besides, who is to say that this tiara is not authentic? If it is, then these things Jeffrey suggests are indubitably true. Mr. Ogilvie does buy it, for twenty thousand dollars, and that is why poor Jeffrey had in his possession so much cash money."

He flourished a pink hand at me, nodded his dyed head vigorously, and finished with:

"*Voilà!* That is it!"

"Did you hear from Main after he got back?" I asked.

The dealer smiled as if my question tickled him, turning his head so that the smile was directed at his wife.

"Did we, Enid, darling?" he passed on the question.

She pouted and shrugged her shoulders indifferently.

"The first we knew he had returned," Gungen interpreted these gestures to me, "was Monday morning, when we heard of his death. Is it not so, my dove?"

His dove murmured, "Yes," and left her chair, saying, "You'll excuse me? I have a letter to write."

"Certainly, my dear," Gungen told her as he and I stood up.

She passed close to him on her way to the door. His small nose twitched over his dyed mustache and he rolled his eyes in a caricature of ecstasy.

"What a delightful scent, my precious!" he exclaimed. "What a heavenly odor! What a song to the nostrils! Has it a name, my love?"

"Yes," she said, pausing in the doorway, not looking back.

"And it is?"

"*Désir du Cœur,*" she replied over her shoulder as she left us.

Bruno Gungen looked at me and giggled.

I sat down again and asked him what he knew about Jeffrey Main.

"Everything, no less," he assured me. "For a dozen years, since he was a boy of eighteen he has been my right eye, my right hand."

"Well, what sort of man was he?"

Bruno Gungen showed me his pink palms side by side.

"What sort is any man?" he asked over them.

That didn't mean anything to me, so I kept quiet, waiting.

"I shall tell you," the little man began presently. "Jeffrey had the eye and the taste for this traffic of mine. No man living save myself alone has a judgment in these matters which I would prefer to Jeffrey's. And, honest, mind you! Let nothing I say mislead you on that point. Never a lock have I to which Jeffrey had not also the key, and might have it forever, if he had lived so long.

"But there is a but. In his private life, rascal is a word that only does him justice. He drank, he gambled, he loved, he spent—dear God, how he spent! He was, in this drinking and gaming and loving and spending, a most promiscuous fellow, beyond doubt. With moderation he had nothing to do. Of the moneys he got by inheritance, of the fifty thousand dollars or more his wife had when they were married, there is no remainder. Fortunately, he was well insured—else his wife would have been left penniless. Oh, he was a true Heliogabalus, that fellow!"

Bruno Gungen went down to the front door with me when I left. I said, "Good night," and walked down the gravel path to where I had left my car. The night was clear, dark, moonless. High hedges were black walls on both sides of the Gungen place. To the left there was a barely noticeable hole in the blackness—a dark-gray hole—oval—the size of a face.

I got into my car, stirred up the engine and drove away. Into the first cross-street I turned, parked the machine, and started back toward Gungen's afoot. I was curious about that face-size oval.

When I reached the corner, I saw a woman coming toward me from the direction of Gungen's. I was in the shadow of a wall. Cautiously, I backed away from the corner until I came to a gate with brick buttresses sticking out. I made myself flat between them.

The woman crossed the street, went on up the driveway, toward the car-line. I couldn't make out anything about her, except that she was a woman. Maybe she was coming from Gungen's grounds, maybe not. Maybe it was her face I had seen against the hedge, maybe not. It was a heads or tails proposition. I guessed yes and tailed her up the drive.

Her destination was a drugstore on the car line. Her business there was with the telephone. She spent ten minutes at it. I didn't go into the store to try for an earful, but stayed on the other side of the street, contenting myself with a good look at her.

She was a girl of about twenty-five, medium in height, chunky in build, with pale gray eyes that had little pouches under them, a thick nose and a prominent lower lip. She had no hat over her brown hair. Her body was wrapped in a long blue cape.

From the drug store I shadowed her back to the Gungen house. She went in the back door. A servant, probably, but not the maid who had opened the door for me earlier in the evening.

I returned to my car, drove back to town, to the office.

"Is Dick Foley working on anything?" I asked Fiske, who sits on the Continental Detective Agency's affairs at night.

"No. Did you ever hear the story about the fellow who had his neck operated on?"

With the slightest encouragement, Fiske is good for a dozen stories without a stop, so I said:

"Yes. Get hold of Dick and tell him I've got a shadow job out Westwood Park way for him to start on in the morning."

I gave Fiske—to be passed on to Dick—Gungen's address and a description of the girl who had done the phoning from the drugstore. Then I assured the night man that I had also heard the story about the pickaninny named Opium, and likewise the one about what the old man said to his wife on their golden wedding anniversary. Before he could try me with another, I escaped to my own office, where I composed and coded a telegram to our Los Angeles branch, asking that Main's recent visit to that city be dug into.

The next morning Hacken and Begg dropped in to see me and I gave them Gungen's version of why the twenty thousand had been in cash. The police detectives told me a stool-pigeon had brought them word that Bunky Dahl—a local guerrilla who did a moderate business in hijacking—had been flashing a roll since about the time of Main's death.

"We haven't picked him up yet," Hacken said. "Haven't been able to place him, but we've got a line on his girl. Course, he might have got his dough somewhere else."

At ten o'clock that morning I had to go over to Oakland to testify against a couple of flimflammers who had sold bushels of stock in a sleight-of-hand rubber manufacturing business. When I got back to the Agency, at six that evening, I found a wire from Los Angeles on my desk.

Jeffrey Main, the wire told me, had finished his business with Ogilvie Saturday afternoon, had checked out of his hotel immediately, and had left on the Owl that evening, which would have put him in San Francisco early Sunday morning. The hundred-dollar bills with which Ogilvie had paid for the tiara had been new ones, consecutively numbered, and Ogilvie's bank had given the Los Angeles operative the numbers.

Before I quit for the day, I phoned Hacken, gave him these numbers, as well as the other dope in the telegram.

"Haven't found Dahl yet," he told me.

Dick Foley's report came in the next morning. The girl had left the Gungen house at 9:15 the previous night, had gone to the corner of Miramar Avenue and Southwood Drive, where a man was waiting for her in a Buick coupe. Dick described him: Age about 30; height about five feet ten; slender, weight about 140; medium complexion; brown hair and eyes; long, thin face with pointed chin; brown hat, suit and shoes and gray overcoat.

The girl got into the car with him and they drove out to the beach, along the Great Highway for a little while, and then back to Miramar and Southwood, where the girl got out. She seemed to be going back to the house, so Dick let her go and tailed the man in the Buick down to the Futurity Apartments in Mason Street.

The man stayed in there for half an hour or so and then came out with another man and two women. This second man was of about the same age as the first, about five feet eight inches tall, would weigh about a hundred and seventy pounds, had brown hair and eyes, a dark complexion, a flat, broad face with high cheek bones, and wore a blue suit, gray hat, tan overcoat, black shoes, and a pear-shaped pearl tie-pin.

One of the women was about twenty-two years old, small, slender and blonde. The other was probably three or four years older, red-haired, medium in height and build, with a turned-up nose.

The quartet had got in the car and gone to the Algerian Café, where they had stayed until a little after one in the morning. Then they had returned to the Futurity Apartments. At half-past three the two men had left, driving the Buick to a garage in Post Street, and then walking to the Mars Hotel.

When I had finished reading this I called Mickey Linehan in from the operatives' room, gave him the report and instructions:

"Find out who these folks are."

Mickey went out. My phone rang.

Bruno Gungen: "Good morning. May you have something to tell me today?"

"Maybe," I said. "You're downtown?"

"Yes, in my shop. I shall be here until four."

"Right. I'll be in to see you this afternoon."

At noon Mickey Linehan returned. "The first bloke," he reported, "the one Dick saw with the girl, is named Benjamin Weel. He owns the Buick and lives in the Mars—room 410. He's a salesman, though it's not known what of. The other man is a friend of his who has been staying with him for a couple of days. I couldn't get anything on him. He's not registered. The two women in the Futurity are a couple of hustlers. They live in apartment 303. The larger one goes by the name of Mrs. Effie Roberts. The little blonde is Violet Evarts."

"Wait," I told Mickey, and went back into the file room, to the index-card drawers.

I ran through the W's—*Weel, Benjamin, alias Coughing Ben, 36,312 W.*

The contents of folder No. 36,312W told me that Coughing Ben Weel had been arrested in Amador County in 1916 on a highgrading charge and had been sent to San Quentin for three years. In 1922 he had been picked up again in Los Angeles and charged with trying to blackmail a movie actress, but the case had fallen through. His description fit the one Dick had given of the man in the Buick. His photograph—a copy of the one taken by the Los Angeles police in '22—showed a sharp-featured young man with a chin like a wedge.

I took the photo back to my office and showed it to Mickey.

"This is Weel five years ago. Follow him around a while."

When the operative had gone I called the police detective bureau. Neither Hacken nor Begg was in. I got hold of Lewis, in the identification department.

"What does Bunky Dahl look like?" I asked him.

"Wait a minute," Lewis said, and then: "32, 67½, 174, medium, brown, brown, broad flat face with prominent cheek-bones, gold bridge work in lower left jaw, brown mole under right ear, deformed little toe on right foot."

"Have you a picture of him to spare?"

"Sure."

"Thanks, I'll send a boy down for it."

I told Tommy Howd to go down and get it, and then went out for some food. After luncheon I went up to Gungen's establishment in Post Street. The little dealer was gaudier than ever this afternoon in a black coat that was even more padded in the shoulders and tighter in the waist than his dinner coat had been the other night, striped gray pants, a vest that leaned toward magenta, and a billowy satin tie wonderfully embroidered with gold thread.

We went back through his store, up a narrow flight of stairs to a small cube of an office on the mezzanine floor.

"And now you have to tell me?" he asked when we were seated, with the door closed.

"I've got more to ask than tell. First, who is the girl with the thick nose, the thick lower lip, and the pouches under grey eyes, who lives in your house?"

"That is one Rose Rubury." His little painted face was wrinkled in a satisfied smile. "She is my dear wife's maid."

"She goes riding with an ex-convict."

"She does?" He stroked his dyed goatee with a pink hand, highly pleased. "Well, she is my dear wife's maid, that she is."

"Main didn't drive up from Los Angeles with a friend, as he told his wife. He came up on the train Saturday night—so he was in town twelve hours before he showed up at home."

Bruno Gungen giggled, cocking his delighted face to one side.

"Ah!" he tittered. "We progress! We progress! Is it not so?"

"Maybe. Do you remember if this Rose Rubury was in the house on Sunday night—say from eleven to twelve?"

"I do remember. She was. I know it certainly. My dear wife was not feeling well that night. My darling had gone out early that Sunday morning, saying she was going to drive out into the country with some friends—what friends I do not know.

But she came home at eight o'clock that night complaining of a distressing headache. I was quite frightened by her appearance, so that I went often to see how she was, and thus it happens that I know her maid was in the house all of that night, until one o'clock, at least."

"Did the police show you the handkerchief they found with Main's wallet?"

"Yes." He squirmed on the edge of his chair, his face like the face of a kid looking at a Christmas tree.

"You're sure it's your wife's?"

His giggle interfered with his speech, so he said, "Yes," by shaking his head up and down until the goatee seemed to be a black whiskbroom brushing his tie.

"She could have left it at the Mains' some time when she was visiting Mrs. Main," I suggested.

"That is not possible," he corrected me eagerly. "My darling and Mrs. Main are not acquainted."

"But your wife and Main were acquainted?"

He giggled and brushed his tie with his whisker again.

"How well acquainted?"

He shrugged his padded shoulders up to his ears.

"I know not," he said merrily. "I employ a detective."

"Yeah?" I scowled at him. "You employ this one to find out who killed and robbed Main—and for nothing else. If you think you're employing him to dig up your family secrets, you're as wrong as Prohibition."

"But why? But why?" He was flustered. "Have I not the right to know? There will be no trouble over it, no scandal, no divorce suing, of that be assured. Even Jeffrey is dead, so it is what one calls ancient history. While he lived I knew nothing, was blind. After he died I saw certain things. For my own satisfaction—that is all, I beg you to believe—I should like to know with certainty."

"You won't get it out of me," I said bluntly. "I don't know anything about it except what you've told me, and you can't hire me to go further into it. Besides, if you're not going to do anything about it, why don't you keep your hands off—let it sleep?"

"No, no, my friend." He had recovered his bright-eyed cheerfulness. "I am not an old man, but I am fifty-two. My dear wife is eighteen, and a truly lovely person." He giggled. "This thing happened. May it not happen again? And would it not be the part of husbandly wisdom to have—shall I say— a hold on her? A rein? A check? Or if it never happen again, still might not one's dear wife be the more docile for certain information which her husband possesses?"

"It's your business." I stood up, laughing. "But I don't want any part of it."

"Ah, do not let us quarrel!" He jumped up and took one of my hands in his. "If you will not, you will not. But there remains the criminal aspect of the situation—the aspect that has engaged you thus far. You will not forsake that? You will fulfil your engagement there? Surely?"

"Suppose—just suppose—it should turn out that your wife had a hand in Main's death. What then?"

"That"—he shrugged, holding his hands out, palms up— "would be a matter for the law."

"Good enough. I'll stick—if you understand that you're entitled to no information except what touches your 'criminal aspect.' "

"Excellent! And if it so happens you cannot separate my darling from that—"

I nodded. He grabbed my hand again, patting it. I took it away from him and returned to the Agency.

A memorandum on my desk asked me to phone detective-sergeant Hacken. I did.

"Bunky Dahl wasn't in on the Main job," the hatchet-faced man told me. "He and a pal named Coughing Ben Weel were putting on a party in a roadhouse near Vallejo that night. They were there from around ten until they were thrown out after two in the morning for starting a row. It's on the up-and-up. The guy that gave it to me is right—and I got a check-up on it from two others."

I thanked Hacken and phoned Gungen's residence, asking for Mrs. Gungen, asking her if she would see me if I came out there.

"Oh, yes," she said. It seemed to be her favorite expression, though the way she said it didn't express anything.

Putting the photos of Dahl and Weel in my pocket, I got a taxi and set out for Westwood Park. Using Fatima-smoke on my brains while I rode, I concocted a wonderful series of lies to be told my client's wife—a series that I thought would get me the information I wanted.

A hundred and fifty yards or so up the drive from the house I saw Dick Foley's car standing.

A thin, pasty-faced maid opened the Gungens' door and took me into a sitting room on the second floor, where Mrs. Gungen put down a copy of *The Sun Also Rises* and waved a cigarette at a nearby chair. She was very much the expensive doll this afternoon in a Persian orange dress, sitting with one foot tucked under her in a brocaded chair.

Looking at her while I lighted a cigarette, remembering my first interview with her and her husband, and my second one with him, I decided to chuck the tale-of-woe I had spent my ride building.

"You've a maid—Rose Rubury," I began. "I don't want her to hear what's said."

She said, "Very well," without the least sign of surprise, added, "Excuse me a moment," and left her chair and the room.

Presently she was back, sitting down with both feet tucked under her now.

"She will be away for at least half an hour."

"That will be long enough. This Rose is friendly with an ex-convict named Weel."

The doll face frowned, and the plump painted lips pressed themselves together. I waited, giving her time to say something. She didn't say it. I took Weel's and Dahl's pictures out and held them out to her.

"The thin-faced one is your Rose's friend. The other's a pal of his—also a crook."

She took the photographs with a tiny hand that was as steady as mine, and looked at them carefully. Her mouth became smaller and tighter, her brown eyes darker. Then, slowly, her face cleared, she murmured, "Oh, yes," and returned the pictures to me.

"When I told your husband about it"—I spoke deliberately—"he said, 'She's my wife's maid,' and laughed."

Enid Gungen said nothing.

"Well?" I asked. "What did he mean by that?"

"How should I know?" she sighed.

"You know your handkerchief was found with Main's empty wallet." I dropped this in a by-the-way tone, pretending to be chiefly occupied putting cigarette ash in a jasper tray that was carved in the form of a lidless coffin.

"Oh, yes," she said wearily, "I've been told that."

"How do you think it happened?"

"I can't imagine."

"I can," I said, "but I'd rather know positively. Mrs. Gungen, it would save a lot of time if we could talk plain language."

"Why not?" she asked listlessly. "You are in my husband's confidence, have his permission to question me. If it happens to be humiliating to me—well, after all, I am only his wife. And it is hardly likely that any new indignities either of you can devise will be worse than those to which I have already submitted."

I grunted at this theatrical speech and went ahead.

"Mrs. Gungen, I'm only interested in learning who robbed and killed Main. Anything that points in that direction is valuable to me, but only in so far as it points in that direction. Do you understand what I mean?"

"Certainly," she said. "I understand you are in my husband's employ."

That got us nowhere. I tried again:

"What impression do you suppose I got the other evening, when I was here?"

"I can't imagine."

"Please try."

"Doubtless"—she smiled faintly—"you got the impression that my husband thought I had been Jeffrey's mistress."

"Well?"

"Are you"—her dimples showed; she seemed amused—"asking me if I really was his mistress?"

"No—though of course I'd like to know."

"Naturally you would," she said pleasantly.

"What impression did you get that evening?" I asked.

"I?" She wrinkled her forehead. "Oh, that my husband had hired you to prove that I had been Jeffrey's mistress." She repeated the word mistress as if she liked the shape of it in her mouth.

"You were wrong."

"Knowing my husband, I find that hard to believe."

"Knowing myself, I'm sure of it," I insisted. "There's no uncertainty about it between your husband and me, Mrs. Gungen. It is understood that my job is to find who stole and killed—nothing else."

"Really?" It was a polite ending of an argument of which she had grown tired.

"You're tying my hands," I complained, standing up, pretending I wasn't watching her carefully. "I can't do anything now but grab this Rose Rubury and the two men and see what I can squeeze out of them. You said the girl would be back in half an hour?"

She looked at me steadily with her round brown eyes.

"She should be back in a few minutes. You're going to question her?"

"But not here," I informed her. "I'll take her down to the Hall of Justice and have the men picked up. Can I use your phone?"

"Certainly. It's in the next room." She crossed to open the door for me.

I called Davenport 20 and asked for the detective bureau.

Mrs. Gungen, standing in the sitting room, said, so softly I could barely hear it:

"Wait."

Holding the phone, I turned to look through the door at her. She was pinching her red mouth between thumb and finger, frowning. I didn't put down the phone until she took the hand from her mouth and held it out toward me. Then I went back into the sitting-room.

I was on top. I kept my mouth shut. It was up to her to make the plunge. She studied my face for a minute or more before she began:

"I won't pretend I trust you." She spoke hesitantly, half as if to herself, "You're working for my husband, and even the money would not interest him so much as whatever I had done. It's a choice of evils—certain on the one hand, more than probable on the other."

She stopped talking and rubbed her hands together. Her round eyes were becoming indecisive. If she wasn't helped along she was going to balk.

"There's only the two of us," I urged her. "You can deny everything afterward. It's my word against yours. If you don't tell me—I know now I can get it from the others. Your calling me from the phone lets me know that. You think I'll tell your husband everything. Well, if I have to fry it out of the others, he'll probably read it all in the papers. Your one chance is to trust me. It's not as slim a chance as you think. Anyway, it's up to you."

A half-minute of silence.

"Suppose," she whispered, "I should pay you to——"

"What for? If I'm going to tell your husband, I could take your money and still tell him, couldn't I?"

Her red mouth curved, her dimples appeared and her eyes brightened.

"That is reassuring," she said. "I shall tell you. Jeffrey came back from Los Angeles early so we could have the day together in a little apartment we kept. In the afternoon two men came in—with a key. They had revolvers. They robbed Jeffrey of the money. That was what they had come for. They seemed to know all about it and about us. They called us by name, and taunted us with threats of the story they would tell if we had them arrested.

"We couldn't do anything after they had gone. It was a ridiculously hopeless plight they had put us in. There wasn't anything we could do—since we couldn't possibly replace the money. Jeffrey couldn't even pretend he had lost it or had been robbed of it while he was alone. His secret early return to San Francisco would have been sure to throw suspicion on him. Jeffrey lost his head. He wanted me to run away with him. Then he wanted to go to my husband and tell him the truth. I wouldn't permit either course—they were equally foolish.

"We left the apartment, separating, a little after seven. We weren't, the truth is, on the best of terms by then. He wasn't—now that we were in trouble—as—— No, I shouldn't say that."

She stopped and stood looking at me with a placid doll's face that seemed to have got rid of all its troubles by simply passing them to me.

"The pictures I showed you are the two men?" I asked.

"Yes."

"This maid of yours knew about you and Main? Knew about the apartment? Knew about his trip to Los Angeles and his plan to return early with the cash?"

"I can't say she did. But she certainly could have learned most of it by spying and eavesdropping and looking through my— I had a note from Jeffrey telling me about the Los Angeles trip, making the appointment for Sunday morning. Perhaps she could have seen it. I'm careless."

"I'm going now," I said. "Sit tight till you hear from me. And don't scare up the maid."

"Remember, I've told you nothing," she reminded me as she followed me to the sitting-room door.

From the Gungen house I went direct to the Mars Hotel. Mickey Linehan was sitting behind a newspaper in a corner of the lobby.

"They in?" I asked him.

"Yep."

"Let's go up and see them."

Mickey rattled his knuckles on door number 410. A metallic voice asked: "Who's there?"

"Package," Mickey replied in what was meant for a boy's voice.

A slender man with a pointed chin opened the door. I gave him a card. He didn't invite us into the room, but he didn't try to keep us out when we walked in.

"You're Weel?" I addressed him while Mickey closed the door behind us, and then, not waiting for him to say yes, I turned to the broad-faced man sitting on the bed. "And you're Dahl?"

Weel spoke to Dahl, in a casual, metallic voice:

"A couple of gum-shoes."

The man on the bed looked at us and grinned.

I was in a hurry.

"I want the dough you took from Main," I announced.

They sneered together, as if they had been practicing.

I brought out my gun.

Weel laughed harshly.

"Get your hat, Bunky," he chuckled. "We're being taken into custody."

"You've got the wrong idea," I explained. "This isn't a pinch. It's a stick-up. Up go the hands!"

Dahl's hands went up quick. Weel hesitated until Mickey prodded him in the ribs with the nose of a .38-special.

"Frisk 'em," I ordered Mickey.

He went through Weel's clothes, taking a gun, some papers, some loose money, and a money-belt that was fat. Then he did the same for Dahl.

"Count it," I told him.

Mickey emptied the belts, spit on his fingers and went to work.

"Nineteen thousand, one hundred and twenty-six dollars and sixty-two cents," he reported when he was through.

With the hand that didn't hold my gun, I felt in my pocket for the slip on which I had written the numbers of the hundred-dollar bills Main had got from Ogilvie. I held the slip out to Mickey.

"See if the hundreds check against this."

He took the slip, looked, said, "They do."

"Good—pouch the money and the guns and see if you can turn up any more in the room."

Coughing Ben Weel had got his breath by now.

"Look here!" he protested. "You can't pull this, fellow! Where do you think you are? You can't get away with this!"

"I can try," I assured him. "I suppose you're going to yell, *Police!* Like hell you are! The only squawk you've got coming is at your own dumbness in thinking because your squeeze on the woman was tight enough to keep her from having you copped, you didn't have to worry about anything. I'm playing the same game you played with her and Main—only mine's better, because you can't get tough afterward without facing stir. Now shut up!"

"No more jack," Mickey said. "Nothing but four postage stamps."

"Take 'em along," I told him. "That's practically eight cents. Now we'll go."

"Hey, leave us a couple of bucks," Weel begged.

"Didn't I tell you to shut up?" I snarled at him, backing to the door, which Mickey was opening.

The hall was empty. Mickey stood in it, holding his gun on Weel and Dahl while I backed out of the room and switched the key from the inside to the outside. Then I slammed the door, twisted the key, pocketed it, and we went downstairs and out of the hotel.

Mickey's car was around the corner. In it, we transferred our spoils—except the guns—from his pockets to mine. Then he got out and went back to the Agency. I turned the car toward the building in which Jeffrey Main had been killed.

Mrs. Main was a tall girl of less than twenty-five, with curled brown hair, heavily-lashed gray-blue eyes, and a warm, full-featured face. Her ample body was dressed in black from throat to feet.

She read my card, nodded at my explanation that Gungen had employed me to look into her husband's death, and took me into a gray and white living room.

"This is the room?" I asked.

"Yes." She had a pleasant, slightly husky voice.

I crossed to the window and looked down on the grocer's roof, and on the half of the back street that was visible. I was still in a hurry.

"Mrs. Main," I said as I turned, trying to soften the abruptness of my words by keeping my voice low, "after your husband was dead, you threw the gun out the window. Then you stuck the handkerchief to the corner of the wallet and threw that. Being lighter than the gun, it didn't go all the way to the alley, but fell on the roof. Why did you put the hand-kerchief——?"

Without a sound she fainted.

I caught her before she reached the floor, carried her to a sofa, found Cologne and smelling salts, applied them.

"Do you know whose handkerchief it was?" I asked when she was awake and sitting up.

She shook her head from left to right.

"Then why did you take that trouble?"

"It was in his pocket. I didn't know what else to do with it. I thought the police would ask about it. I didn't want anything to start them asking questions."

"Why did you tell the robbery story?"

No answer.

"The insurance?" I suggested.

She jerked up her head, cried defiantly:

"Yes! He had gone through his own money and mine. And then he had to—to do a thing like that. He——"

I interrupted her complaint:

"He left a note, I hope—something that will be evidence." Evidence that she hadn't killed him, I meant.

"Yes." She fumbled in the bosom of her black dress.

"Good," I said, standing. "The first thing in the morning, take that note down to your lawyer and tell him the whole story."

I mumbled something sympathetic and made my escape.

Night was coming down when I rang the Gungens' bell for the second time that day. The pasty-faced maid who opened the door told me Mr. Gungen was at home. She led me upstairs.

Rose Rubury was coming down the stairs. She stopped on the landing to let us pass. I halted in front of her while my guide went on toward the library.

"You're done, Rose," I told the girl on the landing. "I'll give you ten minutes to clear out. No word to anybody. If you don't like that—you'll get a chance to see if you like the inside of the can."

"Well—the idea!"

"The racket's flopped." I put a hand into a pocket and showed her one wad of the money I had got at the Mars Hotel. "I've just come from visiting Coughing Ben and Bunky."

That impressed her. She turned and scurried up the stairs.

Bruno Gungen came to the library door, searching for me. He looked curiously from the girl—now running up the steps to the third story—to me. A question was twisting the little man's lips, but I headed it off with a statement:

"It's done."

"Bravo!" he exclaimed as we went into the library. "You hear that, my darling? It is done!"

His darling, sitting by the table, where she had sat the other night, smiled with no expression in her doll's face, and murmured, "Oh, yes," with no expression in her words.

I went to the table and emptied my pockets of money.

"Nineteen thousand, one hundred and twenty-six dollars and seventy cents, including the stamps," I announced. "The other eight hundred and seventy-three dollars and thirty cents is gone."

"Ah!" Bruno Gungen stroked his spade-shaped black beard with a trembling pink hand and pried into my face with hard bright eyes. "And where did you find it? By all means sit down and tell us the tale. We are famished with eagerness for it, eh, my love?"

His love yawned, "Oh, yes!"

"There isn't much story," I said. "To recover the money I had to make a bargain, promising silence. Main was robbed Sunday afternoon. But it happens that we couldn't convict the robbers if we had them. The only person who could identify them—won't."

"But who killed Jeffrey?" The little man was pawing my chest with both pink hands. "Who killed him that night?"

"Suicide. Despair at being robbed under circumstances he couldn't explain."

"Preposterous!" My client didn't like the suicide.

"Mrs. Main was awakened by the shot. Suicide would have canceled his insurance—would have left her penniless. She threw the gun and wallet out the window, hid the note he left, and framed the robber story."

"But the handkerchief!" Gungen screamed. He was all worked up.

"That doesn't mean anything," I assured him solemnly, "except that Main—you said he was promiscuous—had probably been fooling with your wife's maid, and that she—like a lot of maids—helped herself to your wife's belongings."

He puffed up his rouged cheeks, and stamped his feet, fairly dancing. His indignation was as funny as the statement that caused it.

"We shall see!" He spun on his heel and ran out of the room, repeating over and over, "We shall see!"

Enid Gungen held a hand out to me. Her doll face was all curves and dimples.

"I thank you," she whispered.

"I don't know what for," I growled, not taking the hand. "I've got it jumbled so anything like proof is out of the question. But he can't help knowing—didn't I practically tell him?"

"Oh, that!" She put it behind her with a toss of her small head. "I'm quite able to look out for myself so long as he has no definite proof."

I believed her.

Bruno Gungen came fluttering back into the library, frothing at the mouth, tearing his dyed goatee, raging that Rose Rubury was not to be found in the house.

The next morning Dick Foley told me the maid had joined Weel and Dahl and had left for Portland with them.

This King Business

THE TRAIN from Belgrade set me down in Stefania, capital of Muravia, in early afternoon—a rotten afternoon. Cold wind blew cold rain in my face and down my neck as I left the square granite barn of a railroad station to climb into a taxicab.

English meant nothing to the chauffeur, nor French. Good German might have failed. Mine wasn't good. It was a hodgepodge of grunts and gargles. This chauffeur was the first person who had ever pretended to understand it. I suspected him of guessing, and I expected to be taken to some distant suburban point. Maybe he was a good guesser. Anyhow, he took me to the Hotel of the Republic.

The hotel was a new six-story affair, very proud of its elevators, American plumbing, private baths, and other modern tricks. After I had washed and changed clothes I went down to the café for luncheon. Then, supplied with minute instructions in English, French, and sign-language by a highly uniformed head porter, I turned up my raincoat collar and crossed the muddy plaza to call on Roy Scanlan, United States *chargé d'affaires* in this youngest and smallest of the Balkan States.

He was a pudgy man of thirty, with smooth hair already far along the gray route, a nervous, flabby face, plump white hands that twitched, and very nice clothes. He shook hands with me, patted me into a chair, barely glanced at my letter of introduction, and stared at my necktie while saying:

"So you're a private detective from San Francisco?"

"Yes."

"And?"

"Lionel Grantham."

"Surely not!"

"Yes."

"But he's—" The diplomat realized he was looking into my eyes, hurriedly switched his gaze to my hair, and forgot what he had started to say.

"But he's what?" I prodded him.

659

"Oh!"—with a vague upward motion of head and eyebrows—"not that sort."

"How long has he been here?" I asked.

"Two months. Possibly three or three and a half."

"You know him well?"

"Oh, no! By sight, of course, and to talk to. He and I are the only Americans here, so we're fairly well acquainted."

"Know what he's doing here?"

"No, I don't. He just happened to stop here in his travels, I imagine, unless, of course, he's here for some special reason. No doubt there's a girl in it—she is General Radnjak's daughter—though I don't think so."

"How does he spend his time?"

"I really haven't any idea. He lives at the Hotel of the Republic, is quite a favorite among our foreign colony, rides a bit, lives the usual life of a young man of family and wealth."

"Mixed up with anybody who isn't all he ought to be?"

"Not that I know of, except that I've seen him with Mahmoud and Einarson. They are certainly scoundrels, though they may not be."

"Who are they?"

"Nubar Mahmoud is private secretary to Doctor Semich, the President. Colonel Einarson is an Icelander, just now virtually the head of the army. I know nothing about either of them."

"Except that they are scoundrels?"

The *chargé d'affaires* wrinkled his round white forehead in pain and gave me a reproachful glance.

"Not at all," he said. "Now, may I ask, of what is Grantham suspected?"

"Nothing."

"Then?"

"Seven months ago, on his twenty-first birthday, this Lionel Grantham got hold of the money his father had left him—a nice wad. Till then the boy had had a tough time of it. His mother had, and has, highly developed middle-class notions of refinement. His father had been a genuine aristocrat in the old manner—a hard-souled, soft-spoken individual who got what he wanted by simply taking it; with a liking for old wine and young women, and plenty of both, and for cards and dice and running horses—and fights, whether he was in them or watching them.

"While he lived the boy had a he-raising. Mrs. Grantham thought her husband's tastes low, but he was a man who had things his own way. Besides, the Grantham blood was the best in America. She was a woman to be impressed by that. Eleven years ago—when Lionel was a kid of ten—the old man died. Mrs. Grantham swapped the family roulette wheel for a box of dominoes and began to convert the kid into a patent-leather Galahad.

"I've never seen him, but I'm told the job wasn't a success. However, she kept him bundled up for eleven years, not even letting him escape to college. So it went until the day when he was legally of age and in possession of his share of his father's estate. That morning he kisses Mamma and tells her casually that he's off for a little run around the world—alone. Mamma does and says all that might be expected of her, but it's no good. The Grantham blood is up. Lionel promises to drop her a postcard now and then, and departs.

"He seems to have behaved fairly well during his wandering. I suppose just being free gave him all the excitement he needed. But a few weeks ago the Trust Company that handles his affairs got instructions from him to turn some railroad bonds into cash and ship the money to him in care of a Belgrade bank. The amount was large—over the three million mark—so the Trust Company told Mrs. Grantham about it. She chucked a fit. She had been getting letters from him— from Paris, without a word said about Belgrade.

"Mamma was all for dashing over to Europe at once. Her brother, Senator Walbourn, talked her out of it. He did some cabling, and learned that Lionel was neither in Paris nor in Belgrade, unless he was hiding. Mrs. Grantham packed her trunks and made reservations. The Senator headed her off again, convincing her that the lad would resent her interference, telling her the best thing was to investigate on the quiet. He brought the job to the Agency. I went to Paris, learned that a friend of Lionel's there was relaying his mail, and that Lionel was here in Stefania. On the way down I stopped off in Belgrade and learned that the money was being sent here to him—most of it already has been. So here I am."

Scanlan smiled happily.

"There's nothing I can do," he said. "Grantham is of age, and it's his money."

"Right," I agreed, "and I'm in the same fix. All I can do is poke around, find out what he's up to, try to save his dough if he's being gypped. Can't you give me even a guess at the answer? Three million dollars—what could he put it into?"

"I don't know." The *chargé d'affaires* fidgeted uncomfortably. "There's no business here that amounts to anything. It's purely an agricultural country, split up among small landowners—ten, fifteen, twenty acre farms. There's his association with Einarson and Mahmoud, though. They'd certainly rob him if they got the chance. I'm positive they're robbing him. But I don't think they would. Perhaps he isn't acquainted with them. It's probably a woman."

"Well, whom should I see? I'm handicapped by not knowing the country, not knowing the language. To whom can I take my story and get help?"

"I don't know," he said gloomily. Then his face brightened. "Go to Vasilije Djudakovich. He is Minister of Police. He is the man for you! He can help you, and you may trust him. He has a digestion instead of a brain. He'll not understand a thing you tell him. Yes, Djudakovich is your man!"

"Thanks," I said, and staggered out into the muddy street.

I found the Minister of Police's offices in the Administration Building, a gloomy concrete pile next to the Executive Residence at the head of the plaza. In French that was even worse than my German, a thin, white-whiskered clerk, who looked like a consumptive Santa Claus, told me His Excellency was not in. Looking solemn, lowering my voice to a whisper, I repeated that I had come from the United States *chargé d'affaires*. This hocus-pocus seemed to impress Saint Nicholas. He nodded understandingly and shuffled out of the room. Presently he was back, bowing at the door, asking me to follow him.

I tailed him along a dim corridor to a wide door marked "15." He opened it, bowed me through it, wheezed, "*Asseyez-vous, s'il vous plaît,*" closed the door and left me. I was in an office, a large, square one. Everything in it was large. The

four windows were double-size. The chairs were young
benches, except the leather one at the desk, which could have
been the rear half of a touring car. A couple of men could
have slept on the desk. Twenty could have eaten at the table.

A door opposite the one through which I had come
opened, and a girl came in, closing the door behind her, shutting out a throbbing purr, as of some heavy machine, that had
sounded through.

"I'm Romaine Frankl," she said in English, "His Excellency's secretary. Will you tell me what you wish?"

She might have been any age from twenty to thirty, something less than five feet in height, slim without boniness, with
curly hair as near black as brown can get, black-lashed eyes
whose gray irises had black rims, a small, delicate-featured
face, and a voice that seemed too soft and faint to carry as
well as it did. She wore a red woolen dress that had no shape
except that which her body gave it, and when she moved—to
walk or raise a hand—it was as if it cost her no energy—as if
someone else were moving her.

"I'd like to see him," I said while I was accumulating this
data.

"Later, certainly," she promised, "but it's impossible now."
She turned, with her peculiar effortless grace, back to the
door, opening it so that the throbbing purr sounded in the
room again. "Hear?" she said. "He's taking his nap."

She shut the door against His Excellency's snoring and
floated across the room to climb up in the immense leather
chair at the desk.

"Do sit down," she said, wriggling a tiny forefinger at a
chair beside the desk. "It will save time if you will tell me your
business, because, unless you speak our tongue, I'll have to
interpret your message to His Excellency."

I told her about Lionel Grantham and my interest in him,
in practically the same words I had used on Scanlan, winding
up:

"You see, there's nothing I can do except try to learn what
the boy's up to and give him a hand if he needs it. I can't go
to him—he's too much Grantham, I'm afraid, to take kindly
to what he'd think was nursemaid stuff. Mr. Scanlan advised
me to come to the Minister of Police for help."

"You were fortunate." She looked as if she wanted to make a joke about my country's representative but weren't sure how I'd take it. "Your *chargé d'affaires* is not always easy to understand."

"Once you get the hang of it, it's not hard," I said. "You just throw out all his statements that have *no's* or *not's* or *nothing's* or *don't's* in them."

"That's it! That's it, exactly!" She leaned toward me, laughing. "I've always known there was some key to it, but nobody's been able to find it before. You've solved our national problem."

"For reward, then, I should be given all the information you have about Grantham."

"You should, but I'll have to speak to His Excellency first."

"You can tell me unofficially what you think of Grantham. You know him?"

"Yes. He's charming. A nice boy, delightfully naive, inexperienced, but really charming."

"Who are his friends here?"

She shook her head and said:

"No more of that until His Excellency wakes. You're from San Francisco? I remember the funny little street cars, and the fog, and the salad right after the soup, and Coffee Dan's."

"You've been there?"

"Twice. I was in the United States for a year and a half, in vaudeville, bringing rabbits out of hats."

We were still talking about that half an hour later when the door opened and the Minister of Police came in.

The oversize furniture immediately shrank to normal, the girl became a midget, and I felt like somebody's little boy.

This Vasilije Djudakovich stood nearly seven feet tall, and that was nothing to his girth. Maybe he wouldn't weigh more than five hundred pounds, but, looking at him, it was hard to think except in terms of tons. He was a blond-haired, blond-bearded mountain of meat in a black frock coat. He wore a necktie, so I suppose he had a collar, but it was hidden all the way around by the red rolls of his neck. His white vest was the size and shape of a hoop-skirt, and in spite of that it strained at the buttons. His eyes were almost invisible between the cushions of flesh around them, and were shaded into a colorless darkness, like water in a deep well. His mouth was a fat red oval among the yellow hairs of his whiskers and mustache. He came into the room slowly, ponderously, and I was surprised that the floor didn't creak.

Romaine Frankl was watching me attentively as she slid out of the big leather chair and introduced me to the Minister. He gave me a fat, sleepy smile and a hand that had the general appearance of a naked baby, and let himself down slowly into the chair the girl had quit. Planted there, he lowered his head until it rested on the pillows of his several chins, and then he seemed to go to sleep.

I drew up another chair for the girl. She took another sharp look at me—she seemed to be hunting for something in my face—and began to talk to him in what I suppose was the native lingo. She talked rapidly for about twenty minutes, while he gave no sign that he was listening or that he was even awake.

When she was through, he said: "*Da.*" He spoke dreamily, but there was a volume to the syllable that could have come from no place smaller than his gigantic belly. The girl turned to me, smiling.

"His Excellency will be glad to give you every possible assistance. Officially, of course, he does not care to interfere in the affairs of a visitor from another country, but he realizes the importance of keeping Mr. Grantham from being victimized while here. If you will return tomorrow afternoon, at, say, three o'clock . . ."

I promised to do that, thanked her, shook hands with the mountain again, and went out into the rain.

Back at the hotel, I had no trouble learning that Lionel Grantham occupied a suite on the sixth floor and was in it at that time. I had his photograph in my pocket and his description in my head. I spent what was left of the afternoon and the early evening waiting for a look at him. At a little after seven I got it.

He stepped out of the elevator, a tall, flat-backed boy with a supple body that tapered from broad shoulders to narrow hips, carried erectly on long, muscular legs—the sort of frame that tailors like. His pink, regular-featured, really handsome face wore an expression of aloof superiority that was too marked to be anything else than a cover for youthful self-consciousness.

Lighting a cigarette, he passed into the street. The rain had stopped, though clouds overhead promised more shortly. He turned down the street afoot. So did I.

We went to a much gilded restaurant two blocks from the hotel, where a gypsy orchestra played on a little balcony stuck insecurely high on one wall. All the waiters and half the diners seemed to know the boy. He bowed and smiled to this side and that as he walked down to a table near the far end, where two men were waiting for him.

One of them was tall and thick-bodied, with bushy dark hair and a flowing dark mustache. His florid, short-nosed face wore the expression of a man who doesn't mind a fight now and then. This one was dressed in a green and gold military uniform, with high boots of the shiniest black leather. His companion was in evening clothes, a plump, swarthy man of medium height, with oily black hair and a suave, oval face.

While young Grantham joined this pair I found a table some distance from them for myself. I ordered dinner and looked around at my neighbors. There was a sprinkling of uniforms in the room, some dress coats and evening gowns, but most of the diners were in ordinary daytime clothes. I saw a couple of faces that were probably British, a Greek or two, a few Turks. The food was good and so was my appetite. I was smoking a cigarette over a tiny cup of syrupy coffee when Grantham and the big florid officer got up and went away.

I couldn't have got my bill and paid it in time to follow them, without raising a disturbance, so I let them go. Then I settled for my meal and waited until the dark, plump man they had left behind called for his check. I was in the street a minute ahead of him, standing, looking up toward the dimly electric-lighted plaza with what was meant for the expression of a tourist who didn't quite know where to go next.

He passed me, going up the muddy street with the soft, careful-where-you-put-your-foot tread of a cat.

A soldier—a bony man in sheepskin coat and cap, with a gray mustache bristling over gray, sneering lips—stepped out of a dark doorway and stopped the swarthy man with whining words.

The swarthy man lifted hands and shoulders in a gesture that held both anger and surprise.

The soldier whined again, but the sneer on his gray mouth became more pronounced. The plump man's voice was low, sharp, angry, but he moved a hand from pocket to soldier, and the brown of Muravian paper money showed in the hand. The soldier pocketed the money, raised a hand in a salute, and went across the street.

When the swarthy man had stopped staring after the soldier, I moved toward the corner around which sheepskin coat and cap had vanished. My soldier was a block and a half down the street, striding along with bowed head. He was in a hurry. I got plenty of exercise keeping up with him. Presently the city began to thin out. The thinner it got, the less I liked this expedition. Shadowing is at its best in daytime, downtown in a familiar large city. This was shadowing at its worst.

He led me out of the city along a cement road bordered by few houses. I stayed as far back as I could, so he was a faint, blurred shadow ahead. He turned a sharp bend in the road. I hustled toward the bend, intending to drop back again as soon as I had rounded it. Speeding, I nearly gummed the works.

The soldier suddenly appeared around the curve, coming toward me.

A little behind me a small pile of lumber on the roadside was the only cover within a hundred feet. I stretched my short legs thither.

Irregularly piled boards made a shallow cavity in one end of the pile, almost large enough to hold me. On my knees in the mud I hunched into that cavity.

The soldier came into sight through a chink between boards. Bright metal gleamed in one of his hands. A knife, I thought. But when he halted in front of my shelter I saw it was a revolver of the old-style nickel-plated sort.

He stood still, looking at my shelter, looking up the road and down the road. He grunted, came toward me. Slivers stung my cheek as I rubbed myself flatter against the timber-ends. My gun was with my blackjack—in my gladstone bag, in my room in my hotel. A fine place to have them now! The soldier's gun was bright in his hand.

Rain began to patter on boards and ground. The soldier turned up the collar of his coat as he came. Nobody ever did anything I liked more. A man stalking another wouldn't have done that. He didn't know I was there. He was hunting a hiding place for himself. The game was even. If he found me, he had the gun, but I had seen him first.

His sheepskin coat rasped against the wood as he went by me, bending low as he passed my corner for the back of the pile, so close to me that the same raindrops seemed to be hitting both of us. I undid my fists after that. I couldn't see him, but I could hear him breathing, scratching himself, even humming.

A couple of weeks went by.

The mud I was kneeling in soaked through my pants-legs, wetting my knees and shins. The rough wood filed skin off my face very time I breathed. My mouth was as dry as my knees were wet, because I was breathing through it for silence.

An automobile came around the bend, headed for the city. I heard the soldier grunt softly, heard the click of his gun as he cocked it. The car came abreast, went on. The soldier blew out his breath and started scratching himself and humming again.

Another couple of weeks passed.

Men's voices came through the rain, barely audible, louder, quite clear. Four soldiers in sheepskin coats and hats walked down the road the way we had come, their voices presently shrinking into silence as they disappeared around the curve.

In the distance an automobile horn barked two ugly notes. The soldier grunted—a grunt that said clearly: "Here it is." His feet slopped in the mud, and the lumber pile creaked under his weight. I couldn't see what he was up to.

White light danced around the bend in the road, and an automobile came into view—a high-powered car going cityward with a speed that paid no attention to the wet slipperiness of the road. Rain and night and speed blurred its two occupants, who were in the front seat.

Over my head a heavy revolver roared. The soldier was working. The speeding car swayed crazily along the wet cement, its brakes screaming.

When the sixth shot told me the nickel-plated gun was probably empty, I jumped out of my hollow.

The soldier was leaning over the lumber pile, his gun still pointing at the skidding car while he peered through the rain.

He turned as I saw him, swung the gun around to me, snarled an order I couldn't understand. I was betting the gun was empty. I raised both hands high over my head, made an astonished face, and kicked him in the belly.

He folded over on me, wrapping himself around my leg. We both went down. I was underneath, but his head was against my thigh. His cap fell off. I caught his hair with both hands and yanked myself into a sitting position. His teeth went into my leg. I called him disagreeable things and put my thumbs in the hollows under his ears. It didn't take much pressure to teach him that he oughtn't to bite people. When he lifted his face to howl, I put my right fist in it, pulling him into the punch with my left hand in his hair. It was a nice solid sock.

I pushed him off my leg, got up, took a handful of his coat collar, and dragged him out into the road.

White light poured over us. Squinting into it, I saw the automobile standing down the road, its spotlight turned on me and my sparring partner. A big man in green and gold came into the light—the florid officer who had been one of Grantham's companions in the restaurant. An automatic was in one of his hands.

He strode over to us, stiff-legged in his high boots, ignored the soldier on the ground, and examined me carefully with sharp little dark eyes. "British?" he asked.

"American."

He bit a corner of his mustache and said meaninglessly: "Yes, that is better."

His English was guttural, with a German accent.

Lionel Grantham came from the car to us. His face wasn't as pink as it had been.

"What is it?" he asked the officer, but he looked at me.

"I don't know," I said. "I took a stroll after dinner and got mixed up on my directions. Finding myself out here, I decided

I was headed the wrong way. When I turned around to go back I saw this fellow duck behind the lumber pile. He had a gun in his hand. I took him for a stick-up, so I played Indian on him. Just as I got to him he jumped up and began spraying you people. I reached him in time to spoil his aim. Friend of yours?"

"You're an American," the boy said. "I'm Lionel Grantham. This is Colonel Einarson. We're very grateful to you." He screwed up his forehead and looked at Einarson. "What do you think of it?"

The officer shrugged his shoulders, growled, "One of my children—we'll see," and kicked the ribs of the man on the ground.

The kick brought the soldier to life. He sat up, rolled over on hands and knees, and began a broken, long-winded entreaty, plucking at the Colonel's tunic with dirty hands.

"Ach!" Einarson knocked the hands down with a tap of pistol barrel across knuckles, looked with disgust at the muddy marks on his tunic, and growled an order.

The soldier jumped to his feet, stood at attention, got another order, did an about-face, and marched to the automobile. Colonel Einarson strode stiff-legged behind him, holding his automatic to the man's back. Grantham put a hand on my arm.

"Come along," he said. "We'll thank you properly and get better acquainted after we've taken care of this fellow."

Colonel Einarson got into the driver's seat, with the soldier beside him. Grantham waited while I found the soldier's revolver. Then we got into the rear seat. The officer looked doubtfully at me out of his eye-corners, but said nothing. He drove the car back the way it had come. He liked speed, and we hadn't far to go. By the time we were settled in our seats the car was whisking us through a gateway in a high stone wall, with a sentry on each side presenting arms. We did a sliding half-circle into a branching driveway and jerked to a standstill in front of a square whitewashed building.

Einarson prodded the soldier out ahead of him. Grantham and I got out. To the left a row of long, low buildings showed pale gray in the rain—barracks. The door of the square, white building was opened by a bearded orderly in green. We went in. Einarson pushed his prisoner across the small reception hall and through the open door of a bedroom. Grantham and I followed them in. The orderly stopped in the doorway, traded some words with Einarson, and went away, closing the door.

The room we were in looked like a cell, except that there were no bars over the one small window. It was a narrow room, with bare, whitewashed walls and ceiling. The wooden floor, scrubbed with lye until it was almost as white as the walls, was bare. For furniture there was a black iron cot, three folding chairs of wood and canvas, and an unpainted chest of drawers, with comb, brush, and a few papers on top. That was all.

"Be seated, gentlemen," Einarson said, indicating the camp chairs. "We'll get at this thing now."

The boy and I sat down. The officer laid his pistol on the top of the chest of drawers, rested one elbow beside the pistol, took a corner of his mustache in one big red hand, and addressed the soldier. His voice was kindly, paternal. The soldier, standing rigidly upright in the middle of the floor, replied, whining, his eyes focused on the officer's with a blank, in-turned look.

They talked for five minutes or more. Impatience grew in the Colonel's voice and manner. The soldier kept his blank abjectness. Einarson ground his teeth together and looked angrily at the boy and me.

"This pig!" he exclaimed, and began to bellow at the soldier.

Sweat sprang out on the soldier's gray face, and he cringed out of his military stiffness. Einarson stopped bellowing at him and yelled two words at the door. It opened and the bearded orderly came in with a short, thick, leather whip. At a nod from Einarson he put the whip beside the automatic on the top of the chest of drawers and went out.

The soldier whimpered. Einarson spoke curtly to him. The soldier shuddered, began to unfasten his coat with shaking fingers, pleading all the while with whining, stuttering words. He took off his coat, his green blouse, his gray undershirt, letting them fall on the floor, and stood there, his hairy, not exactly clean body naked from the waist up. He worked his fingers together and cried.

Einarson grunted a word. The soldier stiffened at attention, hands at sides, facing us, his left side to Einarson.

Slowly Colonel Einarson removed his own belt, unbuttoned his tunic, took it off, folded it carefully, and laid it on the cot. Beneath it he wore a white cotton shirt. He rolled the sleeves up above his elbows and picked up the whip. "This pig!" he said again.

Lionel Grantham stirred uneasily on his chair. His face was white, his eyes dark.

Leaning his left elbow on the chest of drawers again, playing with his mustache-end with his left hand, standing indolently cross-legged, Einarson began to flog the soldier. His right arm raised the whip, brought the lash whistling down to the soldier's back, raised it again, brought it down again. It was especially nasty because he was not hurrying himself, not exerting himself. He meant to flog the man until he got what he wanted, and he was saving his strength so that he could keep it up as long as necessary.

With the first blow the terror went out of the soldier's eyes. They dulled sullenly and his lips stopped twitching. He stood woodenly under the beating, staring over Grantham's head. The officer's face had also become expressionless. Anger was gone. He showed no pleasure in his work, not even that of relieving his feelings. His air was the air of a stoker shoveling coal, of a carpenter sawing a board, of a stenographer typing a letter. Here was a job to be done in a workmanlike manner, without haste or excitement or wasted effort, without either enthusiasm or repulsion. It was nasty, but it taught me respect for this Colonel Einarson.

Lionel Grantham sat on the edge of his folding chair, staring at the soldier with white-ringed eyes. I offered the boy a cigarette, making an unnecessary complicated operation out of lighting it and my own—to break up his score-keeping. He had been counting the strokes, and that wasn't good for him.

The whip curved up, swished down, cracked on the naked back—up, down, up, down. Einarson's florid face took on the damp glow of moderate exercise. The soldier's gray face was a lump of putty. He was facing Grantham and me. We couldn't see the marks of the whip.

Grantham said something to himself in a whisper. Then he gasped:

"I can't stand this!"

Einarson didn't look around from his work.

"Don't stop it now," I muttered. "We've gone this far."

The boy got up unsteadily and went to the window, opened it and stood looking out into the rainy night. Einarson paid no attention to him. He was putting more weight into the whipping now, standing with his feet far apart, leaning forward a little, his left hand on his hip, his right carrying the whip up and down with increasing swiftness.

The soldier swayed and a sob shook his hairy chest. The whip cut—cut—cut. I looked at my watch. Einarson had been at it for forty minutes, and looked good for the rest of the night.

The soldier moaned and turned toward the officer. Einarson did not break the rhythm of his stroke. The lash cut the man's shoulder. I caught a glimpse of his back—raw meat. Einarson spoke sharply. The soldier jerked himself to attention again, his left side to the officer. The whip went on with its work—up, down, up, down, up, down.

The soldier flung himself on hands and knees at Einarson's feet and began to pour out sob-broken words. Einarson looked down at him, listening carefully, holding the lash of the whip in his left hand, the butt still in his right. When the man had finished, Einarson asked questions, got answers, nodded, and the soldier stood up. Einarson put a friendly hand on the man's shoulder, turned him around, looked at his mangled red back, and said something in a sympathetic tone. Then he called the orderly in and gave him some orders. The soldier, moaning as he bent, picked up his discarded clothes and followed the orderly out of the bedroom.

Einarson tossed the whip up on top of the chest of drawers and crossed to the bed to pick up his tunic. A leather pocketbook slid from an inside pocket to the floor. When he recovered it, a soiled newspaper clipping slipped out and floated across to my feet. I picked it up and gave it back to him—a photograph of a man, the Shah of Persia, according to the French caption under it.

"That pig!" he said—meaning the soldier, not the Shah—
as he put on his tunic and buttoned it. "He has a son, also
until last week of my troops. This son drinks too much of
wine. I reprimand him. He is insolent. What kind of army is
it without discipline? Pigs! I knock this pig down, and he pro-
duces a knife. Ach! What kind of army is it where a soldier
may attack his officers with knives? After I—personally, you
comprehend—have finished with this swine, I have him
court-martialed and sentenced to twenty years in the prison.
This elder pig, his father, does not like that. So he will shoot
me tonight. Ach! What kind of army is that?"

Lionel Grantham came away from his window. His young
face was haggard. His young eyes were ashamed of the hag-
gardness of his face.

Colonel Einarson made me a stiff bow and a formal
speech of thanks for spoiling the soldier's aim—which I
hadn't—and saving his life. Then the conversation turned to
my presence in Muravia. I told them briefly that I had held
a captain's commission in the military intelligence department during the war. That much was the truth, and that was
all the truth I gave them. After the war—so my fairy tale
went—I had decided to stay in Europe, had taken my discharge there and had drifted around, doing odd jobs at one
place and another. I was vague, trying to give them the impression that those odd jobs had not always, or usually, been
ladylike. I gave them more definite—though still highly
imaginary—details of my recent employment with a French
syndicate, admitting that I had come to this corner of the
world because I thought it better not to be seen in Western
Europe for a year or so.

"Nothing I could be jailed for," I said, "but things could
be made uncomfortable for me. So I roamed over into
Mitteleuropa, learned that I might find a connection in
Belgrade, got there to find it a false alarm, and came on down
here. I may pick up something here. I've got a date with the
Minister of Police tomorrow. I think I can show him where
he can use me."

"The gross Djudakovich!" Einarson said with frank contempt. "You find him to your liking?"

"No work, no eat," I said.

"Einarson," Grantham began quickly, hesitated, then said: "Couldn't we—don't you think——" and didn't finish.

The Colonel frowned at him, saw I had noticed the frown, cleared his throat, and addressed me in a gruffly hearty tone:

"Perhaps it would be well if you did not too speedily engage yourself to this fat minister. It may be—there is a possibility that we know of another field where your talents might find employment more to your taste—and profit."

I let the matter stand, saying neither yes nor no.

We returned to the city in the officer's car. He and Grantham sat in the rear. I sat beside the soldier who drove. The boy and I got out at our hotel. Einarson said good night and was driven away as if he were in a hurry.

"It's early," Grantham said as we went indoors. "Come up to my room."

I stopped at my own room to wash off the mud I'd gathered around the lumber stack and to change my clothes, and then went up with him. He had three rooms on the top floor, overlooking the plaza.

He set out a bottle of whisky, a syphon, lemons, cigars, and cigarettes, and we drank, smoked, and talked. Fifteen or twenty minutes of the talk came from no deeper than the mouth on either side—comments on the night's excitement, our opinions of Stefania, and so on. Each of us had something to say to the other. Each was weighing the other before he said it. I decided to put mine over first.

"Colonel Einarson was spoofing us tonight," I said.

"Spoofing?" The boy sat up straight, blinking.

"His soldier shot for money, not revenge."

"You mean——?" His mouth stayed open.

"I mean the little dark man you ate with gave the soldier money."

"Mahmoud! Why, that's—— You are sure?"

"I saw it."

He looked at his feet, yanking his gaze away from mine as if he didn't want me to see that he thought I was lying.

"The soldier may have lied to Einarson," he said presently, still trying to keep me from knowing he thought me the liar. "I can understand some of the language, as spoken by the educated Muravians, but not the country dialect the soldier talked, so I don't know what he said, but he may have lied, you know."

"Not a chance," I said. "I'd bet my pants he told the truth."

He continued to stare at his outstretched feet, fighting to hold his face cool and calm. Part of what he was thinking slipped out in words:

"Of course, I owe you a tremendous debt for saving us from——"

"You don't. You owe that to the soldier's bad aim. I didn't jump him till his gun was empty."

"But——" His young eyes were wide before mine, and if I had pulled a machine gun out of my cuff he wouldn't have been surprised. He suspected me of everything on the blotter. I cursed myself for overplaying my hand. There was nothing to do now but spread the cards.

"Listen, Grantham. Most of what I told you and Einarson about myself is the bunk. Your uncle, Senator Walbourn, sent me down here. You were supposed to be in Paris. A lot of your dough was being shipped to Belgrade. The Senator was leery of the racket, didn't know whether you were playing a game or somebody was putting over a fast one. I went to Belgrade, traced you here, and came here, to run into what I ran into. I've traced the money to you, have talked to you. That's all I was hired to do. My job's done—unless there's anything I can do for you now."

"Not a thing," he said very calmly. "Thanks, just the same." He stood up, yawning. "Perhaps I'll see you again before you leave."

"Yeah." It was easy for me to make my voice match his in indifference: I hadn't a cargo of rage to hide. "Good night."

I went down to my room, got into bed, and went to sleep.

I slept till late the next morning and then had breakfast in my room. I was in the middle of it when knuckles tapped my door. A stocky man in a wrinkled gray uniform, set off with a short, thick sword, came in, saluted, gave me a square white envelope, looked hungrily at the American cigarettes on my table, smiled and took one when I offered them, saluted again, and went out.

The square envelope had my name written on it in a small, very plain and round, but not childish, handwriting. Inside was a note from the same pen:

> The Minister of Police regrets that departmental affairs prevent his receiving you this afternoon.

It was signed "Romaine Frankl," and had postscript:

> If it's convenient for you to call on me after nine this evening, perhaps I can save you some time.
>
> R. F.

Below this an address was written.

I put the note in my pocket and called: "Come in," to another set of knocking knuckles.

Lionel Grantham entered. His face was pale and set.

"Good morning," I said, making it cheerfully casual, as if I attached no importance to last night's rumpus. "Had breakfast yet? Sit down, and——"

"Oh, yes, thanks. I've eaten." His handsome red face was reddening. "About last night—I was——"

"Forget it! Nobody likes to have his business pried into."

"That's good of you," he said, twisting his hat in his hands. He cleared his throat. "You said you'd—ah—help me if I wished."

"Yeah. I will. Sit down."

He sat down, coughed, ran his tongue over his lips.

"You haven't said anything to anyone about last night's affair with the soldier?"

"No," I said.

"Will you not say anything about it?"

"Why?"

He looked at the remains of my breakfast and didn't answer. I lit a cigarette to go with my coffee and waited. He stirred uneasily in his chair and without looking up, asked:

"You know Mahmoud was killed last night?"

"The man in the restaurant with you and Einarson?"

"Yes. He was shot down in front of his house a little after midnight."

"Einarson?"

The boy jumped.

"No!" he cried. "Why do you say that?"

"Einarson knew Mahmoud had paid the soldier to wipe him out, so he plugged Mahmoud, or had him plugged. Did you tell him what I told you last night?"

"No." He blushed. "It's embarrassing to have one's family sending a guardian after one."

I made a guess:

"He told you to offer me the job he spoke of last night, and to caution me against talking about the soldier. Didn't he?"

"Y-e-s."

"Well, go ahead and offer."

"But he doesn't know you're——"

"What are you going to do, then?" I asked. "If you don't make me the offer, you'll have to tell him why."

"Oh, Lord, what a mess!" he said wearily, putting elbows on knees, face between palms, looking at me with the harried eyes of a boy finding life too complicated.

He was ripe for talk. I grinned at him, finished my coffee, and waited.

"You know I'm not going to be led home by an ear," he said with a sudden burst of rather childish defiance.

"You know I'm not going to try to take you," I soothed him.

We had some more silence after that. I smoked while he held his head and worried. After a while he squirmed in his chair, sat stiffly upright, and his face turned perfectly crimson from hair to collar.

"I'm going to ask for your help," he said, pretending he didn't know he was blushing. "I'm going to tell you the whole foolish thing. If you laugh, I'll—— You won't laugh, will you?"

"If it's funny I probably will, but that needn't keep me from helping you."

"Yes, do laugh! It's silly! You ought to laugh!" He took a deep breath. "Did you ever—did you ever think you'd like to be a——" he stopped, looked at me with a desperate sort of shyness, pulled himself together, and almost shouted the last word—"king?"

"Maybe. I've thought of a lot of things I'd like to be, and that might be one of 'em."

"I met Mahmoud at an embassy ball in Constantinople," he dashed into the story, dropping his words quickly as if glad to get rid of them. "He was President Semich's secretary. We got quite friendly, though I wasn't especially fond of him. He persuaded me to come here with him, and introduced me to Colonel Einarson. Then they—there's really no doubt that the country is wretchedly governed. I wouldn't have gone into it if that hadn't been so.

"A revolution was being prepared. The man who was to lead it had just died. It was handicapped, too, by a lack of money. Believe this—it wasn't all vanity that made me go into it. I believed—I still believe—that it would have been—will be—for the good of the country. The offer they made me was that if I would finance the revolution I could be—could be king.

"Now wait! The Lord knows it's bad enough, but don't think it sillier than it is. The money I have would go a long way in this small, impoverished country. Then, with an American ruler, it would be easier—it ought to be—for the country to borrow in America or England. Then there's the political angle. Muravia is surrounded by four countries, any one of which is strong enough to annex it if it wants. Muravia has stayed independent so far only because of the jealousy among its stronger neighbors and because it hasn't a seaport.

"But with an American ruler—and if loans in America and England were arranged, so we had their capital invested here—there would be a change in the situation. Muravia would be in a stronger position, would have at least some slight claim on the friendship of stronger powers. That would be enough to make the neighbors cautious.

"Albania, shortly after the first World War, thought of the same thing, and offered its crown to one of the wealthy American Bonapartes. He didn't want it. He was an older man and had already made his career. I did want my chance when it came. There were"—some of the embarrassment that had left him during his talking returned—"there were kings back in the Grantham lines. We trace our descent from James the Fourth, of Scotland. I wanted—it was nice to think of carrying the line back to a crown.

"We weren't planning a violent revolution. Einarson holds the army. We simply had to use the army to force the Deputies—those who were not already with us—to change the form of government and elect me king. My descent would make it easier than if the candidate were one who hadn't royal blood in him. It would give me a certain standing in spite—in spite of my being young, and—and the people really want a king, especially the peasants. They don't think they're really entitled to call themselves a nation without one. A president means nothing to them—he's simply an ordinary man like themselves. So, you see, I—— It was—— Go ahead, laugh! You've heard enough to know how silly it is!" His voice was high-pitched, screechy. "Laugh! Why don't you laugh?"

"What for?" I asked. "It's crazy, God knows, but not silly. Your judgment was gummy, but your nerve's all right. You've been talking as if this were all dead and buried. Has it flopped?"

"No, it hasn't," he said slowly, frowning, "but I keep thinking it has. Mahmoud's death shouldn't change the situation, yet I've a feeling it's all over."

"Much of your money sunk?"

"I don't mind that. But—well—suppose the American newspapers get hold of the story, and they probably will. You know how ridiculous they could make it. And then the others who'll know about it—my mother and uncle and the Trust Company. I won't pretend I'm not ashamed to face them. And then——" His face got red and shiny. "And then Valeska—Miss Radnjak—her father was to have led the revolution. He did lead it—until he was murdered. She is—I never could be good enough for her." He said this in a peculiarly idiotic tone of awe. "But I've hoped that perhaps by carrying on her father's work, and if I had something besides mere money to offer her—if I had done something—made a place for myself—perhaps she'd—you know."

I said: "Uh-huh."

"What shall I do?" he asked earnestly. "I can't run away. I've got to see it through for her, and to keep my own self-respect. But I've got the feeling that it's all over. You offered to help me. Help me. Tell me what I ought to do!"

"You'll do what I tell you—if I promise to bring you through with a clean face?" I asked, just as if steering millionaire descendants of Scotch kings through Balkan plots were an old story to me, merely part of the day's work.

"Yes!"

"What's the next thing on the revolutionary program?"

"There's a meeting tonight. I'm to bring you."

"What time?"

"Midnight."

"I'll meet you here at eleven thirty. How much am I supposed to know?"

"I was to tell you about the plot, and to offer you whatever inducements were necessary to bring you in. There was no definite arrangement as to how much or how little I was to tell you."

At nine thirty that night a cab set me down in front of the address the Minister of Police's secretary had given in her note. It was a small two-story house in a badly paved street on the city's eastern edge. A middle-aged woman in very clean, stiffly starched, ill-fitting clothes opened the door for me. Before I could speak, Romaine Frankl, in a sleeveless pink satin gown, floated into sight behind the woman, smiling, holding out a small hand to me.

"I didn't know you'd come," she said.

"Why?" I asked, with a great show of surprise at the notion that any man would ignore an invitation from her, while the servant closed the door and took my coat and hat.

We were standing in a dull-rose-papered room, finished and carpeted with oriental richness. There was one discordant note in the room—an immense leather chair.

"We'll go upstairs," the girl said, and addressed the servant with words that meant nothing to me, except the name Marya. "Or would you"—she turned to me and English again—"prefer beer to wine?"

I said I wouldn't, and we went upstairs, the girl climbing ahead of me with her effortless appearance of being carried. She took me into a black, white, and gray room that was very daintily furnished with as few pieces as possible, its otherwise perfect feminine atmosphere spoiled by the presence of another of the big padded chairs.

The girl sat on a gray divan, pushing away a stack of French and Austrian magazines to make a place for me beside her. Through an open door I could see the painted foot of a Spanish bed, a short stretch of purple counterpane, and half of a purple-curtained window.

"His Excellency was very sorry," the girl began, and stopped.

I was looking—not staring—at the big leather chair. I knew she had stopped because I was looking at it, so I wouldn't take my eyes away.

"Vasilije," she said, more distinctly than was really necessary, "was very sorry he had to postpone this afternoon's appointment. The assassination of the President's secretary—you heard of it?—made us put everything else aside for the moment."

"Oh, yes, that fellow Mahmoud—" slowly shifting my eyes from the leather chair to her. "Found out who killed him?"

Her black-ringed, black-centered eyes seemed to study me from a distance while she shook her head, jiggling the nearly black curls.

"Probably Einarson," I said.

"You haven't been idle." Her lower lids lifted when she smiled, giving her eyes a twinkling effect.

The servant Marya came in with wine and fruit, put them on a small table beside the divan, and went away. The girl poured wine and offered me cigarettes in a silver box. I passed them up for one of my own. She smoked a king-size Egyptian cigarette—big as a cigar. It accentuated the smallness of her face and hand—which is probably why she favored that size.

"What sort of revolution is this they've sold my boy?" I asked.

"It was a very nice one until it died."

"How come it died?"

"It—do you know anything about our history?"

"No."

"Well, Muravia came into existence as a result of the fear and jealousy of four countries. The nine or ten thousand square miles that make this country aren't very valuable land. There's little here that any of those four countries especially wanted, but no three of them would agree to let the fourth have it. The only way to settle the thing was to make a separate country out of it. That was done in 1923.

"Doctor Semich was elected the first president, for a ten-year term. He is not a statesman, not a politician, and never will be. But since he was the only Muravian who had ever been heard of outside his own town, it was thought that his election would give the new country some prestige. Besides, it was a fitting honor for Muravia's only great man. He was not meant to be anything but a figurehead. The real governing was to be done by General Danilo Radnjak, who was elected vice-president, which, here, is more than equivalent to Prime Minister. General Radnjak was a capable man. The army worshiped him, the peasants trusted him, and our *bourgeoisie* knew him to be honest, conservative, intelligent, and as good a business administrator as a military one.

"Doctor Semich is a very mild, elderly scholar with no knowledge whatever of worldly affairs. You can understand him from this—he is easily the greatest of living bacteriologists, but he'll tell you, if you are on intimate terms with him, that he doesn't believe in the value of bacteriology at all. 'Mankind must learn to live with bacteria as with friends,' he'll say. 'Our bodies must adapt themselves to diseases, so there will be little difference between having tuberculosis, for example, or not having it. That way lies victory. This making war on bacteria is a futile business. Futile but interesting. So we do it. Our poking around in laboratories is perfectly useless—but it amuses us.'

"Now when this delightful old dreamer was honored by his countrymen with the presidency, he took it in the worst possible way. He determined to show his appreciation by locking up his laboratory and applying himself heart and soul to running the government. Nobody expected or wanted that. Radnjak was to have been the government. For a while he did control the situation, and everything went well.

"But Mahmoud had designs of his own. He was Doctor Semich's secretary, and he was trusted. He began calling the President's attentions to various trespasses of Radnjak's on the presidential powers. Radnjak, in an attempt to keep Mahmoud from control, made a terrible mistake. He went to Doctor Semich and told him frankly and honestly that no one expected him, the President, to give all his time to executive business, and that it had been the intention of his countrymen to give him the honor of being the first president rather than the duties.

"Radnjak had played into Mahmoud's hands—the secretary became the actual government. Doctor Semich was now thoroughly convinced that Radnjak was trying to steal his authority, and from that day on Radnjak's hands were tied. Doctor Semich insisted on handling every governmental detail himself, which meant that Mahmoud handled it, because the President knows as little about statesmanship today as he did when he took office. Complaints—no matter who made them—did no good. Doctor Semich considered every dissatisfied citizen a fellow-conspirator of Radnjak's. The more Mahmoud was criticized in the Chamber of Deputies, the more faith Doctor Semich had in him. Last year the situation became intolerable, and the revolution began to form.

"Radnjak headed it, of course, and at least ninety percent of the influential men in Muravia were in it. The attitude of people as a whole, it is difficult to judge. They are mostly peasants, small landowners, who ask only to be let alone. But there's no doubt they'd rather have a king than a president, so the form was to be changed to please them. The army, which worshiped Radnjak, was in it. The revolution matured slowly. General Radnjak was a cautious, careful man, and, as this is not a wealthy country, there was not much money available.

"Two months before the date set for the outbreak, Radnjak was assassinated. And the revolution went to pieces, split up into half a dozen factions. There was no other man strong enough to hold them together. Some of these groups still meet and conspire, but they are without general influence, without real purpose. And this is the revolution that has been sold Lionel Grantham. We'll have more information in a day or two, but what we've learned so far is that Mahmoud, who spent a month's vacation in Constantinople, brought Grantham back here with him and joined forces with Einarson to swindle the boy.

"Mahmoud was very much out of the revolution, of course, since it was aimed at him. But Einarson had been in it with his superior, Radnjak. Since Radnjak's death Einarson has succeeded in transferring to himself much of the allegiance that the soldiers gave the dead general. They do not love the Icelander as they did Radnjak, but Einarson is spectacular, theatrical—has all the qualities that simple men like to see in their leaders. So Einarson had the army and could get enough of the late revolution's machinery in his hands to impress Grantham. For money he'd do it. So he and Mahmoud put on a show for your boy. They used Valeska Radnjak, the general's daughter, too. She, I think, was also a dupe. I've heard that the boy and she are planning to be king and queen. How much did he invest in this farce?"

"Maybe as much as three million American dollars."

Romaine Frankl whistled softly and poured more wine.

"How did the Minister of Police stand, when the revolution was alive?" I asked.

"Vasilije," she told me, sipping wine between phrases, "is a peculiar man, an original. He is interested in nothing except his comfort. Comfort to him means enormous amounts of food and drink and at least sixteen hours of sleep each day, and not having to move around much during his eight waking hours. Outside of that he cares for nothing. To guard his comfort he has made the police department a model one. They've got to do their work smoothly and neatly. If they don't, crimes will go unpunished, people will complain, and those complaints might disturb His Excellency. He might even have to shorten his afternoon nap to attend a conference or meeting. That wouldn't do. So he insists on an organization that will keep crime down to a minimum, and catch the perpetrators of that minimum. And he gets it."

"Catch Radnjak's assassin?"

"Killed resisting arrest ten minutes after the murder."

"One of Mahmoud's men?"

The girl emptied her glass, frowning at me, her lifted lower lids putting a twinkle in the frown.

"You're not so bad," she said slowly, "but now it's my turn to ask: Why did you say Einarson killed Mahmoud?"

"Einarson knew Mahmoud had tried to have him and Grantham shot earlier in the evening."

"Really?"

"I saw a soldier take money from Mahmoud, ambush Einarson and Grantham, and miss 'em with six shots."

She clicked a fingernail against her teeth.

"That's not like Mahmoud," she objected, "to be seen paying for his murders."

"Probably not," I agreed. "But suppose his hired man decided he wanted more pay, or maybe he'd only been paid part of his wages. What better way to collect than to pop out and ask for it in the street a few minutes before he was scheduled to turn the trick?"

She nodded, and spoke as if thinking aloud:

"Then they've got all they expect to get from Grantham, and each was trying to hog it by removing the other."

"Where you go wrong," I told her, "is in thinking that the revolution is dead."

"But Mahmoud wouldn't, for three million dollars, conspire to remove himself from power."

"Right! Mahmoud thought he was putting on a show for the boy. When he learned it wasn't a show—learned Einarson was in earnest—he tried to have him knocked off."

"Perhaps." She shrugged her smooth bare shoulders. "But now you're guessing."

"Yes? Einarson carries a picture of the Shah of Persia. It's worn, as if he handled it a lot. The Shah of Persia is a Russian soldier who went in there after the war, worked himself up until he had the army in his hands, became dictator, then Shah. Correct me if I'm wrong. Einarson is an Icelandic soldier who came in here after the war and has worked himself up until he's got the army in his hands. If he carries the Shah's picture and looks at it often enough to have it shabby from handling, does it mean he hopes to follow his example? Or doesn't it?"

Romaine Frankl got up and roamed around the room, moving a chair two inches here, adjusting an ornament there, shaking out the folds of a window curtain, pretending a picture wasn't quite straight on the wall, moving from place to place with the appearance of being carried—a graceful small girl in pink satin.

She stopped in front of a mirror, moved a little to one side so she could see my reflection in it, and fluffed her curls while saying almost absently:

"Very well, Einarson wants a revolution. What will your boy do?"

"What I tell him."

"What will you tell him?"

"Whatever pays best. I want to take him home with all his money."

She left the mirror and came over to me, rumpled my hair, kissed my mouth, and sat on my knees, holding my face be tween small warm hands.

"Give me a revolution, nice man!" Her eyes were black with excitement, her voice throaty, her mouth laughing, her body trembling. "I detest Einarson. Use him and break him for me. But give me a revolution!"

I laughed, kissed her, and turned her around on my lap so her head would fit against my shoulder.

"We'll see," I promised. "I'm to meet the folks at midnight. Maybe I'll know then."

"You'll come back after the meeting?"

"Try to keep me away!"

I got back to the hotel at eleven thirty, loaded my hips with gun and blackjack, and went upstairs to Grantham's suite. He was alone, but said he expected Einarson. He seemed glad to see me.

"Tell me, did Mahmoud go to any of the meetings?" I asked.

"No. His part in the revolution was hidden even from most of those in it. There were reasons why he couldn't appear."

"There were. The chief one was that everybody knew he didn't want any revolts, didn't want anything but money."

Grantham chewed his lower lip and said: "Oh, Lord, what a mess!"

Colonel Einarson arrived, in a dinner coat, but very much the soldier, the man of action. His hand-clasp was stronger than it needed to be. His little dark eyes were hard and bright.

"You are ready, gentlemen?" he addressed the boy and me as if we were a multitude. "Excellent! We shall go now. There will be difficulties tonight. Mahmoud is dead. There will be those of our friends who will ask: 'Why now revolt?' Ach!" He yanked a corner of his flowing dark mustache. "I will answer that. Good souls, our confrères, but given to timidity. There is no timidity under capable leadership. You shall see!" And he yanked his mustache again. This military gent seemed to be feeling Napoleonic this evening. But I didn't write him off as a musical-comedy revolutionist—I remembered what he had done to the soldier.

We left the hotel, got into a machine, rode seven blocks, and went into a small hotel on a side street. The porter bowed to the belt when he opened the door for Einarson. Grantham and I followed the officer up a flight of stairs, down a dim hall. A fat, greasy man in his fifties came bowing and clucking to meet us. Einarson introduced him to me— the proprietor of the hotel. He took us into a low-ceilinged room where thirty or forty men got up from chairs and looked at us through tobacco smoke.

Einarson made a short, very formal speech which I couldn't understand, introducing me to the gang. I ducked my head at them and found a seat beside Grantham. Einarson sat on his other side. Everybody else sat down again, in no especial order.

Colonel Einarson smoothed his mustache and began to talk to this one and that, shouting over the clamor of other voices when necessary. In an undertone Lionel Grantham pointed out the more important conspirators to me—a dozen or more members of the Chamber of Deputies, a banker, a brother of the Minister of Finance (supposed to represent that official), half a dozen officers (all in civilian clothes tonight), three professors from the university, the president of a labor union, a newspaper publisher and his editor, the secretary of a students' club, a politician from out in the country, and a handful of small-business men.

The banker, a white-bearded fat man of sixty, stood up and began a speech, staring intently at Einarson. He spoke deliberately, softly, but with a faintly defiant air. The Colonel didn't let him get far.

"Ach!" Einarson barked and reared up on his feet. None of the words he said meant anything to me, but they took the pinkness out of the banker's cheeks and brought uneasiness into the eyes around us.

"They want to call it off," Grantham whispered in my ear. "They won't go through with it now. I know they won't."

The meeting became rough. A lot of people were yelping at once, but nobody talked down Einarson's bellow. Everybody was standing up, either very red or very white in the face. Fists, fingers, and heads were shaking. The Minister of Finance's brother—a slender, elegantly dressed man with a long, intelligent face—took off his nose glasses so savagely that they broke in half, screamed words at Einarson, spun on his heel, and walked to the door.

He pulled it open and stopped.

The hall was full of green uniforms. Soldiers leaned against the wall, sat on their heels, stood in little groups. They hadn't guns—only bayonets in scabbards at their sides. The Minister of Finance's brother stood very still at the door, looking at the soldiers.

A brown-whiskered, dark-skinned, big man, in coarse clothes and heavy boots, glared with red-rimmed eyes from the soldiers to Einarson, and took two heavy steps toward the Colonel. This was the country politician. Einarson blew out his lips and stepped forward to meet him. Those who were between them got out of the way.

Einarson roared and the countryman roared. Einarson made the most noise, but the countryman wouldn't stop on that account.

Colonel Einarson said: "Ach!" and spat in the countryman's face.

The countryman staggered back a step and one of his paws went under his brown coat. I stepped around Einarson and shoved the muzzle of my gun in the countryman's ribs.

Einarson laughed, called two soldiers into the room. They took the countryman by the arms and led him out. Somebody closed the door. Everybody sat down. Einarson made another speech. Nobody interrupted him. The white-whiskered banker made another speech. The Minister of Finance's brother rose to say half a dozen polite words, staring near-sightedly at Einarson, holding half of his broken glasses in each slender hand. Grantham, at a word from Einarson, got up and talked. Everybody listed very respectfully.

Einarson spoke again. Everybody got excited. Everybody talked at once. It went on for a long time. Grantham explained to me that the revolution would start early Thursday morning—it was now early Wednesday morning—and that the details were now being arranged for the last time. I doubted that anybody was going to know anything about the details, with all this hub-bub going on. They kept it up until half-past three. The last couple of hours I spent dozing in a chair, tilted back against the wall in a corner.

Grantham and I walked back to our hotel after the meeting. He told me we were to gather in the plaza at four o'clock the next morning. It would be daylight by six, and by then the government buildings, the President, most of the officials and Deputies who were not on our side, would be in our hands. A meeting of the Chamber of Deputies would be held under the eyes of Einarson's troops, and everything would be done as swiftly and regularly as possible.

I was to accompany Grantham as a sort of bodyguard, which meant, I imagined, that both of us were to be kept out of the way as much as possible. That was all right with me.

I left Grantham at the fifth floor, went to my room, ran cold water over my face and hands, and then left the hotel again. There was no chance of getting a cab at this hour, so I set out afoot for Romaine Frankl's house. I had a little excitement on the way.

A wind was blowing in my face as I walked. I stopped and put my back to it to light a cigarette. A shadow down the street slid over into a building's shadow. I was being tailed, and not very skillfully. I finished lighting my cigarette and went on my way until I came to a sufficiently dark side street. Turning into it, I stopped in a street-level dark doorway.

A man came puffing around the corner. My first crack at him went wrong—the blackjack took him too far forward, on the cheek. The second one got him fairly behind the ear. I left him sleeping there and went on to Romaine Frankl's house.

The servant Marya, in a woolly gray bathrobe, opened the door and sent me up to the black, white, and gray room, where the Minister's secretary, still in the pink gown, was

propped up among cushions on the divan. A tray full of cigarette butts showed how she'd been spending her time.

"Well?" she asked as I moved her over to make a seat for
myself beside her.

"Thursday morning at four we revolute."

"I knew you'd do it," she said, patting my hand.

"It did itself, though there were a few minutes when I
could have stopped it by simply knocking our Colonel behind
the ear and letting the rest of them tear him apart. That re-
minds me—somebody's hired man tried to follow me here
tonight."

"What sort of a man?"

"Short, beefy, forty—just about my size and age."

"But he didn't succeed?"

"I slapped him flat and left him sleeping there."

She laughed and pulled my ear.

"That was Gopchek, our very best detective. He'll be
furious."

"Well, don't sic any more of 'em on me. You can tell him
I'm sorry I had to hit him twice, but it was his own fault. He
shouldn't have jerked his head back the first time."

She laughed, then frowned, finally settling on an expression
that held half of each. "Tell me about the meeting," she commanded.

I told her what I knew. When I had finished she pulled my
head down to kiss me, and held it down to whisper:

"You do trust me, don't you, dear?"

"Yeah. Just as much as you trust me."

"That's far from being enough," she said, pushing my face
away.

Marya came in with a tray of food. We pulled the table
around in front of the divan and ate.

"I don't quite understand you," Romaine said over a stalk
of asparagus. "If you don't trust me why do you tell me
things? As far as I know, you haven't done much lying to
me. Why should you tell me the truth if you've no faith in
me?"

"My susceptible nature," I explained. "I'm so overwhelmed
by your beauty and charm that I can't refuse you anything."

"Don't!" she exclaimed, suddenly serious. "I've capitalized

that beauty and charm in half the countries in the world. Don't say things like that to me ever again. It hurts, because—because——" She pushed her plate back, started to reach for a cigarette, stopped her hand in midair, and looked at me with disagreeable eyes. "I love you," she said.

I took the hand that was hanging in the air, kissed the palm of it, and asked:

"You love me more than anyone else in the world?"

She pulled the hand away from me.

"Are you a bookkeeper?" she demanded. "Must you have amounts, weights, and measurements for everything?"

I grinned at her and tried to go on with my meal. I had been hungry. Now, though I had eaten only a couple of mouthfuls, my appetite was gone. I tried to pretend I still had the hunger I had lost, but it was no go. The food didn't want to be swallowed. I gave up the attempt and lighted a cigarette.

She used her left hand to fan away the smoke between us.

"You don't trust me," she insisted. "Then why do you put yourself in my hands?"

"Why not? You can make a flop of the revolution. That's nothing to me. It's not my party, and its failure needn't mean that I can't get the boy out of the country with his money."

"You don't mind a prison, an execution, perhaps?"

"I'll take my chances," I said. But what I was thinking was: if, after twenty years of scheming and slickering in big-time cities, I let myself get trapped in this hill village, I'd deserve all I got.

"And you've no feeling at all for me?"

"Don't be foolish." I waved my cigarette at my uneaten meal. "I haven't had anything to eat since eight o'clock last night."

She laughed, put a hand over my mouth, and said:

"I understand. You love me, but not enough to let me interfere with your plans. I don't like that. It's effeminate."

"You going to turn out for the revolution?" I asked.

"I'm not going to run through the streets throwing bombs, if that's what you mean."

"And Djudakovich?"

"He sleeps till eleven in the morning. If you start at four, you'll have seven hours before he's up." She said all this perfectly seriously. "Get it done in that time. Or he might decide to stop it."

"Yeah? I had a notion he wanted it."

"Vasilije wants nothing but peace and comfort."

"But listen, sweetheart," I protested. "If your Vasilije is any good at all, he can't help finding out about it ahead of time. Einarson and his army are the revolution. These bankers and deputies and the like that he's carrying with him to give the party a responsible look are a lot of movie conspirators. Look at 'em! They hold their meetings at midnight, and all that kind of foolishness. Now that they're actually signed up to something, they won't be able to keep from spreading the news. All day they'll be going around trembling and whispering together in odd corners."

"They've been doing that for months," she said. "Nobody pays any attention to them. And I promise you Vasilije shan't hear anything new. I certainly won't tell him, and he never listens to anything anyone else says."

"All right." I wasn't sure it was all right, but it might be. "Now this row is going through—if the army follows Einarson?"

"Yes, and the army will follow him."

"Then, after it's over, our real job begins?"

She rubbed a flake of cigarette ash into the table cloth with a small pointed finger, and said nothing.

"Einarson's got to be dumped," I continued.

"We'll have to kill him," she said thoughtfully. "You'd better do it yourself."

I saw Einarson and Grantham that evening, and spent several hours with them. The boy was fidgety, nervous, without confidence in the revolution's success, though he tried to pretend he was taking things as a matter of course. Einarson was full of words. He gave us every detail of the next day's plans. I was more interested in him than in what he was saying. He could put the revolution over, I thought, and I was willing to leave it to him. So while he talked I studied him, combing him over for weak spots.

I took him physically first—a tall, thick-bodied man in his prime, not as quick as he might have been, but strong and tough. He had an amply jawed, short-nosed, florid face that a fist wouldn't bother much. He wasn't fat, but he ate and drank too much to be hardboiled, and your florid man can seldom stand much poking around the belt. So much for the gent's body.

Mentally, he wasn't a heavyweight. His revolution was crude stuff. It would get over chiefly because there wasn't much opposition. He had plenty of will-power, I imagined, but I didn't put a big number on that. People who haven't much brains have to develop will-power to get anywhere. I didn't know whether he had guts or not, but before an audience I guessed he'd make a grand showing, and most of this act would be before an audience. Off in a dark corner I had an idea he would go watery. He believed in himself—absolutely. That's ninety percent of leadership, so there was no flaw in him there. He didn't trust me. He had taken me in because as things turned out it was easier to do so than to shut the door against me.

He kept on talking about his plans. There was nothing to talk about. He was going to bring his soldiers in town in the early morning and take over the government. That was all the plan that was needed. The rest of it was the lettuce around the dish, but this lettuce part was the only part we could discuss. It was dull.

At eleven o'clock Einarson stopped talking and left us, making this sort of speech:

"Until four o'clock, gentlemen, when Muravia's history begins." He put a hand on my shoulder and commanded me: "Guard His Majesty!"

I said, "Uh-huh," and immediately sent His Majesty to bed. He wasn't going to sleep, but he was too young to confess it, so he went off willingly enough. I got a taxi and went out to Romaine's.

She was like a child the night before a picnic. She kissed me and she kissed the servant Marya. She sat on my knees, beside me, on the floor, on all the chairs, changing her location every half-minute. She laughed and talked incessantly, about the revolution, about me, about herself, about anything at all. She nearly strangled herself trying to talk while swallowing wine. She lit her big cigarettes and forgot to smoke them, or forgot to stop smoking them until they scorched her lips. She sang lines from songs in half a dozen languages.

I left at three o'clock. She went down to the door with me, pulled my head down to kiss my eyes and mouth.

"If anything goes wrong," she said, "come to the prison. We'll hold that until——"

"If it goes wrong enough I'll be brought there," I promised.

She wouldn't joke now.

"I'm going there now," she said. "I'm afraid Einarson's got my house on his list."

"Good idea," I said. "If you hit a bad spot get word to me."

I walked back to the hotel through the dark streets—the lights were turned off at midnight—without seeing a single other person, not even one of the gray-uniformed policemen. By the time I reached home rain was falling steadily.

In my room I changed into heavier clothes and shoes, dug an extra gun—an automatic—out of my bag and hung it in a shoulder holster. Then I filled my pocket with enough ammunition to make me bow-legged, picked up hat and rain-coat, and went upstairs to Lionel Grantham's suite.

"It's ten to four," I told him. "We might as well go down to the plaza. Better put a gun in your pocket."

He hadn't slept. His handsome young face was as cool and pink and composed as it had been the first time I saw him, though his eyes were brighter now. He got into an overcoat, and we went downstairs.

Rain drove into our faces as we went toward the center of the dark plaza. Other figures moved around us, though none came near. We halted at the foot of an iron statue of somebody on a horse.

A pale young man of extraordinary thinness came up and began to talk rapidly, gesturing with both hands, sniffing every now and then, as if he had a cold in his head. I couldn't understand a word he said.

The rumble of other voices began to compete with the patter of rain. The fat, white-whiskered face of the banker who had been at the meeting appeared suddenly out of the darkness and went back into it just as suddenly, as if he didn't want to be recognized. Men I hadn't seen before gathered around us, saluting Grantham with a sheepish sort of respect. A little man in a too big cape ran up and began to tell us something in a cracked, jerky voice. A thin, stooped man with glasses freckled by raindrops translated the little man's story into English:

"He says the artillery has betrayed us, and guns are being mounted in the government buildings to sweep the plaza at daybreak." There was an odd sort of hopefulness in his voice, and he added: "In that event we can, naturally, do nothing."

"We can die," Lionel Grantham said gently.

There wasn't the least bit of sense to that crack. Nobody was here to die. They were all here because it was so unlikely that anybody would have to die, except perhaps a few of Einarson's soldiers. That's the sensible view of the boy's speech. But it's God's own truth that even I—a middle-aged detective who had forgotten what it was like to believe in fairies—felt suddenly warm inside my wet clothes. And if anybody had said to me: "This boy is a real king," I wouldn't have argued the point.

An abrupt hush came in the murmuring around us, leaving only the rustle of rain, and the tramp, tramp, tramp of orderly marching up the street—Einarson's men. Everybody commenced to talk at once, happily, expectantly, cheered by the approach of those whose part it was to do the heavy work.

An officer in a glistening slicker pushed through the crowd—a small, dapper boy with too large a sword. He saluted Grantham elaborately, and said in English, of which he seemed proud:

"Colonel Einarson's respects, Mister, and this progress goes betune."

I wondered what the last word meant.

Grantham smiled and said: "Convey my thanks to Colonel Einarson."

The banker appeared again, bold enough now to join us. Others who had been at the meeting appeared. We made an inner group around the statue, with the mob around us—more easily seen now in the gray of early morning. I didn't see the countryman into whose face Einarson had spat.

The rain soaked us. We shifted our feet, shivered, and talked. Daylight came slowly, showing more and more who stood around us wet and curious-eyed. On the edge of the crowd men burst into cheers. The rest of them took it up. They forgot their wet misery, laughed and danced, hugged and kissed one another. A bearded man in a leather coat came to us, bowed to Grantham, and explained that Einarson's own regiment could be seen occupying the Administration Building.

Day came fully. The mob around us opened to make way for an automobile that was surrounded by a squad of cavalrymen. It stopped in front of us. Colonel Einarson, holding a bare sword in his hand, stepped out of the car, saluted, and held the door open for Grantham and me. He followed us in, smelling of victory like a chorus girl of Coty. The cavalrymen closed around the car again, and we were driven to the Administration Building, through a crowd that yelled and ran red-faced and happy after us. It was all quite theatrical.

"The city is ours," said Einarson, leaning forward in his seat, his sword's point on the car floor, his hands on its hilt. "The President, the Deputies, nearly every official of importance, is taken. Not a single shot fired, not a window broken!"

He was proud of his revolution, and I didn't blame him. I wasn't sure that he might not have brains, after all. He had had sense enough to park his civilian adherents in the plaza until his soldiers had done their work.

We got out at the Administration Building, walking up the steps between rows of infantrymen at present-arms, rain sparkling on their fixed bayonets. More green-uniformed soldiers presented arms along the corridors. We went into an elaborately furnished dining-room, where fifteen or twenty officers stood up to receive us. There were lots of speeches made. Everybody was triumphant. All through breakfast there was much talking. I didn't understand any of it.

After the meal we went to the Deputies' Chamber, a large, oval room with curved rows of benches and desks facing a raised platform. Besides three desks on the platform, some twenty chairs had been put there, facing the curved seats. Our breakfast party occupied these chairs. I noticed that Grantham

and I were the only civilians on the platform. None of our fellow conspirators were there, except those who were in
Einarson's army. I wasn't so fond of that.

Grantham sat in the first row of chairs, between Einarson
and me. We looked down on the Deputies. There were perhaps a hundred of them distributed among the curved
benches, split sharply in two groups. Half of them, on the
right side of the room, were revolutionists. They stood up
and hurrahed at us. The other half, on the left, were prisoners. Most of them seemed to have dressed hurriedly.

Around the room, shoulder to shoulder against the wall
except on the platform and where the doors were, stood
Einarson's soldiers.

An old man came in between two soldiers—a mild-eyed old
gentleman, bald, stooped, with a wrinkled, clean-shaven,
scholarly face.

"Doctor Semich," Grantham whispered.

The President's guards took him to the center one of the
three desks on the platform. He paid no attention to us who
were sitting on the platform, and he did not sit down.

A red-haired Deputy—one of the revolutionary party—got
up and talked. His fellows cheered when he had finished. The
president spoke—three words in a very dry, very calm voice,
and left the platform to walk back the way he had come, the
two soldiers accompanying him.

"Refused to resign," Grantham informed me.

The red-haired Deputy came up on the platform and took
the center desk. The legislative machinery began to grind.
Men talked briefly, apparently to the point—revolutionists.
None of the prisoner Deputies rose. A vote was taken. A few
of the in-wrongs didn't vote. Most of them seemed to vote
with the ins.

"They've revoked the constitution," Grantham whispered.

The Deputies were hurrahing again—those who were there
voluntarily. Einarson leaned over and mumbled to Grantham
and me:

"That is as far as we may safely go today. It leaves all in our
hands."

"Time to listen to a suggestion?" I asked.

"Yes."

"Will you excuse us a moment?" I said to Grantham, and got up and walked to one of the rear corners of the platform.

He thought it over. Some of the color washed out of his face, and a little rippling movement appeared in the flesh of his chin. I crowded him along by moving the raincoat enough to show him the muzzle of the gun that actually was there in my left hand. I had the big heaver—he hadn't nerve enough to take a chance on dying in his hour of victory.

He strode across the platform to the desk at which the red-head sat, drove the red-head away with a snarl and a gesture, leaned over the desk, and bellowed down into the chamber. I stood a little to one side of him, a little behind, so no one could get between us.

No Deputy made a sound for a long minute after the Colonel's bellow had stopped. Then one of the anti-revolutionists jumped to his feet and yelped bitterly. Einarson pointed a long brown finger at him. Two soldiers left their places by the wall, took the Deputy roughly by neck and arms, and dragged him out. Another Deputy stood up, talked, and was removed. After the fifth drag-out everything was peaceful. Einarson put a question and got a unanimous answer.

He turned to me, his gaze darting from my face to my rain-coat and back, and said: "That is done."

"We'll have the coronation now," I commanded.

I missed most of the ceremony. I was busy keeping my hold on the florid officer, but finally Lionel Grantham was officially installed as Lionel the First, King of Muravia. Einarson and I congratulated him, or whatever it was, together. Then I took the officer aside.

"We're going to take a walk," I said. "No foolishness. Take me out of a side door."

I had him now, almost without needing the gun. He would have to deal quietly with Grantham and me—kill us without any publicity—if he were to avoid being laughed at—this man who had let himself be stuck up and robbed of a throne in the middle of his army.

We went roundabout from the Administration Building to the Hotel of the Republic without meeting anyone who knew us. The population was all in the plaza. We found the hotel deserted. I made him run the elevator to my floor, and herded him to my room.

I tried the door, found it unlocked, let go the knob, and told him to go in. He pushed the door open and stopped.

Romaine Frankl was sitting crosslegged in the middle of my bed, sewing a button on one of my union suits.

I prodded Einarson into the room and closed the door. Romaine looked at him and at the automatic that was now uncovered in my hand. With burlesque disappointment she said:

"Oh, you haven't killed him yet!"

Colonel Einarson stiffened. He had an audience now—one that saw his humiliation. He was likely to do something. I'd have to handle him with gloves, or—maybe the other way was better. I kicked him on the ankle and snarled: "Get over in the corner and sit down!"

He spun around to me. I jabbed the muzzle of the pistol in his face, grinding his lip between it and his teeth. When his head jerked back I slammed him in the belly with my other fist. He grabbed for air with a wide mouth. I pushed him over to a chair in one corner.

Romaine laughed and shook a finger at me, saying: "You're a rowdy!"

"What else can I do?" I protested, chiefly for my prisoner's benefit. "When somebody's watching him he gets notions that he's a hero. I stuck him up and made him crown the boy king. But this bird has still got the army, which is the government. I can't let go of him, or both Lionel the Once and I will gather lead. It hurts me more than it does him to have to knock him around, but I can't help myself. I've got to keep him sensible."

"You're doing wrong by him," she replied. "You've got no right to mistreat him. The only polite thing for you to do is to cut his throat in a gentlemanly manner."

"Ach!" Einarson's lungs were working again.

"Shut up," I yelled at him, "or I'll knock you double-jointed."

He glared at me, and I asked the girl: "What'll we do with him? I'd be glad to cut his throat, but the trouble is, his army might avenge him, and I'm not a fellow who likes to have anybody's army avenging on him."

"We'll give him to Vasilije," she said, swinging her feet over the side of the bed and standing up. "He'll know what to do."

"Where is he?"

"Upstairs in Grantham's suite, finishing his morning nap."

Then she said lightly, casually, as if she hadn't been thinking seriously about it: "So you had the boy crowned?"

"I did. You want it for your Vasilije? Good! We want five million American dollars for our abdication. Grantham put in three to finance the doings, and he deserves a profit. He's been regularly elected by the Deputies. He's got no real backing here, but he can get support from the neighbors. Don't overlook that. There are a couple of countries not a million miles away that would gladly send in an army to support a legitimate king in exchange for whatever concessions they liked. But Lionel the First isn't unreasonable. He thinks it would be better for you to have a native ruler. All he asks is a decent provision from the government. Five million is low enough, and he'll abdicate tomorrow. Tell that to your Vasilije."

She went around me to avoid passing between my gun and its target, stood on tiptoe to kiss my ear, and said:

"You and your king are brigands. I'll be back in a few minutes."

She went out.

"Ten millions," Colonel Einarson said.

"I can't trust you now," I said. "You'd pay us off in front of a firing squad."

"You can trust this pig Djudakovich?"

"He's got no reason to hate us."

"He will when he's told of you and his Romaine."

I laughed.

"Besides, how can he be king? Ach! What is his promise to pay if he cannot become in a position to pay? Suppose even I am dead. What will he do with my army? Ach! You have seen the pig! What kind of king is he?"

"I don't know," I said truthfully. "I'm told he was a good Minister of Police because inefficiency would spoil his comfort. Maybe he'd be a good king for the same reason. I've seen him once. He's a bloated mountain, but there's nothing ridiculous about him. He weighs a ton, and moves without shaking the floor. I'd be afraid to try on him what I did to you."

This insult brought the soldier up on his feet, very tall and straight. His eyes burned at me while his mouth hardened in a thin line. He was going to make trouble for me before I was rid of him.

The door opened and Vasilije Djudakovich came in, followed by the girl. I grinned at the fat Minister. He nodded without smiling. His little dark eyes moved coldly from me to Einarson.

The girl said:

"The government will give Lionel the First a draft for four million dollars, American, on either a Vienna or Athens bank, in exchange for his abdication." She dropped her official tone and added: "That's every nickel I could get out of him."

"You and your Vasilije are a couple of rotten bargain hunters," I complained. "But we'll take it. We've got to have a special train to Saloniki—one that will put us across the border before the abdication goes into effect."

"That will be arranged," she promised.

"Good! Now to do all this your Vasilije has got to take the army away from Einarson. Can he do it?"

"Ach!" Colonel Einarson reared up his head, swelled his thick chest. "That is precisely what he has got to do!"

The fat man grumbled sleepily through his yellow beard. Romaine came over and put a hand on my arm.

"Vasilije wants a private talk with Einarson. Leave it to him."

I agreed and offered Djudakovich my automatic. He paid no attention to the gun or to me. He was looking with a clammy sort of patience at the officer. I went out with the girl and closed the door. At the foot of the stairs I took her by the shoulders.

"Can I trust your Vasilije?" I asked.

"Oh my dear, he could handle half a dozen Einarsons."

"I don't mean that. He won't try to gyp me?"

"Why should you start worrying about that now?"

"He doesn't seem to be exactly all broken out with friendliness."

She laughed, and twisted her face around to bite at one of my hands.

"He's got ideals," she explained. "He despises you and your king for a pair of adventurers who are making a profit out of his country's troubles. That's why he's so sniffy. But he'll keep his word."

Maybe he would, I thought, but he hadn't given me his word—the girl had.

"I'm going over to see His Majesty," I said. "I won't be long then I'll join you up in his suite. What was the idea of the sewing act? I had no buttons off."

"You did," she contradicted me, rummaging in my pocket for cigarettes. "I pulled one off when one of our men told me you and Einarson were headed this way. I thought it would look domestic."

I found my king in a wine and gold drawing-room in the Executive Residence, surrounded by Muravia's socially and politically ambitious. Uniforms were still in the majority, but a sprinkling of civilians had finally got to him, along with their wives and daughters. He was too occupied to see me for a few minutes, so I stood around, looking the folks over. Particularly one—a tall girl in black, who stood apart from the others, at a window.

I noticed her first because she was beautiful in face and body, and then I studied her more closely because of the expression in the brown eyes with which she watched the new king. If ever anybody looked proud of anybody else, this girl did of Grantham. The way she stood there, alone, by the window, and looked at him—he would have had to be at least a combination of Apollo, Socrates, and Alexander to deserve half of it. Valeska Radnjak, I supposed.

I looked at the boy. His face was proud and flushed, and every two seconds turned toward the girl at the window while he listened to the jabbering of the worshipful group around him. I knew he wasn't any Apollo-Socrates-Alexander, but he managed to look the part. He had found a spot in the world that he liked. I was half sorry he couldn't hang on to it, but my regrets didn't keep me from deciding that I had wasted enough time.

I pushed through the crowd toward him. He recognized me with the eyes of a park sleeper being awakened from sweet dreams by a night-stick on his shoe-soles. He excused himself to the others and took me down a corridor to a room with stained glass windows and richly carved office furniture.

"This was Doctor Semich's office," he told me. "I shall——"

"You'll be in Greece by tomorrow," I said bluntly.

He frowned at his feet, a stubborn frown.

"You ought to know you can't hold on," I argued. "You may think everything is going smoothly. If you do, you're deaf, dumb, and blind. I put you in with the muzzle of a gun against Einarson's liver. I've kept you in this long by kidnaping him. I've made a deal with Djudakovich—the only strong man I've seen here. It's up to him to handle Einarson. I can't hold him any longer. Djudakovich will make a good king, if he wants to. He promises you four million dollars and a special train and safe-conduct to Salo-niki. You go out with your head up. You've been a king. You've taken a country out of bad hands and put it into good—this fat guy is real. And you've made yourself a million profit."

"No. You go. I shall see it through. These people have trusted me, and I shall——"

"My God, that's old Doc Semich's line! These people haven't trusted you—not a bit of it. I'm the people who trusted you. I made you king, understand? I made you king so you could go home with your chin up—not so you could stay here and make an ass of yourself! I bought help with promises. One of them was that you'd get out within twenty-four hours. You've got to keep the promises I made in your name. The people trusted you, huh? You were crammed down their throats, my son! And I did the cramming! Now I'm going to uncram you. If it happens to be tough on your romance—if your Valeska won't take any price less than this dinky country's throne—"

"That's enough." His voice came from some point at least fifty feet above me. "You shall have your abdication. I don't want the money. You will send word to me when the train is ready."

"Write the get-out now," I ordered.

He went over to the desk, found a sheet of paper, and with a steady hand wrote that in leaving Muravia he renounced his

throne and all rights to it. He signed the paper *Lionel Rex* and
gave it to me. I pocketed it and began sympathetically:

"I can understand your feelings, and I'm sorry that—"

He put his back to me and walked out. I returned to the
hotel.

At the fifth floor I left the elevator and walked softly to the
door of my room. No sound came through. I tried the door,
found it unlocked, and went in. Emptiness. Even my clothes
and bags were gone. I went up to Grantham's suite.

Djudakovich, Romaine, Einarson, and half the police force
were there.

Colonel Einarson sat very erect in an armchair in the middle
of the room. Dark hair and mustache bristled. His chin was
out, muscles bulged everywhere in his florid face, his eyes
were hot—he was in one of his finest scrapping moods. That
came of giving him an audience.

I scowled at Djudakovich, who stood on wide-spread
giant's legs with his back to a window. Why hadn't the fat
fool known enough to keep Einarson off in a lonely corner,
where he could be handled?

Romaine floated around and past the policemen who stood
or sat everywhere in the room, and came to where I stood,
inside the door.

"Are your arrangements all made?" she asked.

"Got the abdication in my pocket."

"Give it to me."

"Not yet," I said. "First I've got to know that your Vasilije
is as big as he looks. Einarson doesn't look squelched to me.
Your fat boy ought to have known he'd blossom out in front
of an audience."

"There's no telling what Vasilije is up to," she said lightly,
"except that it will be adequate."

I wasn't as sure of that as she was. Djudakovich rumbled a
question at her, and she gave him a quick answer. He rumbled some more—at the policemen. They began to go away
from us, singly, in pairs, in groups. When the last one had
gone the fat man pushed words out between his yellow
whiskers at Einarson. Einarson stood up, chest out, shoulders
back, grinning confidently under his dark mustache.

"What now?" I asked the girl.

"Come along and you'll see," she said.

The four of us went downstairs and out the hotel's front door. The rain had stopped. In the plaza was gathered most of Stefania's population, thickest in front of the Administration Building and Executive Residence. Over their heads we could see the sheepskin caps of Einarson's regiment, still around those buildings as he had left them.

We—or at least Einarson—were recognized and cheered as we crossed the plaza. Einarson and Djudakovich went side by side in front, the soldier marching, the fat giant waddling. Romaine and I went close behind them. We headed straight for the Administration Building.

"What is he up to?" I asked irritably.

She patted my arm, smiled excitedly, and said: "Wait and see."

There didn't seem to be anything else to do—except worry.

We arrived at the foot of the Administration Building's stone steps. Bayonets had an uncomfortably cold gleam in the early evening light as Einarson's troops presented arms. We climbed the steps. On the broad top step Einarson and Djudakovich turned to face soldiers and citizens below. The girl and I moved around behind the pair. Her teeth were chattering, her fingers were digging into my arm, but her lips and eyes were smiling recklessly.

The soldiers who were around the Executive Residence came to join those already before us, pushing back the citizens to make room. Another detachment came up. Einarson raised his hand, bawled a dozen words, growled at Djudakovich, and stepped back.

Djudakovich spoke, a drowsy, effortless roar that could have been heard as far as the hotel. As he spoke, he took a paper out of his pocket and held it before him. There was nothing theatrical in his voice or manner. He might have been talking about anything not too important. But—looking at his audience, you'd have known it was important.

The soldiers had broken ranks to crowd nearer, faces were reddening, a bayoneted gun was shaken aloft here and there. Behind them the citizens were looking at one another with frightened faces, jostling each other, some trying to get nearer, some trying to get away.

Djudakovich talked on. The turmoil grew. A soldier pushed through his fellows and started up the steps, others at his heels.

Einarson cut in on the fat man's speech, stepping to the edge of the top step, bawling down at the upturned faces, with the voice of a man accustomed to being obeyed.

The soldiers on the steps tumbled down. Einarson bawled again. The broken ranks were slowly straightened, flourished guns were grounded. Einarson stood silent a moment, glowering at his troops, and then began an address. I couldn't understand his words any more than I had the fat man's, but there was no question about his impressiveness. And there was no doubt that the anger was going out of the faces below.

I looked at Romaine. She shivered and was no longer smiling. I looked at Djudakovich. He was as still and as emotionless as the mountain he resembled.

I wished I knew what it was all about, so I'd know whether it was wisest to shoot Einarson and duck through the apparently empty building behind us or not. I could guess that the paper in Djudakovich's hand had been evidence of some sort against the Colonel, evidence that would have stirred the soldiers to the point of attacking him if they hadn't been too accustomed to obeying him.

While I was wishing and guessing, Einarson finished his address, stepped to one side, pointed a finger at Djudakovich, barked an order.

Down below, soldiers' faces were indecisive, shifty-eyed, but four of them stepped briskly out at their colonel's order and came up the steps. "So," I thought, "my fat candidate has lost! Well, he can have the firing squad. The back door for mine." My hand had been holding the gun in my coat pocket for a long time. I kept it there while I took a slow step back, drawing the girl with me.

"Move when I tell you," I muttered.

"Wait!" she gasped. "Look!"

The fat giant, sleepy-eyed as ever, put out an enormous paw and caught the wrist of Einarson's pointing hand. Pulled

Einarson down. Let go the wrist and caught the Colonel's shoulder. Lifted him off his feet with that one hand that held his shoulder. Shook him at the soldiers below. Shook Einarson at them with one hand. Shook his piece of paper—whatever it was—at them with the other. And I'm damned if one seemed any more strain on his arms than the other!

While he shook them—man and paper—he roared sleepily, and when he had finished roaring he flung his two handfuls down to the wild-eyed ranks. Flung them with a gesture that said, *"Here is the man and here is the evidence against him. Do what you like."*

And the soldiers who had cringed back into ranks at Einarson's command when he stood tall and domineering above them, did what could have been expected when he was tossed down to them.

They tore him apart—actually—piece by piece. They dropped their guns and fought to get at him. Those farther away climbed over those nearer, smothering them, trampling them. They surged back and forth in front of the steps, an insane pack of men turned wolves, savagely struggling to destroy a man who must have died before he had been down half a minute.

I put the girl's hand off my arm and went to face Djudakovich.

"Muravia's yours," I said. "I don't want anything but our draft and train. Here's the abdication."

Romaine swiftly translated my words and then Djudakovich's:

"The train is ready now. The draft will be delivered there. Do you wish to go over for Grantham?"

"No. Send him down. How do I find the train?"

"I'll take you," she said. "We'll go through the building and out a side door."

One of Djudakovich's detectives sat at the wheel of a car in front of the hotel. Romaine and I got in it. Across the plaza tumult was still boiling. Neither of us said anything while the car whisked us through darkening streets.

Presently she asked very softly: "And now you despise me?"

"No." I reached for her. "But I hate mobs, lynchings—they sicken me. No matter how wrong the man is, if a mob's against him, I'm for him. The only thing I ever pray to God for is a chance some day to squat down behind a machine gun with a lynching party in front of me. I had no use for Einarson, but I wouldn't have given him that! Well, what's done is done. What was the document?"

"A letter from Mahmoud. He had left it with a friend to be given to Vasilije if anything ever happened to him. He knew Einarson, it seems, and prepared his revenge. The letter confessed his—Mahmoud's—part in the assassination of General Radnjak, and said that Einarson was also implicated. The army worshiped Radnjak, and Einarson wanted the army."

"Your Vasilije could have used that to chase Einarson out—without feeding him to the wolves," I complained.

"Vasilije was right. Bad as it was, that was the way to do it. It's over and settled forever, with Vasilije in power. An Einarson alive, an army not knowing he had killed their idol—too risky. Up to the end Einarson thought he had power enough to hold his troops, no matter what they knew. He——"

"All right—it's done. And I'm glad to be through with this king business. Kiss me."

She did, and whispered:

"When Vasilije dies—and he can't live long, the way he eats—I'm coming to San Francisco."

"You're a cold-blooded hussy," I said.

Lionel Grantham, ex-king of Muravia, was only five minutes behind us in reaching our train. He wasn't alone. Valeska Radnjak, looking as much like the queen of something as if she had been, was with him. She didn't seem to be all broken up over the loss of her throne.

The boy was pleasant and polite enough to me during our rattling trip to Saloniki, but obviously not very comfortable in my company. His bride-to-be didn't know anybody but the boy existed, unless she happened to find someone else directly in front of her. So I didn't wait for their wedding, but left Saloniki on a boat that pulled out a couple of hours after we arrived.

I left the draft with them, of course. They decided to take out Lionel's three millions and return the fourth to Muravia. And I went back to San Francisco to quarrel with my boss over what he thought were unnecessary five- and ten-dollar items in my expense account.

Fly Paper

I T WAS a wandering daughter job.

The Hambletons had been for several generations a wealthy and decently prominent New York family. There was nothing in the Hambleton history to account for Sue, the youngest member of the clan. She grew out of childhood with a kink that made her dislike the polished side of life, like the rough. By the time she was twenty-one, in 1926, she definitely preferred Tenth Avenue to Fifth, grifters to bankers, and Hymie the Riveter to the Honorable Cecil Windown, who had asked her to marry him.

The Hambletons tried to make Sue behave, but it was too late for that. She was legally of age. When she finally told them to go to hell and walked out on them there wasn't much they could do about it. Her father, Major Waldo Hambleton, had given up all the hopes he ever had of salvaging her, but he didn't want her to run into any grief that could be avoided. So he came into the Continental Detective Agency's New York office and asked to have an eye kept on her.

Hymie the Riveter was a Philadelphia racketeer who had moved north to the big city, carrying a Thompson submachine-gun wrapped in blue-checkered oil cloth, after a disagreement with his partners. New York wasn't so good a field as Philadelphia for machine-gun work. The Thompson lay idle for a year or so while Hymie made expenses with an automatic, preying on small-time crap games in Harlem.

Three or four months after Sue went to live with Hymie he made what looked like a promising connection with the first of the crew that came into New York from Chicago to organize the city on the western scale. But the boys from Chi didn't want Hymie; they wanted the Thompson. When he showed it to them, as the big item in his application for employment, they shot holes in the top of Hymie's head and went away with the gun.

Sue Hambleton buried Hymie, had a couple of lonely weeks in which she hocked a ring to eat, and then got a job as hostess in a speakeasy run by a Greek named Vassos.

One of Vassos' customers was Babe McCloor, two hundred and fifty pounds of hard Scotch-Irish-Indian bone and muscle, a black-haired, blue-eyed, swarthy giant who was resting up after doing a fifteen-year hitch in Leavenworth for ruining most of the smaller post offices between New Orleans and Omaha. Babe was keeping himself in drinking money while he rested by playing with pedestrians in dark streets.

Babe liked Sue. Vassos liked Sue. Sue liked Babe. Vassos didn't like that. Jealousy spoiled the Greek's judgment. He kept the speakeasy door locked one night when Babe wanted to come in. Babe came in, bringing pieces of the door with him. Vassos got his gun out, but couldn't shake Sue off his arm. He stopped trying when Babe hit him with the part of the door that had the brass knob on it. Babe and Sue went away from Vassos' together.

Up to that time the New York office had managed to keep in touch with Sue. She hadn't been kept under constant surveillance. Her father hadn't wanted that. It was simply a matter of sending a man around every week or so to see that she was still alive, to pick up whatever information he could from her friends and neighbors, without, of course, letting her know she was being tabbed. All that had been easy enough, but when she and Babe went away after wrecking the gin mill, they dropped completely out of sight.

After turning the city upside-down, the New York office sent a journal on the job to the other Continental branches throughout the country, giving the information above and enclosing photographs and descriptions of Sue and her new playmate. That was late in 1927.

We had enough copies of the photographs to go around, and for the next month or so whoever had a little idle time on his hands spent it looking through San Francisco and Oakland for the missing pair. We didn't find them. Operatives in other cities, doing the same thing, had the same luck.

Then, nearly a year later, a telegram came to us from the New York office. Decoded, it read:

> Major Hambleton today received telegram
> from daughter in San Francisco *quote* Please wire
> me thousand dollars care apartment two hundred

six number six hundred one Eddis Street *stop* I will
come home if you will let me *stop* Please tell me if
I can come but please please wire money anyway
unquote Hambleton authorizes payment of money
to her immediately *stop* Detail competent operative
to call on her with money and to arrange for her
return home *stop* If possible have man and woman
operative accompany her here *stop* Hambleton
wiring her *stop* Report immediately by wire.

II

The Old Man gave me the telegram and a check, saying:
"You know the situation. You'll know how to handle it."

I pretended I agreed with him, went down to the bank,
swapped the check for a bundle of bills of several sizes, caught
a street car, and went up to 601 Eddis Street, a fairly large
apartment building on the corner of Larkin.

The name on Apartment 206's vestibule mail box was J. M.
Wales.

I pushed 206's button. When the locked door buzzed off I
went into the building, past the elevator to the stairs, and up
a flight. 206 was just around the corner from the stairs.

The apartment door was opened by a tall, slim man of
thirty-something in neat dark clothes. He had narrow dark
eyes set in a long pale face. There was some gray in the dark
hair brushed flat to his scalp.

"Miss Hambleton," I said.

"Uh—what about her?" His voice was smooth, but not too
smooth to be agreeable.

"I'd like to see her."

His upper eyelids came down a little and the brows over
them came a little closer together. He asked, "Is it—?" and
stopped, watching me steadily.

I didn't say anything. Presently he finished his question:
"Something to do with a telegram?"

"Yeah."

His long face brightened immediately. He asked:
"You're from her father?"

"Yeah."

He stepped back and swung the door wide open, saying:

"Come in. Major Hambleton's wire came to her only a few minutes ago. He said someone would call."

We went through a small passageway into a sunny living-room that was cheaply furnished, but neat and clean enough.

"Sit down," the man said, pointing at a brown rocking chair.

I sat down. He sat on the burlap-covered sofa facing me. I looked around the room. I didn't see anything to show that a woman was living there.

He rubbed the long bridge of his nose with a longer fore-finger and asked slowly:

"You brought the money?"

I said I'd feel more like talking with her there.

He looked at the finger with which he had been rubbing his nose, and then up at me, saying softly:

"But I'm her friend."

I said, "Yeah?" to that.

"Yes," he repeated. He frowned slightly, drawing back the corners of his thin-lipped mouth. "I've only asked whether you've brought the money."

I didn't say anything.

"The point is," he said quite reasonably, "that if you brought the money she doesn't expect you to hand it over to anybody except her. If you didn't bring it she doesn't want to see you. I don't think her mind can be changed about that. That's why I asked if you had brought it."

"I brought it."

He looked doubtfully at me. I showed him the money I had got from the bank. He jumped up briskly from the sofa.

"I'll have her here in a minute or two," he said over his shoulder as his long legs moved him toward the door. At the door he stopped to ask: "Do you know her? Or shall I have her bring means of identifying herself?"

"That would be best," I told him.

He went out, leaving the corridor door open.

III

In five minutes he was back with a slender blonde girl of twenty-three in pale green silk. The looseness of her small mouth and the puffiness around her blue eyes weren't yet pronounced enough to spoil her prettiness.

I stood up.

"This is Miss Hambleton," he said.

She gave me a swift glance and then lowered her eyes again, nervously playing with the strap of a handbag she held.

"You can identify yourself?" I asked.

"Sure," the man said. "Show them to him, Sue."

She opened the bag, brought out some papers and things, and held them up for me to take.

"Sit down, sit down," the man said as I took them.

They sat on the sofa. I sat in the rocking chair again and examined the things she had given me. There were two letters addressed to Sue Hambleton here, her father's telegram welcoming her home, a couple of receipted department store bills, an automobile driver's license, and a savings account pass book that showed a balance of less than ten dollars.

By the time I had finished my examination the girl's embarrassment was gone. She looked levelly at me, as did the man beside her. I felt in my pocket, found my copy of the photograph New York had sent us at the beginning of the hunt, and looked from it to her.

"Your mouth could have shrunk, maybe," I said, "but how could your nose have got that much longer?"

"If you don't like my nose," she said, "how'd you like to go to hell?" Her face had turned red.

"That's not the point. It's a swell nose, but it's not Sue's." I held the photograph out to her. "See for yourself."

She glared at the photograph and then at the man.

"What a smart guy you are," she told him.

He was watching me with dark eyes that had a brittle shine to them between narrow-drawn eyelids. He kept on watching me while he spoke to her out the side of his mouth, crisply:

"Pipe down."

She piped down. He sat and watched me. I sat and watched him. A clock ticked seconds away behind me. His eyes began shifting their focus from one of my eyes to the other. The girl sighed.

He said in a low voice: "Well?"

I said: "You're in a hole."

"What can you make out of it?" he asked casually.

"Conspiracy to defraud."

The girl jumped up and hit one of his shoulders angrily with the back of a hand, crying:

"What a smart guy you are, to get me in a jam like this. It was going to be duck soup—yeh! Eggs in the coffee—yeh! Now look at you. You haven't even got guts enough to tell this guy to go chase himself." She spun around to face me, pushing her red face down at me—I was still sitting in the rocker—snarling: "Well, what are you waiting for? Waiting to be kissed good-by? We don't owe you anything, do we? We didn't get any of your lousy money, did we? Outside, then. Take the air. Dangle."

"Stop it, sister," I growled. "You'll bust something."

The man said:

"For God's sake stop that bawling, Peggy, and give somebody else a chance." He addressed me: "Well, what do you want?"

"How'd you get into this?" I asked.

He spoke quickly, eagerly:

"A fellow named Kenny gave me that stuff and told me about this Sue Hambleton, and her old man having plenty. I thought I'd give it a whirl. I figured the old man would either wire the dough right off the reel or wouldn't send it at all. I didn't figure on this send-a-man stuff. Then when his wire came, saying he was sending a man to see her, I ought to have dropped it.

"But hell! Here was a man coming with a grand in cash. That was too good to let go of without a try. It looked like there still might be a chance of copping, so I got Peggy to do Sue for me. If the man was coming today, it was a cinch he belonged out here on the Coast, and it was an even bet he wouldn't know Sue, would only have a description of her. From what Kenny had told me about her, I knew Peggy would come pretty close to fitting her description. I still don't see how you got that photograph. Television? I only wired the old man yesterday. I mailed a couple of letters to Sue, here, yesterday, so we'd have them with the other identification stuff to get the money from the telegraph company on."

"Kenny gave you the old man's address?"

"Sure he did."

"Did he give you Sue's?"

"No."

"How'd Kenny get hold of the stuff?"

"He didn't say."

"Where's Kenny now?"

"I don't know. He was on his way east, with something else on the fire, and couldn't fool with this. That's why he passed it on to me."

"Big-hearted Kenny," I said. "You know Sue Hambleton?"

"No," emphatically. "I'd never even heard of her till Kenny told me."

"I don't like this Kenny," I said, "though without him your story's got some good points. Could you tell it leaving him out?"

He shook his head slowly from side to side, saying:

"It wouldn't be the way it happened."

"That's too bad. Conspiracies to defraud don't mean as much to me as finding Sue. I might have made a deal with you."

He shook his head again, but his eyes were thoughtful, and his lower lip moved up to overlap the upper a little.

The girl had stepped back so she could see both of us as we talked, turning her face, which showed she didn't like us, from one to the other as we spoke our pieces. Now she fastened her gaze on the man, and her eyes were growing angry again.

I got up on my feet, telling him:

"Suit yourself. But if you want to play it that way I'll have to take you both in."

He smiled with indrawn lips and stood up.

The girl thrust herself in between us, facing him.

"This is a swell time to be dummying up," she spit at him. "Pop off, you lightweight, or I will. You're crazy if you think I'm going to take the fall with you."

"Shut up," he said in his throat.

"Shut me up," she cried.

He tried to, with both hands. I reached over her shoulders and caught one of his wrists, knocked the other hand up.

She slid out from between us and ran around behind me, screaming:

"Joe does know her. He got the things from her. She's at the St. Martin on O'Farrell Street—her and Babe McCloor."

While I listened to this I had to pull my head aside to let Joe's right hook miss me, had got his left arm twisted behind him, had turned my hip to catch his knee, and had got the palm of my left hand under his chin. I was ready to give his chin the Japanese tilt when he stopped wrestling and grunted:

"Let me tell it."

"Hop to it," I consented, taking my hands away from him and stepping back.

He rubbed the wrist I had wrenched, scowling past me at the girl. He called her four unlovely names, the mildest of which was "a dumb twist," and told her:

"He was bluffing about throwing us in the can. You don't think old man Hambleton's hunting for newspaper space, do you?" That wasn't a bad guess.

He sat on the sofa again, still rubbing his wrist. The girl stayed on the other side of the room, laughing at him through her teeth.

I said: "All right, roll it out, one of you."

"You've got it all," he muttered. "I glaumed that stuff last week when I was visiting Babe, knowing the story and hating to see a promising layout like that go to waste."

"What's Babe doing now?" I asked.

"I don't know."

"Is he still puffing them?"

"I don't know."

"Like hell you don't."

"I don't," he insisted. "If you know Babe you know you can't get anything out of him about what he's doing."

"How long have he and Sue been here?"

"About six months that I know of."

"Who's he mobbed up with?"

"I don't know. Any time Babe works with a mob he picks them up on the road and leaves them on the road."

"How's he fixed?"

"I don't know. There's always enough grub and liquor in the joint."

Half an hour of this convinced me that I wasn't going to get much information about my people here.

I went to the phone in the passageway and called the Agency. The boy on the switchboard told me MacMan was in the operatives' room. I asked to have him sent up to me, and went back to the living-room. Joe and Peggy took their heads apart when I came in.

MacMan arrived in less than ten minutes. I let him in and told him:

"This fellow says his name's Joe Wales, and the girl's supposed to be Peggy Carroll who lives upstairs in 421. We've got them cold for conspiracy to defraud, but I've made a deal with them. I'm going out to look at it now. Stay here with them, in this room. Nobody goes in or out, and nobody but you gets to the phone. There's a fire-escape in front of the window. The window's locked now. I'd keep it that way. If the deal turns out O.K. we'll let them go, but if they cut up on you while I'm gone there's no reason why you can't knock them around as much as you want."

MacMan nodded his hard round head and pulled a chair out between them and the door. I picked up my hat.

Joe Wales called:

"Hey, you're not going to uncover me to Babe, are you? That's got to be part of the deal."

"Not unless I have to."

"I'd just as leave stand the rap," he said. "I'd be safer in jail."

"I'll give you the best break I can," I promised, "but you'll have to take what's dealt you."

IV

Walking over to the St. Martin—only half a dozen blocks from Wales's place—I decided to go up against McCloor and the girl as a Continental op who suspected Babe of being in on a branch bank stick-up in Alameda the previous week. He hadn't been in on it—if the bank people had described half-correctly the men who had robbed them—so it wasn't likely my supposed suspicions would frighten him much. Clearing himself, he might give me some information I could use. The chief thing I wanted, of course, was a look at the girl, so I could report to her father that I had seen her. There was no reason for supposing that she and Babe knew her father was trying to keep an eye on her. Babe had a record. It was natural enough for sleuths to drop in now and then and try to hang something on him.

The St. Martin was a small three-story apartment house of red brick between two taller hotels. The vestibule register showed, *R. K. McCloor, 313*, as Wales and Peggy had told me.

I pushed the bell button. Nothing happened. Nothing happened any of the four times I pushed it. I pushed the button labeled *Manager*.

The door clicked open. I went indoors. A beefy woman in a pink-striped cotton dress that needed pressing stood in an apartment doorway just inside the street door.

"Some people named McCloor live here?" I asked.

"Three-thirteen," she said.

"Been living here long?"

She pursed her fat mouth, looked intently at me, hesitated, but finally said: "Since last June."

"What do you know about them?"

She balked at that, raising her chin and her eyebrows.

I gave her my card. That was safe enough; it fit in with the pretext I intended using upstairs.

Her face, when she raised it from reading the card, was oily with curiosity.

"Come in here," she said in a husky whisper, backing through the doorway.

I followed her into her apartment. We sat on a Chesterfield and she whispered:

"What is it?"

"Maybe nothing." I kept my voice low, playing up to her theatricals. "He's done time for safe-burglary. I'm trying to get a line on him now, on the off chance that he might have been tied up in a recent job. I don't know that he was. He may be going straight for all I know." I took his photograph—front and profile, taken at Leavenworth—out of my pocket. "This him?"

She seized it eagerly, nodded, said, "Yes, that's him, all right," turned it over to read the description on the back, and repeated, "Yes, that's him, all right."

"His wife is here with him?" I asked.

She nodded vigorously.

"I don't know her," I said. "What sort of looking girl is she?"

She described a girl who could have been Sue Hambleton. I couldn't show Sue's picture, that would have uncovered me if she and Babe heard about it.

I asked the woman what she knew about the McCloors. What she knew wasn't a great deal; paid their rent on time, kept irregular hours, had occasional drinking parties, quarreled a lot.

"Think they're in now?" I asked. "I got no answer on the bell."

"I don't know," she whispered. "I haven't seen either of them since night before last, when they had a fight."

"Much of a fight?"

"Not much worse than usual."

"Could you find out if they're in?" I asked.

She looked at me out of the ends of her eyes.

"I'm not going to make any trouble for you," I assured her. "But if they've blown I'd like to know it, and I reckon you would too."

"All right, I'll find out." She got up, patting a pocket in which keys jingled. "You wait here."

"I'll go as far as the third floor with you," I said, "and wait out of sight there."

"All right," she said reluctantly.

On the third floor, I remained by the elevator. She disappeared around a corner of the dim corridor, and presently a muffled electric bell rang. It rang three times. I heard her keys jingle and one of them grate in a lock. The lock clicked. I heard the doorknob rattle as she turned it.

Then a long moment of silence was ended by a scream that filled the corridor from wall to wall.

I jumped for the corner, swung around it, saw an open door ahead, went through it, and slammed the door shut behind me.

The scream had stopped.

I was in a small dark vestibule with three doors besides the one I had come through. One door was shut. One opened into a bathroom. I went to the other.

The fat manager stood just inside it, her round back to me. I pushed past her and saw what she was looking at.

Sue Hambleton, in pale yellow pajamas trimmed with black lace, was lying across a bed. She lay on her back. Her arms were stretched out over her head. One leg was bent under her, one stretched out so that its bare foot rested on the floor. That bare foot was whiter than a live foot could be. Her face was white as her foot, except for a mottled swollen area from the right eyebrow to the right cheek-bone and dark bruises on her throat.

"Phone the police," I told the woman, and began poking into corners, closets and drawers.

It was late afternoon when I returned to the Agency. I asked the file clerk to see if we had anything on Joe Wales and Peggy Carroll, and then went into the Old Man's office.

He put down some reports he had been reading, gave me a nodded invitation to sit down, and asked:

"You've seen her?"

"Yeah. She's dead."

The Old Man said, "Indeed," as if I had said it was raining, and smiled with polite attentiveness while I told him about it—from the time I had rung Wales's bell until I had joined the fat manager in the dead girl's apartment.

"She had been knocked around some, was bruised on the face and neck," I wound up. "But that didn't kill her."

"You think she was murdered?" he asked, still smiling gently.

"I don't know. Doc Jordan says he thinks it could have been arsenic. He's hunting for it in her now. We found a funny thing in the joint. Some thick sheets of dark gray paper were stuck in a book—*The Count of Monte Cristo*—wrapped in a month-old newspaper and wedged into a dark corner between the stove and the kitchen wall."

"Ah, arsenical fly paper," the Old Man murmured. "The Maybrick-Seddons trick. Mashed in water, four to six grains of arsenic can be soaked out of a sheet—enough to kill two people."

I nodded, saying:

"I worked on one in Louisville in 1916. The mulatto janitor saw McCloor leaving at half-past nine yesterday morning. She was probably dead before that. Nobody's seen him since.

Earlier in the morning the people in the next apartment had heard them talking, her groaning. But they had too many fights for the neighbors to pay much attention to that. The landlady told me they had a fight the night before that. The police are hunting for him."

"Did you tell the police who she was?"

"No. What do we do on that angle? We can't tell them about Wales without telling them all."

"I dare say the whole thing will have to come out," he said thoughtfully. "I'll wire New York."

I went out of his office. The file clerk gave me a couple of newspaper clippings. The first told me that, fifteen months ago, Joseph Wales, alias Holy Joe, had been arrested on the complaint of a farmer named Toomey that he had been taken for twenty-five hundred dollars on a phoney "Business Opportunity" by Wales and three other men. The second clipping said the case had been dropped when Toomey failed to appear against Wales in court—bought off in the customary manner by the return of part or all of his money. That was all our files held on Wales, and they had nothing on Peggy Carroll.

V

MacMan opened the door for me when I returned to Wales's apartment.

"Anything doing?" I asked him.

"Nothing—except they've been bellyaching a lot."

Wales came forward, asking eagerly:

"Satisfied now?"

The girl stood by the window, looking at me with anxious eyes.

I didn't say anything.

"Did you find her?" Wales asked, frowning. "She was where I told you?"

"Yeah," I said.

"Well, then." Part of his frown went away. "That lets Peggy and me out, doesn't—" He broke off, ran his tongue over his lower lip, put a hand to his chin, asked sharply: "You didn't give them the tip-off on me, did you?"

I shook my head, no.

He took his hand from his chin and asked irritably:

"What's the matter with you, then? What are you looking like that for?"

Behind him the girl spoke bitterly.

"I knew damned well it would be like this," she said. "I knew damned well we weren't going to get out of it. Oh, what a smart guy you are!"

"Take Peggy into the kitchen, and shut both doors," I told MacMan. "Holy Joe and I are going to have a real heart-to-heart talk."

The girl went out willingly, but when MacMan was closing the door she put her head in again to tell Wales:

"I hope he busts you in the nose if you try to hold out on him."

MacMan shut the door.

"Your playmate seems to think you know something," I said.

Wales scowled at the door and grumbled: "She's more help to me than a broken leg." He turned his face to me, trying to make it look frank and friendly. "What do you want? I came clean with you before. What's the matter now?"

"What do you guess?"

He pulled his lips in between his teeth.

"What do you want to make me guess for?" he demanded. "I'm willing to play ball with you. But what can I do if you won't tell me what you want? I can't see inside your head."

"You'd get a kick out of it if you could."

He shook his head wearily and walked back to the sofa, sitting down bent forward, his hands together between his knees.

"All right," he sighed. "Take your time about asking me. I'll wait for you."

I went over and stood in front of him. I took his chin between my left thumb and fingers, raising his head and bending my own down until our noses were almost touching. I said:

"Where you stumbled, Joe, was in sending the telegram right after the murder."

"He's dead?" It popped out before his eyes had even had time to grow round and wide.

The question threw me off balance. I had to wrestle with my forehead to keep it from wrinkling, and I put too much calmness in my voice when I asked:

"Is who dead?"

"Who? How do I know? Who do you mean?"

"Who did you think I meant?" I insisted.

"How do I know? Oh, all right! Old man Hambleton, Sue's father."

"That's right," I said, and took my hand away from his chin.

"And he was murdered, you say?" He hadn't moved his face an inch from the position into which I had lifted it. "How?"

"Arsenic—fly paper."

"Arsenic fly paper." He looked thoughtful. "That's a funny one."

"Yeah, very funny. Where'd you go about buying some if you wanted it?"

"Buying it? I don't know. I haven't seen any since I was a kid. Nobody uses fly paper here in San Francisco anyway. There aren't enough flies."

"Somebody used some here," I said, "on Sue."

"Sue?" He jumped so that the sofa squeaked under him.

"Yeah. Murdered yesterday morning—arsenical fly paper."

"Both of them?" he asked incredulously.

"Both of who?"

"Her and her father."

"Yeah."

He put his chin far down on his chest and rubbed the back of one hand with the palm of the other.

"Then I am in a hole," he said slowly.

"That's what," I cheerfully agreed. "Want to try talking yourself out of it?"

"Let me think."

I let him think, listening to the tick of the clock while he thought. Thinking brought drops of sweat out on his gray-white face. Presently he sat up straight, wiping his face with a fancily colored handkerchief.

"I'll talk," he said. "I've got to talk now. Sue was getting ready to ditch Babe. She and I were going away. She— Here, I'll show you."

He put his hand in his pocket and held out a folded sheet of thick notepaper to me. I took it and read:

Dear Joe:—
    I can't stand this much longer—we've simply got to go soon. Babe beat me again tonight. Please, if you really love me, let's make it soon.

                                 Sue

The handwriting was a nervous woman's, tall, angular, and piled up.

"That's why I made the play for Hambleton's grand," he said. "I've been shatting on my uppers for a couple of months, and when that letter came yesterday I just had to raise dough somehow to get her away. She wouldn't have stood for tapping her father though, so I tried to swing it without her knowing."

"When did you see her last?"

"Day before yesterday, the day she mailed that letter. Only I saw her in the afternoon—she was here—and she wrote it that night."

"Babe suspect what you were up to?"

"We didn't think he did. I don't know. He was jealous as hell all the time, whether he had any reason to be or not."

"How much reason did he have?"

Wales looked me straight in the eye and said:

"Sue was a good kid."

I said: "Well, she's been murdered."

He didn't say anything.

Day was darkening into evening. I went to the door and pressed the light button. I didn't lose sight of Holy Joe Wales while I was doing it.

As I took my finger away from the button, something clicked at the window. The click was loud and sharp.

I looked at the window.

A man crouched there on the fire-escape, looking in through glass and lace curtain. He was a thick-featured dark man whose size identified him as Babe McCloor. The muzzle of a big black automatic was touching the glass in front of him. He had tapped the glass with it to catch our attention.

He had our attention.

There wasn't anything for me to do just then. I stood there and looked at him. I couldn't tell whether he was looking at me or at Wales. I could see him clearly enough, but the lace curtain spoiled my view of details like that. I imagined he wasn't neglecting either of us, and I didn't imagine the lace curtain hid much from him. He was closer to the curtain than we, and I had turned on the room's lights.

Wales, sitting dead still on the sofa, was looking at Mc-Cloor. Wales's face wore a peculiar, stiffly sullen expression. His eyes were sullen. He wasn't breathing.

McCloor flicked the nose of his pistol against the pane, and a triangular piece of glass fell out, tinkling apart on the floor. It didn't, I was afraid, make enough noise to alarm MacMan in the kitchen. There were two closed doors between here and there.

Wales looked at the broken pane and closed his eyes. He closed them slowly, little by little, exactly as if he were falling asleep. He kept his stiffly sullen blank face turned straight to the window.

McCloor shot him three times.

The bullets knocked Wales down on the sofa, back against the wall. Wales's eyes popped open, bulging. His lips crawled back over his teeth, leaving them naked to the gums. His tongue came out. Then his head fell down and he didn't move any more.

When McCloor jumped away from the window I jumped to it. While I was pushing the curtain aside, unlocking the window and raising it, I heard his feet land on the cement paving below.

MacMan flung the door open and came in, the girl at his heels.

"Take care of this," I ordered as I scrambled over the sill. "McCloor shot him."

VI

Wales's apartment was on the second floor. The fire-escape ended there with a counter-weighted iron ladder that a man's weight would swing down into a cement-paved court.

I went down as Babe McCloor had gone, swinging down on the ladder till within dropping distance of the court, and then letting go.

There was only one street exit to the court. I took it.

A startled looking, smallish man was standing in the middle of the sidewalk close to the court, gaping at me as I dashed out.

I caught his arm, shook it.

"A big guy running." Maybe I yelled. "Where?"

He tried to say something, couldn't, and waved his arm at billboards standing across the front of a vacant lot on the other side of the street.

I forgot to say, "Thank you," in my hurry to get over there.

I got behind the billboards by crawling under them instead of going to either end, where there were openings. The lot was large enough and weedy enough to give cover to anybody who wanted to lie down and bushwhack a pursuer—even anybody as large as Babe McCloor.

While I considered that, I heard a dog barking at one corner of the lot. He could have been barking at a man who had run by. I ran to that corner of the lot. The dog was in a board-fenced backyard, at the corner of a narrow alley that ran from the lot to a street.

I chinned myself on the board fence, saw a wire-haired terrier alone in the yard, and ran down the alley while he was charging my part of the fence.

I put my gun back into my pocket before I left the alley for the street.

A small touring car was parked at the curb in front of a cigar store some fifteen feet from the alley. A policeman was talking to a slim dark-faced man in the cigar store doorway.

"The big fellow that come out of the alley a minute ago," I said. "Which way did he go?"

The policeman looked dumb. The slim man nodded his head down the street, said, "Down that way," and went on with his conversation.

I said, "Thanks," and went on down to the corner. There was a taxi phone there and two idle taxis. A block and a half below, a street car was going away.

"Did the big fellow who came down here a minute ago take a taxi or the street car?" I asked the two taxi chauffeurs who were leaning against one of the taxis.

The rattier looking one said:

"He didn't take a taxi."

I said:

"I'll take one. Catch that street car for me."

The street car was three blocks away before we got going. The street wasn't clear enough for me to see who got on and off it. We caught it when it stopped at Market Street.

"Follow along," I told the driver as I jumped out.

On the rear platform of the street car I looked through the glass. There were only eight or ten people aboard.

"There was a great big fellow got on at Hyde Street," I said to the conductor. "Where'd he get off?"

The conductor looked at the silver dollar I was turning over in my fingers and remembered that the big man got off at Taylor Street. That won the silver dollar.

I dropped off as the street car turned into Market Street. The taxi, close behind, slowed down, and its door swung open.

"Sixth and Mission," I said as I hopped in.

McCloor could have gone in any direction from Taylor Street. I had to guess. The best guess seemed to be that he would make for the other side of Market Street.

It was fairly dark by now. We had to go down to Fifth Street to get off Market, then over to Mission, and back up to Sixth. We got to Sixth Street without seeing McCloor. I couldn't see him on Sixth Street—either way from the crossing.

"On up to Ninth," I ordered, and while we rode told the driver what kind of man I was looking for.

We arrived at Ninth Street. No McCloor. I cursed and pushed my brains around.

The big man was a yegg. San Francisco was on fire for him. The yegg instinct would be to use a rattler to get away from trouble. The freight yards were in this end of town. Maybe he would be shifty enough to lie low instead of trying to powder. In that case, he probably hadn't crossed Market Street at all. If he stuck, there would still be a chance of picking him up tomorrow. If he was high-tailing, it was catch him now or not at all.

"Down to Harrison," I told the driver.

We went down to Harrison Street, and down Harrison to Third, up Bryant to Eighth, down Brannan to Third again, and over to Townsend—and we didn't see Babe McCloor.

"That's tough, that is," the driver sympathized as we stopped across the street from the Southern Pacific passenger station.

"I'm going over and look around in the station," I said. "Keep your eyes open while I'm gone."

When I told the copper in the station my trouble he introduced me to a couple of plain-clothes men who had been planted there to watch for McCloor. That had been done after Sue Hambleton's body was found. The shooting of Holy Joe Wales was news to them.

I went outside again and found my taxi in front of the door, its horn working over-time, but too asthmatically to be heard indoors. The ratty driver was excited.

"A guy like you said come up out of King Street just now and swung on a No. 16 car as it pulled away," he said.

"Going which way?"

"That-away," pointing southeast.

"Catch him," I said, jumping in.

The street car was out of sight around a bend in Third Street two blocks below. When we rounded the bend, the street car was slowing up, four blocks ahead. It hadn't slowed up very much when a man leaned far out and stepped off. He was a tall man, but didn't look tall on account of his shoulder spread. He didn't check his momentum, but used it to carry him across the sidewalk and out of sight.

We stopped where the man had left the car.

I gave the driver too much money and told him:

"Go back to Townsend Street and tell the copper in the station that I've chased Babe McCloor into the S. P. yards."

VII

I thought I was moving silently down between two strings of box cars, but I had gone less than twenty feet when a light flashed in my face and a sharp voice ordered:

"Stand still, you."

I stood still. Men came from between cars. One of them spoke my name, adding: "What are you doing here? Lost?" It was Harry Pebble, a police detective.

I stopped holding my breath and said:

"Hello, Harry. Looking for Babe?"

"Yes. We've been going over the rattlers."

"He's here. I just tailed him in from the street."

Pebble swore and snapped the light off.

"Watch, Harry," I advised. "Don't play with him. He's packing plenty of gun and he's cut down one boy tonight."

"I'll play with him," Pebble promised, and told one of the men with him to go over and warn those on the other side of the yard that McCloor was in, and then to ring for reinforcements.

"We'll just sit on the edge and hold him in till they come," he said.

That seemed a sensible way to play it. We spread out and waited. Once Pebble and I turned back a lanky bum who tried to slip into the yard between us, and one of the men below us picked up a shivering kid who was trying to slip out. Otherwise nothing happened until Lieutenant Duff arrived with a couple of carloads of coppers.

Most of our force went into a cordon around the yard. The rest of us went through the yard in small groups, working it over car by car. We picked up a few hoboes that Pebble and his men had missed earlier, but we didn't find McCloor.

We didn't find any trace of him until somebody stumbled over a railroad bull huddled in the shadow of a gondola. It took a couple of minutes to bring him to, and he couldn't talk then. His jaw was broken. But when we asked if McCloor had slugged him, he nodded, and when we asked in which direction McCloor had been headed, he moved a feeble hand to the east.

We went over and searched the Santa Fe yards.

We didn't find McCloor.

VIII

I rode up to the Hall of Justice with Duff. MacMan was in the captain of detectives' office with three or four police sleuths.

"Wales die?" I asked.

"Yep."

"Say anything before he went?"

"He was gone before you were through the window."

"You held on to the girl?"

"She's here."

"She say anything?"

"We were waiting for you before we tapped her," detective-sergeant O'Gar said, "not knowing the angle on her."

"Let's have her in. I haven't had any dinner yet. How about the autopsy on Sue Hambleton?"

"Chronic arsenic poisoning."

"Chronic? That means it was fed to her little by little, and not in a lump?"

"Uh-huh. From what he found in her kidney, intestines, liver, stomach and blood, Jordan figures there was less than a grain of it in her. That wouldn't be enough to knock her off. But he says he found arsenic in the tips of her hair, and she'd have to be given some at least a month ago for it to have worked out that far."

"Any chance that it wasn't arsenic that killed her?"

"Not unless Jordan's a bum doctor."

A policewoman came in with Peggy Carroll.

The blonde girl was tired. Her eyelids, mouth corners and body drooped, and when I pushed a chair out toward her she sagged down in it.

O'Gar ducked his grizzled bullet head at me.

"Now, Peggy," I said, "tell us where you fit into this mess."

"I don't fit into it." She didn't look up. Her voice was tired. "Joe dragged me into it. He told you."

"You his girl?"

"If you want to call it that," she admitted.

"You jealous?"

"What," she asked, looking up at me, her face puzzled, "has that got to do with it?"

"Sue Hambleton was getting ready to go away with him when she was murdered."

The girl sat up straight in the chair and said deliberately:

"I swear to God I didn't know she was murdered."

"But you did know she was dead," I said positively.

"I didn't," she replied just as positively.

I nudged O'Gar with my elbow. He pushed his undershot jaw at her and barked:

"What are you trying to give us? You knew she was dead. How could you kill her without knowing it?"

While she looked at him I waved the others in. They crowded close around her and took up the chorus of the sergeant's song. She was barked, roared, and snarled at plenty in the next few minutes.

The instant she stopped trying to talk back to them I cut in again.

"Wait," I said, very earnestly. "Maybe she didn't kill her."

"The hell she didn't," O'Gar stormed, holding the center of the stage so the others could move away from the girl without their retreat seeming too artificial. "Do you mean to tell me this baby—"

"I didn't say she didn't," I remonstrated. "I said maybe she didn't."

"Then who did?"

I passed the question to the girl: "Who did?"

"Babe," she said immediately.

O'Gar snorted to make her think he didn't believe her.

I asked, as if I were honestly perplexed:

"How do you know that if you didn't know she was dead?"

"It stands to reason he did," she said. "Anybody can see that. He found out she was going away with Joe, so he killed her and then came to Joe's and killed him. That's just exactly what Babe would do when he found it out."

"Yeah? How long have *you* known they were going away together?"

"Since they decided to. Joe told me a month or two ago."

"And you didn't mind?"

"You've got this all wrong," she said. "Of course I didn't mind. I was being cut in on it. You know her father had the bees. That's what Joe was after. She didn't mean anything to him but an in to the old man's pockets. And I was to get my dib. And you needn't think I was crazy enough about Joe or anybody else to step off in the air for them. Babe got next and fixed the pair of them. That's a cinch."

"Yeah? How do you figure Babe would kill her?"

"That guy? You don't think he'd—"

"I mean, how would he go about killing her?"

"Oh!" She shrugged. "With his hands, likely as not."

"Once he'd made up his mind to do it, he'd do it quick and violent?" I suggested.

"That would be Babe," she agreed.

"But you can't see him slow-poisoning her—spreading it out over a month?"

Worry came into the girl's blue eyes. She put her lower lip between her teeth, then said slowly:

"No, I can't see him doing it that way. Not Babe."

"Who can you see doing it that way?"

She opened her eyes wide, asking:

"You mean Joe?"

I didn't say anything.

"Joe might have," she said persuasively. "God only knows what he'd want to do it for, why he'd want to get rid of the kind of meal ticket she was going to be. But you couldn't always guess what he was getting at. He pulled plenty of dumb ones. He was too slick without being smart. If he was going to kill her, though, that would be about the way he'd go about it."

"Were he and Babe friendly?"

"No."

"Did he go to Babe's much?"

"Not at all that I know about. He was too leary of Babe to take a chance on being caught there. That's why I moved upstairs, so Sue could come over to our place to see him."

"Then how could Joe have hidden the fly paper he poisoned her with in her apartment?"

"Fly paper!" Her bewilderment seemed honest enough.

"Show it to her," I told O'Gar.

He got a sheet from the desk and held it close to the girl's face.

She stared at it for a moment and then jumped up and grabbed my arm with both hands.

"I didn't know what it was," she said excitedly. "Joe had some a couple of months ago. He was looking at it when I came in. I asked him what it was for, and he smiled that wisenheimer smile of his and said, 'You make angels out of it,' and wrapped it up again and put it in his pocket. I didn't pay much attention to him: he was always fooling with some kind of tricks that were supposed to make him wealthy, but never did."

"Ever see it again?"

"No."

"Did you know Sue very well?"

"I didn't know her at all. I never even saw her. I used to keep out of the way so I wouldn't gum Joe's play with her."

"But you know Babe?"

"Yes, I've been on a couple of parties where he was. That's all I know him."

"Who killed Sue?"

"Joe," she said. "Didn't he have that paper you say she was killed with?"

"Why did he kill her?"

"I don't know. He pulled some awful dumb tricks some-times."

"You didn't kill her?"

"No, no, no!"

I jerked the corner of my mouth at O'Gar.

"You're a liar," he bawled, shaking the fly paper in her face. "You killed her." The rest of the team closed in, throwing accusations at her. They kept it up until she was groggy and the policewoman beginning to look worried.

Then I said angrily:

"All right. Throw her in a cell and let her think it over." To her: "You know what you told Joe this afternoon: this is no time to dummy up. Do a lot of thinking tonight."

"Honest to God I didn't kill her," she said.

I turned my back to her. The policewoman took her away.

"Ho-hum," O'Gar yawned. "We gave her a pretty good ride at that, for a short one."

"Not bad," I agreed. "If anybody else looked likely, I'd say she didn't kill Sue. But if she's telling the truth, then Holy Joe did it. And why should he poison the goose that was going to lay nice yellow eggs for him? And how and why did he cache the poison in their apartment? Babe had the motive, but damned if he looks like a slow-poisoner to me. You can't tell, though; he and Holy Joe could even have been working together on it."

"Could," Duff said. "But it takes a lot of imagination to get that one down. Anyway you twist it, Peggy's our best bet so far. Go up against her again, hard, in the morning?"

"Yeah," I said. "And we've got to find Babe."

The others had had dinner. MacMan and I went out and got ours. When we returned to the detective bureau an hour later it was practically deserted of the regular operatives.

"All gone to Pier 42 on a tip that McCloor's there," Steve Ward told us.

"How long ago?"

"Ten minutes."

MacMan and I got a taxi and set out for Pier 42. We didn't get to Pier 42.

On First Street, half a block from the Embarcadero, the taxi suddenly shrieked and slid to a halt.

"What—?" I began, and saw a man standing in front of the machine. He was a big man with a big gun. "Babe," I grunted, and put my hand on MacMan's arm to keep him from getting his gun out.

"Take me to—" McCloor was saying to the frightened driver when he saw us. He came around to my side and pulled the door open, holding the gun on us.

He had no hat. His hair was wet, plastered to his head. Little streams of water trickled down from it. His clothes were dripping wet.

He looked surprised at us and ordered:

"Get out."

As we got out he growled at the driver:

"What the hell you got your flag up for if you had fares?"

The driver wasn't there. He had hopped out the other side and was scooting away down the street. McCloor cursed him and poked his gun at me, growling:

"Go on, beat it."

Apparently he hadn't recognized me. The light here wasn't good, and I had a hat on now. He had seen me for only a few seconds in Wales's room.

I stepped aside. MacMan moved to the other side.

McCloor took a backward step to keep us from getting him between us and started an angry word.

MacMan threw himself on McCloor's gun arm.

I socked McCloor's jaw with my fist. I might just as well have hit somebody else for all it seemed to bother him.

He swept me out of his way and pasted MacMan in the mouth. MacMan fell back till the taxi stopped him, spit out a tooth, and came back for more.

I was trying to climb up McCloor's left side.

MacMan came in on his right, failed to dodge a chop of the gun, caught it square on the top of the noodle, and went down hard. He stayed down.

I kicked McCloor's ankle, but couldn't get his foot from under him. I rammed my right fist into the small of his back and got a left-handful of his wet hair, swinging on it. He shook his head, dragging me off my feet.

He punched me in the side and I could feel my ribs and guts flattening together like leaves in a book.

I swung my fist against the back of his neck. That bothered him. He made a rumbling noise down in his chest, crunched my shoulder in his left hand, and chopped at me with the gun in his right.

I kicked him somewhere and punched his neck again.

Down the street, at the Embarcadero, a police whistle was blowing. Men were running up First Street toward us.

McCloor snorted like a locomotive and threw me away from him. I didn't want to go. I tried to hang on. He threw me away from him and ran up the street.

I scrambled up and ran after him, dragging my gun out.

At the first corner he stopped to squirt metal at me—three shots. I squirted one at him. None of the four connected.

He disappeared around the corner. I swung wide around it, to make him miss if he were flattened to the wall waiting for me. He wasn't. He was a hundred feet ahead, going into a space between two warehouses. I went in after him, and out after him at the other end, making better time with my hundred and ninety pounds than he was making with his two-fifty.

He crossed a street, turning up, away from the waterfront. There was a light on the corner. When I came into its glare he wheeled and leveled his gun at me. I didn't hear it click, but I knew it had when he threw it at me. The gun went past with a couple of feet to spare and raised hell against a door behind me.

McCloor turned and ran up the street. I ran up the street after him.

I put a bullet past him to let the others know where we were. At the next corner he started to turn to the left, changed his mind, and went straight on.

I sprinted, cutting the distance between us to forty or fifty feet, and yelped:

"Stop or I'll drop you."

He jumped sidewise into a narrow alley.

I passed it on the jump, saw he wasn't waiting for me, and went in. Enough light came in from the street to let us see each other and our surroundings. The alley was blind—walled on each side and at the other end by tall concrete buildings with steel-shuttered windows and doors.

McCloor faced me, less than twenty feet away. His jaw stuck out. His arms curved down free of his sides. His shoulders were bunched.

"Put them up," I ordered, holding my gun level.

"Get out of my way, little man," he grumbled, taking a stiff-legged step toward me. "I'll eat you up."

"Keep coming," I said, "and I'll put you down."

"Try it." He took another step, crouching a little. "I can still get to you *with* slugs in me."

"Not where I'll put them." I was wordy, trying to talk him into waiting till the others came up. I didn't want to have to kill him. We could have done that from the taxi. "I'm no Annie Oakley, but if I can't pop your kneecaps with two shots at this distance, you're welcome to me. And if you think smashed kneecaps are a lot of fun, give it a whirl."

"Hell with that," he said and charged.

I shot his right knee.

He lurched toward me.

I shot his left knee.

He tumbled down.

"You would have it," I complained.

He twisted around, and with his arms pushed himself into a sitting position facing me.

"I didn't think you had sense enough to do it," he said through his teeth.

IX

I talked to McCloor in the hospital. He lay on his back in bed with a couple of pillows slanting his head up. The skin was pale and tight around his mouth and eyes, but there was nothing else to show he was in pain.

"You sure devastated me, bo," he said when I came in.

"Sorry," I said, "but—"

"I ain't beefing. I asked for it."

"Why'd you kill Holy Joe?" I asked, off-hand, as I pulled a chair up beside the bed.

"Uh-uh—you're tooting the wrong ringer."

I laughed and told him I was the man in the room with Joe when it happened.

McCloor grinned and said:

"I thought I'd seen you somewheres before. So that's where it was. I didn't pay no attention to your mug, just so your hands didn't move."

"Why'd you kill him?"

He pursed his lips, screwed up his eyes at me, thought something over, and said:

"He killed a broad I knew."

"He killed Sue Hambleton?" I asked.

He studied my face a while before he replied: "Yep."

"How do you figure that out?"

"Hell," he said, "I don't have to. Sue told me. Give me a butt."

I gave him a cigarette, held a lighter under it, and objected:

"That doesn't exactly fit in with other things I know. Just what happened and what did she say? You might start back with the night you gave her the goog."

He looked thoughtful, letting smoke sneak slowly out of his nose, then said:

"I hadn't ought to hit her in the eye, that's a fact. But, see, she had been out all afternoon and wouldn't tell me where she'd been, and we had a row over it. What's this—Thursday

morning? That was Monday, then. After the row I went out
and spent the night in a dump over on Army Street. I got
home about seven the next morning. Sue was sick as hell, but
she wouldn't let me get a croaker for her. That was kind of
funny, because she was scared stiff."

McCloor scratched his head meditatively and suddenly
drew in a great lungful of smoke, practically eating up the rest
of the cigarette. He let the smoke leak out of mouth and nose
together, looking dully through the cloud at me. Then he
said bruskly:

"Well, she went under. But before she went she told me
she'd been poisoned by Holy Joe."

"She say how he'd given it to her?"

McCloor shook his head.

"I'd been asking her what was the matter, and not getting
anything out of her. Then she starts whining that she's
poisoned. 'I'm poisoned, Babe,' she whines. 'Arsenic. That
damned Holy Joe,' she says. Then she won't say anything
else, and it's not a hell of a while after that that she kicks off."

"Yeah? Then what'd you do?"

"I went gunning for Holy Joe. I knew him but didn't know
where he jungled up, and didn't find out till yesterday. You
was there when I came. You know about that. I had picked
up a boiler and parked it over on Turk Street, for the getaway.
When I got back to it, there was a copper standing close to it.
I figured he might have spotted it as a hot one and was waiting to see who came for it, so I let it alone, and caught a
street car instead, and cut for the yards. Down there I ran into
a whole flock of hammer and saws and had to go overboard
in China Basin, swimming up to a pier, being ranked again by
a watchman there, swimming off to another, and finally getting through the line only to run into another bad break. I
wouldn't of flagged that taxi if the *For Hire* flag hadn't been
up."

"You knew Sue was planning to take a run-out on you with
Joe?"

"I don't know it yet," he said. "I knew damned well she
was cheating on me, but I didn't know who with."

"What would you have done if you had known that?" I
asked.

"Me?" He grinned wolfishly. "Just what I did."

"Killed the pair of them," I said.

He rubbed his lower lip with a thumb and asked calmly:

"You think I killed Sue?"

"You did."

"Serves me right," he said. "I must be getting simple in my old age. What the hell am I doing barbering with a lousy dick? That never got nobody nothing but grief. Well, you might just as well take it on the heel and toe now, my lad. I'm through spitting."

And he was. I couldn't get another word out of him.

X

The Old Man sat listening to me, tapping his desk lightly with the point of a long yellow pencil, staring past me with mild blue, rimless-spectacled, eyes. When I had brought my story up to date, he asked pleasantly:

"How is MacMan?"

"He lost two teeth, but his skull wasn't cracked. He'll be out in a couple of days."

The Old Man nodded and asked:

"What remains to be done?"

"Nothing. We can put Peggy Carroll on the mat again, but it's not likely we'll squeeze much more out of her. Outside of that, the returns are pretty well all in."

"And what do you make of it?"

I squirmed in my chair and said: "Suicide."

The Old Man smiled at me, politely but skeptically.

"I don't like it either," I grumbled. "And I'm not ready to write it in a report yet. But that's the only total that what we've got will add up to. That fly paper was hidden behind the kitchen stove. Nobody would be crazy enough to try to hide something from a woman in her own kitchen like that. But the woman might hide it there.

"According to Peggy, Holy Joe had the fly paper. If Sue hid it, she got it from him. For what? They were planning to go away together, and were only waiting till Joe, who was on the nut, raised enough dough. Maybe they were afraid of Babe, and had the poison there to slip him if he tumbled to their

plan before they went. Maybe they meant to slip it to him before they went anyway.

"When I started talking to Holy Joe about murder, he
thought Babe was the one who had been bumped off. He was
surprised, maybe, but as if he was surprised that it had happened so soon. He was more surprised when he heard that
Sue had died too, but even then he wasn't so surprised as
when he saw McCloor alive at the window.

"She died cursing Holy Joe, and she knew she was poisoned, and she wouldn't let McCloor get a doctor. Can't that
mean that she had turned against Joe, and had taken the poison herself instead of feeding it to Babe? The poison was hidden from Babe. But even if he found it, I can't figure him as
a poisoner. He's too rough. Unless he caught her trying to
poison him and made her swallow the stuff. But that doesn't
account for the month-old arsenic in her hair."

"Does your suicide hypothesis take care of that?" the Old
Man asked.

"It could," I said. "Don't be kicking holes in my theory.
It's got enough as it stands. But, if she committed suicide this
time, there's no reason why she couldn't have tried it once
before—say after a quarrel with Joe a month ago—and failed
to bring it off. That would have put the arsenic in her.
There's no real proof that she took any between a month ago
and day before yesterday."

"No real proof," the Old Man protested mildly, "except
the autopsy's finding—chronic poisoning."

I was never one to let experts' guesses stand in my way. I
said:

"They base that on the small amount of arsenic they found
in her remains—less than a fatal dose. And the amount they
find in your stomach after you're dead depends on how much
you vomit before you die."

The Old Man smiled benevolently at me and asked:

"But you're not, you say, ready to write this theory into a
report? Meanwhile what do you purpose doing?"

"If there's nothing else on tap, I'm going home, fumigate
my brains with Fatimas, and try to get this thing straightened
out in my head. I think I'll get a copy of *The Count of Monte
Cristo* and run through it. I haven't read it since I was a kid.

It looks like the book was wrapped up with the fly paper to make a bundle large enough to wedge tightly between the wall and stove, so it wouldn't fall down. But there might be something in the book. I'll see anyway."

"I did that last night," the Old Man murmured.

I asked: "And?"

He took a book from his desk drawer, opened it where a slip of paper marked a place, and held it out to me, one pink finger marking a paragraph.

"Suppose you were to take a millegramme of this poison the first day, two millegrammes the second day, and so on. Well, at the end of ten days you would have taken a centigramme: at the end of twenty days, increasing another millegramme, you would have taken three hundred centigrammes; that is to say, a dose you would support without inconvenience, and which would be very dangerous for any other person who had not taken the same precautions as yourself. Well, then, at the end of the month, when drinking water from the same carafe, you would kill the person who had drunk this water, without your perceiving otherwise than from slight inconvenience that there was any poisonous substance mingled with the water."

"That does it," I said. "That does it. They were afraid to go away without killing Babe, too certain he'd come after them. She tried to make herself immune from arsenic poisoning by getting her body accustomed to it, taking steadily increasing doses, so when she slipped the big shot in Babe's food she could eat it with him without danger. She'd be taken sick, but wouldn't die, and the police couldn't hang his death on her because she too had eaten the poisoned food.

"That clicks. After the row Monday night, when she wrote Joe the note urging him to make the getaway soon, she tried to hurry up her immunity, and increased her preparatory doses too quickly, took too large a shot. That's why she cursed Joe at the end: it was his plan."

"Possibly she overdosed herself in an attempt to speed it along," the Old Man agreed, "but not necessarily. There are people who can cultivate an ability to take large doses of arsenic without trouble, but it seems to be a sort of natural gift with them, a matter of some constitutional peculiarity.

Ordinarily, any one who tried it would do what Sue Hambleton did—slowly poison themselves until the cumulative effect was strong enough to cause death."

Babe McCloor was hanged, for killing Holy Joe Wales, six months later.

The Farewell Murder

I WAS the only one who left the train at Farewell.

A man came through the rain from the passenger shed. He was a small man. His face was dark and flat. He wore a gray waterproof cap and a gray coat cut in military style.

He didn't look at me. He looked at the valise and gladstone bag in my hands. He came forward quickly, walking with short, choppy steps.

He didn't say anything when he took the bags from me. I asked:

"Kavalov's?"

He had already turned his back to me and was carrying my bags towards a tan Stutz coach that stood in the roadway beside the gravel station platform. In answer to my question he bowed twice at the Stutz without looking around or checking his jerky half-trot.

I followed him to the car.

Three minutes of riding carried us through the village. We took a road that climbed westward into the hills. The road looked like a seal's back in the rain.

The flat-faced man was in a hurry. We purred over the road at a speed that soon carried us past the last of the cottages sprinkled up the hillside.

Presently we left the shiny black road for a paler one curving south to run along a hill's wooded crest. Now and then this road, for a hundred feet or more at a stretch, was turned into a tunnel by tall trees' heavily leafed boughs interlocking overhead.

Rain accumulated in fat drops on the boughs and came down to thump the Stutz's roof. The dulness of rainy early evening became almost the blackness of night inside these tunnels.

The flat-faced man switched on the lights, and increased our speed.

He sat rigidly erect at the wheel. I sat behind him. Above his military collar, among the hairs that were clipped short on the nape of his neck, globules of moisture made tiny shining points. The moisture could have been rain. It could have been sweat.

We were in the middle of one of the tunnels.

The flat-faced man's head jerked to the left, and he screamed:

"A-a-a-a-a-a!"

It was a long, quivering, high-pitched bleat, thin with terror.

I jumped up, bending forward to see what was the matter with him.

The car swerved and plunged ahead, throwing me back on the seat again.

Through the side window I caught a one-eyed glimpse of something dark lying in the road.

I twisted around to try the back window, less rain-bleared.

I saw a black man lying on his back in the road, near the left edge. His body was arched, as if its weight rested on his heels and the back of his head. A knife handle that couldn't have been less than six inches long stood straight up in the air from the left side of his chest.

By the time I had seen this much we had taken a curve and were out of the tunnel.

"Stop," I called to the flat-faced man.

He pretended he didn't hear me. The Stutz was a tan streak under us. I put a hand on the driver's shoulder.

His shoulder squirmed under my hand, and he screamed "A-a-a-a-a!" again as if the dead black man had him.

I reached past him and shut off the engine.

He took his hands from the wheel and clawed up at me. Noises came from his mouth, but they didn't make any words that I knew.

I got a hand on the wheel. I got my other forearm under his chin. I leaned over the back of his seat so that the weight of my upper body was on his head, mashing it down against the wheel.

Between this and that and the help of God, the Stutz hadn't left the road when it stopped moving.

I got up off the flat-faced man's head and asked:

"What the hell's the matter with you?"

He looked at me with white eyes, shivered, and didn't say anything.

"Turn it around," I said. "We'll go back there."

He shook his head from side to side, desperately, and made some more of the mouth-noises that might have been words if I could have understood them.

"You know who that was?" I asked.

He shook his head.

"You do," I growled.

He shook his head.

By then I was beginning to suspect that no matter what I said to this fellow I'd get only head-shakes out of him.

I said:

"Get away from the wheel, then. I'm going to drive back there."

He opened the door and scrambled out.

"Come back here," I called.

He backed away, shaking his head.

I cursed him, slid in behind the wheel, said, "All right, wait here for me," and slammed the door.

He retreated backwards slowly, watching me with scared, whitish eyes while I backed and turned the coach.

I had to drive back farther than I had expected, something like a mile.

I didn't find the black man.

The tunnel was empty.

If I had known the exact spot in which he had been lying, I might have been able to find something to show how he had been removed. But I hadn't had time to pick out a landmark, and now any one of four or five places looked like the spot.

With the help of the coach's lamps I went over the left side of the road from one end of the tunnel to the other.

I didn't find any blood. I didn't find any footprints. I didn't find anything to show that anybody had been lying in the road. I didn't find anything.

It was too dark by now for me to try searching the woods.

I returned to where I had left the flat-faced man.

He was gone.

It looked, I thought, as if Mr. Kavalov might be right in thinking he needed a detective.

II

Half a mile beyond the place where the flat-faced man had deserted me, I stopped the Stutz in front of a grilled steel gate that blocked the road. The gate was padlocked on the inside. From either side of it tall hedging ran off into the woods. The upper part of a brown-roofed small house was visible over the hedge-top to the left.

I worked the Stutz's horn.

The racket brought a gawky boy of fifteen or sixteen to the other side of the gate. He had on bleached whipcord pants and a wildly striped sweater. He didn't come out to the middle of the road, but stood at one side, with one arm out of sight as if holding something that was hidden from me by the hedge.

"This Kavalov's?" I asked.

"Yes, sir," he said uneasily.

I waited for him to unlock the gate. He didn't unlock it. He stood there looking uneasily at the car and at me.

"Please, mister," I said, "can I come in?"

"What—who are you?"

"I'm the guy that Kavalov sent for. If I'm not going to be let in, tell me, so I can catch the six-fifty back to San Francisco."

The boy chewed his lip, said, "Wait till I see if I can find the key," and went out of sight behind the hedge.

He was gone long enough to have had a talk with somebody.

When he came back he unlocked the gate, swung it open, and said:

"It's all right, sir. They're expecting you."

When I had driven through the gate I could see lights on a hilltop a mile or so ahead and to the left.

"Is that the house?" I asked.

"Yes, sir. They're expecting you."

Close to where the boy had stood while talking to me through the gate, a double-barrel shotgun was propped up against the hedge.

I thanked the boy and drove on. The road wound gently uphill through farm land. Tall, slim trees had been planted at regular intervals on both sides of the road.

The road brought me at last to the front of a building that looked like a cross between a fort and a factory in the dusk. It was built of concrete. Take a flock of squat cones of various sizes, round off the points bluntly, mash them together with the largest one somewhere near the center, the others grouped around it in not too strict accordance with their sizes, adjust the whole collection to agree with the slopes of a hilltop, and you would have a model of the Kavalov house. The windows were steel-sashed. There weren't very many of them. No two were in line either vertically or horizontally. Some were lighted.

As I got out of the car, the narrow front door of this house opened.

A short, red-faced woman of fifty or so, with faded blonde hair wound around and around her head, came out. She wore a high-necked, tight-sleeved, gray woolen dress. When she smiled her mouth seemed wide as her hips.

She said:

"You're the gentleman from the city?"

"Yeah. I lost your chauffeur somewhere back on the road."

"Lord bless you," she said amiably, "that's all right."

A thin man with thin dark hair plastered down above a thin, worried face came past her to take my bags when I had lifted them out of the car. He carried them indoors.

The woman stood aside for me to enter, saying:

"Now I suppose you'll want to wash up a little bit before you go in to dinner, and they won't mind waiting for you the few minutes you'll take if you hurry."

I said, "Yeah, thanks," waited for her to get ahead of me again, and followed her up a curving flight of stairs that climbed along the inside of one of the cones that made up the building.

She took me to a second-story bedroom where the thin man was unpacking my bags.

"Martin will get you anything you need," she assured me from the doorway, "and when you're ready, just come on downstairs."

I said I would, and she went away. The thin man had finished unpacking by the time I had got out of coat, vest, collar and shirt. I told him there wasn't anything else I needed, washed up in the adjoining bathroom, put on a fresh shirt and collar, my vest and coat, and went downstairs.

The wide hall was empty. Voices came through an open doorway to the left.

One voice was a nasal whine. It complained:

"I will not have it. I will not put up with it. I am not a child, and I will not have it."

This voice's t's were a little too thick for t's, but not thick enough to be d's.

Another voice was a lively, but slightly harsh, barytone. It said cheerfully:

"What's the good of saying we won't put up with it, when we are putting up with it?"

The third voice was feminine, a soft voice, but flat and spiritless. It said:

"But perhaps he did kill him."

The whining voice said: "I do not care. I will not have it."

The barytone voice said, cheerfully as before: "Oh, won't you?"

A doorknob turned farther down the hall. I didn't want to be caught standing there listening. I advanced to the open doorway.

III

I was in the doorway of a low-ceilinged oval room furnished and decorated in gray, white and silver. Two men and a woman were there.

The older man—he was somewhere in his fifties—got up from a deep gray chair and bowed ceremoniously at me. He was a plump man of medium height, completely bald, dark-skinned and pale-eyed. He wore a wax-pointed gray mustache and a straggly gray imperial.

"Mr. Kavalov?" I asked.

"Yes, sir." His was the whining voice.

I told him who I was. He shook my hand and then introduced me to the others.

The woman was his daughter. She was probably thirty. She had her father's narrow, full-lipped mouth, but her eyes were dark, her nose was short and straight, and her skin was almost colorless. Her face had Asia in it. It was pretty, passive, unintelligent.

The man with the barytone voice was her husband. His name was Ringgo. He was six or seven years older than his wife, neither tall nor heavy, but well setup. His left arm was in splints and a sling. The knuckles of his right hand were darkly bruised. He had a lean, bony, quick-witted face, bright dark eyes with plenty of lines around them, and a good-natured hard mouth.

He gave me his bruised hand, wriggled his bandaged arm at me, grinned, and said:

"I'm sorry you missed this, but the future injuries are yours."

"How did it happen?" I asked.

Kavalov raised a plump hand.

"Time enough it is to go into that when we have eaten," he said. "Let us have our dinner first."

We went into a small green and brown dining-room where a small square table was set. I sat facing Ringgo across a silver basket of orchids that stood between tall silver candlesticks in the center of the table. Mrs. Ringgo sat to my right, Kavalov to my left. When Kavalov sat down I saw the shape of an automatic pistol in his hip pocket.

Two men servants waited on us. There was a lot of food and all of it was well turned out. We ate caviar, some sort of consommé, sand dabs, potatoes and cucumber jelly, roast lamb, corn and string beans, asparagus, wild duck and hominy cakes, artichoke-and-tomato salad, and orange ice. We drank white wine, claret, Burgundy, coffee and *crème de menthe*.

Kavalov ate and drank enormously. None of us skimped.

Kavalov was the first to disregard his own order that nothing be said about his troubles until after we had eaten. When he had finished his soup he put down his spoon and said:

"I am not a child. I will not be frightened."

He blinked pale, worried eyes defiantly at me, his lips pouting between mustache and imperial.

Ringgo grinned pleasantly at him. Mrs. Ringgo's face was as serene and inattentive as if nothing had been said.

"What is there to be frightened of?" I asked.

"Nothing," Kavalov said. "Nothing excepting a lot of idiotic and very pointless trickery and play-acting."

"You can call it anything you want to call it," a voice grumbled over my shoulder, "but I seen what I seen."

The voice belonged to one of the men who was waiting on the table, a sallow, youngish man with a narrow, slack-lipped face. He spoke with a subdued sort of stubbornness, and without looking up from the dish he was putting before me.

Since nobody else paid any attention to the servant's clearly audible remark, I turned my face to Kavalov again. He was trimming the edge of a sand dab with the side of his fork.

"What kind of trickery and play-acting?" I asked.

Kavalov put down his fork and rested his wrists on the edge of the table. He rubbed his lips together and leaned over his plate towards me.

"Supposing"—he wrinkled his forehead so that his bald scalp twitched forward—"you have done injury to a man ten years ago." He turned his wrists quickly, laying his hands palms-up on the white cloth. "You have done this injury in the ordinary business manner—you understand?—for profit. There is not anything personal concerned. You do not hardly know him. And then supposing he came to you after all those ten years and said to you: 'I have come to watch you die.'" He turned his hands over, palms down. "Well, what would you think?"

"I wouldn't," I replied, "think I ought to hurry up my dying on his account."

The earnestness went out of his face, leaving it blank. He blinked at me for a moment and then began eating his fish. When he had chewed and swallowed the last piece of sand dab he looked up at me again. He shook his head slowly, drawing down the corners of his mouth.

"That was not a good answer," he said. He shrugged, and spread his fingers. "However, you will have to deal with this Captain Cat-and-mouse. It is for that I engaged you."

I nodded.

Ringgo smiled and patted his bandaged arm, saying:

"I wish you more luck with him than I had."

Mrs. Ringgo put out a hand and let the pointed fingertips touch her husband's wrist for a moment.

I asked Kavalov:

"This injury I was to suppose I had done: how serious was it?'

He pursed his lips, made little wavy motions with the fingers of his right hand, and said:

"Oh—ah—ruin."

"We can take it for granted, then, that your captain's really up to something?"

"Good God!" said Ringgo, dropping his fork. "I wouldn't like to think he'd broken my arm just in fun."

Behind me the sallow servant spoke to his mate:

"He wants to know if we think the captain's really up to something."

"I heard him," the other said gloomily. "A lot of help he's going to be to us."

Kavalov tapped his plate with a fork and made angry faces at the servants.

"Shut up," he said. "Where is the roast?" He pointed the fork at Mrs. Ringgo. "Her glass is empty." He looked at the fork. "See what care they take of my silver," he complained, holding it out to me. "It has not been cleaned decently in a month."

He put the fork down. He pushed back his plate to make room for his forearms on the table. He leaned over them, hunching his shoulders. He sighed. He frowned. He stared at me with pleading pale eyes.

"Listen," he whined. "Am I a fool? Would I send to San Francisco for a detective if I did not need a detective? Would I pay you what you are charging me, when I could get plenty good enough detectives for half of that, if I did not require the best detective I could secure? Would I require so expensive a one if I did not know this captain for a completely dangerous fellow?"

I didn't say anything. I sat still and looked attentive.

"Listen," he whined. "This is not April-foolery. This captain means to murder me. He came here to murder me. He will certainly murder me if somebody does not stop him from it."

"Just what has he done so far?" I asked.

"That is not it." Kavalov shook his bald head impatiently. "I do not ask you to undo anything that he has done. I ask you to keep him from killing me. What has he done so far? Well, he has terrorized my people most completely. He has broken Dolph's arm. He has done these things so far, if you must know."

"How long has this been going on? How long has he been here?"

"A week and two days."

"Did your chauffeur tell you about the black man we saw in the road?"

Kavalov pushed his lips together and nodded slowly.

"He wasn't there when I went back," I said.

He blew out his lips with a little puff and cried excitedly:

"I do not care anything about your black men and your roads. I care about not being murdered."

"Have you said anything to the sheriff's office?" I asked, trying to pretend I wasn't getting peevish.

"That I have done. But to what good? Has he threatened me? Well, he has told me he has come to watch me die. From him, the way he said it, that is a threat. But to your sheriff it is not a threat. He has terrorized my people. Have I proof that he has done that? The sheriff says I have not. What absurdity! Do I need proof? Don't I know? Must he leave fingerprints on the fright he causes? So it comes to this: the sheriff will keep an eye on him. 'An eye,' he said, mind you. Here I have twenty people, servants and farm hands, with forty eyes. And he comes and goes as he likes. An eye!"

"How about Ringgo's arm?" I asked.

Kavalov shook his head impatiently and began to cut up his lamb.

Ringgo said:

"There's nothing we can do about that. I hit him first." He looked at his bruised knuckles. "I didn't think he was that tough. Maybe I'm not as good as I used to be. Anyway, a dozen people saw me punch his jaw before he touched me. We performed at high noon in front of the post office."

"Who is this captain?"

"It's not him," the sallow servant said. "It's that black devil."

Ringgo said:

"Sherry's his name, Hugh Sherry. He was a captain in the British army when we knew him before—quarter-masters department in Cairo. That was in 1917, all of twelve years ago. The commodore"—he nodded his head at his father-in-law—"was speculating in military supplies. Sherry should have been a line officer. He had no head for desk work. He wasn't timid enough. Somebody decided the commodore wouldn't have made so much money if Sherry hadn't been so careless. They knew Sherry hadn't made any money for himself. They cashiered Sherry at the same time they asked the commodore please to go away."

Kavalov looked up from his plate to explain:

"Business is like that in wartime. They wouldn't let me go away if I had done anything they could keep me there for."

"And now, twelve years after you had him kicked out of the army in disgrace," I said, "he comes here, threatens to kill you, so you believe, and sets out to spread panic among your people. Is that it?"

"That is not it," Kavalov whined. "That is not it at all. I did not have him kicked out of any armies. I am a man of business. I take my profits where I find them. If somebody lets me take a profit that angers his employers, what is their anger to me? Second, I do not believe he means to kill me. I know that."

"I'm trying to get it straight in my mind."

"There is nothing to get straight. A man is going to murder me. I ask you not to let him do it. Is not that simple enough?"

"Simple enough," I agreed, and stopped trying to talk to him.

Kavalov and Ringgo were smoking cigars, Mrs. Ringgo and I cigarettes over *crème de menthe* when the red-faced blonde woman in gray wool came in.

She came in hurriedly. Her eyes were wide open and dark. She said:

"Anthony says there's a fire in the upper field."

Kavalov crunched his cigar between his teeth and looked pointedly at me.

I stood up, asking:

"How do I get there?"

"I'll show you the way," Ringgo said, leaving his chair.

"Dolph," his wife protested, "your arm."

He smiled gently at her and said:

"I'm not going to interfere. I'm only going along to see how an expert handles these things."

IV

I ran up to my room for hat, coat, flashlight and gun.

The Ringgos were standing at the front door when I started downstairs again.

He had put on a dark raincoat, buttoned tight over his injured arm, its left sleeve hanging empty. His right arm was around his wife. Both of her bare arms were around his neck. She was bent far back, he far forward over her. Their mouths were together.

Retreating a little, I made more noise with my feet when I came into sight again. They were standing apart at the door, waiting for me. Ringgo was breathing heavily, as if he had been running. He opened the door.

Mrs. Ringgo addressed me:

"Please don't let my foolish husband be too reckless."

I said I wouldn't, and asked him:

"Worth while taking any of the servants or farm hands along?"

He shook his head.

"Those that aren't hiding would be as useless as those that are," he said. "They've all had it taken out of them."

He and I went out, leaving Mrs. Ringgo looking after us from the doorway. The rain had stopped for the time, but a black muddle overhead promised more presently.

Ringgo led me around the side of the house, along a narrow path that went downhill through shrubbery, past a group of small buildings in a shallow valley, and diagonally up another, lower, hill.

The path was soggy. At the top of the hill we left the path, going through a wire gate and across a stubby field that was both gummy and slimy under our feet. We moved along swiftly. The gumminess of the ground, the sultriness of the night air, and our coats, made the going warm work.

When we had crossed this field we could see the fire, a spot of flickering orange beyond intervening trees. We climbed a low wire fence and wound through the trees.

A violent rustling broke out among the leaves overhead, starting at the left, ending with a solid thud against a tree trunk just to our right. Then something *plopped* on the soft ground under the tree.

Off to the left a voice laughed, a savage, hooting laugh.

The laughing voice couldn't have been far away. I went after it.

The fire was too small and too far away to be of much use to me: blackness was nearly perfect among the trees.

I stumbled over roots, bumped into trees, and found nothing. The flashlight would have helped the laugher more than me, so I kept it idle in my hand.

When I got tired of playing peekaboo with myself, I cut through the woods to the field on the other side, and went down to the fire.

The fire had been built in one end of the field, a dozen feet or less from the nearest tree. It had been built of dead twigs and broken branches that the rain had missed, and had nearly burnt itself out by the time I reached it.

Two small forked branches were stuck in the ground on opposite sides of the fire. Their forks held the ends of a length of green sapling. Spitted on the sapling, hanging over the fire, was an eighteen-inch-long carcass, headless, tailless, footless, skinless, and split down the front.

On the ground a few feet away lay an airedale puppy's head, pelt, feet, tail, insides, and a lot of blood.

There were some dry sticks, broken in convenient lengths, beside the fire. I put them on as Ringgo came out of the woods to join me. He carried a stone the size of a grapefruit in his hand.

"Get a look at him?" he asked.

"No. He laughed and went."

He held out the stone to me, saying:

"This is what was chucked at us."

Drawn on the smooth gray stone, in red, were round blank eyes, a triangular nose, and a grinning, toothy mouth—a crude skull.

I scratched one of the red eyes with a fingernail, and said:

"Crayon."

Ringgo was staring at the carcass sizzling over the fire and at the trimmings on the ground.

"What do you make of that?" I asked.

He swallowed and said:

"Mickey was a damned good little dog."

"Yours?"

He nodded.

I went around with my flashlight on the ground. I found some footprints, such as they were.

"Anything?" Ringgo asked.

"Yeah." I showed him one of the prints. "Made with rags tied around his shoes. They're no good."

We turned to the fire again.

"This is another show," I said. "Whoever killed and cleaned the pup knew his stuff; knew it too well to think he could cook him decently like that. The outside will be burnt before the inside's even warm, and the way he's put on the spit he'd fall off if you tried to turn him."

Ringgo's scowl lightened a bit.

"That's a little better," he said. "Having him killed is rotten enough, but I'd hate to think of anybody eating Mickey, or even meaning to."

"They didn't," I assured him. "They were putting on a show. This the sort of thing that's been happening?"

"Yes."

"What's the sense of it?"

He glumly quoted Kavalov:

"Captain Cat-and-mouse."

I gave him a cigarette, took one myself, and lighted them with a stick from the fire.

He raised his face to the sky, said, "Raining again; let's go back to the house," but remained by the fire, staring at the cooking carcass. The stink of scorched meat hung thick around us.

"You don't take this very seriously yet, do you?" he asked presently, in a low, matter-of-fact voice.

"It's a funny layout."

"He's cracked," he said in the same low voice. "Try to see this. Honor meant something to him. That's why we had to trick him instead of bribing him, back in Cairo. Less than ten years of dishonor can crack a man like that. He'd go off and hide and brood. It would be either shoot himself when the blow fell—or that. I was like you at first." He kicked at the fire. "This is silly. But I can't laugh at it now, except when I'm around Miriam and the commodore. When he first showed up I didn't have the slightest idea that I couldn't handle him. I had handled him all right in Cairo. When I discovered I couldn't handle him I lost my head a little. I went down and picked a row with him. Well, that was no good either. It's the silliness of this that makes it bad. In Cairo he was the kind of man who combs his hair before he shaves, so his mirror will show an orderly picture. Can you understand some of this?"

"I'll have to talk to him first," I said. "He's staying in the village?"

"He has a cottage on the hill above. It's the first one on the left after you turn into the main road." Ringgo dropped his cigarette into the fire and looked thoughtfully at me, biting his lower lip. "I don't know how you and the commodore are going to get along. You can't make jokes with him. He doesn't understand them, and he'll distrust you on that account."

"I'll try to be careful," I promised. "No good offering this Sherry money?"

"Hell, no," he said softly. "He's too cracked for that."

We took down the dog's carcass, kicked the fire apart, and trod it out in the mud before we returned to the house.

V

The country was fresh and bright under clear sunlight the next morning. A warm breeze was drying the ground and chasing raw-cotton clouds across the sky.

At ten o'clock I set out afoot for Captain Sherry's. I didn't have any trouble finding his house, a pinkish stuccoed bungalow with a terra cotta roof, reached from the road by a cobbled walk.

A white-clothed table with two places set stood on the tiled veranda that stretched across the front of the bungalow.

Before I could knock, the door was opened by a slim black man, not much more than a boy, in a white jacket. His features were thinner than most American negroes', aquiline, pleasantly intelligent.

"You're going to catch colds lying around in wet roads," I said, "if you don't get run over."

His mouth-ends ran towards his ears in a grin that showed me a lot of strong yellow teeth.

"Yes, sir," he said, buzzing his s's, rolling the r, bowing. "The *capitaine* have waited breakfast that you be with him. You do sit down, sir I will call him."

"Not dog meat?"

His mouth-ends ran back and up again and he shook his head vigorously.

"No, sir." He held up his black hands and counted the fingers. "There is orange and kippers and kidneys grilled and eggs and marmalade and toast and tea or coffee. There is not dog meat."

"Fine," I said, and sat down in one of the wicker armchairs on the veranda.

I had time to light a cigarette before Captain Sherry came out.

He was a gaunt tall man of forty. Sandy hair, parted in the middle, was brushed flat to his small head, above a sunburned face. His eyes were gray, with lower lids as straight as ruler-edges. His mouth was another hard straight line under a close-clipped sandy mustache. Grooves like gashes ran from his nostrils past his mouth-corners. Other grooves, just as deep, ran down his cheeks to the sharp ridge of his jaw. He wore a gaily striped flannel bathrobe over sand-colored pajamas.

"Good morning," he said pleasantly, and gave me a semi-salute. He didn't offer to shake hands. "Don't get up. It will be some minutes before Marcus has breakfast ready. I slept late. I had a most abominable dream." His voice was a deliberately languid drawl. "I dreamed that Theodore Kavalov's throat had been cut from here to here." He put bony fingers under his ears. "It was an atrociously gory business. He bled and screamed horribly, the swine."

I grinned up at him, asking:

"And you didn't like that?"

"Oh, getting his throat cut was all to the good, but he bled and screamed so filthily." He raised his nose and sniffed. "That's honeysuckle somewhere, isn't it?"

"Smells like it. Was it throat-cutting that you had in mind when you threatened him?"

"When I threatened him," he drawled. "My dear fellow, I did nothing of the sort. I was in Udja, a stinking Moroccan town close to the Algerian frontier, and one morning a voice spoke to me from an orange tree. It said: 'Go to Farewell, in California, in the States, and there you will see Theodore Kavalov die.' I thought that a capital idea. I thanked the voice, told Marcus to pack, and came here. As soon as I arrived I told Kavalov about it, thinking perhaps he would die then and I wouldn't be hung up here waiting. He didn't, though, and too late I regretted not having asked the voice for a definite date. I should hate having to waste months here."

"That's why you've been trying to hurry it up?" I asked.

"I beg your pardon?"

"*Schrecklichkeit,*" I said, "rocky skulls, dog barbecues, vanishing corpses."

"I've been fifteen years in Africa," he said. "I've too much faith in voices that come from orange trees where no one is to try to give them a hand. You needn't fancy I've had anything to do with whatever has happened."

"Marcus?"

Sherry stroked his freshly shaven cheeks and replied:

"That's possible. He has an incorrigible bent for the ruder sort of African horse-play. I'll gladly cane him for any misbehavior of which you've reasonably definite proof."

"Let me catch him at it," I said, "and I'll do my own caning."

Sherry leaned forward and spoke in a cautious undertone:

"Be sure he suspects nothing till you've a firm grip on him. He's remarkably effective with either of his knives."

"I'll try to remember that. The voice didn't say anything about Ringgo?"

"There was no need. When the body dies, the hand is dead."

Black Marcus came out carrying food. We moved to the table and I started on my second breakfast.

Sherry wondered whether the voice that had spoken to him from the orange tree had also spoken to Kavalov. He had asked Kavalov, he said, but hadn't received a very satisfactory answer. He believed that voices which announced deaths to people's enemies usually also warned the one who was to die. "That is," he said, "the conventional way of doing it, I believe."

"I don't know," I said. "I'll try to find out for you. Maybe I ought to ask him what he dreamed last night, too."

"Did he look nightmarish this morning?"

"I don't know. I left before he was up."

Sherry's eyes became hot gray points.

"Do you mean," he asked, "that you've no idea what shape he's in this morning, whether he's alive or not, whether my dream was a true one or not?"

"Yeah."

The hard line of his mouth loosened into a slow delighted smile.

"By Jove," he said, "That's capital! I thought—you gave me the impression of knowing positively that there was nothing to my dream, that it was only a meaningless dream."

He clapped his hands sharply.

Black Marcus popped out of the door.

"Pack," Sherry ordered. "The bald one is finished. We're off."

Marcus bowed and backed grinning into the house.

"Hadn't you better wait to make sure?" I asked.

"But I am sure," he drawled, "as sure as when the voice spoke from the orange tree. There is nothing to wait for now: I have seen him die."

"In a dream."

"Was it a dream?" he asked carelessly.

When I left, ten or fifteen minutes later, Marcus was making noises indoors that sounded as if he actually was packing.

Sherry shook hands with me, saying:

"Awfully glad to have had you for breakfast. Perhaps we'll meet again if your work ever brings you to northern Africa. Remember me to Miriam and Dolph. I can't sincerely send condolences."

Out of sight of the bungalow, I left the road for a path along the hillside above, and explored the country for a higher spot from which Sherry's place could be spied on. I found a pip, a vacant ramshackle house on a jutting ridge off to the northeast. The whole of the bungalow's front, part of one side, and a good stretch of the cobbled walk, including its juncture with the road, could be seen from the vacant house's front porch. It was a rather long shot for naked eyes, but with field glasses it would be just about perfect, even to a screen of over-grown bushes in front.

When I got back to the Kavalov house Ringgo was propped up on gay cushions in a reed chair under a tree, with a book in his hand.

"What do you think of him?" he asked. "Is he cracked?"

"Not very. He wanted to be remembered to you and Mrs. Ringgo. How's the arm this morning?"

"Rotten. I must have let it get too damp last night. It gave me hell all night."

"Did you see Captain Cat-and-mouse?" Kavalov's whining voice came from behind me. "And did you find any satisfaction in that?"

I turned around. He was coming down the walk from the house. His face was more gray than brown this morning, but what I could see of his throat, above the v of a wing collar, was uncut enough.

"He was packing when I left," I said. "Going back to Africa."

VI

That day was Thursday. Nothing else happened that day.

Friday morning I was awakened by the noise of my bedroom door being opened violently.

Martin, the thin-faced valet, came dashing into my room and began shaking me by the shoulder, though I was sitting up by the time he reached my bedside.

His thin face was lemon-yellow and ugly with fear.

"It's happened," he babbled. "Oh, my God, it's happened!"

"What's happened?"

"It's happened. It's happened."

I pushed him aside and got out of bed. He turned suddenly and ran into my bathroom. I could hear him vomiting as I pushed my feet into slippers.

Kavalov's bedroom was three doors below mine, on the same side of the building.

The house was full of noises, excited voices, doors opening and shutting, though I couldn't see anybody.

I ran down to Kavalov's door. It was open.

Kavalov was in there, lying on a low Spanish bed. The bed-clothes were thrown down across the foot.

Kavalov was lying on his back. His throat had been cut, a curving cut that paralleled the line of his jaw between points an inch under his ear lobes.

Where his blood had soaked into the blue pillow case and blue sheet it was purple as grape-juice. It was thick and sticky, already clotting.

Ringgo came in wearing a bathrobe like a cape.

"It's happened," I growled, using the valet's words.

Ringgo looked dully, miserably, at the bed and began cursing in a choked, muffled, voice.

The red-faced blonde woman—Louella Qually, the house-keeper—came in, screamed, pushed past us, and ran to the bed, still screaming. I caught her arm when she reached for the covers.

"Let things alone," I said.

"Cover him up. Cover him up, the poor man!" she cried.

I took her away from the bed. Four or five servants were in the room by now. I gave the housekeeper to a couple of them, telling them to take her out and quiet her down. She went away laughing and crying.

Ringgo was still staring at the bed.

"Where's Mrs. Ringgo?" I asked.

He didn't hear me. I tapped his good arm and repeated the question.

"She's in her room. She—she didn't have to see it to know what had happened."

"Hadn't you better look after her?"

He nodded, turned slowly, and went out.

The valet, still lemon-yellow, came in.

"I want everybody on the place, servants, farm hands, everybody downstairs in the front room," I told him. "Get them all there right away, and they're to stay there till the sheriff comes."

"Yes, sir," he said and went downstairs, the others following him.

I closed Kavalov's door and went across to the library, where I phoned the sheriff's office in the county seat. I talked to a deputy named Hilden. When I had told him my story he said the sheriff would be at the house within half an hour.

I went to my room and dressed. By the time I had finished, the valet came up to tell me that everybody was assembled in the front room—everybody except the Ringgos and Mrs. Ringgo's maid.

I was examining Kavalov's bedroom when the sheriff arrived. He was a white-haired man with mild blue eyes and a mild voice that came out indistinctly under a white mustache. He had brought three deputies, a doctor and a coroner with him.

"Ringgo and the valet can tell you more than I can," I said when we had shaken hands all around. "I'll be back as soon as I can make it. I'm going to Sherry's. Ringgo will tell you where he fits in."

In the garage I selected a muddy Chevrolet and drove to the bungalow. Its doors and windows were tight, and my knocking brought no answer.

I went back along the cobbled walk to the car, and rode down into Farewell. There I had no trouble learning that Sherry and Marcus had taken the two-ten train for Los Angeles the afternoon before, with three trunks and half a dozen bags that the village expressman had checked for them.

After sending a telegram to the Agency's Los Angeles branch, I hunted up the man from whom Sherry had rented the bungalow.

He could tell me nothing about his tenants except that he was disappointed in their not staying even a full two weeks. Sherry had returned the keys with a brief note saying he had been called away unexpectedly.

I pocketed the note. Handwriting specimens are always convenient to have. Then I borrowed the keys to the bungalow and went back to it.

I didn't find anything of value there, except a lot of fingerprints that might possibly come in handy later. There was nothing there to tell me where my men had gone.

I returned to Kavalov's.

The sheriff had finished running the staff through the mill.

"Can't get a thing out of them," he said. "Nobody heard anything and nobody saw anything, from bedtime last night, till the valet opened the door to call him at eight o'clock this morning, and saw him dead like that. You know any more than that?"

"No. They tell you about Sherry?"

"Oh, yes. That's our meat, I guess, huh?"

"Yeah. He's supposed to have cleared out yesterday afternoon, with his black man, for Los Angeles. We ought to be able to find the work in that. What does the doctor say?"

"Says he was killed between three and four this morning, with a heavyish knife—one clean slash from left to right, like a left-handed man would do it."

"Maybe one clean cut," I agreed, "but not exactly a slash. Slower than that. A slash, if it curved, ought to curve up, away from the slasher, in the middle, and down towards him at the ends—just the opposite of what this does."

"Oh, all right. Is this Sherry a southpaw?"

"I don't know." I wondered if Marcus was. "Find the knife?"

"Nary hide nor hair of it. And what's more, we didn't find anything else, inside or out. Funny a fellow as scared as Kavalov was, from all accounts, didn't keep himself locked up tighter. His windows were open. Anybody could of got in them with a ladder. His door wasn't locked."

"There could be half a dozen reasons for that. He—"

One of the deputies, a big-shouldered blond man, came to the door and said:

"We found the knife."

The sheriff and I followed the deputy out of the house, around to the side on which Kavalov's room was situated. The knife's blade was buried in the ground, among some shrubs that bordered a path leading down to the farm hands' quarters.

The knife's wooden handle—painted red—slanted a little toward the house. A little blood was smeared on the blade, but the soft earth had cleaned off most. There was no blood on the painted handle, and nothing like a fingerprint.

There were no footprints in the soft ground near the knife. Apparently it had been tossed into the shrubbery.

"I guess that's all there is here for us," the sheriff said. "There's nothing much to show that anybody here had anything to do with it, or didn't. Now we'll look after this here Captain Sherry."

I went down to the village with him. At the post office we learned that Sherry had left a forwarding address: General Delivery, St. Louis, Mo. The postmaster said Sherry had received no mail during his stay in Farewell.

We went to the telegraph office, and were told that Sherry had neither received nor sent any telegrams. I sent one to the Agency's St. Louis branch.

The rest of our poking around in the village brought us nothing—except we learned that most of the idlers in Farewell had seen Sherry and Marcus board the southbound two-ten train.

Before we returned to the Kavalov house a telegram came from the Los Angeles branch for me:

> Sherry's trunks and bags in baggage room here not yet called for are keeping them under surveillance.

When we got back to the house I met Ringgo in the hall, and asked him:

"Is Sherry left-handed?"

He thought, and then shook his head.

"I can't remember," he said. "He might be. I'll ask Miriam. Perhaps she'll know—women remember things like that."

When he came downstairs again he was nodding:

"He's very nearly ambidextrous, but uses his left hand more than his right. Why?"

"The doctor thinks it was done with a left hand. How is Mrs. Ringgo now?"

"I think the worst of the shock is over, thanks."

VII

Sherry's baggage remained uncalled for in the Los Angeles passenger station all day Saturday. Late that afternoon the sheriff made public the news that Sherry and the black were wanted for murder, and that night the sheriff and I took a train south.

Sunday morning, with a couple of men from the Los Angeles police department, we opened the baggage. We didn't find anything except legitimate clothing and personal belongings that told us nothing.

That trip paid no dividends.

I returned to San Francisco and had bales of circulars printed and distributed.

Two weeks went by, two weeks in which the circulars brought us nothing but the usual lot of false alarms.

Then the Spokane police picked up Sherry and Marcus in a Stevens Street rooming house.

Some unknown person had phoned the police that one Fred Williams living there had a mysterious black visitor nearly every day, and that their actions were very suspicious. The Spokane police had copies of our circular. They hardly needed the H.S. monograms on Fred Williams' cuff links and handkerchiefs to assure them that he was our man.

After a couple of hours of being grilled, Sherry admitted his identity, but denied having murdered Kavalov.

Two of the sheriff's men went north and brought the prisoners down to the county seat.

Sherry had shaved off his mustache. There was nothing in his face or voice to show that he was the least bit worried.

"I knew there was nothing more to wait for after my dream," he drawled, "so I went away. Then, when I heard the dream had come true, I knew you johnnies would be hot after me—as if one can help his dreams—and I—ah—sought seclusion."

He solemnly repeated his orange-tree-voice story to the sheriff and district attorney. The newspapers liked it.

He refused to map his route for us, to tell us how he had spent his time.

"No, no," he said. "Sorry, but I shouldn't do it. It may be I shall have to do it again some time, and it wouldn't do to reveal my methods."

He wouldn't tell us where he had spent the night of the murder. We were fairly certain that he had left the train before it reached Los Angeles, though the train crew had been able to tell us nothing.

"Sorry," he drawled. "But if you chaps don't know where I was, how do you know that I was where the murder was?"

We had even less luck with Marcus. His formula was:

"Not understand the English very good. Ask the *capitaine*. I don't know."

The district attorney spent a lot of time walking his office floor, biting his finger nails, and telling us fiercely that the case was going to fall apart if we couldn't prove that either Sherry or Marcus was within reach of the Kavalov house at, or shortly before or after, the time of the murder.

The sheriff was the only one of us who hadn't a sneaky feeling that Sherry's sleeves were loaded with assorted aces. The sheriff saw him already hanged.

Sherry got a lawyer, a slick looking pale man with hornrim glasses and a thin twitching mouth. His name was Schaeffer. He went around smiling to himself and at us.

When the district attorney had only thumb nails left and was starting to work on them, I borrowed a car from Ringgo and started following the railroad south, trying to learn where Sherry had left the train. We had mugged the pair, of course, so I carried their photographs with me.

I displayed those damned photographs at every railroad stop between Farewell and Los Angeles, at every village within twenty miles of the tracks on either side, and at most of the houses in between. And it got me nothing.

There was no evidence that Sherry and Marcus hadn't gone through to Los Angeles.

Their train would have put them there at ten-thirty that night. There was no train out of Los Angeles that would have carried them back to Farewell in time to kill Kavalov. There were two possibilities: an airplane could have carried them back in plenty of time; and an automobile might have been able to do it, though that didn't look reasonable.

I tried the airplane angle first, and couldn't find a flyer who had had a passenger that night. With the help of the Los Angeles police and some operatives from the Continental's Los Angeles branch, I had everybody who owned a plane— public or private—interviewed. All the answers were no.

We tried the less promising automobile angle. The larger taxicab and hire-car companies said, "No." Four privately owned cars had been reported stolen between ten and twelve o'clock that night. Two of them had been found in the city the next morning: they couldn't have made the trip to Farewell and back. One of the others had been picked up in San Diego the next day. That let that one out. The other was still loose, a Packard sedan. We got a printer working on post card descriptions of it.

To reach all the small-fry taxi and hire-car owners was quite a job, and then there were the private car owners who might have hired out for one night. We went into the newspapers to cover these fields.

We didn't get any automobile information, but this new line of inquiry—trying to find traces of our men here a few hours before the murder—brought results of another kind.

At San Pedro (Los Angeles's seaport, twenty-five miles away) a negro had been arrested at one o'clock on the morning of the murder. The negro spoke English poorly, but had papers to prove that he was Pierre Tisano, a French sailor. He had been arrested on a drunk and disorderly charge.

The San Pedro police said that the photograph and description of the man we knew as Marcus fit the drunken sailor exactly.

That wasn't all the San Pedro police said.

Tisano had been arrested at one o'clock. At a little after two o'clock, a white man who gave his name as Henry Somerton had appeared and had tried to bail the negro out. The desk sergeant had told Somerton that nothing could be done till morning, and that, anyway, it would be better to let Tisano sleep off his jag before removing him. Somerton had readily agreed to that, had remained talking to the desk sergeant for more than half an hour, and had left at about three. At ten o'clock that morning he had reappeared to pay the black man's fine. They had gone away together.

The San Pedro police said that Sherry's photograph—without the mustache—and description were Henry Somerton's.

Henry Somerton's signature on the register of the hotel to which he had gone between his two visits to the police matched the handwriting in Sherry's note to the bungalow's owner.

It was pretty clear that Sherry and Marcus had been in San Pedro—a nine-hour train ride from Farewell—at the time that Kavalov was murdered.

Pretty clear isn't quite clear enough in a murder job: I carried the San Pedro desk sergeant north with me for a look at the two men.

"Them's them, all righty," he said.

VIII

The district attorney ate up the rest of his thumb nails.

The sheriff had the bewildered look of a child who had held a balloon in his hand, had heard a pop, and couldn't understand where the balloon had gone.

I pretended I was perfectly satisfied.

"Now we're back where we started," the district attorney wailed disagreeably, as if it was everybody's fault but his, "and with all those weeks wasted."

The sheriff didn't look at the district attorney, and didn't say anything.

I said:

"Oh, I wouldn't say that. We've made some progress."

"What?"

"We know that Sherry and the dinge have alibis."

The district attorney seemed to think I was trying to kid him. I didn't pay any attention to the faces he made at me, and asked:

"What are you going to do with them?"

"What can I do with them but turn them loose? This shoots the case to hell."

"It doesn't cost the county much to feed them," I suggested. "Why not hang on to them as long as you can, while we think it over? Something new may turn up, and you can always drop the case if nothing does. You don't think they're innocent, do you?"

He gave me a look that was heavy and sour with pity for my stupidity.

"They're guilty as hell, but what good's that to me if I can't get a conviction? And what's the good of saying I'll hold them? Damn it, man, you know as well as I do that all they've got to do now is ask for their release and any judge will hand it to them."

"Yeah," I agreed. "I'll bet you the best hat in San Francisco that they don't ask for it."

"What do you mean?"

"They want to stand trial," I said, "or they'd have sprung that alibi before we dug it up. I've an idea that they tipped off the Spokane police themselves. And I'll bet you that hat that you get no *habeas corpus* motions out of Schaeffer."

The district attorney peered suspiciously into my eyes.

"Do you know something that you're holding back?" he demanded.

"No, but you'll see I'm right."

I was right. Schaeffer went around smiling to himself and making no attempt to get his clients out of the county prison.

Three days later something new turned up.

A man named Archibald Weeks, who had a small chicken farm some ten miles south of the Kavalov place, came to see the district attorney. Weeks said he had seen Sherry on his—Weeks's—place early on the morning of the murder.

Weeks had been leaving for Iowa that morning to visit his parents. He had got up early to see that everything was in order before driving twenty miles to catch an early morning train.

At somewhere between half-past five and six o'clock he had gone to the shed where he kept his car, to see if it held enough gasoline for the trip.

A man ran out of the shed, vaulted the fence, and dashed away down the road. Weeks chased him for a short distance, but the other was too speedy for him. The man was too well-dressed for a hobo: Weeks supposed he had been trying to steal the car.

Since Weeks's trip east was a necessary one, and during his absence his wife would have only their two sons—one seventeen, one fifteen—there with her, he had thought it wisest not to frighten her by saying anything about the man he had surprised in the shed.

He had returned from Iowa the day before his appearance in the district attorney's office, and after hearing the details of the Kavalov murder, and seeing Sherry's picture in the papers, had recognized him as the man he had chased.

We showed him Sherry in person. He said Sherry was the man. Sherry said nothing.

With Weeks's evidence to refute the San Pedro police's, the district attorney let the case against Sherry come to trial. Marcus was held as a material witness, but there was nothing to weaken his San Pedro alibi, so he was not tried.

Weeks told his story straight and simply on the witness stand, and then, under cross-examination, blew up with a loud bang. He went to pieces completely.

He wasn't, he admitted in answer to Schaeffer's questions, quite as sure that Sherry was the man as he had been before. The man had certainly, the little he had seen of him, looked something like Sherry, but perhaps he had been a little hasty in saying positively that it was Sherry. He wasn't, now that he had had time to think it over, really sure that he had actually got a good look at the man's face in the dim morning light. Finally, all that Weeks would swear to was that he had seen a man who had seemed to look a little bit like Sherry.

It was funny as hell.

The district attorney, having no nails left, nibbled his finger-bones.

The jury said, "Not guilty."

Sherry was freed, forever in the clear so far as the Kavalov murder was concerned, no matter what might come to light later.

Marcus was released.

The district attorney wouldn't say good-bye to me when I left for San Francisco.

IX

Four days after Sherry's acquittal, Mrs. Ringgo was shown into my office.

She was in black. Her pretty, unintelligent, Oriental face was not placid. Worry was in it.

"Please, you won't tell Dolph I have come here?" were the first words she spoke.

"Of course not, if you say not," I promised and pulled a chair over for her.

She sat down and looked big-eyed at me, fidgeting with her gloves in her lap.

"He's so reckless," she said.

I nodded sympathetically, wondering what she was up to.

"And I'm so afraid," she added, twisting her gloves. Her chin trembled. Her lips formed words jerkily: "They've come back to the bungalow."

"Yeah?" I sat up straight. I knew who *they* were.

"They can't," she cried, "have come back for any reason except that they mean to murder Dolph as they did father. And he won't listen to me. He's so sure of himself. He laughs and calls me a foolish child, and tells me he can take care of himself. But he can't. Not, at least, with a broken arm. And they'll kill him as they killed father. I know it. I know it."

"Sherry hates your husband as much as he hated your father?"

"Yes. That's it. He does. Dolph was working for father, but Dolph's part in the—the business that led up to Hugh's trouble was more—more active than father's. Will you—will you keep them from killing Dolph? Will you?"

"Surely."

"And you mustn't let Dolph know," she insisted, "and if he does find out you're watching them, you mustn't tell him I got you to. He'd be angry with me. I asked him to send for you, but he—" She broke off, looking embarrassed: I supposed her husband had mentioned my lack of success in keeping Kavalov alive. "But he wouldn't."

"How long have they been back?"

"Since the day before yesterday."

"Any demonstrations?"

"You mean things like happened before? I don't know. Dolph would hide them from me."

"I'll be down tomorrow," I promised. "If you'll take my advice you'll tell your husband that you've employed me, but I won't tell him if you don't."

"And you won't let them harm Dolph?"

I promised to do my best, took some money away from her, gave her a receipt, and bowed her out.

Shortly after dark that evening I reached Farewell.

X

The bungalow's windows were lighted when I passed it on my way uphill. I was tempted to get out of my coupé and do some snooping, but was afraid that I couldn't out-Indian Marcus on his own grounds, and so went on.

When I turned into the dirt road leading to the vacant house I had spotted on my first trip to Farewell, I switched off the coupé's lights and crept along by the light of a very white moon overhead.

Close to the vacant house I got the coupé off the path and at least partly hidden by bushes.

Then I went up on the rickety porch, located the bungalow, and began to adjust my field glasses to it.

I had them partly adjusted when the bungalow's front door opened, letting out a slice of yellow light and two people.

One of the people was a woman.

Another least turn of the set-screw and her face came clear in my eyes—Mrs. Ringgo.

She raised her coat collar around her face and hurried away down the cobbled walk. Sherry stood on the veranda looking after her.

When she reached the road she began running uphill, towards her house.

Sherry went indoors and shut the door.

I took the glasses away from my eyes and looked around for a place where I could sit. The only spot I could find where sitting wouldn't interfere with my view of the bungalow was the porch-rail. I made myself as comfortable as possible there, with a shoulder against the corner post, and prepared for an evening of watchful waiting.

Two hours and a half later a man turned into the cobbled walk from the road. He walked swiftly to the bungalow, with a cautious sort of swiftness, and he looked from side to side as he walked.

I suppose he knocked on the door.

The door opened, throwing a yellow glow on his face, Dolph Ringgo's face.

He went indoors. The door shut.

My watch-tower's fault was that the bungalow could only be reached from it roundabout by the path and road. There was no way of cutting cross-country.

I put away the field glasses, left the porch, and set out for the bungalow. I wasn't sure that I could find another good spot for the coupé, so I left it where it was and walked.

I was afraid to take a chance on the cobbled walk.

Twenty feet above it, I left the road and moved as silently as I could over sod and among trees, bushes and flowers. I knew the sort of folks I was playing with: I carried my gun in my hand.

All of the bungalow's windows on my side showed lights, but all the windows were closed and their blinds drawn. I didn't like the way the light that came through the blinds helped the moon illuminate the surrounding ground. That had been swell when I was up on the ridge getting cock-eyed squinting through glasses. It was sour now that I was trying to get close enough to do some profitable listening.

I stopped in the closest dark spot I could find—fifteen feet from the building—to think the situation over.

Crouching there, I heard something.

It wasn't in the right place. It wasn't what I wanted to hear. It was the sound of somebody coming down the walk towards the house.

I wasn't sure that I couldn't be seen from the path. I turned my head to make sure. And by turning my head I gave myself away.

Mrs. Ringgo jumped, stopped dead still in the path, and then cried:

"Is Dolph in there? Is he? Is he?"

I was trying to tell her that he was by nodding, but she made so much noise with her *Is he's* that I had to say "Yeah" out loud to make her hear.

I don't know whether the noise we made hurried things up indoors or not, but guns had started going off inside the bungalow.

You don't stop to count shots in circumstances like those, and anyway these were too blurred together for accurate score-keeping, but my impression was that at least fifty of them had been fired by the time I was bruising my shoulder on the front door.

Luckily, it was a California door. It went in the second time I hit it.

Inside was a reception hall opening through a wide arched doorway into a living-room. The air was hazy and the stink of burnt powder was sharp.

Sherry was on the polished floor by the arch, wriggling sidewise on one elbow and one knee, trying to reach a Luger that lay on an amber rug some four feet away. His upper teeth were sunk deep into his lower lip, and he was coughing little stomach coughs as he wriggled.

At the other end of the room, Ringgo was upright on his knees, steadily working the trigger of a black revolver in his good hand. The pistol was empty. It went snap, snap, snap, snap foolishly, but he kept on working the trigger. His broken arm was still in the splints, but had fallen out of the sling and was hanging down. His face was puffy and florid with blood. His eyes were wide and dull. The white bone handle of a knife stuck out of his back, just over one hip, its blade all the way in. He was clicking the empty pistol at Marcus.

The black boy was on his feet, feet far apart under bent knees. His left hand was spread wide over his chest, and the black fingers were shiny with blood. In his right hand he held a white bone-handled knife—its blade a foot long—held it, knife-fighter fashion, as you'd hold a sword. He was moving toward Ringgo, not directly, but from side to side, obliquely, closing in with shuffling steps, crouching, his hand turning the knife restlessly, but holding the point always towards Ringgo. Marcus's eyes were bulging and red-veined. His mouth was a wide grinning crescent. His tongue, far out, ran slowly around and around the outside of his lips. Saliva trickled down his chin.

He didn't see us. He didn't hear us. All of his world just then was the man on his knees, the man in whose back a knife—brother of the one in the black hand—was wedged.

Ringgo didn't see us. I don't suppose he even saw the black. He knelt there and persistently worked the trigger of his empty gun.

I jumped over Sherry and swung the barrel of my gun at the base of Marcus's skull. It hit. Marcus dropped.

Ringgo stopped working the gun and looked surprised at me.

"That's the idea; you've got to put bullets in them or they're no good," I told him, pulled the knife out of Marcus's hand, and went back to pick up the Luger that Sherry had stopped trying to get.

Mrs. Ringgo ran past me to her husband.

Sherry was lying on his back now. His eyes were closed.

He looked dead, and he had enough bullet holes in him to make death a good guess.

Hoping he wasn't dead, I knelt beside him—going around him so I could kneel facing Ringgo—and lifted his head up a little from the floor.

Sherry stirred then, but I couldn't tell whether he stirred because he was still alive or because he had just died.

"Sherry," I said sharply. "Sherry."

He didn't move. His eyelids didn't even twitch.

I raised the fingers of the hand that was holding up his head, making his head move just a trifle.

"Did Ringgo kill Kavalov?" I asked the dead or dying man.

Even if I hadn't known Ringgo was looking at me I could have felt his eyes on me.

"Did he, Sherry?" I barked into the still face.

The dead or dying man didn't move.

I cautiously moved my fingers again so that his dead or dying head nodded, twice.

Then I made his head jerk back, and let it gently down on the floor again.

"Well," I said, standing up and facing Ringgo, "I've got you at last."

XI

I've never been able to decide whether I would actually have gone on the witness stand and sworn that Sherry was alive when he nodded, and nodded voluntarily, if it had been necessary for me to do so to convict Ringgo.

I don't like perjury, but I knew Ringgo was guilty, and there I had him.

Fortunately, I didn't have to decide.

Ringgo believed Sherry had nodded, and then, when Marcus gave the show away, there was nothing much for Ringgo to do but try his luck with a plea of guilty.

We didn't have much trouble getting the story out of Marcus. Ringgo had killed his beloved *capitaine*. The black boy was easily persuaded that the law would give him his best revenge.

After Marcus had talked, Ringgo was willing to talk.

He stayed in the hospital until the day before his trial opened. The knife Marcus had planted in his back had permanently paralyzed one of his legs, though aside from that he recovered from the stabbing.

Marcus had three of Ringgo's bullets in him. The doctors fished two of them out, but were afraid to touch the third. It didn't seem to worry him. By the time he was shipped north to begin an indeterminate sentence in San Quentin for his part in the Kavalov murder he was apparently as sound as ever.

Ringgo was never completely convinced that I had ever suspected him before the last minute when I had come charging into the bungalow.

"Of course I had, right along," I defended my skill as a sleuth. That was while he was still in the hospital. "I didn't believe Sherry was cracked. He was one hard, sane-looking scoundrel. And I didn't believe he was the sort of man who'd be worried much over any disgrace that came his way. I was willing enough to believe that he was out for Kavalov's scalp, but only if there was some profit in it. That's why I went to sleep and let the old man's throat get cut. I figured Sherry was scaring him up—nothing more—to get him in shape for a big-money shakedown. Well, when I found out I had been wrong there I began to look around.

"So far as I knew, your wife was Kavalov's heir. From what I had seen, I imagined your wife was enough in love with you to be completely in your hands. All right, you, as the husband of his heir, seemed the one to profit most directly by Kavalov's death. You were the one who'd have control of his fortune when he died. Sherry could only profit by the murder if he was working with you."

"But didn't his breaking my arm puzzle you?"

"Sure. I could understand a phoney injury, but that seemed carrying it a little too far. But you made a mistake there that helped me. You were too careful to imitate a left-hand cut on Kavalov's throat; did it by standing by his head, facing his body when you cut him, instead of by his body, facing his head, and the curve of the slash gave you away. Throwing the knife out the window wasn't so good, either. How'd he happen to break your arm? An accident?"

"You can call it that. We had that supposed fight arranged to fit in with the rest of the play, and I thought it would be fun to really sock him. So I did. And he was tougher than I thought, tough enough to even up by snapping my arm. I suppose that's why he killed Mickey too. That wasn't on the schedule. On the level, did you suspect us of being in cahoots?"

I nodded.

"Sherry had worked the game up for you, had done everything possible to draw suspicion on himself, and then, the day before the murder, had run off to build himself an alibi. There couldn't be any other answer to it: he had to be working with you. There it was, but I couldn't prove it. I couldn't prove it till you were trapped by the thing that made the whole game possible—your wife's love for you sent her to hire me to protect you. Isn't that one of the things they call ironies of life?"

Ringgo smiled ruefully and said:

"They should call it that. You know what Sherry was trying on me, don't you?"

"I can guess. That's why he insisted on standing trial."

"Exactly. The scheme was for him to dig out and keep going, with his alibi ready in case he was picked up, but staying uncaught as long as possible. The more time they wasted hunting him, the less likely they were to look elsewhere, and the colder the trail would be when they found he wasn't their man. He tricked me there. He had himself picked up, and his lawyer hired that Weeks fellow to egg the district attorney into not dropping the case. Sherry wanted to be tried and acquitted, so he'd be in the clear. Then he had me by the neck. He was legally cleared forever. I wasn't. He had me. He was supposed to get a hundred thousand dollars for his part. Kavalov had left Miriam something more than three million dollars. Sherry demanded one-half of it. Otherwise, he said, he'd go to the district attorney and make a complete confession. They couldn't do anything to him. He'd been acquitted. They'd hang me. That was sweet."

"You'd have been wise at that to have given it to him," I said.

"Maybe. Anyway I suppose I would have given it to him if Miriam hadn't upset things. There'd have been nothing else to do. But after she came back from hiring you she went to see Sherry, thinking she could talk him into going away. And he lets something drop that made her suspect I had a hand in her father's death, though she doesn't even now actually believe that I cut his throat.

"She said you were coming down the next day. There was nothing for me to do but go down to Sherry's for a show-down that night, and have the whole thing settled before you came poking around. Well, that's what I did, though I didn't tell Miriam I was going. The showdown wasn't going along very well, too much tension, and when Sherry heard you outside he thought I had brought friends, and—fireworks."

"What ever got you into a game like that in the first place?" I asked. "You were sitting pretty enough as Kavalov's son-in-law, weren't you?"

"Yes, but it was tiresome being cooped up in that hole with him. He was young enough to live a long time. And he wasn't always easy to get along with. I'd no guarantee that he wouldn't get up on his ear and kick me out, or change his will, or anything of the sort.

"Then I ran across Sherry in San Francisco, and we got to talking it over, and this plan came out of it. Sherry had brains. On the deal back in Cairo that you know about, both he and I made plenty that Kavalov didn't know about. Well, I was a chump. But don't think I'm sorry that I killed Kavalov. I'm sorry I got caught. I'd done his dirty work since he picked me up as a kid of twenty, and all I'd got out of it was damned little except the hopes that since I'd married his daughter I'd probably get his money when he died—if he didn't do something else with it."

They hanged him.

Woman in the Dark

PART ONE — THE FLIGHT

HER right ankle turned under her and she fell. The wind blowing downhill from the south, whipping the trees beside the road, made a whisper of her exclamation and snatched her scarf away into the darkness. She sat up slowly, palms on the gravel pushing her up, and twisted her body sidewise to release the leg bent beneath her.

Her right slipper lay in the road close to her feet. When she put it on she found its heel was missing. She peered around, then began to hunt for the heel, hunting on hands and knees uphill into the wind, wincing a little when her right knee touched the road. Presently she gave it up and tried to break the heel off her left slipper, but could not. She replaced the slipper and rose with her back to the wind, leaning back against the wind's violence and the road's steep sloping. Her gown clung to her back, flew fluttering out before her. Hair lashed her cheeks. Walking high on the ball of her right foot to make up for the missing heel, she hobbled on down the hill.

At the bottom of the hill there was a wooden bridge, and, a hundred yards beyond, a sign that could not be read in the darkness marked a fork in the road. She halted there, not looking at the sign but around her, shivering now, though the wind had less force than it had had on the hill. Foliage to her left moved to show and hide yellow light. She took the left-hand fork.

In a little while she came to a gap in the bushes beside the road and sufficient light to show a path running off the road through the gap. The light came from the thinly curtained window of a house at the other end of the path.

She went up the path to the door and knocked. When there was no answer she knocked again.

A hoarse unemotional masculine voice said: "Come in."

She put her hand on the latch; hesitated. No sound came from within the house. Outside the wind was noisy everywhere. She knocked once more, gently.

783

The voice said exactly as before: "Come in."

She opened the door. The wind blew it in sharply, her hold on the latch dragging her with it so that she had to cling to the door with both hands to keep from falling. The wind went past her into the room, to balloon curtains and scatter the sheets of a newspaper that had been on a table. She forced the door shut and, still leaning against it, said: "I am sorry." She took pains with her words to make them clear notwithstanding her accent.

The man cleaning a pipe at the hearth said: "It's all right." His copperish eyes were as impersonal as his hoarse voice. "I'll be through in a minute." He did not rise from his chair. The edge of the knife in his hand rasped inside the brier bowl of his pipe.

She left the door and came forward, limping, examining him with perplexed eyes under brows drawn a little together. She was a tall woman and carried herself proudly, for all she was lame and the wind had tousled her hair and the gravel of the road had cut and dirtied her hands and bare arms and the red crêpe of her gown.

She said, still taking pains with her words: "I must go to the railroad. I have hurt my ankle on the road. Eh?"

He looked up from his work then. His sallow, heavily featured face, under coarse hair nearly the color of his eyes, was definitely neither hostile nor friendly. He looked at the woman's face, at her torn skirt. He did not turn his head to call: "Hey, Evelyn."

A girl—slim maturing body in tan sport clothes, slender sunburned face with dark bright eyes and dark short hair—came into the room through a doorway behind him.

The man did not look around at her. He nodded at the woman in red and said: "This—"

The woman interrupted him: "My name is Luise Fischer."

The man said: "She's got a bum leg."

Evelyn's dark prying eyes shifted their focus from the woman to the man—she could not see his face—and to the woman again. She smiled, speaking hurriedly: "I'm just leaving. I can drop you at Mile Valley on my way home."

The woman seemed about to smile. Under her curious gaze Evelyn suddenly blushed and her face became defiant while it reddened. The girl was pretty. Facing her the woman had become beautiful; her eyes were long, heavily lashed, set well apart under a smooth broad brow, her mouth was not small but sensitively carved and mobile, and in the light from the open fire the surfaces of her face were as clearly defined as sculptured planes.

The man blew through his pipe, forcing out a small cloud of black powder. "No use hurrying," he said. "There's no train till six." He looked up at the clock on the mantelpiece. It said ten thirty-three. "Why don't you help her with her leg?"

The woman said: "No, it is not necessary. I—" She put her weight on her injured leg and flinched, steadying herself with a hand on the back of a chair.

The girl hurried to her, stammering contritely: "I—I didn't think. Forgive me." She put an arm around the woman and helped her into the chair.

The man stood up to put his pipe on the mantelpiece beside the clock. He was of medium height, but his sturdiness made him look shorter. His neck, rising from the V of a gray sweater, was short, powerfully muscled. Below the sweater he wore loose gray trousers and heavy brown shoes. He clicked his knife shut and put it in his pocket before turning to look at Luise Fischer.

Evelyn was on her knees in front of the woman, pulling off her right stocking, making sympathetic clucking noises, chattering nervously: "You've cut your knee too. Tch-tch-tch! And look how your ankle's swelling. You shouldn't't've tried to walk all that distance in these slippers." Her body hid the woman's bare leg from the man. "Now sit still and I'll fix it up in a minute." She pulled the torn red skirt down over the bare leg.

The woman's smile was polite. She said carefully: "You are very kind."

The girl ran out of the room.

The man had a paper package of cigarettes in his hand. He shook it until three cigarettes protruded half an inch and held them out to her. "Smoke?"

"Thank you." She took a cigarette, put it between her lips, and looked at his hand when he held a match to it. His hand was thick-boned, muscular, but not a laborer's. She looked through her lashes at his face while he was lighting his cigarette. He was younger than he had seemed at first glance—perhaps no older than thirty-two or three—and his features, in the flare of his match, seemed less stolid than disciplined.

"Bang it up much?" His tone was merely conversational.

"I hope I have not." She drew up her skirt to look first at her ankle, then at her knee. The ankle was perceptibly though not greatly swollen; the knee was cut once deeply, twice less seriously. She touched the edges of the cuts gently with a forefinger. "I do not like pain," she said very earnestly.

Evelyn came in with a basin of steaming water, cloths, a roll of bandage, salve. Her dark eyes widened at the man and woman, but were hidden by lowered lids by the time their faces had turned toward her. "I'll fix it now. I'll have it all fixed in a minute." She knelt in front of the woman again, nervous hand sloshing water on the floor, body between Luise Fischer's leg and the man.

He went to the door and looked out, holding the door half a foot open against the wind.

The woman asked the girl bathing her ankle: "There is not a train before it is morning?" She pursed her lips thoughtfully. "No."

The man shut the door and said: "It'll be raining in an hour." He put more wood on the fire, then stood—legs apart, hands in pockets, cigarette dangling from one side of his mouth—watching Evelyn attend to the woman's leg. His face was placid.

The girl dried the ankle and began to wind a bandage around it, working with increasing speed, breathing more rapidly now. Once more the woman seemed about to smile at the girl, but instead she said, "You are very kind."

The girl murmured, "It's nothing."

Three sharp knocks sounded on the door.

Luise Fischer started, dropped her cigarette, looked swiftly around the room with frightened eyes. The girl did not raise her head from her work. The man, with nothing in his face or manner to show he had noticed the woman's fright, turned his face toward the door and called in his hoarse matter-of-fact voice: "All right. Come in."

The door opened and a spotted great Dane came in, followed by two tall men in dinner clothes. The dog walked straight to Luise Fischer and nuzzled her hand. She was looking at the two men who had just entered. There was no timidity, no warmth in her gaze.

One of the men pulled off his cap—it was a gray tweed matching his topcoat—and came to her smiling. "So this is where you landed?" His smile vanished as he saw her leg and the bandages. "What happened?" He was perhaps forty years old, well groomed, graceful of carriage, with smooth dark hair, intelligent dark eyes—solicitous at the moment—and a close-clipped dark mustache. He pushed the dog aside and took the woman's hand.

"It is not serious, I think." She did not smile. Her voice was cool. "I stumbled in the road and twisted my ankle. These people have been very—"

He turned to the man in the gray sweater, holding out his hand, saying briskly: "Thanks ever so much for taking care of *Fräulein* Fischer. You're Brazil, aren't you?"

The man in the sweater nodded. "And you'd be Kane Robson."

"Right." Robson jerked his head at the man who still stood just inside the door. "Mr. Conroy."

Brazil nodded. Conroy said, "How do you do," and advanced toward Luise Fischer. He was an inch or two taller than Robson—who was nearly six feet himself—and some ten years younger, blond, broad-shouldered, and lean, with a beautifully shaped small head and remarkably symmetrical features. A dark overcoat hung over one of his arms and he carried a black hat in his hand. He smiled down at the woman and said: "Your idea of a lark's immense."

She addressed Robson: "Why have you come here?"

He smiled amiably, raised his shoulders a little. "You said you weren't feeling well and were going to lie down. When Helen went up to your room to see how you were, you weren't there. We were afraid you had gone out and something had happened to you." He looked at her leg, moved his shoulders again. "Well, we were right."

Nothing in her face responded to his smile. "I am going to the city," she told him. "Now you know."

"All right, if you want to"—he was good-natured—"but you can't go like that." He nodded at her torn evening dress. "We'll take you back home, where you can change your clothes and pack a bag and—" He turned to Brazil. "When's the next train?"

Brazil said: "Six." The dog was sniffing at his legs.

"You see," Robson said blandly, speaking to the woman again. "There's plenty of time."

She looked down at her clothes and seemed to find them satisfactory. "I go like this," she replied.

"Now look here, Luise," Robson began again, quite reasonably. "You've got hours before train time—time enough to get some rest and a nap and to—"

She said simply: "I have gone."

Robson grimaced impatiently, half humorously, and turned his palms out in a gesture of helplessness. "But what are you going to do?" he asked in a tone that matched the gesture. "You're not going to expect Brazil to put you up till train time and then drive you to the station?"

She looked at Brazil with level eyes and asked calmly: "Is it too much?"

Brazil shook his head carelessly. "Uh-uh."

Robson and Conroy turned together to look at Brazil. There was considerable interest in their eyes, but no visible hostility. He bore the inspection placidly.

Luise Fischer said coolly, with an air of finality: "So."

Conroy looked questioningly at Robson, who sighed wearily and asked: "Your mind's made up on this, Luise?"

"Yes."

Robson shrugged again, said: "You always know what you want." Face and voice were grave. He started to turn away toward the door, then stopped to ask: "Have you got enough money?" One of his hands went to the inner breast pocket of his dinner jacket.

"I want nothing," she told him.

"Right. If you want anything later let me know. Come on, Dick."

He went to the door, opened it, twisted his head around to direct a brisk "Thanks, good night" at Brazil, and went out.

Conroy touched Luise Fischer's forearm lightly with three fingers, said "Good luck" to her, bowed to Evelyn and Brazil, and followed Robson out.

The dog raised his head to watch the two men go out. The girl Evelyn stared at the door with despairing eyes and worked her hands together. Luise Fischer told Brazil: "You will be wise to lock your door."

He stared at her for a long moment, brooding, and while no actual change seemed to take place in his expression all his facial muscles stiffened. "No," he said finally, "I won't lock it."

The woman's eyebrows went up a little, but she said nothing. The girl spoke, addressing Brazil for the first time since Luise Fischer's arrival. Her voice was peculiarly emphatic. "They were drunk."

"They've been drinking," he conceded. He looked thoughtfully at her, apparently only then noticing her perturbation. "You look like a drink would do *you* some good."

She became confused. Her eyes evaded his. "Do—do you want one?"

"I think so." He looked inquiringly at Luise Fischer, who nodded and said: "Thank you."

The girl went out of the room. The woman leaned forward a little to look intently up at Brazil. Her voice was calm enough, but the deliberate slowness with which she spoke made her words impressive: "Do not make the mistake of thinking Mr. Robson is not dangerous."

He seemed to weigh this speech almost sleepily; then, regarding her with a slight curiosity, he asked: "I've made an enemy?"

Her nod was sure.

He accepted that with a faint grin, offering her his cigarettes again, asking: "Have you?"

She stared through him as if studying some distant thing and replied slowly: "Yes, but I have lost a worse friend."

Evelyn came in carrying a tray that held glasses, mineral water, and a bottle of whisky. Her dark eyes, glancing from man to woman, were inquisitive, somewhat furtive. She went to the table and began to mix drinks.

Brazil finished lighting his cigarette and asked: "Leaving him for good?"

For the moment during which she stared haughtily at him it seemed that the woman did not intend to answer his question; but suddenly her face was distorted by an expression of utter hatred and she spit out a venomous "*Ja!*"

He set his glass on the mantelpiece and went to the door. He went through the motions of looking out into the night; yet he opened the door a bare couple of inches and shut it immediately, and his manner was so far from nervous that he seemed preoccupied with something else.

He turned to the mantelpiece, picked up his glass, and drank. Then, his eyes focused contemplatively on the lowered glass, he was about to speak when a telephone bell rang behind a door facing the fireplace. He opened the door, and as soon as he had passed out of sight his hoarse unemotional voice could be heard. "Hello? . . . Yes. . . . Yes, Nora. . . . Just a moment." He reëntered the room saying to the girl: "Nora wants to talk to you." He shut the bedroom door behind her.

Luise said: "You cannot have lived here long if you did not know Kane Robson before tonight."

"A month or so; but of course he was in Europe till he came back last week"—he paused—"with you." He picked up his glass. "Matter of fact, he is my landlord."

"Then you—" She broke off as the bedroom door opened. Evelyn stood in the doorway, hands to breast, and cried: "Father's coming—somebody phoned him I was here." She hurried across the room to pick up hat and coat from a chair.

Brazil said: "Wait. You'll meet him on the road if you go now. You'll have to wait till he gets here, then duck out back and beat him home while he's jawing at me. I'll stick your car down at the foot of the back road." He drained his glass and started for the bedroom door.

"But you won't"—her lip quivered—"won't fight with him? Promise me you won't."

"I won't." He went into the bedroom, returning almost immediately with a soft brown hat on his head and one of his arms in a raincoat. "It'll only take me five minutes." He went out the front door.

Luise Fischer said: "Your father does not approve?"

The girl shook her head miserably. Then suddenly she turned to the woman, holding her hands out in an appealing gesture, lips—almost colorless—moving jerkily as her words tumbled out: "You'll be here. Don't let them fight. They mustn't."

The woman took the girl's hands and put them together between her own, saying: "I will do what I can, I promise you."

"He mustn't get in trouble again," the girl moaned. "He mustn't!"

The door opened and Brazil came in.

"That's done," he said cheerfully, and took off his raincoat, dropping it on a chair, putting his damp hat on it. "I left it at the end of the fence." He picked up the woman's empty glass and his own and went to the table. "Better slide out to the kitchen in case he pops in suddenly." He began to pour whisky into the glasses.

The girl wet her lips with her tongue, said. "Yes, I guess so," indistinctly, smiled timidly, pleadingly, at Luise Fischer, hesitated, and touched his sleeve with her fingers. "You—you'll behave?"

"Sure." He did not stop preparing their drinks.

"I'll call you up tomorrow." She smiled at Luise Fischer and moved reluctantly toward the door.

Brazil gave the woman her glass, pulled a chair around to face her more directly, and sat down.

"Your little friend," the woman said, "she loves you very much."

He seemed doubtful. "Oh, she's just a kid," he said.

"But her father," she suggested, "he is not nice—eh?"

"He's cracked," he replied carelessly, then became thoughtful. "Suppose Robson phoned him?"

"Would he know?"

He smiled a little. "In a place like this everybody knows all about everybody."

"Then about me," she began, "you—"

She was interrupted by a pounding on the door that shook it on its hinges and filled the room with thunder. The dog came up stiff-legged on its feet.

Brazil gave the woman a brief grim smile and called: "All right. Come in." His hoarse voice was unemotional.

The door was violently opened by a medium-sized man in a glistening black rubber coat that hung to his ankles. Dark eyes set too close together burned under the down-turned brim of a gray hat. A pale bony nose jutted out above ragged short-cut grizzled mustache and beard. One fist gripped a heavy applewood walking stick.

"Where is my daughter?" this man demanded. His voice was deep, powerful, resounding.

Brazil's face was a phlegmatic mask. "Hello, Grant," he said.

The man in the doorway took another step forward. "Where is my daughter?"

The dog growled and showed its teeth. Luise Fischer said: "Franz!" The dog looked at her and moved its tail sidewise an inch or two and back.

Brazil said: "Evelyn's not here."

Grant glared at him. "Where is she?"

Brazil was placid. "I don't know."

"That's a lie!" Grant's eyes darted their burning gaze around the room. The knuckles of his hand holding the stick were white. "Evelyn!" he called.

Luise Fischer, smiling as if entertained by the bearded man's rage, said: "It is so, Mr. Grant. There is nobody else here."

He glanced briefly at her, with loathing in his mad eyes. "Bah! The strumpet's word confirms the convict's!" He strode to the bedroom door and disappeared inside.

Brazil grinned. "See? He's cracked. He always talks like that—like a guy in a bum book."

She smiled at him and said: "Be patient."

"I'm being," he said dryly.

Grant came out of the bedroom and stamped across to the rear door, opening it and disappearing through it.

Brazil emptied his glass and put it on the floor beside his chair. "There'll be more fireworks when he comes back."

When the bearded man returned to the room he stalked in silence to the front door, pulled it open, and holding the latch with one hand, banging the ferrule of his walking stick on the floor with the other, roared at Brazil: "For the last time, I'm telling you not to have anything to do with my daughter! I shan't tell you again." He went out, slamming the door.

Brazil exhaled heavily and shook his head. "Cracked," he sighed. "Absolutely cracked."

Luise Fischer said: "He called me a strumpet. Do people here—"

He was not listening to her. He had left his chair and was picking up his hat and coat. "I want to slip down and see if she got away all right. If she gets home first she'll be O.K. Nora—that's her stepmother—will take care of her. But if she doesn't— I won't be long." He went out the back way.

Luise Fischer kicked off her remaining slipper and stood up, experimenting with her weight on her injured leg. Three tentative steps proved her leg stiff but serviceable. She saw then that her hands and arms were still dirty from the road and, exploring, presently found a bathroom opening off the bedroom. She hummed a tune to herself while she washed and, in the bedroom again, while she combed her hair and brushed her clothes—but broke off impatiently when she failed to find powder or lipstick. She was studying her reflection in a tall looking-glass when she heard the outer door opening.

Her face brightened. "I am here," she called, and went into the other room.

Robson and Conroy were standing inside the door.

"So you are, my dear," Robson said, smiling at her start of surprise. He was paler than before and his eyes were glassier, but he seemed otherwise unchanged. Conroy, however, was somewhat disheveled; his face was flushed and he was obviously rather drunk.

The woman had recovered composure. "What do you want?" she demanded bluntly.

Robson looked around. "Where's Brazil?"

"What do you want?" she repeated.

He looked past her at the open bedroom door, grinned, and crossed to it. When he turned from the empty room she sneered at him. Conroy had gone to the fireplace, where the great Dane was lying, and was standing with his back to the fire watching them.

Robson said: "Well, it's like this, Luise: you're going back home with me."

She said: "No."

He wagged his head up and down, grinning. "I haven't got my money's worth out of you yet." He took a step toward her.

She retreated to the table, caught up the whisky bottle by its neck. "Do not touch me!" Her voice, like her face, was cold with fury.

The dog rose growling.

Robson's dark eyes jerked sidewise to focus on the dog, then on Conroy—and one eyelid twitched—then on the woman again.

Conroy—with neither tenseness nor furtiveness to alarm woman or dog—put his right hand into his overcoat pocket, brought out a black pistol, put its muzzle close behind one of the dog's ears, and shot the dog through the head. The dog tried to leap, fell on its side, and its legs stirred feebly. Conroy, smiling foolishly, returned the pistol to his pocket.

Luise Fischer spun around at the sound of the shot. Screaming at Conroy, she raised the bottle to hurl it. But Robson caught her wrist with one hand, wrenched the bottle away with the other. He was grinning, saying, "No, no, my sweet," in a bantering voice.

He put the bottle on the table again, but kept his grip on her wrist.

The dog's legs stopped moving.

Robson said: "All right. Now are you ready to go?"

She made no attempt to free her wrist. She drew herself up straight and said very seriously: "My friend, you do not know me yet if you think I am going with you."

Robson chuckled. "You don't know me if you think you're not," he told her.

The front door opened and Brazil came in. His sallow face was phlegmatic, though there was a shade of annoyance in his eyes. He shut the door carefully behind him, then addressed his guests. His voice was that of one who complains without anger. "What the hell is this?" he asked. "Visitors' day? Am I supposed to be running a road house?"

Robson said: "We are going now. *Fräulein* Fischer's going with us."

Brazil was looking at the dead dog, annoyance deepening in his copperish eyes. "That's all right if she wants to," he said indifferently.

The woman said: "I am not going."

Brazil was still looking at the dog. "That's all right too," he muttered, and with more interest: "But who did this?" He walked over to the dog and prodded its head with his foot. "Blood all over the floor," he grumbled.

Then, without raising his head, without the slightest shifting of balance or stiffening of his body, he drove his right fist up into Conroy's handsome drunken face.

Conroy fell away from the fist rigidly, with unbent knees, turning a little as he fell. His head and one shoulder struck the stone fireplace, and he tumbled forward, rolling completely over, face upward, on the floor.

Brazil whirled to face Robson.

Robson had dropped the woman's wrist and was trying to get a pistol out of his overcoat pocket. But she had flung herself on his arm, hugging it to her body, hanging with her full weight on it, and he could not free it, though he tore her hair with his other hand.

Brazil went around behind Robson, struck his chin up with a fist so he could slide his forearm under it across the taller man's throat. When he had tightened the forearm there and had his other hand wrapped around Robson's wrist, he said: "All right. I've got him."

Luise Fischer released the man's arm and fell back on her haunches. Except for the triumph in it, her face was as businesslike as Brazil's.

Brazil pulled Robson's arm up sharply behind his back. The pistol came up with it, and when the pistol was horizontal Robson pulled the trigger. The bullet went between his back and Brazil's chest, to splinter the corner of a bookcase in the far end of the room.

Brazil said: "Try that again, baby, and I'll break your arm. Drop it!"

Robson hesitated, let the pistol clatter down on the floor. Luise Fischer scrambled forward on hands and knees to pick it up. She sat on a corner of the table holding the pistol in her hand.

Brazil pushed Robson away from him and crossed the room, to kneel beside the man on the floor, feeling his pulse, running hands over his body, rising with Conroy's pistol, which he thrust into a hip pocket.

Conroy moved one leg, his eyelids fluttered sleepily, and he groaned.

Brazil jerked a thumb at him and addressed Robson curtly: "Take him and get out."

Robson went over to Conroy, stooped to lift his head and shoulders a little, shaking him and saying irritably: "Come on, Dick, wake up. We're going."

Conroy mumbled, "I'm a' ri'," and tried to lie down again.

"Get up, get up," Robson snarled, and slapped his cheeks.

Conroy shook his head and mumbled: "Do' wan'a."

Robson slapped the blond face again. "Come on, get up, you louse."

Conroy groaned and mumbled something unintelligible.

Brazil said impatiently: "Get him out anyway. The rain'll bring him around."

Robson started to speak, changed his mind, picked up his hat from the floor, put it on, and bent over the blond man again. He pulled him up into something approaching a sitting position, drew one limp arm over his shoulder, got a hand around Conroy's back and under his armpit, and rose, slowly lifting the other on unsteady legs beside him.

Brazil held the front door open. Half dragging, half carrying Conroy, Robson went out.

Brazil shut the door, leaned his back against it, and shook his head in mock resignation.

Luise Fischer put Robson's pistol down on the table and stood up. "I am sorry," she said gravely. "I did not mean to bring to you all this—"

He interrupted her carelessly: "That's all right." There was some bitterness in his grin, though his tone remained careless. "I go on like this all the time. God! I need a drink."

She turned swiftly to the table and began to fill glasses.

He looked her up and down reflectively, sipped, and asked: "You walked out just like that?"

She looked down at her clothes and nodded yes.

He seemed amused. "What are you going to do?"

"When I go to the city? I shall sell these things"—she moved her hands to indicate her rings—"and then—I do not know."

"You mean you haven't any money at all?" he demanded.

"That is it," she replied coolly.

"Not even enough for your ticket?"

She shook her head no, raised her eyebrows a little, and her calmness was almost insolence. "Surely that is a small amount you can afford to lend me."

"Sure," he said, and laughed. "But you're a pip."

She did not seem to understand him.

He drank again, then leaned forward. "Listen, you're going to look funny riding the train like that." He flicked two fingers at her gown. "Suppose I drive you in and I've got some friends that'll put you up till you get hold of some clothes you can go out in?"

She studied his face carefully before replying: "If it is not too much trouble for you."

"That's settled, then," he said. "Want to catch a nap first?"

He emptied his glass and went to the front door, where he made a pretense of looking out at the night.

As he turned from the door he caught her expression, though she hastily put the frown off her face. His smile, voice were mockingly apologetic: "I can't help it. They had me away for a while—in prison, I mean—and it did that to me. I've got to keep making sure I'm not locked in." His smile became more twisted. "There's a name for it—claustrophobia—but that doesn't make it any better."

"I am sorry," she said. "Was it—very long ago?"

"Plenty long ago when I went in," he said dryly, "but only a few weeks ago that I got out. That's what I came up here for—to try to get myself straightened out, see how I stood, what I wanted to do."

"And?" she asked softly.

"And what? Have I found out where I stand, what I want to do? I don't know." He was standing in front of her, hands in pockets, lowering down at her. "I suppose I've just been waiting for something to turn up, something I could take as a sign which way I was to go. Well, what turned up was you. That's good enough. I'll go along with you."

He took his hands from his pockets, leaned down, lifted her to her feet, and kissed her savagely.

For a moment she was motionless. Then she squirmed out of his arms and struck at his face with curved fingers. She was white with anger.

He caught her hand, pushed it down carelessly, and growled: "Stop it. If you don't want to play you don't want to play, that's all."

"That is exactly all," she said furiously.

"Fair enough." There was no change in his face, none in his voice.

Presently she said: "That man—your little friend's father—called me a strumpet. Do people here talk very much about me?"

He made a deprecatory mouth. "You know how it is. The Robsons have been the big landowners, the local gentry, for generations, and anything they do is big news. Everybody knows everything they do and so—"

"And what do they say about me?"

He grinned. "The worst, of course. What do you expect? They know him."

"And what do you think?"

"About you?"

She nodded. Her eyes were intent on his.

"I can't very well go round panning people," he said, "only I wonder why you ever took up with him. You must've seen him for the rat he is."

"I did not altogether," she said simply. "And I was stranded in a little Swiss village."

"Actress?"

She nodded. "A singer."

The telephone bell rang.

He went unhurriedly into the bedroom. His unemotional voice came out: "Hello? . . . Yes, Evelyn. . . . Yes." There was a long pause. "Yes; all right, and thanks."

He returned to the other room as unhurriedly as he had left, but at the sight of him Luise Fischer half rose from the table. His face was pasty, yellow, glistening with sweat on forehead and temples, and the cigarette between fingers of his right hand was mashed and broken.

"That was Evelyn. Her father's justice of the peace. Conroy's got a fractured skull—dying. Robson just phoned he's going down to swear out a warrant. That damned fireplace. I can't live in a cell again!"

PART TWO — THE POLICE CLOSE IN

Luise came to him with her hands out. "But you are not to blame. They can't   "

"You don't get it," his monotonous voice went on. He turned away from her toward the front door, walking mechanically. "This is what they sent me up for the other time. It was a drunken free-for-all in a road house, with bottles and everything, and a guy died. I couldn't say they were wrong in tying it on me." He opened the door, made his automatic pretense of looking out, shut the door, and moved back toward her.

"It was manslaughter that time. They'll make it murder if this guy dies. See? I'm on record as a killer." He put a hand up to his chin. "It's air-tight."

"No, no." She stood close to him and took one of his hands. "It was an accident that his head struck the fireplace. I can tell them that. I can tell them what brought it all about. They cannot—"

He laughed with bitter amusement, and quoted Grant: " 'The strumpet's word confirms the convict's.' "

She winced.

"That's what they'll do to me," he said, less monotonously now. If he dies I haven't got a chance. If he doesn't they'll hold me without bail till they see how it's coming out—assault with intent to kill or murder. What good'll your word be? Robson's mistress leaving him with me! Tell the truth and it'll only make it worse. They've got me"—his voice rose—"and I can't live in a cell again!" His eyes jerked around toward the door. Then he raised his head with a rasping noise in his throat that might have been a laugh. "Let's get out of here. I'll go screwy indoors tonight."

"Yes," she said eagerly, putting a hand on his shoulder, watching his face with eyes half frightened, half pitying. "We will go."

"You'll need a coat." He went into the bedroom.

She found her slippers, put on the right one, and held the left one out to him when he returned. "Will you break off the heel?"

He draped the rough brown overcoat he carried over her shoulders, took the slipper from her, and wrenched off the heel with a turn of his wrist. He was at the front door by the time she had her foot in the slipper.

She glanced swiftly once around the room and followed him out. . . .

She opened her eyes and saw daylight had come. Rain no longer dabbled the coupé's windows and windshield and the automatic wiper was still. Without moving she looked at Brazil. He was sitting low and lax on the seat beside her, one hand on the steering wheel, the other holding a cigarette on his knee. His sallow face was placid and there was no weariness in it. His eyes were steady on the road ahead.

"Have I slept long?" she asked.

He smiled at her. "An hour this time. Feel better?" He raised the hand holding the cigarette to switch off the head-lights.

"Yes." She sat up a little, yawning. "Will we be much longer?"

"An hour or so." He put a hand in his pocket and offered her cigarettes.

She took one and leaned forward to use the electric lighter in the dashboard. "What will you do?" she asked when the cigarette was burning.

"Hide out till I see what's what."

She glanced sidewise at his placid face, said: "You too feel better."

He grinned somewhat shamefacedly. "I lost my head back there, all right."

She patted the back of his hand once gently, and they rode in silence for a while. Then she asked: "We are going to those friends of whom you spoke?"

"Yes."

A dark coupé with two uniformed policemen in it came toward them, went past. The woman looked sharply at Brazil. His face was expressionless.

She touched his hand again, approvingly.

"I'm all right outdoors," he explained. "It's walls that get me."

She screwed her head around to look back. The policemen's car had passed out of sight.

Brazil said: "They didn't mean anything." He lowered the window on his side and dropped his cigarette out. Air blew in fresh and damp. "Want to stop for coffee?"

"Had we better?"

An automobile overtook them, crowded them to the edge of the road in passing, and quickly shot ahead. It was a black sedan traveling at the rate of sixty-five or more miles an hour. There were four men in it, one of whom looked back at Brazil's car.

Brazil said: "Maybe it'd be safer to get under cover as soon as we can; but if you're hungry—"

"No; I too think we should hurry."

The black sedan disappeared around a bend in the road.

"If the police should find you, would"—she hesitated— "would you fight?"

"I don't know," he said gloomily. "That's what's the matter with me. I never know ahead of time what I'd do." He lost some of his gloominess. "There's no use worrying. I'll be all right."

They rode through a crossroads settlement of a dozen houses, bumped over railroad tracks, and turned into a long straight stretch of road paralleling the tracks. Halfway down the level stretch, the sedan that had passed them was stationary on the edge of the road. A policeman stood beside it—between it and his motorcycle—and stolidly wrote on a leaf of a small book while the man at the sedan's wheel talked and gestured excitedly.

Luise Fischer blew breath out and said: "Well, they were not police."

Brazil grinned.

Neither of them spoke again until they were riding down a suburban street. Then she said: "They—your friends—will not dislike our coming to them like this?"

"No," he replied carelessly; "they've been through things themselves."

The houses along the suburban street became cheaper and meaner, and presently they were in a shabby city street where grimy buildings with cards saying "Flats to Let" in their windows stood among equally grimy factories and warehouses. The street into which Brazil after a little while steered the car was only slightly less dingy and the rental signs were almost as many.

He stopped the car in front of a four-story red brick building with broken brownstone steps. "This is it," he said, opening the door.

She sat looking at the building's unlovely face until he came around and opened the door on her side. Her face was inscrutable. Three dirty children stopped playing with the skeleton of an umbrella to stare at her as she went with him up the broken steps.

The street door opened when he turned the knob, letting them into a stuffy hallway where a dim light illuminated stained wall paper of a once vivid design, ragged carpet, and a worn brass-bound staircase.

"Next floor," he said, and went up the stairs behind her.

Facing the head of the stairs was a door shiny with new paint of a brown peculiarly unlike any known wood. Brazil went to this door and pushed the bell button four times— long, short, long, short. The bell rang noisily just inside the door.

After a moment of silence vague rustling noises came through the door, followed by a cautious masculine voice: "Who's there?"

Brazil put his head close to the door and kept his voice low: "Brazil."

The fastenings of the door rattled and it was opened by a small wiry blond man of about forty in crumpled green cotton pyjamas. His feet were bare. His hollow-cheeked and sharp-featured face wore a cordial smile and his voice was cordial. "Come in, kid," he said. "Come in." His small pale eyes appraised Luise Fischer from head to foot while he was stepping back to make way for them.

Brazil put a hand on the woman's arm and urged her forward saying: "Miss Fischer, this is Mr. Link."

Link said, "Pleased to meet you," and shut the door behind them.

Luise Fischer bowed.

Link slapped Brazil on the shoulder. "I'm glad to see you, kid. We were wondering what had happened to you. Come on in."

He led them into a living room that needed airing. There were articles of clothing lying around, sheets of newspaper here and there, a few not quite empty glasses and coffeecups, and a great many cigarette stubs. Link took a vest off a chair, threw it across the back of another, and said: "Take off your things and set down, Miss Fischer."

A very blonde full-bodied woman in her late twenties said, "My God, look who's here!" from the doorway and ran to Brazil with wide arms, hugging him violently, kissing him on the mouth. She had on a pink wrapper over a pink silk nightgown and green mules decorated with yellow feathers.

Brazil said, "Hello, Fan," and put his arms around her. Then, turning to Luise Fischer, who had taken off her coat: "Fan, this is Miss Fischer. Mrs. Link."

Fan went to Luise Fischer with her hand out. "Glad to know you," she said, shaking hands warmly. "You look tired, both of you. Sit down and I'll get you some breakfast, and maybe Donny'll get you a drink after he covers up his nakedness."

Luise Fischer said, "You are very kind," and sat down.

Link said, "Sure, sure," and went out.

Fan asked: "Been up all night?"

"Yes," Brazil said. "Driving most of it." He sat down on the sofa.

She looked sharply at him. "Anything the matter you'd just as lief tell me about?"

He nodded. "That's what we came for."

Link, in bath robe and slippers now, came in with a bottle of whisky and some glasses.

Brazil said: "The thing is, I slapped a guy down last night and he didn't get up."

"Hurt bad?"

Brazil made a wry mouth. "Maybe dying."

Link whistled, said: "When you slap 'em, boy, they stay slapped."

"He cracked his head on the fireplace," Brazil explained. He scowled at Link.

Fan said: "Well, there's no sense of worrying about it now. The thing to do is get something in your stomachs and get some rest. Come on, Donny, pry yourself loose from some of that booze." She beamed on Luise Fischer. "You just sit still and I'll have some breakfast in no time at all." She hurried out of the room.

Link, pouring whisky, asked: "Anybody see it?"

Brazil nodded. "Uh-huh—the wrong people." He sighed wearily. "I want to hide out a while, Donny, till I see how it's coming out."

"This dump's yours," Link said. He carried glasses of whisky to Luise Fischer and Brazil. He looked at the woman whenever she was not looking at him.

Brazil emptied his glass with a gulp.

Luise Fischer sipped and coughed.

"Want a chaser?" Link asked.

"No, I thank you," she said. "This is very good. I caught a little cold from the rain." She held the glass in her hand, but did not drink again.

Brazil said: "I left my car out front. I ought to bury it."

"I'll take care of that, kid," Link promised.

"And I'll want somebody to see what's happening up Mile Valley way."

Link wagged his head up and down. "Harry Klaus is the mouthpiece for you. I'll phone him."

"And we both want some clothes."

Luise Fischer spoke: "First I must sell these rings."

Link's pale eyes glistened. He moistened his lips and said: "I know the—"

"That can wait a day," Brazil said. "They're not hot, Donny. You don't have to fence them."

Donny seemed disappointed.

The woman said: "But I have no money for clothes until—"

Brazil said: "We've got enough for that."

Donny, watching the woman, addressed Brazil: "And you know I can always dig up some for you, kid."

"Thanks. We'll see." Brazil held out his empty glass, and when it had been filled said: "Hide the car, Donny."

"Sure." The blond man went to the telephone in an alcove and called a number.

Brazil emptied his glass. "Tired?" he asked.

She rose, went over to him, took the whisky glass out of his hand and put it on the table with her own, which was still almost full.

He chuckled, asked: "Had enough trouble with drunks last night?"

"Yes," she replied, not smiling, and returned to her chair.

Donny was speaking into the telephone: "Hello, Duke? . . . Listen; this is Donny. There's a ride standing outside my joint." He described Brazil's coupé. "Will you stash it for me? . . . Yes. . . . Better switch the plates too. . . . Yes, right away, will you? . . . Right." He hung up the receiver, turned back to the others saying:

"Voily!"

"Donny!" Fan called from elsewhere in the flat.

"Coming!" He went out.

Brazil leaned toward Luise Fischer and spoke in a low voice: "Don't give him the rings."

She stared at him in surprise. "But why?"

"He'll gyp you to hell and gone."

"You mean he will cheat me?"

He nodded, grinning.

"But you say he is your friend. You are trusting him now."

"He's O.K. on a deal like this," he assured her. "He'd never turn anybody up. But dough's different. Anyhow, even if he didn't trim you, anybody he sold them to would think they were stolen and wouldn't give half of what they're worth."

"Then he is a—" She hesitated.

"A crook. We were cellmates a while."

She frowned and said: "I do not like this."

Fan came to the door, smiling, saying: "Breakfast is served."

In the passageway Brazil turned and took a tentative step toward the front door, but checked himself when he caught

Luise Fischer's eye, and, grinning a bit sheepishly, followed her and the blonde woman into the dining room.

Fan would not sit down with them. "I can't eat this early," she told Luise Fischer. "I'll get you a hot bath ready and fix your bed, because I know you're all in and'll be ready to fall over as soon as you're done."

She went out, paying no attention to Luise Fischer's polite remonstrances.

Donny stuck a fork into a small sausage and said: "Now, about them rings. I can—"

"That can wait," Brazil said. "We've got enough to go on a while."

"Maybe; but it's just as well to have a get-away stake ready in case you need it all of a sudden." Donny put the sausage into his mouth. "And you can't have too big a one."

He chewed vigorously. "Now, for instance, you take the case of Shuffling Ben Devlin. You remember Ben? He was in the carpenter shop. Remember? The big guy with the gam?"

"I remember," Brazil replied without enthusiasm.

Donny stabbed another sausage. "Well, Ben was in a place called Finehaven once and—"

"He was in a place called the pen when we knew him," Brazil said.

"Sure; that's what I'm telling you. It was all on account of Ben thought—"

Fan came in. "Everything's ready whenever you are," she told Luise Fischer.

Luise Fischer put down her coffee cup and rose. "It is a lovely breakfast," she said, "but I am too tired to eat much."

As she left the room Donny was beginning again: "It was all on account of—"

Fan took her to a room in the rear of the flat where there was a wide wooden bed with smooth white covers turned down. A white nightgown and a red wrapper lay on the bed. On the floor there was a pair of slippers. The blonde woman halted at the door and gestured with one pink hand. "If there's anything else you need, just sing out. The bathroom's just across the hall and I turned the water on."

"Thank you," Luise Fischer said; "you are very kind. I am imposing on you most—"

Fan patted her shoulder. "No friend of Brazil's can ever impose on me, darling. Now you get your bath and a good sleep, and if there's anything you want, yell." She went out and shut the door.

Luise Fischer, standing just inside the door, looked slowly, carefully around the cheaply furnished room, and then, going to the side of the bed, began to take off her clothes. When she had finished she put on the red wrapper and the slippers and, carrying the nightgown over her arm, crossed the hallway to the bathroom. The bathroom was warm with steam. She ran cold water into the tub while she took the bandages off her knee and ankle.

After she had bathed she found fresh bandages in the cabinet over the basin, and rewrapped her knee but not her ankle. Then she put on nightgown, wrapper, and slippers, and returned to the bedroom. Brazil was there, standing with his back to her, looking out a window.

He did not turn around. Smoke from his cigarette drifted back past his head.

She shut the door slowly, leaning against it, the faintest of contemptuous smiles curving her mobile lips.

He did not move.

She went slowly to the bed and sat on the side farthest from him. She did not look at him but at a picture of a horse on the wall. Her face was proud and cold. She said: "I am what I am, but I pay my debts." This time the deliberate calmness of her voice was insolence. "I brought this trouble to you. Well, now if you can find any use for me—" She shrugged.

He turned from the window without haste. His copperish eyes, his face were expressionless. He said: "O.K." He rubbed the fire of his cigarette out in an ash tray on the dressing table and came around the bed to her.

She stood up straight and tall awaiting him.

He stood close to her for a moment, looking at her with eyes that weighed her beauty as impersonally as if she had been inanimate. Then he pushed her head back rudely and kissed her.

She made neither sound nor movement of her own, submitting completely to his caress, and when he released her and stepped back her face was as unaffected, as masklike, as his.

He shook his head slowly. "No, you're no good at your job." And suddenly his eyes were burning and he had her in his arms and she was clinging to him and laughing softly in her throat while he kissed her mouth and cheeks and eyes and forehead.

Donny opened the door and came in. He leered knowingly at them as they stepped apart, and said: "I just phoned Klaus. He'll be over as soon's he's had breakfast."

"O.K.," Brazil said.

Donny, still leering, withdrew, shutting the door.

"Who is this Klaus?" Luise Fischer asked.

"Lawyer," Brazil replied absent-mindedly. He was scowling thoughtfully at the floor. "I guess he's our best bet, though I've heard things about him that—" He broke off impatiently. "When you're in a jam you have to take your chances." His scowl deepened. "And the best you can expect is the worst of it."

She took his hand and said earnestly: "Let us go away from here. I do not like these people. I do not trust them."

His face cleared and he put an arm around her again, but abruptly turned his attention to the door when a bell rang beyond it.

There was a pause; then Donny's guarded voice could be heard asking: "Who is it?"

The answer could not be heard.

Donny's voice, raised a little: "Who?"

Nothing was heard for a short while after that. The silence was broken by the creaking of a floor board just outside the bedroom door. The door was opened by Donny. His pinched face was a caricature of alertness. "Bulls," he whispered. "Take the window." He was swollen with importance.

Brazil's face jerked around to Luise Fischer.

"Go!" she cried, pushing him toward the window. "I will be all right."

"Sure," Donny said; "me and Fan'll take care of her. Beat it, kid, and slip us the word when you can. Got enough dough?"

"Uh-huh." Brazil was kissing Luise Fischer.

"Go, go!" she gasped.

His sallow face was phlegmatic. He was laconic. "Be seeing you," he said, and pushed up the window. His foot was over the sill by the time the window was completely raised. His other foot followed the first immediately, and, turning on his chest, he lowered himself, grinning cheerfully at Luise Fischer for an instant before he dropped out of sight.

She ran to the window and looked down. He was rising from among weeds in the unkempt back yard. His head turned swiftly from right to left. Moving with a swiftness that seemed mere unhesitancy, he went to the left-hand fence, up it, and over into the next dooryard.

Donny took her arm and pulled her from the window. "Stay away from there. You'll tip his mitt. He's all right, though Christ help the copper he runs into—if they're close."

Something heavy was pounding on the flat's front door. A heavy authoritative voice came through: "Open up!"

Donny sneered in the general direction of the front door. "I guess I better let 'em in or they'll be making toothpicks of my front gate." He seemed to be enjoying the situation.

She stared at him with blank eyes.

He looked at her, looked at the floor and at her again, and said defensively: "Look—I love the guy. I love him!"

The pounding on the front door became louder.

"I guess I better," Donny said, and went out.

Through the open window came the sound of a shot. She ran to the window and, hands on sill, leaned far out.

Fifty feet to the left, on the top of a long fence that divided the long row of back yards from the alley behind, Brazil was poised, crouching. As Luise Fischer looked, another shot sounded and Brazil fell down out of sight into the alley behind the fence. She caught her breath with a sob.

The pounding on the flat's front door suddenly stopped. She drew her head in through the window. She took her hands from the sill. Her face was an automaton's. She pulled the window down without seeming conscious of what she was doing, and was standing in the center of the room looking critically at her finger nails when a tired-faced huge man in wrinkled clothes appeared in the doorway.

He asked: "Where's he at?"

She looked up at him from her finger nails as she had looked at her finger nails. "Who?"

He sighed wearily. "Brazil." He went to a closet door, opened it. "You the Fischer woman?" He shut the door and moved toward the window, looking around the room, not at her, with little apparent interest.

"I am Luise Fischer," she said to his back.

He raised the window and leaned out. "How's it, Tom?" he called to someone below. Whatever answer he received was inaudible in the room.

Luise Fischer put attentiveness off her face as he turned to her. "I ain't had breakfast yet," he said.

Donny's voice came through the doorway from another part of the flat: "I tell you I don't know where he's gone to. He just dropped the dame here and high-tailed. He didn't tell me nothing. He—"

A metallic voice said "I bet you!" disagreeably. There was the sound of a blow.

Donny's voice: "If I did know I wouldn't tell you, you big crum! Now sock me again."

The metallic voice: "If that's what you want." There was the sound of another blow.

Fan's voice, shrill with anger, screamed, "Stop that, you—" and ceased abruptly.

The huge man went to the bedroom door and called toward the front of the flat: "Never mind, Ray." He addressed Luise Fischer: "Get some clothes on."

"Why?" she asked coolly.

"They want you back in Mile Valley."

"For what?" She did not seem to think it was true.

"I don't know," he grumbled impatiently. "This ain't my job. We're just picking you up for them. Something about some rings that belonged to a guy's mother and disappeared from the house the same time you did."

She held up her hands and stared at the rings. "But they didn't. He bought them for me in Paris and—"

The huge man scowled wearily. "Well, don't argue with me about it. It's none of my business. Where was this fellow Brazil meaning to go when he left here?"

"I do not know." She took a step forward, holding out her hand in an appealing gesture. "Is he—"

"Nobody ever does," he complained, ignoring the question he had interrupted. "Get your clothes on." He held a hand out to her. "Better let me take care of the junk."

She hesitated, then slipped the rings from her fingers and dropped them into his hand.

"Shake it up," he said. "I ain't had breakfast yet." He went out and shut the door.

She dressed hurriedly in the clothes she had taken off a short while before, though she did not again put on the one stocking she had worn down from Brazil's house. When she had finished, she went quietly, with a backward glance at the closed door, to the window, and began slowly, cautiously to raise the sash.

The tired-faced huge man opened the door. "Good thing I was peeping through the keyhole," he said patiently. "Now come on."

Fan came into the room behind him. Her face was very pink; her voice was shrill. "What're you picking on her for?" she demanded. "She didn't do anything. Why don't you—"

"Stop it, stop it," the huge man begged. His weariness seemed to have become almost unbearable. "I'm only a copper told to bring her in on a larceny charge. I got nothing to do with it, don't know anything about it."

"It is all right, Mrs. Link," Luise Fischer said with dignity. "It will be all right."

"But you can't go like that," Fan protested, and turned to the huge man. "You got to let her put on some decent clothes."

He sighed and nodded. "Anything, if you'll only hurry it up and stop arguing with me."

Fan hurried out.

Luise Fischer addressed the huge man: "He too is charged with larceny?"

He sighed. "Maybe one thing, maybe another," he said spiritlessly.

She said: "He has done nothing."

"Well, I haven't neither," he complained.

Fan came in with some clothes, a blue suit and hat, dark slippers, stockings, and a white blouse.

"Just keep the door open," the huge man said. He went out of the room and stood leaning against an opposite wall, where he could see the windows in the bedroom.

Luise Fischer changed her clothes, with Fan's assistance, in a corner of the room where they were hidden from him.

"Did they catch him?" Fan whispered.

"I do not know."

"I don't think they did."

"I hope they did not."

Fan was kneeling in front of Luise Fischer, putting on her stockings. "Don't let them make you talk till you've seen Harry Klaus," she whispered rapidly. "You tell them he's your lawyer and you got to see him first. We'll send him down and he'll get you out all right." She looked up abruptly. "You didn't cop them, did you?"

"Steal the rings?" Luise Fischer asked in surprise.

"I didn't think so," the blonde woman said. "So you won't have to—"

The huge man's weary voice came to them: "Come on— cut out the barbering and get into the duds."

Fan said: "Go take a run at yourself."

Luise Fischer carried her borrowed hat to the looking-glass and put it on; then, smoothing down the suit, looked at her reflection. The clothes did not fit her so badly as might have been expected.

Fan said: "You look swell."

The man outside the door said: "Come on."

Luise Fischer turned to Fan. "Good-by and I—"

The blonde woman put her arms around her. "There's nothing to say and you'll be back here in a couple of hours. Harry'll show those saps they can't put anything like this over on you."

The huge man said: "Come on."

Luise Fischer joined him and they went toward the front of the flat.

As they passed the living-room door Donny, rising from the sofa, called cheerfully: "Don't let them worry you, baby. We'll—"

A tall man in brown put a hand over Donny's face and pushed him back on the sofa.

Luise Fischer and the huge man went out. A police-department automobile was standing in front of the house where Brazil had left his coupé. A dozen or more adults and children were standing around it, solemnly watching the door through which she came.

A uniformed policeman pushed some of them aside to make passageway for her and her companion and got into the car behind them. "Let her go, Tom," he called to the chauffeur, and they drove off.

The huge man shut his eyes and groaned softly. "God, I'm *schwach!*"

They rode seven blocks and halted in front of a square red brick building on a corner. The huge man helped her out of the automobile and took her between two large frosted globes into the building and into a room where a bald fat man in uniform sat behind a high desk.

The huge man said: "It's that Luise Fischer for Mile Valley." He took a hand from a pocket and tossed her rings on the desk. "That's the stuff, I guess."

The bald man said: "Nice picking. Get the guy?"

"Hospital, I guess."

Luise Fischer turned to him: "Was he—was he badly hurt?"

The huge man grumbled: "I don't know about it. Can't I guess?"

The bald man called: "Luke!"

A thin white-mustached policeman came in.

The fat man said: "Put her in the royal suite."

Luise Fischer said: "I wish to see my lawyer."

The three men looked unblinkingly at her.

"His name is Harry Klaus," she said. "I wish to see him."

Luke said: "Come back this way."

She followed him down a bare corridor to the far end, where he opened a door and stood aside for her to go through. The room into which the door opened was a small one furnished with cot, table, two chairs, and some magazines. The window was large, fitted with a heavy wire grating.

In the center of the room she turned to say again: "I wish to see my lawyer."

The white-mustached man shut the door and she could hear him locking it.

Two hours later he returned with a bowl of soup, some cold meat and a slice of bread on a plate, and a cup of coffee.

She had been lying on the cot, staring at the ceiling. She rose and faced him imperiously. "I wish to see—"

"Don't start that again," he said irritably. "We got nothing to do with you. Tell it to them Mile Valley fellows when they come for you."

He put the food on the table and left the room. She ate everything he had brought her.

It was late afternoon when the door opened again. "There you are," the white-mustached man said, and stood aside to let his companions enter. There were two of them, men of medium height, in dull clothes, one thick-chested and florid, the other less heavy, older.

The thick-chested florid one looked Luise Fischer up and down and grinned admiringly at her. The other said: "We want you to come back to the Valley with us, Miss Fischer." She rose from her chair and began to put on her hat and coat.

"That's it," the older of the two said approvingly. "Don't give us no trouble and we won't give you none."

She looked curiously at him.

They went to the street and got into a dusty blue sedan. The thick-chested man drove. Luise Fischer sat behind him, beside the older man. They retraced the route she and Brazil had taken that morning.

Once, before they left the city, she had said: "I wish to see my lawyer. His name is Harry Klaus."

The man beside her was chewing gum. He made noises with his lips, then told her politely enough:

"We can't stop now."

The man at the wheel spoke before she could reply. He did not turn his head. "How come Brazil socked him?"

Luise said quickly: "It was not his fault. He was—"

The older man, addressing the man at the wheel, interrupted her: "Let it alone, Pete. Let the D.A. do his own work."

Pete said: "Oke."

The woman turned to the man beside her. "Was—was Brazil hurt?"

He studied her face for a long moment, then nodded slightly. "Stopped a slug, I hear."

Her eyes widened. "He was shot?"

He nodded again.

She put both hands on his forearm. "How badly?"

He shook his head. "I don't know."

Her fingers dug into his arm. "Did they arrest him?"

"I can't tell you, miss. Maybe the District Attorney wouldn't like me to." He smacked his lips over his gum-chewing.

"But please!" she insisted. "I must know."

He shook his head again. "We ain't worrying you with a lot of questions. Don't be worrying us."

PART THREE — CONCLUSION

It was nearly nine o'clock by the dial in the dashboard, and quite dark, when Luise Fischer and her captors passed a large square building whose illuminated sign said "Mile Valley Lumber Co." and turned into what was definitely a town street, though its irregularly spaced houses were not many. Ten minutes later the sedan came to rest at the curb in front of a gray public building. The driver got out. The other man held the door open for Luise. They took her into a ground-floor room in the gray building.

Three men were in the room. A sad-faced man of sixty-some years, with ragged white hair and mustache, was tilted back in a chair with his feet on a battered yellowish desk. He wore a hat but no coat. A pasty-faced young blond man, straddling a chair in front of the filing cabinet on the other side of the room, was saying, "So the traveling salesman asked the farmer if he could put him up for the night and—" but broke off when Luise Fischer and her companions came in.

The third man stood with his back to the window. He was a slim man of medium height, not far past thirty, thin-lipped, pale, flashily dressed in brown and red. His collar was very tight. He advanced swiftly toward Luise Fischer, showing white teeth in a smile. "I'm Harry Klaus. They wouldn't let me see you down there, so I came on up to wait for you." He spoke rapidly and with assurance. "Don't worry. I've got everything fixed."

The story-teller hesitated, changed his position. The two men who had brought Luise Fischer up from the city looked at the lawyer with obvious disapproval.

Klaus smiled again with complete assurance. "You know she's not going to tell you anything at all till we've talked it over, don't you? Well, what the hell, then?"

The man at the desk said: "All right, all right." He looked at the two men standing behind the woman. "If Tuft's office is empty let 'em use that."

"Thanks." Harry Klaus picked up a brown briefcase from a chair, took Luise Fischer's elbow in his hand, and turned her to follow the thick-chested florid man.

He led them down the corridor a few feet to an office that was similar to the one they had just left. He did not go in with them. He said, "Come on back when you're finished," and, when they had gone in, slammed the door.

Klaus jerked his head at the door. "A lot of whittlers," he said cheerfully. "We'll stand them on their heads." He tossed his briefcase on the desk. "Sit down."

"Brazil?" she asked. "He is—"

His shrug lifted his shoulders almost to his ears. "I don't know. Can't get anything out of these people."

"Then—?"

"Then he got away," he said.

"Do you think he did?"

He shrugged his shoulders again. "We can always hope."

"But one of those policemen told me he had been shot and—"

"That don't have to mean anything but that they hope they hit him." He put his hands on her shoulders and pushed her down in a chair. "There's no use of worrying about Brazil till we know whether we've got anything to worry about." He drew another chair up close to hers and sat in it. "Let's worry about you now. I want the works—no song and dance—just what happened, the way it happened."

She drew her brows together in a puzzled frown. "But you told me everything—"

"I told you everything was all fixed, and it is." He patted her knee. "I've got the bail all fixed so you can walk out of here as soon as they get through asking you questions. But we've got to decide what kind of answers you're going to give them." He looked sharply at her from under his hat brim. "You want to help Brazil, don't you?"

"Yes."

"That's the stuff." He patted her knee again and his hand remained on it. "Now give me everything from the beginning."

"You mean from when I first met Kane Robson?"

He nodded.

She crossed her knees, dislodging his hand. Staring at the opposite wall as if not seeing it, she said earnestly: "Neither of us did anything wrong. It is not right that we should suffer."

"Don't worry." His tone was light, confident. "I'll get the pair of you out of it." He proffered her cigarettes in a shiny case.

She took a cigarette, leaned forward to hold its end in the flame from his lighter, and, still leaning forward, asked: "I will not have to stay here tonight?"

He patted her cheek. "I don't think so. It oughtn't to take them more than an hour to grill you." He dropped his hand to her knee. "And the sooner we get through here the sooner you'll be through with them."

She took a deep breath and sat back in her chair. "There is not a lot to say," she began, pronouncing her words carefully so they were clear in spite of her accent. "I met him in a little place in Switzerland. I was without any money at all, any friends. He liked me and he was rich." She made a little gesture with the cigarette in her hand. "So I said yes."

Klaus nodded sympathetically and his fingers moved on her knee.

"He bought me clothes, that jewelry, in Paris. They were not his mother's and he gave them to me."

The lawyer nodded again and his fingers moved again on her knee.

"He brought me over here then and"—she put the burning end of her cigarette on the back of his hand—"I stayed at his—"

Klaus had snatched his hand from her knee to his mouth, was sucking the back of his hand. "What's the matter with you?" he demanded indignantly, the words muffled by the hand to his mouth. He lowered the hand and looked at the burn. "If there's something you don't like, you can say so, can't you?"

She did not smile. "I no speak Inglis good," she said, burlesquing a heavy accent. "I stayed at his house for two weeks—not quite two weeks—until—"

"If it wasn't for Brazil you could take your troubles to another lawyer!" He pouted over his burnt hand.

"Until last night," she continued, "when I could stand him no longer. We quarreled and I left. I left just as I was, in evening clothes, with . . . ."

She was finishing her story when the telephone bell rang. The attorney went to the desk and spoke into the telephone: "Hello? . . . Yes. . . . Just a couple of minutes more. . . . That's right. Thanks." He turned. "They're getting impatient."

She rose from her chair saying: "I have finished. Then the police came and he escaped through the window and they arrested me about those rings."

"Did you do any talking after they arrested you?"

She shook her head. "They would not let me. Nobody would listen to me. Nobody cared."

A young man in blue clothes that needed pressing came up to Luise Fischer and Klaus as they left the courthouse. He took off his hat and tucked it under an arm. "Mith Fither, I'm from the Mile Valley Potht. Can you—"

Klaus, smiling, said: "There's nothing now. Look me up at the hotel in the morning and I'll give you a statement." He handed the reporter a card. He cleared his throat. "We're hunting food now. Maybe you'll tell us where to find it—and join us."

The young man's face flushed. He looked at the card in his hand and then up at the lawyer. "Thank you, Mithter Klauth, I'll be glad to. The Tavern'th jutht around the corner. It'th the only plathe that'th any good that'th open now."

He turned to indicate the south. "My name'th George Dunne."

Klaus shook his hand and said, "Glad to know you," Luise Fischer nodded and smiled, and they went down the street.

"How's Conroy?" Klaus asked.

"He hathn't come to yet," the young man replied. "They don't know yet how bad it ith."

"Where is he?"

"Thtill at Robthon'th. They're afraid to move him."

They turned the corner. Klaus asked: "Any news of Brazil?"

The reporter craned his neck to look past Luise Fischer at the lawyer. "I thought you'd know."

"Know what?"

"What—whatever there watli to know. Thith ith it."

He led them into a white-tiled restaurant. By the time they were seated at a table the dozen or more people at counter and tables were staring at Luise Fischer and there was a good deal of whispering among them.

Luise Fischer, sitting in the chair Dunne had pulled out for her, taking one of the menus from the rack on the table, seemed neither disturbed by nor conscious of anyone's interest in her. She said: "I am very hungry."

A plump bald-headed man with a pointed white beard, sitting three tables away, caught Dunne's eye as the young man went around to his chair, and beckoned with a jerk of his head.

Dunne said, "Pardon me—it'th my both," and went over to the bearded man's table.

Klaus said: "He's a nice boy."

Luise Fischer said: "We must telephone the Links. They have surely heard from Brazil."

Klaus pulled the ends of his mouth down, shook his head. "You can't trust these county-seat telephone exchanges."

"But—"

"Have to wait till tomorrow. It's late anyhow." He looked at his watch and yawned. "Play this kid. Maybe he knows something."

Dunne came back to them. His face was flushed and he seemed embarrassed.

"Anything new?" Klaus asked.

The young man shook his head violently. "Oh, no!" he said with emphasis.

A waiter came to their table. Luise Fischer ordered soup, a steak, potatoes, asparagus, a salad, cheese, and coffee. Klaus ordered scrambled eggs and coffee. Dunne pie and milk.

When the waiter stepped back from the table Dunne's eyes opened wide. He stared past Klaus. Luise Fischer turned her head to follow the reporter's gaze. Kane Robson was coming into the restaurant. Two men were with him. One of them— a fat pale youngish man—smiled and raised his hat.

Luise Fischer addressed Klaus in a low voice: "It's Robson."

The lawyer did not turn his head. He said, "That's all right," and held his cigarette case out to her.

She took a cigarette without removing her gaze from Robson. When he saw her he raised his hat and bowed and smiled ironically. Then he said something to his companions and, leaving them, came toward her. His face was pale; his dark eyes glittered.

She was smoking by the time he reached her table. He said, "Hello, darling," and sat in the empty chair facing her across the table. He turned his head to the reporter for an instant to say a careless "Hello, Dunne."

Luise Fischer said: "This is Mr. Klaus. Mr. Robson."

Robson did not look at the lawyer. He addressed the woman: "Get your bail fixed up all right?"

"As you see."

He smiled mockingly. "I meant to leave word that I'd put it up if you couldn't get it anywhere else, but I forgot."

There was a moment of silence. Then she said: "I shall send for my clothes in the morning. Will you have Ito pack them?"

"*Your* clothes?" He laughed. "You didn't have a stitch besides what you had on when I picked you up. Let your new man buy you new clothes."

Young Dunne blushed and looked at the tablecloth in embarrassment. Klaus's face was, except for the brightness of his eyes, expressionless.

Luise Fischer said softly: "Your friends will miss you if you stay away too long."

"Let them. I want to talk to you, Luise." He addressed Dunne impatiently: "Why don't you two go play in a corner somewhere?"

The reporter jumped up from his chair stammering: "Th-thertainly, Mr. Robthon."

Klaus looked questioningly at Luise Fischer. Her nod was barely perceptible. He rose and left the table with Dunne.

Robson said: "Come back with me and I'll call off all this foolishness about the rings."

She looked curiously at him. "You want me back knowing I despise you?"

He nodded, grinning. "I can get fun out of even that."

She narrowed her eyes, studying his face. Then she asked: "How is Dick?"

His face and voice were gay with malice. "He's dying fast enough."

She seemed surprised. "You hate him?"

"I don't hate him—I don't love him. You and he were too fond of each other. I won't have my male and female parasites mixing like that."

She smiled contemptuously. "So. Then suppose I go back with you. What?"

"I explain to these people that it was all a mistake about the rings, that you really thought I had given them to you. That's all." He was watching her closely. "There's no bargaining about your boy friend Brazil. He takes what he gets."

Her face showed nothing of what she might be thinking. She leaned across the table a little toward him and spoke carefully: "If you were as dangerous as you think you are, I would be afraid to go back with you—I would rather go to prison. But I am not afraid of you. You should know by this time that you will never hurt me very much, that I can take very good care of myself."

"Maybe you've got something to learn," he said quickly; then, recovering his consciously matter-of-fact tone: "Well, what's the answer?"

"I am not a fool," she said. "I have no money, no friends who can help me. You have both and I am not afraid of you. I try to do what is best for myself. First I try to get out of this trouble without you. If I cannot then I come back to you."

"If I'll have you."

She shrugged her shoulders. "Yes, certainly that."

*

Luise Fischer and Harry Klaus reached the Links' flat late the next morning.

Fan opened the door for them. She put her arms around Luise Fischer. "See, I told you Harry would get you out all right." She turned her face quickly toward the lawyer and demanded: "You didn't let them hold her all night?"

"No," he said; "but we missed the last train and had to stay at the hotel."

They went into the living room.

Evelyn Grant rose from the sofa. She came to Luise Fischer saying: "It's my fault. It's all my fault!" Her eyes were red and swollen. She began to cry again. "He had told me about Donny—Mr. Link—and I thought he'd come here and I tried to phone him and papa caught me and told the police. And I only wanted to help him and—"

From the doorway Donny snarled: "Shut up. Stop it. Pipe down." He addressed Klaus petulantly: "She's been doing this for an hour. She's got me screwy."

Fan said: "Lay off the kid. She feels bad."

Donny said: "She ought to." He smiled at Luise Fischer. "Hello, baby. Everything O.K.?"

She said: "How do you do? I think it is."

He looked at her hands. "Where's the rings?"

"We had to leave them up there."

"I told you!" His voice was bitter. "I told you you'd ought to let me sold them." He turned to Klaus. "Can you beat that?"

The lawyer did not say anything.

Fan had taken Evelyn to the sofa and was soothing her.

Luise Fischer asked: "Have you heard from—"

"Brazil?" Donny said before she could finish her question. He nodded. "Yep. He's O.K." He glanced over his shoulder at the girl on the sofa, then spoke rapidly in a low voice. "He's at the Hilltop Sanatorium outside of town—supposed to have D.T.s. You know he got plugged in the side. He's O.K., though—Doc Barry'll keep him under cover and fix him up good as new. He—"

Luise Fischer's eyes were growing large. She put a hand to her throat. "But he—Dr. Ralph Barry?" she demanded.

Donny wagged his head up and down. "Yep. He's a good guy. He'll—"

"But he is a friend of Kane Robson's!" she cried. "I met him there at Robson's house." She turned to Klaus. "He was with him in the restaurant last night—the fat one."

The men stared at her.

She caught Klaus's arm and shook him. "That is why he was there last night—to see Kane—to ask him what he should do."

Fan and Evelyn had risen from the sofa and were listening.

Donny began: "Aw, maybe it's O.K. Doc's a good guy. I don't think he—"

"Cut it out!" Klaus growled. "This is serious—serious as hell." He scowled thoughtfully at Luise Fischer. "No chance of a mistake on this?"

"No."

Evelyn thrust herself between the two men to confront Luise Fischer. She was crying again, but was angry now.

"Why did you have to get him into all this? Why did you have to come to him with your troubles? It's your fault that they'll put him in prison and he'll go crazy in prison! If it hadn't been for you none of this would have happened. You—"

Donny touched Evelyn's shoulder. "I think I'll take a sock at you," he said.

She cringed away from him.

Klaus said: "For God's sake let's stop this fiddledeedee and decide what we'd better do." He scowled at Luise Fischer again. "Didn't Robson say anything to you about it last night?"

She shook her head.

Donny said: "Well, listen. We got to get him out of there. It don't—"

"That's easy," Klaus said with heavy sarcasm. "If he's in wrong there"—he shrugged—"it's happened already. We've got to find out. Can you get to see him?"

Donny nodded. "Sure."

"Then go. Wise him up—find out what the layout is."

Donny and Luise Fischer left the house by the back door, went through the yard to the alley behind, and down the alley for two blocks. They saw nobody following them.

"I guess we're in the clear," Donny said, and led the way down a cross street.

On the next corner there was a garage and repair shop. A small dark man was tinkering with an engine.

"Hello, Tony," Donny said. "Lend me a boat."

The dark man looked curiously at Luise Fischer while saying: "Surest thing you know. Take the one in the corner."

They got into a black sedan and drove away.

"It ain't far," Donny said. Then: "I'd like to pull him out of there."

Luise Fischer was silent.

After half an hour Donny turned the machine into a road at the end of which a white building was visible. "That's her," he said.

Leaving the sedan in front of the building, they walked under a black-and-gold sign that said Hilltop Sanatorium into an office.

"We want to see Mr. Lee," Donny told the nurse at the desk. "He's expecting us."

She moistened her lips nervously and said: "It's two hundred and three, right near the head of the stairs."

They went up a dark flight of stairs to the second floor. "This is it," Donny said, halting. He opened the door without knocking and waved Luise Fischer inside.

Besides Brazil, lying in bed, his sallowness more pronounced than usual, there were two men in the room. One of them was the huge tired-faced man who had arrested Luise Fischer. He said: "I oughtn't let you people see him."

Brazil half rose in bed and stretched a hand out toward Luise Fischer.

She went around the huge man to the bed and took Brazil's hand. "Oh, I'm sorry—sorry!" she murmured.

He grinned without pleasure. "Hard luck, all right. And I'm scared stiff of those damned bars."

She leaned over and kissed him.

The huge man said: "Come on, now. You got to get out. I'm liable to catch hell for this."

Donny took a step toward the bed. "Listen, Brazil. Is there—"

The huge man put out a hand and wearily pushed Donny back. "Go 'way. There's nothing for you to hang around here for." He put a hand on Luise Fischer's shoulder. "Go ahead, please, will you? Say good-by to him now—and maybe you can see him afterwards."

She kissed Brazil again and stood up.

He said: "Look after her, will you, Donny?"

"Sure," Donny promised. "And don't let them worry you. I'll send Harry over to see you and—"

The huge man groaned. "Is this going to keep up all day?"

He took Luise Fischer's arm and put her and Donny out.

They went in silence down to the sedan, and neither spoke until they were entering the city again. Then Luise Fischer said: "Will you kindly lend me ten dollars?"

"Sure." Donny took one hand from the wheel, felt in his pants pocket, and gave her two five-dollar bills.

Then she said: "I wish to go to the railroad station."

He frowned. "What for?"

"I want to go to the railroad station," she repeated.

When they reached the station she got out of the sedan.

"Thank you very much," she said. "Do not wait. I will come over later."

Luise Fischer went into the railroad station and to the news stand, where she bought a package of cigarettes. Then she went to a telephone booth, asked for long distance, and called a Mile Valley number.

"Hello, Ito? . . . Is Mr. Robson there? This is *Fräulein* Fischer. . . . Yes." There was a pause. "Hello, Kane. . . . Well, you have won. You might have saved yourself the delay if you had told me last night what you knew. . . . Yes. . . . Yes, I am."

She put the receiver on its prong and stared at it for a long moment. Then she left the booth, went to the ticket window, and said:

"A ticket to Mile Valley—one way—please."

The room was wide and high-ceilinged. Its furniture was Jacobean. Kane Robson was sprawled comfortably in a deep chair. At his elbow was a small table on which were a crystal-and-silver coffee service, a crystal-and-silver decanter—half full—some glasses, cigarettes, and an ash tray. His eyes glittered in the light from the fireplace.

Ten feet away, partly facing him, partly the fireplace, Luise Fischer sat, more erectly, in a smaller chair. She was in a pale negligee and had pale slippers on her feet.

Somewhere in the house a clock struck midnight. Robson heard it out attentively before he went on speaking: "And you are making a great mistake, my dear, in being too sure of yourself."

She yawned. "I slept very little last night," she said. "I am too sleepy to be frightened."

He rose grinning at her. "I didn't get any either. Shall we take a look at the invalid before we turn in?"

A nurse—a scrawny middle-aged woman in white—came into the room, panting. "Mr. Conroy's recovering consciousness, I do believe," she said.

Robson's mouth tightened and his eyes, after a momentary flickering, became steady. "Phone Dr. Blake," he said. "He'll want to know right away." He turned to Luise Fischer. "I'll run up and stay with him till she is through phoning."

Luise Fischer rose. "I'll go with you."

He pursed his lips. "I don't know. Maybe the excitement of too many people—the surprise of seeing you back here again—might not be good for him."

The nurse had left the room.

Ignoring Luise Fischer's laughter, he said: "No; you had better stay here, my dear."

She said: "I will not."

He shrugged. "Very well, but—" He went upstairs without finishing the sentence.

Luise Fischer went up behind him, but not with his speed. She arrived at the sick-room doorway, however, in time to catch the look of utter fear in Conroy's eyes, before they closed, as his bandaged head fell back on the pillow.

Robson, standing just inside the door, said softly: "Ah, he's passed out again." His eyes were unwary.

Her eyes were probing.

They stood there and stared at each other until the Japanese butler came to the door and said: "A Mr. Brazil to see *Fräulein* Fischer."

Into Robson's face little by little came the expression of one considering a private joke. He said: "Show Mr. Brazil into the living room. *Fräulein* Fischer will be down immediately. Phone the deputy sheriff."

Robson smiled at the woman. "Well?"

She said nothing.

"A choice?" he asked.

The nurse came in. "Dr. Blake is out, but I left word."

Luise Fischer said: "I do not think Mr. Conroy should be left alone, Miss George." . . .

Brazil was standing in the center of the living room, balancing himself on legs spread far apart. He held his left arm tight to his side, straight down. He had on a dark overcoat that was buttoned high against his throat. His face was a ghastly yellow mask in which his eyes burned redly. He said through his teeth: "They told me you'd come back. I had to see it." He spit on the floor. "Strumpet!"

She stamped a foot. "Do not be a fool. I—" She broke off as the nurse passed the doorway. She said sharply: "Miss George, what are you doing?"

The nurse said: "Mr. Robson said he thought I might be able to reach Dr. Blake on the phone at Mrs. Webber's."

Luise Fischer turned, paused to kick off her slippers, and ran up the steps on stockinged feet. The door to Conroy's room was shut. She flung it open.

Robson was leaning over the sick man. His hands were on the sick man's bandaged head, holding it almost face down in the pillow.

His thumbs were pressing the back of the skull. All his weight seemed on his thumbs. His face was insane. His lips were wet.

Luise Fischer screamed, "Brazil!" and flung herself at Robson and clawed at his legs.

Brazil came into the room, lurching blindly, his left arm tight to his side. He swung his right fist, missed Robson's head by a foot, was struck twice in the face by Robson, did not seem to know it, and swung his right fist into Robson's belly. The woman's grip on Robson's ankles kept him from recovering his balance. He went down heavily.

The nurse was busy with her patient, who was trying to sit up in bed. Tears ran down his face. He was sobbing: "He stumbled over a piece of wood while he was helping me to the car, and he hit me on the head with it."

Luise Fischer had Brazil sitting upon the floor with his back to the wall, wiping his face with her handkerchief.

He opened one eye and murmured: "The guy was screwy, wasn't he?"

She put an arm around him and laughed with a cooing sound in her throat. "All men are."

Robson had not moved.

There was a commotion and three men came in.

The tallest one looked at Robson and then at Brazil and chuckled.

"There's our lad that don't like hospitals," he said. "It's a good thing he didn't escape from a gymnasium or he might've hurt somebody."

Luise Fischer took off her rings and put them on the floor beside Robson's left foot.

Two Sharp Knives

O N MY way home from the regular Wednesday night poker game at Ben Kamsley's I stopped at the railroad station to see the 2:11 come in—what we called putting the town to bed—and as soon as this fellow stepped down from the smoking-car I recognized him. There was no mistaking his face, the pale eyes with lower lids that were as straight as if they had been drawn with a ruler, the noticeably flat-tipped bony nose, the deep cleft in his chin, the slightly hollow grayish cheeks. He was tall and thin and very neatly dressed in a dark suit, long dark overcoat, derby hat, and carried a black Gladstone bag. He looked a few years older than the forty he was supposed to be. He went past me towards the street steps.

When I turned around to follow him I saw Wally Shane coming out of the waiting-room. I caught Wally's eye and nodded at the man carrying the black bag. Wally examined him carefully as he went by. I could not see whether the man noticed the examination. By the time I came up to Wally the man was going down the steps to the street.

Wally rubbed his lips together and his blue eyes were bright and hard. "Look," he said out of the side of his mouth, "that's a ringer for the guy we got—"

"That's the guy," I said, and went down the steps behind him.

Our man started towards one of the taxicabs at the curb, then saw the lights of the Deerwood Hotel two blocks away, shook his head at the taxi driver, and went up the street afoot.

"What do we do?" Wally asked. "See what he's—?"

"It's nothing to us. We take him. Get my car. It's at the corner of the alley."

I gave Wally the few minutes he needed to get the car and then closed in. "Hello, Furman," I said when I was just behind the tall man.

His face jerked around to me. "How do you—" He halted. "I don't believe I—" He looked up and down the street. We had the block to ourselves.

829

"You're Lester Furman, aren't you?" I asked.

He said "Yes" quickly.

"Philadelphia?"

He peered at me in the light that was none too strong where we stood. "Yes."

"I'm Scott Anderson," I said, "Chief of Police here. I—"

His bag thudded down on the pavement. "What's happened to her?" he asked hoarsely.

"Happened to who?"

Wally arrived in my car then, abruptly, skidding into the curb. Furman, his face stretched by fright, leaped back away from me. I went after him, grabbing him with my good hand, jamming him back against the front wall of Henderson's warehouse. He fought with me there until Wally got out of the car. Then he saw Wally's uniform and immediately stopped fighting.

"I'm sorry," he said weakly. "I thought—for a second I thought maybe you weren't the police. You're not in uniform and— It was silly of me. I'm sorry."

"It's all right," I told him. "Let's get going before we have a mob around us." Two cars had stopped just a little beyond mine and I could see a bellboy and a hatless man coming towards us from the direction of the hotel.

Furman picked up his bag and went willingly into my car ahead of me. We sat in the rear, Wally drove.

We rode a block in silence, then Furman asked, "You're taking me to police headquarters?"

"Yes."

"What for?"

"Philadelphia."

"I—" he cleared his throat, "—I don't think I understand you."

"You understand that you're wanted in Philadelphia, don't you, for murder?"

He said indignantly, "That's ridiculous. Murder! That's—" He put a hand on my arm, his face close to mine, and instead of indignation in his voice there now was a desperate sort of earnestness. "Who told you that?"

"I didn't make it up. Well, here we are. Come on, I'll show you."

We took him into my office. George Propper, who had been dozing in a chair in the front office, followed us in. I found the Trans-American Detective Agency circular and handed it to Furman. In the usual form it offered fifteen hundred dollars for the arrest and conviction of Lester Furman, alias Lloyd Fields, alias J. D. Carpenter, for the murder of Paul Frank Dunlap in Philadelphia on the 26th of the previous month.

Furman's hands holding the circular were steady and he read it carefully. His face was pale, but no muscles moved in it until he opened his mouth to speak. He tried to speak calmly. "It's a lie." He did not look up from the circular.

"You're Lester Furman, aren't you?" I asked.

He nodded, still not looking up.

"That's your description, isn't it?"

He nodded.

"That's your photograph, isn't it?"

He nodded, and then, staring at his photograph on the circular, he began to tremble—his lips, his hands, his legs.

I pushed a chair up behind him and said, "Sit down," and he dropped down on it and shut his eyes, pressing the lids together. I took the circular from his limp hands.

George Propper, leaning against a side of the doorway, turned his loose grin from me to Wally and said, "So that's that and so you lucky stiffs split a grand and a half reward money. Lucky Wally! If it ain't vacations in New York at the city's expense it's reward money."

Furman jumped up from the chair and screamed, "It's a lie. It's a frame-up. You can't prove anything. There's nothing to prove. I never killed anybody. I won't be framed. I won't be—"

I pushed him down on the chair again. "Take it easy," I told him. "You're wasting your breath on us. Save it for the Philadelphia police. We're just holding you for them. If anything's wrong it's there, not here."

"But it's not the police. It's the Trans-American De—"

"We turn you over to the police."

He started to say something, broke off, sighed, made a little hopeless gesture with his hands, and tried to smile. "Then there's nothing I can do now?"

"There's nothing any of us can do till morning," I said. "We'll have to search you, then we won't bother you any more till they come for you."

In the black Gladstone bag we found a couple of changes of clothes, some toilet articles, and a loaded .38 automatic. In his pockets we found a hundred and sixty-some dollars, a book of checks on a Philadelphia bank, business cards and a few letters that seemed to show he was in the real estate business, and the sort of odds and ends that you usually find in men's pockets.

While Wally was putting these things in the vault I told George Propper to lock Furman up.

George rattled keys in his pocket and said, "Come along, darling. We ain't had anybody in our little hoosegow for three days. You'll have it all to yourself, just like a suite in the Ritz."

Furman said, "Good night and thank you," to me and followed George out.

When George came back he leaned against the door frame again and asked, "How about you big-hearted boys cutting me in on a little of that blood money?"

Wally said, "Sure. I'll forget that two and a half you been owing me three months."

I said, "Make him as comfortable as you can, George. If he wants anything sent in, O.K."

"He's valuable, huh? If it was some bum that didn't mean a nickel to you. . . . Maybe I ought to take a pillow off my bed for him." He spit at the cuspidor and missed. "He's just like the rest of 'em to me."

I thought, "Any day now I'm going to forget that your uncle is county chairman and throw you back in the gutter." I said, "Do all the talking you want, but do what I tell you."

It was about four o'clock when I got home—my farm was a little outside the town—and maybe half an hour after that before I went to sleep. The telephone woke me up at five minutes past six.

Wally's voice: "You better come down, Scott. The fellow Furman's hung himself."

"What?"

"By his belt—from a window bar—deader'n hell."

"All right. I'm on my way. Phone Ben Kamsley I'll pick him up on my way in."

"No doctor's going to do this man any good, Scott."

"It won't hurt to have him looked at," I insisted. "You'd better phone Douglassville too." Douglassville was the county seat.

"O.K."

Wally phoned me back while I was dressing to tell me that Ben Kamsley had been called out on an emergency case and was somewhere on the other side of town, but that his wife would get in touch with him and tell him to stop at head-quarters on his way home.

When, riding into town, I was within fifty or sixty feet of the Red Top Diner, Heck Jones ran out with a revolver in his hand and began to shoot at two men in a black roadster that had just passed me.

I leaned out and yelled, "What's it?" at him while I was turning my car.

"Holdup," he bawled angrily. "Wait for me." He let loose another shot that couldn't have missed my front tire by more than an inch and galloped up to me, his apron flapping around his fat legs. I opened the door for him, he squeezed his bulk in beside me, and we set off after the roadster.

"What gets me," he said when he had stopped panting, "is they done it like a joke. They come in, they don't want noth-ing but ham and eggs and coffee and then they get kind of kidding together under their breath and then they put the guns on me like a joke."

"How much did they take?"

"Sixty or thereabouts, but that ain't what gripes me so much. It's them doing it like a joke."

"Never mind," I said. "We'll get 'em."

We very nearly didn't, though. They led us a merry chase. We lost them a couple of times and finally picked them up more by luck than anything else, a couple of miles over the state line.

We didn't have any trouble taking them, once we had caught up to them, but they knew they had crossed the state line and they insisted on regular extradition or nothing, so we had to carry them on to Badington and stick them in the jail there until the necessary papers could be sent through. It was ten o'clock before I got a chance to phone my office.

Hammill answered the phone and told me Ted Carroll, our district attorney, was there, so I talked to Ted—though not as much as he talked to me.

"Listen, Scott," he asked excitedly, "what is all this?"

"All what?"

"This fiddle-de-dee, this hanky-panky."

"I don't know what you mean," I said. "Wasn't it suicide?"

"Sure it was suicide, but I wired the Trans-American and they phoned me just a few minutes ago and said they'd never sent out any circulars on Furman, didn't know about any murder he was wanted for. All they knew about him was he used to be a client of theirs."

I couldn't think of anything to say except that I would be back in Deerwood by noon. And I was.

Ted was at my desk with the telephone receiver clamped to his ear, saying, "Yes. . . . Yes. . . . Yes," when I went into the office. He put down the receiver and asked, "What happened to you?"

"A couple of boys knocked over the Red Top Diner and I had to chase 'em almost to Badington."

He smiled with one side of his mouth. "The town getting out of your hands?" He and I were on opposite sides of the fence politically and we took our politics seriously in Candle County.

I smiled back at him. "Looks like it—with one felony in six months."

"And this." He jerked a thumb towards the rear of the building, where the cells were.

"What about this? Let's talk about this."

"It's plenty wrong," he said. "I just finished talking to the Philly police. There wasn't any Paul Frank Dunlap murdered there that they know about; they've got no unexplained murder on the 26th of last month." He looked at me as if it were my fault. "What'd you get out of Furman before you let him hang himself?"

"That he was innocent."

"Didn't you grill him? Didn't you find out what he was doing in town? Didn't you—"

"What for?" I asked. "He admitted his name was Furman, the description fit him, the photograph was him, the Trans-American's supposed to be on the level. Philadelphia wanted him: I didn't. Sure, if I'd known he was going to hang himself— You said he'd been a client of the Trans-American. They tell you what the job was?"

"His wife left him a couple of years ago and he had them hunting for her for five or six months, but they never found her. They're sending a man up tonight to look it over." He stood up. "I'm going to get some lunch." At the door he turned his head over his shoulder to say, "There'll probably be trouble over this."

I knew that; there usually is when somebody dies in a cell.

George Propper came in grinning happily. "So what's become of that fifteen hundred fish?"

"What happened last night?" I asked.

"Nothing. He hung hisself."

"Did you find him?"

He shook his head. "Wally took a look in there to see how things was before he went off duty and found him."

"You were asleep, I suppose."

"Well, I was catching a nap, I guess," he mumbled; "but everybody does that sometimes—even Wally sometimes when he comes in off his beat between rounds—and I always wake up when the phone rings or anything. And suppose I had been awake. You can't hear a guy hanging hisself."

"Did Kamsley say how long he'd been dead?"

"He done it about five o'clock, he said he guessed. You want to look at the remains? They're over at Fritz's undertaking parlor."

I said, "Not now. You'd better go home and get some more sleep, so your insomnia won't keep you awake tonight."

He said, "I feel almost as bad about you and Wally losing all that dough as you do," and went out; went out chuckling.

Ted Carroll came back from lunch with the notion that perhaps there was some connection between Furman and the two men who had robbed Heck Jones. That didn't seem to make much sense, but I promised to look into it. Naturally, we never did find any such connection.

That evening a fellow named Rising, assistant manager of

the Trans-American Detective Agency's Philadelphia branch, arrived. He brought the dead man's lawyer, a scrawny, asthmatic man named Wheelock, with him. After they had identified the body we went back to my office for a conference.

It didn't take me long to tell them all I knew, with the one additional fact I had picked up during the afternoon, which was that the police in most towns in our corner of the state had received copies of the reward circular.

Rising examined the circular and called it an excellent forgery: paper, style, type were all almost exactly those ordinarily used by his agency.

They told me the dead man was a well-known, respectable and prosperous citizen of Philadelphia. In 1928 he had married a twenty-two-year-old girl named Ethel Brian, the daughter of a respectable, if not prosperous, Philadelphia family. They had a child born in 1930, but it lived only a few months. In 1931 Furman's wife had disappeared and neither he nor her family had heard of her since, though he had spent a good deal of money trying to find her. Rising showed me a photograph of her, a small-featured, pretty blonde with a weak mouth and large, somewhat staring, eyes.

"I'd like to have a copy made," I said.

"You can keep that. It's one of them that we had made. Her description's on the back."

"Thanks. And he didn't divorce her?"

Rising shook his head with emphasis. "No, sir. He was a lot in love with her and he seemed to think the kid's dying had made her a little screwy and she didn't know what she was doing." He looked at the lawyer. "That right?"

Wheelock made a couple of asthmatic sounds and said, "That is my belief."

"You said he had money. About how much, and who gets it?"

The scrawny lawyer wheezed some more, said, "I should say his estate will amount to perhaps a half a million dollars, left in its entirety to his wife."

That gave me something to think about, but the thinking didn't help me out then.

They couldn't tell me why he had come to Deerwood. He seemed to have told nobody where he was going, had simply told his servants and his employees that he was leaving town for a day or two. Neither Rising nor Wheelock knew of any enemies he had. That was the crop.

And that was still the crop at the inquest the next day. Everything showed that somebody had framed Furman into our jail and that the frame-up had driven him to suicide. Nothing showed anything else. And there had to be something else, a lot else.

Some of the else began to show up immediately after the inquest. Ben Kamsley was waiting for me when I left the undertaking parlor, where the inquest had been held. "Let's get out of the crowd," he said. "I want to tell you something."

"Come on over to the office."

We went over there. He shut the door, which usually stayed open, and sat on a corner of my desk. His voice was low: "Two of those bruises showed."

"What bruises?"

He looked curiously at me for a second, then put a hand on the top of his head. "Furman—up under the hair—there were two bruises."

I tried to keep from shouting. "Why didn't you tell me?"

"I am telling you. You weren't here that morning. This is the first time I've seen you since."

I cursed the two hoodlums who had kept me away by sticking up the Red Top Diner and demanded, "Then why didn't you spill it when you were testifying at the inquest?"

He frowned. "I'm a friend of yours. Do I want to put you in a spot where people can say you drove this chap to suicide by third-degreeing him too rough?"

"You're nuts," I said. "How bad was his head?"

"That didn't kill him, if that's what you mean. There's nothing the matter with his skull. Just a couple of bruises nobody would notice unless they parted the hair."

"It killed him just the same," I growled. "You and your *friendship* that—"

The telephone rang. It was Fritz. "Listen, Scott," he said, "there's a couple ladies here that want a look at that fellow. Is it all right?"

"Who are they?"

"I don't know 'em—strangers."

"What do they want to see him for?"

"I don't know. Wait a minute."

A woman's voice came over the wire: "Can't I please see him?" It was a very pleasant, earnest voice.

"Why do you want to see him?" I asked.

"Well, I"—there was a long pause—"I am"—a shorter pause, and when she finished the sentence her voice was not much more than a whisper—"his wife."

"Oh, certainly," I said. "I'll be right over."

I hurried out.

Leaving the building, I ran into Wally Shane. He was in civilian clothes, since he was off duty. "Hey, Scott!" He took my arm and dragged me back into the vestibule, out of sight of the street. "A couple of dames came into Fritz's just as I was leaving. One of 'em's Hotcha Randall, a baby with a record as long as your arm. You know she's one of that mob you had me in New York working on last summer."

"She know you?"

He grinned. "Sure. But not by my right name, and she thinks I'm a Detroit rum-runner."

"I mean did she know you just now?"

"I don't think she saw me. Anyways, she didn't give me a tumble."

"You don't know the other one?"

"No. She's a blonde, kind of pretty."

"O.K.," I said. "Stick around a while, but out of sight. Maybe I'll be bringing them back with me." I crossed the street to the undertaking parlor.

Ethel Furman was prettier than her photograph had indicated. The woman with her was five or six years older, quite a bit larger, handsome in a big, somewhat coarse way. Both of them were attractively dressed in styles that hadn't reached Deerwood yet.

The big woman was introduced to me as Mrs. Crowder. I said, "I thought your name was Randall."

She laughed. "What do you care, Chief? I'm not hurting your town."

I said, "Don't call me Chief. To you big-city slickers I'm the Town Whittler. We go back through here."

Ethel Furman didn't make any fuss over her husband when

she saw him. She simply looked gravely at his face for about three minutes, then turned away and said, "Thank you," to me.

"I'll have to ask you some questions," I said, "so if you'll come across the street . . ."

She nodded. "And I'd like to ask you some." She looked at her companion. "If Mrs. Crowder will—"

"Call her Hotcha," I said. "We're all among friends. Sure, she'll come along, too."

The Randall woman said, "Aren't you the cut-up?" and took my arm.

In my office I gave them chairs and said, "Before I ask you anything I want to tell you something. Furman didn't commit suicide. He was murdered."

Ethel Furman opened her eyes wide. "Murdered?"

Hotcha Randall said as if she had had the words on the tip of her tongue right along, "We've got alibis. We were in New York. We can prove it."

"You're likely to get a chance to, too," I told her. "How'd you people happen to come down here?"

Ethel Furman repeated, "Murdered?" in a dazed tone.

The Randall woman said, "Who's got a better right to come down here? She was still his wife, wasn't she? She's entitled to some of his estate, isn't she? She's got a right to look out for her own interests, hasn't she?"

That reminded me of something. I picked up the telephone and told Hammill to have somebody get hold of the lawyer Wheelock—he had stayed over for the inquest, of course—before he left town and tell him I wanted to see him. "And is Wally around?"

"He's not here. He said you told him to keep out of sight. I'll find him, though."

"Right. Tell him I want him to go to New York tonight. Send Mason home to get some sleep: he'll have to take over Wally's night trick."

Hammill said, "Oke," and I turned back to my guests.

Ethel Furman had come out of her daze. She leaned forward and asked, "Mr. Anderson, do you think I had—had anything to do with Lester's—with his death?"

"I don't know. I know he was killed. I know he left you something like half a million."

The Randall woman whistled softly. She came over and put
a diamond-ringed hand on my shoulder. "Dollars?"

When I nodded, the delight went out of her face, leaving
it serious. "All right, Chief," she said, "now don't be a
clown. The kid didn't have a thing to do with whatever you
think happened. We read about him committing suicide in
yesterday morning's paper, and about there being something
funny about it, and I persuaded her she ought to come
down and—"

Ethel Furman interrupted her friend: "Mr. Anderson, I
wouldn't have done anything to hurt Lester. I left him because I wanted to leave him, but I wouldn't have done anything to him for money or anything else. Why, if I'd wanted
money from him all I'd've had to do would've been to ask
him. Why, he used to put ads in papers telling me if I wanted
anything to let him know, but I never did. You can—his
lawyer—anybody who knew anything about it can tell you
that."

The Randall woman took up the story: "That's the truth,
Chief. For years I've been telling her she was a chump not to
tap him, but she never would. I had a hard enough time getting her to come for her share now he's dead and got nobody
else to leave it to."

Ethel Furman said, "I wouldn't've hurt him."

"Why'd you leave him?"

She moved her shoulders. "I don't know how to say it. The
way we lived wasn't the way I wanted to live. I wanted—I
don't know what. Anyway, after the baby died I couldn't
stand it any more and cleared out, but I didn't want anything
from him and I wouldn't've hurt him. He was always good to
me. I was—I was the one that was wrong."

The telephone rang. Hammill's voice: "I found both of
'em. Wally's home. I told him. The old guy Wheelock is on
his way over."

I dug out the phony reward circular and showed it to Ethel
Furman. "This is what got him into the can. Did you ever see
that picture before?"

She started to say "No"; then a frightened look came into
her face. "Why, that's—it can't be. It's—it's a snapshot I
had—have. It's an enlargement of it."

"Who else has one?"

Her face became more frightened, but she said, "Nobody that I know of. I don't think anybody else could have one."

"You've still got yours?"

"Yes. I don't remember whether I've seen it recently—it's with some old papers and things—but I must have it."

I said, "Well, Mrs. Furman, it's stuff like that that's got to be checked up, and neither of us can dodge it. Now there are two ways we can play it. I can hold you here on suspicion till I've had time to check things up, or I can send one of my men back to New York with you for the check-up. I'm willing to do that if you'll speed things up by helping him all you can and if you'll promise me you won't try any tricks."

"I promise," she said. "I'm as anxious as you are to—"

"All right. How'd you come down?"

"I drove," the Randall woman said. "That's my car, the big green one across the street."

"Fine. Then he can ride back with you, but remember, no funny business."

The telephone rang again while they were assuring me there would be no funny business. Hammill: "Wheelock's here."

"Send him in."

The lawyer's asthma nearly strangled him when he saw Ethel Furman. Before he could get himself straightened out I asked, "This is really Mrs. Furman?"

He wagged his head up and down, still wheezing.

"Fine," I said. "Wait for me. I'll be back in a little while." I herded the two women out and across the street to the green car. "Straight up to the end of the street and then two blocks left," I told the Randall woman, who was at the wheel.

"Where are we going?" she asked.

"To see Shane, the man who's going to New York with you."

Mrs. Dober, Wally's landlady, opened the door for us.

"Wally in?" I asked.

"Yes, indeedy, Mr. Anderson. Go right on up." She was staring with wide-eyed curiosity at my companions while talking to me.

We went up a flight of stairs and I knocked on his door.

"Who is it?" he called.

"Scott."

"Come on in."

I pushed the door open and stepped aside to let the women in.

Ethel Furman gasped, "Harry!" and stepped back, treading on my foot.

Wally had a hand behind him, but my gun was already out in my hand. "I guess you win," he said.

I said I guessed I did and we all went back to headquarters.

"I'm a sap," he complained when he and I were alone in my office. "I knew it was all up as soon as I saw those two dames going into Fritz's. Then, when I was ducking out of sight and ran into you, I was afraid you'd take me over with you, so I had to tell you one of 'em knew me, figuring you'd want to keep me under cover for a little while anyhow—long enough for me to get out of town. And then I didn't have sense enough to do it.

"I drop in home to pick up a couple of things before I scram and that call of Hammill's catches me and I fall for it plenty. I figure I'm getting a break. I figure you're not on yet and are going to send me back to New York as the Detroit rum-runner again to see what dope I can get out of these folks and I'll be sitting pretty. Well, you fooled me, brother, or didn't— Listen, Scott, you didn't just stumble into that accidentally, did you?"

"No. Furman had to be murdered by a copper. A copper was most likely to know reward circulars well enough to make a good job of forging one. Who printed that for you?"

"Go on with your story," he said. "I'm not dragging anybody in with me. It was only a poor mug of a printer that needed dough."

"O.K. Only a copper would be sure enough of the routine to know how things would be handled. Only a copper—one of my coppers—would be able to walk into his cell, bang him across the head and string him up on the— Those bruises showed, you know."

"They did? I wrapped the blackjack in a towel, figuring it would knock him out without leaving a mark anybody'd find under the hair. I seem to've slipped up a lot."

"So that narrows it down to my coppers," I went on,

"and—well—you told me you knew the Randall woman, and there it was, only I figured you were working with them. What got you into this?"

He made a sour mouth. "What gets most saps in jams? A yen for easy dough. I'm in New York, see, working on that Dutton job for you, palling around with bootleggers and racketeers, passing for one of them; and I get to figuring that here my work takes as much brains as theirs, and is as tough and dangerous as theirs, but they're taking in big money and I'm working for coffee and doughnuts. That kind of stuff gets you; anyway, it got me.

"Then I run into this Ethel and she goes for me like a house afire. I like her, too, so that's dandy; but one night she tells me about this husband of hers and how much dough he's got and how nuts he is about her and how he's still trying to find her, and I get to thinking. I think she's nuts enough about me to marry me. I still think she'd marry me if she didn't know I killed him. Divorcing him's no good, because the chances are she wouldn't take any money from him and, anyway, it would only be part. So I got to thinking about suppose he died and left her the roll.

"That was more like it. I ran down to Philly a couple of afternoons and looked him up and everything looked fine. He didn't even have anybody else close enough to leave more than a little of his dough to. So I did it. Not right away; I took my time working out the details, meanwhile writing to her through a fellow in Detroit.

"And then I did it. I sent those circulars out—to a lot of places—not wanting to point too much at this one. And when I was ready I phoned him, telling him if he'd come to the Deerwood Hotel that night, sometime between then and the next night, he'd hear from Ethel. And, like I thought, he'd've fallen for any trap that was baited with her. You picking him up at the station was a break. If you hadn't, I'd've had to discover he was registered at the hotel that night. Anyway, I'd've killed him and pretty soon I'd've started drinking or something and you'd've fired me and I'd've gone off and married Ethel and her half-million under my Detroit name." He made the sour mouth again. "Only I guess I'm not as sharp as I thought I was."

"Maybe you are," I said, "but that doesn't always help. Old man Kamsley, Ben's father, used to have a saying, 'To a sharp knife comes a tough steak.' I'm sorry you did it, Wally. I always liked you."

He smiled wearily. "I know you did," he said. "I was counting on that."

OTHER WRITINGS

The Thin Man:
An Early Typescript

T HE TRAIN went north among the mountains. The dark
man crossed the tracks to the ticket-window and said:
"Can you tell me how to get to Mr. Wynant's place? Mr.
Walter Irving Wynant's."

The man within stopped writing on a printed form. His
eyes became brightly inquisitive behind tight rimless spectacles. His voice was eager. "Are you a newspaper reporter?"

"Why?" The dark man's eyes were very blue. They looked
idly at the other. "Does it make any difference?"

"Then you ain't," the ticket-agent said. He was disappointed. He looked at a clock on a wall. "Hell, I ought to've
known that. You wouldn't've had time to get here." He
picked up the pencil he had put down.

"Know where his place is?"

"Sure. Up there on the hill." The ticket-agent waved his
pencil vaguely westward. "All the taxi-drivers know it, but if
it's Wynant you want to see you're out of luck."

"Why?"

The ticket-agent's mien brightened. He put his forearms
on the counter, hunching his shoulders, and said: "Because
the fact is he went and murdered everybody on the place and
jumped in the river not more than an hour ago."

The dark man exclaimed, "No!" softly.

The ticket-agent smacked his lips. "Uh-huh—killed all
three of them—the whole shooting match—chopped them
up in pieces with an ax and then tied a weight around his own
neck and jumped in the river."

The dark man asked solemnly: "What'd he do that for?"

A telephone-bell began to ring behind the ticket-agent.
"You don't know him or you wouldn't have to ask," he
replied as he reached for the telephone. "Crazy as they
make them and always was. The only wonder is he didn't do
it long before this." He said, "Hello," into the telephone.

The dark man went through the waiting-room and down-stairs to the street. The half a dozen automobiles parked near the station were apparently private cars. A large red and white sign in the next block said *Taxi*. The dark man walked under the sign into a small grimy office where a bald fat man was reading a newspaper.

"Can I get a taxi?" the dark man asked.

"All out now, brother, but I'm expecting one of them back any minute. In a hurry?"

"A little bit."

The bald man brought his chair down on all its legs and lowered his newspaper. "Where do you want to go?"

"Wynant's."

The bald man dropped his newspaper and stood up, saying heartily: "Well, I'll run you up there myself." He covered his baldness with a sweat-stained brown hat.

They left the office and—after the fat man had paused at the real-estate-office next door to yell, "Take care of my phone if it rings, Toby"—got into a dark sedan, took the left turn at the first crossing, and rode uphill towards the west.

When they had ridden some three hundred yards the fat man said in a tone whose casualness was belied by the shine of his eyes: "That must be a hell of a mess up there and no fooling."

The dark man was lighting a cigarette. "What happened?" he asked.

The fat man looked sharply sidewise at him. "Didn't you hear?"

"Only what the ticket-agent told me just now"—the dark man leaned forward to return the lighter to its hole in the dashboard—"that Wynant had killed three people with an ax and then drowned himself."

The fat man laughed scornfully. "Christ, you can't beat Lew," he said. "If you sprained your ankle he could get a broken back out of it. Wynant didn't kill but two of them—the Hopkins woman got away because it was her that phoned—and he choked them to death and then shot himself. I bet you if you'd go back there right now Lew'd tell you there was a cool half a dozen of them killed and likely as not with dynamite."

The dark man took his cigarette from his mouth. "Then he wasn't right about Wynant being crazy?"

"Yes," the fat man said reluctantly, "but nobody could go wrong on that."

"No?"

"Nope. Holy hell! didn't he used to come down to town in his pajamas last summer? And then when people didn't like it and got Ray to say something to him about it didn't he get mad and stop coming in at all? Don't he make as much fuss about people trespassing on his place as if he had a gold mine there? Didn't I see him with my own eyes heave a rock at a car that had gone past him raising dust once?"

The dark man smiled meagerly. "I don't know any of the answers," he said. "I didn't know him."

Beside a painted warning against trespass they left their graveled road for an uneven narrow crooked one of dark earth running more steeply uphill to the right. Protruding undergrowth brushed the sedan's sides and now and then an overhanging tree-branch its top. Their speed made their ride rougher than it need have been.

"This is his place," the fat man said. He sat stiffly at the wheel fighting the road's unevenness. His eyes were shiny, expectant.

The house they presently came to was a rambling structure of grey native stone and wood needing grey paint under low Dutch roofs. Five cars stood in the clearing in front of the house. The man who sat at the wheel of one of them, and the two men standing beside it, stopped talking and watched the sedan draw up.

"Here we are," the fat man said and got out. His manner had suddenly become important. He put importance in the nod he gave the three men.

The dark man, leaving the other side of the sedan, went towards the house. The fat man hurried to walk beside him.

A man came out of the house before they reached it. He was a middle-aged giant in baggy worn clothes. His hair was grey, his eyes small, and he chewed gum. He said, "Howdy, Fern," to the fat man and, looking steadily at the dark man, stood in the path confronting them squarely.

Fern said, "Hello, Nick," and then told the dark man: "This is Sheriff Petersen." He narrowed one eye shrewdly and addressed the Sheriff again: "He came up to see Wynant."

Sheriff Nick Petersen stopped chewing. "What's the name?" he asked.

The dark man said: "John Guild."

The Sheriff said: "So. Now what were you wanting to see Wynant about?"

The man who had said his name was John Guild smiled. "Does it make any difference now he's dead?"

The Sheriff asked, "What?" with considerable force.

"Now that he's dead," Guild repeated patiently. He put a fresh cigarette between his lips.

"How do you know he's dead?" The Sheriff emphasized "you."

Guild looked with curious blue eyes at the giant. "They told me in the village," he said carelessly. He moved his cigarette an inch to indicate the fat man. "He told me."

The Sheriff frowned skeptically, but when he spoke it was to utter a vague "Oh." He chewed his gum. "Well, what was it you were wanting to see him about?"

Guild said: "Look here: is he dead or isn't he?"

"Not that I know of."

"Fine," Guild said, his eyes lighting up. "Where is he?"

"I'd like to know," the Sheriff replied gloomily. "Now what is it you want with him?"

"I'm from his bank. I want to see him on business." Guild's eyes became drowsy. "It's confidential business."

"So?" Sheriff Petersen's frown seemed to hold more discomfort than annoyance. "Well, none of his business is confidential from me any more. I got a right to know anything and everything that anybody knows about him."

Guild's eyes narrowed a little. He blew smoke out.

"I have," the Sheriff insisted in a tone of complaint. "Listen, Guild, you haven't got any right to hide any of his business from me. He's a murderer and I'm responsible for law and order in this county."

Guild pursed his lips. "Who'd he kill?"

"This here Columbia Forrest," Petersen said, jerking a thumb at the house, "shot her stone dead and lit out for God only knows where."

"Didn't kill anybody else?"

"My God," the Sheriff asked peevishly, "ain't that enough?"

"Enough for me, but down in the village they've got it all very plural." Guild stared thoughtfully at the Sheriff. "Got away clean?"

"So far," Petersen grumbled, "but we're phoning descriptions of him and his car around." He sighed, moved his big shoulders uncomfortably. "Well, come on now, let's have it. What's your business with him?" but when Guild would have replied the giant said: "Wait a minute. We might as well go in and get hold of Boyer and Ray and get it over with at one crack."

Leaving the fat man, Guild and the Sheriff went indoors, into a pleasantly furnished tan room in the front of the house, where they were soon joined by two more men. One of these was nearly tall as the Sheriff, a raw-boned blond man in his early thirties, hard of jaw and mouth, somber of eye. One was younger, shorter, with boyishly rosy cheeks, quick dark eyes, and smoothed dark hair. When the Sheriff introduced them to Guild he said the taller one was Ray Callaghan, a Deputy Sheriff, the other District Attorney Bruce Boyer. He told them John Guild was a fellow who wanted to see Wynant.

The youthful District Attorney, standing close to Guild, smiled ingratiatingly and asked: "What business are you in, Mr. Guild?"

"I came up to see Wynant about his bank-account," the dark man replied slowly.

"What bank?"

"Seaman's National of San Francisco."

"I see. Now what did you want to see him about? I mean, what was there about his account that you had to come up here to see him about?"

"Call it an over-draft," Guild said with deliberate evasiveness.

The District Attorney's eyes became anxious.

Guild made a small gesture with the brown hand holding his cigarette. "Look here, Boyer," he said, "if you want me to go all the way with you you ought to go all the way with me."

Boyer looked at Petersen. The Sheriff met his gaze with noncommittal eyes. Boyer turned back to Guild. "We're not hiding anything from you," he said earnestly. "We've nothing to hide."

Guild nodded. "Swell. What happened here?"

"Wynant caught the Forrest girl getting ready to leave him and he shot her and jumped in his car and drove away," he said quickly. "That's all there is to it."

"Who's the Forrest girl?"

"His secretary."

Guild pursed his lips, asked: "Only that?"

The raw-boned Deputy Sheriff said, "None of that, now!" in a strained croaking voice. His pale eyes were bloodshot and glaring.

The Sheriff growled, "Take it easy there, Ray," avoiding his Deputy's eyes.

The District Attorney glanced impatiently at the Deputy Sheriff. Guild stared gravely, attentively at him.

The Deputy Sheriff's face flushed a little and he shifted his feet. He spoke to the dark man again, in the same croaking voice: "She's dead and you might just as well talk decently about her."

Guild moved his shoulders a little. "I didn't know her," he said coldly. "I'm trying to find out what happened." He stared for a moment longer at the raw-boned man and then shifted his gaze to Boyer. "What was she leaving him for?"

"To get married. She told him when he caught her packing after she came back from town and—and they had a fight and when she wouldn't change her mind he shot her."

Guild's blue eyes moved sidewise to focus on the raw-boned Deputy Sheriff's face. "She was living with Wynant, wasn't she?" he asked bluntly.

"You son of a bitch!" the Deputy Sheriff cried hoarsely and struck with his right fist at Guild's face.

Guild avoided the fist by stepping back with no appearance of haste. He had begun to step back before the fist started towards his face. His eyes gravely watched the fist go past his face.

Big Petersen lurched against his Deputy, wrapping his arms around him. "Cut it out, Ray," he grumbled. "Why don't you behave yourself? This is no time to be losing your head."

The Deputy Sheriff did not struggle against him.

"What's the matter with him?" Guild asked the District Attorney. There was no resentment in his manner. "In love with her or something?"

Boyer nodded furtively, then frowned and shook his head in a warning gesture.

"That's all right," Guild said. "Where'd you get your information about what happened?"

"From the Hopkinses. They look after the place for Wynant. They were in the kitchen and heard the whole fight. They ran upstairs when they heard the shots and he stood them off with the gun and told them he'd come back and kill them if they told anybody before he'd an hour's start, but they phoned Ray as soon as he'd gone."

Guild tossed the stub of his cigarette into the fireplace and lit a fresh one. Then he took a card from a brown case brought from an inner pocket and gave the card to Boyer.

John Guild
Associated Detective Bureaus, Inc.
Frost Building, San Francisco

"Last week Wynant deposited a ten-thousand-dollar New York check in his account at the Seaman's National Bank," Guild said. "Yesterday the bank learned the check had been raised from one thousand to ten. The bank's nicked for six thousand on the deal."

"But in the case of an altered check," Boyer said, "I understand——"

"I know," Guild agreed, "the bank's not responsible—theoretically—but there are usually loopholes and it's—— Well, we're working for the insurance company that covers the Seaman's and it's good business to go after him and recover as much as we can."

"I'm glad that's they way you feel about it," the District Attorney said with enthusiasm. "I'm mighty glad you're going to work with us." He held out his hand.

"Thanks," Guild said as he took the hand. "Let's look at the Hopkinses and the body."

CHAPTER TWO

Columbia Forrest had been a long-limbed smoothly slender young woman. Her body, even as it lay dead in a blue sport suit, seemed supple. Her short hair was a faintly reddish brown. Her features were small and regular, appealing in their lack of strength. There were three bullet-holes in her left temple. Two of them touched. The third was down beside the eye.

Guild put the tip of his dark forefinger lightly on the edge of the lower hole. "A thirty-two," he said. "He made sure: any of the three would have done it." He turned his back on the corpse. "Let's see the Hopkinses."

"They're in the dining-room, I think," the District Attorney said. He hesitated, cleared his throat. His young face was worried. He touched Guild's elbow with the back of one hand and said: "Go easy with Ray, will you? He was a little bit—or a lot, I guess—in love with her and it's tough on him."

"The Deputy?"

"Yes, Ray Callaghan."

"That's all right if he doesn't get in the way," Guild said carelessly. "What sort of person is this Sheriff?"

"Oh, Petersen's all right."

Guild seemed to consider this statement critically. Then he said: "But he's not what you'd call a feverish manhunter?"

"Well, no, that's not—you know—a sheriff has other things to do most of the time, but even if he'd just as lief have somebody else do the work he won't interfere." Boyer moistened his lips and leaned close to the dark man. His face was boyishly alight. "I wish you'd—I'm glad you're going to work with me on this, Guild," he said in a low earnest voice. "I—this is my first murder and I'd like to—well—show them"—he blushed—"that I'm not as young as some of them said."

"Fair enough. Let's see the Hopkinses—in here."

The District Attorney studied Guild's dark face uneasily for a moment, started to say something, changed his mind, and left the room.

A man and a woman came with him when he returned. The man was probably fifty years old, of medium stature, with thin greying hair above a round phlegmatic face. He wore tan trousers held up by new blue suspenders and a faded blue shirt open at the neck. The woman was of about the same age, rather short, plump, and dressed neatly in grey. She wore gold-rimmed spectacles. Her eyes were round and pale and bright.

The District Attorney shut the door and said: "This is Mr. and Mrs. Hopkins, Mr. Guild." He addressed them: "Mr. Guild is working with me. Please give him all the assistance you can."

The Hopkinses nodded in unison.

Guild asked: "How'd this happen?" He indicated with a small backward jerk of his head the dead young woman.

Hopkins said, "I always knew he'd do something like that sometime," while his wife was saying: "It was right in this room and they were talking so loud you could hear it all over the place."

Guild shook his cigarette at them. "One at a time." He spoke to the man: "How'd you know he was going to do it?"

The woman replied quickly: "Oh, he was crazy-jealous of her all the time—if she got out of his sight for a minute—and when she came back from the city and told him she was going to leave to get married he——"

Again Guild used his cigarette to interrupt her. "What do you think? Is he really crazy?"

"He was then, sir," she said. "Why, when we ran in here when we heard the shooting and he told us to keep our mouths shut he was—his eyes—you never saw anything like them in your life—nor his voice either and he was shaking and jerking like he was going to fall apart."

"I don't mean that," Guild explained. "I mean, is he crazy?" Before the woman could reply he put another question to her: "How long have you been with him?"

"Going on about ten months, ain't it, Willie?" she asked her husband.

"Yes," he agreed, "since last fall."

"That's right," she told Guild. "It was last November."

"Then you ought to know whether he's crazy. Is he?"

"Well, I'll tell you," she said slowly, wrinkling her forehead. "He was certainly the most peculiar person you ever heard tell of, but I guess geniuses are like that and I wouldn't want to say he was out and out crazy except about her." She looked at her husband.

He said tolerantly: "Sure, all geniuses are like that. It's—it's eccentric."

"So you think he was a genius," Guild said. "Did you read the things he wrote?"

"No, sir," Mrs. Hopkins said, squirming, "though I did try sometimes, but it was too—I couldn't make heads or tails of it—much—but I ain't an educated woman and——"

"Who was she going to marry?" Guild asked.

Mrs. Hopkins shook her head vigorously. "I don't know. I didn't catch the name if she said it. It was him that was talking so loud."

"What'd she go to town for?"

Mrs. Hopkins shook her head again. "I don't know that either. She used to go in every couple of weeks and he always got mad about it."

"She drive in?"

"Mostly she did, but she didn't yesterday, but she drove out in that new blue car out there."

Guild looked questioningly at the District Attorney, who said: "We're trying to trace it now. It's apparently a new one, but we ought to know whose it is soon."

Guild nodded and returned his attention to the Hopkinses. "She went to San Francisco by train yesterday and came back in this new car at what time today?"

"Yes, sir. At about three o'clock, I guess it was, and she started packing." She pointed at the traveling bags and clothing scattered around the room. "And he came in and the fuss started. I could hear them downstairs and I went to the window and beckoned at Willie—Mr. Hopkins, that is—and we stood at the foot of the stairs, there by the dining-room-door and listened to them."

Guild turned aside to mash his cigarette in a bronze tray on a table. "She usually stay over-night when she went to the city?"

"Mostly always."

"You must have some idea of what she went to the city for," Guild insisted.

"No, I haven't," the woman said earnestly. "We never did know, did we, Willie? Jealous like he was, I guess if she was going in to see some fellow she wouldn't be likely to tell anybody that might tell him, though the Lord knows I can keep my mouth shut as tight as anybody. I've seen the——"

Guild stopped lighting a fresh cigarette to ask: "How about her mail? You must've seen that sometimes."

"No, Mr. Gould, we never did, and that's a funny thing, because all the time we've been here I never saw any mail for her except magazines and never knew her to write any."

Guild frowned. "How long had she been here?"

"She was here when we came. I don't know how long she'd been here, but it must've been a long time."

Boyer said: "Three years. She came here in March three years ago."

"How about her relatives, friends?"

The Hopkinses shook their heads. Boyer shook his head. "His?"

Mrs. Hopkins shook her head again. "He didn't have any. That's what he would always say, that he didn't have a relative or a friend in the world."

"Who's his lawyer?"

Mrs. Hopkins looked blank. "If he's got one I don't know it, Mr. Gould. Maybe you could find something like that in his letters and things."

"That'll do," Guild said abruptly around the cigarette in his mouth, and opened the door for the Hopkinses. They left the room.

He shut the door behind them and with his back against it looked around the room, at the blanketed dead figure on the bed, at the clothing scattered here and there, at the three traveling bags, and finally at the bloodstained center of the light blue rug.

Boyer watched him expectantly.

Staring at the bloodstain, Guild asked: "You've notified the police in San Francisco?"

"Oh, yes, we've sent his description and the description and license-number of his car all over—from Los Angeles to Seattle and as far east as Salt Lake."

"What is the number?" Guild took a pencil and an envelope from his pockets.

Boyer told him, adding: "It's a Buick coupe, last year's."

"What does he look like?"

"I've never seen him, but he's very tall—well over six feet— and thin. Won't weigh more than a hundred and thirty, they say. You know he's tubercular: that's how he happened to come up here. He's about forty-five years old, sunburned, but sallow, with brown eyes and very dark brown hair and whiskers. He's got whiskers—maybe five or six inches long— thick and shaggy, and his eyebrows are thick and shaggy. There's a lot of pictures of him in his room. You can help yourself to them. He had on a baggy grey tweed suit and a soft grey hat and heavy brown shoes. His shoulders are high and straight and he walks on the balls of his feet with long steps. He doesn't smoke or drink and he has a habit of talking to himself."

Guild put away his pencil and envelope. "Had your finger-print people go over the place yet?"

"No, I——"

"It might help in case he's picked up somewhere and we're doubtful. I suppose we can get specimens of his handwriting. Anyway we'll be able to get them from the bank. We'll try to——"

Someone knocked on the door.

"Come in," Boyer called.

The door opened to admit a man's head. He said: "They want you on the phone."

The District Attorney followed the man downstairs. During his absence Guild smoked and looked somberly around the room.

The District Attorney came back saying: "The car belongs to a Charles Fremont, on Guerrero Street, in San Francisco."

"What number." Guild brought out his pencil and envelope again. Boyer told him the number and he wrote it down. "I think I'll trot back right now and see him."

The District Attorney looked at his watch. "I wonder if I couldn't manage to get away to go with you," he said.

Guild pursed his lips. "I don't think you ought to. One of us ought to be here looking through his stuff, gathering up the loose ends. I haven't seen anybody else we ought to trust with it."

Though Boyer seemed disappointed he said, "Righto," readily enough. "You'll keep in touch with me?"

"Sure. Let me have that card I gave you and I'll put my home address and phone-number on it." Guild's eyes became drowsy. "What do you say I drive Fremont's car in?"

The District Attorney wrinkled his forehead. "I don't know," he said slowly. "It might— Oh, sure, if you want. You'll phone me as soon as you've seen him—let me know what's what?"

"Um-hmm."

CHAPTER THREE

A red-haired girl in white opened the door.

Guild said: "I want to see Mr. Charles Fremont."

"Yes, sir," the girl said amiably in a resonant throaty voice. "Come in."

She took him into a comfortably furnished living-room to the right of the entrance. "Sit down. I'll call my brother." She went through another doorway and her voice could be heard singing: "Charley, a gentleman to see you."

Upstairs a hard masculine voice replied: "Be right down."

The red-haired girl came back to the room where Guild was. "He'll be down in a minute," she said.

Guild thanked her.

"Do sit down," she said, sitting on an end of the sofa. Her legs were remarkably beautiful.

He sat in a large chair facing her across the room, but got up again immediately to offer her cigarettes and to hold his lighter to hers. "What I wanted to see your brother about," he said as he sat down again, "was to ask if he knows a Miss Columbia Forrest."

The girl laughed.."He probably does," she said. "She's— They're going to be married tomorrow."

Guild said: "Well, that's——" He stopped when he heard footsteps running down stairs from the second floor.

A man came into the room. He was a man of perhaps thirty-five years, a little above medium height, trimly built, rather gaily dressed in grey with lavender shirt, tie, and protruding pocket-handkerchief. His face was lean and good-looking in a shrewd tight-lipped fashion.

"This is my brother," the girl said.

Guild stood up. "I'm trying to get some information about Miss Columbia Forrest," he said and gave Charles Fremont one of his cards.

The curiosity that had come into Fremont's face with Guild's words became frowning amazement when he had read Guild's card. "What——?"

Guild was saying: "There's been some trouble up at Hell Bend."

Fremont's eyes widened in his paling face. "Wynant has——?"

Guild nodded. "He shot Miss Forrest this afternoon."

The Fremonts stared at each other's blank horrified faces. She said through the fingers of one hand, trembling so she stuttered: "I t-t-told you, Charlie!"

Charles Fremont turned savagely on Guild. "How bad is she hurt? Tell me!"

The dark man said: "She's dead."

Fremont sobbed and sat down with his face in his hands. His sister knelt beside him with her arms around him. Guild stood watching them.

Presently Fremont raised his head. "Wynant?" he asked.

"Gone."

Fremont let his breath out in a low groan. He sat up straight, patting one of his sister's hands, freeing himself from her arms. "I'm going up there now," he told her, rising.

Guild had finished lighting a cigarette. He said: "That's all right, but you'll do most good by telling me some things before you go."

"Anything I can," Fremont promised readily.

"You were to be married tomorrow?"

"Yes. She was down here last night and stayed with us and I persuaded her. We were going to leave here tomorrow morning and drive up to Portland—where we wouldn't have to wait three days for the license—and then go up to Banff. I've just wired the hotel there for reservations. So she took the car—the new one we were going in—to go up to Hell Bend and get her things. I asked her not to—we both tried to persuade her—because we knew Wynant would make trouble, but—but we never thought he would do anything like this."

"You know him pretty well?"

"No, I've only seen him once—about three weeks ago—when he came to see me."

"What'd he come to see you for?"

"To quarrel with me about her—to tell me to stay away from her."

Guild seemed about to smile. "What'd you say to that?"

Fremont drew his thin lips back tight against his teeth. "Do I look like I'd tell him anything except to go to hell?" he demanded.

The dark man nodded. "All right. What do you know about him?"

"Nothing."

Guild frowned. "You must know something. She'd've talked about him."

Anger went out of Fremont's lean face, leaving it gloomy. "I didn't like her to," he said, "so she didn't."

"Why?"

"Jesus!" Fremont exclaimed. "She was living up there. I was nuts about her. I knew he was. What the hell?" He bit his lip. "Do you think that was something I liked to talk about?"

Guild stared thoughtfully at the other man for a moment and then addressed the girl: "What'd she tell you?"

"Not anything. She didn't like to talk about him any more than Charley liked to have her."

Guild drew his brows together. "What'd she stay with him for then?"

Fremont said painfully: "She was going to leave. That's why he killed her."

The dark man put his hands in his pockets and walked down the room to the front windows and back, squinting a little in the smoke rising from his cigarette. "You don't know where he's likely to go? who he's likely to connect with? how we're likely to find him?"

Fremont shook his head. "Don't you think I'd tell you if I knew?" he asked bitterly.

Guild did not reply to that. He asked: "Where are her people?"

"I don't know. I think she's got a father still alive in Texas somewhere. I know she's an only child and her mother's dead."

"How long have you known her?"

"Four—nearly five months."

"Where'd you meet her?"

"In a speakeasy on Powell Street, a couple of blocks beyond the Fairmont. She was in a party with some people I know— Helen Robier—I think she lives at the Cathedral—and a fellow named MacWilliams."

Guild walked to the windows again and back. "I don't like this," he said aloud, but apparently not to the Fremonts. "It doesn't make sense. It's— Look here." He halted in front of them and took some photographs from his pocket. "Are these good pictures of her?" He spread three out fanwise. "I've only seen her dead."

The Fremonts looked and nodded together. "The middle one especially," the girl said. "You have one of those, Charley."

Guild put the dead girl's photographs away and displayed two of a bearded man. "Are they good of him?"

The girl said, "I've never seen him," but her brother nodded and said: "They look like him."

Guild seemed dissatisfied with the answers he had been given. He put the photographs in his pocket again. "Then it's not that," he said, "but there's something funny somewhere."

He scowled at the floor, looked up quickly. "You people aren't putting up some kind of game on me, are you?"

Charles Fremont said: "Don't be a sap."

"All right, but there's something wrong somewhere."

The girl spoke: "What? Maybe if you'd tell us what you think is wrong——"

Guild shook his head. "If I knew what was wrong I could find out for myself what made it wrong. Never mind, I'll get it. I want the names and addresses of all the friends she had, the people she knew that you know of."

"I've told you Helen Robier lives—I'm pretty sure—at the Cathedral," Fremont said. "MacWilliams works in the Russ Building, for a stockbroker, I think. That's all I know about him and I don't believe Columbia knows—" he swallowed "—knew him very well. They're the only ones I know."

"I don't believe they're all you know," Guild said.

"Please, Mr. Guild," the girl said, coming around to his side, "don't be unfair to Charley. He's trying to help you— we're both trying—but——" She stamped her foot and cried angrily, tearfully: "Can't you have some consideration for him now?"

Guild said: "Oh, all right." He reached for his hat. "I drove your car down," he told Fremont. "It's out front now."

"Thank you, Guild."

Something struck one of the front windows, knocking a triangle of glass from its lower left-hand corner in on the floor. Charles Fremont, facing the window, yelled inarticulately and threw himself down on the floor. A pistol was fired through the gap in the pane. The bullet went over Fremont's head and made a small hole in the green plastered wall there.

Guild was moving towards the street-door by the time the bullet-hole appeared in the wall. A black pistol came into his right hand. Outside, that block of Guerrero Street was deserted. Guild went swiftly, though with many backward glances, to the nearest corner. From there he began to retrace his steps slowly, stopping to peer into shadowy door-ways and the dark basement-entrances under the high front steps.

Charles Fremont came out to join him. Windows were being raised along the street and people were looking out.

"Get inside," Guild said curtly to Fremont. "You're the one he's gunning for. Get inside and phone the police."

"Elsa's doing that now. He's shaved his whiskers off, Guild."

"That'd be the first thing he did. Go back in the house."

Fremont said, "No," and went with Guild as he searched the block. They were still at it when the police arrived. They did not find Wynant. Around a corner two blocks from the Fremonts' house they found a year-old Buick coupe bearing the license-numbers Boyer had given Guild—Wynant's car.

CHAPTER FOUR

After dinner, which Guild ate alone at Solari's in Maiden Lane, he went to an apartment in Hyde Street. He was admitted by a young woman whose pale tired face lighted up as she said: "Hello, John. We've been wondering what had become of you."

"Been away. Is Chris home?"

"I'd let you in anyhow," she said as she pushed the door farther open.

They went back to a square bookish room where a thick-set man with rumpled sandy hair was half buried in an immense shabby chair. He put his book down, reached for the tall glass of beer at his elbow, and said jovially: "Enter the sleuth. Get some more beer, Kay. I've been wanting to see you, John. What do you say you do some detective-story reviews for my page—you know—The Detective Looks at Detective Fiction?"

"You asked me that before," Guild said. "Nuts."

"It's a good idea, though," the thick-set man said cheerfully. "And I've got another one. I was going to save it till I got around to writing a detective story, but you might be able to use it in your work sometime, so I'll give it to you free."

Guild took the glass of beer Kay held out to him, said, "Thanks," to her and then to the man: "Do I have to listen to it?"

"Yes. You see, this fellow's suspected of a murder that requires quite a bit of courage. All the evidence points right at him—that kind of thing. But he's a great lover of Sam Johnson—got his books all over the place—so you know he didn't do it, because only timid men—the kind that say, 'Yes, sir,' to their wives and, 'Yes, Ma'am,' to policemen—love Johnson. You see, he's only loved for his boorishness and the boldness of his rudeness and bad manners and that's the kind of thing that appeals to——"

"So I look for a fellow named Sam Johnson and he's guilty?" the dark man said.

Kay said: "Chris has one of his nights."

Chris said: "Sneer at me and be damned to you, but there's a piece of psychology that might come in handy some day. Remember it. It's a law. Love of Doctor Johnson is the mark of the pathologically meek."

Guild made a face. "God knows I'm earning me beer," he said and drank. "If you've got to talk, talk about Walter Irving Wynant. That'll do me some good maybe."

"Why?" Chris asked. "How?"

"I'm hunting for him. He slaughtered his secretary this afternoon and lit out for parts unknown."

Kay exclaimed: "Not really!"

Chris said: "The hell he did!"

Guild nodded and drank more beer. "He only paused long enough to take a shot at the fellow his secretary was supposed to marry tomorrow."

Chris and Kay looked at each other with delighted eyes.

Chris lay back in his chair. "Can you beat that? But, you know, I'm not nearly as surprised as I ought to be. The last time I saw him I thought there was something wrong there, though he always was a bit on the goofy side. Remember I said something to you about it, Kay? And it's a cinch this magazine stuff he's been doing lately is woozy. Even parts of his last book— No, I'm being smart-alecky now. I'll stick to what I wrote about his book when it came out: in spite of occasional flaws his 'departmentalization' comes nearer supplying an answer to Pontius Pilate's question than anything ever offered by anybody else."

"What kind of writing does he do?" Guild asked.

"This sort of thing." Chris rose grunting, went to one of his bookcases, picked out a bulky black volume entitled, in large gold letters, *Knowledge and Belief*, opened it at random, and read: "Science is concerned with percepts. A percept is a defined, that is a limited, difference. The scientific datum that white occurs means that white is the difference between a certain perceptual field and the rest of the perceiver. If you look at an unbroken expanse of white you perceive white because your perception of it is limited to your visual field: the surrounding, contrasting, extra-visual area of non-white gives you your percept of white. These are not scientific definitions. They cannot be. Science cannot define, cannot limit, itself. Definitions of science must be philosophical definitions. Science cannot know what it cannot know. Science cannot know there is anything it does not know. Science deals with percepts and not with non-percepts. Thus, Einstein's theory of relativity—that the phenomena of nature will be the same, that is not different, to two observers who move with any uniform velocity whatever relative to one another—is a philosophical, and not a scientific, hypothesis.

"Philosophy, like science, cannot define, cannot limit, itself. Definitions of philosophy must be made from a viewpoint that will bear somewhat the same relation to philosophy that the philosophical viewpoint bears to science. These definitions may be——"

"That'll be enough of that," Guild said.

Chris shut the book with a bang. "That's the kind of stuff he writes," he said cheerfully and went back to his chair and beer.

"What do you know about him?" Guild asked. "I mean outside his writing. Don't start that again. I want to know if he was only crazy with jealousy or has blown his top altogether—and how to catch up with him either way."

"I haven't seen him for six or seven months or maybe longer," Chris said. "He always was a little cracked and unsociable as hell. Maybe just erratic, maybe worse than that."

"What do you know about him?"

"What everybody knows," Chris said depreciatively. "Born somewhere in Devonshire. Went to Oxford. Went native in India and came out with a book on economics—a pretty good book, but visionary. Married an actress named Hana Drix—or something like that—in Paris and lived with her there for three or four years and came out of it with his second book. I think they had a couple of children. After she divorced him he went to Africa and later, I believe, to South America. Anyway he did a lot of traveling and then settled down in Berlin long enough to write his *Speculative Anthropology* and to do some lecturing. I don't know where he was during the War. He popped up over here a couple of years later with a two-volume piece of metaphysics called *Conscious Drifting.* He's been in America ever since—the last five or six years up in the mountains here doing that *Knowledge and Belief.*"

"How about relatives, friends?"

Chris shook his tousled head. "Maybe his publishers would know—Dale & Dale."

"And as a critic you think——"

"I'm no critic," Chris said. "I'm a reviewer."

"Well, as whatever you are, you think his stuff is sane?"

Chris moved his thick shoulders in a lazy shrug. "Parts of his books I know are damned fine. Other parts—maybe they're over my head. Even that's possible. But the magazine stuff he's been doing lately—since *Knowledge and Belief*—I know is tripe and worse. The paper sent a kid up to get an interview out of him a couple of weeks ago—when everybody was making the fuss over that Russian anthropologist—and he came back with something awful. We wouldn't have run it if it hadn't been for the weight Wynant's name carries and the kid's oaths that he had written it exactly as it was given to him. I'd say it was likely enough his mind's cracked up."

"Thanks," Guild said, and reached for his hat, but both the others began questioning him then, so they sat there and talked and smoked and drank beer until midnight was past.

In his hotel-room Guild had his coat off when the telephone-bell rang. He went to the telephone. "Hello. . . . Yes. . . . Yes." He waited. "Yes? . . . Yes, Boyer. . . . He showed up at Fremont's and took a shot at him. . . . No, no harm done except that he made a clean sneak. . . . Yes, but we found his car. . . . Where? . . . Yes, I know where it is. . . . What time? . . . . Yes, I see. . . . Tomorrow? What time? . . . Fine. Suppose you pick me up here at my hotel. . . . Right."

He left the telephone, started to unbutton his vest, stopped, looked at the watch on his wrist, put his coat on again, picked up his hat, and went out.

At California Street he boarded an eastbound cable-car and rode over the top of the hill and down it to Chinatown, leaving the car at Grant Avenue. Rain nearly fine as mist was beginning to blow down from the north. Guild went out beyond the curb to avoid a noisy drunken group coming out of a Chinese restaurant, walked a block, and halted across the street from another restaurant. This was a red brick building that tried to seem oriental by means of much gilding and colored lighting, obviously pasted-on corbelled cornices and three-armed brackets marking its stories—some carrying posts above in the shape of half-pillars—and a tent-shaped terra cotta roof surmounted by a mast bearing nine aluminumed rings. There was a huge electric sign—*Manchu*.

He stood looking at this gaudy building until he had lit a cigarette. Then he went over to it. The girl in the cloak-room would not take his hat. "We close at one," she said.

He looked at the people getting into an elevator, at her again. "They're coming in."

"That's upstairs. Have you a card?"

He smiled. "Of course I have. I left it in my other suit."

She looked severely blank.

He said, "Oh, all right, sister," gave her a silver dollar, took his hat-check, and squeezed himself into the crowded elevator.

At the fourth floor he left the elevator with the others and went into a large shabby oblong room where, running out from a small stage, an oblong dance-floor was a peninsula among tables waited on by Chinese in dinner clothes. There were forty or fifty people in the place. Some of them were dancing to music furnished by a piano, a violin, and a French horn.

Guild was given a small table near a shuttered window. He ordered a sandwich and coffee.

The dance ended and a woman with a middle-aged harpy's face and a beautiful satin-skinned body sang a modified version of *Christopher Colombo*. There was another dance after that. Then Elsa Fremont came out to the center of the dance-floor and sang *Hollywood Papa*. Her low-cut green gown set off the red of her hair and brought out the greenness of her narrowly lanceolate eyes. Guild smoked, sipped coffee, and watched her. When she was through he applauded with the others.

She came straight to his table, smiling, and said: "What are you doing here?" She sat down facing him.

He sat down again. "I didn't know you worked here."

"No?" Her smile was merry, her eyes skeptical.

"No," he said, "but maybe I should have known it. A man named Lane, who lives near Wynant in Hell Bend, saw him coming in this place early this evening."

"That would be downstairs," the girl said. "We don't open up here till midnight."

"Lane didn't know about the murder till he got home late tonight. Then he phoned the District Attorney and told him he'd seen Wynant and the D.A. phoned me. I thought I'd drop in just on the off-chance that I might pick up something."

Frowning a little, she asked: "Well?"

"Well, I found you here."

"But I wasn't downstairs earlier this evening," she said. "What time was it?"

"Half an hour before he took his shot at your brother."

"You see"—triumphantly—"you know I was home then talking to you."

"I know that one," Guild said.

CHAPTER FIVE

At ten o'clock next morning Guild went into the Seaman's National Bank, to a desk marked *Mr. Coler, Assistant Cashier*. The sunburned blond man who sat there greeted Guild eagerly.

Guild sat down and said: "Saw the papers this morning, I suppose."

"Yes. Thank the Lord for insurance."

"We ought to get him in time to get some of it back,"

Guild said. "I'd like to get a look at his account and whatever canceled checks are on hand."

"Surely." Coler got up from his desk and went away. When he came back he was carrying a thin pack of checks in one hand, a sheet of typed paper in the other. Sitting down, he looked at the sheet and said: "This is what happened: on the second of the month Wynant deposited that ten-thousand-dollar check on——"

"Bring it in himself?"

"No. He always mailed his deposits. It was a Modern Publishing Company check on the Madison Trust Company of New York. He had a balance of eleven hundred sixty-two dollars and fifty-five cents: the check brought it up to eleven thousand and so on. On the fifth a check"—he took one from the thin pack—"for nine thousand dollars to the order of Laura Porter came through the clearing house." He looked at the check. "Dated the third, the day after he deposited his check." He turned the check over. "It was deposited in the Golden Gate Trust Company." He passed it across the desk to Guild. "Well, that left him with a balance of twenty-one hundred sixty-two dollars and fifty-five cents. Yesterday we received a wire telling us the New York check had been raised from one thousand to ten."

"Do you let your customers draw against out-of-town checks like that before they've had time to go through?"

Coler raised his eyebrows. "Old accounts of the standing of Mr. Wynant—yes."

"He's got a swell standing now," Guild said. "What other checks are there in there?"

Coler looked through them. His eyes brightened. He said: "There are two more Laura Porter ones—a thousand and a seven hundred and fifty. The rest seem to be simply salaries and household expenses." He passed them to Guild.

Guild examined the checks slowly one by one. Then he said: "See if you can find out how long this has been going on and how much of it."

Coler willingly rose and went away. He was gone half an hour. When he returned he said: "As near as I can learn, she's been getting checks for several months at least and has been getting about all he deposited, with not much more than enough left over to cover his ordinary expenses."

Guild said, "Thanks," softly through cigarette-smoke.

From the Seaman's National Bank, Guild went to the Golden Gate Trust Company in Montgomery Street. A girl stopped typewriting to carry his card into the cashier's office and presently ushered him into the office. There he shook hands with a round white-haired man who said: "Glad to see you, Mr. Guild. Which of us criminals are you looking for now?"

"I don't know whether I'm looking for any this time. You've got a depositor named Laura Porter. I'd like to get her address."

The cashier's smile set. "Now, now, I'm always willing to do all I can to help you chaps, but——"

Guild said: "She may have had something to do with gypping the Seaman's National out of eight thou."

Curiosity took some of the stiffness from the cashier's smile.

Guild said: "I don't know that she had a finger in it, but it's because I think she might that I'm here. All I want's her address—now—and I won't want anything else unless I'm sure."

The cashier rubbed his lips together, frowned, cleared his throat, finally said: "Well, if I give it to you you'll understand it's——"

"Strictly confidential," Guild said, "just like the information that the Seaman's been nicked."

Five minutes later he was leaving the Golden Gate Trust Company carrying, in a pocket, a slip of paper on which was written *Laura Porter, 1157 Leavenworth.*

He caught a cable car and rode up California Street. When his car passed the Cathedral Apartments he stood up suddenly and he left the car at the next corner, walking back to the apartment-building.

At the desk he said: "Miss Helen Robier."

The man on the other side of the counter shook his head. "We've nobody by that name—unless she's visiting someone."

"Can you tell me if she lived here—say—five months ago?"

"I'll try." He went back and spoke to another man. The other man came over to Guild. "Yes," he said, "Miss Robier did live here, but she's dead."

"Dead?"

"She was killed in an automobile accident the Fourth of July."

Guild pursed his lips. "Have you a MacWilliams here?"

"No."

"Ever have one?"

"I don't think so. I'll look it up." When he came back he was positive. "No."

Outside the Cathedral, Guild looked at his watch. It was a quarter to twelve. He walked over to his hotel. Boyer rose from a chair in the lobby and came to meet him, saying: "Good morning. How are you? Anything new?"

Guild shrugged. "Some things that might mean something. Let's do our talking over a lunch-table." He turned beside the District Attorney and guided him into the hotel grill.

When they were seated and had given their orders he told Boyer about his conversation with the Fremonts, the shot that had interrupted them, and their search for Wynant that had resulted in their finding his car; about his conversation with Chris—"Christopher Maxim," he said, "book-critic on the *Dispatch*"; about his visit to the Manchu and his meeting Elsa Fremont there; and about his visits that morning to the two banks and the apartment-house. He spoke rapidly, wasting few words, missing no salient point.

"Do you suppose Wynant went to that Chinese restaurant, knowing the girl worked there, to find out where she and her brother lived?" Boyer asked when Guild had finished.

"Not if he'd been at Fremont's house raising hell a couple of weeks ago."

Boyer's face flushed. "That's right. Well, do you——?"

"Let me know what's doing on your end," Guild said, "and maybe we can do our supposing together. Wait till this waiter gets out of the way."

When their food had been put in front of them and they were alone again the District Attorney said: "I told you about Lane seeing Wynant going in this Chinese place."

Guild said, "Yes. How about the finger-prints?" and put some food in his mouth.

"I had the place gone over and we took the prints of everybody we knew had been there, but the matching-up hadn't been done when I left early this morning."

"Didn't forget to take the dead girl's?"

"Oh, no. And you were in there: you can send us yours."

"All right, though I made a point of not touching anything. Any reports from the general alarm?"

"None."

"Anyway, we know he came to San Francisco. How about the circulars?"

"They're being printed now—photo, description, handwriting specimens. We'll get out a new batch when we've got his finger-prints: I wanted to get something out quick."

"Fine. I asked the police here to get us some of his prints off the car. What else happened on your end?"

"That's about all."

"Didn't get anything out of his papers?"

"Nothing. Outside of what seemed to be notes for his work there wasn't a handful of papers. You can look at them yourself when you come up."

Guild, eating, nodded as if he were thoroughly satisfied. "We'll go up for a look at Miss Porter first thing this afternoon," he said, "and maybe something'll come of that."

"Do you suppose she was blackmailing him?"

"People have blackmailed people," Guild admitted.

"I'm just talking at random," the District Attorney said a bit sheepishly, "letting whatever pops into my mind come out."

"Keep it up," Guild said encouragingly.

"Do you suppose she could be a daughter he had by that actress wife in Paris?"

"We can try to find out what happened to her and the children. Maybe Columbia Forrest was his daughter."

"But you know what the situation was up there," Boyer protested. "That would be incest."

"It's happened before," Guild said gravely. "That's why they've got a name for it."

*

Guild pushed the button beside Laura Porter's name in the vestibule of a small brown stone apartment-building at 1157 Leavenworth Street. Boyer, breathing heavily, stood beside him. There was no response. There was no response the second and third times he pushed the button, but when he touched the one labeled *Manager* the door-lock buzzed.

They opened the door and went into a dim lobby. A door straight ahead of them opened and a woman said: "Yes? What is it?" She was small and sharp-featured, grey-haired, hook-nosed, bright-eyed.

Guild advanced towards her saying: "We wanted to see Miss Laura Porter—three ten—but she doesn't answer the bell."

"I don't think she's in," the grey-haired woman said. "She's not in much. Can I take a message?"

"When do you expect her back?"

"I don't know, I'm sure."

"Do you know when she went out?"

"No, sir. Sometimes I see my people when they come in and go out and sometimes I don't. I don't watch them and Miss Porter I see less than any."

"Oh, she's not here most of the time?"

"I don't know, mister. So long as they pay their rent and don't make too much noise I don't bother them."

"Them? Does she live with somebody?"

"No. I meant them—all my people here."

Guild turned to the District Attorney. "Here. One of your cards."

Boyer fumbled for his cards, got one of them out, and handed it to Guild, who gave it to the woman.

"We want a little information about her," the dark man said in a low confidential voice while she was squinting at the card in the dim light. "She's all right as far as we know, but——"

The woman's eyes, when she raised them, were wide and inquisitive. "What is it?" she asked.

Guild leaned down towards her impressively. "How long has she been here?" he asked in a stage whisper.

"Almost six months," she replied. "It is six months."

"Does she have many visitors?"

"I don't know. I don't remember ever seeing any, but I don't pay much attention and when I see people coming in here I don't know what apartment they're going to."

Guild straightened, put his left hand out, and pressed an electric-light-button, illuminating the lobby. He put his right hand to his inner coat-pocket and brought out pictures of Wynant and his dead secretary. He gave them to the woman. "Ever see either of these?"

She looked at the man's picture and shook her head. "No," she said, "and that ain't a man I'd ever forget if I'd once seen him." She looked at Columbia Forrest's picture. "That!" she cried. "That *is* Miss Porter!"

CHAPTER SIX

Boyer looked round-eyed at Guild.

The dark man, after a little pause, spoke to the woman. "That's Columbia Forrest," he said, "the girl who was killed up in Hell Bend yesterday."

The woman's eyes became round as the District Attorney's. "Well!" she exclaimed, looking at the photograph again, "I never would've thought she was a thief. Why, she was such a pleasant mild-looking little thing——"

"A thief?" Boyer asked incredulously.

"Why, yes." She raised puzzled eyes from the photograph. "At least that's what the paper says, about her going——"

"What paper?"

"The afternoon paper." Her face became bright, eager. "Didn't you see it?"

"No. Have you——?"

"Yes. I'll show you." She turned quickly and went through the doorway open behind her.

Guild, pursing his lips a little, raising his eyebrows, looked at Boyer.

The District Attorney whispered loudly: "She wasn't blackmailing him? She was stealing from him?"

Guild shook his head. "We don't know anything yet," he said.

The woman hurried back to them carrying a newspaper. She turned the newspaper around and thrust it into Guild's hand, leaning over it, tapping the paper with a forefinger. "There it is." Her voice was metallic with excitement. "That's it. You read that."

Boyer went around behind the dark man to his other side, where he stood close to him, almost hanging on his arm, craning for a better view of the paper.

They read:

MURDERED SECRETARY KNOWN
TO N.Y. POLICE

NEW YORK, Sept. 8 (A.P.).—Columbia Forrest, in connection with whose murder at Hell Bend, Calif., yesterday the police are now searching for Walter Irving Wynant, famous scientist, philosopher and author, was convicted of shoplifting in New York City three years ago, according to former police magistrate Erle Gardner.

Ex-magistrate Gardner stated that the girl pleaded guilty to a charge brought against her by two department stores and was given a six-month sentence by him, but that the sentence was suspended due to the intervention of Walter Irving Wynant, who offered to reimburse the stores and to give her employment as his secretary. The girl had formerly been a typist in the employ of a Wall St. brokerage house.

Boyer began to speak, but Guild forestalled him by addressing the woman crisply: "That's interesting. Thanks a lot. Now we'd like a look at her rooms."

The woman, chattering with the utmost animation, took them upstairs and unlocked the door of apartment 310. She went into the apartment ahead of them, but the dark man, holding the corridor-door open, said pointedly: "We'll see you again before we leave." She went away reluctantly and Guild shut the door.

"Now we're getting somewhere," Boyer said.

"Maybe we are," Guild agreed.

Words ran swiftly from the District Attorney's mouth. "Do

you suppose she handled the details of his banking and forged those Laura Porter checks and juggled his books to cover them? The chances are he didn't spend much and thought he had a fat balance. Then when she had his account drained she raised the last check, drew against it, and was running away?"

"Maybe, but——" Guild stared thoughtfully at the District Attorney's feet.

"But what?"

Guild raised his eyes. "Why didn't she run away while she was away instead of driving back there in another man's car to tell him she was going away with another man?"

Boyer had a ready answer. "Thieves are funny and women are funny and when you get a woman thief there's no telling what she'll do or why. She could've had a quarrel with him and wanted to rub it in that she was going. She could have forgotten something up there. She might've had some idea of throwing suspicion away from the bank-account-juggling for awhile. She could've had any number of reasons, they need not've been sensible ones. She could've——"

Guild smiled politely. "Let's see what the place'll tell us."

On a table in the living-room they found a flat brass key that unlocked the corridor-door. Nothing else they found anywhere except in the bathroom seemed to interest them. In the bathroom, on a table, they found an obviously new razor holding a blade freshly spotted with rust, an open tube of shaving-cream from which very little had been squeezed, a new shaving-brush that had been used and not rinsed, and a pair of scissors. Hanging over the edge of the tub beside the table was a face-towel on which smears of lather had dried.

Guild blew cigarette-smoke at these things and said: "Looks like our thin man came here to get rid of his whiskers."

Boyer, frowning in perplexity, asked: "But how would he know?"

"Maybe he got it out of her before he killed her and let himself in with the key on the table—hers." Guild pointed his cigarette at the scissors. "They make it look like him and not—well—Fremont for instance. He'd need them for the whiskers and the things are new, as if he'd bought them on his way here." He bent over to examine the table, the inside of the tub, the floor. "Though I don't see any hairs."

"What does it mean, then—his coming here?" the District Attorney asked anxiously.

The dark man smiled a little. "Something or other, maybe," he said. He straightened from his examination of the floor. "He could've been careful not to drop any of his whiskers when he hacked them off, though God knows why he'd try." He looked thoughtfully at the shaving-tools on the table. "We ought to do some more talking to her boy friend."

Downstairs they found the manager waiting in the lobby for them. She stood in front of them using a bright smile to invite speech.

Guild said: "Thanks a lot. How far ahead is her rent paid?"

"Up to the fifteenth of the month it's paid."

"Then it won't cost you anything to let nobody in there till then. Don't and if you go in don't touch anything. There'll be some policemen up. Sure you didn't see a man in there early last night?"

"Yes, sir, I'm sure I didn't see anybody go in there or come out of there, though the Lord knows they could if they had a key without me——"

"How many keys did she have?"

"I only gave her one, but she could've had them made, all she wanted to, and likely enough did if she was—— What'd she do, mister?"

"I don't know. She get much mail?"

"Well, not so very much and most of that looked like ads and things."

"Remember where any of it was from?"

The woman's face colored. "That I don't. I don't look at my people's mail like that. I was always one to mind my own business as long as they paid their rent and don't make so much noise that other people——"

"That's right," Guild said. "Thanks a lot." He gave her one of his cards. "I'll probably be back, but if anything happens—anything that looks like it might have anything to do with her—will you call me up? If I'm not there leave the message."

"Yes, sir, I certainly will," she promised. "Is there——?"

"Thanks a lot," Guild said once more and he and the District Attorney went out.

They were sitting in the District Attorney's automobile when Boyer asked: "What do you suppose Wynant left the key there for, if it was hers and he used it?"

"Why not? He only went there to shave and maybe frisk the place. He wouldn't take a chance on going there again and leaving it there was easier than throwing it away."

Boyer nodded dubiously and put the automobile in motion. Guild directed him to the vicinity of the Golden Gate Trust Company, where they parked the automobile. After a few minutes' wait they were shown into the white-haired cashier's office.

He rose from his chair as they entered. Neither his smile nor his bantering "You are shadowing me" concealed his uneasy curiosity.

Guild said: "Mr. Bliss, this is Mr. Boyer, District Attorney of Whitfield County."

Boyer and Bliss shook hands. The cashier motioned his visitors into chairs.

Guild said: "Our Laura Porter is the Columbia Forrest that was murdered up at Hell Bend yesterday."

Bliss's face reddened. There was something akin to indignation in the voice with which he said: "That's preposterous, Guild."

The dark man's smile was small with malice. "You mean as soon as anybody becomes one of your depositors they're sure of a long and happy life?"

The cashier smiled then. "No, but——" He stopped smiling. "Did she have any part in the Seaman's National swindle?"

"She did," Guild replied and added, still with smiling malice, "unless you're sure none of your clients could possibly touch anybody else's nickels."

The cashier, paying no attention to the latter part of Guild's speech, squirmed in his chair and looked uneasily at the door.

The dark man said: "We'd like to get a transcript of her account and I want to send a handwriting man down for a look at her checks, but we're in a hurry now. We'd like to know when she opened her account, what references she gave, and how much she's got in it."

Bliss pressed one of the buttons on his desk, but before anyone came into the room he rose with a muttered "Excuse me" and went out.

Guild smiled after him. "He'll be ten pounds lighter before he learns whether he's been gypped or not and twenty if he finds he has."

When the cashier returned he shut the door, leaned back against it, and spoke as if he had rehearsed his words. "Miss Porter's account shows a balance of thirty-eight dollars and fifty cents. She drew out twelve thousand dollars in cash yesterday morning."

"Herself?"

"Yes."

Guild addressed Boyer: "We'll show the teller her photo on the way out just to be doubly sure." He turned to the cashier again: "And about the date she opened it and the references she gave?"

The white-haired man consulted a card in his hand. "She opened her account on November the eighth, last year," he said. "The references she gave were Francis X. Kearny, proprietor of the Manchu Restaurant on Grant Avenue, and Walter Irving Wynant."

CHAPTER SEVEN

"The Manchu's only five or six blocks from here," Guild told Boyer as they left the Golden Gate Trust Company. "We might as well stop in now and see what we can get out of Francis Xavier Kearny."

"Do you know him?"

"Uh-uh, except by rep. He's in solid with the police here and is supposed to be plenty tough."

The District Attorney nodded. He chewed his lips in frowning silence until they reached his automobile. Then he said: "What we've learned today seems to tie him, her, the Fremonts, and Wynant all up together."

"Yes," Guild agreed, "it seems to."

"Or do you suppose she could have given Wynant's name because she knew, being his secretary, she could catch the bank's letter of inquiry and answer it without his knowing anything about it?"

"That sounds reasonable enough," the dark man said, "but there's Wynant's visit to the Manchu yesterday."

The District Attorney's frown deepened. "What do you suppose Wynant was up to—if he was in it with them?"

"I don't know. I know somebody's got the twelve thousand she drew out yesterday. I know I want six of it for the Seaman's National. Turn left at the next corner."

They went into the Manchu Restaurant together. A smiling Chinese waiter told them Mr. Kearny was not in, was not expected until nine o'clock that night. They could not learn where he might be found before nine o'clock. They left the restaurant and got into Boyer's automobile again.

"Guerrero Street," Guild said, "though we ought to stop first at a booth where I can phone the police about the Leavenworth Street place and the office to pick up cancelled checks from both banks, so we'll know if any of them are forgeries." He cupped his hands around the cigarette he was lighting. "This'll do. Pull in here."

The District Attorney turned the automobile in at the Mark Hopkins.

Guild, saying, "I'll hurry," jumped out and went indoors. When he came out ten minutes later his face was thoughtful. "The police didn't find any finger-prints on Wynant's car," he said. "I wonder why."

"He could've taken the trouble to——"

"Uh huh," the dark man agreed, "but I'm wondering why he did. Well, on to Guerrero Street. If Fremont's not back from Hell Bend we'll see what we can shake the girl down for. She ought to know where Kearny hangs out in the daytime."

A Filipino maid opened the Fremonts' door.

"Is Mr. Charles Fremont in?" Guild asked.

"No, sir."

"Miss Fremont?"

"I'll see if she's up yet."

The maid took them into the living-room and went up-stairs.

Guild pointed at the broken window-pane. "That's where the shot was taken at him." He pointed at the hole in the green wall. "That's where it hit." He took a misshapen bullet from his vest-pocket and showed it to Boyer. "It."

Boyer's face had become animated. He moved close to Guild and began to talk in a low excited voice. "Do you suppose they could all have been in some game together and Wynant discovered that his secretary was double-crossing him besides getting ready to go off with——"

Guild jerked his head at the hall-door. "Sh-h-h."

Light footsteps ran down the stairs and Elsa Fremont in a brightly figured blue *haori* coat over light green silk pajamas entered the room. "Good morning," she said, holding a hand out to Guild. "It is for me anyway." She used her other hand to partly cover a yawn. "We didn't close the jernt till nearly eight this morning."

Guild introduced the District Attorney to her, then asked: "Your brother go up to Hell Bend?"

"Yes. He was leaving when I got home." She dropped down on the sofa with a foot drawn up under her. Her feet were stockingless in blue embroidered slippers. "Do sit down."

The District Attorney sat in a chair facing her. The dark man went over to the sofa to sit beside her. "We've just come from the Manchu," he said.

Her lanceolate eyes became a little narrower. "Have a nice lunch?" she asked.

Guild smiled and said: "We didn't go there for that."

She said: "Oh." Her eyes were clear and unwary now.

Guild said: "We went to see Frank Kearny."

"Did you?"

"See him? No."

"There's not much chance of finding him there during the day," she said carelessly, "but he's there every night."

"So we were told." Guild took cigarettes from his pocket and held them out to her. "Where do you think we could find him now?"

The girl shook her red head as she took a cigarette. "You can search me. He used to live in Sea Cliff, but I don't know where he moved to." She leaned forward as Guild held his lighter to her cigarette. "Won't whatever you want to see him about wait till night?" she asked when her cigarette was burning.

Guild offered his cigarettes to the District Attorney, who shook his head and murmured: "No, thanks."

The dark man put a cigarette between his lips and set fire to it before he answered the girl's question. Then he said: "We wanted to find out what he knows about Columbia Forrest."

Elsa Fremont said evenly: "I don't think Frank knew her at all."

"Yes, he did, at least as Laura Porter."

Her surprise seemed genuine. She leaned towards Guild. "Say that again."

"Columbia Forrest," Guild said in a deliberately monotonous voice, "had an apartment on Leavenworth Street where she was known as Laura Porter and Frank Kearny knew her."

The girl, frowning, said earnestly: "If you didn't seem to know what you're talking about I wouldn't believe it."

"But you do believe it?"

She hesitated, finally said: "Well, knowing Frank, I'll say it's possible."

"You didn't know about the Leavenworth Street place?"

She shook her head, meeting his gaze with candid eyes. "I didn't."

"Did you know she'd ever gone as Laura Porter?"

"No."

"Ever hear of Laura Porter?"

"No."

Guild drew smoke in and breathed it out. "I think I believe you," he said in a casual tone. "But your brother must have known about it."

She frowned at the cigarette in her hand, at the foot she was not sitting on, and then at Guild's dark face. "You don't have to believe me," she said slowly, "but I honestly don't think he did."

Guild smiled politely. "I can believe you and still think you're wrong," he said.

"I wish," she said naively, "you'd believe me and think I'm right."

Guild moved his cigarette in a vague gesture. "What does your brother do, Miss Fremont?" he asked. "For a living, I mean?"

"He's managing a couple of fighters now," she said, "only one of them isn't. The other's Sammy Deep."

Guild nodded. "The Chinese bantam."

"Yes. Charley thinks he's got a champ in him."

"He's a good boy. Who's the other?"

"A stumble-bum named Terry Moore. If you go to fights much you're sure to've seen him knocked out."

Boyer spoke for the first time since he had declined a cigarette. "Miss Fremont, where were you born?"

"Right here in San Francisco, up on Pacific Avenue."

Boyer seemed disappointed. He asked: "And your brother?"

"Here in San Francisco too."

Disappointment deepened in the District Attorney's young face and there was little hopefulness in his voice asking: "Was your mother also an actress, an entertainer?"

The girl shook her head with emphasis. "She was a school-teacher. Why?"

Boyer's explanation was given more directly to Guild. "I was thinking of Wynant's marriage in Paris."

The dark man nodded. "Fremont's too old. He's only ten or twelve years younger than Wynant." He smiled guilelessly. "Want another idea to play with? Fremont and the dead girl have the same initials—C.F."

Elsa Fremont laughed. "More than that," she said, "they had the same birthdays—May twenty-seventh—though of course Charley is older."

Guild smiled carelessly at this information while the District Attorney's eyes took on a troubled stare.

The dark man looked at his watch. "Did your brother say how long he was going to stay in Hell Bend?" he asked.

"No."

Guild spoke to Boyer. "Why don't you call up and see if he's there. If he is, ask him to wait for us. If he's left, we'll wait here for him."

The District Attorney rose from his chair, but before he could speak the girl was asking anxiously: "Is there anything special you want to see Charley about? Anything I could tell you?"

"You said you didn't know," Guild said. "It's the Laura Porter angle we want to find out about."

"Oh." Some of her anxiety went away.

"Your brother knows Frank Kearny, doesn't he?" Guild asked.

"Oh, yes. That's how I happened to go to work there."

"Is there a phone here we can use?"

"Certainly." She jumped up and, saying, "Back here," opened a door into an adjoining room. When the District Attorney had passed through she shut the door behind him and returned to her place on the sofa beside Guild. "Have you learned anything else?" she asked, "anything besides about her being known as Laura Porter and having the apartment?"

"Some odds and ends," he said, "but it's too early to say what they'll add up to when they're sorted. I didn't ask you whether Kearny and Wynant know each other, did I?"

She shook her head from side to side. "If they do I don't know it. I don't. I'm telling you the truth, Mr. Guild."

"All right, but Wynant was seen going into the Manchu."

"I know, but——" She finished the sentence with a jerk of her shoulders. She moved closer to Guild on the sofa. "You don't think Charley has done anything he oughtn't've done, do you?"

Guild's face was placid. "I won't lie to you," he said. "I think everybody connected with the job has done things they oughtn't've done."

She made an impatient grimace. "I believe you're just trying to make things confusing, to make work for yourself," she said, "so you'll be looking like you're doing something even if you can't find Wynant. Why don't you find him?" Her voice was rising. "That's all you've got to do. Why don't you find him instead of trying to make trouble for everybody else? He's the only one that did anything. He killed her and tried to kill Charley and he's the one you want—not Charley, not me, not Frank. Wynant's the one you want."

Guild laughed indulgently. "You make it sound simple as hell," he told her. "I wish you were right."

Her indignation faded. She put a hand on his hand. Her eyes held a frightened gleam. "There isn't anything else, is there?" she asked, "something we don't know about?"

Guild put his other hand over to pat the back of hers. "There is," he assured her pleasantly. "There's a lot none of us knows and what we do know don't make sense."

"Then——"

The District Attorney opened the door and stood in the doorway. He was pale and he was sweating. "Fremont isn't up there," he said blankly. "He didn't go up there."

Elsa Fremont said, "Jesus Christ!" under her breath.

CHAPTER EIGHT

Night was settling between the mountains when Guild and Boyer arrived at Hell Bend. The District Attorney drove into the village, saying: "We'll go to Ray's. We can come back to Wynant's later if you want to."

"All right," Guild said, "unless Fremont might be there."

"He won't if he came up to see the body. She's at Schumach's funeral parlor."

"Inquest tomorrow?"

"Yes, unless there's some reason for putting it off."

"There's none that I know of," Guild said. He looked side-wise at Boyer. "You'll see that as little as possible comes out at the inquest?"

"Oh, yes!"

They were in Hell Bend now, running between irregularly spaced cottages towards lights that glittered up along the rail-road, but before they reached the railroad they turned off to the right and stopped before a small square house where softer lights burned behind yellow blinds.

Callaghan, the raw-boned blond Deputy Sheriff, opened the door for them. He said, "Hello, Bruce," to the District Attorney and nodded politely if without warmth at Guild.

They went indoors, into an inexpensively furnished room where three men sat at a table playing stud poker and a huge

German sheep dog lay attentive in a corner. Boyer spoke to the three men and introduced Guild while the Deputy Sheriff sat down at the table and picked up his cards.

One of the men—thin, bent, old, white-haired, white-mustached—was Callaghan's father. Another—stocky, broad-browed over wide-spaced clear eyes, sunburned almost dark as Guild—was Ross Lane. The third—small, pale, painfully neat—was Schumach, the undertaker.

Boyer turned from the introductions to Callaghan. "You're sure Fremont didn't show up?"

The Deputy Sheriff replied without looking up from his cards. "He didn't show up at Wynant's place. King's been there all day. And he didn't show up at Ben's to—to see her. Where else'd he go if he came up here?" He pushed a chip out on the table. "I'll crack it." He had two kings in his hand.

Schumach pushed a chip out and said: "No, sir, he didn't show up to look at the *corpus delicti.*"

Lane dropped his cards face-down on the table. The elder Callaghan put in a chip and picked up the rest of the deck.

His son said, "Three cards," and then to Boyer: "You can phone King if you want." He moved his head to indicate the telephone by the door.

Boyer looked questioningly at Guild, who said: "Might as well."

Guild addressed a question to Lane while the other three men at the table were making their bets and Boyer was using the telephone. "You're the man who saw Wynant going into the Manchu?"

"Yes." Lane's voice was a quiet bass.

"Was anybody with him?"

Lane said, "No," with certainty, then hesitated thoughtfully and added: "unless they went in ahead of him. I don't think so, but it's possible. He was just going in when I saw him and it could've happened that he'd stopped to shut his car-door or take his key out or something and whoever was with him had gone on ahead."

"Did you see enough of him to make sure it was him?"

"I couldn't go wrong on that, even if I did see only his back. My place being next to his, I guess I've seen a lot more of him than most people around here and then, tall and skinny, with those high shoulders and that funny walk, you couldn't miss him. Besides, his car was there."

"Had he cut his whiskers off, or was he still wearing them?"

Lane opened his eyes wide and laughed. "By God, I don't know," he said. "I heard he shaved them, but I never thought of that. You've got me there. His back was to me and I wouldn't't've seen them unless they happened to be sticking out sideways or I got a slanting look at him. I don't remember seeing them, yet I might've and thought nothing of it. If I'd seen his face without them it's a cinch I'd've noticed, but—— You've got me there, brother."

"Know him pretty well?"

Lane picked up the cards the younger Callaghan dealt him and smiled. "Well, I don't guess anybody could say they know him pretty well." He spread his cards apart to look at them.

"Did you know the Forrest girl pretty well?"

The Deputy Sheriff's face began to redden. He said somewhat sharply to the undertaker: "Can you do it?"

The undertaker rapped the table with his knuckles to say he could not.

Lane had a pair of sixes and a pair of fours. He said, "I'll do it," pushed out a chip and replied to the dark man's question: "I don't know just what you mean by that. I knew her. She used to come over sometimes and watch me work the dogs when I had them over in the field near their place."

Boyer had finished telephoning and had come to stand beside Guild. He explained: "Ross raises and trains police dogs."

The elder Callaghan said: "I hope she didn't have you going around talking to yourself like she had Ray." His voice was a nasal whine.

His son slammed his cards down on the table. His face was red and swollen. In a loud accusing tone he began: "I guess I ought to go around chasing after——"

"Ray! Ray!" A stringy white-haired woman in faded blue had come a step in from the next room. Her voice was chiding. "You oughtn't to——"

"Well, make him stop jawing about her, then," the Deputy Sheriff said. "She was as good as anybody else and a lot better than most I know." He glowered at the table in front of him.

In the uncomfortable silence that followed, Boyer said: "Good evening, Mrs. Callaghan. How are you?"

"Just fine," she said. "How's Lucy?"

"She's always well, thanks. This is Mr. Guild, Mrs. Callaghan."

Guild bowed murmuring something polite. The woman ducked her head at him and took a backward step. "If you can't play cards without rowing I wish you'd stop," she told her son and husband as she withdrew.

Boyer addressed Guild: "King, the Deputy stationed at Wynant's place, says he hasn't seen anything of Fremont all day."

Guild looked at his watch. "He's had eleven hours to make it in," he said. He smiled pleasantly. "Or eleven hours start if he headed in another direction."

The undertaker leaned over the table. "You think——?"

"I don't know," Guild said. "I don't know anything. That's the hell of it. We don't know anything."

"There's nothing to know," the Deputy Sheriff said querulously, "except that Wynant was jealous and killed her and ran away and you haven't been able to find him."

Guild, staring bleakly at the younger Callaghan, said nothing.

Boyer cleared his throat. "Well, Ray," he began, "Mr. Guild and I have found quite a bit of confusing evidence in the——"

The elder Callaghan prodded his son with a gnarled forefinger. "Did you tell them about that Smoot boy?"

The Deputy Sheriff pulled irritably away from his father's finger. "That don't amount to nothing," he said, "and, besides, what chance've I got to tell anything with all the talking you've been doing?"

"What was it?" Boyer asked eagerly.

"It don't amount to nothing. Just that this kid—maybe you know him, Pete Smoot's boy—had a telegram for Wynant and took it up to his house. He got there at five minutes after two. He wrote down the time because nobody answered the door and he had to poke the telegram under the door."

"This was yesterday afternoon?" Guild asked.

"Yes," the Deputy Sheriff said gruffly. "Well, the kid says the blue car, the one she drove out from the city in, was there then and Wynant's wasn't."

"He knew Wynant's car?" Guild asked.

Pointedly ignoring Guild, the Deputy Sheriff said: "He says there wasn't any other car there, either in the shed or outside. He'd've seen it if there was. So he put the telegram under the door, got on his bike, and rode back to the telegraph office. Coming back along the road he says he saw the Hopkinses cutting across the field. They'd been down at Hooper's buying Hopkins a suit. The kid says they didn't see him and they were too far from the road for him to holler at them about the telegram." The Deputy Sheriff's face began to redden again. "So if that's right, and I guess it is, they'd've got back to the house, I reckon, around twenty past two—not before that, anyway." He picked up the cards and began to shuffle them, though he had dealt the last hand. "You see, that—well—it don't mean anything or help us any."

Guild had finished lighting a cigarette. He asked Callaghan, before Boyer could speak: "What do you figure? She was alone in the house and didn't answer the kid's knock because she was hurrying to get her packing done before Wynant came home? Or because she was already dead?"

Boyer began in a tone of complete amazement: "But the Hopkinses said——"

Guild said: "Wait. Let Callaghan answer."

Callaghan said in a voice hoarse with anger: "Let Callaghan answer if he wants to, but he don't happen to want to, and what do you think of that?" He glared at Guild. "I got nothing to do with you." He glared at Boyer. "You got nothing to do with me. I'm a deputy sheriff and Petersen's my boss. Go to him for anything you want. Understand that?"

Guild's dark face was impassive. His voice was even. "You're not the first deputy sheriff that ever tried to make a name for himself by holding back information." He started to put his cigarette in his mouth, lowered it, and said: "You got the Hopkinses' call. You were first on the scene, weren't you? What'd you find there that you've kept to yourself?"

Callaghan stood up. Lane and the undertaker rose hastily from their places at the table.

Boyer said: "Now, wait, gentlemen, there's no use of our quarreling."

Guild, smiling, addressed the Deputy Sheriff blandly: "You're not in such a pretty spot, Callaghan. You had a yen for the girl. You were likely to be just as jealous as Wynant when you heard she was going off with Fremont. You've got a childish sort of hot temper. Where were you around two o'clock yesterday afternoon?"

Callaghan, snarling unintelligible curses, lunged at Guild.

Lane and the undertaker sprang between the two men, struggling with the Deputy Sheriff. Lane turned his head to give the growling dog in the corner a quieting command. The elder Callaghan did not get up, but leaned over the table whining remonstrances at his son's back. Mrs. Callaghan came in and began to scold her son.

Boyer said nervously to Guild: "I think we'd better go."

Guild shrugged. "Whatever you say, though I would like to know where he spent the early part of yesterday afternoon." He glanced calmly around the room and followed Boyer to the front door.

Outside, the District Attorney exclaimed: "Good God! You don't think Ray killed her!"

"Why not?" Guild snapped the remainder of his cigarette to the middle of the roadbed in a long red arc. "I don't know. Somebody did and I'll tell you a secret. I'm damned if I think Wynant did."

CHAPTER NINE

Hopkins and a tall younger man with a reddish mustache came out of Wynant's house when Boyer stopped his automobile in front of it.

The District Attorney got down on the ground saying: "Good evening, gentlemen." Indicating the red-mustached man, he said to Guild: "This is Deputy Sheriff King, Mr. Guild. Mr. Guild," he explained, "is working with me."

The Deputy Sheriff nodded, looking the dark man up and down. "Yes," he said, "I been hearing about him. Howdy, Mr. Guild."

Guild's nod included Hopkins and King.

"No sign of Fremont yet?" Boyer asked.

"No."

Guild spoke: "Is Mrs. Hopkins still up?"

"Yes, sir," her husband said, "she's doing some sewing."

The four men went indoors.

Mrs. Hopkins, sitting in a rocking chair hemming an un-bleached linen handkerchief, started to rise, but sank back in her chair with a "How do you do" when Boyer said: "Don't get up. We'll find chairs."

Guild did not sit down. Standing by the door, he lit a ciga-rette while the others were finding seats. Then he addressed the Hopkinses: "You told us it was around three o'clock yes-terday afternoon that Columbia Forrest got back from the city."

"Oh, no, sir!" The woman dropped her sewing on her knees. "Or at least we never meant to say anything like that. We meant to say it was around three o'clock when we heard them—him—quarreling. You can ask Mr. Callaghan what time it was when I called him up and——"

"I'm asking you," Guild said in a pleasant tone. "Was she here when you got back from the village—from buying the suit—at two-twenty?"

The woman peered nervously through her spectacles at him. "Well, yes, sir, she was, if that's what time it was. I thought it was later, Mr. Gould, but if you say that's what time it was I guess you know, but she'd only just got home."

"How do you know that?"

"She said so. She called downstairs to know if it was us coming in and she said she'd just that minute got home."

"Was there a telegram under the door when you came in?"

The Hopkinses looked at each other in surprise and shook their heads. "No, there was not," the man said.

"Was he here?"

"Mr. Wynant?"

"Yes. Was he here when you got home?"

"Yes. I—I think he was?"

"Do you know?"

"Well, it—" she looked appealingly at her husband—"he was here when we heard them fighting not much after that, so he must've been——"

"Or did he come in after you got back?"

"Not—we didn't see him come in."

"Hear him?"

She shook her head certainly. "No, sir."

"Was his car here when you got back?"

The woman started to say Yes, stopped midway, and looked questioningly at her husband. His round face was uncomfortably confused. "We—we didn't notice," she stammered.

"Would you have heard him if he'd driven up while you were here?"

"I don't know, Mr. Gould. I think—I don't know. If I was in the kitchen with the water running and Willie—Mr. Hopkins that is—don't hear any too good anyway. Maybe we——"

Guild turned his back to her and addressed the District Attorney. "There's no sense to their story. If I were you I'd throw them in the can and charge them with the murder."

Boyer gaped. Hopkins's face went yellow. His wife leaned over her sewing and began to cry. King stared at the dark man as at some curio seen for the first time.

The District Attorney was the first to speak. "But—but why?"

"You don't believe them, do you?" Guild asked in an amused tone.

"I don't know. I——"

"If it was up to me I'd do it," Guild said good-naturedly, "but if you want to wait till we locate Wynant, all right. I want to get some more specimens of Wynant's and the girl's handwriting." He turned back to the Hopkinses and asked casually: "Who was Laura Porter?"

The name seemed to mean nothing to them. Hopkins shook his head dumbly. His wife did not stop crying.

"I didn't think you knew," Guild said. "Let's go up and get those scratch samples, Boyer."

The District Attorney's face, as he went upstairs with Guild, was a theater where anxiety played. He stared at the dark man with troubled pleading eyes. "I—I wish you'd tell me why you think Wynant didn't do it," he said in a wheedling voice, "and why you think Ray and the Hopkinses are mixed up in it." He made a despairing gesture with his hands. "What do you really think, Guild? Do you really suspect these people or are you——?" His face flushed under the dark man's steady unreadable gaze and he lowered his eyes.

"I suspect everybody," Guild said in a voice that was devoid of feeling. "Where were you between two and three o'clock yesterday afternoon?"

Boyer jumped and a look of fear came into his young face. Then he laughed sheepishly and said: "Well, I suppose you're right. I want you to understand, Guild, that I keep asking you things not because I think you're off on the wrong track, but because I think you know so much more about this kind of thing than I do."

Guild was in San Francisco by two o'clock in the morning. He went straight to the Manchu.

Elsa Fremont was singing when he stepped out of the elevator. She was wearing a taffeta gown—snug of bodice, billowy of skirt—whereon great red roses were printed against a chalky blue background, with two rhinestone buckles holding a puffy sash in place. The song she sang had a recurring line, *Boom, chisel, chisel!*

When she had finished her second encore she started towards Guild's table, but two men and a woman at an intervening table stopped her, and it was ten minutes or more before she joined him. Her eyes were dark, her face and voice nervous. "Did you find Charley?"

Guild, on his feet, said: "No. He didn't go up to Hell Bend."

She sat down twisting her wrist-scarf, nibbling her lip, frowning.

The dark man sat down asking: "Did you think he'd gone there?"

She jerked her head up indignantly. "I told you I did. Don't you ever believe anything that anybody tells you?"

"Sometimes I do and am wrong," Guild said. He tapped a

cigarette on the table. "Wherever he's gone, he's got a new car and an all-day start."

She put her hands on the table suddenly, palms up in a suppliant gesture. "But why should he want to go anywhere else?"

Guild was looking at her hands. "I don't know, but he did." He bent his head further over her hands as if studying their lines. "Is Frank Kearny here now and can I talk to him?"

She uttered a brief throaty laugh. "Yes." Letting her hands lie as they were on the table, she turned her head and caught a passing waiter's attention. "Lee, ask Frank to come here." She looked at the dark man again, somewhat curiously. "I told him you wanted to see him. Was that all right?"

He was still studying her palms. "Oh, yes, sure," he said good-naturedly. "That would give him time to think."

She laughed again and took her hands off the table.

A man came to the table. He was a full six feet tall, but the width of his shoulders made him seem less than that. His face was broad and flat, his eyes small, his lips wide and thick, and when he smiled he displayed crooked teeth set apart. His age could have been anything between thirty-five and forty-five.

"Frank, this is Mr. Guild," Elsa Fremont said.

Kearny threw his right hand out with practiced heartiness. "Glad to know you, Guild."

They shook hands and Kearny sat down with them. The orchestra was playing *Love Is Like That* for dancers.

"Do you know Laura Porter?" Guild asked Kearny.

The proprietor shook his ugly head. "Never heard of her. Elsa asked me."

"Did you know Columbia Forrest?"

"No. All I know is she's the girl that got clipped up there in Whitfield County and I only know that from the papers and from Elsa."

"Know Wynant?"

"No, and if somebody saw him coming in here all I got to say is that if lots of people I don't know didn't come in here I couldn't stay in business."

"That's all right," Guild said pleasantly, "but here's the thing: when Columbia Forrest opened a bank-account seven months ago under the name of Laura Porter you were one of the references she gave the bank."

Kearny's grin was undisturbed. "That might be, right enough," he said, "but that still don't mean I know her." He put out a long arm and stopped a waiter. "Tell Sing to give you that bottle and bring ginger ale set-ups." He turned his attention to Guild again. "Look it, Guild. I'm running a joint. Suppose some guy from the Hall or the Municipal Building that can do me good or bad, or some guy that spends with me, comes to me and says he's got a friend—or a broad—that's hunting a job or wants to open some kind of account or get a bond, and can they use my name? Well, what the hell! It happens all the time."

Guild nodded. "Sure. Well, who asked you to OK Laura Porter?"

"Seven months ago?" Kearny scoffed. "A swell chance I got of remembering! Maybe I didn't even hear her name then."

"Maybe you did. Try to remember."

"No good," Kearny insisted. "I tried when Elsa first told me about you wanting to see me."

Guild said: "The other name she gave was Wynant's. Does that help?"

"No. I don't know him, don't know anybody that knows him."

"Charley Fremont knows him."

Kearny moved his wide shoulders carelessly. "I didn't know that," he said.

The waiter came, gave the proprietor a dark quart bottle, put glasses of cracked ice on the table, and began to open bottles of ginger ale.

Elsa Fremont said: "I told you I didn't think Frank knew anything about any of them."

"You did," the dark man said, "and now he's told me." He made his face solemnly thoughtful. "I'm glad he didn't contradict you."

Elsa stared at him while Kearny put whisky and the waiter ginger ale into the glasses.

The proprietor, patting the stopper into the bottle again, asked: "Is it your idea this fellow Wynant's still hanging around San Francisco?"

Elsa said in a low hoarse voice: "I'm scared! He tried to shoot Charley before. Where"—she put a hand on the dark man's wrist—"where is Charley?"

Before Guild could reply Kearny was saying to her: "It might help if you'd do some singing now and then for all that dough you're getting." He watched her walk out on the dance-floor and said to Guild: "The kid's worried. Think anything happened to Charley? Or did he have reasons to scram?"

"You people should ask me things," Guild said and drank.

The proprietor picked up his glass. "People can waste a lot of time," he said reflectively, "once they get the idea that people that don't know anything do." He tilted his glass abruptly, emptying most of its contents into his throat, set the glass down, and wiped his mouth with the back of his hand. "You sent a friend of mine over a couple of months ago—Deep Ying."

"I remember," Guild said. "He was the fattest of the three *boo how doy* who tried to spread their tong war out to include sticking up a Japanese bank."

"There was likely a tong angle to it, guns stashed there or something."

The dark man said, "Maybe," indifferently and drank again.

Kearny said: "His brother's here now."

Some of Guild's indifference went away. "Was he in on the job too?"

The proprietor laughed. "No," he said, "but you never can tell how close brothers are and I thought you'd like to know."

The dark man seemed to weigh this statement carefully. Then he said: "In that case maybe you ought to point him out to me."

"Sure." Kearny stood up grinning, raised a hand, and sat down.

Elsa Fremont was singing *Kitty From Kansas City.*

A plump Chinese with a round smooth merry face came between tables to their table. He was perhaps forty years old, of less than medium stature, and though his grey suit was of good quality it did not fit him. He halted beside Kearny and said: "How you do, Frank."

The proprietor said: "Mr. Guild, I want you to meet a friend of mine, Deep Kee."

"I'm your friend, you bet you." The Chinese, smiling broadly, ducked his head vigorously at both men.

Guild said: "Kearny tells me you're Deep Ying's brother."

"You bet you." Deep Kee's eyes twinkled merrily. "I hear about you, Mr. Guild. Number one detective. You catch 'em my brother. You play trick on 'em. You bet you."

Guild nodded and said solemnly: "No play trick on 'em, no catch 'em. You bet you."

The Chinese laughed heartily.

Kearny said: "Sit down and have a drink."

Deep Kee sat down beaming on Guild, who was lighting a cigarette, while the proprietor brought his bottle from beneath the table.

A woman at the next table, behind Guild, was saying oratorically: "I can always tell when I'm getting swacked because the skin gets tight across my forehead, but it don't ever do me any good because by that time I'm too swacked to care whether I'm getting swacked or not."

Elsa Fremont was finishing her song.

Guild asked Deep Kee: "You know Wynant?"

"Please, no."

"A thin man, tall, used to have whiskers before he cut them off," Guild went on. "Killed a woman up at Hell Bend."

The Chinese, smiling, shook his head from side to side.

"Ever been in Hell Bend?"

The smiling Chinese head continued to move from side to side.

Kearny said humorously: "He's a high-class murderer, Guild. He wouldn't take a job in the country."

Deep Kee laughed delightedly.

Elsa Fremont came to the table and sat down. She seemed tired and drank thirstily from her glass.

The Chinese, smiling, bowing, leaving his drink barely tasted, went away. Kearny, looking after him, told Guild: "That's a good guy to have liking you."

"Tong gunman?"

"I don't know. I know him pretty well, but I don't know that. You know how they are."

"I don't know," Guild said.

A quarrel had started in the other end of the room. Two men were standing cursing each other over a table. Kearny screwed himself around in his chair to stare at them for a moment. Then, grumbling, "Where do these bums think they are?" he got up and went over to them.

Elsa Fremont stared moodily at her glass. Guild watched Kearny go to the table where the two men were cursing, quiet them, and sit down with them.

The woman who had talked about the skin tightening on her forehead was now saying in the same tone: "Character actress—that's the old stall. She's just exactly the same kind of character actress I was. She's doing bits—when she can get them."

Elsa Fremont, still staring at her glass, whispered: "I'm scared."

"Of what?" Guild asked as if moderately interested.

"Of Wynant, of what he might——" She raised her eyes, dark and harried. "Has he done anything to Charley, Mr. Guild?"

"I don't know."

She put a tight fist on the table and cried angrily: "Why don't you do something? Why don't you find Wynant? Why don't you find Charley? Haven't you got any blood, any heart, any guts? Can't you do anything but sit there like a——" She broke off with a sob. Anger went out of her face and the fingers that had been clenched opened in appeal. "I—I'm sorry. I didn't mean—— But, oh, Mr. Guild, I'm so——" She put her head down and bit her lower lip.

Guild, impassive, said: "That's all right."

A man rose drunkenly from a nearby table and came up behind Elsa's chair. He put a fat hand on her shoulder and said: "There, there, darling." He said to Guild: "You cannot annoy this little girl in this way. You cannot. You ought to be ashamed of yourself, a man of your complexion." He leaned forward sharply, peering into Guild's face. "By Jesus, I believe you're a mulatto. I really do."

Elsa, squirming from under the fat drunken hand, flung a "Let me alone" up at the man. Guild said nothing. The fat man looked uncertainly from one to the other of them until a hardly less drunken man, mumbling unintelligible apologies, came and led him away.

Elsa looked humbly at the dark man. "I'm going to tell Frank I'm going," she said in a small tired voice. "Will you take me home?"

"Sure."

They rose and moved towards the door. Kearny was standing by the elevator.

"I don't feel like working tonight, Frank," the girl told him. "I'm going to knock off."

"Oke," he said. "Give yourself a hot drink and some aspirin." He held his hand out to Guild. "Glad I met you. Drop in any time. Anything I can ever do for you, let me know. You going to take the kid home? Swell! Be good."

CHAPTER TEN

Elsa Fremont was a dusky figure beside Guild in a taxicab riding west up Nob Hill. Her eyes glittered in a splash of light from a street-lamp. She drew breath in and asked: "You think Charley's run away, don't you?"

"It's likely," Guild said, "but maybe he'll be home when we get there."

"I hope so," she said earnestly. "I do hope so, but—I'm afraid."

He looked obliquely at her. "You've said that before. Mean you're afraid something's happened to him or will happen to you?"

She shivered. "I don't know. I'm just afraid." She put a hand in his, asking plaintively: "Aren't you ever going to catch Wynant?"

"Your hand's cold," he said.

She pulled her hand away. Her voice was not loud: intensity made it shrill. "Aren't you ever human?" she demanded. "Are you always like this? Or is it a pose?" She drew herself far back in a corner of the taxicab. "Are you a damned corpse?"

"I don't know," the dark man said. He seemed mildly puzzled. "I don't know what you mean."

She did not speak again, but sulked in her corner until they reached her house. Guild sat at ease and smoked until the taxicab stopped. Then he got out saying: "I'll stop long enough to see if he's home."

The girl crossed the sidewalk and unlocked the door while he was paying the chauffeur. She had gone indoors leaving the door open when he mounted the front steps. He followed her in. She had turned on ground-floor lights and was calling upstairs: "Charley!" There was no answer.

She uttered an impatient exclamation and ran upstairs. When she came down again she moved wearily. "He's not in," she said. "He hasn't come."

Guild nodded without apparent disappointment. "I'll give you a ring when I wake up," he said, stepping back towards the street-door, "or if I get any news of him."

She said quickly: "Don't go yet, please, unless you have to. I don't—I wish you'd stay a little while."

He said, "Sure," and they went into the living-room.

When she had taken off her coat she left him for a few minutes, going into the kitchen, returning with Scotch whisky, ice, lemons, glasses, and a siphon of water. They sat on the sofa with drinks in their hands.

Presently, looking inquisitively at him, she said: "I really meant what I said in the cab. Aren't you actually human? Isn't there any way anybody can get to you, get to the real inside you? I think you're the most—" she frowned, selecting words "—most untouchable, unreal, person I've ever known. Trying to—to really come in contact with you is just like trying to hold a handful of smoke."

Guild, who had listened attentively, now nodded. "I think I know what you're trying to say. It's an advantage when I'm working."

"I didn't ask you that," she protested, moving the glass in her hand impatiently. "I asked you if that's the way you really are or if you just do it."

He smiled and shook his head noncommittally.

"That isn't a smile," she said. "It's painted on." She leaned to him swiftly and kissed him, holding her mouth to his mouth for an appreciable time. When she took her mouth from his her narrow green eyes examined his face carefully. She made a moue. "You're not even a corpse—you're a ghost."

Guild said pleasantly, "I'm working," and drank from his glass.

Her face flushed. "Do you think I'm trying to make you?" she asked hotly.

He laughed at her. "I'd like it if you were, but I didn't mean it that way."

"You wouldn't like it," she said. "You'd be scared."

"Uh-uh," he explained blandly. "I'm working. It'd make you easier for me to handle."

Nothing in her face responded to his bantering. She said, with patient earnestness: "If you'd only listen to me and believe me when I tell you I don't know any more what it's all about than you do, if that much. You're just wasting your time when you ought to be finding Wynant. I don't know anything. Charley doesn't. We'd both tell you if we did. We've both already told you all we know. Why can't you believe me when I tell you that?"

"Sorry," Guild said lightly. "It don't make sense." He looked at his watch. "It's after five. I'd better run along."

She put a hand out to detain him, but instead of speaking she stared thoughtfully at her dangling wrist-scarf and worked her lips together.

Guild lit another cigarette and waited with no appearance of impatience.

Presently she shrugged her bare shoulders and said: "It doesn't make any difference." She turned her head to look uneasily behind her. "But will you—will you do something for me before you go? Go through the house and see that everything is all right. I'm—I'm nervous, upset."

"Sure," he said readily, and then, suggestively: "If you've got anything to tell me, the sooner the better for both of us."

"No, no, there's nothing," she said. "I've told you everything."

"All right. Have you got a flashlight?"

She nodded and brought him one from the next room.

When Guild returned to the living-room Elsa Fremont was standing where he had left her. She looked at his face and anxiety went out of her eyes. "It was silly of me," she said, "but I do thank you."

He put the flashlight on the table and felt for his cigarettes. "Why'd you ask me to look?"

She smiled in embarrassment and murmured: "It was a silly notion."

"Why'd you bring me home with you?" he asked.

She stared at him with eyes in which fear was awakening. "Wh-what do you mean? Is there——?"

He nodded.

"What is it?" she cried. "What did you find?"

He said: "I found something wrong down in the cellar."

Her hand went to her mouth.

"Your brother," he said.

She screamed: "What?"

"Dead."

The hand over her mouth muffled her voice: "K-killed?"

He nodded. "Suicide, from the looks of it. The gun could be the one the girl was killed with. The——" He broke off and caught her arm as she tried to run past him towards the door. "Wait. There's plenty of time for you to look at him. I want to talk to you."

She stood motionless staring at him with open blank eyes.

He said: "And I want you to talk to me."

She did not show she had heard him.

He said: "Your brother did kill Columbia Forrest, didn't he?"

Her eyes held their blank stare. Her lips barely moved. "You fool, you fool," she muttered in a tired flat voice.

He was still holding her arm. He ran the tip of his tongue over his lips and asked in a low persuasive tone: "How do you know he didn't?"

She began to tremble. "He couldn't've," she cried. Life had come back to her voice and face now. "He couldn't've."

"Why?"

She jerked her arm out of his hand and thrust her face up towards his. "He couldn't've, you idiot. He wasn't there. You can find out where he was easily enough. You'd've found out long before this if you'd had any brains. He was at a meeting of the Boxing Commission that afternoon, seeing about a permit or something for Sammy. They'll tell you that. They'll have a record of it."

The dark man did not seem surprised. His blue eyes were meditative under brows drawn a little together. "He didn't kill her, but he committed suicide," he said slowly and with an air of listening to himself say it. "That don't make sense too."

From the Memoirs of a Private Detective

1

WISHING to get some information from members of the W.C.T.U. in an Oregon city, I introduced myself as the secretary of the Butte Civic Purity League. One of them read me a long discourse on the erotic effects of cigarettes upon young girls. Subsequent experiments proved this trip worthless.

2

A man whom I was shadowing went out into the country for a walk one Sunday afternoon and lost his bearings completely. I had to direct him back to the city.

3

House burglary is probably the poorest paid trade in the world; I have never known anyone to make a living at it. But for that matter few criminals of any class are self-supporting unless they toil at something legitimate between times. Most of them, however, live on their women.

4

I know an operative who while looking for pickpockets at the Havre de Grace race track had his wallet stolen. He later became an official in an Eastern detective agency.

5

Three times I have been mistaken for a Prohibition agent, but never had any trouble clearing myself.

6

Taking a prisoner from a ranch near Gilt Edge, Mont., to Lewistown one night, my machine broke down and we had to sit there until daylight. The prisoner, who stoutly affirmed his innocence, was clothed only in overalls and shirt. After shivering all night on the front seat his morale was low, and I had no difficulty in getting a complete confession from him while walking to the nearest ranch early the following morning.

7

Of all the men embezzling from their employers with whom I have had contact, I can't remember a dozen who smoked, drank, or had any of the vices in which bonding companies are so interested.

8

I was once falsely accused of perjury and had to perjure myself to escape arrest.

9

A detective agency official in San Francisco once substituted "truthful" for "voracious" in one of my reports on the grounds that the client might not understand the latter. A few days later in another report "simulate" became "quicken" for the same reason.

10

Of all the nationalities haled into the criminal courts, the Greek is the most difficult to convict. He simply denies everything, no matter how conclusive the proof may be; and nothing so impresses a jury as a bare statement of fact, regardless of the fact's inherent improbability or obvious absurdity in the face of overwhelming contrary evidence.

11

I know a man who will forge the impressions of any set of fingers in the world for $50.

12

I have never known a man capable of turning out first-rate work in a trade, a profession or an art, who was a professional criminal.

13

I know a detective who once attempted to disguise himself thoroughly. The first policeman he met took him into custody.

14

I know a deputy sheriff in Montana who, approaching the cabin of a homesteader for whose arrest he had a warrant, was confronted by the homesteader with a rifle in his hands. The deputy sheriff drew his revolver and tried to shoot over the homesteader's head to frighten him. The range was long and a strong wind was blowing. The bullet knocked the rifle from the homesteader's hands. As time went by the deputy sheriff came to accept as the truth the reputation for expertness that this incident gave him, and he not only let his friends enter him in a shooting contest, but wagered everything he owned upon his skill. When the contest was held he missed the target completely with all six shots.

15

Once in Seattle the wife of a fugitive swindler offered to sell me a photograph of her husband for $15. I knew where I could get one free, so I didn't buy it.

16

I was once engaged to discharge a woman's housekeeper.

17

The slang in use among criminals is for the most part a conscious, artificial growth, designed more to confuse outsiders than for any other purpose, but sometimes it is singularly expressive; for instance, *two-time loser*—one who has been convicted twice; and the older *gone to read and write*—found it advisable to go away for a while.

18

Pocket-picking is the easiest to master of all the criminal trades. Anyone who is not crippled can become an adept in a day.

19

In 1917, in Washington, D.C., I met a young woman who did not remark that my work must be very interesting.

20

Even where the criminal makes no attempt to efface the prints of his fingers, but leaves them all over the scene of the crime, the chances are about one in ten of finding a print that is sufficiently clear to be of any value.

21

The chief of police of a Southern city once gave me a description of a man, complete even to a mole on his neck, but neglected to mention that he had only one arm.

22

I know a forger who left his wife because she had learned to smoke cigarettes while he was serving a term in prison.

23

Second only to "Dr. Jekyll and Mr. Hyde" is "Raffles" in the affections of the daily press. The phrase "gentleman crook" is used on the slightest provocation. A composite portrait of the gentry upon whom the newspapers have bestowed this title would show a laudanum-drinker, with a large rhinestone horseshoe aglow in the soiled bosom of his shirt below a bow tie, leering at his victim, and saying: "Now don't get scared, lady, I ain't gonna crack you on the bean. I ain't a rough-neck!"

24

The cleverest and most uniformly successful detective I have ever known is extremely myopic.

25

Going from the larger cities out into the remote rural communities, one finds a steadily decreasing percentage of crimes that have to do with money and a proportionate increase in the frequency of sex as a criminal motive.

26

While trying to peer into the upper story of a roadhouse in northern California one night—and the man I was looking for was in Seattle at the time—part of the porch roof crumbled under me and I fell, spraining an ankle. The proprietor of the roadhouse gave me water to bathe it in.

27

The chief difference between the exceptionally knotty problem confronting the detective of fiction and that facing the real detective is that in the former there is usually a paucity of clues, and in the latter altogether too many.

28

I know a man who once stole a Ferris-wheel.

29

That the law-breaker is invariably soon or late apprehended is probably the least challenged of extant myths. And yet the files of every detective bureau bulge with the records of unsolved mysteries and uncaught criminals.

"Suggestions to Detective Story Writers"

A FELLOW who takes detective stories seriously, I am annoyed by the stupid recurrence of these same blunders in book after book. It would be silly to insist that nobody who has not been a detective should write detective stories, but it is certainly not unreasonable to ask any one who is going to write a book of any sort to make some effort at least to learn something about his subject. Most writers do. Only detective story writers seem to be free from a sense of obligation in this direction, and, curiously, the more established and prolific detective story writers seem to be the worst offenders. Nearly all writers of Western tales at least get an occasional glimpse of their chosen territory from a car-window while en route to Hollywood; writers of sea stories have been seen on the waterfront; surely detective story writers could afford to speak to policemen now and then.

Meanwhile, a couple of months' labor in this arena has convinced me that the following suggestions might be of value to somebody:

(1) There was an automatic revolver, the Webley-Fosbery, made in England some years ago. The ordinary automatic pistol, however, is not a revolver. A pistol, to be a revolver, must have something on it that revolves.

(2) The Colt's .45 automatic pistol has no chambers. The cartridges are put in a magazine.

(3) A silencer may be attached to a revolver, but the effect will be altogether negligible. I have never seen a silencer used on an automatic pistol, but am told it would cause the pistol to jam. A silencer may be used on a single-shot target pistol or on a rifle, but both would still make quite a bit of noise. "Silencer" is a rather optimistic name for this device which has generally fallen into disuse.

(4) When a bullet from a Colt's .45, or any firearm of approximately the same size and power, hits you, even if not in a fatal spot, it usually knocks you over. It is quite upsetting at any reasonable range.

(5) A shot or stab wound is simply felt as a blow or push at first. It is some little time before any burning or other painful sensation begins.

(6) When you are knocked unconscious you do not feel the blow that does it.

(7) A wound made after the death of the wounded is usually recognizable as such.

(8) Finger-prints of any value to the police are seldom found on anybody's skin.

(9) The pupils of many drug-addicts' eyes are apparently normal.

(10) It is impossible to see anything by the flash of an ordinary gun, though it is easy to imagine you have seen things.

(11) Not nearly so much can be seen by moonlight as you imagine. This is especially true of colors.

(12) All Federal snoopers are not members of the Secret Service. That branch is chiefly occupied with pursuing counterfeiters and guarding Presidents and prominent visitors to our shores.

(13) A sheriff is a county officer who usually has no official connection with city, town or State police.

(14) Federal prisoners convicted in Washington, D.C., are usually sent to the Atlanta prison and not to Leavenworth.

(15) The California State prison at San Quentin is used for convicts serving first terms. Two-time losers are usually sent to Folsom.

(16) Ventriloquists do not actually "throw" their voices and such doubtful illusions as they manage depend on their gestures. Nothing at all could be done by a ventriloquist standing behind his audience.

(17) Even detectives who drop their final g's should not be made to say "anythin' "—an oddity that calls for vocal acrobatics.

(18) "Youse" is the plural of "you."

(19) A trained detective shadowing a subject does not ordinarily leap from doorway to doorway and does not hide behind trees and poles. He knows no harm is done if the subject sees him now and then.

—

A few weeks ago, having no books on hand that I cared to talk much about, I listed in this column nineteen suggestions to detective story writers. Those suggestions having been received with extreme enthusiasm—to the extent at least of one publisher offering me a hundred dollars for a slightly more complete list—I, not needing that particular hundred dollars at the moment, herewith present a few more suggestions at the mere usual space rate:

(20) The current practice in most places in the United States is to make the coroner's inquest an empty formality in which nothing much is brought out except that somebody has died.

(21) Fingerprints are fragile affairs. Wrapping a pistol or other small object up in a handkerchief is much more likely to obliterate than to preserve any prints it may have.

(22) When an automatic pistol is fired the empty cartridge-shell flies out the right-hand side. The empty cartridge-case remains in a revolver until ejected by hand.

(23) A lawyer cannot impeach his own witness.

(24) The length of time a corpse has been a corpse can be approximated by an experienced physician, but only approximated, and the longer it has been a corpse, the less accurate the approximation is likely to be.

CHRONOLOGY

NOTE ON THE TEXTS

NOTES

Chronology

915

1894   Samuel Dashiell Hammett born May 27 on "Hopewell and Aim," tobacco farm of paternal grandfather Samuel Hammett in St. Mary's County, Maryland, second of three children of Richard Thomas Hammett and Annie Bond Dashiell. (Hammett family has been in America since the 17th century, Dashiell family since the 18th. Mother, who suffers from chronic tuberculosis, is of French Huguenot ancestry but converted to Catholicism on marrying Hammett. Father works on family tobacco farm and pursues career in local politics with little success.) Baptized a Catholic at St. Nicholas Church.

1895–97   Family, including older sister, Aronia, and younger brother, Richard, moves briefly to Philadelphia.

1898–1907   Family settles in Baltimore, where father works as clerk and later as salesman, bus conductor, factory foreman, and security guard. Hammett attends Public School 72.

1908–14   Attends Baltimore Polytechnic Institute in 1908. Leaves school after less than a year to work as newsboy, office boy and freight clerk for B&O Railroad, and clerk for Poe and Davies stockbrokerage. Family struggles financially. Paternal grandfather dies in 1911.

1915–17   Works as detective for Baltimore office of Pinkerton detective agency, located in the Continental Building. Learns job from older employee James Wright (later described by Hammett as model for his character the Continental Op).

1918   Leaves Pinkerton to enlist in army. Undergoes basic training at Camp Mead, Maryland; in July is assigned to a motor ambulance company. In October, complains of flu-like symptoms and is hospitalized with high fever; diagnosed with bronchopneumonia and released after 20 days.

1919   Hospitalized again in February; is diagnosed with tuberculosis and given discharge from army with small disability pension. Moves back with family. Despite frail condition, returns to work at Pinkerton; after six months is again hospitalized. Bureau of War Risk Insurance reviews his case and grants him a higher pension.

1920   Leaves home permanently in May; travels to Spokane, Washington, where he resumes work for Pinkerton. Serves as Pinkerton operative in Idaho and Montana, becoming involved as strikebreaker in Anaconda miners' strike. Health deteriorates; admitted in November to Cushman Hospital in Tacoma.

1921   Falls in love with nurse Josephine ("Jose") Dolan. After four months, is transferred to treatment center at Camp Kearny, near San Diego, California. Mother dies in April; Hammett does not return to Baltimore for funeral. Learns from Jose that she is pregnant; by letter, they agree to marry. Released from Camp Kearny in May, but physical condition remains fragile (will continue to suffer cyclical recurrence of lung problems). Moves to San Francisco in June. Marries Jose on July 7 at Saint Mary's Cathedral. Settles with Jose in apartment on Eddy Street and resumes work for Pinkerton. Daughter Mary Jane born October 15 (Hammett will later tell several people that she was not his biological child).

1922–23   Serious relapse makes it impossible for Hammett to work; reluctantly asks his family for financial help. With subsidy from Veterans Bureau, studies stenography and writing at Munson's Business College; decides to seek work in advertising. In October 1922 first published short story, "The Parthian Shot," appears in *The Smart Set*; publishes four more pieces in the magazine over the next year, including autobiographical "From the Memoirs of a Private Detective," based on his Pinkerton experience. Publishes "The Road Home," his first contribution to *Black Mask*, under pseudonym Peter Collinson in December 1922. In *Black Mask* story "Arson Plus" (October 1923) introduces anonymous operative later known as the Continental Op (the Op will be the protagonist of 28 stories and two novels).

1924–25   Wife and daughter go to live with her family in Montana for six months. Regularly publishes stories in *Black Mask*, including "The Tenth Clew," "The House in Turk Street," "The Whosis Kid," "The Scorched Face," and "Dead Yellow Women." Starts and then abandons a novel, "The Secret Emperor."

1926   Takes full-time job as advertising manager for jeweler Albert Samuels. Daughter Josephine Rebecca born May 24. Hammett, who has been drinking heavily for years, suffers lung hemorrhage and collapses at work in July. Diagnosed with hepatitis and is unable to continue working. Lives apart from family. Receives literary encouragement from Joseph T. Shaw, who assumes editorship of *Black Mask* in November.

1927   Begins reviewing crime fiction for *Saturday Review of Literature* in January (continues to publish there for next three years). After hiatus of a year, resumes writing fiction; continues series of Continental Op stories for *Black Mask* with "The Big Knock-Over" (February), "$106,000 Blood Money" (May), and "The Main Death" (June). Jose moves with children to San Anselmo in spring (family will live together only sporadically over next two years). Begins novel *Red Harvest* (originally titled "Poisonville"); first episode is serialized as "The Cleansing of Poisonville" in the November issue of *Black Mask*.

1928   Submits completed manuscript of novel to Alfred A. Knopf in February; Blanche Knopf offers publication but suggests revisions, including toning down of violence; Hammett agrees to some changes, and then makes extensive revisions in collaboration with Knopf editor Harry Block. Receives offer of scriptwriting work from William Fox Studios and goes to Hollywood in June, but no deal materializes. Completes second novel *The Dain Curse* in June (serialized in *Black Mask*, Nov. 1928–Feb. 1929). By end of year, completes his next novel, *The Maltese Falcon*.

1929   *Red Harvest* is published in February; Paramount buys movie rights. Knopf accepts *The Dain Curse* but requests extensive changes, which Hammett makes reluctantly. Hammett's health improves, and he moves into new, more expensive apartment with writer and actress Nell Martin, with whom he maintains longtime relationship. Manuscript of *The Maltese Falcon* is accepted by Knopf with requests for only minor revisions. *The Dain Curse* is published in July to favorable reviews and sells better than *Red Harvest*. *The Maltese Falcon* is serialized in *Black Mask* (Sept. 1929–Jan. 1930). Hammett and Martin travel to New York in the fall for extended stay; he works on new novel, *The Glass Key*.

1930   *The Maltese Falcon* is published in February; it receives excellent reviews from influential critics, including Will Cuppy and Franklin P. Adams, and is reprinted seven times in the course of the year. Paramount releases film *Roadhouse Nights*, loosely derived from *Red Harvest*. Hammett completes *The Glass Key* (serialized in *Black Mask*, March–June). Takes job as regular reviewer of crime fiction for the *New York Evening Post*. Warner Brothers acquires movie rights to *The Maltese Falcon* in June. At urging of David O. Selznick, Hammett is offered writing contract with Paramount, which he fulfills with hastily written seven-page story outline. Works on several other projects, and leaves Paramount at end of year. Meets Lillian Hellman, then married to writer Arthur Kober, at Hollywood party in November; they become lovers (relationship continues for the rest of their lives although they are frequently separated and often have other partners).

1931   Remains in Hollywood through the spring. Sees other writers socially, including Arthur Kober and Lillian Hellman, Dorothy Parker, and S. J. Perelman and his wife, Laura; drinks heavily and has many affairs. Writes treatment of an original Sam Spade story for Darryl Zanuck at Warner Brothers, but after receiving $10,000 for the story, it is rejected. *City Streets*, film based on Hammett's initial Paramount story, released in April. *The Glass Key* is published by Knopf in April, receiving strong reviews and selling well. Hammett moves to New York. Forms friendly relationship with William Faulkner. Completes first 65 pages of an early version of *The Thin Man*, then puts it aside. A film version of *The Maltese Falcon*, starring Ricardo Cortez and Bebe Daniels, is released by Warner Brothers in May.

1932   Found guilty in absentia on June 30 of battery and attempted rape in civil suit brought against him by actress Elise De Vianne, who is awarded $2,500 in damages.

Works on a second version of *The Thin Man*. Unable to pay his bill at Hotel Pierre, leaves surreptitiously and goes to live at Sutton Club Hotel on East 56th Street, which is managed by Nathanael West.

1933   Publishes novella "Woman in the Dark" as a three-part serial in *Liberty*. Finishes *The Thin Man* in May (condensed version appears in December *Redbook*). Travels with Hellman to Florida Keys for extended stay in fishing camp, where he helps her with her play *The Children's Hour*. Rents house in Huntington, Long Island, in summer.

1934   *The Thin Man* is published by Knopf in January. MGM movie version of the novel, starring William Powell and Myrna Loy, is released in June (five other movies featuring the novel's protagonists, Nick and Nora Charles, will be released between 1934 and 1947). *Secret Agent X-9*, King Features comic strip with script credited to Hammett and art by Alex Raymond, first appears in January (Hammett's byline is dropped after fifteen months). Publishes three stories in *Collier's*, January–March. Spends spring in Florida Keys with Hellman. Signs contract with MGM in October for a second movie in *Thin Man* series; stays at the Beverly Wilshire Hotel and socializes with friends, including Herbert Asbury, Nunnally Johnson, Joel Sayre, Arthur Kober, and Edward G. Robinson. Drinks heavily.

1935   Submits draft of story to MGM in January. Meets Gertrude Stein, who admires his work greatly, at dinner party in April. In June signs three-year contract with MGM, paying him minimum of $1,000 per week as writer and executive (Hammett frequently fails to meet terms of contract and is periodically taken off salary). Runs up heavy debts and is sued over the next several years by various creditors. Has brief affair with Laura Perelman during summer. In the fall divides time between Los Angeles and New York. Universal releases movie *Mister Dynamite*, starring Edmund Lowe, based on a Hammett story originally written in 1931; Paramount releases film version of *The Glass Key* starring George Raft and Edward Arnold.

1936   Meets Raymond Chandler at *Black Mask* dinner in January. Begins long-term affair with Pru Whitfield, wife of

Black Mask writer Raoul Whitfield. Becomes increasingly involved with Communist Party, which he joins as a secret member. Stays with Hellman on Tavern Island near Norwalk, Connecticut, during spring. Moves to Princeton, New Jersey, in October. *Satan Met a Lady*, a second film version of *The Maltese Falcon* starring Warren William and Bette Davis, released by Warner Brothers. *After the Thin Man*, based on Hammett's story, opens in December. Released from contract with Knopf after he fails to deliver promised novel.

1937   Returns to Hollywood in April to work on third *Thin Man* movie, under new agreement that pays him only for completed work. Publicly supports the Anti-Nazi League and the Western Writers Congress, and donates money to Abraham Lincoln Brigade fighting in Spain in support of Loyalist government. Becomes active in movement to gain recognition from studios for Screen Writers Guild. Begins 14-month period of abstinence from drinking. Jose Hammett files for mail-order divorce in Sonora, Mexico, court (after Hammett's death, divorce is ruled illegal and Jose is recognized as entitled to widow's benefits).

1938   Completes treatment for *Another Thin Man*. Along with other writers including Hellman, Langston Hughes, Dorothy Parker, and Malcolm Cowley, signs statement in defense of Moscow purge trials in April. Becomes ill after resuming drinking and is flown back to New York to enter Lenox Hill Hospital; moves into Plaza Hotel after his release in June. Signs contract with Bennett Cerf of Modern Library for new novel. Tells friends that he is at work on novel tentatively titled "My Brother Felix." Stays with Hellman on Tavern Island during summer and early fall, where he gives her detailed assistance on revisions of her play *The Little Foxes*. Speaks at anti-Nazi rallies sponsored by Communist Party in New York in November. MGM rejects his scenario for a *Thin Man* sequel.

1939   MGM cancels Hammett's contract in July. Modern Library announces new Hammett novel, "There Was a Young Man," for publication in the fall, but he does not deliver a manuscript. Hammett becomes member of editorial board of Equality Publishers, press sponsored by the Communist Party whose declared aim is "to defend democracy and combat anti-Semitism and Fascism" (press publishes monthly magazine *Equality* but ceases publication after signing of Nazi-Soviet pact in late August). Becomes a regular guest at Hardscrabble Farm, 130-acre property purchased by Hellman in Pleasantville, New York. *Another Thin Man* opens in November.

1940   Helps publisher Ralph Ingersoll in assembling staff for his newspaper *PM*; after public protests over Communist influence on the paper, Ingersoll repudiates Hammett in memo to stockholders. Serves as national chairman of Committee on Election Rights—1940, organization seeking to get Communist candidates on local ballots, and supports presidential campaign of Communist Party general secretary Earl Browder.

1941   In accordance with Communist policy shift following Nazi-Soviet pact, publicly opposes lend-lease policy of aid to Britain and American entry into war. (Becomes a supporter of the war effort following the shift in the Communist Party line after the German attack on the Soviet Union in June.) Elected president of League of American Writers. Receives $500 a week for nominal authorship of NBC radio serial *The Adventures of the Thin Man*, for which he does no writing. John Huston films highly successful adaptation of *The Maltese Falcon*, starring Humphrey Bogart and Mary Astor.

1942   Works on screen adaptation of Hellman's play *Watch on the Rhine*, with Hellman making extensive revisions (Hammett receives primary screen credit when film opens in September 1943). Returns advance on unwritten novel to Random House in March. Knopf issues all five novels as *The Complete Dashiell Hammett*. A second film version of *The Glass Key*, starring Brian Donlevy and Alan Ladd, opens. After previous rejections on health grounds, Hammett is accepted into the army as a private; he is inducted in September and undergoes Signal Corps Training at Fort Monmouth, New Jersey, where his tasks include composing lessons for trainees and giving orientation lectures.

1943   To avoid further dental problems, has all his teeth pulled at army hospital in March. Promoted to corporal in May.

Sent in June to Camp Shenango in Transfer, Pennsylvania, a facility used by the army to isolate soldiers with subversive political views. After he has been there a week, camp is dispersed following protest by Eleanor Roosevelt, and Hammett is sent to Fort Lawton near Tacoma, Washington, and then to Fort Randall, Alaska. Assigned to provide orientation for troops in the Aleutian Islands, arrives in September on small volcanic island of Adak. Starts a camp newspaper, *The Adakian*, under orders of Brigadier General Harry Thompson.

1944   First issue of *The Adakian* published in January (Hammett continues as editor for 15 months, contributing 13 signed articles). Establishes editorial staff that includes future journalists Bernard Kalb and Eliot Asinof and that is racially integrated, despite the overall segregation of the armed forces. Promoted to sergeant in August. *The Battle of the Aleutians*, pamphlet co-written by Hammett, published for distribution to troops. Sent on tour of the Aleutians to give educational lectures to servicemen.

1945   Joins training unit at Fort Richardson, near Anchorage. Promoted to master sergeant in June, and discharged in September. Moves to New York, living in apartment on East 66th Street. Lives on royalties from three radio serials based on his characters.

1946   Divides time between New York apartment and Hardscrabble Farm. Elected president of Communist-sponsored Civil Rights Congress of New York in June (position is nominal), and named a trustee of CRC bail fund. Begins teaching courses in mystery writing at Jefferson School of Social Sciences, devoted to "Marxism as the philosophy and social science of the working class" (continues teaching there until 1956).

1947   Moves to apartment in Greenwich Village. Hires full-time housekeeper, Rose Evans, who assumes close management of Hammett's affairs. Resumes contact with his brother Richard. Daughter Mary Jane stays with Hammett for an extended period; both drink heavily.

1948   Hammett's father, whom he had recently visited for the first time in nearly two decades, dies in Maryland in

March. Warner Brothers brings lawsuit against radio series *The Adventures of Sam Spade* on grounds that Warners owns all broadcast rights to *The Maltese Falcon*; Hammett files complaint seeking to affirm his right to use of the name Sam Spade. Health breaks after long period of heavy drinking and he is admitted to Lenox Hill Hospital; quits drinking permanently when warned that his life is in immediate danger if he continues.

1949   Lives mostly at Hardscrabble Farm. Loses suit against Warners regarding *Adventures of Sam Spade*; studio files plagiarism complaint against Hammett. Elected to board of trustees of Jefferson School of Social Sciences in August. Civil Rights Congress posts bail in November for eleven Communist leaders appealing convictions under the Smith Act of 1940 for conspiring to advocate the violent overthrow of the U.S. government.

1950   Goes to Hollywood to work on screenplay of William Wyler's *Detective Story*, but is unable to write. Lives with Jose during six-month stay, and enjoys company of daughter Josephine. Works with Hellman on her play *The Autumn Garden*.

1951   Visits Josephine and her daughter Ann in Los Angeles; returns with them for stay at Hardscrabble Farm. When four of the Communists convicted for Smith Act violations fail to surrender to authorities, subpoenas are issued for the trustees of the Civil Rights Congress bail fund. Hammett appears before U.S. District Court Judge Sylvester Ryan on July 9 and repeatedly invokes the Fifth Amendment when questioned about the CRC, the bail fund, and the whereabouts of the fugitives. At the conclusion of his testimony, Ryan finds him guilty of contempt of court and sentences him to six months in prison. Serves his sentence at the Federal House of Detention in New York until September, when he is moved to the federal prison in Ashland, Kentucky. Released on December 9 with time off for good behavior. Health is further damaged by imprisonment. Warner Brothers suit decided in Hammett's favor in December (studio's appeal is rejected in 1954).

1952   Finds himself impoverished due to cancellation of radio shows based on his work and liens on his income by

Internal Revenue Service for back taxes owed since 1943;
all his books are out of print. Takes up residence at Ka-
tonah, New York, on estate of friend Dr. Samuel Rosen,
living rent-free in gatekeeper's cottage. Writes 12,500
words of a novel which he abandons (it is published as
"Tulip" in *The Big Knockover*, a collection of Hammett's
stories published in 1966).

1953   Subpoenaed by Senator Joseph McCarthy to testify before his subcommittee of the Committee on Government
Operations, where he is questioned about purchase of his
books for libraries by U.S. State Department, and
whether he ever donated royalties from such sales to the
Communist Party. When asked by McCarthy whether he
thinks it reasonable for the government to purchase and
distribute books by Communists when it is fighting Communism, Hammett replies: "If I were fighting Communism, I don't think I would do it by giving people any
books at all."

1955   Called to testify in February before New York State Joint
Legislative Committee about his involvement with Civil
Rights Congress; during questioning says, "Communism
to me is not a dirty word. When you are working for the
advance of mankind it never occurs to you whether a guy
is a Communist." Suffers heart attack while visiting Lillian Hellman on Martha's Vineyard in August.

1956   Questioned by F.B.I. in March about his ability to pay tax
judgment of over $140,000; Hammett asserts that he has
no income or savings. In an interview given to the *Washington Daily News* the same month, states: "I stopped
writing because I was repeating myself. It is the beginning
of the end when you discover you have style." Fails to appear in court to answer federal suit for back taxes.

1957–61   Ordered to pay $104,795 in back taxes for the years
1950–54 in February 1957. Health continues to deteriorate
severely; moves into Lillian Hellman's New York apartment in spring of 1958. Granted small pension by Veterans
Administration in May 1959 on grounds of severe respira-
tory illness. Goes out in public for last time in February
1960 to see opening of Hellman's play *Toys in the Attic*.

Dies of lung cancer on January 10, 1961, at Lenox Hill Hospital. Funeral is held at Frank E. Campbell funeral home in New York. Buried at Arlington National Cemetery on January 13.

Note on the Texts

This volume presents, in the order of their first publication, a selection of 24 crime stories by Dashiell Hammett, followed by "The Thin Man: An Early Typescript" (an unfinished novel in ten chapters), and two short pieces about detective work and detective fiction.

All of the stories included in this volume appeared initially in magazines, principally in the pulp *Black Mask* (titled *The Black Mask* until early in 1927), where Hammett also first published *Red Harvest* (1929), *The Dain Curse* (1929), *The Maltese Falcon* (1930), and *The Glass Key* (1931). For a brief period, Hammett considered revising his stories and collecting them in book form. In a letter of June 16, 1929, to Harry Block, his editor at Alfred A. Knopf, he suggested two possible volumes, *The Continental Op* (a collection of stories featuring his character of the same name) and *The Big Knock-Over* (to include "The Big Knock-Over"and the related story "$106,000 Blood Money"). "I'd want to rewrite the stories," he told Block, "and there are possibly fifty or sixty thousand words out of the quarter-million that I'd throw out as not worth bothering about. In the remainder there are some good stories, and altogether I think they'd give a more complete and true picture of the detective at work than has been given anywhere else." Within a month, however, Hammett had reconsidered; "I don't think I want to do anything with them," he wrote Block again on July 14, 1929.

Hammett continued to decline Knopf proposals over subsequent years to publish story collections, but he did allow his stories to appear in print elsewhere: in magazine anthologies, in newspaper syndication (through King Features), and in paperback collections, the first series of which was published by Lawrence E. Spivak in New York beginning in 1943, edited by Ellery Queen (a pseudonym used jointly by Frederick Dannay and Manfred B. Lee). Two stories included in this volume, "The Golden Horseshoe" and "Dead Yellow Women," appeared in a British hardcover collection, *The Dashiell Hammett Omnibus* (London: Cassell, 1950), along with Hammett's novels.

Numerous textual changes, large and small (including alterations to titles, substantial verbal revision, and the omission of sentences and paragraphs), are introduced in these later reprintings. In almost all cases, Hammett is known not to have been or is not likely to have been responsible for these changes. As William F. Nolan comments in *Hammett: A Life at the Edge* (1983), "Aside from the money he received from these collections of his early fiction, Hammett had nothing to do with them. He did not revise the works as they went into book form." He did suggest, in a letter to Lillian Hellman written from the Aleutian Islands on July 26, 1944, that the story "Two Sharp Knives" be retitled "To a Sharp Knife" when it appeared in book form; the latter was Hammett's original title, the former "thought up by *Collier's*" where the story was first published.

With one exception, this volume reprints Hammett's stories from their initial magazine printings. No copy is known to be extant of the issue of the pulp magazine *Mystery Stories* in which "This King Business" initially appeared, in January 1928; it is reprinted here from *The Creeping Siamese* (New York: Lawrence E. Spivak, 1950), the first book version. Two stories in this volume, "Arson Plus" and "Slippery Fingers," were published in *Black Mask* under the pseudonym Peter Collinson.

The following list gives details about the first serial and first book versions of each of the stories included in this volume; when the first book version is a collection of the work of various authors, the first appearance in a Hammett collection is also noted:

Arson Plus
The Black Mask 6.13 (October 1, 1923): 25–36.
Woman in the Dark. New York: Lawrence E. Spivak, 1951.

Slippery Fingers
The Black Mask 6.14 (October 15, 1923): 96–103.
Woman in the Dark. New York: Lawrence E. Spivak, 1951.

Crooked Souls
The Black Mask 6.14 (October 15, 1923): 35–44.

The Tenth Clew
The Black Mask 6.19 (January 1, 1924): 3–23.
The Return of the Continental Op. New York: Lawrence E. Spivak, 1945. [As "The Tenth Clue"]

Zigzags of Treachery
The Black Mask 6.23 (March 1, 1924): 80–102.
The Continental Op. New York: Lawrence E. Spivak, 1945.

The House in Turk Street
The Black Mask 7.2 (April 15, 1924): 9–22.
Hammett Homicides. New York: Lawrence E. Spivak, 1946.

The Girl with the Silver Eyes
The Black Mask 7.4 (June 1924): 45–70.
Hammett Homicides. New York: Lawrence E. Spivak, 1946.

Women, Politics and Murder
The Black Mask 7.7 (September 1924): 67–83.
The Continental Op. New York: Lawrence E. Spivak, 1945. [As
    "Death on Pine Street"]

The Golden Horseshoe
The Black Mask 7.9 (November 1924): 37–62.
Dead Yellow Women. New York: Lawrence E. Spivak, 1947.

Nightmare Town
Argosy All-Story Weekly 165.4 (December 27, 1924): 502–26.
Nightmare Town. New York: Lawrence E. Spivak, 1948.

The Whosis Kid
The Black Mask 8.1 (March 1925): 7–32.
The Return of the Continental Op. New York: Lawrence E.
    Spivak, 1945.

The Scorched Face
The Black Mask 8.3 (May 1925): 9–31.
Nightmare Town. New York: Lawrence E. Spivak, 1948.

Dead Yellow Women
The Black Mask 8.9 (November 1925): 9–39.
Dead Yellow Women. New York: Lawrence E. Spivak, 1947.

The Gutting of Couffignal
The Black Mask 8.10 (December 1925): 30–48.
The Return of the Continental Op. New York: Lawrence E.
    Spivak, 1945.

The Assistant Murderer
The Black Mask 8.12 (February 1926): 57–59.
The Adventures of Sam Spade and Other Stories. New York:
    Lawrence E. Spivak, 1944.

Creeping Siamese
The Black Mask 9.1 (March 1926): 38–47.
The Creeping Siamese. New York: Lawrence E. Spivak, 1950.

The Big Knock-Over
Black Mask 9.12 (February 1927): 7–38.
$106,000 Blood Money. New York: Lawrence E. Spivak, 1943.

$106,000 Blood Money
Black Mask 10.3 (May 1927): 9–34.
$106,000 Blood Money. New York: Lawrence E. Spivak, 1943.

The Main Death
Black Mask 10.4 (June 1927): 44–57.
Hammett Homicides. New York: Lawrence E. Spivak, 1946.

This King Business
Mystery Stories (January 1928).
The Creeping Siamese. New York: Lawrence E. Spivak, 1950.

Fly Paper
Black Mask 12.6 (August 1929): 7–26.
Best Stories from Ellery Queen's Mystery Magazine. New York: Detective Book Club, 1944.
The Continental Op. New York: Lawrence E. Spivak, 1945.

The Farewell Murder
Black Mask 12.12 (February 1930): 9–30.
The Best American Mystery Stories of the Year. New York: John Day, 1932.
The Continental Op. New York: Lawrence E. Spivak, 1945.

Woman in the Dark
Liberty 10.14 (April 8, 1933): 5–11; 10.15 (April 15, 1933): 12–18; 10.16 (April 22, 1933): 44–49.
Woman in the Dark. New York: Lawrence E. Spivak, 1951.

Two Sharp Knives
Collier's 93.2 (January 13, 1934): 12–13.
The Avon Annual. New York: Avon, 1945. [As "To a Sharp Knife"]
Hammett Homicides. New York: Lawrence E. Spivak, 1946.

"The Thin Man: An Early Typescript" has been reprinted from Hammett's original typescript, in the Guymon Collection, Mary Norton Clapp Library, Occidental College Library, Los Angeles. A handwritten note accompanying the typescript, signed by Hammett and dated Hardscrabble Farm, Pleasantville, N.Y., January 14, 1942, explains the unfinished novel's relation to *The Thin Man* (1934):

> In 1930 I started writing a book entitled "The Thin Man." By the time I had written these 65 pages my publisher and I agreed that it might be wise to postpone the publication of "The Glass Key"—scheduled for that fall—until the following spring. This meant that "The Thin Man" could not be published until the fall of 1931. So—having plenty of time—I put these 65 pages aside and went to Hollywood for a year. One thing and/or another intervening after that, I didn't return to work

on the story until a couple of more years had passed—
and then I found it easier, or at least generally more satisfactory, to keep only the basic idea of the plot and
otherwise to start anew. Some of the incidents in this
original version I later used in "After The Thin Man," a
motion picture sequel, but—except for that and for the
use of the characters' names Guild and Wynant—this
unfinished manuscript has a clear claim to virginity.

The unfinished "Thin Man" remained unpublished during Hammett's lifetime, and no other manuscript version is known to be extant; it first appeared in print in its entirety in *City Magazine* 9.17
(November 4, 1975): 1–12 (insert).

"From the Memoirs of a Private Detective" is reprinted here from
The Smart Set (March 1923, pages 87–90), where it was first published; Hammett did not make further revisions to this work.

"'Suggestions to Detective Story Writers'" has been assembled
from two installments of "The Crime Wave," a book-review column
Hammett contributed to the *New York Evening Post* between April
and October of 1930; its first section (from 910.1 to 911.39 in this volume) reprints all but the title, list of books reviewed, and opening
paragraph of the review of June 7, 1930, and its second (from 912.1
onward in this volume) reprints the penultimate section of the review of July 5, 1930. The title has been supplied for this volume.
Hammett did not revise "The Crime Wave" columns after their initial appearances.

This volume presents the texts of the original printings and the
typescript chosen for inclusion here, but it does not attempt to re-
produce features of their design and layout. The texts are printed
without change, except for the correction of typographical errors.
Spelling, punctuation, and capitalization often are expressive features
and they are not altered, even when inconsistent or irregular. The
following is a list of typographical errors corrected, cited by page and
line number: 4.23, [no quotation mark] The; 8.25, "It; 11.3, com-
plection; 15.8, talk,; 15.13, womai; 19.2, $2.60;; 28.19, came old; 36.17,
"No,"; 50.19, mit; 50.34, wreck! [no quotation mark]; 54.9, back;
54.36, going."; 67.14, busines; 72.38, with out; 84.21, unpleasand;
85.8, minutes."; 91.1, same; 91.10, Estop; 91.17, that; 96.20, direcion;
102.12, in you; 104.1, police;; 104.21, Homocide; 105.21, Stacy; 108.9,
Mrs. Ledwich; 114.20, Francico; 114.28, layed; 114.33, wan't; 115.19,
Francico; 115.21, afrad; 121.2, clear. [no quotation mark]; 123.17, "No,
"No; 126.7, trousers. [no quotation mark]; 131.6, wet; 131.14, way;
141.37, heathen"; 174.35, that."; 178.36, lense; 183.3, "I; 183.35, 'gone;
194.27, "O'Gar; 204.19, "'It; 223.18, *Tiajuana*; 227.14, CHAPTER III;

233.7, architect'; 237.20, he hair; 238.34, mind; 240.34, wrie; 241.37, gablers; 259.24, CHAPTER IX; 262.29, no,; 263.1, Ed.; 290.18, *mele*; 316.24, paralled; 318.4, eves; 353.1, night; 364.32, 'And; 377.17, tead; 401.38, gun off; 417.21, run; 473.4, surprnse; 484.1, it color; 484.9, cold His; 484.19–20, in conspicuous; 502.40, Goodbody's; 504.26, wouldn't spilled; 506.10, Falsoner's; 514.1, street; 514.9, "What; 516.32, crediors; 525.9, there?; 525.34, Peninsular; 526.18, 1; 530.2, we; 530.9, our our; 530.32, sick?"; 532.16, self-defense.; 533.5, him. [no quotation mark]; 533.31, can over; 578.28, upstairs"; 579.1, up!'; 600.33, "I ... days."; 609.21, troup; 614.24, "I; 629.22, five- ; 637.20, come; 663.33, took; 715.19, levely; 742.36, doing?; 752.29, wouldn't,'; 753.3, husbands; 772.32, Week's; 782.4, [no quotation marks] Then; 825.17, repeated,; 833.24, get's; 835.14–15, became; 865.34–35, occassional; 871.11, depositer; 873.22, up. [no quotation marks]; 879.4, where; 879.19, County. [no quotation marks]; 883.7, murmurred; 891.5, Wyanant; 900.25, earnestly. I; 906.17, or.

Notes

In the notes below, the reference numbers denote page and line of this volume (the line count includes chapter headings). No note is made for material included in standard desk-reference books such as Webster's *Collegiate, Biographical,* and *Geographical* dictionaries. For further information and references to other studies, see Diane Johnson, *Dashiell Hammett: A Life* (New York: Random House, 1983); Richard Layman, *Dashiell Hammett: A Descriptive Bibliography* (Pittsburgh: University of Pittsburgh Press, 1979); Richard Layman, *Shadow Man: The Life of Dashiell Hammett* (New York: Harcourt Brace Jovanovich, 1981); Richard Layman and Julie M. Rivett, eds., *Selected Letters of Dashiell Hammett, 1921–1960* (New York: Counterpoint, 2001); Joan Mellen, *Hellman and Hammett: The Legendary Passion of Lillian Hellman and Dashiell Hammett* (New York: HarperCollins, 1996); and William F. Nolan, *Hammett: A Life at the Edge* (New York: Congdon & Weed, 1983).

18.35   Hiram Johnson]   Johnson (1866–1945) was governor of California (1911–17) and Theodore Roosevelt's presidential running mate on the Progressive ticket in 1912. He later served four terms as senator.

82.4   badger-game]   Confidence game in which the victim is lured into a compromising sexual situation and then subjected to blackmail or extortion.

98.2   Stevenson monument]   The monument to Robert Louis Stevenson in Portsmouth Square, San Francisco.

164.25   piking]   Cheating; conning.

168.30   Bull Montana]   Italian-born wrestler and movie actor whose films included *When the Clouds Roll By* (1919), *The Lost World* (1925), and *Son of the Sheik* (1926).

222.8   scratcher]   Forger.

229.24   keno goose]   Container from which, in the game of keno, numbered balls are released.

234.10–11   carrying a beautiful bun]   Drunk.

249.3   bungstarter]   Wooden mallet used for opening a cask.

252.10–11   read and write]   Rhyming slang: fight.

290.18   *mere*]   Short warclub, usually made of jade.

336.23   *lechón*]   Pig.

348.12   kick]   Bag for holding loot.

373.7   soaked]   Pawned.

395.31   *Ta Jen*]   Great man; a term of respect and also an official rank in the Chinese bureaucracy.

402.14   settlement worker]   Provider of social services or charitable assistance through a settlement house.

405.14–15   clan feuds . . . the "Four Brothers" used to stage]   The Four Brothers was a Chinese clan amalgamated from four lineages (Lau, Quan, Cheung, and Chew) and embroiled in an extended gang war in New York, 1909–10, in which at least 12 people were killed.

407.22   Coxey's Army]   Group of unemployed workers, led by Jacob Coxey (1854–1951), who traveled to Washington, D.C., in 1894 to demonstrate in favor of paper money and the funding of public works projects.

442.19   highbinders]   Chinese extortion gangs in San Francisco preying on gamblers and prostitutes.

444.3–4   Taoukwang]   Daoguang (1782–1850), Chinese emperor who, following the Chinese defeat in the first Opium War (1839–42), opened five treaty ports to British merchants and ceded Hong Kong to Great Britain.

452.26   *The Lord of the Sea*]   Novel (1901) by M. P. Shiel.

498.10   knock-down]   Introduction.

547.2   cush]   Money; profit.

571.33   push]   Gang.

574.33   bingavast]   Get away.

579.3   Zonite]   Brand name of a liquid antiseptic douche.

582.16   rhino]   Money.

593.7   *schmierkäse*]   Cream cheese.

640.14   *cacoethes carpendi*]   Mania for finding fault.

645.27   highgrading]   Stealing ore, or dealing in stolen ore.

649.8   *The Sun Also Rises*]   Novel (1926) by Ernest Hemingway.

662.38–39   "*Asseyez-vous, s'il vous plaît,*"]   "Please be seated."

718.26   puffing]   Blowing safes with explosives.

722.29   *The Count of Monte Cristo*]   Novel (1844) by Alexandre Dumas.

722.33   Maybrick-Seddons trick] Florence Maybrick was convicted in 1889 of poisoning her husband, James Maybrick, with arsenic extracted from fly paper; her death sentence was commuted and she was released after 15 years' imprisonment. Frederick Seddon was hanged in 1912 for the murder, by means of repeated exposure to arsenic-coated flypaper, of Eliza Barrow the previous year; Seddon's wife, Maggie, was acquitted.

726.11   shatting on my uppers] Broke.

729.32–33   to powder] To run away.

761.27   *Schrecklichkeit*] Terror.

813.13   *schwach*] Weak; faint.

865.36   Pontius Pilate's question] "What is truth?"; cf. John 18:38.

882.15   *haori*] Knee-length Japanese coat.

897.22   *boo how doy*] Enforcer for Chinese tongs; often translated as "hatchet man."

908.24   Raffles] Gentleman burglar depicted in stories by E. W. Hornung collected in *The Amateur Cracksman* (1895) and other volumes.

Library of Congress Cataloging-in-Publication Data

Hammett, Dashiell, 1894–1961
  [Selections. 2001]
  Crime stories and other writings/Dashiell Hammett.
    p. cm.—(The Library of America ; 125)

Includes bibliographical references (p.).
ISBN 1–931082–00–6 (alk. paper)
  1. Detective and mystery stories, American. I. Title. II. Series.

PS3515.A4347 A6 2001
813'.52—dc21   00 054594

THE LIBRARY OF AMERICA SERIES

The Library of America fosters appreciation and pride in America's literary heritage by publishing, and keeping permanently in print, authoritative editions of its best and most significant writing. An independent nonprofit organization, it was founded in 1979 with seed money from the National Endowment for the Humanities and the Ford Foundation.

1. Herman Melville, *Typee, Omoo, Mardi* (1982)
2. Nathaniel Hawthorne, *Tales and Sketches* (1982)
3. Walt Whitman, *Poetry and Prose* (1982)
4. Harriet Beecher Stowe, *Three Novels* (1982)
5. Mark Twain, *Mississippi Writings* (1982)
6. Jack London, *Novels and Stories* (1982)
7. Jack London, *Novels and Social Writings* (1982)
8. William Dean Howells, *Novels 1875–1886* (1982)
9. Herman Melville, *Redburn, White-Jacket, Moby-Dick* (1983)
10. Nathaniel Hawthorne, *Collected Novels* (1983)
11. Francis Parkman, *France and England in North America*, vol. I (1983)
12. Francis Parkman, *France and England in North America*, vol. II (1983)
13. Henry James, *Novels 1871–1880* (1983)
14. Henry Adams, *Novels, Mont Saint Michel, The Education* (1983)
15. Ralph Waldo Emerson, *Essays and Lectures* (1983)
16. Washington Irving, *History, Tales and Sketches* (1983)
17. Thomas Jefferson, *Writings* (1984)
18. Stephen Crane, *Prose and Poetry* (1984)
19. Edgar Allan Poe, *Poetry and Tales* (1984)
20. Edgar Allan Poe, *Essays and Reviews* (1984)
21. Mark Twain, *The Innocents Abroad, Roughing It* (1984)
22. Henry James, *Essays, American & English Writers* (1984)
23. Henry James, *European Writers & The Prefaces* (1984)
24. Herman Melville, *Pierre, Israel Potter, The Confidence-Man, Tales & Billy Budd* (1985)
25. William Faulkner, *Novels 1930–1935* (1985)
26. James Fenimore Cooper, *The Leatherstocking Tales*, vol. I (1985)
27. James Fenimore Cooper, *The Leatherstocking Tales*, vol. II (1985)
28. Henry David Thoreau, *A Week, Walden, The Maine Woods, Cape Cod* (1985)
29. Henry James, *Novels 1881–1886* (1985)
30. Edith Wharton, *Novels* (1986)
31. Henry Adams, *History of the United States during the Administrations of Jefferson* (1986)
32. Henry Adams, *History of the United States during the Administrations of Madison* (1986)
33. Frank Norris, *Novels and Essays* (1986)
34. W. E. B. Du Bois, *Writings* (1986)
35. Willa Cather, *Early Novels and Stories* (1987)
36. Theodore Dreiser, *Sister Carrie, Jennie Gerhardt, Twelve Men* (1987)
37. Benjamin Franklin, *Writings* (1987)
38. William James, *Writings 1902–1910* (1987)
39. Flannery O'Connor, *Collected Works* (1988)
40. Eugene O'Neill, *Complete Plays 1913–1920* (1988)
41. Eugene O'Neill, *Complete Plays 1920–1931* (1988)
42. Eugene O'Neill, *Complete Plays 1932–1943* (1988)
43. Henry James, *Novels 1886–1890* (1989)
44. William Dean Howells, *Novels 1886–1888* (1989)
45. Abraham Lincoln, *Speeches and Writings 1832–1858* (1989)
46. Abraham Lincoln, *Speeches and Writings 1859–1865* (1989)
47. Edith Wharton, *Novellas and Other Writings* (1990)
48. William Faulkner, *Novels 1936–1940* (1990)
49. Willa Cather, *Later Novels* (1990)
50. Ulysses S. Grant, *Personal Memoirs and Selected Letters* (1990)

51. William Tecumseh Sherman, *Memoirs* (1990)
52. Washington Irving, *Bracebridge Hall, Tales of a Traveller, The Alhambra* (1991)
53. Francis Parkman, *The Oregon Trail, The Conspiracy of Pontiac* (1991)
54. James Fenimore Cooper, *Sea Tales: The Pilot, The Red Rover* (1991)
55. Richard Wright, *Early Works* (1991)
56. Richard Wright, *Later Works* (1991)
57. Willa Cather, *Stories, Poems, and Other Writings* (1992)
58. William James, *Writings 1878–1899* (1992)
59. Sinclair Lewis, *Main Street & Babbitt* (1992)
60. Mark Twain, *Collected Tales, Sketches, Speeches, & Essays 1852–1890* (1992)
61. Mark Twain, *Collected Tales, Sketches, Speeches, & Essays 1891–1910* (1992)
62. *The Debate on the Constitution: Part One* (1993)
63. *The Debate on the Constitution: Part Two* (1993)
64. Henry James, *Collected Travel Writings: Great Britain & America* (1993)
65. Henry James, *Collected Travel Writings: The Continent* (1993)
66. *American Poetry: The Nineteenth Century,* Vol. 1 (1993)
67. *American Poetry: The Nineteenth Century,* Vol. 2 (1993)
68. Frederick Douglass, *Autobiographies,* (1994)
69. Sarah Orne Jewett, *Novels and Stories* (1994)
70. Ralph Waldo Emerson, *Collected Poems and Translations* (1994)
71. Mark Twain, *Historical Romances* (1994)
72. John Steinbeck, *Novels and Stories 1932–1937* (1994)
73. William Faulkner, *Novels 1942–1954* (1994)
74. Zora Neale Hurston, *Novels and Stories* (1995)
75. Zora Neale Hurston, *Folklore, Memoirs, and Other Writings* (1995)
76. Thomas Paine, *Collected Writings* (1995)
77. *Reporting World War II: American Journalism 1938–1944* (1995)
78. *Reporting World War II: American Journalism 1944–1946* (1995)
79. Raymond Chandler, *Stories and Early Novels* (1995)
80. Raymond Chandler, *Later Novels and Other Writings* (1995)
81. Robert Frost, *Collected Poems, Prose, & Plays* (1995)
82. Henry James, *Complete Stories 1892–1898* (1996)
83. Henry James, *Complete Stories 1898–1910* (1996)
84. William Bartram, *Travels and Other Writings* (1996)
85. John Dos Passos, *U.S.A.* (1996)
86. John Steinbeck, *The Grapes of Wrath and Other Writings 1936–1941* (1996)
87. Vladimir Nabokov, *Novels and Memoirs 1941–1951* (1996)
88. Vladimir Nabokov, *Novels 1955–1962* (1996)
89. Vladimir Nabokov, *Novels 1969–1974* (1996)
90. James Thurber, *Writings and Drawings* (1996)
91. George Washington, *Writings* (1997)
92. John Muir, *Nature Writings* (1997)
93. Nathanael West, *Novels and Other Writings* (1997)
94. *Crime Novels: America Noir of the 1930s and 40s* (1997)
95. *Crime Novels: America Noir of the 1950s* (1997)
96. Wallace Stevens, *Collected Poetry and Prose* (1997)
97. James Baldwin, *Early Novels and Stories* (1998)
98. James Baldwin, *Collected Essays* (1998)
99. Gertrude Stein, *Writings 1903–1932* (1998)
100. Gertrude Stein, *Writings 1932–1946* (1998)
101. Eudora Welty, *Complete Novels* (1998)
102. Eudora Welty, *Stories, Essays, & Memoir* (1998)
103. Charles Brockden Brown, *Three Gothic Novels* (1998)
104. *Reporting Vietnam: American Journalism 1959–1969* (1998)
105. *Reporting Vietnam: American Journalism 1969–1975* (1998)
106. Henry James, *Complete Stories 1874–1884* (1999)
107. Henry James, *Complete Stories 1884–1891* (1999)

108. *American Sermons: The Pilgrims to Martin Luther King Jr.* (1999)
109. James Madison, *Writings* (1999)
110. Dashiell Hammett, *Complete Novels* (1999)
111. Henry James, *Complete Stories 1864–1874* (1999)
112. William Faulkner, *Novels 1957–1962* (1999)
113. John James Audubon, *Writings & Drawings* (1999)
114. *Slave Narratives* (2000)
115. *American Poetry: The Twentieth Century,* Vol. 1 (2000)
116. *American Poetry: The Twentieth Century,* Vol. 2 (2000)
117. F. Scott Fitzgerald, *Novels and Stories 1920–1922* (2000)
118. Henry Wadsworth Longfellow, *Poems and Other Writings* (2000)
119. Tennessee Williams, *Plays 1937–1955* (2000)
120. Tennessee Williams, *Plays 1957–1980* (2000)
121. Edith Wharton, *Collected Stories 1891–1910* (2001)
122. Edith Wharton, *Collected Stories 1911–1937* (2001)
123. *The American Revolution: Writings from the War of Independence* (2001)
124. Henry David Thoreau, *Collected Essays and Poems* (2001)
125. Dashiell Hammett, *Crime Stories and Other Writings* (2001)
126. Dawn Powell, *Novels 1930–1942* (2001)
127. Dawn Powell, *Novels 1944–1962* (2001)
128. Carson McCullers, *Complete Novels* (2001)
129. Alexander Hamilton, *Writings* (2001)

This book is set in 10 point Linotron Galliard,
a face designed for photocomposition by Matthew Carter
and based on the sixteenth-century face Granjon. The paper is
acid-free Ecusta Nyalite and meets the requirements for permanence
of the American National Standards Institute. The binding
material is Brillianta, a woven rayon cloth made by
Van Heek-Scholco Textielfabrieken, Holland.
The composition is by The Clarinda
Company. Printing and binding by
R.R.Donnelley & Sons Company.
Designed by Bruce Campbell.